WINCHESTER UNDEAD

WINCHESTER STORM and WINCHESTER TRIUMPH

« DAVE LUND »

PERMUTED
PRESS

A PERMUTED PRESS BOOK
ISBN: 978-1-68261-884-4

Winchester Undead:
Winchester Storm (Book Five) and Winchester Triumph (Book Six)
© 2019 by Dave Lund
All Rights Reserved

Cover photography by Dave Lund of www.f8industries.net
Cover design by Cody Corcoran

PERMUTED
PRESS

Permuted Press, LLC
New York · Nashville
permutedpress.com

Published in the United States of America

WINCHESTER: STORM

The flames danced across the lunar landscape of the desert night.

Movement caught his eye; spinning quickly toward the movement, Bexar raised his rifle. Three people outside the fence were running toward the gate. The tip of the red triangle in the optic tracked just ahead of the leader. Two smooth pulls on the trigger, and the first person fell; the second person tripped over the body. Bexar drove the rifle to the person at the rear, who stopped and turned to run away. Another two shots and the rounds pierced his back, blood erupting out of his chest where the rounds exited, the man crumpling to the ground in mid-stride. The remaining person of the assaulting force stood, arms raised. An odd-looking tube was slung across his body; it looked vaguely familiar to Bexar, but he wasn't sure why. Anger pierced the air between them. A fraction of a second passed, but for Bexar it felt like ten minutes. Through the reticle all he saw were the eyes and the hatred they held. A single squeeze of the trigger and the back of the attacker's skull exploded in a shower of bone and brain matter. Bexar scanned left and right. Nothing else moved; no other threats arrived.

CHAPTER 1

April 1, Year 1

Andrew banked the bright yellow Aviat Husky left and deftly held the aircraft in a lazy orbit above the scraggly lake in the Ozarks. Bentonville, Arkansas, as far as he could tell, belonged to the dead. *Which is too bad,* Andrew thought as he glanced at the twin-needled fuel gauge. Avgas was hard to come by, but regular unleaded gas with an octane booster seemed to be working fine. He reached into the back seat and felt in his bag for the big spiral bound Hema road atlas. It wasn't good airmanship using a road atlas to fly his way cross country; certain hazards definitely applied, such as tall towers now unlit. It was true IFR flying for a country pilot like himself... *I Follow Roads.* When disorientated Andrew would push his bush plane down, skimming the rooftops of the cars on the largest highways he could find, looking for highway signs and road signs to help him figure out his location.

With the wings level, Andrew held the aircraft impossibly slow in the crisp air above the lake. If his altimeter was still correct, he was roughly seven thousand feet above sea level, and with his uncalibrated eyeball he would call it closer to five thousand feet above the lake. Oreo nudged his hand as he dug for the atlas; a quick scratch between his best friend's ears and the atlas came out of the bag. Squinting, he read the small print naming the lake *Beaver Lake.*

The atlas didn't name the little community below him, nor did it show a little airplane to indicate an airport, but the black tarmac stood out from the brown trees and roof tops. Smoke billowed softly from a few of the chimneys, blowing lazily south. Replacing the atlas in the bag by Oreo, he dug around and found his binoculars. The runway numbers were easily seen without them, *thirty-one and thirteen; chimney smoke trailing south.* The choice was easy to land toward the north. What grabbed Andrew's attention wasn't the smoke or the runway; it was a small boat a few hundred yards off the shore to the east of the runway.

Banking the aircraft over and again starting a lazy orbit, Andrew peered through the binoculars at the man in the boat, who was pulling in a floating jug line and looked up at the circling aircraft and waved.

"That's a good sign, Oreo. He's waving at us."

Oreo nudged Andrew on the shoulder with his snout, which was responded to with another scratch between the ears. The engine sputtered, Andrew reached for the fuel selector and cycled the tanks, smoothly adjusting the throttle and pushing the light aircraft's nose forward. A few more coughs and the spinning propeller outside of his windscreen slowed and jerked to a stop, a white tip of one of the propeller blades staring at him in defiance.

"Well, shit. Like it or not buddy, this is where we land."

Andrew's bush-plane-turned-glider edged through the air, nearly silent, the passing wind the only noise in the cockpit. With no radio to listen to, no other pilots to broadcast, no mayday call to claim his ownership of the small landing strip, and no other airplanes to jockey for position, all he had to do was land safely.

"Crunch this one in, and this community better be friendlier than that one in Tennessee."

Oreo whimpered and looked out of the window. Sitting straight in the seat behind Andrew, his eyes were open and bright, ears perked up. With more flight hours as the dog-second-in-command than most people pilots log in a lifetime, Oreo showed blazing awareness to their tense situation.

Andrew cut across the middle of the field from the east, banked, and made a sweeping left turn to put the big tundra tires on the tarmac and let the aircraft roll to a stop to save wear on the brakes. The engine off from fuel starvation long before putting the tires on the ground, Andrew turned off the ignition to save the battery and flipped open the clam-shell window and door, and stuck wheel chocks under one tire while turning a three-sixty, scanning for any threats... living or dead.

CHAPTER 2

Chivo lay near the cliff's edge, a wool blanket pulled over him to break his form up if he were seen from a distance. This was nothing like the ghillie suit he would have preferred to have, but it was better than nothing. Since the night more than a week ago when Doc was killed, the group hadn't had another run in with the other survivors' splinter group, which was the good news. The bad news was that his hand still ached, and Bexar was still in a cast. With a pencil and a notebook, Chivo took his time to plot all the dirt roads between the compound and where their truck lay in burned ruin. He was just too far to see the truck with any sort of detail; the truck was roughly a mile and a half away. He could see its rough shape, and he could tell that it had burned, but he couldn't tell if the debris around it included his rifle case. South of the compound lay the Interstate. After his previous experience with that section of road, Chivo wanted nothing to do with it until he absolutely had to go back there. The enormous horde of dead had thinned out over the past few days, still not as bad as the night of the attack or the day they'd wrecked the truck, but still enough of the reanimated corpses that it would be suicide to go down there.

The past two days Chivo had lain near the cliff's edge at different times during the day, using the different angles of the day's light to better observe and take notes. His first duty, though, was a range card for his M4 on the approach to the compound from the west, up the driveway or over the rocky ground. His distances and elevations were set. With the shorter distances of fire to protect the compound, he was confident in his ability to quickly respond to another attack. His self-imposed duty now was to map a way to the truck that, with Angel's help, he could reach the truck via horseback or on foot if need be. The big Barrett 50-caliber rifle would be a huge asset for counter-insurgency operations against the splinter survivor group, assuming the rifle survived.

Chivo, relating the current situation more along his original missions in Northern Afghanistan, thought of the survivor groups as tribes. The list of people in the friendly tribe read only twelve names when they were pulled off the Interstate and out of the clutches of death. The list, now one person short after Doc was killed, still had promise and had some along for the ride. Chivo's focus wandered through his internal lists, moving each piece into a plan to stabilize the tribes and get out of dodge sooner than later.

Angel, some tactical skills, skilled with horses and designer of the compound and Guillermo, friendly registered nurse and now the defacto group medic since Doc died are the tribal leaders, the first family. John is the beer guy and the quartermaster of dry foods. Brian is the group armorer with general tactical knowledge. Heath takes care of the systems in the compound. Marylyn and Frances, another couple, are both in charge of long-term food storage, meal planning, and inventory. Coach, no real name known, heads security. Stan is the group's mechanic and general handyman. Gary has no real skills that I've seen, but his ability to tell a story is incredible. His daily journal might be of interest to a future historian, if there are any left to care. Jennifer is a bit of a mad-scientist seamstress. She's the one who modified Bexar's pants for the cast and Doc. Doc is dead. If this tribe is going to barter with the other tribe, they need to barter skills, not goods, if at all possible. Jennifer and Stan are the most valuable for that task. Surely every other tribe in the region needs something repaired, something sewn, and something patched.

He and Bexar had wasted enough time sitting in Utah, so close to Groom Lake and reuniting Bexar with his wife, Jessie, but even as anxious as Bexar was to get moving, he needed to be out of the cast on his leg first. Luckily, he was starting to put a little weight on his leg and cast, if only for short periods, but it was a start.

Rifle, insurgents, vehicle, and leave.

Simple plan, only three parts and a drive, but Chivo knew that even the simplest of plans often didn't survive first contact with the enemy.

Yuma, AZ

Aymond sat in the back of the hardened ordinance storage structure. Near the covered aircraft storage and flight line, just a year ago the air would have been full of Marine Aviators ripping across the desert sky, but now all they had was silence and the soft hum of the Chinese radar truck. The remaining men of his Marines Special Operations Team, or MSOT, had settled into the new routine of their new temporary home. Enterprising as they were, they'd found a cache of HESCO barriers and a front-end loader that Jones was able to get running. A little over a week ago, they'd left San Diego in a rush and in ruins, hopefully slowing the Chinese invasion, but Aymond doubted it. He needed more than the eight of them who remained alive to fight off an invasion; he needed more Marines or anyone who could carry a rifle really.

I need patriots, minutemen ready to fill the gap between the Chinese and the dead.

Walking into the hard mid-day sun, Aymond squinted from the contrast. Even in April, the air was already warm, and, as much fun as he'd had while temporarily stationed at the Marine Corps Air Station Yuma when he was a young Marine, he really didn't want to stick around for the triple-digit temperatures of summer. HESCO formed a protective U-shaped wall around the north, west, and south sides of the group of hardened bunkers. A chain-link fence with barbed wire surrounded them, but chain-link wouldn't stop the Zeds, and chain-link would give them no protection if the PLA somehow showed up.

Hammer and Gonzo were on a recon patrol in one of the M-ATVs with Kirk. Jones manned the radar truck, marker-smudged tape placed over the Chinese labels with what the switches did, as best as the men could figure out. Aymond monitored the radio, ready to shake loose Davis, Snow, and Chuck from their sleep cycle if Hammer and his merry band of raiders ran into trouble. The second M-ATV sat at the ready, loaded for the war they would bring as the Quick Reaction Force. Happy stood on the top of the HESCO near the radar truck and east-facing entrance, binoculars to his eyes as he scanned the housing complexes in the distance.

The early patrols found signs of survivors having been on base at some point, improvised positions, obvious signs of battle, but so far no other living person had been found.

"Anything yet?"

"Nothing but Zeds, Chief, although I'm fairly sure this is where they come to check the accuracy of carpenter levels."

Beaver Lake, AR

"I know he waved, but keep cool. Like sirens luring sailors, we can't trust until we verify."

Oreo nudged Andrew's hand.

"Yeah, I agree."

Andrew pulled one of the bags out of the small cargo hold, a backpack that looked like something a high school kid would have stuffed in a locker, shouldered the bag, and jogged to the broken split-rail fence line and to the metal building off the end of the runway. Panting from jogging uphill, he noticed his breath hung in the cool air. Each of the four roll-up garage doors was locked in place. The regular door on the side of the building was locked too. Oreo whimpered softly. Andrew looked at his dog and then in the direction he was looking.

"Come on," Andrew tersely whispered as he ran to the back of the building and into the tree line. He took the backpack off and lay still in the shadows among the trees. Oreo lay on the ground next to him, sniffing the air, ears forward toward the road going down the hill, and he tilted his head as dogs do when trying to decipher something unexpected. A house on their left appeared vacant and closed; another house directly across the road, partially hidden by the trees did not. Taking in his surroundings, Andrew saw faint smoke rising from the chimney. His heart was beating behind his ears, straining to listen to any sound outside his own body, but the more he attempted to listen the less he could hear.

Oreo's tail swept back and forth before he sat up and suddenly ran out of the trees toward the house. Tail wagging, he stopped across the road where the driveway met and sat eagerly. A little girl, who appeared to be no older than ten, walked from behind the trees and overgrown brush. A pistol that seemed impossibly large for her small body tugged at her belt, and in her hands she held a rifle that appeared to be a Ruger 10/22 with a camouflaged stock colored in bright pink.

At sight of her, Oreo stretched and waited like an eager puppy. The girl looked at Oreo and smiled and said something Andrew couldn't hear, but Oreo trotted to her and sat in front of her to enjoy a happy scratch behind his ears. The girl knelt and looked at the tag on his collar, "Oreo is your name? Did you fly that plane here, or who are you here with?"

The girl scanned the wood line, squinting with the look of a seasoned hunter. Andrew took a deep breath, stood, and walked around the side of the building into view. The girl reacted immediately and raised her rifle. Oreo trotted off toward Andrew who stood a few hundred feet away with his hands out and away from his body.

"Mister, don't you move uh inch."

"My name is Andrew, and I won't, and this is Oreo, who you just met."

"What'cha doin' here?"

"Ran out of gas, and it's sort of hard to pull to the side of the road when you're five thousand feet up."

The girl didn't say anything; she glanced over her shoulder at a much older man who walked up the driveway.

"Gran'pa, this man says he ran out of gas."

The man nodded and squinted, examining Andrew. "Where you from there, mister?"

"You don't have to call me mister, mister. The whole world calls me Andrew."

"What?"

"The old country song, you know? Well, sorry, no, my name is Andrew. This is Oreo. We're from Florida."

"Wha'cha flying around for?"

"Just searching, looking for others."

"We've had some problems with *others*, Andrew."

"Yeah, well, so have I."

"Come on up here so we don't have to holler at one'nuther. We don't wanna be attract'n those damn things."

Andrew walked slowly toward the man and the girl with his hands open and away from his side, her rifle still trained on him. The last thing he wanted to do was spook someone and get shot at... again. Andrew stopped in the middle of the road, about twenty feet from the girl and the man. Oreo never stopped wagging his tail as he walked to the girl and nudged her in the leg to get another ear scratch.

"Where ya head'n?"

"Truth be told, I'm not really sure. I'm just wandering here and there hoping to find something, someone who can fix this mess. I guess I'm looking for help, the military, the government, someone or anyone who can tell me that *they* are on top of it, and we'll all be OK."

"Son, I'm afraid that just ain't gonna be the case ... why don't you lower your rifle, princess. My name's Warren, and this little one is my granddaughter, Mary."

Andrew smiled and nodded at each in greeting. Mary, now with a hand free, finally acknowledged Oreo's insistence and petted him. Warren glanced at Oreo and then stared at the plane. "We ain't got no hundred low lead for your plane."

"It'll run on car gas. I have some bottles of octane booster in the cabin I mix with the gasoline."

Warren nodded slowly and looked at the sky for a moment. "Well, come on inside, and we can talk trading. First, I'll trade you lunch for news or stories, and then we can talk about get'n some gas for your plane."

"Sounds like a plan, Warren. Thank you."

They walked in silence, Mary and Oreo ahead of them with his tail wagging while her ponytail bounced with each step. Warren frowned and glanced over his shoulder toward the parked Husky bush plane.

Groom Lake, NV

The peaceful desert morning and cool air grew worse with every passing minute. Bill struggled to finish the riggings for the homebuilt antenna he hoped would give him the chance to communicate over the horizon with other survivors, if only he could complete his task. A radio is nothing without the right antenna.

"I like the fresh air and all, but seriously, fuck this weather."

"Erin, darling, relax. We're outside, and Brit isn't with us... so what if it's windy."

"Jessie, it isn't the wind. It's the damn sand that's blowing!"

Jessie shrugged and walked against the howling wind sandblasting the small group on the desert floor. Wind ripped across the mountains and into the dry lakebed, picking up sand and some surprisingly large rocks. Bill's antenna was finally erected, but it took so long that the nice weather had changed dramatically since he first started.

It isn't that it took so long; it's that the weather changed that suddenly. First zombies, now extreme weather... Erin's right.

Jessie coughed. Goggles that the world had previously seen on the dusty helmets of military men and women in the first Iraqi war were pulled tight against her face, and a dark shemagh was wrapped over her head and around her mouth in a vain attempt to keep the dust out of her lungs. The last thing Jessie needed was to get a lungful of dust and spend the rest of her pregnancy below ground with miner's lung.

Erin usually liked to lay on the roofrack of the FJ with the big Barrett rifle, but today she opted to stand on the ground, or attempt to in the gusting winds, with her short-barreled M4. It didn't seem to matter what firearm Erin had in her young hands, she was not only fast but wickedly accurate.

I'd hate to piss her off.

Since the first time Sarah had ridden up on her motorcycle and warned that her daughter was holding over-watch with a rifle, Jessie'd had a bit of a soft spot for Erin. Although a young girl who should be worried about school dances and homework, the bouncing ponytailed country girl in jeans was a stone-cold machine, constructed in the ruins of society out of necessity.

Jessie frowned, not that anyone could see it, and looked at Sarah, who was standing next to Bill. *She has the intelligence, poise, and confidence that I know my little Keeley had; she just never had a chance to grow into it.*

Bill moved in more of a fast waddle than a walk back toward the FJ. Sarah circled her hand above her head, meaning *Time to leave.*

At least none of the damned had shown their undead faces this time, Jessie thought.

The last time anyone had seen Brit was shortly after the first attempt to erect Bill's homebrewed radio antenna. Jake said he'd spoken with her, and she'd said she had the flu. Sarah and Jessie thought she was too embarrassed to be seen in the public spaces after nearly getting bit. Erin took it upon herself to passingly "mention" the episode to all who ventured near her. When Sarah asked her to stop, that it would cause nothing but discord, Erin gave her mother the middle finger and walked off.

The interior of the FJ was warm, which was nice, but not as nice as being free from the sand and dirt that flowed across the dry lake like a monsoon. With every bounce, every jostle, dirt floated off their clothing and covered the inside of the well-used overlanding-rig-turned-bug-out-vehicle.

"So after testing the antenna and the radios, the airmen will broadcast a loop on shortwave that they recorded detailing how to construct a spark-gap radio. The secondary shortwave channel will have a looped ten-minute tutorial on CW," Bill explained.

"What's CW?"

"Continuous wave, what they used to call Morse code."

"Huh." Sarah's look was one of curiosity. Although she would have enjoyed a longer explanation, she really didn't want one as long as Bill was ready to give. She didn't want a lesson; she wanted the cliff notes, which Bill seemed physically incapable of providing for any subject. The rest of the slow ride was passed in silence. Driving the Toyota, Jessie wanted to drive much faster, but visibility was not much beyond the end of the hood due to the dust storm. Eventually they drove into the gaping cavern of the hanger that housed the main entrance to the underground facility. Jason was standing by the blast door, happily returned to his previous job as greeter. *He needs a blue vest... and maybe some shopping carts to go with his shotgun.* Jessie smirked at the thought.

SSC, Ennis, TX

Sweat stung her eyes. Panting and trying to catch her breath, Amanda moved with all the energy she could muster. This time she would make it. This time she would succeed. She had to succeed—she could not fail. Failure could be death. Amanda dove under the big armored truck. Rolling to the other side, she stood quickly and jumped as high as she could with her hands stretched far above her head.

Her feet fell to the pavement, her knees bending to absorb the impact. Amanda touched the cold tarmac and jumped as hard as she could, hands reaching toward the roof of the MRAP and back down to the asphalt.

One... two... three... four...

Amanda counted out twenty burpees before dropping to her hands to bang out twenty-five push-ups. On her feet, she began the circuit again. Every single day she worked one of a half-dozen of her own workouts of the day. The extensive facility had a well-equipped gym, a weight room that would make a Division I football program proud, but what she shunned in pushing iron, Amanda made up for in conditioning and body strength. She had a plan. It was a simple plan, but it would require the best of her. Outside the protection of the concrete-lined walls deep underground was the real world, the world that belonged to the dead, and the world she'd unwittingly inherited by being the last one alive in the Presidential line of succession. No, the citizens, her fellow citizens and the U.S. Constitution she'd sworn to protect needed a leader, a strong leader to bring them through this dark time. History would remember her name as someone who gave beyond their best, or history would remember nothing at all but the empty ruins of an extinct civilization.

CHAPTER 3

"Brian, do it again, please."

Brian moved with the practiced poise of someone who had once been an athlete. Obviously his mind retained the vigor of his youth, but the body of a middle-aged man simply didn't respond as quickly, as gracefully as a younger man, nor did it recover as quickly from such a physical experience as the end of the world as we know it.

A butter knife in Chivo's hand was the closest thing that the group could come up with for an analogue to a rubberized training knife, but with Chivo, they would be as safe as they could be for the new training.

Chivo glanced suddenly to his left over Brian's shoulder, who in response turned his head to follow Chivo's gaze and look of surprise. In less than a blink of an eye, Chivo's ruse worked, and he was in Brian's guard, knife to his throat. "Had you scanned the surroundings before we started?" Chivo asked.

"Yeah."

"Then why did you look when you knew nothing was there?"

"I don't know."

Chivo nodded. "Know what you know and act accordingly."

These sorts of Yogi-isms seemed to gush forth unwittingly from Chivo when he was playing the role of instructor. Ever the quiet professional, he had no problem teaching his peers and fellow Special Forces soldiers, but teaching civilians was a different ballgame altogether. It required an air of overt confidence that Chivo typically tried to play off, but at least with Guillermo and Angel's group of survivors, preppers who did it right, he found eager and willing students.

"OK, Brian, set it up again."

These people have no idea. Their war is coming. It will be brutal, and they will have to be ready to fight. Fight or surrender; if not against this enemy, the opposing group of survivors, it will be the next one or the ones after that. The dead don't envy the living; they have no mind but to feed. No, the fall of man will be from man's own mind and flesh... Lord help us all.

Chivo lunged at Brian with the butter knife. Brian stepped off line with a sharp block to the radial, rotating through with an elbow to Chivo's face. The knife fell from Chivo's hand, and his hand bent into a hard wrist lock, which Brian used to simulate breaking his elbow.

"Good job," Chivo said, while shaking his hand and retrieving the dropped butter knife.

Step by step. Knife defense, disarming, escape, survival, fighting... this is an unconventional force of conventional people.

Chivo's face betrayed nothing, but he doubted whether their new friends and one-time saviors would be able to become saviors unto themselves.

Lost Bridge Village, Beaver Lake, AR

Burning wood popped and hissed in the fireplace. With the fire pushed to one side, the other side glowing with the white hot coals gave heat to a medium-sized dutch oven. The living room's dark shadows belied the afternoon sunlight outside. Wool blankets were tacked to the walls, stretched over the windows, and old newspaper in thick crumpled clumps filled the space between the blankets and the windows; the homemade insulation helped to keep the fire's meager heat from escaping the home too quickly.

"Come summer, we're gonna have to pull down the blankets and hope to get some air through, but these modern homes just weren't meant for it."

Andrew nodded, wrapping his hands around the mug of hot tea, a wonderful treat after the weeks of hopping from camp to camp via his airplane.

"You're not the first to say that to me, Warren. A number of others I've found have all said the same. They wished for the old homes, but with that said, the old homes aren't as well insulated, and many of them are near the center of towns, historic homes and neighborhoods. It goes without saying that being close to downtown anywhere is a bad idea."

"Most folks been accommodating?"

"Eh, well, I'd say most have been cautious. Some groups were quite reluctant to allow an outsider in their midst; one couple seemed to want to cook Oreo here for dinner. I couldn't even imagine. Needless to say we took flight very quickly after that suggestion. It isn't all death and despair though. I found a group of farmers in Georgia who'd banded together and have established an intermittent mail route between about a half-dozen smaller camps. They even have a trade day every other Sunday!"

"Amazing, how can they do that safely? We tried to venture out toward Rogers, near Bentonville, using the lake, but all we found were the dead. Not one sign of another living soul that way. The other way up the lake are a few other groups. All in all they been the friendly sort, but then some of 'em we knew before too. The damnedest thing was ole' Highway 12. One day, I saw what had to be a thousand of the dead marching 'cross the bridge. They even pushed some cars over the edge and into the water, the dead going with them. They sank like the cars, but I don't think we'll be swimming in the water come summer. Not with the dead mucking about in the water."

"You should see the giant migrations of dead; massive, miles long. Some of the other groups have seen them, a couple even talked about other groups they had contact with wiped off the earth by the mass of migrating dead."

"You bump across any government or military or anything like'n that yet?"

Andrew tilted his head. "Sort of. Nothing what I would have hoped for, but I've seen some groups of military vehicles, tents, and such. I've steered clear; they make me a little uneasy, Warren, and truth be told that is what I'm searching for. There are survivors, more survivors than I could have imagined when I flew out the first time, but nothing is organized. I don't know if it could be organized. There just aren't the resources or the people... I take that back, there might be enough people if we had someplace safe to center the efforts. A leader, a mission, equipment, and purpose, but no, so far everyone is just trying to keep their friends, their families, and their own little communities alive as long as they can."

"What about them fellers over in Nevada? You listen to them yet?"

"Listen how? I don't understand, the others said there was an EMP, and my radios didn't work anymore."

"I suppose that's true, Andrew, but... Princess, go grab my shortwave out of the pantry. Some things survived. I don't know why, but this guy was in an old metal ammo can in my garage, stuffed in with my hunting gear. Bought it years ago for the weather radio, but it picks up the shortwave stuff too."

Mary left her warm and cozy place sitting on the hearth to quickly return, handing Warren a crank-powered radio before returning to her warm spot and checking on the meal cooking in the dutch oven. Oreo yawned and lay back against her legs.

Warren cranked the radio while explaining the looped broadcasts, starting with the BBC news broadcast from just after the attack, which had since gone off the air. "Then some station came on blabbering nonsense, just a bunch of numbers or letters, and then it disappeared, no idea what was the reason, but strange all around."

Stopping, Warren extended the antenna and turned on the radio. "The reception is better at night, but maybe we can find you som'thing right now, and then we can try again after supper."

The radio hissed, static rolling between each change in frequency before Warren stopped on a tinny voice that sounded miles away with the weak reception "... the letter D is dash, dot, dot; the letter E is dot; the letter F is dot, dot, dash, dot..."

"Hey, that's Morse code!"

Warren nodded. "Sure'nuff is. First time I've heard that on the radio. Usually they talk about how they're a safe haven, all are welcome. They also say we got ourselves a new President... a woman."

Andrew quickly dug around in his pockets before pulling out a bright orange Field Notes notebook and a pen. "Would you mind letting it play. I want to write this all down. Maybe they'll start over, and we can get what we missed."

Warren nodded and set the radio on the end table next to his recliner. The transmission continued through the alphabet, following some basic protocols for when transmitting so messages could be understood. An example broadcast of Morse code was transmitted very slowly along with what it all meant.

"This has been an official United States of America radio broadcast, authorized by the President of the United States Amanda Lampton and broadcast from the safe facility in Groom Lake, Nevada. For information on how to construct a radio and antenna out of parts scavenged from everyday items you can find in your home or neighborhood, please tune to the shortwave frequency..."

"President Amanda Lampton is her name, so they say. Ever heard of her, Andrew?"

"Warren, I have no idea, but if you wouldn't mind, I would like to try to make contact. Would you change the frequency so we can get the assembly instructions?"

Warren looked at Mary. His soft eyes betrayed a kindhearted man contained behind the hard weathered face. Her possible future broke his heart every time he considered it. Silently nodding in response, Warren tuned the radio to the second frequency, turned the generating crank a few more times, and set it back on the end table. Andrew smiled, excitement from a glimmer of hope twinkling in his eyes as he took careful notes in his small durable notebook.

CHAPTER 4

The beep crackle of a radio transmission snapped Aymond awake. The hardened structure that was his berth inside their HESCO built firebase was the safest he had felt since leaving the Mountain Warfare Training Center. Faintly glowing, the hands of his analog wrist watch, a classic military field watch, showed 0400.

Rifle fire filled the radio transmission. Aymond was not awake enough to understand the words, but the gunfire in the background coming through the handset vividly brought back memories of deployments in northern Afghanistan.

What the hell?

"No copy, say again your last, over!"

Now standing, Aymond squinted in the darkness at the other Marines that weren't on patrol or holding fire watch.

"Chief, contact, PLA, request QRF, repeat Quebec Romeo Foxtrot, how copy?"

"Good copy!"

Aymond turned his head and yelled "QRF, SHAKE IT LOOSE!"

A small chorus of mumbled "fucks" was heard as the Marines leapt off their cots, shrugging on their battle rattle and slinging rifles.

"Clear copy, QRF, location, status, over?"

"The eight north of the river, at business eight, mounted patrol, one dozen APCs, one radar truck, about a platoon in strength, how copy?"

"Clear copy, strobe friendly, ETA ten mikes."

"Roger, ten mikes, out."

The hard thump of a 50-caliber rifle was heard in rapid succession over the last radio transmission. Hammer, Happy, and Snow were the patrol team in contact. Jones and Chuck held fire watch, leaving Gonzo, Kirk, Davis, and Aymond in a rest cycle with one M-ATV and their lone radar truck. Jones and Chuck came running toward the M-ATV, Gonzo already behind the wheel, the diesel engine rumbling and ready to go. Two minutes later, the armored truck tore out of the compound, leaving it open, unguarded, and in a condition Aymond would have preferred not to leave it, but there were only nine Marines left, counting himself. Master Gunnery Sergeant Aymond had no other choice.

Kirk spun the remote turret that commanded the mounted M2, a 50-caliber machine gun, forward. Next to the heavy automatic weapon were the sensors and camera. The Marines in contact were instructed and knew to deploy IR strobes that the rest of the MSOT could see with their NODs, or night optic devices, assuming that these Chinese and Korean forces were like the ones they'd fought in California, without any night-vision capability. The problem was that unlike the previously contacted units, this PLA unit was operating at night.

SSC, Ennis, TX

Amanda jogged past her chosen MRAP in the cold tunnel, the overhead lighting casting hard shadows. If not for her familiarity with the tunnel and daily workout routine, she would have been concerned with all the dark spaces, but in the weeks that they had been in the secret underground facility not a single walking corpse had threatened them.

No, my threat is from a single walking man... I can't believe how stupid I was.

Frowning, Amanda quickened her pace, sweat falling from her face, steaming in the cool air. Upon reaching the paved-off wall at the end of the tunnel, beyond which lay the publicly known section of tunnels that had been filled with gravel and water; she turned and began her jog back to the main facility. What started off as a one-mile jog with more walking than jogging weeks ago was now a steady five-mile run. Amanda, who was now in the best shape of her life, felt fear and uncertainty fall away from her thoughts. With each footfall, her plan became clearer, and her resolve strengthened.

Tomorrow morning, tomorrow is the day.

A faint smile slipped through her mask to her face. Passing her chosen MRAP, she ran her fingers along the hull as she passed.

Foreign and domestic...

The oath of office... Clint had sworn her in as President, with video-conferenced witnesses from Groom Lake... but the oath, a blur at the time, still resonated in her mind.

Foreign AND domestic... domestic, created by the Presidents before me... the Constitution... back to the basics... the basics.

The plan she'd made secretly from Clint's eyes, due to her burgeoning distrust of him, had to happen. She would make it happen, and it would begin in twenty-four hours. The list of items she had prepped scrolled through her thoughts, and she checked items off the list as she visualized the memory of placing each into the MRAP for her journey.

Groom Lake is well stocked. I just have to get there. All I have to worry about is ammo, fuel, and some food and water; the rest they will have in their stores.

Reaching the makeshift pull-up bars, Amanda stopped and caught her breath before jumping up and hanging from the athletic-tape-wrapped steel bar.

Groom Lake, NV

Jake sat in the mess hall slowly sipping at his black coffee while he read the *Alien Dispatch*, which was the Groom Lake newspaper of sorts. Every other day, the front and back printed sheet of copy paper was produced for all the residents. Containing what little news they had, the rest of the copy was full of stories, jokes, and a surprisingly engaging serialization about "what really happened in Roswell." A few people griped that the paper and copier toner used to produce the paper was a waste, but besides beans and bullets, the facility had a surprisingly large cache of office supplies. Which made a little sense in contrast to the square footage given to office space, cube farms still smeared with the dried gore of the original undead outbreak in the facility that Cliff had singlehandedly cleared.

It really seemed like Cliff should have returned by now.

The thought hung in Jake's mind as he watched a trio of women walk into the mess hall. Earlier than the usual crowd; only a few dozen people sat in small groups across the expansive room. *Her husband too... Cliff, her husband, and the other guy; the ragtag rescue party's radio traffic was weeks ago.* Jessie was barely beginning to show her pregnancy, which Jake found to be a strange juxta-position of visuals: a pregnant woman with tactical kit and a rifle. It was one he wasn't accustomed to seeing but realized that it was the current and their future in their post-apocalyptic life.

Even in contrast to the other survivors, those women have an intense vibe radiating in every direction.

Jake tried not to stare as they walked between the tables. The women were armed, but everyone was armed at all times as a standing rule. The rifles, maga-zines, and tactical gear weren't what set them apart from the rest. It was their bearing, their focus, and even the way they walked that screamed of an intensity that the others didn't have, except for Cliff and the lost Para-Rescue Jumpers. They were similar, except they weren't pregnant. Fading inward to his thoughts, Jake didn't realize at first that the women were walking toward his table.

"Morning, Jake, we have a question."

Blinking and returning to the present, Jake set his coffee on the table. "I'm sorry, could you repeat that?"

"We said good morning and that we have a question."

"Well, good morning to you, Jessie, Sarah, and Ms. Erin. What is your question?"

"Bill told us that no one has fully explored the facility. The weather topside turned miserable yesterday, bad sandstorm across the lake bed, so we think the underground facility should be explored to create a map of sorts."

Jake nodded. Jessie was correct in that none of them knew the full layout of the facility, where every door went, what every room was, only that Cliff said he had cleared the entire facility and that it was safe. So far he was right, except Cliff wasn't here, and so now they had no idea.

"You'll need a full access key card."

"That's why we're talking to you."

Jake pulled the lanyard over his head, which held his ID card with his photo printed on it like some high school student, and handed it to Jessie. "If you find a door that won't open for my ID, then I don't know what to tell you."

Jessie put the lanyard around her neck. "Any hints before we get started?"

Jake described the layout of the facility as far as he understood it. "The labs are all the way down on level seven, but who knows. Cliff told me there was only enough food for two hundred people to survive on for a year, but he was wrong, well, not wrong but not right. There's enough MREs in the supply level to feed that many for perhaps longer than a year, but the dry storage we found is what we are eating now."

"Which will last how long with this many people?"

"The estimate is nearly five years, and we have fourteen hundred thirty-nine and a half residents," Jake said with a smile, glancing at Jessie's stomach.

Erin stood turned away from the table, listening to the conversation while watching for any threats that could approach the group. "How's that work out with all the bunk rooms?" she asked.

"Those weren't bunk rooms. Those rooms were all office spaces, cube farms, and, before you ask, I have no idea why, but strangely the supply cache had all the collapsible bunks and bedding. It was almost like the planners guessed that something like this would happen."

"I'll bet it wasn't a guess."

Jake sighed. "Probably not. Supposedly the labs on seven were working on the problem we currently have. I can't remember what Cliff called the project name, but there was only one of the scientists still alive when he arrived. His name was Lance, but he was killed in a lab accident."

"Like he blew up?"

"No, Erin, he was bit."

Saint George, UT

"Sure, but that's a big what if."

"I know it is, mano, but we've got to try. I mean we owe our lives to these guys. We repay that debt and the pop smoke, though first, I need to get my rifle."

"If it survived the wreck."

"Sure, Schrodinger's cat, right? It neither survived or was destroyed until we open the box."

"You have issues, dude."

"My biggest issue is your lack of balls and being a pussy about your leg."

"Hey!"

Chivo smiled, their whispered discussion before the rest of the house woke up being exactly what they needed. A plan, a means, and a bad attitude; everything required for success was put into motion.

"So get Angel, his guys, the horses, and we boogie down to the crash site and then come back. Then I can recon the other group. Kill those fuckers, find new wheels, and we get you to Area 51."

"What if we don't find new wheels?"

"Then we steal the horses."

"That's how you get hung, guy."

"I'm already hung, so what?"

Bexar smirked and shook his head. "OK, fine, Señor Machismo, so what's your timeline?"

"Five days? Seven tops. If my rifle survived, then I can simply put the other group under from across town. If it didn't, I'll have to improvise."

"More napalm?"

"Hell no, well, maybe, mano, you never know. We have to stay loose, improvise."

"Why do I feel like every time you improvise, something blows the fuck up?"

"Remember, smile, be kind..."

"... and be ready to blow everyone the fuck up?"

"Exactly."

Lost Bridge Village, AR

Oreo nudged Andrew, waking the pilot from a comfortable sleep on the sofa near the fireplace. Once Andrew sat up, Oreo walked to the back door and sat, tail happily swishing back and forth across the tile.

"OK, buddy, sniff it out first though."

Andrew pulled his boots on before unlocking and opening the back door, stepping onto the back porch with Oreo. Muzzle in the air, Oreo sniffed the air before deciding it was safe to go out into the grass for his morning constitution. The eastern sky glowed with the coming sunrise. When they stepped back into the house, Warren was in the living room, stirring the white coals in the fireplace before setting a blue enamel kettle on the glowing embers.

"Good morning, Pilot Andrew and Oreo."

"You're up early, Warren."

"If you have the chance to grow into an old man like myself, you'll find that early is normal. Besides, we need to get started early so we can meet up with the others by the lake."

"And do what?"

"Welp, 'ole Tom used to be one of the radio hams, I'd bet he'd want to look at the plans you wrote down yesterday. Then we find someone you can barter with for some gas-o-leen. Once Mary wakes and after breakfast, we'll head on down there, but for now I want you to tell me whereabouts them other survivors with the trade days were located."

Yuma, AZ

The hard fast thumping of the big M2 tore the air apart around the M-ATV. Nothing else sounded like one, and there was a reason why Ma Deuce has seen every war the U.S. has officially and unofficially fought in since John Browning designed it in the early twentieth century. Roughly five hundred rounds per minute ripped through all that stood in front of it in the practiced short controlled bursts fired by Kirk.

Twilight was beginning to break into dawn, removing the MSOT advantage of night optic devices. One of the APCs lay in ruin on the bridge; another had fallen off into the river after trying to evade the third, which lay burning to the north, blocking any escape the PLA forces had wanted to take. At least two dozen of the dismounts lay in ruin on the bridge in view. It was unknown how many were killed in the downed armored vehicles, but Aymond knew one thing for sure: there were nine more APCs, a radar truck, and some of the PLA bodies were starting to get up again. Quite undermanned and underarmed to be a true quick reaction force, the arrival of the second M-ATV helped Hammer and Snow break contact and gain some ground while the PLA's attention was diverted. It was all taking too long. They were stuck in a drawn-out battle, something they could not keep up for much longer.

"Hammer, kill the radar truck if you can, over!"

"Roger!"

Another 50-caliber round tore through the air, this time from the east, center punching the big rectangular antenna of the radar truck and rendering it useless.

"Good kill!"

Small arms fire thumped against the armored hull of the M-ATV.

"Chief, we've got to get moving or we're not going to have much of our ride left!"

Aymond nodded, his face set in stone, no emotion showing, just the hard eyes of an experienced operator thinking through a problem.

"Hammer, Snow, Happy, haul ass east on the eight, rendezvous at the Avenue 3E bridge, how copy?"

"Uh, Chief, Happy has the truck and is on the west side of the bridge."

Aymond grunted, the first outward sign of any emotion given during the battle. "Clear copy, Hammer. Happy, pop green smoke to pull attention away from Hammer and Snow, and then get north to Hammer and Snow. I don't care how you do it, just do it, how copy?"

"I'm clear, Chief, green smoke going out the door now, moving!"

"Kirk, one more burst, and then stop until I tell you different. Jones, get us moving back south. Go slow at first. We're going to rabbit them through town to our rendezvous point. Everyone clear?"

Various grunts and noises of positive affirmation could be heard among the Marines overcrowding the already cramped interior. The big M2 fell silent, and Jones sat stationary, the truck facing the north. Without the added benefit of the electronically zoomed display that Kirk had at the remote turret station, the APCs on the bridge appeared tiny. Slowly, green smoke began rising into the desert air to the west.

"Chief, it looks like they're splitting the mounted patrol into two groups."

Aymond nodded. "Kirk, give them a few more bursts to keep their attention."

The only answer given was the sound of Ma Deuce sending 50-caliber freedom prizes to the newly welcomed guests of America.

"Jones, pull forward about half a click. Then, Kirk, open up again. If they don't take the bait, then we'll have to drive back, motivate them a little, and then disengage and haul ass."

The heavy truck lurched forward more nimbly than would be expected before the tires chirped to a stop on the baked asphalt. The heavy machine gun opened fire again, and the staccato notes of return fire hitting the armor welcomed their presence.

"OK, turn us around and haul ass. Kirk, give our friends one more burst after we get moving, and then keep an eye on our six. I'm not really sure of the top speed of those APCs, but I want them kept close enough to feel like they're winning, but far enough away that they don't hard-kill the truck."

"Aye, Chief."

Jones shot forward, turning the wheel and bounding over the center median before slowing and speeding up again like someone trying to entice the fish to bite the bait on their line.

"We have six of the nine in pursuit, Chief."

Aymond nodded and keyed the radio. "Three unaccounted for, Hammer."

"Roger!"

Jones drove south on Business I-8 and into the heart of Yuma. "Chief, this is going to go right by our FOB."

"Yeah, I know, Jones. Assuming this works, we'll go back for the radar truck and our gear. If it doesn't, then we'll have to improvise a bit."

Internally, Aymond cringed. Improvising wasn't something he preferred to do. He planned and tasked, with plans to back up other plans and plans to back the back-up-plans.

"Save your ammo, Kirk, as long as they keep up the chase."

"Got it, Chief."

Jones swung the big truck from curb to curb, dodging Zeds and abandoned vehicles in the road. Aymond watched the road signs go by, trying to imagine the layout of the town he used to be familiar with.

"Jones, left now!"

Jones ripped the steering wheel hard left, the big M-ATV leaning on the long travel suspension, tires squealing on the pavement.

"Sorry, I remembered what street we needed when I saw the shopping center."

Jones shrugged, the classic shrug of an indifferent grunt just doing what he's told.

"Chief, they made the turn."

"Good, Kirk, maybe they think we're trying to shake them."

"Uhhh... maybe, they've sped up and are gaining on us now."

Aymond keyed the radio. "Snow, SITREP."

"Situation is we're rolling; the report is that we didn't toss smoke because Hammer left the APCs with glory holes for the Zeds to fuck them through."

Aymond nodded. The smoke was a diversion; he was hoping to make the Chinese and Koreans believe there were more of them, or that air support was coming in to chew them up. Anything, as long as it distracted them long enough for the Marines' play to unfold and disappear.

"ETA?"

Happy keyed the radio. "Call it five mikes, five clicks."

Aymond didn't have to say be careful; running one hundred kilometers an hour or roughly sixty miles per hour on the Interstate would have been slow last year. This year it was ludicrously fast while trying to dodge Zeds and vehicles.

"Jones, speed up and then take Pacific southbound. Try to keep it at about fifty clicks."

"Roger that, Chief."

The M-ATV sped up slightly before braking hard to make the right turn onto Pacific Avenue.

"Take it to Business 8 and turn left, and then we're going to go left on 3E, clear, Jones?"

"Clear, Chief."

Aymond looked at his watch and then at the map in his head, calculating the time for their path and Happy's path. *This might just work.*

"Happy, when you get to the bridge, park it, set a hasty ambush, and check in."

"Clear, good copy."

Aymond's overloaded truck swung left back onto Business I-8, running alongside the north fence line of the air station. As they passed the end of the main runway, the intersection of Avenue 3E was in view. Discipline kept Aymond from keying the radio to request another situation report. He knew the SITREP would come when it came; he had to trust his teammates.

Jones turned the truck north on 3E, speeding back up once he was pointed in the right direction.

"Jones, once Kirk gives the word that the PLA made the turn, I want you to floor it."

"The lead vehicle just made the turn, Chief."

Jones didn't wait for any other instruction; his right foot slapped the accelerator pedal to the floor, and the big turbo diesel roared. They were quickly nearing the railroad tracks and then the bridge for the hasty ambush. With nothing but radio silence, Aymond was internally wishing for the radio call to come across the speaker.

"We're set, Chief!"

Cold, with no emotion in his voice, Aymond replied, "Roger. Keep your speed, Jones. Once we clear the overpass, try to make a turn off and get us up on the highway."

Jones nodded.

The bridges flew overhead, a gray concrete blur as Jones stood on the brakes, frowning at the abuse his truck was taking. They would need to get comfortable and give him at least three days to work over the M-ATV in a location that had the tools and parts he needed or the truck would end up as a combat loss. They already had too many asses in the truck for seats; the remaining three Marines would make one truck nearly impossible to travel with as a team.

Skipping the desert to avoid having to drive through some fences, Jones made the turn off onto the north frontage by bounding through the ditch and back onto the pavement. Reaching the Interstate, Jones bounced the truck through the center median as he raced to the other truck, Kirk already bringing the mounted M2 into the fray.

Five APCs lay in ruin, charred corpses falling out of the trucks that were burning. The second truck's 50-caliber M2 caught the pursuing PLA by surprise and at close range. The heavy rounds punched through the armored personnel carrier's light armor like cardboard.

Aymond keyed the mic. "OK, back to the FOB. We get the other truck, get our gear, and we get our asses out of Yuma. If the PLA have radio contact, then it might be raining APCs in a short time."

SSC, Ennis, TX

Steam filled the cavernous shower room. Like a high school locker room, stainless-steel shower heads protruded from the tiled walls and columns.

More like a damn prison.

Hot water poured off Amanda's nude form. Her hands against the tile wall, her head and neck under the shower spray, Amanda felt her tight muscles begin to release from the morning's PT session. She examined what she could see. With her legs lean and muscular and her stomach flat, this was the best shape she had ever been in and the hardest exercise program that she had ever attempted. Apparently, after the world ends and you're trapped in an underground prison sheltering you from the storm that rages on the surface, there's time to exercise.

Clint often joined her in the shower. Today he didn't, and she was thankful he didn't. Amanda knew she was leaving tomorrow, and she wasn't sure if she was capable of keeping up the ruse much longer. Especially if her boyfriend... ex-boyfriend... was trying to get laid.

Using the checklist in her mind, she clicked off all the items that she had loaded into her MRAP. There wasn't much, just the essentials of some food, water, fuel, and as much ammo as she could scavenge without being noticed.

The little notebook in the pocket of her battle rattle held the long key code to open the main door on the surface, the secret rising platform built into a forgotten shed in a small park on a small lake in the middle of Texas. If she found any other survivors, she could write down the number and give it to them with directions to the facility. Clint be damned, she was going to save her country at all costs.

With a flick of her wrist, the shower went from steaming hot to ice cold, sending a momentary shiver through her body at the sudden change, Amanda took a deep breath and felt awake, more alive than she had in weeks. Everything felt more real now that she had an actual plan and she was going to be able to actually help people. Turning the water off, Amanda pulled the crappy military-issue towel from the hook on the wall, brushed away most of the water, and wrapped her hair into the towel before picking up her rifle, which hung by the sling from another hook on the wall. As she walked past the sinks and mirrors, she stopped to admire her fit athletic body. The scars of child bearing shone red against her pale skin. Her heart sank momentarily while thinking about her children. Frowning, Amanda walked into the bunk area adjoining the showers and to her footlocker. Digging through the contents, she came up with a pair of scissors that she had pulled from the supply cache after first arriving.

Standing in front of the mirrors over the sinks once again, Amanda removed her towel and began cutting at her long hair.

Lost Bridge Village, AR

Warren walked near Andrew. Oreo kept watch up ahead with Mary as they walked down the hill alongside the tiny airstrip. Mary was nearly twenty yards in front of them. Oreo's ears were perked up and on watch duty, his tail wagging slightly; he would nudge Mary every so often to have his head scratched. In her hands, she held the pink rifle from the day before. Warren had his rifle slung over his shoulder nonchalantly as if this was all perfectly normal for life in the United States.

Well, it is normal now.

"Our little community here kept together before the end, but looking back I should have pushed to organize everyone better. We lost a lot of people to the dead at first. Welp, we're nearly there, just a bit further now."

They passed by a fenced-off pool and building.

"What's that, Warren?"

"That was the civic center. Now we use it mostly for our weekly meetings. Outside of that, the pool is practically worthless, so much chlorine in it that it would pro'bly damn near kill a man if he tried to live by drinking much of it."

"Couldn't you distill it?"

"Sure'n we could, but don't need to really. A few of us have wells dug, and the rest can take water from the lake. We made filter buckets out of rocks and sand to pour water through, and then we boil the water to kill off anything we can't see. Works all right."

"Seems like you and the others were well prepped when the end came."

"Welp, we was thinking we was, but sure enough, we have so much that would make life better if we had it."

Mary stopped at a driveway, the home's backyard ending at the shoreline. A lone metal tower behind the house stood out of the tops of the trees against the blue sky. She waited with Oreo for Warren and Andrew to walk up as well.

"OK, little one, go'n ahead and knock."

Mary walked up the drive and knocked smartly on the front door. A few moments later, a balding middle-aged man who looked like he'd lost a significant amount of weight recently opened the door. He smiled at Mary, looked puzzled by Oreo, and was shocked when he saw Andrew standing with Warren.

"Morn'n, Warren, Mary. Who's the stranger?"

"He flew in yesterday. His name is Andrew."

"Flew? How'd you fly in here, flap your arms real hard?"

"He's got an areoplane up on the strip, out of gas and needs unleaded, but he's met other survivors... he also has something for you to look at."

"Like what?"

"Plans for a homemade radio, picked it up on the shortwave, them peoples over in Nevada broadcast it along with instructions on Morse code."

"CW, yes, sir, I know it already. Y'all come inside and let me see the plans you wrote down. We'll see what it is, and then we'll try to find some gasoline for your plane. It's just that what we've got left, we're trying to keep for the boats so we can fish and eat."

Andrew nodded. "I can respect that. Just remember that fuel goes bad, and fuel with ethanol in it goes bad even faster."

"Yup, we know," Will said with a hard glance at Warren, who acted like he didn't hear the discussion.

As they walked into the house, candlelight flickered in the living room. Dark curtains hung over the windows in Will's house just like they did at Warren's house.

"What kind of radio you have in your plane? Does it still work?"

"I have nothing. It didn't work, so I took it out to save weight."

"Huh. Well most of my shit got fried by the EMP... sorry, Mary. My radios were fried by the EMP. All I have left are a couple of cheap Chinese dual-band handhelds, for all the good they'll do you with only four watts of power and no way to charge them. Besides, who you going to talk to on two meter? All the repeaters are down, too, at least all the ones I could reach with those little things."

Andrew joined Will as he brought the candle from the living room and sat down at the dining room table. After handing Will the notebook and his notes, they all watched in silence as Will copied the notes onto a legal pad, nodding his head with a crooked smile.

"Yes, sir, top band with a spark-gap radio... this will work, this will work just fine. We're gonna have to get creative to build this antenna. First, we need to build a power source."

"They have directions for that too. I wrote them on the next page."

Will nodded and turned to the next page, reading intently.

"No, that design won't work. Well it will work, but it will just be hard to use. I have a better idea."

Saint George, UT

"Let's get a move on, vaquero."

Chivo grunted at Angel's remark. Angel led the afternoon's happy trail ride of two. Chivo followed Angel as they rode down the jagged desert hillside about a quarter mile north of the compound. This was the flattest descent and the only one the horses could take to head east without going back to the Interstate. Moments later, the horses' hooves clopped along the sunbaked asphalt of the now-defunct neighborhood.

"We cleared about half of these homes before giving up on finding anything useful. We evaluated the risk for the reward and decided to leave whatever forgotten supplies sat in these homes until we needed them, assuming that there is even anything worth needing left in the first place. I think our perspective of what we need might change in a couple years."

Chivo nodded, the reins of his horse held softly, which both surprised and didn't surprise Angel. Angel had heard rumors that Special Forces in Afghanistan had been using horses. It seemed like a random skill for a top-level operator to have, but Angel knew he was biased since he loved his horses. Snaking their way through yards with desert landscapes and crossing unfinished cul-de-sacs with half-built homes made it feel like they could be riding horses on Mars, except for the random homes in which the dead thumped against the windows trying to get out at a fresh kill as it passed. Trapped in their homes for all eternity. Chivo didn't know which was worse, living in the new world or the possibility of never quite being able to die.

Reaching the eastern edge of the subdivision, the pair were again crossing red dirt and desert. This time, they were close to I-15, much closer than Chivo would have liked, but the geography made them take this route. If they'd taken a different route further north, it would have added hours to their journey, increasing their time of exposure to danger and leaving the compound less protected longer than if they were there.

Chivo looked at the shimmering Interstate. The dead still owned this stretch of road, but their numbers were thinning with each passing day. He knew that every day that lapsed was another day that the other group could launch another surprise attack. Next time, they might not be so lucky as to only lose one member of the group. Operations such as this were a delicate balancing act, running down the high wire at full speed with no net to catch you. One little mistake could be the end. Chivo felt his horse tense up, quarters quivering, close enough to the dead to smell the rotting stench. The air around them buzzed with black flies. Petting the side of his horse's neck, Chivo tried to keep his mount as calm as he could. If his horse bucked him off, he would fall off the high wire. If the horse bolted, he would fall off the high wire. If a number of things out of his immediate control happened, he would fall off the high wire.

Rounding the edge of the hillside, their path turned more northerly and away from the teeming mass of death to the south. Truck yards full of CONEX containers sat in their path; the chain-link fences, CMU-made walls, and barbed wire fought to keep intruders out of the trucking firm's property, which made sense before the end.

"Angel, you guys could scavenge all these fences and build an outer perimeter or a series of concentric rings. The cliff on one side trumps it all, but adding layers of security will slow down future attacks."

Angel looked at the fences, nodding. "That's a good idea, but it would be hard to accomplish on horseback. We need a truck or a trailer that we could team the horses to, but we don't have any harnesses for such a thing."

"Then get a truck."

"Sure, but you had a truck, and look where you are now."

Chivo shrugged and kept riding as they passed outside a trailer park wall; they turned to ride around the side of a duplex and into another subdivision. This was their last hurrah before reaching the wrecked truck. More homes held the dead, or so it seemed, for the sounds of the dead throwing their bodies and their heads against the windows to get out increased in frequency. Some of the homes were burned-out shells. The lack of emergency services after the fall of society left homes to burn to the slabs and fire to spread as the wind blew it. Modern cars sat dormant in the twin driveways of the duplexes, except for one lone old Beetle that had been converted into a Baja-style Bug. Chivo didn't say anything, but he made a mental note to check the car on the way back.

Eventually, the pair reached the back of the squat convenience store and gas station on the corner, the last bit of cover before possibly having to enter the open area and be dangerously close to the Interstate and the chumming swarm of death it held. Dismounting, Chivo handed his reins to Angel. Still around the back of the convenience store, Chivo snuck around the edge to check for any threats before really reconning the area. The traffic lights were knocked over, the truck was a burned-out shell, and the bodies of the undead had melted and charred into the blackened pavement near the truck where they had caught fire. The scene was as gruesome as Chivo had ever seen in a long professional career of unique combat experiences. Binoculars now held up to his eyes, he scanned the scene in more detail. The fuel cans were nowhere to be found, presumably burned into the pavement, but Chivo expected nothing less with such a fire. Following the line from the damaged bridge railing where the truck had taken flight to where the truck crashed, he continued scanning along that path to find where the contents of the truck bed might have landed.

In the rock-lawn landscaping of the convenience store lay his prize, a long Pelican case, still latched. Behind one of the large rocks in the landscaping was a bit of green poking out. Chivo hoped it was some of their gear. Angel and his husband had a lot of gear cached, but anything extra would be an added benefit. Besides, Chivo didn't want to use up too much of the group's resources. They might need them after he and Bexar left.

Chivo returned to Angel and the horses. "Tie'em off. I found it. I'm going to dart out there to get it; I need you to hold cover for me just in case I missed something."

"Got it." Angel tied the reins to the electrical box on the back of the building and took a kneeling position on the edge of the corner. Chivo gave him a thumbs up and darted in a low crouch to a space between two palm trees in the store's landscaping. Waiting and scanning for a moment before darting again, Chivo reached the Pelican rifle case and found one of the gear bags they had brought from Cortez. Shouldering the bag, holding the rifle case, Chivo made one hard sprint for the building. Dead were falling off the bridge to a hard crunch on the burned pavement below. Trying to reach their new prize, the dead streamed out into the open from around the gas station across the street, their awkward, shambling gait slow but never ending. Chivo could hear them, but he didn't look back to see them as he sprinted, not slowing down until he passed Angel and the relative safety of the back of the building.

"No times to check your gear now, a bunch of dead are giving chase to the little Mexican that could."

Chivo smirked, tied the rifle case to the side of the saddle, and wedged the gear bag under his elbows and sort of in his lap. They left in a slow trot to gain some distance from the advancing dead, which made it around to the back of the convenience store just as they left.

Groom Lake, NV

The concrete at the bottom of the stairwell was darkly stained, blood smeared the walls, and it all smelled wretched. Jessie coughed and threw up at the smell. Leaning over the handrail of the stairs, she finished with a couple of dry heaves before spitting and trying to wipe the spittle and snot from her red face.

"Sorry. Pregnant nose."

"What?" Erin looked perplexed.

Sarah smirked. "Pregnancy is weird. You have to pee all the time, you can't remember what you were doing or why you came into a room in the first place, and your nose is really sensitive. Morning sickness is a cruel joke. It is really all-day sickness and with your newly found superpower of supersmell, it doesn't take much to set off losing what food you were able to keep down in the first place."

"That sounds horrible."

"It is," Jessie gasped, still trying to regain her bearings. "OK, well I think I'm done with that for now. The bottom floor is supposed to be the lab. Let's see what's behind door number one."

Jessie held the keycard against the RF reader, and the little LED light on the reader turned from red to green, the door lock releasing with an audible click. Jessie opened the door and held it open. Darkness greeted them. Erin loudly slapped her hand against the door frame a couple of times, but nothing stirred in the darkness.

"We should have brought something to hold the door open with."

"Mom has a point."

"She does, so if we see a door stop or something that we can use for one, grab it, and we'll take it with us."

Sarah and Erin nodded in agreement with Jessie as they switched on the lights mounted on their rifles. The bright lights piercing the dark room brought no surprises. No alien corpses, no dead, nothing but a dank-smelling foyer that could have been in any government building in America. Erin stepped into the dark room, flicking the light switch on the wall up and on, only to be greeted by another locked door with an RF reader for access.

Two for two, Jake's ID opened the doors they'd found, and the trio of women found themselves in the most secret lab of the U.S. government. It was empty, and Erin was again disappointed that there were no aliens.

"You would think with all the technology and the secrecy that there would have to be an alien in the mix somewhere."

Jessie looked at Erin as they pulled open the cabinets looking for anything interesting.

"Come on, what about the pyramids? Didn't you ever see that guy on TV talking about that?"

"The guy with the crazy hair?"

"Yeah."

Sarah raised her hands in front of her face like she was on TV. "But what if… aliens."

Jessie and Sarah both started laughing, until Jessie snorted, and then all three of them began laughing so hard that Jessie had to sit down.

Catching their breath, they turned out the lights and shut the doors behind them as they left. Standing in the stairwell once again, looking at the dark stains and now puke on the floor, Erin asked the question that all three of them were thinking: "Has anyone seen a zombie go upstairs before?"

Jessie shook her head. "No, but it doesn't matter. Always take the high ground. Make them fight up to you if they're dead or alive. Now I need to get out of this horrible stairwell before the dry heaves start up again."

Starting up the stairs, Jessie wondered how this pregnancy would go. Keeley's was easy, or at least her memory of the pregnancy was that it was easy. She knew about the blessing of giving birth; once you hold your newborn in your hands for the first time, all the memories of the terrible trials of pregnancy and childbirth begin fading away.

SSC, Ennis, TX

Amanda sat on her bunk eating her dinner. After her shower and haircut, she'd cleaned her rifle and pistol, disassembling each magazine one at a time to clean them and check the springs. Her gear reassembled and ready for the morning, she ate quietly and wondered where Clint had been; she hadn't seen him all day. The facility was quite large for being underground, but being the only two people in it meant that you tended to bump into each other a lot unless you disappeared on purpose. Even when she tried to do that, Clint would magically find her, *accidently* of course, and inquire as to what she was doing. Today he had been a ghost, until he walked into the bunkroom.

"I see you got your hair done. Get your nails did too?"

Amanda held up a hand, calloused from the pull-up bar and weight room, in front of her face and feigned blowing on her fingernails, which were cut short and unpainted.

"Yup! Now I'm just waiting for my facial and cucumber wrap while I eat my organic locally sourced MRE while wearing a pistol on my hip."

"There you go; the President deserves to be pampered a bit now and again."

"Where were you all day? Run to the store or something while I was getting my hair done?"

"Nope, I took the day off and spent it on the lake fishing."

"Seriously?"

"No, but I did spend some time up top pulling down some of the HESCO, so it looked more weathered and wouldn't give us up with SATINT."

"With what?"

"Satellite intelligence,. Remember, I have to assume that the Chinese and Koreans are jamming our ability to update imagery, but they probably still have full access to theirs. We need to keep ourselves under a dark rock for a good while until everything blows over, and having the entry gate completely blocked would stick out like a poodle at the dog track."

"Did you contact Groom Lake and warn them?"

"No, you know we can't do that. We have to run completely dark. Cliff knew what was up; he should have warned them before he left."

"He didn't know he wasn't coming back."

"Well, he should have finished up his task by now; hopefully he'll be back in the next few days. Depending on his outcome, we might be able to come out of the shadows."

"Why is that?"

Clint's expression didn't change, but he didn't answer.

"No, seriously, what was his mission, or what is his mission? After all we've been through together you still keep secrets."

"Don't we all?"

Amanda tried to keep her facial expression neutral, but she doubted she did it as well as Clint, who seemed to flip his emotions off and on like a light switch. "Honey, I'm an open book, and you're always a dark hallway."

"I'm sure."

Clint striped out of his utilities and walked into the shower room naked, dark scars on his back betraying his fit body.

Shit. He knows something is up. Will he try to stop me? Should I leave early? What if he blocked the exit while he was topside?

Her mind spun faster and faster before she finally took a few deep breaths and realized there was nothing she could do about it at the moment. If she tried to leave now, it would tip her hand. If she waited until just before sunrise as planned, nothing changed, except if her path was blocked. If Clint had taken steps to stop her, she might have a chance to figure it all out before he realized she was trying to leave.

So many problems, and all of it caused by one asshole at the end of the world.

Yuma, AZ

"Marines, we have a choice. We can't go west because that's where we came from. I don't want to go south because we'll quickly be in Mexico, and we need to find friendly forces to help bring the fight back to the tangos. Do we go north or east?"

Aymond stood next to the loaded trucks, which idled loudly, his team standing in a half circle around him.

"We don't have much time to chat about this, gentlemen. We have to assume the PLA is about to make it rain and we're out of umbrellas."

"Did you actually just say that out loud, Chief," Gonzo replied.

A mixed response of "north" and laughter was all that came after from the rest of the men.

"OK, north it is, but why north?"

"Fucking Vegas, Chief. We're going to get us some shore leave and party."

"Sure, Happy, of all the places in the world that survived, Vegas would be it."

"We could also see the Hoover Dam, Chief."

"I've always wanted to hit up Area 51; I want to see some spaceships."

"And aliens."

"Hammer, Snow, fine. You two can hold hands and go be fucking tourists in the ruins of our country. Maybe as high rollers, you'll get comped a room. The rest of us are going north with purpose. Load it up!"

Nothing else was said. The Marines took their spots in the two M-ATVs, while Jones took the driver's seat of the radar truck. They drove out of their HESCO-lined position to the wilds unknown. Aymond wondered if the Hoover Dam might be a good place to take a low-key defensive position under all that concrete, before realizing it would be catastrophic if the dam were bombed or if it failed for some reason.

Pulling out onto Highway 95 and pointed northbound, Kirk finally asked, "So where are we headed, Chief?"

"You chuckleheads want to go to Vegas, we'll go to Vegas, but I want to see if any PJs are hanging around Nellis. We could use some of them in our merry band of raiders."

"That we could, Chief, that we could."

Lost Bridge Village, AR

Andrew enjoyed the best dinner that he and Oreo had eaten in some time and all out of a household fireplace, cooked in a single Dutch oven. It was amazing. Either it was amazing or his standards had slipped significantly since the fall of man; regardless, he felt welcomed and happy amongst his newly acquainted fellow survivors, which was better than some of the receptions he'd had in the past few weeks.

"Andrew, where was you saying that you saw the military units?"

"I'm not sure they were actually military units. They were driving military vehicles in a short convoy and appeared to be wearing camouflage uniforms, but I gave them a wide margin for fear they weren't military and weren't friendly. Overall, I've had much better luck landing next to small communities that have built up and walled off."

"Walled, how walled?"

"Well, I've seen a little of everything, Will. The best I saw was a ring of those metal shipping containers that they put on train cars. The guards could walk on top of them and shoot from an elevated position if necessary."

"I can see it. Those containers are hard to come by 'round these parts. Besides we got no way to move something heavy like that."

"Do you need it, with the lake at your back?"

"We need sumth'n. We get about a dozen a week falling down the hillside into our neighborhood here."

"A dozen? You should be so lucky. Tomorrow I can show you my atlas. I've been tracking massive swarming herds of the dead, like bison of the old frontier, roaming the countryside but destroying all they find. I've see cars pushed off bridges, lights knocked down. I even saw a couple houses knocked over from the sheer relentlessness of them all together. Scariest thing I've seen so far. I can't imagine how someone would survive if caught in the middle of a swarm."

Will and Warren both looked at Andrew with surprised expressions.

"The worst part," Andrew continued, "is the smell and the flies. Sweet Jesus, the flies are bad, like a thick dark cloud. I made the mistake of trying to figure out what the pulsing cloud was when I first saw it and flew down next to it all. Took me a solid hour to wipe all the dead flies from my windshield and the leading edges of my wings."

They all sat in silence for a moment, Warren and Will imaging what Andrew was describing and Andrew reliving the scene in vivid detail.

"So, uh, Will, what is your plan for a better power supply for the radio? What's wrong with the one they described?"

"Their plan means that you have to keep cranking with one hand while you tap out your message with'n the other. Nope, I'm going to use a bicycle on a stand to turn an electric motor from my workshop to charge a car battery. All I'm have'n to do is modify the motor and the bicycle and make a stand. The rest is the easy bits."

"So what first?"

"First is you go on back up the hill with Warren before it gets dark. First light, I'll be up to start build'n, and you come on down here and help. Sound good to you, Warren?"

"Yes, sir, it does."

"Great, be see'n you in the morning. God's speed to you all."

Will stood up and scraped the remaining food on his plate back into the Dutch oven, set the plate on the hearth, and walked to the back of the house.

"Mary, it's time to go, Princess."

Mary stood, checked her rifle, and walked to the front door, Oreo plodding along beside her with his tail wagging. Outside the sky was already glowing with the mix of yellow, red, and blue of the setting sun. Nightfall was quickly approaching. Warren and Will knew what all the rest of the survivors knew: the night belonged to the dead. You can't see them, and they can't see you, but they can hear you, and they seemed to have a supernatural ability to triangulate sounds to find you from surprising distances.

Saint George, UT

The firepit glowed, the wood popping and hissing. Chivo's big 50-caliber rifle lay propped up against his chair while he sipped on John's homebrew, a reward for such a successful day. Thanks to the horses, he and Angel were able to redirect the pursuing dead away from their path back to the compound. After testing the rifle, with Bexar sitting at the spotting scope to call out shot placements on targets, Chivo declared the optic sound and the rifle to be in proper working order. The only disappointment was the loss of one of the gear bags, but for such a bad wreck, overall the outcome was quite positive. Guillermo and the others not sitting watch duty finally left them alone after wanting to hear every detail of the day's action. Chivo didn't consider it a day of action at all, but when compared to living in a well-prepped fenced-off compound, he guessed it seem like an adventurous story.

"Like a slug-bug?"

"Yeah, but Baja style, off-road tires and cut-off fenders and such."

"Does it run?"

"Hell if I know, mano. I just saw it today, and we had to make up some shit to keep the dead from following us home like some lost fucking puppy."

"So what next?"

"Next, you get healed up and fast. While you're healing, I'm going to take care of Guillermo and Angel's problematic associates, and then we check the VW and bug out quick like."

"Wow, bug out? Really?"

Chivo smirked. "What, mano, like you wouldn't make that joke if you had the chance."

Bexar said nothing and raised his pint glass as acknowledgement.

CHAPTER 5

Amanda dressed in the dark, putting on utility pants and a T-shirt, the typical uniform of the day at the SSC. Clint appeared to be sleeping in his bunk across the room. She looked at her dark bunk, the white sheets and wool blankets. They had shared a bed, pushing two of the bunks together. After shrugging into the smaller tactical carrier she used day-to-day and slinging her rifle over her shoulder, she looked across the room into the shadows and at the dark form of Clint's body.

I should kill him. If I killed him now, then he couldn't stop me... no.

Frowning, Amanda walked out of the bunkroom as quietly as she could. As angry as she was with Clint, she wouldn't kill him. The ugly honest truth pulsing through her thoughts was that she wasn't all that angry at Clint. She was angry at herself for acting so foolish.

That was the last time. Never again. I have a country to salvage... if there is one left.

Each quiet step through the corridors emboldened her mood, made her more confident that her choice was the only right choice and that she could succeed, would succeed. A few minutes later, she stood next to *her* MRAP. After she unplugged the block heater, Amanda shrugged out of her smaller tactical carrier and put the fatigue jacket on over her T-shirt. Then the heavier armor carrier that she left stashed in the truck went over that. The steam from her breath hung in the cold underground tunnel; each breath sounded thunderous, her heartbeat thumping so loudly in her ears that Amanda worried it would wake Clint. Shaking her head, Amanda climbed into the heavy MRAP and looked at the few cases of MREs, stacks of ammo in green metal cans, and water in the plastic jerry cans that she had cached since first forming her plan.

"Well, shit, here goes nothing."

Switches turned to the on/run selection, a push of a button, and the starter groaned to push the turbo diesel before it coughed to life, thunderously rattling in the tunnel.

Dear God, that's loud. He has to know now. He's going to…

Amanda took a deep breath and rapped her knuckles against the driver's side window, which didn't make a sound. Heavily armored and powerful, as long as she didn't tip the truck over or seriously damage a tire, she thought she would be fine.

After pushing Drive, Amanda drove through the tunnel toward the exit, and her journey began with no sign of Clint.

SSC Command Center

Clint sipped the instant coffee, which had grown cold over the last two hours. A few keystrokes later, the closed-circuit monitor turned from greens and black hues to color, the lights in the bunkroom now illuminated. Amanda's bunk showed empty covers left askew. On his bunk, a pile of pillows lay under the covers. On another monitor, the MRAP drove slowly through the tunnel to the far north exit. He was fairly sure that Amanda didn't know where she was going to emerge on the surface, but Clint knew the exact spot and wished he still had overhead imagery so he could see what Amanda did when she didn't recognize the remnants of the old road. Parts of the steel bridges were still in the lake, which he was sure the fish loved, but the road was gone. Two turns and the country roads would run into the highway. Clint pulled a road atlas out of the bag next to him, trying to remember which highway it was.

Finding the lake and Highway 287, he traced the route he believed Amanda would take to get to Groom Lake and shook his head. Amanda had no idea how perilous the route was. If she was smart enough to stay off the Interstates, she might have a chance. With a small ruler, he traced the route to scale and made some notes.

The direct route takes some twenty-two hours of driving. She will have to refuel at least every three hundred miles, and if she stays off I-40, it could take an extra five hours... probably five days there and then five days back, plus layover—except there would be no return trip.

Clint flipped the pages in the big spiral bound atlas and traced another route, making notes.

Sixteen hours. No return, two days of driving, another day to enter and complete the objective.

A few clicks of the computer mouse and the daily planner calendar for his username appeared on the screen. Clint counted the days off, trying to fit his plan just perfectly.

Groom Lake, NV

Jessie sipped green flavored water. She wasn't sure what it really was or what it was supposed to taste like, but it was made with green-colored powder and tasted like nothing else. Sarah drank dark hot coffee, which Jessie really wanted, but she'd sworn off caffeine for the pregnancy. Erin walked to the table holding a tray; she set it in the middle of the table, three plates for the three of them.

Jessie tried not to smell the powdered eggs covered in processed cheese that Sarah began eating and instead focused on trying to nibble at the food on her plate and keep down some of her dry white toast. Erin ate buttered toast.

Jessie put her toast down and pushed the plate away from her. "Which way do we go today, Erin?"

"Sideways."

Jessie looked puzzled. "Sideways?"

"Yeah, Jason told me that there's supposed to be another bunker toward the north via some tunnels; the computers that run this place are in another room that way too."

Sarah glanced at her daughter and then Jessie, raising her eyebrows, before acting like she couldn't hear the conversation and continuing to blissfully eat.

"When did you see Jason?"

"Last night, after his shift ended."

"Where were we?"

"Uh, sleeping."

Jessie glanced at Sarah, who was still playing the role of a deaf-mute mother, before she directed the conversation back to the beginning.

"Do we know how to get to those tunnels?"

"Not exactly, but *we* might have an idea where a secret door is hidden."

Sarah finally decided to be a part of the conversation. "Why a hidden secret door? We're in a secret hidden facility under a secret base that isn't supposed to exist?"

"Aliens?"

They all had a good laugh, before Jessie stood up and announced she had to pee again and left.

Sarah bussed the table while Erin followed Jessie, beginning a conversation about birthing and what a newborn was like. Jessie stopped, suddenly aware of the connection.

"You're not sleeping with him, are you?"

Erin looked hurt. "No, and if I were, what does it matter?"

Jessie glanced across the room to where Sarah was standing talking to one of Jake's "mayor staff" and then back at Erin.

"I guess you're right. It doesn't matter. It only matters if you get pregnant. Do you want to bring a baby into this... this new life of ours?"

The lights cut out, the soft hiss of the air system being replaced with the capacitor sound of the emergency lighting flickering on.

"See, here we are in the safest place I've found and they can't even keep the fucking lights on."

The doorway's exit sign glowed red above them. Erin shook her head.

"I think about your baby every day, and it isn't even born yet. I don't know what you're going to do. We can't live here forever. Eventually we have to move topside, and we need to be able to hunt, farm, and gather what we need. We're in the fucking desert and... and that just won't work. And, no, I'm not sleeping with him; he's just a friend who misses his dead wife. Everyone we know dies, and now your baby is coming, and your husband isn't even here, so I have to be ready. What the fuck else am I supposed to do?"

Tears streamed down Jessie's face while she gave Erin a hug. "Thank you."

Erin nodded, trying to act like she wasn't wiping her eyes as well. The lights came back on as Sarah made her way to them.

"What was that about?"

"Nothing, Mom. Jessie, don't you still have to pee?"

"Oh, God, yes!" Jessie walked away quickly.

"Are you OK, Erin?"

"Yes, Mom. What did that chick want?"

"That was Marcia; she's looking for Brit, and apparently she hasn't been seen in a few days."

"Good, that bitch should be hiding for her worthlessness. She nearly got bit for being an idiot."

Sarah didn't respond, only sighed as she followed Erin down the passageway to wait for Jessie so they could begin their hunt for the hidden door.

Lost Bridge Village, AR

Mary followed Andrew and Oreo out the front door, her pink rifle at the ready, and the intense glare of her eyes betraying her fierce soul. Satisfied that they were currently free of the undead, with Oreo's agreement, the three walked to Andrew's parked aircraft at the top of the ramp.

"What can you do with such a small plane?"

"We can go just about anywhere. It's a Husky, and it's designed to be abused by pilots in the Alaskan brush country. There are no roads between villages there, so aircraft ferry people, food, supplies, and medicine."

"You can't carry much in that though."

"No, Mary, you can't. It's not like driving a pickup truck or something, but when I say this can land and take off just about anywhere, I'm not kidding. One guy even had a bear attack his plane in the bush once. A buddy flew out a box of duct tape and in a few hours he was flying back to home to complete a repair that would be more pleasing to someone with the FAA."

"What is the FAA?"

"They're... they were in charge of pilots and airplanes in the U.S. before all this went down. See the numbers and letters on the vertical stab—the tail fin?"

"Yeah."

"That's the N-number, like a license plate. The N means this plane is based in the United States."

"Is it hard to fly?"

"Not too hard, just takes practice."

"Can you teach me?"

Andrew looked at Mary, her eyes no longer showing the hard stare of before; her eyes glowed brightly with delightful curiosity.

"We'll have to talk to Warren and find more fuel, but, well, maybe we could start with just a test flight first."

It wasn't a yes, but it wasn't a no either, Andrew couldn't bear to disappoint someone who needed some hope, but airplanes were rotting into the tarmac in their tie-down spots, and who knew how many pilots were even left. The road atlas in his hand, Andrew patted his leg, and Oreo returned to his side from across the airfield. He reached down to pat his friend on the head only to see Oreo startle at the touch. Andrew looked across the field at the tree line and back up the road out of the small lakeside community. He didn't see anything, but he hadn't stayed alive this long by not trusting Oreo. He knew trouble was coming before trouble even knew where it was going.

Quartzsite, AZ

The last watch finished their sleep rotation, and the short-hop from the Yuma overnight spot, a tiny spec of a town on I-10, was complete. Aymond had no desire to drive through the night into the unknown. With the complete lack of air support causing serious problems for his men as seen in the previous battle, he gambled that they could stop even if only traveling a few hours away, even if the PLA may be giving chase. The sun was up, and sleep rotations for a team took longer than sleeping through the night would normally take, but it was essential to get everyone rest and still maintain security.

Aymond stood on top of the lead M-ATV, binoculars to his face, slowly scanning the area. He couldn't tell if the destruction and desolation was just how
this town was or if the Zeds had caused it. Highway 95 North was the road they
needed to be on, but they had to cross I-10 first, which lay about seven hundred
meters to the north. No cars appeared to be on the bridge, which could be a
good sign or could be bad, meaning the bridge was no longer there.

"Ready to roll, Chief!"

"Fuel?"

"Siphoned and served out of those big RVs across the way."

"Roger that, Snow, load it up and roll."

Aymond climbed off the roof and took the front passenger position, pulling
the heavy armored door closed with a thud, noticing the new heavy-looking bags
hanging on the rail outside of the rear bay, a rainbow of colors.

The convoy pulled onto the highway and rattled northbound. Clicking the
comm-link push to talk, Aymond asked, "What's with the new fashionable-
looking rucks hanging off our rigs?"

Snow, passenger in the second M-ATV, replied, "Found some useful shit in
those RVs, Chief, thought we'd bring it along."

"Like what?"

"You know, Chief, a few gallons of milk, some yogurt, just about everything
from the fridges that would survive and add to our morale."

Aymond didn't respond to the joke, the silence growing louder with each
moment. Gonzo stopped the convoy. Aymond keyed again, "Bridge is out. Happy,
Hammer, and funnyman Snow, dismount and see what's up."

Kirk turned the remote turret left and right, looking for any threats. Gonzo
slowly rolled the lead truck to a slow walking pace, giving the dismounted
Marines a place to take cover if needed. Snow stopped at the ragged edge and
looked east and west along I-10 before keying, "Chief, the bridge is demo'ed,
lots of Zeds crushed by it. All the cars on the I-10 are pushed to the ditches, like
a huge dozer came through and destroyed everything.

Aymond thought for a moment. "Did the bridge seem to go east or west?"

"East... Chief, there's another bridge to the east and another bridge to the
west; they're both demo'ed as well."

"Options, gentlemen?"

Happy keyed, "Yeah, Chief, what if we backtrack, hit one of those small roads, go west, and make our way to where the other bridge was. We could use the on- and off-ramps to get around all these damn fences."

Aymond didn't have to ask why he wanted to go west. Aymond wanted to go west, too; a group of Zeds powerful enough to destroy bridges is something they didn't need right now.

"All right boys, mount back up. Do it like Happy said."

Westward the convoy went, passing a trailer park and more RVs before reaching an intersection with a truck stop. What Aymond couldn't figure out was why no Zeds came out of the areas with homes or RVs as they passed.

"Snow, when you went shopping did you find any Zeds?"

"Just a few that were trapped in their coaches, didn't see any out in the wild."

"Guys, if a passing horde of Zeds goes by, do you think it was like the Pied Piper, taking all the walkers out of town?"

Kirk was the first to respond. "Maybe, but let's clear I-10 and then this shit-hole town before we verify any wild guesses."

Aymond knew Kirk had a point.

The convoy easily drove down the Interstate on-ramp, crossed the median at a spot that appeared to be for just such a purpose, and then drove up the off-ramp, turning right and pointing north once again.

The sign said "Main Saint," but there wasn't much to it while they traveled east. Reaching the original route, the convoy turned north again. More RV parks flanked either side of the roadway. For once, Aymond was glad to see abandoned cars in the road, even if they did have to drive around them. It was a blessing in disguise—they weren't on a motivated Zed route. A smattering of businesses passed by, but not a single Zed to be seen. The scene was eerie, and Aymond could feel that he wasn't the only one whose alarm bells were ringing.

Quickly the small town was behind the convoy, and the open desert bloomed before them with nothing but hard, parched asphalt beneath their tires and some mountains in the distance. Forty-five minutes later, the convoy stopped just south of Parker, Arizona. In the town ahead, they could see the dead meandering through the middle of town with no real direction or purpose.

Those were the dead that Aymond was used to seeing; the thought of them somehow teaming up to bring down concrete bridges wasn't one that he wanted to consider.

Ennis, TX

Shortly after the whine of the massive hydraulic and screw set began moving, a crack of light appeared, dirt and sand falling off the edge to the concrete ramp where Amanda sat comfortably in the big MRAP. The crack of light grew and slowly the large heavy door rose, her eyes protested the sudden glare of morning sunlight. Amanda squinted and drove the big armored truck up the ramp and onto the surface.

Her trip to the SSC from Little Rock had been perilous, even with her two specially trained agents. However, that was mostly due to their Gulfstream jet being destroyed and having to acquire civilian vehicles along the route, which were not able to stand up to the abuse of warlike conditions.

This war against the dead, how long will it last? How long will we have to fight? How will we win... what if we don't win?

Amanda had a rough idea where she should be by the general layout of the facility, as far as she understood it. At the gate she could go right or left. Left led to a dirt trail, right led to a small road, so her first decision was an easy one. The huge door to the secret world below closed slowly behind her. After taking a deep breath, her resolve solidified, and onto the road she drove.

Passing unkempt pasture, Amanda took the first road to the right that she came to and traveled in a mostly northern direction. The highway sign said 287. There wasn't a bridge or on-ramp, just a divided rural highway. Indifferent to the stop signs, Amanda crossed and turned left.

I need a road map, so I need a gas station or a truck stop.

With nothing but open country and farmland in her view, the roadmap would have to wait. In her memory of arrival, Amanda had a rough idea of what highways she would be immediately using, and she knew that Highway 287 was her first significant road. Alone with her supplies, with no music to play for the trip, Amanda drove in silence at a blistering forty-five mph, thinking, planning, and contemplating all that had transpired since late December.

The roadway had some disabled traffic and a handful of shuffling undead that she easily passed without incident. The plan was to stay away from the Interstates if at all possible. That had gotten them to the SSC from Little Rock, and it would serve her well here too.

The minutes ticked by, as did the miles covered. The highway carved around the top of Waxahachie, becoming a strange mix of rural and highly developed seemingly at once. The highway signs still stood, which was a help. The blue highway sign had the logos of some gas stations on it for the exit, so she took the exit.

On the frontage road, abandoned cars sat dead in place staggered back from the dark stoplight. As carefully as she could, fearful of getting stuck, she drove the MRAP into the grass between the frontage road and the highway, around the abandoned cars, before bouncing over the concrete island and into the intersection. Stopped momentarily in the intersection, Amanda looked at the gas station on the corner. Three cars were in view at the pumps. The windows were smashed out of the building, but the large green-and-white sign still stood triumphantly. The slap of rotting hands against the rear of the armored truck startled Amanda back into the reality of what she was trying to accomplish. Amanda turned and drove sharply away, heading north before threading the needle between more cars to drive into the driveway of the gas station.

Parked between the gas station and a Waffle House, Amanda left the MRAP running, its nose pointed to the exit onto the frontage road so she could continue. The dead she left in her wake at the intersection were making their way toward her, and more came around from the back of the Waffle House. Amanda knew she didn't have much time.

In a quick walk, Amanda held her M4 at a low ready, scanning the dark interior of the gas station for any signs of movement and then checking around her to keep track of how close the closest threats were. If possible, Amanda wanted to conserve her ammunition; she only had so much with her, and she only had herself, so fire discipline would be up to her alone.

She didn't see any movement in the shadows, but the smell coming from the gas station was horrible. All the food had rotted, the few cartons of milk and anything else in the cooler. The smell mixed with the smell of the corpses chasing her into the pungent smell of the new world. The door was locked, but the glass was broken out of it, so Amanda stepped through the hole where the glass had once been and into the convenience store. Flies inside the store dive-bombed her eyes and ears. Behind the counter, she found a handful of fold-out roadmaps, all sealed in plastic so people couldn't use them to figure out the directions they needed without purchasing one first.

The sound of something hitting the door and then hitting the ground with a hard, hollow thud helped motivate Amanda to speed up her scavenge mission. She grabbed one of each on the rack without paying attention as to what they were maps of. Turning around, she saw a body get up off the floor, pieces of broken glass stuck into the skin of his hands and face. A second corpse tried to step into the small convenience store and tripped over the bottom of the door, falling to the ground with a similar sound as the first, making no attempt to catch himself. Looking past her two new visitors, she saw a small welcoming party forming on the side of the gas station that she had come from. Deciding that discretion was the better part of valor, Amanda stepped through the door on the south side of the store, leaving her trail of undead friends to trip their way through two doors to follow.

Sitting safely in the MRAP once again, Amanda drove out of the driveway and onto the frontage road to resume her westward course. While driving, she looked at each one of the road maps that she had acquired. She had a map for New Mexico, Texas, and Oklahoma, plus specific maps for Dallas/Fort Worth and Houston. Houston and Oklahoma wouldn't be useful to her for this trip, but the maps would be kept, just in case.

Stopping in the middle of the highway next to a sign indicating how far away she was from Dallas and Fort Worth, Amanda tore open the Texas map and the DFW map. It took her a few moments to find Waxahachie on the Texas map; tracing her finger along the line for Highway 287, she turned her attention to the DFW map. She had to go near Fort Worth, but she didn't want to have to go through it.

Groom Lake, NV

"This is where Jason said it would be."

"Maybe Jason was wrong, honey."

"I don't know, Mom, maybe, but maybe we aren't looking at quite the right place."

Jessie listened to Sarah and Erin but stood in the hallway with the door to a janitor's closet standing open. The storage closet had the usual janitorial supplies one would expect, except that it seemed larger than it should be. Stepping past the shelves, she saw why.

"Erin, Sarah, in here."

Past the shelves was a large metal door painted in battleship gray. The little panel on the wall next to it contained a keypad and an RF reader. None of them knew what the numeric code could be, but the door clicked open with the card that Jake had given them.

"This place is spooky."

"After all we've seen and done, Jessie now decides that a secret door in a secret facility at a secret base is what makes it spooky," Sarah quipped with a smirk. Erin laughed.

"You know what? Fuck you both! Why don't one of you lead the way inside." Jessie stood aside and held her arm out like she was holding open the door to a restaurant. Erin stepped into the hallway, followed by Sarah and Jessie. The door closed behind them with a hiss and a heavy thud.

Erin turned around to look back at the door, "OK, now that was spooky."

"See, told you."

"Children, girls, cut it out. We have work to do."

Jessie and Erin both replied sarcastically, "Yes, Mommy."

Gray concrete walls matched the gray metal door at the entrance. The overhead lights were spaced just far enough apart that there were hard shadows on the floor between each of them. After what Erin estimated to be around one hundred feet, the trio reached another gray metal door, a recessed camera above it. This time, there were no handles or knobs, just a smooth flat door, but there was another RF chip reader on the wall, and the small LED turned from red to green after Jessie placed Jake's ID next to the reader. The door slid into the wall instead of swinging out or in to open. Beyond the door on the left side was a bland-looking office full of government furniture, some fake plants, and a fake window painted on the wall. To the right were showers that looked sterile and cold, all completed in sealed concrete. They didn't see any other doors in the office and decided to walk through the shower room to see if there was anything else.

An opening in the concrete snaked around a wall and to another room. This room looked like a smaller version of the supply warehouse in the main facility. As they walked through the facility, the lights flickered on automatically in each area they entered. At each transition to another room, the concrete was raised like a mini-wall about a foot high that they had to step over.

"Think this uses the same power as the main facility? Think this is safe from the rolling blackouts we experience?"

Jessie and Sarah gave noncommittal grunts in return to the questions. Beyond the storeroom was a bleak hallway with hotelesque signs pointing left or right for the bunkroom, dining hall, and common area. Meandering aimlessly and silently, they walked toward the bunkroom first. Appearing to have enough space for about fifty people, the bunkroom was outfitted with the same sort of beds and lockers as theirs was in the main facility. The restroom and showers looked the same, except that there was no obvious delineation for male or female in the bunkroom, restroom, or showers. The dining room was another, and again smaller, copy of the main facility, but the common room was something new. There was a large TV with rows of DVD cases filling shelving along the wall, a pool table that converted into a ping pong table, and a dart board.

Sarah broke the silence first. "Looks like a crappy bar or a low-grade frat house."

"Except that there's no bar to be seen. If I had to live here, I'd need a strong drink handy."

Erin shook her head. "No, don't you two get it? This is supposed to keep a special group of people alive if the first facility gets compromised. The designers expected the first facility to be vulnerable to something. The walls we had to step over? Probably to trip someone if they're not paying attention... this was designed as a refuge if there was an outbreak in the main facility. The little walls are to trip the dead, to slow them down so the survivors could kill them."

"Then why don't we have those in the main facility?"

"I don't know, Mom."

"What if it's because the zombies were too secret, like above top secret or whatever it is, so secret that even those who worked and lived in a secret underground facility at a secret base weren't to be trusted with the information?" Jessie said.

"Now that's damn creepy," Erin said, looking around the room. "If we've found all we can find, then I want to get back to the normal secret-alien-base shit."

Everyone agreed. They quickly finished checking for any more doors and retraced their steps until they were in the welcoming office with the showers. A small sign above the entrance to the showers stated "DECONTAMINATION," but they weren't sure who would be decontaminated from what. The next to last door opened to a dark hallway.

"Were these lights on or off before we stepped into the hall the first time?"

Jessie shrugged. "I don't know, maybe off?"

Erin rolled her eyes, clicked on the weapon light on her rifle, and stepped into the darkness. The other two followed. The RF pad's LED wasn't lit green or red; it appeared to be off. Jessie tapped the ID against it a few times and got no response. Erin pushed on the door and was surprised to find it unsecured. The janitor's closet was dark, and the hallway seen through the open closet door was dark.

"Now *this* is spooky, Jessie." Erin cautiously stepped through the janitor's closet, Sarah and Jessie following.

"Maybe it's just a normal blackout, but we answered our own question. Past the camera door, it is on separate power; the hallway through to here is on this facility's power."

Everyone nodded in agreement with Jessie, not that they could be seen in the darkness.

From deep inside the main facility, they heard screams and rapid gunfire.

MSOT, Parker, AZ

The town seemed to consist completely of low-roofed strip-center shopping, gas stations, and palm trees. Zeds swarmed the convoy as they rolled through the middle of town, but they were too few to be an issue to the Marines. Soon they were crossing the Colorado River to take a left onto Route 62. The convoy climbed along the highway up the desert mountains, and any trace of civilization seemed to fall away. The convoy poked along at fifty mph in a part of Arizona so remote that it seemed even the wildlife commuted.

The minutes ticked by slowly, the hours following. Aymond checked his watch for the sixth time in as many minutes. Eventually they turned right onto Highway 95 and were pointed north again. In the back, the other Marines were sleeping.

"You going to be good to drive longer?"

"Yeah, Chief, no worries."

Aymond nodded and leaned against the door, falling asleep quickly.

It took a moment for his mind to snap back into place. "Chief, time to get up." Gonzo was shaking him.

"What, Gonzo?"

"Chief, we're in Needles, Arizona. The problem is that this highway jumps on Interstate 40 for a while."

"Is it overrun or has a herd of Zeds leveled everything?"

"Don't know yet, we're closing on it right now, wanted you awake for it."

Aymond nodded.

As they approached the overpass for I-40, it appeared to be intact. Gonzo drove under it and turned left, following the highway signs. Taking the ramp onto I-40, they saw that the cars on the Interstate were pushed from the center, but the damage wasn't as intense as they had seen on I-10.

"Same thing, just not as much. Maybe it was a smaller group of Zeds." Gonzo shrugged.

"Well, keep on going; we'll have to figure it out along the way."

Looking out the small bulletproof window, they could see that the town they were passing teemed with Zeds. Most of them didn't appear to notice the convoy passing by, but that could change in an instant. Quickly they were past the town and in the desert, and shortly after that Gonzo followed the signs and turned north on Highway 95. If Aymond was remembering correctly, they wouldn't hit another town until they were just outside of Las Vegas.

Lost Bridge Village, AR

"Bob said to be bringing the parts we got down to the comm'nity build'n before lunch. I'd bring your maps too. I think most everyone is going to be there, and they mean to hear about your travels."

Oreo followed Mary out of the kitchen and into the garage and then followed her back into the house as she carried the box of parts they had assembled the previous evening. It was their contribution to the radio. In the past day and a half, word had spread outside of the circle of Warren, Andrew, Mary, Bob, and Oreo to include the entire small community. Andrew hoped like hell the radio would work. These people were longing for something, anything positive to give them some hope. Now he regretted bringing up the massive herds of the dead, the destruction left in their wake. Nothing good could come from scaring these nice people with his stories. Looking down, Andrew saw Oreo sit at his feet.

They're not stories, it's the truth, guy.

I know, but the truth sucks, buddy.

The new world sucks.

The old world sucked.

OK, but Mary?

She'll be OK, she's more OK than you are.

Andrew looked away from Oreo's stare and at the wall, shaking his head, realizing he had just had a silent discussion with his dog in his mind.

"Warren, that's great. It will be nice to have some conversation with other people for a change." Andrew made a sideways glance at Oreo, who started wagging his tail.

Soon they were out the front door, ponytail and pink rifle leading the way, Oreo prancing along beside her, his ears erect and alert. The sun had begun chasing away the cool morning air, resulting in a beautiful day. In a blink, they were in the big multipurpose room, parts that Bob needed, many of which weren't on the broadcasted list, spread across a handful of folding tables. A few had brought hot Dutch ovens with a bit of a potluck lunch for everyone, and a few held watch by the windows that faced the road. Everyone was armed, and it was obvious that everyone knew one another.

The next few minutes were a bit of a blur, Andrew shaking hands with nearly three dozen men and women. A small group of children sat at a table away from all the frenzy to play a board game. Andrew noticed that all the older kids were also armed with a mix of pistols and small rifles. This wasn't the first group of survivors he'd met in which he encountered strict security rules, but this was one of the first times he wasn't so sure that everyone wasn't like this before the attack.

"How much fuel do you need?"

"Uh... the bladders can hold about fifty gallons, plus my can... fifty-five or so would completely fuel the aircraft, but I'll be thankful for whatever I might be able to trade for or have."

"Where are you from?"

"Have you met others?

"Are there any other close survivors?"

"Have you seen Little Rock? Is there anything left?"

"What about the military, seen any?"

The group of men and women swarmed him, questions flying. The whole scene was overwhelming, and Andrew had experienced it before. All the survivors wanted to hear news, good news especially, but anything from the outside was welcomed. Andrew tried to answer, but before he could even start answering a question another question was asked. The group was nearly shouting questions at him by the time Warren stepped into the middle.

"Now all y'all hold on just a minute. Andrew is our guest, and you all should be treat'n him better than this. Why don't we get the fold'n chairs out. We can all sit while Andrew is nice enough to tell his story and give us any news he can remember. Once he's done, then maybe your questions will have answers."

A handful of muffled sorries were heard as the group released its crushing weight from around the pilot, and were replaced by the sounds of metal folding chairs coming out of the storage room and being set up.

Andrew looked around the room a little bewildered before finding Oreo lying at Mary's feet while she played the board game with the other children, eyes closed but ears up and twitching. *You little bastard, what about me?* Oreo peeked at Andrew with one eye open before letting it droop closed again. Shaking his head slightly, Andrew walked to the chair Warren offered.

"Thank you, Warren... thank all of you for your kindness. Well, let me start by saying things are both better and worse than you think they are out there."

Andrew continued his meandering talk for close to an hour, turning the pages of his atlas to show his notes and marks, describing the other survivor groups, the massive herds of the dead, and every detail he could think to talk about. The group remained silent and quite motionless the entire time, all eyes focused on Andrew and his atlas. After Andrew finished, everyone remained silent. He expected a lot of questions, not this uncomfortable silence, which was thankfully interrupted by Bob.

"I think we're ready to string the wire for the antenna."

Most everyone stood and went outside to see what Bob was going to do for the antenna. Two wooden electric transmission poles stood about one hundred and fifty feet apart from the main driveway down to the edge of the parking lot. The lines weren't live; just like all the electrical lines in the U.S. that Andrew had seen, they had no electricity flowing through them. Bob directed two men on ladders leaning against the poles and another who was on a ladder under the middle of the wire between the poles as they hung the smaller cable Bob was using for the antenna. After about thirty minutes the work was done, and a wire snaked across the parking lot into the building. One of the older kids, a young teenager, was already on the bicycle made into a generator and pedaling in a steady rhythm, shifting gears as the rear wheel spun in a blur. The small bank of car batteries connected together had a lone voltmeter wired at the end, the needle slowly climbing off the zero pin. Bob sat down at the table. The radio looked like something in the background of a mad scientist's lab in a movie, but Bob seemed confident that it wouldn't shock him and would work.

Once the needle reached the mark Bob had drawn on the dial, the battery bank's voltage was high enough to power the radio properly. Bob made sure the power switch was off and counted the coils wired on the stand next to the main box, moving alligator clips to the desired spacing. The group all seemed to hold their breath as Bob arranged his pencil, notebook, and the odd-looking device that he called the "key." Once settled, Bob flipped the switch on the radio.

Nothing happened, and the group stood silent for a moment before starting to grumble, having expected immediate communication to start pouring in, like turning on a car's FM radio. Bob waved his hand dismissively at the grumbles and tapped the key lightly; the wire strung between the insulated ends of spark plugs from his truck buzzed with a visible spark of electricity popping across the gap. A couple people gasped, and a few laughed.

"That's why it's called a *spark-gap* transmitter, folks. "Bob smiled and began slowly tapping out a message, using a handwritten chart next to him with markings for each letter. Finished with the short message, Bob waited and repeated the transmission with no response.

"Warren, did you bring the shortwave?"

"Ye'sir, like you asked."

Warren handed Bob the hand-cranked shortwave radio. After cranking the radio for a couple of minutes, Bob turned it on and tuned it to the original transmission frequency from Groom Lake. Only static was heard. Bob tuned the radio up and down the shortwave bands, but there was nothing but static around the frequencies that Groom Lake had been heard on previously.

"Well, they're a few hours behind us. Maybe they're not up yet. We can try again this evening."

"Maybe they're dead," an anonymous voice called out from the back of the crowd.

"Maybe they are, but even if they are, maybe there are others like us who made a radio. This radio is a wonderful idea; we're not going to give up on it yet."

As the afternoon continued, different children and a few adults took turns on the bicycle to generate power as asked by Bob. Slowly and piece by piece, the crowd left to walk to their homes. By dinner time, the only people who remained were Bob, who continued to transmit and wait patiently, Mary, who napped in the corner with Oreo curled up against her, Warren, and Andrew, who sat quietly, exhausting the topics of conversation of the day.

"Bob, are you going to work into the night, or are you going to actually get some sleep?"

"Andrew, why don't you take Mary and Warren back up to their house. I'm going to keep at it for a while."

Andrew nodded, stood up, and stretched, snacking on the remaining potluck lunch, which substituted for dinner. Warren scooped Mary off the floor and held her in one arm, still sleeping, her head on his shoulder, and picked up her rifle with the other hand. Andrew was a little surprised; Warren was stronger than he appeared. Oreo yawned and plodded along next to them as they sauntered up the hill to Warren's house, slowly racing the setting sun. Both of them knew that Bob would probably stay up all night trying to make contact. They would have to check on him in the morning.

Highway 67, TX

The large MRAP sat idling in the middle of Highway 67 just on the edge of Stephenville, Texas. The start of Amanda's journey, which should have taken no more than a few hours, had taken the entire day. The sun hung low against the horizon. Large dark clouds approaching in the northern sky glowed purple and green, lightning causing the clouds to flash and glow like lightning bugs in a field. The sky above her was clear, but Amanda was confident that her night would be spent being rocked by the looming storm. The atlas she had open in her lap didn't have much detail for the city of Stephenville, but, so far, the map hadn't much detail for any of the towns she had seen roll by her windshield. She had successfully avoided Fort Worth and the surrounding large cities of the DFW Metroplex, but the cost was an entire travel day and being a little lost. Across the field to her right was the end of a runway; a small municipal airport in a small Texas town. The highway, small with only two lanes and shoulders, provided no answer as to what was ahead of her. She knew that another town was near as the yellow sign warned of a reduced speed limit ahead, but she still wasn't exactly sure where she was and what she could do for the night.

The airport would have been Clint's choice - large, open areas, hangers with possible Avgas or gasoline to be found - except that her new ride didn't run on gasoline, it needed diesel, and Amanda wasn't sure that being in a metal building/hangar would be the safest choice for the night with the taunting storm approaching. She had no meteorological schooling on any professional level outside of what she'd read as the SecAg and what life experience had given her growing up in Arkansas. Spring storms were nothing new; lightning was nothing new, but Amanda knew for sure that an approaching storm with emerald-green clouds meant she would probably get some hail fairly soon and maybe see some tornados in the area. As awesome as the big armored MRAP was, tornado proof it was not, although she assumed that it would handle hail just as well if not better than it was supposed to handle small arms fire.

Driving forward, Amanda passed another intersecting small highway and a rather large BBQ joint on the side of the road. This was the heart of Texas cattle country; she assumed that the BBQ had probably been good back when such things still existed. Vague memories of eating BBQ in small shack restaurants while on official visits to Texas felt like a previous life; the smell of smoked brisket seemed to be a ghost of a whiff on the air. She was feeling more discouraged than she'd felt that morning, as fat rain drops started to hit the windshield hard. Muffled by the heavy armor, the sudden impact snapped Amanda out of her daydream and back to the reality she was in, driving slowly on US-67. On her left and right, every structure she saw seemed to be made of a metal building, as if the townspeople expected a tornado to rip the town off the face of Texas and they wanted to have an easy time rebuilding.

The sky turned ominously dark overhead, blotting out the remaining sunlight and requiring her to switch on her headlights and bright auxiliary lights. Amanda rolled through the stop sign, turning left onto Highway 377. The wind gusted, rocking the heavy truck, the trees around her moving back and forth in protest to the increasing wind strength. Dust and debris gusted across the road, and the rainfall increased, falling with hard angry drops and defeating the windshield wipers in their attempt to keep up. Amanda kept driving, slowly. Lightning streaked across the sky, illuminating the road ahead with the ghostly figures of people walking onto the road. Amanda blinked fast, trying to reset her limited vision from the assault of light, the macabre vision imprinted on the back of her mind. Squinting, she tried to see past the edge of the heavy rain that seemed to stop her headlights just past the front bumper. Another streak of lightning, and the hard clap of thunder vibrated through the armor plating almost immediately. The silhouette of an obese man shown in relief against the rain just as the headlights flashed against his mangled face and a split second before she heard the dull thud of his body being slapped to the ground by the heavy front bumper.

Another flash of lightning provided a snapshot of the growing horde of reanimated dead straggling out of the neighborhood on Amanda's left. Steering to the right-hand side of the road, Amanda drove over a highway sign while trying to dodge the next body, but it bounced under the truck and under the left side tires. Sweating, she wasn't sure what she could do except stop, wait, and hope for the best or speed up and do the same. Not one for inaction, Amanda stomped the accelerator to the floor and the big diesel roared, the turbo screaming as the heavy beast of a truck rocked and began to gain momentum.

Bodies bounced off the truck to the left, some falling under the truck, some being caught under the tires, but Amanda had no other options that she could see. If this truck failed, she would find another; if nothing else, she would walk. This was just like the arduous journey to the SSC in the first place, except now her mission was clearer in her mind. She had her own choices, she had her own mission, and no one would lord over her any longer.

Hail hit and bounced off the hood, the windshield, and the roof. The rain kept getting heavier and heavier. Another streak of lightning, and the dark Wal-Mart sign flashed by on her right side, along with an image of hundreds of dead swarming in the parking lot like a frightened herd stampeding on the prairie. Calm washed over her body as she realized that the storm was her ally. The lightning, the hail, the thunder, it confused the dead; they paid no attention to the truck passing by. The businesses and buildings tapered off, and the storm continued to rage, but as Amanda drove past the other side of town the amount of dead she saw went from much too many to nearly none, leaving only the occasional abandoned car or truck on the highway to cause her problems now.

Free from most of the danger from the dead and now trying to get back to finding shelter from the storm, she slowed down. With the next flash of lightning, Amanda saw some sort of church on the right. The wide concrete driveway bore a sign with the name of the Catholic church, but Amanda only saw "Catholic" and assumed the rest. The parking lot was empty, but the gate on the entrance of the drive was open, so entry was fair game for any who passed.

Amanda pulled to the edge of the V-shaped parking lot furthest away from the building, careful to stay on the concrete. She didn't want to chance getting the heavy truck stuck in the mud the storm was surely making. After switching off the wipers and the lights, Amanda turned the switch next to the steering wheel to the OFF position. The truck hissed and groaned as it shut off, but the vibration and the noise were soon replaced by the sound of rain and small hail bouncing off the armored glass and roof. Lightning flashed in a jarred rhythm with seemingly no end. She climbed over the center console to the back area, where instead of troops, gear and supplies occupied the spaces and the seats. Amanda moved a few of the boxes, retrieved an MRE and tore into the sealed package anxiously. It was nearly impossible to see anything but the flashing sky from where she sat, but eventually the hail ceased, the rain turned from squall to steady, and the thunder rolled away with the light show that had brought it. Her first day on the road found her in central Texas, alone and exhausted. Amanda was thankful that she was full, dry, and more comfortable than she had been on her first journey after the attack. Confidence in herself and her plan grew as she drifted into a light sleep.

Groom Lake, NV

The lights flickered on and off, staying on for what felt like only seconds and off for what felt like hours. In reality, the lights were cycling off and on every few minutes. Erin was the first to notice that the cycle was rhythmic, as if deliberate, like a child playing with a light switch. As a team they moved as quickly as they dared, forming a three-man active-shooter response team, just as Bexar had taught Jessie, and Jessie had taught both Sarah and Erin. The small handful of Groom Lake survivors who had attended the training courses thus far were taught the movements too; Jessie hoped that they would find some of those few individuals so they could add to their beleaguered team of tactical women.

With purpose, but not rushing to the detriment of their safety, the trio made their way up decks to where the main "towns" were housed. Each had rightly sheltered in place, keeping the doors locked. The safety protocol that Jake enforced, which had been in place before Jessie and her girls had arrived, appeared to be working. At each of the doors, Erin and Sarah would take a defensive position in the hall while Jessie knocked on the door. An easy and quick passphrase exchange would result in the door opening. Jessie would ask the number accounted for and the number missing and remind the "town" of the lockdown procedure while she made quick notes on the notebook she carried in her pocket.

Once lockdown started, those sheltered in place were supposed to light the emergency lighting in their bunk rooms, if needed, and begin a systematic strip search of everyone to look for any bites or other signs of injury that could be infected with Yama. Two of the towns had completed the procedure; three hadn't, but promised to begin immediately. The goal was to lock down the facility and prevent an outbreak from killing everyone. If one town was killed then at least the rest of the facility would survive. It was also left up to the town to put down any infected in their midst. The needs of the many outweighed the needs of the soon-to-be-dead.

Sarah and Jessie formed the front of the formation as it moved up the hallway. Sarah walked backwards, her rifle hanging on the sling, her pistol out and held with one hand, her free hand holding onto Jessie's belt, giving move-ment, direction, and speed through feel like the hard leash of a service dog. Their weapon lights shone in the darkness and stayed on when the lights came on, as the lights went off just as suddenly and any moment of blindness could result in their death by a stealthy corpse, reanimated and waiting silently as they passed. The dozen bodies on the ground that they had to step over or around so far all had dark holes in their skulls and bite marks on their arms and necks. Some had no bite marks at all that they could see. Jessie realized that an outbreak would be a perfect opportunity to kill someone without cause or conse-quence, just for a grudge or past slight. Only a handful of reanimated corpses had appeared in their path with just a couple more towns to check before the "time-out" portion of the lockdown could begin. Another failsafe was that, once swept, the facility would remain in lockdown for another twelve hours until the all-clear could be sounded.

Those cycles were supposed to be announced over the PA system, but with the power cycling in and out, it seemed unlikely that this would be very organized. It might be the end of the facility if something couldn't be done to stop the system madness.

After a quick and hushed conversation, the three of them were left with only the cafeteria, Jake's offices, and the radio shack to clear, at least of the known facility. Jessie felt confident that they had only begun to unlock the bare surface of secrets to be found here. Sarah and Jessie threw the double doors open. The three-man formation they'd used to move through the confined space of the hallways no longer needed for a large area like the cafeteria, all three of them entered and closed the doors behind them. They would have to clear the hallway again before they left, but that would help prevent someone, dead or alive, from sneaking up on them through the open doors.

Beams of light from the powerful weapon lights they each had pierced the darkness, as they methodically swept the room, moving slowly and purposefully along the walls, away from the fatal funnel of the doorway and staying away from the open center where cover could elude them. The tactics were meant for police officers responding to an active shooter in a school or a building, and seemed a little strange for the risen dead, but they couldn't be sure that there wasn't a shooter lying in wait for them. Tables and chairs were scattered and knocked over. Blood smears on the walls and floor gave off a warning; the lack of any bodies on the floor gave an even stronger one. Jessie bumped an unopened can of Rip-It on the floor. She stopped and paused for a moment. Erin, a few yards behind her, did the same. Momentarily, Sarah, who was across the room, detected that the other lights had stopped moving and stopped as well, sweeping her light across the cafeteria and askew tables. Jessie held the can in front of her weapon light to show Sarah, then threw it into the dark opening of the center serving line.

The loud crash of large serving trays and plastic plates was the result, which was followed immediately by a handful of gurgling moans and more crashing as reanimated survivors of Groom Lake straggled out to meet their end. Erin put each person down one by one until she saw a hand with a red knit mitten appear from the darkness. Waiting, a wry smile stretched across her lips as she saw her favorite of the Groom Lake residents appear. Brit looked bad. It was obvious she had been dead longer than the rest. One gentle squeeze of the trigger and Erin sent the back of Brit's skull and brain matter across the white tile floor, Brit's reanimated body crumpling in place. Jessie wasn't sure, but she thought she heard a faint "fuck you" just as Erin's rifle coughed the last shot.

The rest of the cafeteria was cleared. They found Major Wright outside his office near the radio shack, his throat torn from his neck and blood soaking his uniform as he staggered toward the women down the hall. Jessie put the major down. Jake was locked in his office, as he was supposed to be. Bill and the airmen were found in the radio shack, all the radios unplugged due to the surges of the power switching on and off. All told, nearly three dozen people were dead due to Brit's arrogance and incompetence. Something that Jake felt responsible for after setting everything in motion by entertaining Brit's grudge against Jessie, Sarah, and Erin.

Bill had a quick conversation with Jake followed by Jessie before he led the way to the server farm deep in the bedrock. One by one, they disconnected he network switches from anything that did not appear to be an internal intranet-only connection. This was a drastic measure, one that Bill hadn't wanted to attempt because no one knew what would happen. The facility could be rendered completely dead, nothing could happen, or the madness might be stopped; no one knew for sure.

Once disconnected, the servers were hard-powered with fingers crossed that they would reboot without issue or concern, since neither Jake nor Bill had anyway to log in as a user with any amount of privilege to fix any issues. Slowly the servers appeared to reboot, but there was no way to tell for sure for a few more minutes. After all the activity settled in the server rooms, Bill, Jessie, Sarah, and Erin left for the radio shack. They would either need to start the evacuation process to the top side, retrieving as much gear as they could while establishing safe areas on the surface, or cleanup would begin in the facility. Jessie had no idea what time it was on the surface or what time it was at all, but she knew that it would take them a long time to accomplish a full evacuation. People might die if they moved too fast, and people might die if they moved too slowly.

Eventually, the facility lights came back on, the air system's faint hiss returned, and the lights stayed on, though each of them expected the lights to fail at any moment. Growing more anxious with each passing minute, by the time that Jake announced the all clear they no longer expected the lights to go out. They grew to hope the lights wouldn't.

Exhausted, Jessie, Sarah, and Erin retired to the bunkroom to clean weapons, top off magazines, shower, and sleep. Persons assigned to the cleaning crew were tasked to move the bodies to the service elevator and to the main hanger for disposal by burning by the yet-to -be-formed burn crew. Bill, tired but excitedly awake from the events, returned to the radio shack and began transmitting in the blind on the electronic radio he'd modified to receive and transmit on the correct frequencies to match the radios that might be built if anyone took the shortwave transmissions seriously. The remaining airmen started up the shortwave broadcasts again, along with the other radio equipment.

Bill still used the old Races call sign, his own personal HAM geek humor for the end of the world, but he wasn't sure if anyone was left that would get it. Headphones on, a blank legal pad of paper and a pen sat at the ready while Bill leaned back in the large desk chair with his eyes closed. Faint and scratchy, the first dah and dit of a weak transmission took Bill a second to realize what he heard, but he shot up, pen in hand, and began writing out the letters of the slow transmission.

Waving eagerly, the airmen gathered around Bill to see what the excitement was all about. All the external speakers turned off on all the other radios, Bill set his headphones on the table and turned up his own speaker. The faint scratched transmission of other survivors came across slowly. Bill quickly wrote a note on another sheet of paper and handed it to an airman, who left immediately, note in hand. At the end of the transmission, Bill took an excited breath. It was the same sense of excitement that he'd had the first time he'd made contact with another HAM radio operator on the other side of the world, or like the first time he'd made contact with an astronaut on the space station. Bill's heart raced, and he had to concentrate not to key in the reply too fast. The survivor on the other end of the radio didn't seem like a seasoned CW operator, but there were only a few HAMS before the end of the world.

Back and forth the short messages were sent. Bill also resisted the urge to use the shorthand that was common amongst other HAM radio operators for fear of confusing the person on the other end. By the time Jake arrived in the radio shack, Bill had a short conversation written down. It was only a page long, but it told an incredible story.

Lost Bridge Village, AR

Bob's heavy eyes snapped wide open at the buzzing sound of the received transmission. Instead of the usual dit and dah of a modern CW transmission, the buzzing spark-gap receiver took a little getting used to. Just before he could begin to key a response, a faint transmission responded. Now very awake, heart pounding, Bob wrote down the conversation that ensued from the back and forth transmission. One side was the operator in Groom Lake; the other side was an operator who claimed to be in Montana. Bob had no reason to believe otherwise; this was a momentous day, a momentous week. Not only had Andrew swooped down from the sky to open their small world to the idea of other survivors all across the country, but after building the radio, another group of survivors in another state far away were also alive and transmitting. Bob's heart raced, and he wished he could tell Warren, or Andrew, or anyone, but everyone was long gone, the sun setting hours ago.

Once the bulk of the back and forth of transmissions had slacked off, Bob keyed in his call sign followed by the shorthand "AR" keyed quickly as a single word. Across the country, Bob didn't hear Bill as he yelled with excitement, but the return transmission was fast, clear, and the sort of thing that old HAMs would be excited about, which Bob was, and he assumed that the operator using an old Races-style call sign in Groom Lake was too. Twenty minutes later, and Bob had his contact logged, along with the questions he had answered. Keying his station's signoff from the frequency for the night, Bob left the Groom Lake operator calling himself "Bill" to chat with others, which Bob listened to and transposed to show the others in Lost Bridge Village in the morning. Any chance of going home to sleep was wiped away, Bob being much too excited to even attempt it.

CHAPTER 6

The eastern horizon glowed yellow in the morning twilight. At the kitchen table, Bexar chatted with Gary, who wrote quick notes of the conversation that he would transcribe later. After the initial surprise from the group members wanting to know their story, Gary spoke with Bexar about recording the story of who he was and what had happened after the EMP and after the dead rose to hunt the living. Bexar realized he was sincere and genuinely interested, and for the first time in his life while sober the chains fell free of the locks, the doors opened, and Bexar spoke openly of his time as a Texas peace officer. He talked about all the plans, prepping, and training that went into the group's bug-out plans, the cache site, all the details good and bad: Malachi's death, the attack in The Basin, burying Keeley, his own retaliation and attempt to rescue Jessie. Tears streamed down his face as he spoke nearly in a whisper as all the guilt, remorse, and anguish of being one of the lucky few to live through the past few months washed over him. Gary's soft eyes and gentle words, both encouraging and caring, helped Bexar talk about all the memories and feelings that he was running from.

Guillermo stepped out of the kitchen and set a fresh cup of coffee down on the table before quietly ushering the remaining group members out of the kitchen to give the two some privacy. Gary was a special member of their group, a bit of a misfit crew; Gary's self-imposed title was the "Chief of Good Morale." Professionally, Gary was a licensed therapist, gentle and caring, supportive, not the stereotype of a person most people picture when they think of a thera-pist. Gary was an avid outdoorsman, hunter, shooting enthusiast, and general fitness nut. Long multiday hikes across terrain that most wouldn't want to even fly over was where Gary found his solace. In nature, be it hiking, running, cycling, shooting on a range, or hunting, Gary would have fun no matter what the activity as long as he could be outside. He was one of the last members added to the group, long after John and Brian helped form the original cell, after Heath and Coach joined, after Merylin and Frances began all the intensive food prep, after the other group split off into their own faction, joining just before Jennifer and Doc.

Walking outside, Guillermo found Stan and Chivo readying the horses for another journey, this one an attempt to salvage an old and wayward VW Beetle. Stan, the group mechanic and systems guy, was the obvious choice for Chivo to take. Angel wanted to return with him for tactical reasons, or maybe Angel thought Chivo was cute; Guillermo wasn't sure, but Stan would be more useful in an attempt to resurrect an old car after the end of the world as we know it.

Stan used the solar array to charge a small car battery that was used with some of the equipment. A roll pouch of tools, some lunch, some water, weapons, ammo, a small can of treated gasoline, a can of starter fluid, and the will to succeed were tied onto the horses, and, just after sunrise, the pair left. Walking across the yard and into the open side door of the shop, Guillermo found Heath with an electric motor disassembled on his workbench. Without a word, Guillermo walked up to him and stood, watching the process.

"Hey, Willy, aerator's acting up."

"The what?"

"Aerator. It's the motor that keeps the septic churning to help the biological processes break down all the waste. The spare unit is in place for now, but I'm rebuilding this one so I can place it in storage as the spare. Without it we would need to be on the hunt for another."

"What happens if it all fails completely?"

"Then we're literally up shit creek."

"Heh, OK, Heath, good work, buddy, and thank you for what you do."

Heath smiled and went back to work, Guillermo leaving him be.

The rest of the group was fast at work with their daily chores. Guillermo's chores for the morning were complete. Kitchen rotation was one of his favorites because he got to cook. He had to clean, too, but he didn't have to do any of the harder outdoor chores or sit safety watch at night. Walking back into the house, he found Gary and Bexar still chatting, now sitting on the sofas in the living room. Gary motioned to the rocking chair and nodded, so Guillermo sat.

"You've not just survived, you've battled, fought, scratched, and just flat-out forced yourself to survive damn the odds. It is easy to dismiss things as circumstance or luck, but luck favors the ready, and the ready don't favor luck. You aren't lucky, you're ready. I have no doubt that you will succeed, that you'll rejoin your wife, and your child will survive. I strongly suspect that no matter what could possibly happen your family will be whole, and you'll make sure that child lives to see us reclaim this world for the living."

Guillermo smiled. Gary was really animated, genuinely excited, and he meant what he said. Missing out on the majority of the previous talk, he would have to read the story after Gary transcribed it and wrote it out, with Bexar's approval of course, but something about the gimped survivor cop from Texas really had Gary fired up. This was going to be a good day. It had already started well, and in a few hours Guillermo would start cooking dinner.

I need to ask Merylin and Frances for something they can spare from the cache; a special day today means tonight should have a special meal.

Smiling, Guillermo excused himself. Gary and Bexar were laughing and, if John wandered in at some point, they might start pouring beer even though it wasn't even past eight in the morning.

Stephenville, TX

Stretching her neck, Amanda sat up. The bed of boxes and troop carrier seats wasn't exactly what her weary body needed, but uncomfortable sleep that is relatively safe is better than no sleep at all. Another storm had ripped through the area during the night. The wind had rocked the heavy truck hard enough to cause concern, but all the stress of the previous day left Amanda so weary that she couldn't keep her eyes open for just a little bit of weather. She figured that if the MRAP tipped over she would wake up and deal with it then, but as sturdy as the truck was she would probably be OK inside if that happened.

After snacking on the crackers left over from the previous night's MRE dinner and downing a half-liter of water, Amanda stood to look out the windows. She needed to pee; preferably she could squat against a tire, but if it wasn't safe, she wasn't above hanging her ass over the edge of the turret and peeing on the roof while the dead world watched from below.

The scene outside the heavy bullet-resistant windows was surreal. Half of the church building to the south was gone, and debris filled the parking lot. The metal church buildings at the back of the parking lot were leveled, which was probably the source of much of the debris. Bodies littered the ground. Most of them appeared to be reanimates that were thrown by the storm and hit by debris. Some were mangled, still twitching with movement, the virus holding onto the last vestiges of ability from the destroyed bones and flesh.

"Oh my God."

Amanda released the hatch for the turret, climbed up the slung nylon step and pulled herself onto the roof. Standing on the roof and in the cool air, she turned slowly, looking at the scene around her. It appeared that a tornado had come through or had been close enough to destroy the buildings. Trees had been uprooted and overturned. The few cars and trucks she had seen on the highway were tossed aside like discarded toys. She counted seventeen dead in the parking lot.

I can't fathom being caught in a storm and being struck by a flying reanimated body like a fucked-up remake of The Birds.

The thought caused Amanda to shiver before she grunted, frowning at the destruction. It didn't matter; the seventeen in the parking lot were seventeen that no one would have to deal with in the future after she got the country back on its feet. Holding onto the edge of the turret, Amanda hung her ass over the edge of the truck to pee. There were few moments that she envied men, but being able to stand up and direct pee at will was something she envied at this very moment.

"Fuck it," was all she said after pulling her pants up and tightening her belt. Climbing back into the cab, she pulled the heavy roof latch closed, dogging it in place. Rotating the switch to RUN, Amanda waited for the gauges to come online and for the motor to be ready. She pushed the momentary button for the starter and the turbo diesel belched to life, ready for another day in the modern world of combat against the dead. The fuel gauge showed a half-tank left, so the day could start, but she would need to fuel at the first opportunity so things wouldn't turn into an emergency. After consulting with her road maps, Amanda drove to the end of the driveway and turned right onto the highway. Driving south on Highway 377, the route seemed wrong, but the map showed her connection, Highway 6, would be after the next town, and that would point her back in the right direction. To avoid a direct route involving an Interstate sometimes meant that the wrong direction had to be traveled on a small highway.

Amanda wanted to see Dublin, Texas to see if it had any Irish pubs, but the highway split and routed her away from the city, which was fine since it still intersected Highway 6. Another right turn and into the countryside she went. Instead of a gas station, Amanda was watching for a construction site or farm with a fuel tank on a raised platform. She had a universal key, also known as bolt cutters, in the MRAP, so a padlocked gravity-fed tank of diesel for tractors or road equipment would be even easier to get into than an electrically powered tank of diesel for trucks.

The storm damage in the area along the new highway wasn't as severe as the path of destruction that had been carved out next to her overnight spot. *God smiles on children, drunks, and idiots.*

Smirking for her dumb luck in parking near the future path of a tornado and then surviving without any damage, Amanda figured she must be a favored idiot; she had too many gray hairs to be a child, and a glass of wine felt like an ancient dream. The Texas countryside rolled by her windshield; small homes were carved out between pastures and farmland, and wooded areas dotted the landscape.

The sign said De Leon, home to a celebrated peach and melon festival, with slightly over two thousand residents, but Amanda had to take its word for it because she had never heard of the town. Passing a cattle trailer pulled by a large dually pickup that sat abandoned in the road in the opposite lane, she stopped the truck. In the bed of the truck was a diamond-plate toolbox, but there was also a tank of fuel with a fuel spout. It was common for farmers and ranchers to have up to about a fifty-gallon tank of fuel for farm equipment on a farm truck; they usually all ran on diesel. Most of the pumps were electrically operated with a simple DC-electric motor, which could be a problem, or it could still work. Most of the ranchers wired the pump up themselves by running a hot wire directly to the battery, so it could be possible to run it off the MRAP's battery too. Amanda wasn't sure if the MRAP's system was twelve volt, twenty-four volt, or something else that she couldn't fathom, but she figured the worst that could happen was that it wouldn't work.

Or you catch it all on fire while trying to fuel.

Amanda shook her head and hoped for God's continued providence on her idiot ways. Idling in the middle of the road, she climbed down from the driver's side of her big truck and cleared the immediate area. No dead were seen; nothing seemed to be reacting to the sound of her truck's loud motor. The cap on the auxiliary fuel tank in the bed of the truck was locked with a padlock, as was the nozzle. Returning with the bolt cutters, she quickly relieved the locks of their duty. Unscrewing the cap, she was happy to see the tank was nearly three-quarters full. The placard stated that the tank did hold fifty gallons, so she might net approximately thirty-five gallons. The pump was electric, and it was held in place with worn electrical tape. The pickup was unlocked and unattended; Amanda pulled the release inside the cab and walked to the front to open the hood. The battery connections were a rat's nest of extra wires, a fine example of cheap redneck engineering on an expensive farm truck. The toolbox in the bed of the pickup did not have any jumper cables, but it did have a small spool of thin red electrical wire and a roll of duct tape. The battery for the MRAP was on the wrong side of the truck for an easy connect, so Amanda decided to siphon the fuel out of the unscrewed cap. Ten minutes later, the MRAP was buttoned back up. Amanda drank water in an attempt to get the taste of diesel out of her mouth, but no dead had come to investigate, and the fuel gauge was nearly full.

"Life is good; today will be a wonderful day."

By the time she was in the town, she was exiting it again. Overall, the town looked quiet, as if everyone was on vacation; there wasn't much visible damage to the buildings or anything that she could see. If most of small-town America had survived this well, Amanda held hope for the future chances of the country.

More open country rolled by through the heavy windows. Barely any cars were left on the highway. Only a handful of dead roamed along the deserted Texas highway, nothing of interest appeared, and the town of Gorman scrolled past without incident, as did the next small town. Lulled into a bored sense of safety, Amanda felt like she was nearly standing still, but her map showed progress, progress and I-20 approaching.

Stopping abreast a lonely, small truck stop where Highway 6 crossed I-20, Amanda studied her map. She had two routes marked on her atlas. The first and presumably faster route took I-20 west through Abilene, turning on Highway 84. The second crossed I-20and stayed on Highway 6 until catching Highway 180. The two routes met again near Snyder, Texas, and the safer route would be to stay off the Interstate, but Amanda couldn't put aside the desire to save a little time.

Ahead of her a semi-truck and trailer lay on the berm of the overpass, appearing to have been knocked off the Interstate. A car lay on Highway 6 below the bridge; it also appeared to have been pushed off the bridge. Amanda hadn't seen damage like this before, but it would match what was described weeks ago as damage from one of the massive roaming herds of the dead. Clint said they amassed along the Interstates; his theory was that the dead ended up attracting each other by the sounds of their movement. The larger the group, the louder they were, the more dead would be attracted. Interstates went through large cities, and large cities had lots of people, so it all snowballed together. Like wandering cattle, nothing and no one was in charge, just the herd following the herd in an infinite loop of meandering destruction.

Amanda didn't have the desire or the need to see more or to encounter a herd. She knew it wasn't here right now; she had no idea if it was heading east or west and if she would catch up to it or run into another one. Her choice to take a faster route was immediately removed; the back roads and smaller highways would remain her choice. She drove around the crumpled car, under the overpass, and toward Eastland, Texas.

Lost Bridge Village, AR

Andrew woke up to Oreo nudging him. The room was dark from the heavy blankets over the windows, but the kettle sat on the hearth of the fireplace, and the breakfast fire was already reduced to white coals. Somehow he had slept late, but if he was lucky there was coffee still left in the kettle. He had no idea what time it was, but after checking the house, he found himself alone.

At least they trust me enough to let me sleep unattended; that's nice.

The kettle had coffee. It was a little stale from sitting next to the fire for too long, but as little coffee as Andrew had been able to enjoy over the past few months, any coffee was better than no coffee. Relaxing with Oreo on the couch, sipping the coffee, Andrew looked for his atlas, which was missing. Assuming he'd left it at the community building, Andrew didn't worry about it. This group didn't seem like the type that would steal from him. Another warm sip of the bitter coffee and Andrew felt more relaxed than he had at most of the other survivor camps. Others were better armed, better staffed, and better protected, but this group had better people. Or this group had kinder people at least; they were quite pleasant. The potluck lunch yesterday had been a treat, even if Bob's radio was unsuccessful. At least he'd tried. Some groups wouldn't have even tried; most wouldn't have for lack of a shortwave radio that still worked. Andrew made a mental note to tell others about Groom Lake and the shortwave broadcasts. Even if Bob's radio didn't work, the shortwave broadcasts might be a way to get some new information. He leaned his head back, held his mug in one hand, absentmindedly petted Oreo with the other, and closed his eyes, visualizing the map in his head, trying to decide where to fly next.

Groom Lake?

"What do you say, Oreo, want to fly to Nevada?"

The dog lazily opened his eyes before shutting them again.

"I know, but I want to go to Area 51. That's where that facility is supposed to be. If not, we can look for aliens. That sound fun?"

Oreo gave no response. Andrew tried to remember where Area 51 was located. He thought that it was near Las Vegas because he remembered a *Popular Mechanics* article years ago about people commuting via a private airline from Las Vegas to work in Area 51. He would have to look at his atlas, except that he was sure a top-secret government base wouldn't be marked on it.

Maybe Bob would know. Well, if I am going near Las Vegas, I could roughly follow I-40 west for navigation, stop where I can along the way for fuel, maybe meet more survivors... I need to get fueled up and flying. We've been here for too long, even if they are really nice.

"Hey, Oreo, we could visit the Grand Canyon along the way. That would be cool. See the Hoover Dam. Maybe there are people living near that who have working electricity from the dam. That would be incredible."

Oreo's head snapped up just before Andrew heard the doorknob of the front door rattle. Andrew looked at Oreo, who climbed down and waited with his tail wagging. He figured if Oreo was happy, then he didn't have to worry. Andrew was correct, as Warren and Mary came through the door, Warren carrying his atlas.

Mary gave Oreo a hug and excitedly blurted out, "Bob made contact with Groom Lake and listened to the radio guy there talk to a guy in Montana and another in Minnesota."

"Wow. What did they say?"

Warren had a piece of paper that he had scribbled the notes on. "The one in Minnesota has an odd name and has a small community of survivors right near Minneapolis. Some town called Winnebago or something. The one in Montana is named Dorsey and is near Great Falls. He's saying that it's been bad with the snow'n all. Most of them survivors have been starved. Some drank themselves to death, and others just killed themselves off. He also said they don't be hav'n many of the dead either. Supposed the cold weather is makin'em stiff, and they can't move. He done bugged out to one of them missile silos up there, could you believe it, living below ground like that."

"Really! Hadn't thought of that. Not much of a harsh winter in my part of Florida; the worst is when we have a late frost, and we lose a bunch of oranges."

"This'n guy Dorsey was talking about getting close to six feet of snow this year, hoping to thaw out by July."

"Damn, six feet? Six inches of snow would shut Deland down for a week!"

"No joke, we get snow here, but nuth'n like that, nuth'n even close."

"Warren," Andrew glanced at Mary and back, "do you think I've earned my keep well enough to get some fuel? Oreo and I want to attempt flying out to Groom Lake to that facility."

"What'n for?"

"Well, I've got a bunch of information marked in my atlas, and I'm sure I'll gather more while en route. I'm sure they could use that, and besides I'm curious. I want to see what is left of our government. I want to see if they have a plan, if we have a chance."

"That's fair, and I'm suppose'n we owe some gratitude for giving us the link to the outside world. It was like hell getting Bob to get off the radio and rest. Most of the town is down there; others are taking shifts on the radio, sending messages and listening to others. It's slow'n work, little buzzes here and there that you've got to be writ'n down and such, but it be better than nuth'n. Well, come on down with us again. We can ask the town. Between everyone, we might scrape up enough fuel to get you headed out the right way."

Andrew was grinning from ear to ear as they all headed back down to the community building. If yesterday was a fun get-together, what Andrew found today was an all-out party. It was like the town had won the lotto. An hour later, Andrew's plane was topped off, and his little spare fuel can was full. Half the town watched as Andrew taxied into position and completed a preflight run-up on the ramp. Happy that the magnetos should work and the engine probably wouldn't fail on takeoff, Andrew pushed the power button, and the little aircraft raced down the runway. The tail wheel popped off the ground first before the yellow aircraft floated lazily into the sky, banking right to fly westbound.

Once the sound of the engine was gone, Mary wiped her eyes, sad to see Oreo leave and sad that she didn't get to go flying.

"Grandpa Warren, I want to learn how to fly."

"I'm sorry, baby girl, maybe you'll be hav'n a chance in the future when all this mess is behind us."

Warren picked up Mary and carried her across the road to their house. The brave new world was a sad place, no place for his little princess, and it broke Warren's heart to know that the future was more bleak than the past could have ever imagined.

Saint George, UT

Stan and Chivo rode in silence, the soft clops of the horses' hooves along the desert the only noise besides the occasional snort or fart from the horses. Following the same path that he and Angel had used, the pair eventually arrived at the neighborhood near the truck wreck where Chivo had spied the VW previously. Chivo's rifle sat across his legs so the muzzle wouldn't poke the horse and possibly spur him, the sling across his body keeping it from falling to the ground. He held the reins loosely in his left hand, his right hand gripping the stock of the M4. The last go around he'd had in this area nearly turned south on him. The plan was to clear the house, get the horses and the car into the garage, shut the garage door, and work in relative safety. The houses had practically no backyards, so they couldn't secure the horses in a backyard. The front yards had no fences, so the horses could be attacked by the dead if they were tied up in the front yard. Stan commented that they should bring the horses into the living room and let them rest there. Chivo wasn't opposed to the idea; he just wasn't sure that the horses would fit through the front door very well. Besides, all they needed was a horse to get injured tripping over a sofa or something. Chivo figured that in the worst case they could clear another house and secure them in its garage while they worked in the first. Since the homes were set a bit like duplexes with paired side-by-side driveways, it wouldn't be that hard to do. It would only add a little bit of time. Time in the new world was a strange beast; they had both too much time and not enough time. It all depended on a slight change in circumstance.

The neighborhood was quiet; a few dead thumped against the front windows of homes. Only a couple reanimates were seen out roaming the streets. They weren't worth killing and alerting the area that someone was scavenging from the sound of rifle fire. The second street on his right and five houses down was the Bug. Reaching the driveway, Stan remained in the saddle as mounted security. Chivo tied his reins to the tube bumper of the Baja-beetle and knocked on the front door. A few moments later a wet thump hit the back of the door. Chivo shook his head as the reanimated corpse on the other side of the door continued to step into the shut door with a loud thud each time. Checking the door, he found it locked. After retrieving a lava rock from the desert-style landscaping in the front yard, Chivo threw it through the large front window with a sharp crash. The thumping against the door ended, and a few moments later the reanimated corpse crashed through the broken front window and onto the lawn. As it struggled to get up, Chivo drove his knife through the back of the undead woman's skull. After wiggling the knife to get it loose, Chivo looked at the rotted nude body, the sagging gray flesh, and stepped to the window to clean the blade on the curtains before replacing it in the sheath.

Chivo looked back at Stan, who sat on his horse looking a little wide-eyed. Chivo gave him a wink and stepped into the dark home. In only a few minutes, Stan heard the garage-door latch release before it rolled up to show a garage full of junk.

Stan guided his horse near the edge of the garage, and Chivo appeared behind a mountain of random boxes and a ping pong table holding a silver car key in his hand. "What do you say? Should we try a different garage or not use the garage? What do you think, Chivo?"

"Naw, mano, this is fine, just time for a fucking yard sale... maybe some napalm."

"What?"

"I'm kidding. Give me a hand, and let's push all this shit out into the fucking yard."

Stan climbed off his horse, tied it next to the other one, and helped with the garage reorganization, unceremoniously tossing boxes of Halloween decorations, old clothes, dishes, and everything else imaginable onto the lawn and driveway next door. Fifteen minutes later, a few dead had straggled near, and the garage was empty.

"Stan, there's a little side yard that's paved and there should be room for the horses. I'll take care of these assholes if you move the horses. When you get back, we can push the Bug into the garage and get to fucking work."

Nodding, Stan took the horses around the far side of the house; Chivo unsheathed his knife and jogged toward the closest walking corpse. Stopping in front of the reanimated dead, Chivo took a side step and tripped the old man lunging for him. Once on the ground, the knife plunge was repeated. Rocking the knife back and forth, Chivo couldn't get it to come loose from the man's skull. Frowning, he worked harder as the other two dead came closer and closer, but the knife wouldn't budge.

"Pendejo!" Chivo spun in his crouched position while pulling his pistol clear of the holster and fired twice in rapid succession, each shot striking a zombie in the forehead. He kicked the handle of his knife, which caused the knife to pop loose from the skull. He jogged to where it had skidded to a stop on the asphalt, retrieved it, and headed back to Stan and the Bug. Stan was already trying to push it into the garage. Around them the sound of the dead slamming against doors and windows crescendoed. Once the Bug was in the garage, they shut the door behind them and latched it closed, just as dozens of approaching dead marched up the driveway. The sound of the dead banging against the thin sheet metal garage door rattled the frame.

"Well, mano, hopefully out of sight out of mind for a little while and they'll give it up before they knock the door down."

Stan lit a match, and the darkness of the closed garage pushed against the small flame until it slid behind the glass globe of a camp lantern. The gentle hiss of white gas followed by the poof of the flame catching preceded the warm glow of the dual mantel lamp that Stan hung from the garage door opener on the ceiling.

"At least we don't have to take the deck lid off or worry about jamming our hands into tight places around that tiny motor."

The rear bodywork of the Beetle had been cut away, replaced with a classic-style tube bumper and short-cut rear fenders, with the engine hanging from the transmission in the open air. Stan popped off the cap of the distributor, inspected the rotor, and used a shim to check the gap in the points.

Chivo opened the passenger door and replaced the old car battery under the back seat with the freshly charged battery that they'd brought. Assuming they could drain the tank if it didn't work, Chivo raised the hood and poured about one of the two gallons of gas they'd brought with them into the metal tank, saving the rest in case they actually did need to drain the tank.

One by one, Stan removed each of the four spark plugs and inspected them in the light, checking the spark gap and verifying that they appeared to be in good working order. The oil was dark and used, but Stan didn't see any evidence of water or contamination; if water was in the oil, this entire enterprise would have been for naught. After removing the valve covers, and while using a large crescent wrench, Stan turned the crank via the bolt on the crankshaft pulley, stopping at top dead center and bottom dead center with each turn to check the valve adjustment for each of the four cylinders. None of the valves needed adjustment. While Stan checked the engine and mechanicals, Chivo used two cans of Fix-A-Flat to fill the four small tires. The foaming can of glue wasn't the best choice, but it was a field-expedient choice when you had no other way.

"It looks like ass, but, so far, whoever kept this old Bug kept it in apparent almost-good working order."

Chivo nodded. Even if it wasn't in good working order, the old Bugs were so robust that they would just run anyway. People always said that they were easy to work on. Growing up poor, he'd learned that they were just as hard to work on as anything else, but the design was so good that they would run while forgiving egregious mechanical mistakes on the part of the homegrown mechanic.

After checking that the bowl and float were clean, Stan reassembled the carburetor and pulled out a test light to static test the ignition timing. Once complete, the pair packed up the tools in preparation for starting the car and leaving once everything became really noisy. Both of them knew that the Baja-style stinger exhaust would be really loud since it was just a straight pipe with a flared trumpet end that made the exhaust even louder.

Chivo sat in the driver's seat, a cheap fiberglass bucket seat, pushed in the clutch, turned the key, and gave the gas pedal a quick pump. All they heard was the click of the starter. Chivo tried again, and the motor didn't turn over; again, all they heard was the click of the starter.

"Chivo, flip on the headlights for a sec."

Chivo did as instructed and was surprised to see that even in the darkness of the garage, the headlights were very weak.

"Shit. Let me swap out with the old battery, maybe we'll get lucky."

Stan made quick work of swapping the battery connections. "Try the headlights again."

This time nothing shone at all.

"OK, let me switch them back. I think it'll run, but we might have to push start it."

"It's like I'm back in the old neighborhood, mano, except we never took this long to steal a fucking car."

Stan grunted. He didn't see it as stealing and missed that Chivo's comment was a joke. In his mind, it was salvaging for the good of the group, and it was righteous, not dirty and uncomely like theft. The moral line that was a hard, sharp one in his mind was wide and light gray for Chivo, who was surprised by the sudden appearance of all the tools being tossed into the passenger seat.

"OK, Specialist Hood-rat, I'm going to open the garage door and push you out backwards, so put the tranny in reverse and pop the clutch when I say to."

Chivo glared at Stan, mumbling, "Hood-rat? I'll fucking put your tranny in reverse, fucking mang."

"What?"

"I said it's a great plan, Stan-the-man, fucking outstanding, quit dicking around and let's get your wonderful plan in action."

Stan took down the lantern, turned the gas off, and set the still glowing and hot light on the floorboard of the passenger's side. After pulling the release, he lifted the garage door and let the latch hold it open; it had been some time since they'd heard any reanimated dead banging against the metal.

Some dead shambled down the darkening street. Chivo hadn't realized how long they had been in the garage, but apparently it was more than the couple of hours that it felt like. The sun had already set, and they needed to haul ass back to the compound or setup for the night.

Chivo turned the key to the on position, pushed down on the gear shift, selected reverse, released the parking brake, and held the clutch pedal to the floor. Stan began pushing as hard as he could, the little car gaining speed as it reached the end of the driveway. Chivo didn't wait, it was now or not, so he released the clutch and began pumping the gas pedal. The car lurched against the transmission before roaring to life. Chivo shifted to neutral and yelled at Stan, "We'll come back for the horses tomorrow; there are too many dead fucking about! Get in and let's get home!"

Stan climbed in on top of the tools piled in the passenger seat; Chivo shifted to first and drove away from the assembling welcome party of death, the obnoxiously loud exhaust echoing off the houses. As they passed the far side of the house, Chivo caught a glimpse of one of the horses on the ground, two dead feeding on it, and blood running into the street. The other horse was missing.

Shaking his head, Chivo wasn't sure what he would tell Angel. It wasn't like they could replace the horses before they left for Groom Lake.

The Compound, Saint George, UT

Bexar put his beer in the cup holder of the camp chair and pulled himself onto his good foot. Gingerly, he began putting some weight on the cast, steadying himself by holding onto the chair. He wasn't quite ready yet, but the leg would hold his weight, if unsteadily.

In the morning, I've got to get Guillermo to cut this cast off. I'm sitting around getting drunk and fat when I should be training for survival, for my family's survival.

Out of the corner of his eye, Bexar saw the ghost of a faint streak of light in the sky. Before he could turn his head, the concussion thumped into Bexar's chest with the force of a sledge hammer. Ears ringing, the world came to focus slowly; in view were flames, movement, the moving shadows of people running as seen only by firelight.

The shop... oh God, the shop is on fire!

The Beetle

"What the fuck is that?"

Chivo looked up and right to where Stan was pointing. In the distance, flames licked the night sky. The slow roll of an explosion rumbled through the small car.

"Shit, mano, that's the fucking compound!"

Chivo focused forward; the headlights' faint glow on the roadway made it feel like he was driving by candlelight. Going as fast as he dared, Chivo carefully threaded through the thickening mass of the dead, dodging left and right. The nimble, loud, air-cooled car drove as commanded. All that Chivo and Stan saw of the dead were the backs of their heads, as each pair of dead eyes in the area were pointed toward the beacon calling them home to feed.

The Compound, Saint George, UT

Bexar stood, adrenaline coursing through his veins, ears ringing. He couldn't hear the screaming. Two people lay motionless on the driveway. Angel ran to the first, heavy med bag over his shoulder, and pointed toward the shop. Bexar couldn't hear him, but he saw the shop was well on its way to being fully engulfed.

The flames danced across the lunar landscape of the desert night. Movement caught his eye; spinning quickly toward the movement, Bexar raised his rifle. Three people outside the fence were running toward the gate. The tip of the red triangle in the optic tracked just ahead of the leader. Two smooth pulls on the trigger, and the first person fell; the second person tripped over the body. Bexar drove the rifle to the person at the rear, who stopped and turned to run away. Another two shots and the rounds pierced his back, blood erupting out of his chest where the rounds exited, the man crumpling to the ground in mid-stride. The remaining person of the assaulting force stood, arms raised. An odd-looking tube was slung across his body; it looked vaguely familiar to Bexar, but he wasn't sure why. Anger pierced the air between them. A fraction of a second passed, but for Bexar it felt like ten minutes. Through the reticle all he saw were the eyes and the hatred they held. A single squeeze of the trigger and the back of the attacker's skull exploded in a shower of bone and brain matter. Bexar scanned left and right. Nothing else moved; no other threats arrived.

Bexar could hear yelling. Guillermo was attacking the growing flames of the shop with a fire extinguisher. Years of being a cop didn't make one a firefighter, but it gave Bexar a feel for fires and response. Guillermo was fighting a losing battle. Finally understanding what Angel was yelling, Bexar let his rifle hang on the sling and ran as fast as the cast would let him, the massive adrenaline dump of the attack and battle blocking any pain that he'd had just moments before. As he charged into the open door, thick black smoke poured through, choking him, the heat searing his lungs with each breath. Bexar didn't stop. The light on his rifle shone dimly in the smoke, but he still couldn't see anything but smoke and flame. Bexar stumbled to the floor; looking back, he realized he'd tripped over Heath's body, burned and blackened. Standing and grabbing Heath under his arms, Bexar walked backwards, dragging with all his strength, struggling against the cast on his leg. He made it into the courtyard before collapsing, choking and coughing on smoke and soot. The last thing he saw was Guillermo tackling him with a heavy wool blanket.

The Beetle

Chivo followed Stan's excited instructions and turned onto Twin Lakes. Reaching the long driveway felt like a half hour for Stan; the forty-five miles per hour Chivo drove seemed like a walking pace when it was obvious that the compound was on fire. The main gate was intact. Stan made quick work of the combination lock and chain, opening the gate for Chivo before closing and locking it behind the VW. Chivo didn't wait, but sped off to the end of the drive and towards the fire. Anger flushed through Stan before he realized that Chivo had the training and could probably help immediately with whatever had gone wrong. Stan locked the gate and began running up the long driveway.

Chivo slid to a stop in the courtyard. The shop was fully engulfed and would have to burn itself out. He looked at the fire and the embers floating in the wind. Thankfully the wind was out of the north and was pushing the flames and embers away from the house. Four bodies lay in the courtyard; one was very badly burned, another had an obvious life-ending head wound, and the other's neck lay at an unnatural angle. Ignoring the obvious casualties, Chivo ran to the only remaining patient and found Bexar.

Covered in black soot and unconscious, Bexar lay there, his rifle next to him, the sling removed, and the tactical carrier badly damaged and cut off him. His clothes were in a ruined heap, also expediently removed by a pair of EMS shears. Guillermo knelt over Bexar, latex gloves on, working methodically and quickly, an IV already started. Jennifer stood nearby holding the IV bag above Bexar. Angel ran up to Chivo.

"What the fuck happened, Angel?"

"They attacked again, that's what happened. They blew up the shop, and I think they somehow rigged the propane tanks."

Chivo doubted they could have rigged anything without getting inside the wire, which someone would have noticed.

"Did you mount a patrol, a security sweep?"

"No."

Chivo cursed, "Get me Coach and Brian. We'll do it."

"Coach is dead."

"Fuck, mano. Fine! Just get me Brian. We're going out the side gate to make a sweep. Make sure those fucking bodies don't get up again, and get Bexar and everyone else the fuck inside in case there's another attack!"

Angel turned and yelled for Brian, quickly executing the instructions Chivo gave him. This was not the time to argue, and Angel knew he was right.

Brian hustled over, visibly shaken.

"Brian, I need you to focus, mano. We're going to need to do this the right way or more people might die. I can't babysit you while we do this, and it would help me for you to come along. Can you handle your shit?"

Slowly nodding, Brian turned, looked at the shop, and saw Angel standing over Heath's badly burned body before firing a single shot into the skull. His eyes narrowed as anger burned deep in his soul.

"Yeah, Chivo, fuck 'em all! Let's roll."

The pair jogged to the side gate next to the garage. Brian worked the combination lock, and the pair were outside the wire. Chivo began moving west, quickly putting distance between the fence line and the compound and themselves. Brian followed about a dozen yards behind him, and they each moved methodically and quietly. Brian tried to match Chivo's movement, but Chivo was less than a ghost; he seemed to absorb light and sound, a dark quietness in the desert that was reserved only for master hunters. Halfway to the road, Chivo turned and began moving south. A few moments later, he stopped and melted into a crouched position. Brian stopped and crouched, unable to detect whatever it was that Chivo saw. The moon barely gave enough light to create shadows on the low vegetation. The light of the burning shop a few hundred yards away danced across the desert, and his ears pounded with a heartbeat so loud that he was sure Chivo could hear it.

Movement. Someone was crawling through the desert, coming from the direction of the compound, almost on a straight course for Chivo. Brian froze, holding his breath, trying to be a shadow of a hole in the ground while moving only his eyes back and forth, looking for more movement besides the single person. He didn't see any, and he couldn't even see Chivo's form anymore.

The crawler reached the area where Brian remembered Chivo had been. Waiting, anticipating a rifle shot, all Brian saw was some fast movement before seeing Chivo's hand sticking up and motioning him to come close.

Face down on the ground was a man whose hands and feet were bound with flex cuffs. Chivo's shemagh was wrapped around his eyes and tied, the ends stuffed into his mouth.

"He said that he's the only survivor of the raiding party, that the other three were killed by someone inside the compound after the RPG attack."

The sound of the dead crashing through the desert behind them to the west became more apparent, growing in intensity and size. Chivo was confident that they were about to have a serious problem with all the undead moths heading to the flame. It was still hours until sunrise; once the sun was up, the fire wouldn't be as obvious. Chivo knew that they needed to act quickly or be overrun. The fence would eventually fail, just like the bridge that killed Apollo.

"OK, mano, let's get this fucker back to the compound. We'll tag him and bag him, and then I've got to unfuck the march of the dead."

Chivo stood and pulled the bound man into a sitting position, drew his pistol, and struck the man across the face. His body went limp. Chivo then squatted and pulled the prisoner over his shoulder into a modified fireman's carry. Moving carefully but swiftly, they made their way back to the side gate, passing the three bodies of the remaining raider party.

The Compound, Saint George, UT

Bexar gasped awake. It took him a moment, but he realized that he was lying on the kitchen table; Guillermo was standing next to him, as were Frances and Jennifer. Another moment passed, and then he realized that he was nude and the cast on his leg was gone. Bexar didn't know why he kept waking up nude in strange places, but he was sure it wasn't from being an alcoholic.

"Frances, if you wanted to see me naked, you could have just asked."

Guillermo laughed.

"Honey, if I want to see a dick, Merylin has a whole drawer of them."

Bexar began laughing, which quickly started a coughing fit.

Brian walked into the room. "Guillermo, Chivo caught one of the attackers. He's chained to the flagpole outside."

"Where's Chivo?"

Stan ran into the room. "Chivo left, tore ass out of here in that Beetle we got."

Angel replied, "You got it, good job. What about the horses?"

"I think the horses are a loss. I'm sorry."

Angel scowled, shaking his head.

"I'm sorry, buddy; we were overrun and couldn't get them as we left. On the way back we felt the blast and saw the flames. What the hell happened?"

"They somehow got the shop to catch fire, and I think the propane tanks exploded."

Brian interrupted, "No, the captive said it was an RPG attack. Three of his party were killed. One of them had a launch tube, at least that's what Chivo called it."

To Bexar, the attack felt like a bad dream, lingering after waking up. "I killed three of them before going into the shop."

Angel patted his shoulder.

"As much fun as this is, Guillermo, I don't feel like I'm hurt. Do you have anything I could wear? I want to get up."

Guillermo laid a towel over Bexar's midsection and groin. "The towel will have to do for a few minutes. You aren't hurting because I shot you up with morphine, guy. Heath is about your size, and Jennifer can fix up something to fit tomorrow if it's not quite right. I also gave you some antibiotics in the mix. That's about all we can do for you right now."

"What all is wrong with me then?"

"We'll have to wait and see about your leg. The cast was damaged in the aftermath, so it came off. You have some pretty good burns on your arms and chest. Your gear and your clothes were burned and ruined. I think your rifle is OK. We washed most of the soot off and cleaned the burns. It'll all probably hurt like a son of a bitch tomorrow."

"Such optimism."

"That's easy for you to say, Bexar; you're the one flying on the morphine rocket."

Jennifer walked down the hall and returned a few minutes later with some underwear, a pair of socks, a T-shirt, some heavy-duty work pants, and a pair of work boots. Guillermo helped Bexar sit up. The IV bag hung from the light fixture over his head. Jennifer and Guillermo carefully helped Bexar get into the shirt and underwear before helping him to his room and his bed to rest.

The Beetle

Chivo stopped in the middle of the road at the end of the compound's long driveway, revving the obnoxiously loud engine and honking the horn. The smashed-out tail lights and turn signals kept the vehicle dark, except for the headlights, which Chivo had switched to bright. The dead slowly began shambling toward the loud air-cooled car, and Chivo began slowly threading his way through the undead on the road, making his way down the hillside and back toward the Interstate. He didn't know the area away from the compound at all; the surface streets were a mystery to him, and anything he couldn't see from the powerful optic of his big 50BMG Barrett rifle was unknown. Frank, the captured raider, wouldn't tell him anything about his group's location either—yet. Chivo would take care of that first thing in the morning. He had left Brian with specific instructions to cut off the man's clothes, chain him to the flagpole, and spray him with the hose until he regained consciousness. Once he was awake, Brian was to make sure he didn't fall asleep. Chivo needed the man shaken, cold, tired, and disorientated.

Slowly, Chivo made his way to the frontage road. He took a right and found a tanker semi-truck abandoned on the road, a car wedged under the middle of the tank, the top of the car crushed from the crash. Chivo pulled alongside the tanker, rolled down his window, and fired a half-dozen times into the aluminum side of the tank with his pistol. He wasn't sure what the tanker held, but the red hazard placard told him what was in the tanker was combustible. Liquid spewed out of the tanker, covering the crashed car. Chivo pulled forward and turned around, the dead continuing to swarm to his obnoxiously loud car. The camp lantern from the garage where the VW had been kept still sat on the passenger floorboard. A few moments were all it took to get the dual mantels lit and burning. Chivo stopped next to the tanker and the crashed car to roll down his window again; the air stank of the dead and raw fuel. Smiling, he threw the lantern onto the fuel-slicked roof of the crashed car, which whooshed into flames. Chivo accelerated as hard and fast as the VW would go, dodging the dead the best he could while resisting the urge to watch in the rear-view mirror. The air around him glowed bright orange, shadows of the dead approaching the flames dancing against the hillside; the hard thump of an explosion seemed to propel the car even faster. The tires squealed as he made the left turn to go back up the hill toward the compound and the burning shop, and Chivo was glad to see that the fuel truck burned much more brightly than the burning shop. It appeared that the small strip center near the semi-tanker had also caught fire. Together it might as well have been a bug zapper for the dead. The mass of the dead shifted. Chivo saw more macabre faces shambling down the hill than the backs of heads this time coming up it.

Yup, Bexar, one piece at a time.

CHAPTER 7

Outside of Boulder City, Nevada
April 5, Year 1

The air churned and buzzed with the sounds of flies. Aymond lay on the ground high upon the rocky mound with binoculars to his eyes, scanning the curved roadway; marked units sat idle and abandoned at each end, the police officers who'd placed them long missing.

The rest of the team knelt in a loose defensive position around the M-ATVs and the PLA radar truck. The dome was up and ready to run, but since the device was unknown and the Chinese seemed to purposely keep from walking in front of it, they would only activate the dome if Zeds appeared on the bridge.

Aymond, reasonably sure they were alone, or at least that the PLA or Koreans weren't around yet, stood and began hiking down the south side to where the rest of the team was waiting. As he reached them, the team gathered close enough to hear but remained facing outward in a defensive posture.

"Completely overrun. There are police vehicles on either end, but obviously they appear abandoned. There are no signs of survivors; I have no idea if some are sheltering in the facility below."

"What about the generators?" Happy asked the question that everyone was thinking.

"I have no idea, but some of the exterior lights are on, though the fuses on the transmission lines appear disconnected or blown. We'd have to get a Corps of Engineers team in here to really know, unless one of you dickheads knows anything about electricity."

"I fucked a stripper called White Lightning once."

Muffled smirks and coughing erupted from the group.

"Outstanding, Gonzo, your mom would be so proud."

"That *was* his mom!"

Aymond tried to ignore Hammer, but the whole team was straining, trying not to laugh.

"OK, gentlemen, and you too, Gonzo, saddle up. This is a wash. Time to point north to Nellis."

The convoy lurched out of their spot on Highway 93 near the Hoover Dam, turning right on Lakeshore Road. The route that Snow had mapped out on a civilian road atlas was a meandering, indirect one, but it kept the team from driving through Henderson and it would drop them near Ellis Air Force Base without having to drive through the heart of Las Vegas. Aymond had no idea what they would find in Vegas, but he assumed it wouldn't be magic shows and gambling.

The road loosely followed the far edge of the shore of Lake Mead, passing a few RV parks and establishments along the way. December was apparently high time for the area. The RV parks looked full, a handful of Zeds shambling through the mass of expensive-looking mobile homes, but the convoy passed far enough away that by the time the Zeds turned to follow them, the rising dust was all they caught. They took Lakeshore to Northshore Road, a narrower two-lane roadway with open desert sprinkled with vacationers, which led to Lake Mead Boulevard. The drive with a sports car or a motorcycle would probably have been enjoyable, but lumbering along in an armored truck, even one as advanced as the M-ATV, wasn't exactly deserving of a hot lap on *Top Gear*.

As they exited the mountains, the roadway abruptly crashed into the eastern edge of Las Vegas. Snow stopped and glanced at Aymond in the front passenger seat, holding the civilian road map.

Aymond pointed out of his side window. "Take a right. If we go through open country, we'll run into the southern edge of the base."

Snow nodded and radioed the following trucks with the plan before turning the wheel and crunching onto the rocky desert floor. A few hundred yards later, the convoy bounced across a small paved road and continued northward across the desert, the edge of civilization's rotting City of Light out their left-side windows. Without GPS, an overland route required orienteering skills that the team members possessed, with compasses they had in their kits, but they needed better maps to be accurate. Dead reckoning was all they really needed, just as long as they kept the edge of the city in sight. Much like early explorers sailing down the coast of Africa, they could get home as long as they kept land in view. Little league fields required a minor course correction, as did the gravel quarry, but the fenced-off edge of the air base stopped them in their tracks. Happy made quick work of the fence with his bolt cutters before removing the cross beams to make room for the trucks. The convoy drove slowly onto the tarmac of the runways. A row of angry-looking A-10s sat on the ramp with flat tires. A few members of the team had trained with the PJs at Nellis before and had a good idea where they would be found; the runways and taxiways would lead them right to their doorstep like the yellow brick road.

Aymond scanned the flightline across the acres of concrete and desert. "There's a whole bunch of Zeds on that side, Snow. Keep us over here as long as you can." This didn't look good to Aymond.

Snow didn't speak, but he felt the same disappointment, that this base was like the others that they had visited. He drove to the north end of the runways and across the taxiways to the long ramp leading to where the PJs' helicopters should be tied down. On the tarmac were numerous Zeds who had been killed; they lay motionless, baked by the sun and completely untouched by the buzzards or other wildlife.

"Well someone's been here, Chief, and they were fucking pipe hitters!"

"Let's hope they're still here."

The convoy drove to the edge of the ramp where the PJ facility stood, windows dark. Aymond keyed the radio. "Set a defensive position, and use the radar truck. Chuck, Davis, Gonzo, and Hammer, sweep the two buildings fast, but keep your asses from getting bit."

No one responded verbally, but the flurry of activity was enough to know that the message was received and well understood. The M-ATVs parked in a loose V-formation with the radar truck at the tip, the inside of the protective V being toward the buildings. Jones had the radar truck's dome up and on before the armored war wagons had even turned their motors off. All they could do was standby, hoping that the search team found some friendlies.

Snyder, Texas

The second night away in her MRAP-turned-motorhome was much less eventful than the first. There were no tornados, no driving rain, no dead lit by lightning's flash. The morning had been looking up until now. The fuel gauge meant that Amanda wasn't comfortable moving on until she could top off the heavy truck; the semi-tanker parked at the truck stop was the first choice. What was contained in the still-shiny aluminum tanker trailer was anyone's guess. Amanda wasn't willing to chance accidently putting gasoline or cooking oil or who knows what else into the fuel tank of her rig. She assumed that the placards and numbers on the rig explained what the load was, but Amanda had no knowledge of them and no idea where to find the information in this post-Internet era.

She knew the big saddle-tanks on the semi-truck held diesel fuel and many gallons of it. The trusty length of rubber hose could be her pipeline to success. Across the large parking lot from her chosen truck stop was a squat three-story hotel; no large semi-trucks in the parking lot there, although there was a propane delivery truck with a large tank on the back parked next to the building. None of this mattered, as teeming through the parking lot were the dead, dozens of them converging on the rattling exhaust of her diesel engine. They were beginning to slap against the armored hull. Amanda wasn't worried about her safety yet, and she could slowly drive through the massing swarm, nudging the bodies out of her way and hopefully away from her tires. A spare tire was on the truck, but she had no idea how to get it down or how to jack up the truck, so the spare might as well have been a birthday cake for all the good it would do if she got a flat tire.

She did not have a surplus of fuel, and she had no outside help; the one thing she had at the moment was time. Time to think through the problem piece by piece. If the dead would act like her dogs and chase something she threw, life would be a lot easier. She could throw a stick, the dead would trace the stick in the air as it flew, and follow obediently. After all, they acted like moths to the flame.

Flame... fire!

Familiar as Amanda was with her M4, the big M2 machine gun on the turret was something she had only fired once, the day of the library raid. The hotel and the propane tanker truck loomed large in her windshield. From the highway, she estimated the truck to be about six hundred feet away, and that guess would have to do because there was no way she was going to get outside to pace it off.

If I do nothing, I have to drive off and find other fuel. Worst case I blow everything up, and I have to drive off and find other fuel. Amanda shrugged to herself, ignoring the fact that the worst case would be her vehicle being disabled. She opened the roof hatch and climbed up the sling into the turret. Walking herself through a mental checklist, she pulled the charging handle hard to the rear and let go, switched the safety, moved the big rifle in the mount a little to get the muzzle pointed in the propane truck's general direction, and pushed the make-it-loud button. The air ripped open from the assault of automatic weapons fire. Windows shattered, and pieces of the hotel's façade broke away and fell in chunks. An obese person, long dead, shambled out of his hotel room, falling through the broken window to the parking lot three stories below and into a crumpled heap.

Amanda quickly pushed on the handles, arcing a rain of steel toward the propane truck, squinting in anticipation and ducking behind the armored glass of the turret. The large holes walked up the cab of the truck and the 50-caliber rounds pierced the heavy tank like a laser. Immediately, the propane tank ruptured, venting the pressurized propane—and nothing happened. Instead, every pair of milky-white eyes stared at her as the dead shambled toward the enormous eruption of sound of the M2 ripping the air apart.

"Fuck, that always worked in the damn movies... I need fuel. Fuck!"

She climbed back into the interior of the MRAP, and the roof hatch thunked closed. After dogging the latch and sitting in the driver's seat, Amanda drove across the worn grass median and next to the semi-truck. The side of the MRAP rubbed against the semi-truck, knocking both trucks' side mirrors off. Amanda could get the driver's door open, but it wouldn't open far enough for her to get out. Angry at the dead, angry that a propane truck wouldn't blow up like she'd thought it would, and angry at herself for believing that it would in the first place, Amanda slammed her door closed. After unlatching the roof hatch, Amanda grabbed her hose and climbed out onto the roof again.

Standing on the roof, she could see the situation that she'd created, and it wasn't good, not good at all. More dead streamed from behind the hotel, from across the street, from the fields, and from the highway. Wrapping the hose around her shoulders, Amanda climbed down the side of her armored truck into the small gap between it and the semi. As luck would have it, she'd been able to stop with the fuel filler cap on her tank quite close to the filler cap on the tank of the semi. With no gap between the trucks the dead didn't appear to be able to get to her, so Amanda got to work. She unscrewed her cap and let it hang on the safety chain; she went to unscrew the cap of the semi's saddle tank and found it locked, needing a key to release it. She banged on the driver's door window of the semi and got no response. Trying the door, she found it too was locked.

"Fucking hell."

Angry, Amanda drew her pistol and fired twice into the thin glass of the semi's door window, breaking the glass. After pushing the shattered safety glass window out of the way and unlocking the truck from the inside, she opened the door and squeezed inside. The cab of the truck was disgusting, some unknown goo was in the driver's seat, and the interior smelled worse than it looked, which was saying something. Coughing, Amanda tried the cubby holes and storage areas around the driver's door before finding a single silver key on a cheap truck-stop keychain. Outside the truck, she tried the key in the gas cap and was happy to find it worked.

With the cap now off, one end of the hose went into the semi's fuel tank; she took a few breaths, wrapped her lips around the hose, and pulled with all she had. Spitting fuel out of her mouth, she cursed as diesel splashed on her pants and boots before she got the end of the hose in her tank. Now she waited.

Tucumcari Municipal Airport, NM

Andrew walked across the tarmac. His home for the previous night had been in one of the short rows of hangers. It had felt like a real home for all the time he'd spent in his hanger over the years. Oreo plodded along next to him, happy, alert, and ready, just like always. The two big tanks of aviation fuel for the field had Jet-A and Avgas. The Jet-A was of no use to him, but the Avgas was exactly what he needed for the Husky. For a field in the middle of BFE New Mexico, one of the runways was surprisingly long, and the fuel-delivery system was much more complex than it needed to be, which also meant that the system depended on electric pumps... electric pumps that no longer worked. Although if the tanks worked like the others he had used before, Andrew's guess was that he might still be able to fuel from the tank. The short grip of a pair of bolt cutters stuck out of the top of his backpack, and, after the short walk from the hanger, he and Oreo stood inspecting the fuel tanks.

The tanks were idiot-marked with big bold letters labeling which tank held which fuel. For all the problems of filling a diesel truck with gasoline, fueling a turbine aircraft with Avgas was more annoying and more problematic. Pilots never being ones to trust a guy on the flight line, they liked big markings that they could see from the cockpit to help them feel safe in the knowledge that the correct fuel tank was being used. The filling connection and the output hose were of no use; the output would flow too fast and dump fuel all over everything, not exactly Andrew's first choice. The two vents on top of the tank didn't seem promising either, but small tank access in the middle of the tank on the top was their best bet. This wasn't exactly a gamble; this exact sequence had played out with similar tanks all across the United States during the past few weeks. After cutting the two locks off the cap, an adjustable crescent wrench made quick work of the cap's bolts, and Andrew was able to peer down the small hole into the tank; it smelled like Avgas and not Jet-A, and he could see tiny rays of sunlight shimmering off the fuel surface.

"We're in business, buddy."

Andrew climbed down to where Oreo sat dutifully waiting; the pair walked back to the hanger, started the Husky, and taxied off the tarmac, across the dusty desert ground, and right up next to the tank. After shutting off the engine, Andrew climbed out, loosened the fuel caps, and began siphoning fuel, filling the aircraft's bladders and his small gas can.

"I bet we only have six more months of flying before the fuel all goes bad. Thank God there's no damn ethanol in aviation fuel or we'd be going up shit creek already!"

Oreo yawned; he had heard the same thing repeated at every fuel stop. After sumping his tanks for water, Andrew walked the aircraft for a fast preflight check, climbed in, and taxied back onto the tarmac. The windsock hung limp. With no wind, there was no need to taxi to take off into the wind. Andrew conducted his run-up and magneto checks on the flightline in front of the small airfield's FBO. Once the engine reached a reasonable operating temperature and the final checks were complete, Andrew pushed power and began his take-off roll, bounding across the flightline and taxiway, eschewing the runways all together. Before the fall of society, such foolhardy actions would have left him with some explaining to do to an agency known far and wide for their complete lack of a sense of humor, but now Andrew simply didn't care.

Rolling out toward the west, he flew over the small town of Tucumcari, New Mexico. Keeping his altitude low, Andrew scanned the town with his binoculars for any signs of survivors. An entire section of the town appeared to be ruined by fire; the main drag appeared to be owned by the dead. Andrew didn't see any signs of survivors. If there were any down there, they were alone and on their own. Only desert stretched across the landscape in every direction that he could see. After retrieving the road atlas from his bag and scratching Oreo between the ears, Andrew flipped pages until he found what he needed, making pencil marks and notes along the route and of what the town held. I-40 snaked westward, and he followed it, taking a straighter and faster route overhead than the roadway below could give.

"We should be over Albuquerque in a bit!" Andrew yelled over the engine and wind noise to his K-9 companion. Smiling, Andrew let the yellow aircraft gain altitude and airspeed.

Saint George, UT

To say he felt sore was an understatement; Bexar had a headache and felt hungover. The skin on his arms hurt. Looking in the mirror on the dresser, he saw the burns and scratches. Black soot was still smeared on his face. His leg ached, but he could walk on it, sort of, limping a bit because the leg was tender. Folded neatly on the dresser were more pairs of underwear, socks, a T-shirt, and thick brown work pants with cargo pockets; the tag indicated that some place called Duluth Trading made them. Bexar stared at himself in the mirror, at the injuries, the scars, cuts, and bruises he'd earned since December.

"What is it with me and getting fucking blown up?"

His reflection had no answer. Moving slower than usual, Bexar bent over to put on his new pants and proceeded to get dressed. The pants were a little long and a bit loose, but beggars couldn't be choosers in the brave new world of the dead. The T-shirt fit well. A worn pair of work boots sat on the ground. A belt was on the dresser, along with his pistol, rifle, magazines, and his beloved custom CM Forge knife. The tactical gear was gone, the carrier, mag pouches, all of it. The holster for the pistol wasn't the same one he'd had before, but it fit the weapon and seemed to function.

Bexar press checked the pistol; it was still loaded, as was his rifle. His rifle was filthy and needed to be cleaned. The spare magazines went into the cargo pockets on his pants for now; perhaps Angel had some spare mag pouches, or maybe Jennifer could whip up something with her badass seamstress skills.

In the living room, he found Guillermo and Chivo standing close and speaking in hushed tones. Chivo looked up and waved him over.

"One chair, a cheese cloth or light dish towel, or worse case a T-shirt, a bucket, a hose, and my man Bexar here is all I need to gather the intel that we need to rectify this problem."

Guillermo's eyes were puffy. He was filthy, covered in dirt and soaked in sweat, and he looked exhausted and emotionally defeated, giving only a weak smile for a greeting to Bexar.

"OK. I'll tell the others to stay away."

"Good. Let them know that they don't want to be a part of this."

Guillermo looked up from the floor and at Bexar again. "But I do."

Chivo put his hand on Guillermo's shoulder. "Are you sure?"

"They..." tears rolled down his cheeks, streaking through the dirt, "they did this to us, and I want retribution."

"Retribution will come. Today is only about making sure we can get it."

Guillermo nodded and walked out of the room.

"What happened?"

Chivo looked at Bexar. "You don't remember last night?"

"I remember the shop exploded and burned."

"You pulled Heath out of the shop after it exploded. You don't remember that?"

"Vaguely, like a bad dream."

"Mixing adventures with morphine will do that. Heath died, but you did the right thing."

Bexar's expression didn't change, "Anyone else?"

"Yeah, mano, Gary and Coach got it too."

Bexar shook his head. "So tell me how we're going to fix this."

"We have a prisoner; you and I are going to interview him in an hour or so."

"Bad cop, bad cop again?"

"Something like that, buddy."

Groom Lake, NV

A general assembly, the first full assembly since the Groom Lake survivors had met to see Amanda Lampton sworn in as President, sat noisily in the assembly hall. Some of the residents hadn't been here for the swearing-in ceremony, arriving after the surprise and missing the festivities. The celebration had been vibrant and happy with so many people releasing the fear and anger of the previous months. The only thing that Jake found missing was an open bar, the facility being poorly stocked on spirits, wine, or beer, but some people told him that they were glad about that because this was the longest they had been sober, and they felt like they had new lives. Jake wasn't one to disagree and decided against the previous plans of trying to distill some liquor out of the stored grains.

Jessie, Sarah, and Erin stood in the back of the hall, along with Jason and a handful of the shooters who had completed the first, and thus far only, Alien's Home Tactical Training Academy, as one of the participants had named the basic tactical shooting course.

Jake took the stage to a round of applause. "Thank you, thank all of you. Every single day we live is a day we are winners, winning the war against the onslaught of the dead and the Yama Strain. All of you here today were instrumental in the containment of the outbreak. If it hadn't been for your quick action and adherence to the lockdown rules we have in place, I am confident that more of us would have been taken by Yama."

The crowd applauded for themselves, Jake smiling at the interruption, happy for the positive outlook the residents had.

"We live and learn, just as all of us have done since the attack on December 26th of this past year. We have learned what caused the outbreak, and we have a theory as to why the lights and systems were turning on and off. First the outbreak: Brit Sanchez was aboveground without good reason. She was attacked by a reanimate and was bitten. She failed to follow the rules of safety and further failed by concealing a bite wound from all of us. Her selfishness killed our fellow residents. Her selfishness also resulted in the death of our military commander, Major Jeffery Wright."

An audible gasp was heard, and whispering began immediately. Jake held up his hands.

"This won't happen again. We have a future plan to prevent another outbreak, but before we get to that, we need to talk about the systems. This facility is more complex than we had realized. I know all of you are surprised to hear that a secret underground base at Area 51 is a complex and advanced place, but you'll have to believe me."

Jake winked at the crowd, which chuckled politely in return.

"The systems are all computer controlled. Those computers are connected to other, similar facilities around the United States. Of all those facilities, this one and the one in Texas are the only two that have survived and have survivors living in them. We believe that the Chinese and Koreans were attempting to hack this facility via that network. We physically disconnected the servers from any outside connection. The servers all rebooted and are running. We don't know how all the systems in the facility work, but thankfully the issues with the lights, air systems and everything else have become reliable. That is why we think the systems came back online and why we believe they will remain online for the foreseeable future. Until we find a survivor that has an idea as to how the computers control the facility, we'll work hard to keep the status quo and keep us all safe."

The crowd clapped.

"Now, the new procedures so we don't have another Yama Strain Sanchez infecting our protected survivors. All aboveground working parties will be strip-searched by selected persons before they are allowed re-entry. Just as we quarantine our new friends before they're allowed to take up residence here, we will check each of us for our protection. No one is exempt. Any time an aboveground party returns, a male and a female will conduct physical examinations on the returning members, of the same gender, of course, before they are allowed entry back into the facility."

The applause was slower than before but still there.

"I know some of you have no desire to return topside. I understand and respect that decision. Others are happy to go topside any chance they get; I understand and respect that decision as well. We have many jobs and a place for everyone here, and we are committed to helping you. Today, though, we need twenty volunteers for a special detail, an important detail of honor to help in the respectful cremation of our fallen citizens, our fellow residents and friends."

Hands were raised around the room.

"Thank you all so much for volunteering. Check in with Sarah in the back of the room for the details. In a few minutes, I ask all of you who are not assisting with the detail to join us in the cafeteria. The kitchen staff has prepared a special lunch in remembrance of our fallen friends. Thank you."

Jake gave a curt nod and walked off the stage, the crowd applauding shortly before the room erupted in conversation and movement. The volunteers made their way to the back of the room as instructed. Their day was just beginning, and it wouldn't involve the bland sheet cake that the rest of the residents were going to eat.

As the hall cleared, Sarah addressed the volunteers, thirty in all. "Thank you for volunteering. The task is honorable work, but the work is going to be hard. The victims' bodies have already been moved to the blast door, and we need help carrying them outside. Once outside the hangar, we have a location to the west of the hangar chosen where some of the detail will dig a shallow mass grave. We have acquired some jet fuel from the tanks and have some other material that we'll be using to start the funeral pyre in that grave."

Much to Jessie and Sarah's surprise, none of the volunteers balked at the task, the plan, or asked to be excused. All of them were resolute in the need for the work to be done.

Jessie spoke up. "Don't forget that we will all be strip-searched upon returning. Some privacy partitions are already in place in the hangar constructed out of the office cubicles, and we will do our best to have some small portion of modesty."

"What if someone is bit?"

The question that no one in the assembly had asked, but everyone had thought, was finally said out loud. Erin replied first. "Then that person will be put down."

No one spoke for a few moments. The comment was cold and without feeling, but they knew it was the only answer. A few months before, such a concept would have been outrageous to the point of lunacy. In this new world owned by the dead, it was expected.

Work Party, Groom Lake, NV

"East of the hangar, between the taxiway and runways we'll start by digging a shallow grave. I have to apologize, but all we have are these folding army shovels. I wish we had a backhoe or even full-sized shovels, but this is it, so this is what we'll use. According to the number of bodies that we have, we're guessing that a hole about ten foot by ten foot will work if it's about three feet deep. The rules are simple; everyone digs. When you're on break, you really aren't on break. You can sit and rest, but your rifle will be in your hands, you'll be facing outwards, and you'll call out for any zombies you see. We're not going to have another damn Typhoid Mary here."

Erin interrupted Jessie, "Brit the bitch!"

Jessie glanced at Erin and continued. "Once the hole is dug, we'll douse the bodies with the fuel and light it."

No one else spoke. Some in the small group nodded; others were now a bit annoyed at what they had volunteered for, but now that they stood in the hangar next to the stack of their dead friends, it would be impossible for them to shirk their duties at this point.

"I have no idea how hot the fire has to be to burn bone, but we'll try. When we're done burning the bodies, we'll all take turns shoveling the dirt back into the hole and finishing the burial. Any questions?"

A middle-aged man who appeared to have lost a lot of weight recently spoke up. "Who's going to be checking us before we go back inside? Are we checking one another?"

Sarah spoke up for the answer. "Good question and, no, our greeter guards are in a meeting right now discussing the procedures for the searches. By the time we're done, they should be ready for us."

"If there's nothing else, everyone grab a shovel," Jessie said. "I'll be right behind you with my FJ, water, and snacks, and we'll meet over at the worksite. Sarah is going to mark off the edges, and then we can all get to work. The faster we get started, the sooner we'll be done."

General grumbling faded behind her as Jessie walked to the FJ, loading two blue jugs of water and a box of protein bars from the storeroom.

Nellis Air Force Base, NV

"Chief, no one is here. It appears that there were some survivors, but they're gone now."

Aymond nodded. "Thanks, Hammer. What about supplies?"

"That they've got. It looks like they raided half the base. Damn near a pallet of XM193, like fifty cases of MREs, various M4s, magazines, those massive trauma bags the PJs take on their helicopters, and some other random stuff. Chuck is taking an inventory. We're clear to move inside though."

"Roger that, Hammer. Not many Zeds coming our way, which is surprising. You tell the others to lock it down and head inside, I'm going to check with Chuck and take a look around. Tell the others team meeting in thirty mikes."

Hammer didn't respond. He just walked off to complete his task. Five minutes later, the entire team crowded into the conference room that the PJs had been using as a supply cache, each of them digging through bags and crates of gear, turning on electronics, night-vision goggles, and tactical lights to see if they still worked, and making notes along the way to help Chuck with the full inventory. They didn't have the complete mission-profile load-out containers that the SEAL teams had in California, but this was better than what they'd had on their trucks.

"Hey, Chief, check this out. It's a shortwave radio. My dad used to play with one when I was a kid. You could pick up broadcasts from Europe sometimes. This one has a hand crank to power it up."

"Does it work, Gonzo?"

"Not as hard as his mom's crank works," was called out from the back of the room.

"Fuck you, Chuck! How many sailors did your sister fuck before the clap became applause?"

The rest of the room laughed as Gonzo spun the handle on the radio until it lit up, static coming out of the speakers. "Whoa, everyone, shut the fuck up."

This time he wasn't joking. Everyone got quiet, and radio static filled the room as Gonzo slowly rolled the tuning dial across the bands.

"... secured underground facility, food, shelter, clean water. All survivors are welcome at Groom Lake, Nevada. You can make a radio out of parts from disabled cars, tune..."

The radio transmission faded out to static.

"Get it back, Gonzo!" Chuck was no longer lobbing insults at his teammate's mother; genuine excitement filled his voice.

Gonzo slowly spun the dial, as he paced around the room, trying to find a spot to regain the signal. After a few minutes, the static faded, and the limited energy from turning the handle had been used.

Aymond nodded. "That's like what we heard on the HF weeks ago. I thought it was bullshit. Any of you been to Groom Lake?"

"Do you think we'll find aliens, Chief?"

"No, Happy, I doubt it, but I don't think we're too far away from it. OK, Gonzo, you, Chuck, and Happy finish up with this inventory. First we recon the rest of Nellis, and then it's time we visit a top-secret base."

Snyder, TX

Amanda left the fuel cap on the half-full saddle tank of the semi-truck open. Using one of her spare T-shirts from the supplies, she soaked it in diesel and stuffed it into the tank. The fuel tank of her MRAP was topped off and the cap back on. Dead surrounded the trucks, all of them pawing at the metal sides, trying to get to a fresh meal. The flies were like nothing Amanda had ever experienced. Her shemagh was wrapped tightly around her head and face, sunglasses pushed tight against her eyes, but the flies still found their way into her ears and mouth. Between the diesel fumes and the flies, she could barely breathe. She tossed the hose on top of her MRAP and used some 550-cord to tie it onto the turret handle. She didn't want it in the vehicle stinking up the interior with diesel fumes, although she still had to deal with the fuel spilled on her clothes, which burned against her skin as she sweated. Climbing between the vehicles one last time, Amanda lit the soaked T-shirt sticking out of the semi-truck's saddle tank with her lighter and quickly pulled herself up the side of her truck and into the cab, leaving the turret hatch open, hoping to air it out a little. She would have to change pants soon, but now was not the time. The MRAP in gear, she drove forward, nudging away the dead clawing at her vehicle, some falling under the bumper, others knocked to the ground. She had no time to waste.

Frustrated, Amanda drove faster, running over the dead as she did so, u-turning out of the parking lot to go west before turning north on Highway 84. The mass of the dead were near the semi, so she accelerated quickly, watching in the rearview as the gas tank on the semi-truck spewed flames out of the open filler neck. The dead appeared to ignore her as they zeroed in on the fire like moths to a bug zapper.

They like fire. I like fire. I like that they like fire.

The Compound, Saint George, UT

The group members had been warned that they might not want to watch, but that if they did watch, they would have to be perfectly quiet. The captured attacker from the previous night lay on a folding table completely nude, shivering in the cool air, his hands and feet tied and also tied to the table. The end of the table was propped up on the edge of the fire pit, which had the prisoner laying with his head low at a modest angle and his feet above his head. He writhed against the restraints. A rope around his waist kept him from raising his hips off the table. A black T-shirt served as a blindfold. Chivo had two buckets of water, a dish towel soaking in the cold water of one. Bexar had a hose that was fed from the rain cistern, which had surprisingly good water pressure. Chivo gave Bexar very specific instructions; he was to help hold the towels tight and be quick to refill the water buckets.

Guillermo and a couple others watched from about ten yards away. The group's medical bag sat at Guillermo's feet, his presence and the bag standing by at Chivo's request.

"OK, Frank, this is your first and only chance. What is your group leader's name?"

"Fuck you, spic!"

Chivo's face showed no change, and with absolutely no emotional reaction, he gave a single curt nod to Bexar. Bexar pulled the soaking wet towel out of the bucket and placed it across Frank's mouth, nose, and face. Chivo, bucket in hand, began pouring water on the towel.

"What is your group leader's name, Frank. You can make this stop at any time, but only you can make it stop. What is his name? Just one name will make it stop."

Frank's body writhed against the restraints, his head jerking unsuccessfully back and forth, trying to escape the water. Chivo stopped the flow of water. "The name. Frank, only a name."

Frank's coughs gurgled. "Fuck you."

Chivo nodded to Bexar and began slowly pouring water across Frank's face, mouth, and nose again. Frank struggled, coughing. Chivo stopped, "You can end this, Frank. Only you can end this, and I want you to end this."

"Fuck your mother!"

Chivo's face was completely devoid of any expression. The insults didn't matter, the torture didn't matter; the only thing that mattered to Chivo was obtaining the objective. He poured water on Frank's covered face.

"There is no end until you decide, Frank."

Gasping against the towel, Frank called out, "Dan!"

"See, Frank, that wasn't so hard, was it? Just a simple answer, and you could breathe again. Where is your hideout?"

"No, I can't!"

Chivo nodded to Bexar, and the process began again, Frank struggling and gurgling. The waterboarding interrogation only took thirty minutes, but Chivo learned that the group's hideout was less than a mile as the crow flies to the southwest. There were only four of them left, and they were in dire straits. Nearly out of water, nearly out of food, the only thing they did have was a serious amount of weapons and ammo, as the RPG attack the previous night had shown. Chivo left Frank tied to the table outside in the cool air, where he shivered more in fear than from the cool air. Walking over to Guillermo, he saw that the others had left, unable to watch Chivo's enhanced interrogation techniques.

"OK, Willy, they're close to here; they're very well-armed, and they're almost out of water and food. This is your firebase on an exposed hill, so it's your choice. Do we kill them, or do we save them?"

Guillermo shook his head, his cheeks wet with tears from what he had watched. "It isn't my choice. This requires a group vote."

"Why don't you make it snappy, I either need to get us geared up for an op or geared up for a peace offering between your tribes. Either one you choose, I need to get Frank up and work on becoming his best bud for either plan to work."

Guillermo nodded and walked inside. Chivo gestured with his head, and Bexar followed to where Frank was tied to the table.

"You did good, Frank; you did really good, but understand you're not out of the woods yet. I'm going to take you off this table and let you get dressed, but if you even think about attempting to fight or escape, my man here will kill you before your 50cc brain can even finish the thought. Do you understand?"

A very weak "Yes, sir," was the response. Chivo looked at Bexar, who understood he was to provide hard cover. Like a bizarre felony traffic stop, Bexar pointed his rifle at Frank while Chivo cut him loose, handed him his clothes, and let him dress. Once dressed, Chivo zip-tied Frank's hands behind his back and also to his belt to keep him from being able to move.

Brian walked out of the house alone and headed straight to Chivo, leaned into his ear and whispered, "No peace. Fuck them. They killed... those friends were our family; every person in this group is my family."

Chivo nodded. Brian walked back inside the house. The burned-out shell of what was the workshop still smoked and smoldered a few yards away. First Chivo looked at Bexar and then to Frank. In one fluid motion, Chivo rotated, striking Frank on the side of the neck with the back of his arm, on the common peroneal. Frank collapsed, dazed.

"Help me tie this fucker to the flagpole again; you and I need to chat, and I've got to leave to take care of something before we go take the fight to Frank's group."

Five thousand feet AGL, NM

Andrew descended and banked over the heart of Albuquerque. Massive destruction was all he could see with the naked eye. Using the binoculars, Andrew saw that some bridges had collapsed, but he saw no signs of any survivors. The dead owned the city. Not wanting to waste any more time, he and Oreo continued westward, loosely following I-20 so as to not get lost. Without proper pilot charts, there was no way for Andrew to know where all the airports were located and, just as important, where the tallest radio and communication towers stood. So for his safety, he tried to eyeball it and keep around five thousand feet above ground level.

Before the attack, his Garmin unit would give him the correct altitude above the ground, the altimeter on the dash set to mean sea level. At least he was still able to verify or reset that altimeter at most of the airports that he landed in as they had small signs near the runway with the field elevation. Finding those fields was more difficult than he would have liked, but keeping to his rule to only fly during daylight, Andrew scanned for landing strips. Not that he needed one at any given minute, but if something happened, he would rather land at an airport or private strip than on a highway or in a field. At an airport there was a chance he could scavenge parts from other aircraft to get flying again. On the dash, the indicated airspeed still worked, but without his Garmin, Andrew had no idea what his ground speed was; he didn't even know how far he had flown except for making rough estimates with a road atlas. His Husky could climb, slowly, as high as twenty thousand feet, but Andrew had no supplemental oxygen nor any reason to fly that high. More importantly, the aircraft had a listed range of around eight hundred miles. That wasn't a number he wanted to chance, so when he was roughly half full of fuel, Andrew was on the hunt for a landing strip in hopes of scoring some Avgas.

In this part of the country, the airports were often roughly an "A" shape with long runways from being leftover auxiliary airports for military pilot training, so they weren't too hard to spot from the moderate altitude that he tried to keep.

Andrew located one of the big A-shaped airfields. It had old-looking surfaces with a big "X" on each end of the runways signifying that the runway was out of service, so the dark black tarmac of the primary runway was the obvious choice.

Taxiing near the fuel pumps, Andrew could see that the sign on the FBO said "Winslow." Flipping through the pages of the big spiral-bound atlas, Andrew saw that he was nearing Flagstaff, Arizona. The sun was well past being directly overhead, nearly halfway down the sky toward the horizon. Andrew decided that Winslow was a wonderful place to sleep but decided to fuel his plane first today, unlike the day before.

Today, the roadway scene on I-40 was weird, something like Andrew hadn't yet seen. All the cars were pushed off the roadway, and signs were knocked down. It looked as if a giant bulldozer had come through and destroyed all that was in its path. Andrew's mind flashed back to a favorite childhood movie, remembering that to stop the Nothing, he would have to name the princess.

"Of course, it couldn't be that simple, Oreo."

Oreo cocked his head, as dogs do.

After the fuel tanks were topped off, Andrew eschewed the couple of hangars available on the airport and taxied to the far south end on the unused runway. After walking Oreo for his much-needed break, they sat under the shade of the wings and ate a light dinner while watching the desert sunset. Then they both climbed back into the Husky and secured the door and windows to sleep in the plane. Andrew felt better being as far away from I-40 as he could be after seeing the destruction that day.

Groom Lake, NV

The day was one of hard work; Jessie was exhausted and nauseated, and the memories of her first pregnancy, carrying Keeley, began to come back: the hardships, the sickness, the pain, and the constant need to urinate. As those experiences returned with this pregnancy, she felt a sense of wonderment as to how her mind could forget all the bad parts of pregnancy when she held her little girl in her arms for the first time. Tears streamed down her cheeks, streaking through the dirt and soot from the horrible fire they had to tend, but the day was done. Soon she could shower, send these clothes to the laundry service, and then attempt to eat and sleep. Her back hurt, and she was beginning to really show the pregnancy, which meant that the others in the work party kept taking her shovel away. She wanted to help, but for all the work she attempted, Jessie spent most of her time sitting on the roof rack of the FJ with her rifle in hand watching for threats.

The new facility policy, one that she, Sarah, and Erin had helped Jake write, meant that even though not a single undead menace had appeared for the day, each and every one of them would still have to submit to a complete strip search for bite marks.

After parking the FJ back in the hangar, Jessie walked over to the women's line. She thought it strange that for a work party of their number, the vast majority of the volunteers were women. Just like public restrooms before the end of the world, the women's line was a half-dozen women deep and taking longer than it probably should. Safely hidden from the men behind the row of partitions, they all stood in the nude, waiting, holding their clothes in one arm, their rifles slung across their nude breasts, but none of them felt embarrassed or all that uncomfortable. It would seem that the new world order had given rise to the end of modesty.

"Fuck this," was all Jessie heard; by the time she turned to look, Erin had walked away from the back of the women's line and headed left toward the men's line.

The men's line had a single man currently being searched; neither he nor Jason, who was conducting the search, noticed her waiting for her turn. Soon the man headed to the exit area where he could dress, once again in private and still separated from the women's dressing area.

Jason's face flushed red at the sight of Erin standing in front of him completely nude, clothes tucked under her left arm and holding her rifle in her right hand. He stared at the floor. "Um, Erin, uh... you aren't supposed to be here."

"The women's line was taking too long, and I want to go shower and eat, so here I am."

"I can't do this. I have to check everywhere. I can't... you can't. It's not right... uh, I..."

Erin cut him off, "Just check me! Man the fuck up about it!"

The tension between the two of them was more than this situation; a growing history between them exponentially increased Jason's awkwardness.

"I heard you were the hero of Cortez, so what is your problem with this?"

"My, it, this... no, it isn't this. You know what it is."

"I do, and what's your deal?"

"I... we can't."

"But I know you love me, so why's it such a problem?"

Jason frowned. "I'm nineteen, I'm, you... we... Erin, you're too young."

"I won't be too young forever. Now inspect me for zombie bites so we can all go inside."

Radio Hut, Groom Lake, NV

"Whoa, what the fuck was that?" The airman ripped the headphones from his head and pushed back in his chair. Bill sat at his spark-gap radio, waiting to see if anyone else would transmit; so far he'd had contact with seven different groups or people from all across the United States. It was the best news that they'd had in weeks. People were alive and fighting to survive, but something had to be done quickly or none of them, including him, would survive.

"What was it, Jeremy?"

"Some sort of broadband wave of noise; it's hard to describe."

"Did you get a sound grab of it?"

"Yeah."

"Play it over the external speaker so I can hear it."

Jeremy did as instructed, and the room filled with five seconds of loud broadband sound, like some sound effect from a sci-fi movie.

"That sounds like an encrypted transmission."

Jeremy shook his head. "Doesn't sound like anything I've heard. The digitally encrypted stuff pixelates from the digital encoding."

Bill nodded. "Sure, but this wasn't digital. It was probably made using an old analog trick. Long before you were born and after WWII, agents had recordings, like actual records, not tapes or CDs obviously, that they carried. The record was of random radio-wave spectrum noise from space emitted by the suns and stars, completely random. Copies of that record were kept and sent out to agents in the field. With some basic work that the radio transmission recorded, it was phased with the record, and the agent receiving it would have to reverse the process. Damn near impossible to break, unless the Soviets got their vodka-soaked hands on one of the recordings. Some of the hardest encryption to crack, securing open air transmissions from interception, amazing technology really."

"Did they ever?"

"I think so, but I'm no secret squirrel like you, gents. I'm just an old man who likes playing with radios."

The other airmen laughed.

"Jeremy, play it again, please."

SSC, Ennis, TX

Clint sat at the computer terminal. The one-time cipher wasn't too terribly difficult to remember, but the thumb drive he had carried for six months had to be used with a computer. The thumb drive held more than just text documents or music, although both were present in case someone got suspicious, but no one had ever suspected, none of his teammates, not his boss, not his agency, and his reward would be coming soon.

The radio signal received earlier was encoded and encrypted. Password-protected secret memory sectors on the thumb drive were devoted to radio signals. First, Clint had to run the program from the thumb drive, and then in the program he could apply the MP3 that the jump drive carried. Once those two things were lined up, the message would be easy to read.

A few minutes later, Clint had the message decoded.

Nevada go dark disconnected. Enemy present on West Coast. New mission. Destroy San Diego and enemy.

Although Clint tried to practice, his Korean was rusty and quite subpar for what he needed. However, even if he didn't understand the message correctly, the message was sent simply enough so he knew that the righteous invaders were suffering losses.

The interface of the software only allowed so many characters, so Clint found himself writing poorly and shortly as if he was on Twitter, hashtag-doubleagent.

Targetto Nevada, five days.

Five days was longer than it would have taken Clint to reach Groom Lake, but he assumed that Amanda wouldn't have much of a chance in the wild range-land of the dead, except that Clint had helped to teach her how to survive. With the message encoded, Clint could now wait for his communist brothers and sister to arrive. He would hand over the entire northwestern ICBM field and the best the government had to offer at the SSC.

Radio Hut, Groom Lake, NV

Bill insisted that the radio remain open to scan all the amateur radio bands, which was hard for the changes between the high-frequency frequencies and the seventy-centimeter frequencies. Without warning, a similar sound as before erupted from the studio speakers.

"What the fuck do you think that is?"

"I don't know what they're saying Jeremy, but it's the same kind of transmission. What's the transmission power like?"

"Damn, Bill, it's like ten times as strong."

"So we can assume that either the first was a weak radio or it was a radio that was very far away. The second was a strong radio or one that was much closer than the other. I'd bet money that the first was far away, and the second was much closer."

"Like how far or how close?"

"That I don't know, Mike, but on those frequency ranges it could be China or it could be somewhere else on the continent; the other could have been from next door or a few states over."

"So it was a strong signal, so what."

"So what? So it sounded like a message broadcast on an open channel that was encrypted by adding some type of random noise that can only be decoded by another who has the same random noise sample."

"Who the hell would be sending encrypted signals?"

"The Chinese, the Koreans... I doubt it would be a random survivor community or we would have probably heard it before now."

"Why now?"

"No idea. I'm going to get Jake. This could mean nothing or it could mean something. With the cyber-attack on the facility, I'm leaning toward it means something, and that something isn't good."

Saint George, UT

Bexar sat hunched in the back seat of the tiny VW that Chivo drove. Frank sat next to Chivo, his hands and feet free. Frank had begun to believe that Chivo was his newfound best friend. Bexar held his pistol in his hand, the muzzle against the back of Frank's seat, where it would be harder to miss his target than holding it against his head and much easier to conceal. The last thing they needed was for Frank to understand his precarious situation in remaining amongst the living.

Chivo had explained his plan to Bexar before they left; it wasn't a grandiose plan, just simple and effective. They had no reason to believe that Frank was a strong enough person to lie effectively. After witnessing Chivo's enhanced inter-rogation techniques, Bexar was sure that he would have quickly given in after helping and watching the process. It was not for the faint of heart.

The undead were a bit sparser in the area; they weren't headed for the Interstate, just down the drive, south on Old Dump Road for a few hundred yards, where they turned into a loose industrial park. After turning onto Red Rock Road, Chivo deftly misshifted and caused the car to lurch and die.

"Shit, mano, looks like we have to walk from here. These old fucking cars. I bet the gas is already bad. Fucking ethanol goes bad in a couple of months, and it's been over three."

Frank was a bit wide-eyed. "Um, yeah, well, we're less than a half-mile away if we walk straight there."

Chivo climbed out of the car. Frank joined him, and Bexar holstered his pistol as he climbed out on the driver's side so Frank wouldn't see him do it. Chivo and Bexar retrieved their rifles from the back seat, the car being too small to climb out holding one without getting caught up on everything. The car sat next to the worn caliche drive of a trucking company.

"You guys just going to leave the car here?"

Bexar looked at Chivo. "What do you think? Frank's got a point."

"Hey, mano, you two head up. I'll catch up in a minute. I'll try to get it started. If it's dead for good, I'll leave it and join you in a few."

Frank nodded, Bexar gave thumbs up, and they began walking down Red Rock Road before climbing down a retaining wall and taking the direct route to the hideaway. Once out of sight, Chivo turned south and began sprinting through the trucking company's lot and up the hill on the far end. The top of the hill was a ridge and was flattened, the trucking company using it for storage. He only had a few hundred yards to go, but he had to get there fast, much faster than it would take Bexar and Frank to make the short walk.

Bexar stopped and tied his boot, asking Frank to watch for any approaching dead. A few shambled by in the distance, aimlessly, but none of them appeared close enough to be a threat. Frank stood nervously, shifting from side to side while Bexar was knelt down. When Bexar had silently counted to thirty, slowly tying his boot as he did, he stood and continued the walk. The hardest part of the walk wasn't slowing the pace down. Bexar exaggerated his limp, explaining that his leg had been broken and describing the truck crash. The hardest part of the walk was resisting the urge to look over his shoulder. It would have been pointless. Bexar knew that even if he did look, there was no way he would have been able to see Chivo anyway.

"We're almost there. Once we're safe in the fence line, you can sit and rest for a while."

"Thanks, Frank." Bexar paused. "So why the shop and not the house?"

"We watched everyone for a few days and knew the shop was just a shop, the food was all stored somewhere in the home. We needed the food."

"Why not just ask for it?"

"What if they said no?"

"What if they had said yes, Frank. Then some good people would still be amongst the living."

"Why chance it?"

This parking lot was paved. There were numerous semi-trucks and trailers parked and abandoned, all of them appearing to have been opened and rummaged through. Ahead of them was the storage lot; the tight compound had a u-shape of storage buildings on the north side, a central building, a short fence, and another building on the south side. It was tight, secure, and secluded. If not for the two men standing on the roof of the outer ring of storage buildings, Bexar might not have noticed that it was occupied. Walking out of the parking lot onto the road, Frank stopped and waved to the two men standing guard. Bexar recognized the rifle that one man carried as some sort of AR-15; the other man carried an RPG. The only real experience Bexar had with that was from watching classic action movies from the 1980s, news reports from the wars in the Middle East, and the man he'd killed the night of the attack on the compound. Luckily, when he was still a cop, in his part of Texas most of the turds were armed with ghetto blasters, not explosive rocket-propelled weapons of war.

"We thought you were dead, Frank."

"I did too, Dan."

"Where are the others?"

"They did die."

"You know the rules about outsiders; you just signed this man's death warrant by bringing him here."

"No, you don't understand..."

The RPG carrier's head exploded in a red mist and his body crumpling to the ground, interrupting Frank. Dan, the man with the rifle, turned his head, trying to comprehend what had just happened. His head vanished in a spray of red, blood spewing from his neck as he fell off the roof to the ground below. Frank, shocked and frozen in place, didn't see Bexar unholster his pistol. A single shot to the side of his head, and Frank fell to the ground. The heavy sound of Chivo's 50-caliber rifle echoed off the buildings.

So far Chivo's plan was following the script. Bexar ran as quickly as he could to crouch against the outer wall of the storage units. He stayed still and waited. If Chivo was four for four, then the remaining member would appear quickly. Against the north wall, Bexar was in Chivo's view and the most out of view for the remaining member of Frank's group. One last heavy rifle shot echoed through the area, and Bexar knew they were in the clear, assuming that Frank hadn't lied about the number of people in his group.

Bexar stood and swung his rifle over his back on the sling before taking a few steps back to gain some running room, as much as he could run. A few quick steps and Bexar leapt, using his good leg, his hands grasping the rooftop. Bexar pulled himself up and flopped onto the roof. It wasn't as graceful as he had hoped, but he'd accomplished his goal. While lying prone, he pulled himself to the inside edge of the roof, took out his pistol, and scanned the small courtyard. There was no movement, and no other people appeared. Three bodies lay near him, motionless, thick pools of blood congealing on the roof, some dripping off the edge to the dusty ground below. Each of them was missing the most important piece of anatomy required to reanimate. Bexar wasn't worried about them rising to attack him. His focus was toward any new threats that might appear. Soon the sound of the VW reached his ears as it backfired back to life, the sound of the obnoxious muffler growing closer. It shut off, and Chivo soon joined Bexar on the roof.

"A bunch of dead are making their way toward us, so we shouldn't take too long. Hold cover, I'll go first." Chivo didn't wait for an answer; he slid off the roof, rotating gracefully as he did, silently falling to the ground below. Soon in view, he signaled for Bexar to join him. Bexar fell loudly to the ground with a curse.

"Smooth, esé."

Bexar shrugged. They moved forward as a team, first clearing the large main building and then the second large building. The storage units were last. They were all closed and, at a quick glance, appeared to be latched.

Twenty minutes later, the compound was cleared and deemed safe. Frank had been right, very little food, water, or any other supplies besides crates of stolen military weapons were found. They had thousands of rounds of 5.56, a dozen crates of RPGs, another three cases of hand grenades. This group was loaded for war, and Guillermo's group would have been killed off if not for the crime of being prepared. Chivo didn't blame either group; he could see Frank's group's desperation and Guillermo's group's grievance. If Frank, Dan, and the rest of the group had approached Guillermo for help peacefully they might have had a chance, but they didn't.

"Like the fucking bikers, man."

"At least nothing exploded this time, mano."

"The shop did, and I'm getting really damn tired of being knocked the fuck out by shit exploding."

Chivo smirked. "How're we going to get all this hardware back up the hill?"

"Why don't we let Angel and them figure that out; we did our piece. Except we should take what we want first off the top. We're done here, we're leaving, we need to arm up. In this fucking world, the dead are the easy ones; the living, shit, Chivo, the living are the worst."

"Yeah, mano, it's always people, desperate people who make really desperate choices. Your life, no one's life matters except to provide for their own."

Bexar nodded. "So, are you going to show me how to use these RPGs?"

"Dude, I've taught people who couldn't read or write how to effectively deploy an RPG. You can at least figure out a pop-up book, so you're already a step ahead."

Bexar flipped Chivo off, but he only laughed as he stacked case after case of 5.56 on the ground to take to the car. They needed a full-ton truck. What they had was a car that was light enough to sit in the bed of one.

Groom Lake, NV

"What can we do about it, Bill? I mean, we're not exactly a standing army; we're deep below ground. All we can do is shut the blast door and let it blow over."

"I don't know, Jake, it's just, well... those transmissions really creeped me out. First, one of the numbers stations came back online, then another, and now this. Something is going on, and I don't like it."

"How many different survivors have you made contact with so far?"

"What?" Bill was caught off guard by the sudden change of subject.

"With your radio, what is your count up to now?"

"Between the open HAM radio channels and the spark-gap radio, we've made contact and plotted over a hundred survivors and groups."

"Where are they located?"

"All over. You should come down and see our growing map. All the pins are something to get excited about."

"OK, then reach out to those groups, tell them that you... tell them that *we* believe something is afoot. They can be our early warning system, our NORAD for an impending attack of some sort. Any of them military units?"

"No, a bunch of former military though."

"Well that's a start. If one of our survivors, one of our modern Paul Reveres sounds the alarm, we have to devise a response, some way to get help, to send help, or to be of help. Otherwise, it does us no good."

"I'll make contact, but there just isn't anyway, I mean, what can they do; they're going to ask."

"We'll figure something out. For now, tell them to report anything suspicious."

"See something, say something."

"Heh, yeah, sort of like that, Bill."

Bill looked worried, but he left to do his job. Jake leaned back in his office chair and put his feet on the desk and closed his eyes, concentrating. *Cliff would have known what to do; he always had a plan. He always had a simple plan... simple. We need a simple plan, but I don't have any idea where to even start. We had almost lost the survivors here. If it hadn't been for a high-school-style lockdown drill followed by Jessie and Sarah cleaning house with their rifles, we would have all been dead. We fought our asses off against the damn homegrown cult and still had to be saved in Colorado. Cliff rescued us, and that was against some low-grade assholes, not a trained invading military force.*

Jake shook his head and sat up. He needed to go for a walk and think; for once he was at a complete loss as to what to do or say.

Post, TX

Amanda's map didn't show more than a small speck in the middle of nowhere Texas for Post, but she knew that this was where the turn onto Highway 380 would be located. That much she had marked on her map, but first she had to drive through the town. The sun was beginning to set on the western horizon. She could stop or go, and the smart option would be to stop, even though Amanda was anxious to cover more ground, log more miles, and get another step closer to Groom Lake.

A small lake on her right glistened in the orange glow of the ending day, making her decision for her; a scenic spot would be a nice change. Amanda turned and drove into the small parking lot for the park. American and Texas flags hung, tattered, on the flagpole outside of an old wooden building that had a sign for WIC services on it. Driving over the curb, Amanda parked in a small grove of trees just because she felt slightly safer than sitting out in the open. The nose of the big truck pointed toward the exit; the side windows glowed orange on the left and she could see the lake on the right. Scanning the area, it appeared that she was free from any meandering dead. After turning off the engine and grabbing her rifle and a crushed roll of toilet paper, Amanda climbed out of the truck and stretched before choosing a low brick wall that doubled as a bench as her spot for now.

Finished and feeling relieved, Amanda left it all uncovered; she didn't feel it necessary to bury it or even deal with it. With so few living people left, it really didn't seem like it would matter. A short walk to the lake gave her cool water to rinse her hands off. She hadn't exercised since she'd left, not more than a few pushups in the back of the MRAP. Checking that the area was still clear and safe from the dead, Amanda set her rifle on the ground and started with some light stretching before completing a series of eight-count body builders, which were finished off with some burpees and a few sprints back and forth; she was careful not to wander too far from the MRAP or her rifle.

Sweaty, steam rising off her skin in the cool air, satisfied, and feeling better about her day, she noticed that darkness crept across the ground, the shadows growing faint as the last light of the day fell from view. Amanda retrieved her rifle and climbed into the armored truck to her dinner of a cold MRE and water.

If Groom Lake has real food, any kind of real food, I think I will feel like I've died and gone to heaven.

CHAPTER 8

S4
April 6, Year 1

The commander studied the computer screen with the latest satellite images displayed, and he used the electronic tools to measure the distances. Thirty-five kilometers if they could drive the four-wheeled APC straight over the mountains. Although Groom Lake was a secret facility, the entire area had been used for more than just aircraft development; other secret projects and not-so-secret nuclear weapons tests had been conducted, all contained within the Nevada Test Site. Numerous roads traversed the area, connecting all the different facilities to the nuclear test sites, to the landing fields, and all the other items the corrupt imperialist government demanded. Ironically, the easiest and fastest way for the recon element to get there was to drive on a paved road through the field of craters from all the bomb testing, turning off to a dirt road that would put the team at a good position on the mountain ridge to the southwest of their target. Still approximately five kilometers away from the heart of the complex, they would be close enough to establish the sort of eyes-on-the-ground information that he needed. He needed to know what sort of movement and resistance they could expect. They planned biological-warfare sabotage in a simple form, as they wanted to take everything intact, just as the other complex would be; if they weren't successful, another crater would be added to the numerous others passing by the armored windshield.

Saint George, UT

The compound was a flurry of activity, and the sun was only just now above the horizon. The horses killed by the dead and any chance of fabricating a cart or something else useful destroyed by the RPG attack on the shop, a meeting was held and improvisation was running rampant, just for a single idea. The group meeting the previous evening, after Chivo and Bexar had returned, was one of excitement and lament. The chance to significantly increase the group's weapons, ammo, and general arsenal was alluring. But the difficulty in transporting so many heavy items using an old, worn-out Beetle with an exhaust so loud that more dead would come just for the car show was a problem they couldn't grasp for an outcome. That was until John talked about the steel works and large fabrication shop near Frank's storage-area compound. The fabrication shop had an enormous forklift that ran on diesel, or that was what he assumed, doubting that one that large would run on propane. Regardless, now that morning was upon them, the group opted to send a scavenger party outside the wire and into the wilds of the industrial park for a forklift that may or may not work; if it didn't work, their plan was to search, improvise, and find a solution.

Chivo smiled. These sorts of by-the-seat-of-your-pants operations happened more often than not in the Special Forces world; despite all the training and planning, sometimes the guys would have to head out, hunt for bad guys, and break stuff.

Bexar wore a new chest rig to hold his pistol and rifle magazines. Jennifer had done a wonderful job with the supplies she had on hand. Black and basic, it fit well and seemed to function just as it should. In heavy-duty work pants, work boots, and a T-shirt, Bexar felt more like himself than he had wearing all the high-speed tactical gear that Chivo still wore. For all his days in training, courses, and department in-services, Bexar was still just a cop, not some tactic-cool SWAT guy.

The morning was perfect, with clear skies, cool but not cold. Bexar was ready to get the party started. Brian and Stan were joining the expedition to adventure. Each person carried a small day pack that held water, some snacks, and some medical supplies, all matching; a group standard item. The bags belonging to their lost friends were given to Chivo and Bexar. The VW sat in the courtyard, a small oil drip under the rear of the car staining the concrete, and there it would sit until Chivo and Bexar left for Groom Lake. The one thing they did take was the battery out of the Bug. No one in the group knew anything about forklifts but they all assumed that it probably required a battery to start and run.

After the walk down the long driveway, the jokes and talking came to an end. The seriousness of exiting the relative safety of the fenced compound now became paramount. The gate was opened and then closed behind them and locked. The threat of Frank's group was eliminated, but after some discussion, Chivo convinced them that others might spring up when they least expected it.

The walk down Old Dump Road didn't take long. With a set of borrowed binoculars, Chivo could see movement on the Interstate further down the road, but so far, they hadn't encountered any of the dead face to face. Chivo had a shortcut planned, the layout committed to his memory from his recon and sniper skills the previous day. Cutting through a dirt parking lot, climbing down a short retaining wall, walking through another parking lot of yet another business housed in a dirty metal building, the team of four stood at the chain-link fence of the steel-fabrication business. Large sections of steel pipe, bars, beams, and other pieces of steel sat rusty in the yard.

A whispered discussion as to whether they should split up or move as a team was quickly ended with Chivo's not so tactful statement that they stay together, move together, and work as a team. Quick work with a pair of bolt cutters and Stan had the group inside the fence line. The main fabrication shop, a massive metal building, stood to their right. In a covered area to their left sat an oil-stained, greasy, and dirty forklift larger than some cars.

"Well, John, there's your forklift, mano. Get to work."

John looked at Chivo and then at Stan. Stan shrugged and walked to the forklift. Under faded yellow paint, obscured by rust and dirt, "CATERPILLAR" could barely be discerned on the back of the beast. A large rusted muffler stood erect on the side of the roll cage of an operator's cab. The engine compartment was under a vented cover behind the driver's seat. Stan lifted the engine cover and inspected what they'd found.

"Uh, I have no idea guys... maybe we should just try it first. If that doesn't work, we'll have to figure out where the battery is and swap ours in. Which one of you knows how to run this thing?"

No one spoke; Bexar shrugged. "Can't be too hard, can it? I mean you drive it, and the forks go up and down. Guess I'll try."

After climbing into the operator's position, Bexar was met with three long handles, another on the side of the steering column, a small handful of gauges, and one key sticking out of the dash. If any of the controls had been labeled when the forklift was made, the labels were long gone. With a pedal on the left of the steering column, another on the right, and another long one that looked universally like an accelerator pedal, the big machine was intimidating, more so than Bexar realized before he'd volunteered to be *that* guy.

Holding his breath, Bexar turned the key. A clicking sound came from the engine behind him, which then belched to life, black smoke pouring out of the exhaust stack. If the VW was a problem because it was loud, this massive forklift was a serious problem because it was even louder! After a few moments, the engine settled down into an idle that shook the whole beast. Turning the steering wheel back and forth, Bexar realized that the hydraulic system pushed the rear wheels left and right; the dual front tires were rigidly mounted. Testing each lever, Bexar found that one slid the huge fork assembly left and right, another tilted the whole lifting tower forward and back, and the third raised and lowered the forks.

Bexar yelled over the engine, "Hop on; we need to get our shit and get home before we attract a crowd with this big yellow bastard!"

Chivo stood next to Bexar in the large open cab, steadying himself by holding onto the protective cage over the cab. John and Stan stood on the steps on either side of the cab, holding onto the handles used to climb into the cab. Like a low-budget zombie-killing A-Team, Bexar raised the forks off the ground and drove forward slowly, trying to get the hang of the rear-axle steering. More than once, he had to stop and reverse, getting caught driving into the large pieces of steel in the facility. Amazingly, the forklift turned tightly, almost like a zero-turn lawn mower.

An off-road vehicle it was not, so after driving out of the fabrication facility, Bexar stuck to the paved road, taking the long way around to the south and cutting through a paved parking lot to travel north on Red Rock Road. Every couple of minutes, one of them would have to take a few shots at the approaching dead. The loud old diesel forklift was Saint George's Pied Piper of the living dead. Finally reaching the storage unit and fenced-off compound, Bexar drove the forks into the section of chain-link fence by the parking lot, tilted the forks back and raised them, ripping the fence off the posts and out of the ground. There wasn't room to drive the forklift inside the compound, so Bexar spun it to the left to point toward the road home. Chivo and John pulled the fence off the forks, and Bexar lowered them to the ground and shut off the engine. The sudden silence was unsettling, but not as unsettling as the growing moans of the approaching dead.

"OK, we better make this quick. John, you and Stan are a team. Start grabbing the wooden crates and stack them on the forks, and Bexar and I will do the same. If things go sideways, we can get on the roof and thin the herd if we need to, but I think if we work fast enough, it won't be that big of a problem."

John and Stan didn't have to be told twice. They trotted into the compound, grabbing the first wooden crate they found, carrying it as a team back toward the forklift.

"Won't be a big problem? You had to fucking say it out loud, didn't you?"

"Bexar, it either is or isn't, you superstitious dick. Now get your white ass moving so we can get the fuck out of here before the big problem arrives."

Bexar grunted, walked into the compound, and team-carried one of the crates with RPGs back to the forklift. After the first two loads, each of the two teams was having to put down one of the dead that was getting too close. The sun marched across the sky and was nearly overhead when the last crate was loaded. They had a pile of crates that reached the end of the long forks and was piled high enough that all of them had to team up to lift the last few over their heads to reach the top of the stack. Dozens of the dead lay in crumpled heaps in the parking lot; many more were approaching, slowly shambling with singular focus.

"Fucking pop smoke, mano! Time to roll."

Chivo didn't have say it twice. Everyone climbed aboard the forklift. Bexar couldn't see past the load, and all of them were glad that the engine coughed to life once again. After tilting the lift rearward, Bexar slowly raised the forks until he could see under the stack of wooden crates. Somehow they'd been able to fit every single one of the crates holding weapons, ammo, explosives and who knows what else onto the forklift. Moving slowly, Bexar guided the forklift out of the parking lot, making a right turn onto the road to head for home. Their pace riding the giant old forklift was slower than the group's pace walking down the hill that morning, but it was slightly faster than the growing number of followers. Chivo turned around to face the rear, kneeling on the metal floor, and held his rifle against the driver's cage to steady his aim. One by one, he took careful shots to put down the closest of the following dead. None of them spoke, the loud diesel engine making it annoying trying to yell and hear one another.

What felt like hours later, the forklift turned off Old Dump Road and onto the long asphalt driveway leading to the compound. Stan jumped off the side of the forklift and jogged ahead, not having to run very quickly to outpace the slow-moving beast. With each bump and bounce Bexar held his breath, worried about the teetering load high above the ground, the solid rubber tires offering nothing in the way of any dampening. This forklift wasn't meant to be driven down a road like this, but the dead weren't meant to rise to hunt the living either.

Reaching the gate, Stan stood at the ready, the gate open. The rest of the group members stood just inside the gate, rifles ready. Once the back of the forklift cleared, Stan shut the gate and locked the chain holding it secure. Angel, Guillermo, and the rest of the group stood at the fence, shooting down the dead who stumbled up the drive following the loud yellow beacon.

Parking next to the Beetle, Bexar carefully lowered the forks and set them flat on the ground before shutting off the loud motor. One by one, the rest of the group members came back up the driveway with wide-eyed excitement like kids on Christmas. For preppers and survivors, large quantities of free ammo, rifles, explosives, and uncommon items like some RPGs made for a present that was worth three Christmases and a birthday all rolled into one!

Las Vegas, NV

Aymond sat in the big meeting room the Pararescue Jumpers had in their building. None of them were sure where the PJs had gone; some had obviously been killed, as indicated by the small makeshift memorials they found, but the cache of stored goods was fairly complete: ammo, MREs, water, extra gear, and even some small camping stoves and fuel, which Aymond promptly used this morning to make some instant coffee from the MRE he ate for breakfast.

The shortwave radio broadcast the previous night changed everything. It also really concerned him. If they had picked it up, the PLA might have picked it up too, and they might come looking for whomever was broadcasting it. It wasn't good OpSec on the part of the people in Groom Lake, which was surprising for how secretive the facility had historically been. Even with his top-secret clearance, Aymond had no idea what he would find when they arrived. It could be alien technology or singlewide trailers, he didn't know, and after all they had been through since December, he wouldn't be surprised by either one.

The team's sleep and security rotation would be complete in about two more hours. It was important that all his men got a full night's rest when they could because when the shit hit the fan again, they might have to go days without sleeping. They needed to be rested, well, and strong to face that and come out on top. Happy and Kirk sifted through the stored cache of gear, picking and choosing what they could carry on the M-ATVs along with what they needed. Jones and Gonzo were exploring the hangars close by for any parts or equipment that Jones needed for the trucks or that they could use. Aymond believed in cross-training, but he also believed in letting someone who was highly experienced in a field of knowledge do what they knew best. Jones was an experienced mechanic, better than any of Aymond's men, so it was best he do the job. Gonzo was along to carry anything heavy and to provide extra security.

Absentmindedly, Aymond flipped through the past November's issue of *Popular Mechanics*. It all felt surreal, the way things felt in some sort of dream, and the future felt completely uncertain. There was only one thing that Aymond knew for sure. If they didn't find more people and more help, the United States would fall to either the Chinese or the Zeds. There was no way to win either war by themselves. Aymond tossed the magazine on the table and stood, slinging his rifle and taking his coffee with him. He wanted to check on Jones' and Gonzo's progress.

Jones and Gonzo returned before Aymond could make it past the protective ring of the M-ATVs and the radar truck. They were unsuccessful in finding any useful spare parts, except for a set of tools that Jones said he needed, so the minor excursion was a waste of time. Now that the final sleep rotation was coming to an end, it was time for a team meeting to plan the day. Nellis appeared to be abandoned and left to the Zeds, but Aymond wanted to know for sure. If there were any survivors they would need them. What they needed was an army, or at least a few more Marines, if they were going to have any chance against the PLA.

54

Twenty-five miles southwest of Groom Lake was another dry lake bed in the large sectioned-off piece of government-controlled land; bomb craters large and small to the north spoke to the area's past life as a test facility. However, marked off on the edge of the dry lakebed was a ten-thousand-foot-long runway; next to the same was a newly constructed five-thousand-foot-long paved runway with a handful of newly built hangars, including a large clamshell-opening hangar that harkened back to the days of lighter than air travel.

The big Y-20 seemed to hang in the sky. Flying low and from the southwest, the big cargo plane banked gently to line up for the final approach over the dry lakebed. Since it was heavily loaded, the pilot didn't dare use the shorter paved runway, opting to trust in the rugged design of the new aircraft and the supposed ability to land on unimproved surfaces.

There was discussion about conducting a low-level air drop, but the satellite intelligence suggested that the area was secure, either ignored by or unknown to the rogue group in the underground facility to the northeast. So the safer option of simply landing to offload the vehicles and men was taken.

Soldiers, members of the elite PLA Siberian Tiger unit, quickly exited the tail ramp of their aircraft, forming a defensive line as the first anti-Yama radar truck was released from the tie downs and driven to a position to provide sweeping coverage.

Nearing sunset, the two Chinese APCs drove across the lakebed to the hangars by the paved runway, which would be their command post for the upcoming operation. The radar truck set a position on the southwestern side, the side not shielded by the mountains. Their plan was underway.

In the MRAP, TX

The towns of Brownfield and Plains, Texas may not have had many people living in them before the attacks, but Amanda was sure that there weren't any people living in them now, at least from what she could see. Rumbling along US-380, Amanda dodged only the occasional car and some semi-trucks and was amazed at how flat and open this part of Texas was.

Flatter than flat; someone could watch their dog runaway for three days out here and never lose sight of him.

Abandoned homes and farms dotted the flat landscape; most of them appeared to have been left to rot back into the dirt long before the attack happened. If not for the small sign, Amanda wouldn't have known that after a slight bump in the pavement she was now in New Mexico. She was bored; no music, no one to talk to, nothing to do but listen to the droning diesel engine as she bounced and jarred along a lonesome highway in a part of the country that defined what it was to be in BFE.

The wire fences along the highway still stood. It almost appeared as if nothing was wrong, that the attack had never occurred and the dead weren't stumbling around trying to bite the few who remained amongst the living in the rest of the country. No, if this town had electricity, it would probably be carrying on just fine, minus deliveries for food and other provisions.

If this country has a chance, if the United States can survive, it will be due to the survivors we can find out in the rural areas, hard-scrabble people used to making a life out of desolate areas and through desperate times.

The highway widened from two lanes to four lanes, and the signs warned of a lower speed limit, not that Amanda really cared. The sparse landscape became slightly more cluttered with metal buildings and older homes. Staring out of the driver's side window, Amanda drifted left and right, not really paying attention to the road. She watched for signs of life, chimney smoke, if the homes even had chimneys, anything to give her hope. Movement out of the corner of her eye caught her attention, and she instinctively slammed on the brakes. The heavy armored truck lurching forward snapped Amanda's head forward with it, and she saw a child riding a bicycle in the middle of the road waving at her.

"Holy shit!"

Sitting in the MRAP, now sitting stationary, Amanda stared at the child.

I've lost it. I've only made it to the fourth month after the attack, and I've completely lost my mind.

Squinting, waiting for the child to vanish or to see that it was actually a walking corpse of a child, Amanda waited, holding her breath. The child waved again and rode away, pedaling as fast as he could. Amanda followed slowly, trying not to spook the kid. Quickly the boy took a left, and Amanda wasn't sure if he was trying to get away, just going somewhere, or trying to get her to follow. Curiosity won the argument in her thoughts, so she slowly followed, trying her best to drive casually in a large tan armored military vehicle with a machine gun on top. She drove close enough to keep the boy in sight but without getting so close as to be a threat to anyone watching, if that were even possible.

At the second cross street, the boy rode into the yard of a white house, dropped the bike, and ran into the home. Not sure what to do, Amanda stopped in the middle of the intersection and waited, watching the house. If this was an ambush, she would probably be OK in the truck against whatever small arms the people had, and she could just drive away. But it didn't feel like an ambush should feel, which confused Amanda because she really had no training in any of this stuff. Before she'd just relied on Clint for his expert take on tactical situations. Now it was up to her and her limited experience. The curtains moved behind an open window on the second floor.

If someone were going to ambush travelers, why would they use a kid to lead them to a house? Why wouldn't they just stage it out on the highway?

A woman appeared from the front door holding some sort of rifle that Amanda didn't recognize, except that it had wooden stock and a scope on it. Amanda drove in front of the house, stopped in the middle of the street, and turned the truck off. Waiting, she and the woman stared at each other through the thick glass. Not able to roll down a window, Amanda wasn't sure what to do. The woman didn't move, but she appeared to be trying to talk to her. Amanda nodded and climbed into the back of the truck, stepped up, released the top hatch and climbed into the turret, leaving the M2 pointed away from the woman. She smiled.

"Are you with the Army?"

"No, not exactly."

"Where did ya get that thing?"

"From a base in Texas. What town is this?"

"Tatum. Where are you headed? Is there help coming? Do you have any food or water you could spare? What the hell happened, and why is it taking so long for us to get help?"

Amanda felt like the woman was sincere. "I have some. I'm headed to Nevada. Are there many of you left besides you and the boy?"

"Of course there are."

The blunt answer was given in such a way that it was obvious the woman thought it to be a stupid question. Why would there not be a lot of people left in the little town of Tatum, New Mexico.

Amanda smiled. "Give me a minute to climb down. Would you mind if we sat down and spoke for a while?"

"If you have some food to spare and can tell us when FEMA is going to get off their asses to come help, you're welcome to come inside."

The boy appeared behind the woman, smiling. "James, go get your daddy and tell him we have a visitor. Then go tell Mr. Finch. He's going to want to come by as well."

The boy ran into the yard, jumped on his bicycle, and rode off as fast as he could. After opening the back hatch, Amanda grabbed a case of MREs and climbed down, closing up the MRAP behind her. If she had known that there would be others, Amanda would have packed the entire back of the truck with cases of MREs, but as it was she didn't and hadn't made that plan. She walked into the home, her mind spinning with the thought of how to get some of the supplies stockpiled at the SSC to this town. Then she thought of all the other small towns she had simply driven through. She should have taken the time to explore each of them to look for other survivors, but she didn't. Back and forth the argument went in her mind; she was heartbroken for the people she might have been able to find and help but didn't, too anxious to get to Groom Lake to complete the mission she set out to do in the first place.

Flying Above New Mexico

Andrew trimmed the aircraft and let it fly. The road atlas in his lap, he flipped pages, holding a ruler over one page and then the next. The mountains were passing safely below him, and the sprawling mass of Albuquerque could be seen in the distance. He closed the atlas and stuffed it into the open bag in the back seat, Oreo nudging him again as always. Amazingly, Andrew didn't have to clean much dog waste out of the aircraft, his friend somehow keeping it together for hours at a time, but this was the first time he was actually trying to make a destination quickly. Before he would have lazily followed the Interstates and searched for more survivors and, hopefully, answers to this whole mess, landing where he pleased when it was safe to do so, but now he wanted to get to Area 51 as fast as he could. There was a chance he could make it in a single hop, but without knowing the winds aloft, Andrew had no way to plan his route, to know which altitudes would give him the better winds for speed and efficiency. All of the tools that modern pilots were used to were gone, pushing him back into the stick-and-rudder barn-storming days of aviation history long past.

He adjusted the trim slightly and the small aircraft tilted forward slightly, slowly descending toward the big New Mexico city. So far, every large city that he had flown near appeared to be completely dead and overrun by zombies, but even in this strange new world in which he lived, Andrew still held hope.

The Interstate near the city was completely clear of vehicles; the ones he could see were pushed into the ditches. Descending lower, Andrew banked right and then left, looking out each side window, trying to see as much detail as he could. Shaking his head, Andrew knew that sort of destruction was from a massive horde of the dead. If one came through Albuquerque, then he doubted anyone could have survived; even some of the bridges had collapsed. Flying a northwesterly route over the heart of the city, thick black fog blocked his view, but Andrew knew that it wasn't fog and that hundreds or thousands of the reanimated dead were below the veil of black flies.

Oreo whimpered a little as Andrew began slowly climbing and gaining altitude.

"I know buddy, but we can't stop yet, not there. Try to hold it. I'll stop soon."

Saint George, UT

Each of the wooden crates stood open, and all the new toys of war were spread out in the courtyard. There were rows of green metal cans of ammunition, mostly 5.56 XM193, but larger cans of 7.62 and 50-caliber as well; two crates labeled "30 GRENADE HAND FRAG DELAY M67" stood by themselves, the lids removed. The new gear seemed overwhelming and endless, and it was dangerous to let it sit out in the open. Chivo checked each item, explaining it to Angel and Guillermo, who was writing down what each was, what it was for and how much of it they now had. The hard work of unpacking each of the crates complete, Stan and John went inside to prepare the group's lunch. Merylin and Frances held security positions, standing at the edge of the courtyard near the driveway, their rifles in hand, and Brian sat on the roof of the house with binoculars scanning for any threats. Jennifer was the only one of the group not out in the courtyard. After sitting security during the night, she'd opted to sleep; she was content to find out what all the new toys were later.

The inventory complete, Angel held the yellow pad of paper and clipboard in his hand, reviewing his notes, meticulously checking to make sure he hadn't missed a single detail.

"What are we going to do with RPGs and grenades? I can't imagine those would be all that effective against the zombies?"

Chivo shrugged. "Who knows, Guillermo. They might be, but I know they would be really effective against the living."

"But you took care of that for us."

Bexar shook his head. "Everywhere I've been, I keep finding turds, wolves preying on other survivors. Fuck, I wish I had all this when we were in Big Bend. Things might have gone much differently."

"We don't even know how to use half this stuff. The M-16s sure, but I've never seen a real grenade in person much less used one."

Chivo smiled. "First of all, if you try to pull the cotter pin out with your teeth, you won't have many teeth left, but I'll show everyone this afternoon. If Angel continues to take notes, then you can review them later, practice, and train.

This sort of hardware is hard to come by, and you might be thankful to have it at some point."

Guillermo nodded, looking at the pile of arms that made their prepper compound look like a terrorist commune, and then back at Bexar.

"What about you? Do you know about all this?"

"Nope, but I'm going to pay attention this afternoon. That's for sure!"

Bexar glanced at Chivo, who nodded slightly. Taking his cue, Bexar continued. "With you guys safe, our plan is to leave in the morning."

Angel looked up from his notes and looked at Guillermo, who tilted his head. "That's too bad. The group voted, and you're both welcome to stay. We want you to stay."

"Thank you, but I made a promise to my friend here, and I'm going to make good on it. It's time to finally return him to his pregnant wife."

Groom Lake, NV

Jake, Bill, representatives from each of the different "towns" of Groom Lake, Sarah, and Jessie sat at the conference table. Erin flat out told her mother she wasn't going to "some stupid meeting," and Sarah had half a mind to join her in not attending, but Jessie was going so she felt like she needed to go to give support. Jake smiled and tapped his knuckles on the table. The conversations in the room slowly died off until all eyes were on him.

"Good afternoon, and thank you all for coming. First of all, I wanted to thank Jessie and Sarah again for their help. They may be new members of our community, but they have really made their mark in a short amount of time."

The group clapped politely before Jake continued. "With his new radio setup, Bill has made contact with more survivors. Some have expressed interest in attempting to come join us; others are content to continue to shelter in place, but all have expressed a strong need for help, which I can imagine surprises no one here. However, that is not why I asked all of you to this meeting. We have two issues that may become serious problems if we don't address them. First of all, we have lost all contact with the Texas facility; we haven't heard from Clint or President Lampton in a few days, and we are hoping that they are only experiencing technical difficulties. I would ask that we keep that information only between us. I'm afraid that rumors may get out of hand if we make that public knowledge.

"Second, we intercepted two radio broadcasts that by themselves would be concerning, but in the context of losing communication with Texas, the apparent cyber-attacks on our facility, and some previous radio broadcasts that we've heard, we are quite concerned. Bill?"

Bill fidgeted in his seat and looked at his notes. "At least one numbers station appeared briefly recently, broadcasting for two days, two different messages on two different frequencies."

One woman raised her hand; most of the others looked puzzled.

"Right, umm, *numbers stations* is a generic term for radio stations that began around World War One but really became prevalent during the Cold War. They would broadcast random numbers or letters, sometimes with different tones or other sounds. There were a few conspiracy theories about them. As we sit here in Area 51, I would tend to assume that the theories may have been right; regardless, it was generally assumed by those of us in amateur radio that the stations were broadcasting secret messages to spies or agents. Since the stations were broadcast on the shortwave bands, the recipient could have been just about anywhere. Back in the height of all these stations some other ham-radio operators began DF'ing, or locating the broadcast locations, or at least where the broadcasting antenna was located. Sorry, direction finding or triangulating the locations. Anyways, the numbers stations that appeared recently are now gone; we have no idea who broadcast it, who received it, or what it meant. That alone isn't too big of a deal. I mean, we know that Clint and Cliff are out there. It is possible that others are out there too, trying to do the right thing, but two really strange radio broadcasts really makes me concerned about the numbers stations too. The best way to describe the two other broadcasts are that they were broad spectrum noise on HF, the high-frequency bands, like the radio broadcast equivalent of someone hitting a large gong. One of the broadcasts appeared to have been sent from some distance away, and the other was much closer."

Bill took a drink of water, holding up his hands in response to the questions that started immediately.

"Most likely those were encrypted messages, one being sent and the other being a reply. We have no way of knowing what the messages were. We don't know where they came from exactly, but HF broadcasts, depending on propagation, could have come from nearly anywhere in the world. The one guess I'm willing to take is that the reply message came from within North America, possibly somewhere fairly close to here."

All the representatives from the different Groom Lake cities began asking questions, talking over each other, nearly shouting to be heard. Jake stood and held up his hands to get their attention; once everyone had calmed down, he sat again.

"My concerns aren't really about those radio broadcasts; my concerns are specifically about our underground city surviving. I broke all of this down into bite-sized bits of information so I could understand it better. If Cliff were here, he would have a plan of action, but he isn't, and we can't reach him, so all we have are one another."

Jake stood and walked to the dry-erase board on the wall and began writing. "Some of this most of you probably know; however, a lot of what I'm about to tell you hasn't been told to anyone but myself by Cliff. After this meeting, after we have a plan of action, we will have another full assembly, and I will explain all of what I'm about to tell you to all of our fellow survivors and residents."

All eyes were glued on Jake; the room felt as if it were collectively holding its breath.

"Number one, we know that the Chinese and North Koreans teamed up to attack the United States with an EMP strike followed by overflights that sprayed what we know now to be called the Yama Strain. The name doesn't really matter, all that matters is that it is a tool of mass genocide, a way to kill off an entire country with little damage of war. Cliff assumed that since the attack happened, the Chinese had devised a way to counter Yama. He didn't know if it was a way to stop it or a way to inoculate others from it, but he was confident that the dead would remain the dead. Even the infected dead couldn't be brought back to life; they could only be destroyed. In the depths of this very facility, a group of scientists were working on a solution. The United States government knew about all of this and expected the attack; the problem is that they thought there was more time before it came. Cliff was originally in a facility in Denver under the airport when the attack came. That facility was overrun and went dark, but he somehow escaped and came here, this being the closest backup facility. Besides Texas, there were many other facilities, but Cliff said they were destroyed, except for Texas, as far as we know. Basically, the whole plan that the U.S. government had for what they felt to be an eventuality fell apart; the entire safety net failed, and here we are. Cliff found this facility overrun but lit and operational, unlike the one in Denver, which had completely failed. Systematically, he cleared the entire facility of zombies, the evidence of which can still be seen on the floors and walls in some areas. There was one lone survivor here, Lance, a young scientist still trying to find a solution, an end to Yama. Lance died; Cliff didn't really go into detail about it, but said that with Lance's death any chance to scientifically combat Yama died with him.

"If the attack was the prelude to invasion that we think it could be, then we may be in store for actual war, more attacks. We've done well to save so many people and to provide a safe place to survive and live, but the Chinese must know that we're here by now."

Some gasped, and others shook their heads.

"We have a few ideas and are welcome to any other ideas that any of you have, but as we see it, our options are to continue as we are and hope we're wrong, lock down the blast doors, turn off the radios, and go dark, or train for war with the weapons and gear we have on the fifth level."

"What about the others, all the people out there that have made contact with us, the ones who can't or won't come here, what about them?" someone called out.

The room erupted in conversation, growing louder with each passing second. Jessie stood abruptly, and her chair hit the wall behind her and tipped over with a crash. Everyone turned to look at her in silence.

"We have to tell them. We fucking tell them everything. There is no choice but to tell them the entire story, the history, and the fears. Let them prepare. Let them know. Bill, where are all these people located?"

"Uh, all over. We have a map in the radio hut with pins showing each contact we've made."

"Tell them all, Jake, tell them everything you just told us. Keep repeating it until we can't anymore. Jake, every able-bodied person in this goddamned hole in the ground is going to have to get ready to fight, ready to fight a war, be fully ready, and be ready now. We can't wait until next week or even tomorrow—this isn't going to be our fucking underground Alamo!"

Jessie stormed out of the room, the door slamming behind her; everyone looked at Sarah who was still.

"I agree with her. If I were you, every single one of us would go down to the fifth level and get geared up. If this is going to happen, it could happen today, next month, or next year. We have no idea, but we can't wait helplessly and hope it won't happen. Like she said, we get ready, we stay ready, and we hope it doesn't happen, but we're ready if it does."

Everyone looked at Jake before the room erupted with everyone talking at once. Sarah looked at the room, shook her head, and left to find Jessie and her daughter. If Jake and the others didn't get ready to fight, they needed to be ready to bug out.

Tatum, NM

James was back, his bicycle left in the yard. Sunlight filtered through the windows of the home, and a dozen people sat in the living room. Lisa was the woman who lived there, Amanda learned, and her husband, Joe, came home about thirty minutes after James came back. Everyone who sat in the living room arrived on a bicycle, some of them new-looking, some of them ancient and held together with some unusual repairs.

"After the gas started going bad a bit ago, we all turned to bicycles. Inner tubes are a bit of a problem. We started with using cans of Fix-A-Flat that we got from the gas stations. Eventually we started using small pieces of rubber from the tire shop as inner tubes. Seems to be working OK," Joe explained.

Amanda nodded, her curiosity quenched. As excited as everyone in the room was, all but Amanda held an open MRE in their hands. All of them appeared thin, and their clothes didn't seem to fit them as well as they had. She quickly learned that of the town's original six hundred or so residents roughly two hundred of them were still living. The roaming herds of the dead hadn't come through town and, within the first day of the attack, the citizens of Tatum banded together to have constant patrols to put down any zombies who came through. Mostly, especially at first, the dead that posed a threat were their own fellow residents. There was an outbreak of suicides about six weeks after the attack, which in the end really brought the rest of the survivors together. They pooled their supplies and made sure that everyone had a firearm and a fair share of the supplies necessary to survive, and they held open discussions about depression and survival. For all that they did well as a community, what the entire town was waiting for was help.

Over the previous weeks, small groups would bicycle together further and further out on patrols looking for other survivors, scavenging for anything of use, and hoping to find answers. The clusters of farms around the county were contacted, a few more survivors found among them. Eventually, they bicycled all the way out to Plains and down to Lovington. There were a few survivors in Plains, but the town hadn't done as well as Tatum. Lovington as a town hadn't banded together, but there were three big survivor groups that held roughly four hundred people of the nearly eleven thousand previous residents of the town. The groups were each led by experienced preppers and, surprisingly, each of the groups had good relationships with each other. Amanda was astonished, expecting a splintered town run by three different factions with different leaders and loyalties to be at a bit of a war with one another. They weren't, and had even facilitated a barter system for trading.

Rumors abounded in Tatum and in Lovington, but no one knew exactly what had happened.

Mr. Finch arrived about the time that Joe finished giving the quick history of Tatum and how they had survived.

"Welcome to our little town, Ms...." Mr. Finch paused.

"Lampton, Amanda Lampton."

"Ms. Lampton that's quite the truck you have. How is it that it still works, and where are you getting fuel for it?"

"It was stored in a hardened facility in Texas, but it was designed to survive an EMP anyways, as far as I know. Fuel is always a bit of an issue. I tend to syphon what I can find out of semi-trucks' fuel tanks."

"We had a few older vehicles that still worked after the EMP, but fuel began going bad sort of quickly. Some of the guys who used to work the oil field said it was due to the ethanol, and we've run dry of the diesel fuel we did have. Either way, we're pedaling our way around nowadays. Thank you for the food you could share, but we must know, do you know what happened? How did you survive? How did you get here? Where are you going and why?"

Amanda was waiting for that question. She knew it would come, and she had spent the previous half-hour in an internal debate trying to decide how she would approach it.

"First, I do know what happened. The Chinese and North Korean governments launched an attack on the United States. It began with nuclear missiles detonated high in the atmosphere, which caused an EMP, destroying electronics and the country's electrical infrastructure, as you are already aware. The aircraft you saw fly past after the EMP sprayed what has been named the Yama Strain."

Amanda continued for nearly an hour, explaining that she had been the Secretary of Agriculture, how two agents had come to her house in Little Rock, about the journey to Texas, the facility there and the one in Groom Lake, and the hunt for survivors. Then she extended an open invitation for any to join her on her journey to Nevada, with the intent to return to Texas. Believing that these people, survivors, fellow citizens deserved to know the truth, Amanda left no detail a secret, except that she was now the sworn President of the United States.

Once finished, the room sat in stunned silence, each of the people in the small living room trying to process all the information that was thrown at them, trying to decide how much to believe, if they could believe any of it.

Joe spoke first. "So there is no help coming." It wasn't a question.

Amanda shook her head. "There is nothing in place still functioning that can help, yet."

"And your plan is to drive to Area 51, pick up a group of people, drive back to Texas to get more vehicles, and then shuttle back and forth until all those people are safe underground in Texas? What about people like us?"

"We didn't know about other survivors. Well, some people who had radios that survived were able to contact those in Groom Lake, but no one knows how many people have survived. We don't know how many people died."

Faces around the room, previously elated to have a large meal that equated to more than the typical day's ration of food, now looked defeated. Amanda tried to keep a positive attitude, but the loss of any hope for the future sucked the air out of the room.

Mr. Finch finally spoke. "Thank you, Ms. Lampton. We've survived as a town together so far, and we will survive as a town together into the future, hoping that someday things will get back to some sort of normal that we once knew. Tomorrow we will hold a town hall discussion to let everyone know what we learned from you. If you are going to be staying the night, you are welcome to join us in our meeting tomorrow."

Amanda didn't answer at first. "Mr. Finch, thank you, but it would be best if I continued my journey. Don't give up hope. Don't give up on one another. We will survive, but only if we work together. We now know you are here. I'm sorry we didn't know that before. The task we face is hard but not insurmountable. Once in back in Texas, I will send a truck to you with all we can spare. I'm sorry that there isn't more we can do more quickly."

When she stood to leave, Mr. Finch stood as well. "Ms. Lampton, let me at least walk you to your truck. Joe, I'll be back in a moment."

Mr. Finch went to the front door and held it open for Amanda, and they walked in silence until they came to the back of the MRAP. "Ms. Lampton, how many other cabinet-level secretaries survived?"

Amanda paused before answering. "None of them."

"That's what I thought. Madam President, God's speed."

Amanda shook his hand, opened the back hatch, climbed into her truck, and passed down another case of MREs to Mr. Finch, "We won't fail you."

Mr. Finch nodded and walked back to the house. Amanda climbed into the driver's seat, started the truck, and drove down the block to return to the highway; turning left, she drove west, the sun low enough on the horizon to shine directly into the windshield.

In the Aviat Husky

Oreo's insistence that they land grew, and the day was getting late, so instead of pushing on and being left to an airplane that smelled like dog crap, Andrew saw the single long airstrip near I-40 and decided to take the opportunity to land for the evening. The town, which sat on the opposite side of I-40 from the airfield, wasn't too large, so he didn't think that there would be too big of a problem, or at least he hoped there wouldn't be. If worse came to worst, he could let Oreo relieve himself and they could fly on, landing on a deserted small highway or somewhere else if need be. Although fueling up was also high on Andrew's priority list, second at the moment only to Oreo's situation.

Banking over the airport to make a final turn for landing, Andrew saw a large concrete arrow by the beacon and smiled. This airport was a part of the original air transport system from the late 1920s. Happy to see that some history had survived even the end of the world, Andrew landed and made the turn-off for the FBO and a small group of hangars. Two white tanks sat aboveground, which was a good sign for easier fueling, but first, after the prop stopped spinning, Andrew climbed out and pulled Oreo out of the back seat. Oreo immediately ran to the taxiway sign and peed on it. Andrew scanned the area. There was no sign of movement, no signs of the dead, although this section of I-40 appeared to have been pushed clear by a massive horde, as had the entire stretch of Interstate since Albuquerque. They appeared to be outbound toward the West Coast. Andrew was following in their path, but he had no way of knowing how far ahead of him they were and if he might catch up. Using the available tie downs, Andrew secured his aircraft and began clearing the closest hangar to find a spot for the night.

Nellis Air Force Base, NV

One recon team was out, and the other team split into two shifts for security; so far the reports weren't good. The entire base was overrun, although they did find the Thunderbirds' F-16s sitting on the flightline. The daylight waning, the recon team was heading back in for the night. Aymond debated staying another day or leaving after the sleep rotation in the morning. The shortwave broadcast was back on, someone repeating the same script and advising a channel switch for other information. The other frequency had another person repeating instructions on how to construct some sort of radio and how to use Morse code. It didn't matter. Aymond was glad to know someone else out there survived.

One more day, if there is anyone here, we're going to need them. Then we'll go to Area 51, which I hope is staffed with military personnel. We have a war to fight.

CHAPTER 9

Outside of Magdalena, NM
April 7, Year 1

Amanda woke unrested, her mind having refused to let her sleep peacefully through the night. The survivors in Tatum, all the others she didn't know about, that no one knew about... she had been right. There were survivors, many survivors trying to just live another day all across the country. The longer she took, the more time it took to mount an effort to help, to somehow conquer the reanimated dead, the more of them that would die. After refueling from another abandoned semi-truck's fuel tanks on this side of San Antonio, New Mexico, she drove into the night until she knew she was really making a bad choice due to her emotions by pushing on. She simply stopped in the middle of US-60, turned off the lights, turned off the truck, cracked the roof hatch for some air, and felt utterly and completely alone.

Giving up on sleep, Amanda climbed out onto the roof of the truck. Standing out of the turret, she saw the eastern horizon beginning to glow with the morning twilight, the moon only a sliver of light in the sky. As her eyes adjusted to the darkness, Amanda could see well enough to drive. Scanning the area and confirming that she was actually alone, Amanda climbed down to the pavement, squatting against one of the large wheels before starting her day. She missed the perfect facilities of the SSC, the hot showers and mostly comfortable bunks, but meeting the survivors in Tatum the previous day had galvanized her will, her resolve to win re-energized. Back in the MRAP, Amanda tore open an MRE as she drove. Today was the day, unsafe or not; she wasn't going to stop for the night again, and there simply wasn't any more time to waste.

Saint George, UT

Bexar woke up early, before sunrise, dressed and walked into the garage. The only other person awake was Frances, who was sitting security watch for the last half of the night. He thought it was smart that the group split the nightshift, only five hours per person; the dayshift was seven each. That made the rotation harder with fewer people, but the problem of being too tired during a long shift of sitting in the dark listening to crickets was slightly easier to withstand and still be useful with the shorter shifts. As a rookie, Bexar had worked the nightshift, just as every rookie cop did wherever they might work. The dayshift was for the veteran officers and people trying to buck for a promotion. The nightshift was the fun shift, as long as something was going on. For Bexar, it seemed like every nightshift had something going on; it seemed that without fail he would fall into some sort of fucked-up call. It got bad enough that his sergeant forbade him from making traffic stops after four a.m. because every time he did it would end in a chase, a fight, or having to Taser someone, and other units running code across the city to come help.

Standing alone in the garage over the work bench with his AR disassembled, he slowly cleaned the rifle, inspecting each piece, and removed the bolt carrier and took it apart. Bexar finally realized what his old supervisor had been trying to do. It wasn't about keeping the calm; the reality was that when an officer was a complete shit magnet, the numbers game could catch up, and an officer-involved shooting would follow. Officers never really recover from having to shoot someone. It had been only in the last couple of years that officers were beginning to be encouraged to see a therapist, especially after a critical incident, but before that they were told to man up and truck on. The things that followed were a common script: heavy drinking, failed marriages, and lives ruined for a once proud officer, and that was for the "good" shoots.

Bexar shook his head, absentmindedly dragging the teeth of the small extractor across the back of his hand to see if it left light scratches. Scratches were good; when the extractor became worn, it wouldn't scratch the skin, and failure to extract malfunctions would be soon to follow. The ejector spring felt good, and the gas rings still spun, but they were showing wear.

I should probably switch out parts when we get to Groom Lake and start carrying some spare parts.

He'd always hated cleaning his weapons, a chore, a task after a range day or qualifying, something to be done quickly, efficiently, and be done with. But this morning, Bexar felt a certain amount of Zen in meticulously cleaning and inspecting each part of his rifle before reassembling the bolt carrier and putting it all back in the upper. A light coat of Break-Free covered the bolt carrier and charging handle. After checking the trigger, he set a drop of lube on the edge of the hammer's release, carefully working the hammer back and forth. Someone taught him a long time ago that it helped with a smoother trigger squeeze, and he wasn't sure if it was real or not, but it *felt* like it made a difference, and that was what mattered.

The irony of the concerns about being in an officer-involved shooting wasn't lost on Bexar after reassembling his rifle, making a functionality check, reloading, and making it ready. Not counting the risen dead, he had no idea how many actual living people he'd had to kill in the past few months. Unloading and disassembling his pistol on the bench, Bexar thought about what the number might be and became angry. Angry at each of the bastards that forced him to kill, angry that his little girl was dead, angry that his wife was still miles away, angry that they were going to have to raise a baby in this new and horrible world they lived in. Most of all, he was angry at the bastards that started this whole mess, the faceless attackers, angry that no amount of justice could be taken to reconcile what they had done.

Working faster, Bexar's previous Zen of weapon maintenance left him, and he quickly cleaned, reassembled, and reloaded his pistol, holstering it and walking back into the house. Following the smell of coffee, he found Guillermo sitting at the kitchen table, chatting with Frances, who had apparently finished her shift on security watch.

"Welcome, my friend Bexar, join us." Guillermo gestured to an open chair next to Frances, standing to pour a mug of coffee for the new arrival; two mason jars sat on the table, one with powdered creamer and the other with some artificial sweetener. As preppers go, this group was living the luxurious life. Bexar,

Malachi, and Jack's original group plan of canvas tents and country living paled in comparison.

"What are you going to do after you get there?"

Bexar stared into his coffee, his mind wandering in the steam. "I'm, sorry, what?"

Frances smiled wearily, tired but needing to wind down before going to bed. "After you get to Groom Lake, after you are reunited with your wife, what are your plans?"

"Hopefully live a peaceful and uneventful life; raising a child... I'm not sure if that can happen."

"If you bring your wife back here, I bet it could."

Bexar smiled. "You guys are really trying for the hard sell before we leave, huh?"

Guillermo grinned. "Wouldn't you? Why leave to live in a hole in the ground in Nevada? What about Chivo? What is your friend going to do, settle down underground with your family?"

"I'll probably do what I've done for the last twenty years, mano: Serve my country with unique and secret distinction."

Guillermo stood and brought another mug of coffee to the table. Frances stood. "Merylin is probably waking up, and it's her day to cook. If I want any time with her before she gets to work and I get to sleep, I've got to get it now. Bexar, Chivo, if I'm asleep when you leave, thank you, thank you for everything."

Chivo smiled and thanked her.

"What about you guys? The compound has eight members once we leave. Are you going to keep on with the same plan or try to branch out for something new?"

"We're not sure, Chivo. Our plan is to keep on the same track, but we're always open to new opportunities, like the chance Angel took with you two. That worked out for the better, even if it was a hard road to travel."

The small talk continued back and forth, drifting from scavenging for more working vehicles or somehow finding horses to replace the ones Chivo and Stan had lost to the dead. They talked about the new weapons and possibly changing the security setup and protocols to include them; Chivo thought it lunacy not to.

When you have the ability to deploy automatic weapons and RPGs to deter an invading force, why keep those tools in the back locked away.

"The SEALs do this thing when they encounter a superior force; they fire everything they have, I mean everything, and it is staggering. The enemy force can't respond quickly enough; it's like a sudden wall of death. By the time a counter attack can be mounted, the frogmen have slipped away and disappeared into thin air. While I was in the unit, we tended to use other kinds of support, but we had the Little Birds and the amazing pilots of the 160th. Holy shit, the Night Stalkers would take those fucking helicopters places I wouldn't want to drive a car through, and they would do it in total darkness and in shitty weather. God, I hope they made it through this mess. If we're going to function well enough to destroy the fucking Chinese, we're going to need guys like that."

"Is that where this is going?" Guillermo asked.

"It has to. I don't know what they wanted to accomplish. The only thing that makes any sense whatsoever is the attack being a prelude to invasion, but I don't know how they would conquer the dead to do it. Maybe there's something we don't know. Maybe in a year's time or two years, the bodies of the reanimated dead fall apart. It could be a war of patience and attrition, who knows with those fuckers. Afghanistan I got, I understood those tribes and the centuries of fighting, the same with the drug cartels, and I understood the purpose and the money driving them. This shit we're in now, I can't wrap my brain around it; it's just loco, all of it."

Guillermo shook his head. "Only time will tell?"

"Sure, mano, in a year, maybe two, we'll know. Either things will happen or they won't, and there's shit all we can do except react to it. If there's an invasion, then we need all the survivors and all the equipment we have left to repel it. If it is a war of attrition, we just have to survive, and we'll take the country back. If this was some sort of suicide pact, destroy the world, destroy themselves, or just destroy the world so they have their own slice to themselves, that just doesn't make any sense, but it seems to now. So we're left with the only three things we can do: wait, train, and survive."

Merylin walked into the kitchen, smiled, and began preparing the group breakfast. Each of them had a specific role in the group, but tasks like cooking rotated daily to keep things fair for all. Bexar and Chivo hadn't cooked a single meal since they'd arrived, but Chivo, being experienced with such things, assured Bexar privately that eliminating a threatening rival "tribe" and returning with war booty was all they would have to do even if they stayed for a year.

Chivo excused himself and left to walk outside. The VW sat in the courtyard, next to the massive forklift. The new weapons, ammo, and gear were stored in the garage now that the shop had been destroyed, but the crates remained in the courtyard for the moment. The group had discussed using the crates as crates, or disassembling them to have wood for the fire or wood to construct unknown future projects. A vote hadn't happened yet, so for now, the crates sat empty, stacked against the far fence line. Walking the fence line, Chivo inspected the fence and perimeter.

What they need is a bunch of Hesco barriers, make the compound a true fire base, something that could be defended more easily. Start with the fence line and then gradually extend out the compound's security wall in concentric rings until they "owned" the whole hillside.

A hardened target is a target passed by. Chivo checked the homemade roof rack, the extra gas cans, and their share of the booty, mostly ammo and a few grenades, all unpacked from the bulky crates and jammed into the tiny car. It sat squat on the worn suspension. The best estimate that he had was that it would take them roughly five hours of driving to get to Groom Lake, if everything went right. Roughly two hundred miles, so ten gallons of treated gasoline from the group's stores were in the Beetle's gas tank, and another ten gallons sat in two gas cans on the roof. If twenty gallons wouldn't get them two hundred miles in an old Beetle, then they had issues.

Milan, NM

Oreo nudged Andrew awake, a dusty, dirty couch in the hangar his bed for the night. Andrew pushed his dog away, but Oreo nudged him again, and then Andrew heard voices.

"That's the Husky we saw, so he's got to be in one of the hangars. He isn't anywhere else."

Now wide awake, Andrew leapt off the couch, pistol in his hands; he crept to the hangar's side door, edged against the metal wall and waited, nearly holding his breath. His heartbeat banged in his ears so loud that he was sure that the two men outside could hear it. The doorknob turned, and the door rattled, the deadbolt locked from the inside by Andrew the night before. There was the sound of a key sliding into the lock and then the deadbolt turned with a hard click. The door edged open, daylight burning brightly into the hangar. Andrew shielded his eyes the best he could to keep some of the night vision he had and waited for the men to step inside.

One then the other, both older men in jeans and worn-out tennis shoes, stepped into the dark hangar. Andrew waited, hidden in the shadows behind the opened door. Once inside, Andrew pushed his pistol into the second man's back. "Don't move or I'll kill you." Oreo barked.

"Hey, guy, we're not here to harm you. You're a pilot, and we're pilots, and we live across the Interstate. After we saw your Husky land yesterday, we wanted to come chat. Nothing we have sitting outside will fly again without some work and parts we simply don't have, but really we wanted news, wanted to know if you know anything about what's going on."

Andrew waited for Oreo. If Oreo approved, he would trust his dog. He hadn't been wrong yet. A moment later, Andrew felt a nudge on his leg, and Oreo sat down against him, "My dog says you passed the test. I learned to trust my dog more than I trust people nowadays. Why don't we go outside and chat."

"Sure, or I can push open the hangar doors to get some light in here, your choice."

Moments later the metal doors rattled as the two men pushed them open along the tracks in the concrete, light flooding the hangar and the lone aircraft that sat in it, an older King Air. That plane easily flew higher, faster, and further than his little bush plane, but it took much more fuel and couldn't land on rough fields.

After introductions, Roy and Jay told Andrew the story of their survival in Milan. Twenty-two of them were left after a horrible week last month when a massive group of the dead pushed through on the Interstate. They didn't all stay on I-40; many of them flooded the town, killing thirteen while the rest of the survivors sheltered in place, praying to survive. Canned food kept the remaining twenty-two people alive, days spent scavenging abandoned homes and stores for anything they could find gave them a stockpile to last through the end of the year, but the one thing they didn't have was any information.

Andrew told them about all the other survivors and groups he had met over his travels, about his friends in Arkansas, the home-built radio, Groom Lake, and his desire to get there.

"So Bob built the radio basically out of used car parts?"

"Pretty much. He was a radio geek before the attack and knew what he was doing, so he changed the design a little bit, but that's basically what he did. He made a much better generator design. The antenna was a long run of wire draped over power poles."

"Do you remember what he did well enough to help us build one?"

"I can do you one better, I wrote it all down; it's in the plane."

Both of the men shot up, waiting impatiently for Andrew to take them to the new treasure of information, the ability to have a working radio, a way to talk to the outside world!

Half an hour later, the men were in the hangar, the cowls off the King Air's engines, wrenches turning to remove some of the parts they needed to build a radio. Quickly they decided that the airfield's historic airway beacon would be the perfect perch for the large antenna loop they needed. Promising to return in a few hours while they gathered the rest of the necessary parts and to bring a lunch back, they left Andrew with the key to the padlock on the Avgas tank to refill his plane while he waited.

This was a better experience than he'd had in the weeks before. News was a barterable good, but the directions to build a radio, a chance to communicate, that was more than just a barterable good, it was like having solid gold bars. Andrew wasn't Oprah rich, he was post-apocalyptic rich, which was even better.

After taxiing to the fuel tank and filling the Husky's fuel bladders, he relocked the fuel tank and taxied back to the tie downs to secure the plane. He figured at the least he was going to be remaining in Milan until the afternoon; worst case he might have to spend another night in the hangar. He was close, closer than before and wanted to get closer still to his destination. Not a dusty metal hangar in nowhere New Mexico, but in a real honest-to-God secret underground base that had food, showers, bed, people, and safety. Not that Andrew wanted to stay there forever, but the chance to relax for a couple weeks in what qualified as a five-star resort in the new world was a titillating thought.

Sitting on the tarmac under the shade of the Husky's wing, Andrew flipped through the atlas, ruler in hand. A straight line was roughly five hundred miles and would go right over the Grand Canyon, which was something that Andrew had wanted to see since he was a child. If the winds aloft were in his favor, there was no reason he couldn't make the flight to Groom Lake without refueling, but again, with no way to know, he wasn't about to take that gamble. The Grand Canyon was about the halfway point and could be an interesting stop. He knew that operators in the area offered aerial tours of the Grand Canyon, so there had to be landing strips somewhere nearby, but only the larger airports were shown on the atlas.

Jay and Roy returned, three others in tow, each carrying bags. One of the bags was given to Andrew; it contained a loaf of bread and three sealed mason jars with soup in them. Two cans of dog food were also in the canvas bag.

They didn't offer a can opener, but Andrew had an old P51 opener in his bag for just such an occasion. Oreo waited patiently, drool dripping to the tarmac as Andrew slowly made his way around the opening of the can. Once the top was open, without a proper dish, he simply upended the can onto the tarmac. Oreo didn't mind and quickly ate the gravy-covered processed meat that he had missed for much of the time after the attack. After feeding Oreo, Andrew held the loaf of bread in his hands, a real loaf of bread. Some other survivor groups, the ones that were well-stocked preppers, had the means to make bread, but it had been weeks since he'd had any. Tempted to bite right into the middle of the loaf, Andrew contained himself and tore off a chunk, the chewy meat of the loaf tasting like a piece of heaven, the thick crust tough and crunchy.

Yup, better than Oprah rich... much better.

Andrew sat, enjoying one of the jars of soup and the bread while watching the group build the radio and hang the antenna's wire from the beacon's tower. Finishing the bread, Andrew took Oreo and went to nap under the plane, both with full stomachs, until some yelling woke him up.

After a moment, he realized that it wasn't really yelling, but happily excited people. Andrew correctly guessed that the radio worked, and the group had made contact or were listening to another conversation, writing out the letters of each tapped-out word buzzing on and off in the spark-gap radio. Standing slowly, Andrew walked to the group sitting around a folding table in the hangar, wondering if they were excited enough that they might give him another loaf of bread.

"So it works?"

"Damn straight it works, son! This is amazing, just simply amazing!"

"Bob said it was ancient technology, what the original wireless telegraph operators used, long before voice communications."

"Andrew, we don't care. It works, and we made contact. Now we're listening to another group out of... where are they out of, Susanne?"

"Michigan."

"Wow, out of Michigan, and they're talking to your friends in Nevada. Area 51, I never thought we had aliens there, but I knew we had something. Thank God for that something."

Andrew looked at the sky; the sun was well-past overhead and endlessly marching toward the western horizon. They would be delayed another day, but if they could fly out at first light in the morning, they could stop off at the Grand Canyon, refuel, and land on the dry lakebed of Groom Lake before sunset.

"Jay, you guys wouldn't happen to have any charts or sections you would like to donate? I'm flying off of a road atlas, IFR all the way; I follow roads."

"Son, we've got a whole stack of charts. You can take the lot or pull the ones you want, and you can always come back for the rest if you need them!"

Jay handed him his keys again, pulling up the key to the FBO with a short explanation of where they were stored. Sporty's Pilot Supply it was not, but it was better than he had, so it was the best that could be found.

Smiling, Andrew left the group to find the sectional charts, while their attention stayed unwaveringly on the radio. If they had all thirty-eight, he would take all of them. It was worth the room and worth the weight to be able to know altitudes, where towers were, actually *plan* a flight instead of bumming around the slow routes of the Interstate system hoping to find somewhere to land for the night. With obstacles, elevations, and altitudes marked, he could even fly at night.

That's it, I'm going to take a quick nap, plot the course, and fly out. If I do it right, I should arrive just after sunrise. Groom Lake is marked on the sectional. All I need is sunlight to land.

Outside of Hurricane, UT

Amanda felt exhausted, the long drive taking its toll on her, but as tired as she felt, she was strangely energized. She still had half a tank of fuel left after siphoning more fuel a few hours prior and, according to the signs, she would be coming out of the highway in the middle of nowhere soon. Following Highway 59, in Hurricane she would take Highway 9 for a bit and, unfortunately, end up on I-15, but not for long before she turned off. The Interstates were not her friends, but not since the night of the huge storm and dodging zombies by lightning flashes had she had much issue on the small highways. Surprisingly, this trip was a longer journey than her trek from Little Rock to the SSC, but it was going much smoother and much quicker than before.

Highway 59 descended into the town, and two turns later Amanda was on Highway 9 driving west through the middle of town. Scanning for signs of survivors or any signs, and excited to see more, she continued on, tired, the MRAP swerving back and forth on the roadway some as she stared out of the side windows. The hard thunk of something hitting the front bumper brought her attention forward again.

Outside her windshield stood nearly a virtual wall of meandering death, hundreds if not thousands of the reanimated dead milling about in the roadway. Amanda slammed on the brakes and jerked the wheel right, taking the first side street she saw. At first glance, the streets appeared to be in a grid pattern, and Amanda hoped she was right. In the side-view mirror she saw dead shambling in a slow, methodical pursuit, so she turned left, paralleling the highway, slowing and swerving back and forth. There were less of the dead on this street, but more and more followed the movement and the sound of the heavy diesel engine. More dead streamed out from around buildings and homes, blocking her path once again. Turning left, she drove the truck through a chain-link fence, bouncing across a rock-filled field between her and Highway 9.

Back on the highway, Amanda pointed west, slowing down to nearly a crawl, the truck practically driving with the engine at idle as the heavy steel bumper pushed bodies out of the way or under the truck. Frowning, Amanda scanned the gauges; everything from the oil pressure to the air pressure was where it was supposed to be. Feathering the accelerator pedal until the truck slowly sped up, she glanced at the speedometer which showed a brisk five miles per hour; she continued pushing through the middle of the rioting pack of dead with persistence. If something happened and she got stuck, if the truck failed, if any number of things happened, she would live out the rest of her life surrounded by death in a large armored truck.

Saint George, UT

They were getting a later start than they wanted. Originally planning on leaving first thing in the morning, Chivo went outside again after breakfast to find Stan in the middle of an oil change on the Beetle. Trying to be gracious, Chivo agreed that it was probably a good idea, but Bexar was visibly annoyed. The morning slipped by as more things happened. They agreed to stay for lunch, but would leave immediately thereafter, Bexar nearly shaking from the anticipation and anxiety of wanting to get on the road to get to Jessie.

A far cry from Bexar's beloved Wagoneer with its full-length roof rack, the homemade wooden rack did well to hold their provisions, most of which didn't fit in the interior of the car or under the hood of the trunk. Expecting to arrive in a single day's drive, most of what they carried in the way of gear were weapons of war, including Chivo's favorite rifle to reach out and touch someone from a distance. The rifle and case being much too long to even attempt fitting in the car, it sat tied down on the roof rack like a canoe of death. Four MREs and a gallon of water each was all they decided to bring in the way of provisions, choosing to fill the spaces with the weaponry purloined from Frank's group.

Shortly after lunch, they were finally on their way, the loud exhaust announcing their departure to anyone dead or alive that happened to be in the area.

Remembering how bad things were just before they turned onto the I-15 frontage road, the windows were only rolled down a little way, even without air conditioning, both of them ready to roll them up quickly at the first undead they encountered.

The tires were old, but they would have to work; the car was loud and slow but was keeping a steady pace as they made a right turn onto Saint George Boulevard, the wide four-lane road that cut through town to Highway 18. The palm trees, an apparent favorite of landscapers in the area, looked withered and sickly, and the median was full of weeds. The close-standing businesses and office spaces did not look much better.

"Amazing, isn't it, how fast everything went to shit?" Bexar nearly yelled over the loud muffler.

Chivo nodded, deftly swerving around a small cluster of dead walking in the middle of the roadway. Flat-topped mountains loomed in the distance, and Bexar silently wondered how their little car would do trying to climb up the hillsides. For all the dead that had been seen on the Interstate and surrounding area recently, the heart of town seemed nearly abandoned by the dead, eerily devoid of lingering hordes veiled in thick black curtains of flies.

Twenty minutes after turning north on Highway 18, the vagabond pair of travelers were free of civilization's ruins and once again on the open highway, winding slowly through the desolate desert country side. Small clusters of homes and ranches dotted the distance along the roadside, which left Bexar questioning what someone could do to be a successful rancher in the uninhabited barrens of this region of Utah.

Passing a subdivision, the reanimated dead that they had missed leaving Saint George were found slowly streaming out from around the sides of the houses and toward the highway. Unlike their drive into Saint George, this time they cleared the growing herd of death before the roadway was blocked and a serious problem occurred.

Groom Lake, NV

They had resorted to yelling, the overweight quartermaster trying to protect the cache of supplies that they weren't even finished inventorying yet. Jessie wanted free rein to outfit, arm, and supply every single survivor that lived in the vast underground facility with as much ammo, weaponry, and equipment that they would possibly need to stand their ground against whatever may come. She was done playing the game in piecemeal. It was time to jump feet first into the water and face all that could be with all they had.

"No, even if Jake was standing here ordering me to give you free rein, I would not do it. It isn't fair for the group, it isn't right, and a woman like you doesn't have the first clue how to defend your own home much less a community like we have here!"

Frustrated, Jessie gave the quartermaster a one-fingered salute. Erin, who was with her, stepped close to the overweight man. Her right hand holding a knife, she pressed it against the crotch of the man's jeans, left hand gently brushing the side of his face and simply whispered, "You fuck with us and I'll cut off your dick and shove it down your throat. You don't even have a clue how to defend your pathetic little cock much less all this gear you're hoarding. Walk away and never come back. If I so much as see you in the hallway, you'll have to sit down to piss the rest of your life."

Blood drained from the man's face. He gasped for air, unable to speak, raising his hands in the air as a sign of surrender. Erin felt her right hand get warm and wet. Looking down, she saw that the man had wet himself. "That's just sad, a grown-ass man scared of little ol' me. Run along now, little boy, go on."

The man took two timid steps backwards, away from Erin and the knife she had against his now wet jeans. before he left in a stumbling sprint toward the door.

"Jesus, Erin, remind me not to piss you off."

"I don't think you ever could, Jessie," Erin said with a faint smile.

Ignoring the metal desk piled haphazardly with stacks of papers against the computer, covered in crumbs, and generally disgusting, the pair set out into the dark reaches of the storage area with small notebooks in their hands, donning headlamps to read the box and crate contents, making short notes as they walked, discussing what they thought they would need. Erin wanted more ammo for her 50-caliber rifle and a good spotting scope. Jessie just wanted something, a lot of something, she just wasn't sure what. All the survivors in the underground facility had pistols; they were required to carry them at all times, but the pistols were of all different makes and calibers, a mix of mostly what they'd all brought with them. Rifles were another story. Some had AR-variant-style rifles, some had hunting rifles, a few had some sort of variant of the AK-47, and fewer still, like Jason, had some type of shotgun; although not a rifle, it was at the least a long gun of some sort.

Erin pointed at a large section of wooden crates. "Jessie, I think we should outfit the group with as many of these M-16s as we can, all that don't have some sort of AR. Then at least the magazines and ammo are interchangeable."

"That's a good idea; we had group-standard weapons for the same reasons with our prepper group."

The pair kept walking, reading what they could on the highest shelves of the racking. It felt like they were in a tactical Costco, but instead of five-gallon jugs of ketchup, they had boxes with five thousand rounds of 5.56.

"How did your prepper group start?"

Jessie had waited for these questions to come from Erin for some time, but even expecting and rehearsing the answers to herself time and time again, she got choked up when trying to begin. "My Bexar, we met while I was finishing college. He was working all sorts of odd jobs, and we knew we were in love from the beginning. He grew up with Malachi and Jack, true lifelong friends. They could go months without seeing each other because of life and kids, but when they got together, conversations would seemingly pick up where they had left off, like no time had passed. The jokes, everything. Jake married first, but he and Sandra had dated for years and years. I think even before they went to college. Malachi married last, but he loved that little east Texas girl. For a time she worked in the prison system before she'd had enough of the bullshit that came with it and left. They moved to north Texas, we were in central Texas, and Jack's family was between Dallas and Fort Worth. We all camped together when we had the chance, meeting at random state parks and even out to Big Bend on one occasion, but it was Jack who started us on the idea of prepping. Things got a little out of hand after that, but as crazy as they got with it all, I supported it, Sandra supported it, and I think Amber, Malachi's wife, supported it, although I had the impression she was just mostly playing along. Each of them was good at many varied tasks, but each had their strong points. My Bexar, especially from the training associated with being in law enforcement, was the group's tactics and weapons guy. Malachi was communications and planning; he was a bit OCD about all of that. Jack was good with food storage. Really the three families had the perfect plan."

"If it was perfect, what happened?"

"The fucking dead happened. Bexar heard about the attack from the police dispatcher before it happened and was able to get a group text out to Malachi and Jack before the EMPs hit. He didn't include me on the text because he's forgetful like that, and he abandoned his post and duties to escape home. His motorcycle – he was a motorcycle cop – died near the neighborhood because the EMPs hit. He ran home, we loaded up, and bugged out."

"How did your vehicles still work?"

"We had an old Jeep Wagoneer. God, I hated that thing, but Bexar had it since high school and would probably have divorced me before selling that fucking thing. Anyways, we all had older rigs with no electronics in them for an EMP to kill off. We all left our homes to bugout to a central Texas location where we had all of our supplies. It took us a few days each, but we all got there... sort of. Amber had been shot, died, and turned, biting Malachi. He died that night and was found reanimated the next day. Losing Malachi and Amber was the first big blow to the group."

"Why didn't you stay with your supplies?"

"The goddamn dead! We were still too close to Dallas; the night horizon glowed orange with the huge fires ripping through the city, and out of those fires came the first wave of dead. We threw all we had on the roof racks and bugged out again. We decided to head to Big Bend National Park, and eventually we made it there."

"Where?"

"You know on Texas where the Rio Grande goes down then back up before going down again to the Gulf of Mexico?"

"Yeah."

"Well most of that is a national park. Now that place was the good life! It was surprisingly mostly deserted, not too many dead to clear out... between some solar panels and some ingenuity, we had power to our cabins in the Basin, the mountain area, and we even had running water as it was spring fed. There were javelina and mule tail deer to shoot and eat. Jack even got an ice cream freezer from the store in the park to work on solar power so we could preserve the meat."

"So why here, and why now?"

"We used Malachi's radio, a ham radio, and contacted Cliff, who told us about this place. A fucking biker gang heard us on the radio and attacked us to raid our supplies."

"What happened? Everyone fled, and here you are. Why did you get separated from Bexar?"

"No... we, well, a lot of things went wrong. Our daughter Keeley was killed, and the biker gang kidnapped me. I didn't know if Bexar was alive because he was missing, just vanished, and after realizing I was pregnant and alone, I set off to come here. A lot of fucking good that it did me!"

Jake walked into the cavernous room, looking down each long dark aisle as he passed until he spotted Jessie's and Erin's headlamps and walked up to them with a serious look on his face. "Were you two really going to cut off our quartermaster's penis?"

Erin laughed. "No, but now that he's gone all tattle-tale, I might just have to do it now!"

"Heh, well, I'd ask you not to. He's scared and pissed off and telling everyone about it. After the last outbreak, you all bought some good will, but that won't last if you keep up stuff like that. Anyways, the reason I'm here is that we voted on it, and the towns agree, we fight. But what do we do now?"

"First, we equip. Second, we train. But in the meantime, we figure out what all we have down here in storage. Send us all the people you can spare; we need to figure out everything we've got here, and we have to do it *fast*."

Jake nodded. "OK, let me see who I can scare up and that I trust to help you. I can't have anyone's crotch outty being turned into an inney."

Jake left, and Erin and Jessie continued to chat back and forth. Jessie told her about seeing Bexar in the Basin acting like a madman before she heard what she thought was an explosion; that she was knocked off her feet and into unconsciousness. After that, it was simple planning and building the motivation to actually go.

Erin shook her head. "Damn, and I thought my life was tough."

"Well, to be fair, I don't have Sarah for a mother!"

They both had a much-needed laugh from that; all the while they climbed through crate after crate of weapons and clothing.

Ellis Air Force Base, NV

The team chief, Gunnery Master Sergeant Jerry Aymond, had finally reached his limit. The base was dead, everything was dead, they were done with Nellis, and they needed to leave and point toward Area 51. That might be dead too, but it appeared to be somewhat alive due to the shortwave radio broadcasts. Those transmissions were the first real sign of some sort of surviving civilization that they had found, and the remaining Marines in his MSOT needed good news for a change. Walking out of his makeshift office and into the lounge area that the men had started sleeping in, Aymond cleared his voice loudly, then again, waking the nightwatch patrol.

"Raiders! Load it up to convoy north. We're done here, and it's time we go."

"Think we'll find alien bodies?"

"Who the fuck knows, Happy, but if the recording is true, we'll find people, which I would rather find any day of the week than an alien."

The team quietly worked hard, loading the truck as quickly as they could, stacking the supplies and equipment that they were able to scavenge from the PJs' cache. An hour later, Aymond sat in the passenger seat of the lead M-ATV. With the radar truck taking the middle position, the small convoy drove off the flight line and toward the north. The padlocked chain-link gate to the parking area was quickly disposed of, but the next gate's concrete crash barriers were something they would rather avoid than hassle with. After threading through the parking lot, the heavy block wall gave way to another chain-link fence, which they found had already been cut; it was open wide enough for the vehicles to pass through.

All of them were privy to many secrets; except for Jones, they all held top-secret clearances, but Area 51 was not something they had any knowledge of.

Overall, they only had a vague idea as to where it was, trusting that the directions given on the shortwave radio transmissions were correct. The directions were very general, for groups coming from larger areas. Some highway names were given, but without a way to directly communicate with the facility. With GPS being down, they would once again have to wing it.

The directions were for groups coming from the West Coast areas, using I-15 as a general marker that led them to US-95, which was on the northwest side of Las Vegas. Driving out of the fenced perimeter of Nellis Air Force Base, they found themselves on the northeast side of Las Vegas. A simple road atlas was all they had available; the route appeared easy, Aymond following the little lines he marked on the paper, but he had his concerns. After the recon patrols through the large base, it was obvious that Las Vegas was completely overrun by Zeds. Once they were fully fueled, Aymond scaled off the approximate distance that they would have to travel to reach Groom Lake, and he was pleased to see that they shouldn't need fuel while en route. He was tired of the hop-scotching and waiting; they would drive all night if they had to, but they weren't stopping until the convoy pulled into Area 51.

Enterprise, UT

The easy trip had been anything but easy. The handful of tiny towns that they'd passed along the way appeared deserted. If there were any reanimated dead in the towns, they didn't see any; if there were any survivors, they didn't see any of them either. Eerily alone as they traveled together, like a scene from "On the Beach," the countryside remained intact but devoid of life.

On the dashboard of the old Beetle was one large single gauge. It contained the speedometer, an odometer, a fuel gauge that seemed questionable at best, and two warning lights. The one that was marked "OIL" was off; the one that was marked "TEMP" was on.

Highway 18 crashed into a T-junction at Enterprise, a service station at the far side of the roadway junction, which Bexar guessed probably also served as the community meeting place, grocery store, and supply house. Chivo shifted into neutral and let the VW coast into the parking lot, bouncing across the potholes.

"These old air-cooled VWs have a single fan belt that goes from the crank pulley to the generator, which is bolted to the fan. If we've temped out the motor, this punta is either done or the fan belt broke."

"Where the fuck are we going to find a fan belt for a forty-year-old car?"

"We improvise, mano," Chivo said, stopping the VW in the middle of the parking lot. "It's a simple v-belt. We scavenge one off a tractor, a lawn mower, use some rope, hell, you can whittle one out of a piece of wheat for all I care, but we'll figure it out... FUCK!"

Chivo launched out of the car. Bexar, not sure what the problem was yet, simply followed his lead, getting out, grabbing his rifle and getting ready to fight. It was quickly apparent what the problem was. Again following Chivo's lead, Bexar's knife was in his hand and he was cutting the gear lashed to the roof rack free while Chivo threw green cans of ammunition out onto the pavement from the back of the car as fast as he could, the green cans clattering loudly across the parking lot.

Thick black smoke poured from the back of the car. The Baja modification left the car without a deck lid over the motor, so flames quickly lapped the roof of the car.

"Bexar, get this shit on the other side of the building. Do it quick!"

Leaving the car, which was becoming fully engulfed, Bexar scooped up a handful of gear and Chivo's big rifle case and sprinted to the far side of the convenience store, where he dropped the load. He sprinted back to the car, Chivo passing him in the opposite direction, as the whole back of the car burned, flames reaching high above them. Thick, caustic black smoke filled the air.

Chivo and Bexar passed each other again, Chivo yelling at Bexar, "Stay back there!"

The hand grenades, some of the ammo cans, and a handful of rounds for the RPG they'd brought were still in the car. Chivo ran back behind the convenience store and slid to a stop. Bexar was doubled over, coughing and trying to catch his breath.

"Keep your mouth open!"

A small pop sound preceded the explosion. As the windows shattered, pieces of shrapnel and German steel that was once their car rocketed past their mostly safe position behind the brick wall.

The pressure wave toppled the metal awning over the gas pumps. Ears ringing, Bexar couldn't hear Chivo, who grabbed his head, turning it from side to side, looking at his ears before giving a thumbs up. It dawned on Bexar what Chivo meant to keep his mouth open; it prevented his eardrums from bursting from the explosive concussion. Chivo tapped Bexar on the chest, pointed to his eyes and then pointed out. Pointing to Bexar, he pointed left; pointing to himself, Chivo pointed right and then raised his rifle. Bexar nodded, remembering again what one of the elaborate hand signals he and his motor buddies had made up mocking the SWAT team, which usually involved which taqueria they were going to eat at after working the morning school zones.

Rifle up in the low ready, Bexar followed Chivo around the corner of the building. Staying close, Bexar took responsibility for the left side of view, scanning the fields and the highway; the destruction was incredible. The convenience store was on fire, the fuel pumps were on fire, and it seemed that everything was on fire. Chivo stopped, tapped him, and gestured back to where they had come. The ringing in his ears starting to fade, Bexar could faintly hear the popping sounds of the growing fire. Chivo picked up his rifle case and grabbed a few ammo cans, Bexar picked up what he could carry as well, following Chivo into the desert beyond the burning convenience store, once again moving what they had left away from a growing fire.

Chivo yelled, "At least this time I don't think this damn thing will explode!"

Bexar nodded. "I'm getting really fucking tired of shit blowing up near me!"

"Seriously, you're like an explosion shit magnet. What the fuck is wrong with you?"

"It's my wonderfully pleasant personality."

"Personality like a rabid raccoon!"

They both laughed. The demanding world that now existed was something to be laughed at only because all that anyone could do was laugh. Anything else would result in madness.

In the MRAP, UT

Thick black smoke stood as a lone pillar on the horizon. Ending her quick tour of Central, Utah, where she'd been looking for survivors, Amanda feared that the black smoke was the result of survivors running afoul in their cooking or some other means. She now believed, more than ever before, that the country was full of survivors, enough to repel the dead, to conquer Yama.

On the edge of the town lay a rancher's field. Under an awning, she found a few tractors, and next to the tractors was a metal tank sitting about six feet off the ground, fuel nozzle dangling. The gate was unlocked so, after pushing it open, Amanda drove the big truck along the dirt path to the tractors and the fuel tank. Rust combating the painted surface, barely visible was the stenciled "DIESEL FUEL ONLY" on the front of the tank. Hopeful, Amanda rapped the tank with her knuckles; the tank sounded like it had fuel in it. How much, she had no idea, but with the sun quickly approaching the western horizon, she would take any fuel she could find. Especially if she was going to drive through the night; she was no longer willing to spend another day resting or waiting.

The fuel tank didn't quite top off the MRAP, although it nearly did, but it was quick and easy, taking only about ten minutes. It was much quicker than her usual fueling sequence of siphoning from a semi-truck's saddle tank, with the added blessing of not having to wash the taste of fuel out of her mouth.

Back on the highway and pointed north, she drove toward the growing pillar of thick black smoke, wondering if any others were doing the same.

SSC, Ennis, TX

Clint lifted the last box of MREs he was bringing into the MRAP. Loaded with ammo, food, water, and enough fuel to make the trip without having to scavenge for any of it, he was ready to leave. His first thought was to set some IEDs for any surviving visitors who might arrive, that is if any would be left, but in the last message his handlers were quite specific that they wanted the facility deserted and intact. This was to be one of the primary operating bases for running their new providence once the invasion was complete.

Clint was indifferent; his newly revised mission was peculiar but not totally unexpected. His first thought was to drive to the southern edge of the fields in northern Colorado, but his orders were very explicit in that he was to travel to Montana. That would mean he would have to play a new role instead of just breaking into a dead facility.

Apparently there were other plans for the flights of ICBMs in Colorado and Wyoming. They didn't explain, and he didn't really care. Orders were orders. All it meant was that his travel time would take longer and would involve more snow. Early April was springtime in Texas and could still be very much winter in Montana. Well-provisioned, the stores from the SSC facility gave him the cold-weather gear and even the proper Air Force uniform to wear in case by some miracle some missile crew had survived and was still manning the control panels. If he had been someone in that position, the temptation to rogue launch against Korea and China would have been too great. Since that hadn't happened, Clint didn't expect to find anyone, but the best prepared were always the luckiest.

The soft orange glow of the late afternoon sun edged into the dark tunnel as the hatch opened, grass and dirt falling onto the ramp. The hidden exit was the same that Amanda had used, except that Clint knew exactly where he was and which way he had to travel. His route was meticulously planned, as was each of the rest of the steps. He didn't want to travel far at night, but he had to get started immediately if he was to make his rendezvous on time.

Las Vegas, NV

The journey on Highway 215 around the northern side of the city began easily enough. It was not very developed, not like the thick swarming city to their south, but the highway dove into the heart of the northwest corner of the city. Needing to reach Highway 95 to get pointed north and to their destination, they found the Zeds on the highway a virtual roadblock, forcing the convoy to slow to a virtual crawl as the Zeds bounced off the bumper of Aymond's M-ATV.

Aymond keyed the radio. "We're going to stop. Jones, bring the radar truck alongside my truck. Kirk, think you can get into the back of that thing and get it running?"

"Roger that, Chief, can do."

Jones stopped with the back of the radar truck next to the driver's side front wheel of the lead M-ATV, the remote turret firing controlled bursts, clearing the swarming Zeds, but unable to get the angle needed. The dozen or so in close range, next to the trucks, would have to be killed by hand.

Gonzo opened the driver's door, raising his pistol and firing. Kirk opened the back door and stepped out, doing the same, moving quickly but smoothly. He heard Gonzo's pistol rounds snap past him, dropping Zeds in his path. Kirk turned and fired, clearing his immediate path, careful of his backdrop, not wanting to put a round into the radar truck. As quickly as they had started, it was over. All the doors were closed, the big flat transmitter raising and rotating forward, and the rioting swarm of Zeds fell to the ground. The thick cloud of black flies also fell from the air around them, the radar truck killing them as readily as the Zeds.

"Jones, drive forward slowly and stay in the center of the road. Kirk, rotate the dome as we roll, but keep it facing forward; it even killed the flies, so I don't want to see what it would do to us if it gets pointed back toward us."

"Roger, Master-Guns."

"Gotcha, Chief."

As they drove onward slowly, the sea of dead before them fell. Trying to avoid them the best they could, they drove over the bodies, hoping the bones wouldn't puncture a tire. Heavy rubber-run flat inserts were in the tires, and the onboard air system could keep the tires inflated if there was a minor puncture, but a serious failure would be a show stopper.

The deeper they traveled into the city, closer to their turnoff, the more they found that the city was completely in ruins. It was amazing that Nellis was as intact as it had been. Aymond observed the destruction, the ruins, the swarming Zeds, and the bodies that they drove through, and found himself hoping that they would actually find real people at Area 51.

Groom Lake, NV

Two dozen people now worked in six teams, organizing the massive stores. The numbers of variety of weapons was staggering to Jessie, most of which none of them had any idea how to use, except for the rifles. The M2 machine guns seemed simple enough to use. Even if Major Wright had survived, she doubted he knew how to use most of this gear. What they needed were some survivors who were combat vets, infantry, anybody with the experience to teach them how to use most of this gear. The M-16s were easy enough; the three of them had plenty of experience with AR-15s or M4s. Somehow the group of survivors that had amassed underground in Groom Lake were regular everyday people, the kind of people one would hope would survive the end of the world, but still people with no training or tactics, not that Jessie held her level of training in any sort of high esteem. All she had was a bit more than most of them, which was all they had for now, so that was what they would use.

The remaining airmen worked primarily in the radio hut, electronics and communications being their trained jobs in the Air Force. Since Wright's death, they had mostly stopped wearing their full uniforms. With civilian clothing not being readily available, and no shopping malls to be had, they switched to wearing untucked T-shirts with their utility trousers, practically a hippie rebellion in their world, which Jessie was both happy and sad to see. Happy for her belief that this, of all times, was when people should be comfortable and have some level of happiness where they could find it; but she was sad to see the loss of the only remaining functional piece of the mighty United States military.

Glancing at the clock on the wall, Jessie realized that they had been at it for more than six hours. They had missed lunch, and if they didn't act soon, they would miss dinner as well.

"Hey, Sarah?"

Sarah finished taking notes from the group reporting to her before walking to Jessie.

"Yeah?"

"We've been working for quite some time. I don't want to stop. Think we should see if the mess hall could send down some sort of boxed dinner or something?"

"Sure... Erin!"

"What, Mom?" Erin yelled from somewhere in the darkness.

"I'll be back in a few. Take my place!"

Sarah walked toward the door and handed her clipboard to Jessie, who sat down, absentmindedly rubbing her growing baby belly. She was tired and hungry, her feet swollen and aching, her back ached. and she wished she could go out for a pedicure.

"You going to make it?"

Jessie handed Sarah's clipboard to Erin. "Well I don't really have a choice in the matter, do I?"

Enterprise, UT

Sunset was over, twilight and the starry sky battling for domination overhead. Chivo and Bexar were trying to settle into their overnight accommodations, not far from the still smoldering gas station. The afternoon had been spent locating and clearing a good spot to sleep, after first looking for a usable vehicle. Giving up on finding a vehicle before the end of the day, shelter became the primary goal. Found and cleared, they began moving the surviving gear from the desert field to the metal building they had chosen for the night. Working together, they moved slower than they had the first two times that they moved the gear because the urgency and danger were gone from the situation, outside of the handful of gathering reanimated dead, attracted to the area by the blast and fire, coming from who knows where.

Chivo held his arm out, stopping Bexar. "You see that, mano?"

To the south, bright lights grew out of the desert, slowly coming closer, appearing brighter as they came.

"What the fuck is that?"

"That's a truck."

"No shit, Chivo, but what sort of Mad Max bullshit is it?"

"No, mano, that's a fucking MRAP."

"Like a Cougar?"

"Yeah, well, that's one kind of MRAP."

"The sheriff north of us got one of those surplus for the tactical team; fucking huge."

"And heavy, armored, and armed."

"How do we play this?"

"That's our new ride, mano... I've got a plan."

Groom Lake, NV

Jessie sat at the desk and ate her dinner. The mess hall had sent down enough vegetable soup and "orange drink" for all who toiled deep in the dark corners of the storage area. The soup was good, and the beverage again tasted more like the color than an actual orange. It dawned on Jessie that she would probably never eat an actual orange again unless she happened across one somewhere out in the wilds. Her baby wouldn't have an orange, or limes, or lemonade.

My God, what about scurvy?

Taking a deep breath, Jessie felt distant enough from the situation momentarily to recognize the edge of a soon-to-be-mother freak-out. She was happy that she wasn't far enough along to start nesting yet; she couldn't see if the storage area had baseboards, but if it did she was sure they were filthy. She remembered their little house in Brazos County, their first house; after painting Keeley's room bright blue early on in the pregnancy and then finding out that they were having a girl, Bexar repainted the room for Jessie more than anyone. The baby wouldn't know the difference, but Jessie *had* to have the right paint and crib and covers and decorations... a couple's first baby was a big deal. She laughed to herself. This time her entire pregnancy was a different story.

She was on the fifth level, or five floors underground, but Jessie didn't really know how deep they really were or how stout the underground facility would be against an attack. Tipping up the plastic bowl, finishing the rest of the broth, she watched Sarah run the show. Erin went back and forth between groups, taking notes and also making a pile of gear for the three of them. Watching all the activity, activity she and Sarah were responsible for, Jessie wondered if they were making the right choice. If the SSC went offline, if there was an invasion, would it be better to be holed up in an underground fort on the frontier, or was there a better option?

Originally, their bug-out plan with Malachi and Jack was supposed to work. They had made all the right choices, stored all the right stuff, and built the right vehicles, and everything still went to hell. The plan failed because it was a single plan; it didn't have any contingencies. This plan didn't have a contingency, and she needed one for herself, Sarah, and Erin, and they needed one fast.

"Hey, Erin, could you come here for a moment?"

For all the activity in the vast storage area, the noise level was manageable; Erin heard Jessie from a few hundred feet away and began walking toward her.

"What's up?"

"Tell your mom that you're coming with me for something, and we're going topside. There's something I need to do with the FJ."

"OK, like what?"

"Plan B."

"Isn't that the morning-after pill? A little late for that now."

Jessie glared at Erin, who laughed and jogged away toward Sarah. A few minutes later, they stood in the hangar next to the FJ, wearing what had become their small-group-standard aboveground expedition kit, which contained significantly more gear and ammo than what consisted of their EDC, everyday carry, while underground.

Inside the MRAP, UT

Amanda slowed as she approached a T-intersection. Checking her atlas, she saw she needed to turn left. A lone reanimate stood in the roadway, right in the middle of the intersection. Veering to drive around it, she was startled when it started waving its hands over its head. Amanda slammed on the brakes, the heavy air brakes hissing in protest.

It was a man, not a zombie, and he was yelling at her, waving his arms, trying to get her to come to him. She couldn't hear him in the truck, but it looked like he was yelling "Help." Amanda drove forward, stopping very close to him, his chest barely visible over the high hood. He was yelling help and waving frantically. He wore a pistol, a dirty T-shirt, and pants, but appeared to have nothing else. Amanda left the truck running and cracked open her door to stand on the step to hear what the man was saying.

As she opened the door, her feet were ripped out from under her. Hitting her head on the step as she fell, the world around her went dark.

PLA Reconnaissance Position, NV

After driving north from S4, the APC turned and followed the dirt road, meandering up the western side of the mountain. Reaching their planned desti-nation and confident of the lack of persons alive or dead in their surroundings, the four-man team left the APC just below the military ridgeline. They now lay under netting to break up their outlines and set a rotation behind the powerful tripod-mounted spotting scope. As they slowly scanned each of the buildings, the only movement the team could find was from the dead trapped in what the intelligence reports listed as onsite apartment housing for some of the facility staff. The location they were most interested in was the northeast white hangar next to the edge of the dry lake bed and the numerous other escape routes and hatches around the complex.

Encrypted satellite communications kept the recon team in contact with the small assault force. The elite of the expeditionary special reconnaissance teams of the PLA, the Siberian Tiger unit specialized in survival skills in harsh environments. They were the initial recon and assault team to clear out pockets of resistance and special facilities to be followed by the sweeper and cleanup teams comprised of mixed units from the PLA and the Korean People's Army. This mission was easy: simple sabotage, infect, load up, and fly out. The sweeper teams would come through in the next few months, neutralizing the Yama-infected imperialists.

The assault set to launch just before dawn, the team continued to update their commander with status reports every hour. So far, each of the six reports was a simple one-word transmission indicating that the situation was unchanged and that no enemy imperialist movement was detected on the surface.

Groom Lake, NV

Jason joined Jessie and Erin, at Erin's insistence. Her quick idea turned into another four hours of Erin gathering essential items to take with them. After her plan was outlined, Erin didn't want Jessie to do any heavy lifting, which it was that, heavy, so the three of them drove out of the hangar, looping around to the west and heading south toward the shooting range. Dawn was only a few hours away. Although the canvas wall tent, the only remaining original group-standard tent, was dyed a flat-green color from the natural bright-white color of the canvas, Jessie wanted to find a spot where the tent would be close enough to get to, far enough away to possibly be missed, and amongst enough clutter to possibly be overlooked. Up the hillside from the shooting range stood a tank farm, and those five tall tanks would give Jessie all that she wanted in a discreet intermediary bug-out location.

None of them had any idea what was in the tanks – it could have been flying-saucer fuel for all they knew – but bouncing up the dirt road in the darkness, they couldn't even see the tanks yet, even with the bright off-road lighting that Jack had installed on the FJ; the darkness was a thick veil around them. Jessie drove, with Erin sitting in the passenger seat and Jason behind her. Erin, hyper-vigilant, found her mind wasn't on Jason but on the surrounding darkness. Her "big rifle" rode on the roof rack, which was where she planned to go if the shit hit the fan. With the short-barreled M4 in her hands, she absentmindedly kept tapping her right thumb against the safety, checking that it was flipped up and on safe. Jason's weapon of choice remained his shotgun.

After what felt like an eternity in the darkness, the tanks grew out of the desert hillside ahead of them. Driving to the westernmost side of the tanks, Jessie stopped the FJ and turned off the lights and the engine, and each of them sat quietly in the interior, waiting for any reaction, any shambling dead to approach. Still not having the opportunity to practice with any of the night optic devices that they had located in the storage area, each of them clicked on their headlamps; the dim LED lights left the interior of the bug-out vehicle awash in red light.

Mostly confident that they were alone in the expanse of Groom Lake, they climbed out of the truck.

"Jason, the tent is in the case on the left, and the poles are in that PVC tube," Jessie said, pointing to the roof rack. She began to reach for the PVC tube to start pulling out poles when Erin stopped her, reminding her that she was to hold security; she and Jason would do the work.

Grunting, Jason and Erin flopped the tent out of the case and down from the roof rack, and it fell with a dull thud onto the desert floor. Jessie and Bexar could set the tent up in about an hour, as they found out in Maypearl. They could pull the tent down in ten minutes when pressed, although not as neatly as they would typically. The EMT metal tubing clanked, sounding as loud as gunshots to the three of them in the darkness; they were trying to be quiet, but the tubing simply wouldn't cooperate.

When the metal angle pieces were arranged and the strong tent frame assembled, Jason and Erin pulled the heavy canvas tent over the frame.

"Just like the pioneers, huh, Erin?"

"No wonder they had fucking wagons and donkeys and shit. If this is their state-of-the-art lightweight camping tent, what did they cook with, lead?"

"Cast iron, and, yes, it's heavy too. There's a skillet and a Dutch oven in the case in the back of the truck."

"Isn't a Dutch oven when a guy…"

Jason snorted. "Yes, but it's also a cast-iron pot with a lid."

Erin and Jason kept bantering back and forth, at a whisper. Jessie walked around the bug-out site for another security sweep, but also to get a feel for the layout if she had to come up here in complete darkness.

In the MRAP

Chivo drove. To say he was familiar with the different models of vehicles all classified as the mine-resistant ambush-protected vehicle would be an understatement. Ironically enough, they ambushed and took this one, but the lone driver, a woman they knew and were surprised to find in BFE Utah and alone, lay flat on her back in the rear of the truck. Bexar tended to her. Although she had been knocked out from hitting her head against the thick metal side step, she came around quickly and with a severe headache.

After listening to both of them apologize profusely, Amanda had the pleasure of listening to a lecture on patrol tactics and safely using an MRAP from Chivo. Sipping water, he offered to give her a shot from the medical bag in the truck that he promised would take away all the pain, but Amanda opted to take a handful of 800mg Motrin instead. Chivo smiled slightly. If she was going to eat the 800mg "grunt candy," then maybe she could become a warrior president yet.

Two hours after the ambush, President Lampton was awake, the MRAP was loaded with the remaining provisions that Chivo and Bexar had saved from the doomed VW, and they were once again pointed north, driving through the night at Amanda's insistence. Beginning with the short version of events, Chivo wanted to know all the details about Clint and the two facilities.

"What about Cliff? Clint sent him a message, some sort of random numbers radio broadcast; he was supposed to go to Granite Mountain. We haven't heard from him since you guys radioed your message from Cortez to Bill and them at Groom Lake."

"Fuck Cliff."

"Now, Bexar, sure he fucked us, but he also saved us, so I'd say that leaves him close to neutral," Chivo continued, telling Amanda the whole backstory about Cliff sabotaging their exit and the group in Saint George, which surprised Amanda because she'd driven through the same towns they had, including Saint George, and hadn't seen that survivor group. They also told her about Cliff's partial redemption by saving both of them so Angel and his group could get to them.

"So why didn't the other group..."

"Frank's."

"So why didn't Frank's group just ask for help? If they had helped you, why wouldn't they help them?"

Bexar quietly listened to the conversation, wishing Chivo would speed up; they were closer to Jessie than they had been since Big Bend, and his heart ached to see the love of his life again. Especially now that even President Lampton felt it necessary to overland to Groom Lake, jeopardizing her life for the idea that an attack might be imminent.

"The two groups knew each other, or knew of each other at least, before the attack. Frank's group didn't think Guillermo and Angel would help them, so the story went."

"How did you figure all of that out?"

"We captured one of their members during an attack, and I asked him."

"And he told you?"

"Yes, ma'am."

Bexar chortled. "He fucking waterboarded him... uh, Madam President."

Amanda raised her eyebrows. "Did it work?"

"The enhanced interrogation techniques worked well, ma'am."

Faintly smiling, Amanda thought to tell him to simply call her Amanda, but her pounding head made her want to let him sweat it out a bit longer.

Chivo slowed and stopped after turning south onto Highway 93.

"Dude, why are we stopping?"

"Are you a medic?"

"No, I always called for medics."

"Then chill out for a bit. I know you're excited, but it is time to medically evaluate the President again. You can put your happy ass in that seat for a bit if you can't wait five minutes."

Chivo laughed and slapped Bexar on the ass as he climbed over him to get to the driver's seat. The dash looked about like any semi-truck that Bexar had ever seen. He pushed the yellow diamond valve in, and the parking brakes released; he looked for the gear selector.

"It's a push button, mano," Chivo called from the back.

After pushing the button for drive, they were off at what felt like a breakneck pace from his seat behind the driver's wheel, but topping out at fifty-five miles per hour according to the needle. The powerful lighting turned the dark highway in the middle of nowhere into near daylight. As heavy as the truck was, it felt more nimble behind the wheel than Bexar would have guessed, as he gently swerved around an abandoned semi-truck in the roadway. Smiling, he felt invincible in the big armored truck sitting so high above the passing pavement.

Mercury Highway, NV

"Master Guns, I'm telling you I saw fucking headlights! They turned away from us and then disappeared."

Aymond turned to Kirk, who sat behind the driver's wheel. The entire team having heard Jones' radio transmission, the convoy sat motionless, all their lights extinguished as a precaution. The lighting selector even disabled the brake lights. "We're in the Nevada Test Site. Think it might be a patrol from Area 51?"

"No dice, Chief, why would they flip their lights off if they're a friendly patrol, especially after inviting everyone to come visit on the shortwave?"

"The PLA didn't have night optics."

"The PLA and KPA that we fought *so far* didn't, but who's to say that these guys don't have them?"

Aymond knew Kirk was right and knew the answer before he had even asked it. The trip out of Las Vegas had taken much longer than anticipated, darkness falling on them hours ago; the convoy had remained at a slow speed with the radar truck leading, the dome on and blasting away at nothing but empty desert for a good while. They hadn't seen a single Zed since turning off of Highway 95, so the need for the dome being up and in use seemed moot, especially with possible tangos in the area.

"Gonzo, drop the dome and get back into this truck. Jones, fall into the second position. NODs on, keep the lights off. If they're PLA tangos and headed north, we need to catch them before they get to the base."

Buildings appeared out of the desert, awash in the green-and-black glow of the night optic devices as the team quickly drove by. Jones was the only one who hadn't had a lot of experience with the NODs until the MSOT found him and Simmons holed up in an aircraft hangar, a mechanic not having a high need for using them even if every Marine was a rifleman.

The lead M-ATV's remote turret, controlled again by Gonzo, swept back and forth as they passed buildings and facilities in the secret weapons test area, but the turret always faced toward the front. In the rear M-ATV's remote turret, Snow kept rear watch at the controls. The Marines were in combat patrol mode, although Gonzo secretly wished for a Rip-It to make it feel like old times.

CHAPTER 10

PLA Scout Position, Groom Lake, NV
April 8, Year 1

The reconnaissance team had noted the vehicle in their report a few hours prior, but after the lights were turned off, they didn't see any movement from it again. The four PLA special forces soldiers quietly debated the purpose of being next to the fuel tanks. They would not be safe for any sort of fighting position, although they could be used for a security watch point. The grainy green-and-black world magnified large through the spotting scope didn't have the resolution they needed to see what anyone was doing or how many people were there. Although there had only been a single vehicle, it appeared to be military in nature.

Guard Shack, Groom Lake, NV

"Look, mano, the sign says to stop and dial the number, so we'll stop and dial the number."

"Why should we waste our time with that?"

Amanda answered before Chivo could, "They could have a security patrol or guards."

"She's right."

Bexar conceded defeat on the issue. They all climbed out of the truck and stretched their legs while Chivo dialed the number and made contact with the facility.

"OK, the instructions are to follow this road down the mountain and around the dry lake bed. After reaching the south end of the lake bed, we turn left and drive onto the flightline and into the northeasternmost hangar."

"Couldn't we just drive across the lake bed?"

"I don't know, buddy, but when a secure facility tells you to enter a certain way, you enter a certain way. You don't know what they've got in place."

Bexar took his spot behind the steering wheel again with Chivo riding in the front passenger's seat coaching him on how to navigate the poorly maintained gravel road up the mountain; they were surprised to find that near the guard shack and beyond the fence line the road was nicely paved.

"Who in the world did they get to build a secret paved road into what is arguably the most famous top-secret base in the world?"

"My people, mano."

"Jesus, that's kind of racist."

"Yeah, probably him too."

Both of them laughed while Amanda staring at them with a bit of bemused curiosity. When they had met at the SSC, Bexar was banged up and fairly reserved. This was a different man than before, they both were, and they had obviously been through some tough times together.

Mercury Highway

Aymond watched the craters pass as the convoy ripped through the desert as quickly as they dared. Gonzo and the forward-looking infrared display of the remote turret was their first line of defense through the darkness. Aymond threw out what they'd learned of the invading force from San Diego and their contact with them in Yuma. If they really were chasing a blacked-out enemy patrol and they did have NODs, then he had to assume they would have FLIR capabilities as well. If that was the case, then all they had on their side was surprise. Aymond hoped that would be enough, but hoped even more that Jones had been mistaken.

Wall Tent

After the long ordeal of erecting the tent, from concept to finish, Jessie was exhausted, and she hadn't even done any of the hard work. After the strong winds and sandstorms they had experienced before on the surface, Jessie made sure Jason and Erin hammered a stake into every available loop and that each of the guy-lines were staked and taut. The last thing she needed now was for her tent to take flight and blow away into the desert.

Erin and Jason were tired but sort of wired; two cases of MREs, a five-gallon plastic jug of water, and two cases of 5.56 joined the single case of 50-caliber rounds for Erin's rifle inside the tent. All the prepper provisions, the cast-iron cookware, and the rest remained in the FJ. This was all a hunch on Jessie's part—one she hoped would prove to be untrue. The eastern sky was beginning to lighten with the approaching dawn; Erin convinced Jessie and Jason to wait for dawn. Jessie sat against one of the FJ's wheels, slowly eating one of the MREs. She found it odd, but the MRE was sort of tasty compared to the food they had been eating from the mess hall. She gave the kitchen crew credit for stretching rations and cooking every day, but the improvising apparently gave way to some blandness. Or Jessie was tired and hungry, which was a winning combination to make a bad meal into the best meal of the day.

Erin sat next to Jason a little further down the hill, in front of the tanks, both of them eating an MRE each for breakfast.

He's a little old for her. She's only fifteen, and he's four years older than she is... so is Bexar, Bexar's four years older than me.

Tamping down her suppressed high school teacher instincts, Jessie realized that the law prohibiting a relationship between the two of them no longer existed and, in a few years, as they grew older, the difference in age wouldn't have even batted an eye before the end of the world.

Jessie felt a slight mixture of hope and sadness for Erin; the pickings were sort of slim after the dead started shambling around, but humanity always finds a way. Throughout the known history of civilization, no matter what plague or event befell the weary, they always found a way. Noah had his ark.

Is this our own ark? It's the damned Fort Apache amongst the native undead is what it is, but my John Wayne isn't here yet.

Light flashed to the north, the shockwave of an explosion blasting across Jessie and her motley duo of armed teenagers. Jessie stood, looking at the rising fireball. Erin sprinted toward her, climbed on top of the FJ and ripped open her rifle case. Jason stood still, awestruck by the sight.

In the MRAP

"What the fuck was that?"

"You and things blowing the fuck up, mano. Fuck it, go across the lake bed, go now, go!"

Bexar slowed and turned the wheel left, bouncing over uncut desert toward the edge of the lake bed. Reaching the hard surface, he pushed the accelerator all the way to the floor, the turbocharged diesel roaring in response.

Chivo flipped on the communications radio mounted in the MRAP. The electronic display illuminated dimly and he began punching in commands to the keypad on the front. Bexar only glanced at him, a crashed C-130 passing by their window bringing his attention forward. Racing toward the rising fireball, the quickened adrenaline heartbeat of racing to a robbery in progress or a man with a gun call felt like home, those associations being pushed out over the last few months. Bexar's eyes narrowed; taking a deep breath, he was a man racing to a battle.

MSOT Convoy

"Holy shit, Chief!"

Aymond nodded. Apparently Jones was correct, and they were running behind. The nimble M-ATVs were already racing as fast as they could; the closer they got to the fireball, the closer to the battle, the more careful they would have to be, but until then the trucks kept along at their governed speed, bouncing along the paved road now winding around the mountains. The internal debate about the radar truck in the convoy was one that would have to be decided quickly. If they cached it, they might lose it. There weren't exactly a lot of hiding spots out in the open. If they charged into battle with it, the valuable truck might be a combat loss. It wasn't armored, and Jones could be KIA as well.

Aymond pressed the transmit button on the handheld team radio he wore. "Jones, in the next two klicks, find a spot to stash the radar truck, get on board with the trail unit, advise when back en route."

"Roger, Master Guns."

"Roger, Chief."

Aymond turned to Kirk. "What do you think, high ground or flank?"

"Flank, Chief."

"North or south?"

"That fireball is north of the road, so I say south."

Aymond nodded. "Do it."

In the MRAP

"Who the fuck was that on the radio?"

Chivo smiled. "I don't know, but they weren't fucking speaking Mandarin!"

Amanda unlatched the roof hatch and began to climb up to the turret.

Chivo yelled over the noise, "Lampton, get your ass back in here!"

Amanda looked down at Chivo, who now spoke with a calm, firm voice, "Madam President, why don't you climb down and take my spot. We have friendlies on the net. Bexar drives, you talk on the radio, and I man the turret."

It wasn't a request. Amanda climbed down, Chivo already climbing into the back of the truck yelled forward before climbing into the turret, "Bexar, tell her what you want to say. We're playing this one fast and loose. I don't know ... fuck, treat it like a bad cop situation or some shit. Good luck, mano!"

If they had been wearing proper combat gear, they could have plugged in their headsets, but they lacked proper in-vehicle communication.

Bexar glanced at Amanda. "Say what I say: 'Who are you, and what's your twenty... location?'"

Amanda held the handset and keyed the radio: "Friendly forces, what is your position?"

After some back and forth on the radio, Amanda turned to Bexar. "They're Marines!"

"Yeah, I can hear the radio, too, but now what?"

Amanda returned to the radio. After another series of transmissions, she lowered the handset. The Marines knew they were on the lakebed, and they wanted the MRAP to charge straight for the fire.

MSOT Convoy

Aymond frowned. *Fucking civilians charging into battle, going to have to save their asses...*

The entire team wore the MBITR radios and had heard the radio transmissions; there was a mix of emotions amongst the team in response to the radio traffic. Kirk keyed on the net. "Chief, we're about a klick behind you, over."

"Get out on the lakebed, intercept, and assist the civilians to the north; we're taking the south, over."

"Roger."

Still frowning, Aymond press-checked his rifle, slapped the assist a couple of times to make sure the bolt was all the way forward, and spoke over his shoulder, "Talk to me, Gonzo."

"Shit, Chief, can't see shit with the FLIR, except the fire. Can't see anymore because of the buildings."

Kirk slammed on the brakes, the tires chirping on the tarmac as he turned sharply to race in between what looked like barracks, across the flightline, and into the desert. Gonzo swung the turret as they bounced past the buildings. He yelled, "Got two APCs, about a dozen tangos piling in. Holy shit! Someone just dropped one of the tangos."

"The civilians?"

"No, I see them, looks like an MRAP; they're about a klick and a half out and coming fast."

Aymond keyed the radio. "Two mounted patrols, a dozen combatants visible and bugging out."

The Tanks

Jessie stood on the roof rack. The last time she had done that was the first day she'd met Sarah and Erin. This time she wasn't on the wrong end of Erin's steady aim. Erin had climbed on top of the easternmost tank and lay prone with her rifle. Jason climbed the ladder with the green can of 50-caliber ammunition for her rifle; apparently she thought she would need it.

"Jessie, some truck just hauled ass out into the runways!"

"Shit."

Jessie nearly leapt off the roof. Climbing into the driver's seat, she started the FJ, left the lights off, and drove toward the rising sun, straight across the desert, to the taxiway. Turning north, she floored the old FJ and drove toward the hangar until she saw movement to her right.

That's the truck.

It was large and tracer fire streamed out of the weapon mounted on the roof. Big trucks sat near the hangar and looked like something out of a Chuck Norris movie from the eighties. Trusting her instincts, she turned hard right and raced toward the truck driving across the runways.

The Hangar

The PLA special forces saboteur team's mission was done. The teams came out of the blast door and into what remained of the hangar after their initial attack. Suddenly taking heavy fire, they piled into the armored personnel carriers, turned and drove north as fast as the heavy trucks would accelerate.

In the MRAP

Amanda excitedly repeated what was broadcast on the radio.

Bexar nodded, concentrating on his task. He saw odd-looking armored trucks driving away from the fire. He was going to tell Amanda to ask Chivo what to do, but the big M2 in the turret opened fire, rattling with controlled bursts. Spent shells dinged against the armored roof, some of them falling into the interior of the MRAP.

It took a moment to realize that the sound he heard was enemy fire hitting the windshield. Lights started coming on in the dashboard; glancing down for a moment, Bexar saw one that looked like a tire pressure warning. The others he didn't have time to think about as the truck pulled hard right.

Amanda held the radio handset and repeated the Marine's transmission, yelling, "Friendly coming from our right. He said slow down, the run flats will keep us rolling, and turn off all of your lights."

Shadows of men piling out of the armored trucks still close to the burning hangar danced across the desert floor as muzzle flashes burst from the running men like strobe lights.

Bexar let off the gas and found the button for the lights, turning all of them off. Looking up, he saw a familiar orange streak coming toward the windshield. Out of instinct, he ripped the wheel to the left as something rocketed past him, barely noticing an explosion behind them in the remaining mirror.

The controlled bursts Chivo was using before gave way to long streams of fire. Chivo yelled at Amanda to bring him ammo. To their right, another dark vehicle appeared, which looked vaguely American, but Bexar wasn't exactly an expert on military vehicles. The tracer fire was beginning to be hard to see, dawn giving new perspective to the world around them, but the truck that pulled alongside his position streamed high-cyclic death from its turret-mounted weapon.

Chivo stopped firing; Bexar stopped the truck and could hear a voice calling to cease fire over the radio. An SUV shot across the runways toward the ruined armored trucks, the bodies, and the shell of a hangar. The doors were gone, the roof was mostly gone, and most of the hangar was simply gone, burnt, ravaged by the fast and heavy battle; a thick concrete hump in the back was all that was left. Bodies lay in ruin around the armored trucks that they had been attacking, which smoked, each of them badly damaged.

Is that... is that Jack's FJ? I haven't seen that since The Basin. The bikers had it; we left it there when Chivo's crew pulled my unconscious ass out of that firefight.

"Jesus, my God! Jessie, what the fuck are you doing?"

Bexar slammed his foot to the floor. The truck, both front tires flat, was slow to respond, but began to pick up speed. The hangar appeared to be about a half mile away, and Jack's old Toyota FJ was going to beat him there.

The FJ

Jessie slammed on the brakes, sliding to a stop on the tarmac outside the ruined hangar. The two armored trucks of the attacking force sat destroyed; men and pieces of men lay on the tarmac near them. As the SUV stopped, Jessie climbed out of the truck, held her rifle and walked briskly into the remaining shell of the hangar. The blast door was damaged and open.

"Shit. Sarah!"

Behind her one of the dead PLA stood, shakily stepping toward the interior of the destroyed hangar.

The Tanks

Erin cursed under her breath and squeezed the trigger. Jason couldn't hear anything but the loud ringing in his ears; he was worried that he might not be able to hear again after the massive muzzle blasts of the Barrett rifle being shot in rapid succession. Erin rose up, slapped an empty magazine on the tank, and picked up the fresh one. Jason pulled the rounds out of the green ammo can, each over five inches long. Ten rounds were loaded in the magazine and set next to Erin.

After swapping out magazines again, Erin stopped firing and made very small adjustments back and forth, scanning the scene for more threats. She watched as the truck came to a stop next to the FJ, and four men in uniform, battle gear, and thick beards stepped out of the truck. Concerned, Erin watched as they quickly formed up and cleared the ruined trucks they had all been firing at. Each of the Chinese attackers lay dead for good, their heads ruined by Erin's sharp skills.

Her ears rang loudly too; looking at Jason, she could see him talking but couldn't hear him. She pointed to her ear and shook her head. Jason pointed to himself, to his ears, and also shook his head. She switched out the magazine on her 50-caliber rifle with the fully loaded mag that Jason handed her, then gave him a kiss before stepping toward the ladder. As she climbed down, a rifle as long as she was tall smoking in her arms, he loaded the second magazine and quickly followed. They quickly walked toward the hangar. She was worried about her mom but trusted Jessie.

MSOT

"Clear!"

"Clear!"

"Clear!"

Aymond keyed the radio. "Kirk, get Jones back to the radar truck, and get that damn thing over here. Then go back to where Jones saw the headlights and try to find where these PLA assholes came from."

He saw the damaged MRAP accelerating across the lake bed toward the hangar. The truck ground to a stop against the parking brake and the engine died. The windshield was pockmarked from rifle fire, and both the front tires were flat. The MRAP had seen better days. The driver leapt out of the truck while it was still moving. Ragged and thin, the man yelled, "Jessie, stop!" while sprinting toward the woman, ignoring Aymond and the MSOT, his rifle swinging by the sling as he ran.

The woman turned and fell to her knees. The man slid to a stop, helped her up, and held her tightly. In return, she wrapped her arms around him. In the midst of the damage and ruin, the two held each other, crying.

The Hangar

"Bexar, my sweet Bexar, it's really you. I never gave up; I knew you would come to me!"

"I'm sorry, baby. I'm so sorry. I'm sorry about Keeley, I'm sorry about Big Bend, I'm sorry about Maypearl, I'm sorry about it all."

Tears streaked down Jessie's cheeks. Bexar placed his hand on her stomach, wiping tears off his face as he did so. Chivo walked past the Marines, who stood still both watching the scene unfold and scanning for any new threats. Amanda followed Chivo in joining Bexar and Jessie.

Chivo looked at Jessie gravely. "Ma'am, I want to apologize. I was in Big Bend as a part of the rescue force and saw you, but I thought you were dead. Our orders were to get the survivors, and Bexar was the only one we saw... but I made a promise, and I brought him back to you."

Jessie wrapped her arms around the man. She didn't know him and couldn't even say thank you she was crying so hard, so she just hugged him.

Aymond walked to the group and stood silently for a moment. Once Jessie finally released Chivo to stand next to her husband and hold his hand, Chivo glanced at the uniform, read the name tape, and smiled.

"Master Gunnery Sergeant Aymond, may I present to you the President of the United States, Amanda Lampton." Chivo gestured toward Amanda, who stood there, a large lump on the side of her head, her hair blood-matted, and bruising on her face.

"Bullshit."

A lively discussion began in the ruined shell of the hangar, none of which concerned Bexar; nothing else could, he had his wife back.

Jessie looked over Bexar's shoulder.

"What's wrong, baby?" Bexar turned to see a teenage girl walk toward the hangar, a rifle like Chivo's held across her shoulders, a short- barrel M4 hanging from a sling, A teenage boy with a shotgun was with her. Chivo looked at Erin and chuckled; she responded by flipping him off. Erin walked past Jessie and to the ruined blast door, peering through the entry way, observing dark scorch marks on the interior walls.

"What's her deal, Jess?"

Erin nearly held her breath, trying to listen. Nothing. She could hear nothing at all.

"Bexar, there are over a thousand people down there; the attack might have finally done this place in. The computers were under attack for weeks."

"Jessie, let's just get to Level Five. We get Mom, and we get the fuck out."

"Get out to where, back to Texas? If they know about this place, they have to know about the SSC. They'll be there next if they aren't there right now!"

Jessie turned, walking back toward the FJ to retrieve her chest carrier and spare magazines. Bexar followed along. "You're not going down there."

"Like hell I'm not!"

"I just got you back; I'm not going to lose you again. I can't lose you again!"

"Look, chica, you should stay. You have your Bexar. You have your baby, and I'm going for Mom and coming right back, in and out."

"There is no in and out. The last outbreak was a shitstorm all from one person. There's no telling what's happened now ... you have no idea if she's still on Level Five, it's been hours since we left her there. She could be anywhere in that damn place!"

Jones drove up in the Chinese-made radar truck, which resulted in a lot of rifles being raised and Aymond standing in between the rifles and the truck. "Whoa, easy now, this one is ours."

Chivo spoke first. "What the fuck is that, Aymond, radar?"

"Something like that. We commandeered it from the PLA in San Diego. It kills the Zeds."

Amanda looked surprised. "Sergeant..."

Chivo interrupted her. "Master Gunnery Sergeant. Marines get really testy when you shorten it like that, ma'am."

Amanda gave Chivo a hard sideways look. "Thank you, Chivo. Mr. Aymond, what PLA in San Diego?"

"The short brief is that there is roughly a battalion-sized force of PLA, a container-ship flotilla, and they used airborne to secure the San Diego airport. We destroyed the container ships, blocked the harbor, demo'ed the runways at Halsey Field, and stole the radar truck. Although we had a successful guerilla campaign, we couldn't sustain it, so we began working our way toward the interior looking for other military units."

An explosion rumbled across the mountains. Aymond keyed his radio and spoke quickly. After the reply, Aymond excused himself to climb into the M-ATV as a small yellow aircraft taxied to a stop by the trucks.

Chivo shook his head. "Area 51, a fucking el circo. Aliens are next."

No one else spoke. The aircraft's engine shut off, the propeller jerked to a stop, and a man climbed out of the small plane, joined by a black-and-white dog, tail wagging, "Holy shit, did you guys hear that aircraft crash?"

Aymond looked at the new visitor, the morning being one of constant surprises for the Marine. "We did. Where was it, and what happened?"

"South. There's another dry lake bed down near Mercury; looked big, whatever it was. It wasn't one of yours? I was circling overhead for the last hour waiting for dawn. Dammit! You guys shot the shit out of those guys! That was one hell of a firefight."

Aymond wasn't listening. After the news about the other aircraft, he keyed his radio and spoke rapidly and climbed into the M-ATV with the other MSOT team members. Ordering Jones to stay put with the radar switched on, they drove off rapidly.

Muffled sounds of gunfire could be heard from beyond the ruined blast door.

"It's been a fun morning, but it's time to go." Erin set down her large Barrett, grasping her short-barrel M4. Jason followed her to the door.

Jessie clicked on the headlamp she still wore from the previous night. "Honey, Bexar, are you coming with me or not?"

"Those are my only two choices?"

"That's it."

"If that's it, then there is only one choice. I'm going with. Chivo?"

"Yeah, mano, why the fuck not."

Amanda began walking toward the blast door. Chivo held up his hand. "Corporal..."

"Jones, sir."

"Corporal Jones, welcome to the party. If you wouldn't mind escorting President Lampton to my broke-ass MRAP for her safety until the Master Guns returns? If we don't come back, she will direct you and your team back to another secret facility in Texas with her. I suggest you listen to her. Right, ma'am?"

"Thank you, Chivo," Amanda replied, without masking the sarcasm and annoyance in her voice.

"Now, Mrs. Bexar, if you don't mind, I'd like to go first."

"Chivo, the goat, is it? First of all, I don't know you, and, secondly, you don't know where the hell you're going! I do."

"Baby, he should go first. Chivo and I... we've been through a lot together, trust me."

"Mrs. Bexar, you can whisper directions in my ear as we go." Chivo smiled at Bexar as the reunited and newly expanded team stacked on the door to enter.

Chivo looked over his shoulder. "Slow is smooth, smooth is fast, got it?"

Jessie, Bexar, Erin, and Jason responded in order. Chivo stepped inside, and the rest followed in a tight formation.

54

The reconnaissance patrol watched in horror as the massacre unfolded in front of them, unable to help and not close enough to respond in time to render any aid. All they could do was radio support, directing their teammates' weapons fire to the approaching enemy. This mission was a failure, their team in shambles. A brief report was returned to their command chain via their SATCOM. Returning to their APC, they drove down the mountainside to the awaiting commander. They could hear the jet engines of the transport aircraft already starting in the distance. They all knew what the response was going to be if the team's mission failed; they had to leave immediately. The four men watched in disbelief as their transport lifted off without them, and then smoke began trailing from one of the engines and then another. Just fifty feet off the ground, the tail began to drop, the right wing falling lower, before the aircraft cartwheeled across the lakebed in a growing ball of fire.

Rapidly, the four men formulated a plan and drove toward the south as fast as their APC could maintain.

CHAPTER 11

Near Ulm, Montana
April 8, Year 1

Cliff sat in the MRAP at a rural crossroad, the heater running, thick snow still covering some parts of the countryside. Away from the computers of the SSC, he had a shortwave radio on the console, and a notebook and pen in his hand; he wrote down the seemingly random letters and numbers, a female voice coming across the scratchy transmission.

Transcribing the cypher, Cliff wrote down the coordinates on a smaller piece of paper, retrieved a cigarette lighter from the breast pocket of his flight suit, and lit the first piece of paper on fire, holding it out of the open door until it burnt to his fingers and he let it drop.

Driving another ten minutes south, he turned the MRAP into an unmarked but obvious driveway, drove past a helipad, and stopped at the heavy gate. The missile-alert facility plaque still hung on the fence, the Officer In Charge and the Non-Commissioned Officer In Charge placard slots missing the names that changed with each watch-duty rotation. Glancing at the poles on the corners and the video cameras, he assumed that if the Launch Control Center was still online, and since the Launch Control Support Building was still standing and the fence was still intact, that the cameras were still operational as well.

A loop of wire hung from the red-and-white radio tower, which was odd. Assured by his handlers that the hardwire launch control workaround would actually work, all he had to do was actually get in the facility. For him to accomplish that, it all started with a single button push on the intercom.

WINCHESTER: TRIUMPH

PROLOGUE

Ken made the most out of the shallow defilade. He had to; it was all he had. Lying flat on his stomach, dirt and rocks fell from the sky above. Disorientated, the shockwave of the explosion made the ground ripple under his body, making it feel to Ken that he was both weightless and falling at the same time. Hundreds of yards away, he was still close, much too close to the fighting. The hard snap of rounds passing just inches above his head brought back memories of his youth and the thick jungle air of Southeast Asia. They were shooting at him with the same kind of rifles as they had in *his* war. Ringing deep in his ears prevented Ken from hearing much of anything else after the last mortar round hit so close. Slowly at first, sounds of battle grew from a distance place to fill his ears, before his mind caught up and the bone-sickening crunch of an armored truck taking a direct hit ripped through the tinnitus and snapped the reality of the battle back to Ken's immediate focus. The violent screams of mortar fire fell away from Ken's ears and toward the fortified farmhouse.

Taking a chance, Ken glanced up from what he was sure to be his shallow grave to see a lone man in the distance stand in the ruins of the farmhouse, destroyed by the barrage of falling steel and explosives.

The man wasn't in a uniform; he wasn't one of the damn invaders. Dirt kicked up around the man's feet, rifle rounds trying to find their true mark. Looking left, Ken saw another approaching armored personnel carrier (APC); there had been so many before. A roof hatch opened and a helmet barely poked through the hole. The helmet came up a little further, scanning the battle, pointing and shouting.

Must be an officer.

Thousands of Zeds shambled through the middle of the chaos, the movement and noise disorientating their dead and rotted minds. What remained of the numerous APCs lay in ruin, most of the Zeds were still moving, nauseous black smoke filled the scene, and dozens of Zeds were on fire as a result of the battle. The flames danced on their bodies until enough flesh had burned that the bodies collapsed, still twitching and writhing. Ken looked back at the officer in the hatch of the APC in time to see blood arc through the air from the hole that once was his head and neck, a distant thump of a heavy rifle following seconds later. The body fell into the open hatch, blood still spewing as the APC accelerated sharply. Dismounted soldiers were trying to make their way toward what was left of the driveway that went up the hillside.

"Oh fuck, holy shit..." Ken took some deep breaths, screwed his eyelids shut, and tried to slow his heartrate to focus his thoughts and make a plan. Too many years had passed since Vietnam, but deep in his mind lived the warrior he had been. Slumbering and long dormant, Ken's anger burned hot, scorching the substance of his being. It felt detached, like he could see the battlefield in an overhead view. Only a few seconds had passed, but they might as well have been days or weeks for how time felt. It was time to get to work, it was time to win, and nothing else mattered.

Ken leapt to his feet and ran toward the battle, screaming in rage.

CHAPTER 1

April 8, Year 1

Amanda, hands on her hips, stood in front of the ruined MRAP. Jones uneasily stood next to her, shifting his weight back and forth and nervously scanning the area around them for any new threats. Andrew and Oreo walked in between the hangars, exploring the above-ground facilities at a place Andrew never dreamed he would see and live to tell the tale.

"It would take me a week if I had all the parts, if I had my tools, if the fucking Zeds weren't crawling out of this hole in the ground...uh, excuse me, I mean, I apologize for the language, ma'am."

"Fucking Zeds, Jones, I agree."

Amanda glanced over her shoulder at the remains of the destroyed hangar, the charred hole in the ground where Chivo and Bexar had joined the ragtag-looking group to re-enter the Groom Lake facility after the attack. The light coming from the entrance wasn't noticeable any longer in the midday sun. Looking back at the MRAP, the sun and sand-blasted tail of a crashed C-130 rose over the dry lake bed. In the distance, a dark red cloud churned across the desert.

"Ruins, everything here is in ruins."

"The west coast is worse, ma'am. Zeds everywhere, a lot of stuff burned and destroyed. We would need thousands of trucks like that radar truck to zap all of them."

"Or we need one truck and an unfathomable amount of time. We're short on Chinese-built radar trucks, Jones, society is short on time, and we've been invaded. Yet here we stand waiting."

Amanda glanced at the small yellow aircraft, her mind turning.

Oreo ran to Amanda and Jones, stopping with a muffled bark, nudging the president in the thigh. Amanda looked at the dog, which looked back toward the underground facility's main entrance. Close to a football field away there was movement, someone stepping around the destroyed blast door. Jones glanced to the direction that Aymond and the rest of the MARSOC Marines had left in the remaining M-ATVs then back at the blast door.

"Hey, that's..."

A single rifle shot pierced the unnervingly quiet air. By the blast door, a lone head snapped backward and fell backward to where it had come. Jones looked at Amanda who stood with her rifle shouldered. She slowly lowered the rifle's muzzle and scanned the area before lowering the rifle and letting it hang on the sling across her chest.

"Shit...that was close to 100 meters. Uh, good shot, Madam President."

Amanda didn't show any reaction, but her mind smiled that she would impress a Marine with a well-placed shot. Oreo ran off and she watched the dog, noticing Andrew running toward them waving his arms, yelling and pointing. The wind grew stronger out of the north, but neither Jones nor Amanda could understand what he was trying to say. They looked at the yellow plane, Andrew's plane, which he was pointing at.

"Oh shit, Jones."

Beyond the plane, across the dry lake bed, the red cloud was closing fast and she realized it wasn't a cloud; it was a churning mass of dirt and sand.

"Jones, secure your truck!" Amanda yelled after Jones who was already running toward the open and activated Chinese radar truck. Andrew ran past Amanda, yelling, "give me a hand!" Amanda sprinted behind him to his aircraft. She followed Andrew's lead of kicking the tire chocks from under the large tundra tires of his aircraft.

"Push on the wing strut!"

Amanda pushed. Andrew pulled and held his side firm, spinning the plane toward the second and mostly intact hangar on this flightline. One of the large sliding doors was open, and once the plane was rolling toward the hangar, Andrew sprinted to the hangar doors, which weren't open far enough for the wing to fit. "Just keep pushing" was all he yelled as Andrew pushed hard to open the hangar door.

Pushing, Amanda was gaining speed. As this was her first time to push an aircraft around, she was hesitant but jogged along with the plane, not sure how it would stop. Andrew ran back to his plane and pushed hard. Just as the tail-wheel skipped across the hangar door tracks, he yelled, "Pull!" and grabbed the wing strut. Amanda and Andrew's feet slid on the painted concrete hangar floor as they slowed the aircraft to a stop. They ran to the hangar doors and began pushing them closed just as Jones skidded to a stop inside the hangar.

Papoose Mountain

The PLA cargo aircraft popped and groaned as it still smoldered on the desert floor in the distance. After finding the runway and hangars, Aymond and the rest of his Marine Special Operations Team drove to the top of the mountain that stood in between their location and Groom Lake. Tire tracks and a few remnants of some sort of MRE-style meal they hadn't seen before was all they found, but it was obvious that the mountaintop had been used as an observation post.

"Chief, look at that," Gonzo said, pointing toward the northeast.

The rest of the remaining team members, eight total including Master Gunnery Sergeant Aymond, were forming up by the trucks after searching the immediate area for any other clues or information about the PLA that had been there.

Aymond looked at Gonzo and followed the pointed finger. "Haboob... well shit."

"Load it up. Let's get down to the desert floor and use the mountains as a break. If it isn't too bad, we'll head back to Jones' location and hold tight."

One last time, Aymond scanned Groom Lake with his binoculars, pausing to look at where he had left Jones and the supposed president. The forward edge of the closing wall of dust washed over the lake bed and the hangars. If Jones was still out, if the radar truck was still there, or even if the little yellow plane was still there, Aymond couldn't tell.

The M-ATVs made it a few hundred yards down the dirt road toward the desert floor when the trucks rocked hard from the strong wind. Visibility dropped quickly to nearly zero from all the churning dirt and sand.

The Underground Facility

Jessie glanced at her watch; they had been below ground for nearly three hours and hadn't made it halfway into the facility. The first two levels were still overrun with the dead, no survivors were found, and the small group of the would-be rescue party had no choice but to secure the fire doors to clear the reanimated dead later. It was quickly apparent that if any survivors were to be found—if Sarah was to be found—Jessie, Erin, and crew would have to move quickly, trying to contain the outbreak by amputating the overrun infected areas from the rest of the facility.

"This is really different than the facility in Texas." Bexar wiped his face with the T-shirt he wore, which was soaked from the stress and exertion of the morning.

"It's older, mano. This one was begun in the 1960s," Chivo whispered in response.

"Turn here," Jessie whispered to Chivo, who remained the point man of their motley crew. Jessie followed, directing the group; Bexar was third in line followed by Jason and then Erin at the end, providing rear security for any of the undead that decided to trail along. The lights were still on, which was a blessing that Jessie didn't expect to last. A man staggered out of an open door, the front of his shirt drenched in his own blood, pieces of his neck missing, bite marks on his arms and face. Chivo's single shot echoed in the tight hall, more of the undead thumping against the closed and secured doors behind the team.

"Get the keycard from around his neck; we're going to need it."

As the team crept forward, Chivo stopped for a moment and cut the keycard free, handing the bloody plastic card over his shoulder to Jessie who wiped it on her pants and put it in her pocket. Continuing, they stopped at the closed doorway to the next Groom Lake "town." The team formed a security perimeter and Jessie tapped on the door. The small LED light over the RFID lock shone red, which indicated that the door was locked. Jessie tapped on the door a little harder. Expecting the heavy thuds of the dead, she was surprised to hear the quiet tap of a response.

In a hard whisper, Jessie spoke with the man on the other side.

"Only about half our town, but we're secure. We strip-searched each other for any bites and everyone is clear."

"Is Sarah with your town?"

"No."

"OK, good job. Shelter in place until I release you; we're still in lockdown."

"What about Jake?"

Jessie looked at the bloodied keycard in her hand.

"Jake is dead."

Groom Lake

The hangar rattled, the doors shook, and dust and sand floated in the still air inside the cavernous hangar. Jones, Andrew, Oreo, and Amanda walked slowly in the dark shadows; shining lights, they searched their temporary shelter for anything that could be useful. A ragged collection of vehicles that wouldn't have even been found on the shadiest of used car lots before the attack were parked along the south wall. The western wall, the other end of the hangar, was a work area with tools, parts, and equipment secured behind a fenced-off section with a locked gate. Jones found a side door for pedestrian traffic on the south wall. Next to it was a panel of light switches, which to everyone's surprised worked, bathing the hangar in the humming orange glow of a gymnasium as the lights warmed up.

The middle of the hangar was wide open with guidelines and sections, walking paths and markings on the painted floor. Andrew looked around with a little disappointment. "I was hoping to find a UFO."

Amanda laughed and said, "Tell you what: if we find one, you can keep it."

Oreo appeared unconcerned, his tail wagging, ears up, walking lazily beside Andrew.

"These cars look like hell."

"They still look better off than your ride, Madam President."

"Jones, would you just call me Amanda or Lampton or something less formal?"

"Uh, yes ma'—um...Amanda."

"And you're right...you're a mechanic, look through the vehicles and find the best one; I'm going to need a replacement."

The Underground Facility

"Fall back!"

The stiff staccato sounds of multiple AR-15s and M4 rifles being fired rapidly accented the crack-boom sound of Jason's pump-action shotgun. Enraged moans of the dead grew louder with the advancing horde. Blood-soaked teeth gnashed, eyes gazed completely without emotion, and cold hands clawed at their clothes. The group was now in full retreat, a body hanging limply over Bexar's shoulders as they retreated through the relative safety of the hall.

Prior to disaster, the group paused at one set of the cafeteria doors while Jessie tapped the door and waited for the reply. The double doors were secured by a sturdy leather belt, tying the door handles together. A panicked crying whisper pleaded for help in response. Chivo untied the belt as the soft crying grew to sobbing interrupted by a loud crash and screaming. Now free, the doors burst open, knocking Chivo to the ground, trapping Jessie behind an open door.

Jason and Bexar pushed against the doors, trying to stop the eruption of death-like fingers in a dam, the relentless push of scores of reanimated dead quickly overcoming them. Chivo pushed against the shoulders of a dead woman, her olive drab T-shirt slick with dark blood, her teeth snapped at his hands, but he finally got a foot between him and her. Kicking hard, she fell against the following fellow dead which were crashing over a makeshift protective wall comprised of cafeteria table and chairs.

Chivo rolled away from the doorway while Jason pulled Jessie to her feet. Bexar grabbed the shoulders of the survivor and dragged the man free of the feeding frenzy before pulling the man onto his shoulders. Jessie took the new point position; Erin held the rear, rapidly firing through one and then another magazine of ammunition, rotating her short-barreled rifle with each rapid magazine change. A ballet of death at her fingertip, the rifle rotated forward with her left hand, catching the bolt release as she took aim, bracing the forestock, and firing. Each squeeze of the trigger was another head ruined, another reanimated body falling to the ground.

"Move your ass, girl! El cucuy is closing!" Chivo yelled as he fired past Erin.

Erin turned, flipping him off as she ran past, rejoining the group as they retreated, following Jessie as she moved quickly through what appeared to be an endless maze of look-a-like bland office hallways. Panting, sweating and slick with blood, Bexar had difficulty holding the survivor on his shoulders. Jessie stepped into the open door of a dark janitor's closet, Jason and Erin crowding in with her. Bexar abruptly stopped at the door, Chivo bumping into him before pushing the both of them, along with the unconscious survivor, into the closet, pulling the door closed. A hand caught between the door and door frame bent with a loud crack. Chivo pushed the door open with a hard shove before shutting it again, the reanimated corpse on the other side falling to the ground.

"Great, babe..."

"Shut up, Bexar."

Bexar looked surprised, not that anyone could have seen his face in the darkness, but he did stop talking. A sharp click was heard followed by the hissing air pressure change as the heavy door slid open. The lights inside the secret second facility were already on. Blood trailed along the floor from where they stood toward the interior, disappearing through another closed door.

CHAPTER 2

"I'm sorry, Colonel..."

"Smith."

"I'm sorry, Colonel Smith, but you're not authorized to enter this facility."

Steve Dorsey, Lieutenant Colonel (USAF ret.) as an Air National Guard fighter pilot, wasn't authorized to be in the facility any more than anyone else, except that he was personally invited by Major Matt Stone who coached his son's hockey team. Major Stone of the 12th Missile Squadron manned this flight of Minutemen III ICBMs. Dorsey glanced at the status board; eight of the ten missiles showed a ready status, not that Dorsey could launch them even if he had wanted.

Dorsey glanced at the duty board before keying the intercom again. "Colonel Smith, which Flight is this Missile Alert Facility assigned to?"

The colonel showed no emotion, the frustration in his voice purely for effect. "Lieutenant Colonel, the Flights have been dissolved, the 12th Missile Squadron no longer exists, and the 341st no longer exists. Frankly, none of the Wings remain and the entire command structure is in shambles. There are scant few of us left, communications are compromised and no longer function, and I'm here on order of President Lampton to secure the couple of remaining MAFs."

Glancing at his notebook and scribbled notes, the transmissions from Groom Lake and the communications via the cobbled together radio all spoke of President Lampton, the first women president. There was no mention of any remaining military forces or even any sort of government structure at all in any of the transmissions. Most of the radio messages alluded to the government taking strides to rebuild and they were asking for people to join them to help. That didn't sound like anything even remotely as functional as Smith made it sound.

Dorsey had no idea what the actual protocol was to grant access to the facility. The question about the Flight was a shot in the dark but the best he could come up with. The man he spoke with arrived in an MRAP and appeared to be wearing the correct uniform, as best as he could tell via the low-quality security camera. Something didn't seem right, but nothing seemed right anymore. Not when he shot down the bomber drones, not when he had to bail out four miles short of the runways at Malmstrom, and especially not when he fought his way back to his house over the following weeks. The only positive of it all is that he found Matt when making a scavenging run on the air base and that Matt brought him back to the lonely MAF south of Ulm.

"OK, Colonel, park next to the main garage. Come into the Launch Control Support Building and I'll buzz you through."

The gate clicked and whirred as it slid open. "Colonel" Clint Smith climbed into the running MRAP and drove into the fenced-off facility, the gate sliding closed behind him, and parked next to the oversized garage near an odd-looking outsized ranch-style home.

The Underground Facility

Bexar laid the survivor on the floor as gently as he could. The man wearing an odd mix of military utilities and civilian clothing was fit and had a scraggly looking new beard. He also did not appear to be breathing. Chivo reached down to check the man's pulse when his eyes snapped open and he sat up.

"Shit." Chivo pushed backward and out of the way just before the deafening boom of Jason's shotgun echoed through the gray concrete hallway. Jason shook his head and walked toward Erin, who was already beginning to follow the blood trail. Bexar glanced at the man on the floor, his head ruined by the shotgun blast; the corpse wouldn't get up again. Chivo stood and followed the straggling group. "Come on, mano, the women folk are apparently anxious to keep moving."

Bexar glanced at Chivo who made a face and shrugged and followed the group to the next door, careful not to step in the blood on the floor. Jessie touched the blood-smeared ID card to a reader on the wall next to the closed door, which opened to reveal a bland-looking office with cheap government furniture and fake plants. What really drew Bexar's attention was a fake window and outdoor scene painted on the wall. The blood trailed to the right and into what appeared to be a shower facility. Chivo provided rear security while Bexar followed Jessie, Erin, and Jason with a slightly confused look. The showers exited into a large room with supplies. The blood stopped and was pooled by a gray metal desk. White paper wrappers from bandages littered the floor, but there was no sign of the person who left them.

Chivo began forward toward the tiled room. Erin stepped to the front and touched his arm, stopping him. She held up a hand gesturing to wait a moment. Erin turned and picked up a fake potted plant from near the desk and threw it into the dark room ahead. The loud crash echoed off the tile and was immediately followed by a series of grunts and moans of the dead.

"Well shit."

Erin looked at Chivo and shrugged off his comment. Holding her rifle ready, she waited for the dead to appear from the darkness. Wet-sounding footsteps grew closer until the first reanimated corpse stepped into the light. A man in his 30s, Erin recognized him as one of the work crew they had left in the supply room. Not waiting, Erin fired a single round, pieces of brain and bone speckling the tile as the body crumpled to the floor. More footsteps followed, another corpse approached, ribbons of flesh hanging from her teeth, Erin fired again and another reanimate was downed for good.

A third shape began to emerge from the darkness, but as it crossed into the light, Erin gasped and stood frozen. Chivo glanced at her and raised his rifle.

"No!" Erin screamed.

Chivo stopped and lowered his rifle, a little surprised at Erin's outburst. She raised her rifle and fired, tears falling from her cheeks to the floor. Erin walked to the reanimated woman she had just put down, fell to her knees, and grasped a cold dead hand. She gently kissed it and gingerly set the hand on the woman's chest...her mother's chest.

Jessie put her hand on Erin's shoulder. Erin spun and stood, pushing Jessie to the ground and with a blur, a pistol was in her hand, tears streaked across Erin's face.

"Your fault! This is all your god-dammed fault! If you hadn't wanted to fuck with your tent, this wouldn't have fucking happened!"

Chivo and Bexar were yelling at Erin, both had their rifles up, but Jessie held up a hand toward them. "Wait."

"Erin, I'm so sorry."

Erin punched Jessie in the jaw, holstered the pistol, and walked toward the exit, pushing Bexar out of the way as she passed. Jason stood still, mouth open, and looked back and forth from Erin to Jessie and Sarah's body.

"Well, don't just fucking stand there, mano. Go after her, she's going to need you."

Jason turned and jogged after Erin who held a middle finger in the air over her shoulder as she stepped through the door at the end of the hall and back into the main facility.

Jessie stood and fought back tears before taking a deep breath. "Shit...well, you guys still with me? We have a lot of work to do."

Chivo didn't say a word and simply stepped in front to take point and lead the three of them into the darkness.

In The Stairwell

Jason sprinted up the stairs after Erin, quick gunfire echoing down the concrete and steel. He reached the top flight just as Erin stepped through the door and into the main hallway of the first level. Following in her wake, the remaining reanimated corpses that he saw were left in ruins by her quick trigger. Without a word, Jason trailed closely, head on a swivel while he quickly walked, watching for any threats approaching from the rear and any that Erin didn't see ahead. However, he didn't need to; they were moving too quickly for any dead to catch them from the rear and Erin was too switched on to miss any ahead of them.

Emerging into the remains of the hangar dust-choked the air, the sun was dim through the swirling dirt. Erin scooped up her big .50-caliber rifle from where she had left it on the floor, pulled her shemagh over her mouth and nose and squinted her eyes against the sandstorm. The plane was gone, the Marines weren't there, not that they could tell; visibility was better measured in inches than miles or even feet. Erin walked with determination, disappearing from Jason's view into the swirling red mass.

The hangar doors rattled loudly as Erin pushed one open wide enough to squeeze into the interior. Jason caught up just as she did, dirt and sand erupting into the space behind them. Inside, Jason saw the small yellow plane, the pilot and his dog, the woman who was supposed to be the president, and one of the Marines. The dog trotted toward Erin, stopped short, and sat watching her cross the large space. Amanda tried to talk to her, Erin's middle finger her only reply. Jason jogged to climb into the passenger seat of an old rusting four-wheeled drive Suburban before Erin shifted into reverse.

The tires chirped on the painted concrete. Jones raised his rifle and started toward the big SUV, but Amanda held up her hand. "Let her go, Jones."

Jones looked at Amanda then at the young man and woman who climbed out of the Suburban to push open the hangar door far enough to drive through.

"Mr. Jones, once they're gone, would you and Andrew please push the door close?" Amanda had to practically yell over the rattle of the storm.

"Yes, ma'am."

The taillights disappeared into the storm and the hangar door was pushed closed behind them.

In the Suburban

Erin slowly drove in silence. Now free from the underground facility, her shoulders began to relax, the anger and determination fading from her. She stomped on the brake and put it in park. With her head on the steering wheel, Erin took some deep breaths.

"Would you drive?" Erin whispered.

Jason nodded and they traded seats. He could barely see the end of the hood, much less any further, but he put the selector in drive. "Where to?"

"First, the tent."

Slowly Jason drove, hoping he was going the right way. Erin slid next to Jason on the bench seat, wrapped her fingers in his, kissed the back of his hand, and laid her head on his shoulder, heavy tears falling onto his shirt.

The storm was disorientating. Jason felt like they were tumbling down a cliff, but it was just the winds gusting and pushing the big four-wheel drive. Some patches weren't as dark as others and he would get short glimpses of where they were. He was driving the correct direction, but it was slow going. Without clocks and no way to see the sun, they had no idea how long it took, except that it felt like a trip that lasted hours and hours. To his surprise, Jessie's tent was still standing, shuddering in the wind. Jason parked with the passenger door nearly touching the door flaps. They climbed out and into the tent.

"All the ammo, all the MREs, we take everything," Erin yelled over the wind-shook tent noise.

"What about Jessie? What about the tent?"

"That bitch can get more from where she is and fuck this stupid fucking tent."

Jason arched his eyebrows. Just a few hours before, during the attack, Erin had nearly sacrificed herself to protect Jessie and her unborn child. Things were different now and he didn't know if it would remain that way.

"What then?"

"Then we leave."

"To where?"

"I have an idea, but first we load up this shit, top off the fuel, and go before the fucking Marines get back."

Jason wasn't sure about Erin's plan but he was sure about sticking with her.

Papoose Mountain

What little evidence was left of the PLA recon team was likely destroyed in the massive dust storm. The storm slowed and the air began clearing. Visibility was finally beginning to return to normal. Aymond sat silently in the armored truck, sweltering with the top hatch closed, doors closed, and the engines off. There were no recovery trucks available; if the M-ATVs ingested dust, they could lose another truck and they were already down to two. The radio crackled.

"Chief, the uh...President Lampton is requesting the team returns, over."

"Requesting, Jones?"

"It isn't really a request, Master-Gunns."

Aymond showed no emotion or reaction. "Roger."

After a brief pause, Aymond keyed the radio. "OK, guys, dust off the trucks. Time to head back."

Dirt and sand covered the big armored trucks, but after deployments in Iraq, Afghanistan, and elsewhere in the Middle East, the members of the MSOT were ready for such things. The men climbed out with a couple of stiff brushes to begin cleaning off the engine intake, radiator, mounted weaponry, and windows. The remotely operated turret received the most attention as the optics and sensors needed the extra care. Ten minutes later, the team was traveling north, past the remote radar sites and following the road around the mountain back to the hangars on the dry lake bed.

When they arrived, Jones was outside cleaning the PLA truck the best he could. Some of the other Marines stopped to help while Aymond continued to where Amanda was helping Andrew push the yellow Aviat Husky back onto the ramp.

"Aymond, thank you for returning. I believe the rescue party that went below may need some help; what can we do?"

"Ma'am, my team can take care of it. You, however, should stay topside. What is your goal for all of this? Even if we clear the entire facility, the area is not secure and the cleanup would take a significant amount of time. Perhaps we can find you a more safe location instead?"

Amanda's eyes narrowed slightly. She understood the reluctance in letting her come along with his team, but after all she had been through, president or not, she was tired of the mansplaining. This was the story of her professional life and even in the horrific world of a post-apocalyptic society at war, the prejudice remained. *I should have put Clint in his fucking place and then much of this could have been avoided.*

"Master Gunnery Sergeant Aymond, take your men below and secure the facility. This location is vital to the survival of the United States government and her citizens. Further orders will follow."

Aymond stood unmoving, deciding if he was going to believe what the others had said. Worried that he was aligning with a charlatan war chief, that the remnants of a more legitimate government remained, he weighed his position with what he knew to be true. *Even if she isn't the president, this is a top-secret facility...even the fucking PLA tried to destroy it.*

"Yes, ma'am."

Aymond turned and made a circle over his head, calling the team to circle up on him.

"Gentlemen, what do you think? Is she the president or not? She's ordering us to clear the underground bunker."

A series of non-committal grunts followed.

"Chief, president or not, fuck it; this is dreamland. I want to see if there are any aliens down there."

After the chuckling subsided, Aymond continued, "Thanks, Gonzo, I do too, but we also know that the fucking PLA tried to destroy this place and the people here, so it has to have some sort of tactical advantage or they know something that is dangerous to the invasion forces. That alone makes me want to clear the bunker."

A couple of thumbs up and some nods were the silent response.

"Jones, you and Happy stay topside, form a defensive position, protect our trucks and the Chinese radar truck. Without those, we're mostly fucked. The rest of you gear up; we go below in five mikes."

A mix of "hoorahs" and "kill" were the positive responses, and the team split from the loose huddle and began the preparations. The control tower to the southeast would have been an obvious choice for an observation post, but limited to only Jones and himself, Gonzo opted to lay out a loose semi-circle with the radar truck as the centerpiece. He didn't want to get stuck in a position with no maneuverability and no responsive help on tap if they were attacked by the invasion forces or surrounded by a swarm of Zeds.

Gradually, the rest of the team formed up with Aymond at the burned-out facility entrance. "OK, slow and steady. There are possible survivors, there is the civilian team from earlier, and we can be sure there are Zeds..."

"And aliens."

Aymond glanced at Snow, who smirked. "And maybe aliens. The point is we move slow, steady, and methodically. If we need to rearm, then we hold our position and send runners; however, we are going to put down every damn Zed so we have no surprises. We have no idea how many people were inside, how many are still alive, or how many Zeds there are. If it's completely fucked, we'll pull back and reevaluate the suggestion from Ms. Lampton."

The team stacked up. Hammer took point and the team entered the facility with determined purpose.

The Surface

Amanda watched the Marines disappear into their mission then glanced at the two who remained on the surface. They were a few hundred feet away and appeared to be setting a defensive position. She walked back to the small yellow plane.

"Mr. Pruitt, you mentioned other survivors before...could you tell me about them, please?"

Andrew looked at Oreo who was rubbing his head against Amanda's leg and receiving a happy ear scratch for the effort.

"Uh, what would you like to know?"

"Let us start with some general information. If you had to guess, how many people have you met?"

"Probably a few hundred in all."

"Any military units?"

"Yes, well, no. I mean, I saw some but after encountering some less than friendly types who were in military uniforms, I tended to give them all a wide pass. So I've seen some convoys and groups and stuff, but I didn't really talk to them."

"Do you remember where they are?"

"I can do you one better than that, I have notes and marks on my maps."

Amanda smiled. "That is wonderful. What about other survivors?"

"I have notes and marks for them too."

"Were most of them friendly?"

"Uh, most were, some weren't. It was really odd, but after the Groom Lake radio stuff, people got real happy."

"The shortwave transmissions?"

"No, yes, well, not just that, but they gave out instructions on how to build a radio using some car parts and other junk. It's an odd mix but people can bang out Morse code on them and communicate."

"Wow, I had no idea."

"Really? I mean..."

"No, it's OK. Another member of a secret government organization was trying to keep me safe by keeping us hidden and silent. I missed out on some stuff for it."

"Seriously? That sounds like a terrible movie. What happened?"

"I can't lead if I'm sequestered and being hidden in a hole in the ground."

Andrew nodded.

"So, Andrew, if you know how to make this radio and you know where the groups are, you could visit them with plans for the groups who aren't already communicating, right?"

"Well, yeah, but who would they talk to? The guy on the other side of the radio was supposed to be here."

Amanda stood still, quietly contemplating for a moment. "How far does your aircraft travel without needing to refuel?"

"That depends on the winds aloft and the weight, but 500 miles is a good safe number. That'd take a few hours, but that depends on the winds too. It cruises at about a buck forty, but ground speed can be just about anything depending on what's going on."

"So you could get from here to Dallas in a day or so?"

"Yeah, well, it isn't that easy. I'd need probably at least two fuel stops; I don't like pushing the limits when having to scavenge for gas."

CHAPTER 3

April 8, Year 1
Groom Lake

The old Suburban shook and squeaked as Erin and Jason bounced from the rough dirt track and onto the smooth paved surface. A dark ribbon of roadway cut through the lone desert. They followed the pavement around the mountain and toward the south, passing the ruins of the wrecked PLA cargo aircraft. Only the wind and rumbling drone of the old V8 engine filled the still air inside the cab. Jason drove, not convinced that they were making the right decision, but certain he was with the right person. His wife died escaping the brutal cult in Cortez and it felt like a lifetime ago, even though it had only been a number of weeks, not even half a year. The realities of the new world they lived in was one of fleeting life, with a sudden and early death more likely than not. The pervasive luxuries of mourning; help from the community, friends, and family to make it past the bitterly stark pain of loss had since passed. Their new society was one of lifetimes lived in tense and sparse moments, balanced precipitously on the edge of human extinction. His heart still ached for his wife and he would always love her, but he knew that she would be angry if he died alone. Jason glanced at Erin. She was stoic, the raging emotion of finding her mother and having to put down her reanimated corpse burned deeply. Erin's feelings were pushed so deep, so removed from the surface as to not be noticeable; her face appeared like etched granite in its beauty and terror. Thoughts of running away to start a new life, a new family has been the long dream of youth past. That dream remained, although the reality of running away for a new life is that they would likely be running for the rest of theirs, as short as it would likely be. Jason took Erin's hand, gently caressing her calloused palm with his thumb.

"Let's elope."

Erin turned to look at Jason, silently.

"I mean, we are going to drive by Las Vegas, want to get Elvis to marry us?"

"Zombie Elvis?"

"Well, that's probably all we'll find there."

A faint smile crept onto the corners of Erin's mouth. She intertwined her fingers in his, and Jason continued, "You were right, are right. I love you and our ages don't matter, not now. I don't know how long I have left before my luck fails us, but I want to spend what luck I have left with you."

"You're not allowed to die." Erin slid across the bench seat and rest her head on his shoulder. "I love you."

Jason smiled at her. "Until death does us part."

"No, until death binds us together for eternity."

Groom Lake

"If at first you don't succeed, you're going to die."

"Great pep talk, coach! Really fucking motivational" Bexar sarcastically replied to Chivo.

Their team, now short two members, exited the ironically more secret bunker inside of a secret underground bunker after rearming in the secondary store-room. Inside the concrete and metal stairwell, muffled rifle fire could be heard from an unknown level above them.

"Mrs. Bexar, would the others inside be fighting their way out?"

"They're not supposed to; we have rules in place that locks the facility down like a high school. Doors are shut and locked, people are supposed to keep quiet, and the sweeper team clears floor to floor. Once the all clear is given, then the doors can be unlocked."

"What do they do while locked down?"

"Everyone gets a full physical inspection for bites or other wounds to stop a secondary outbreak."

"Slick, that's not a bad plan. Bexar, how did you ever convince her to marry a serial fuckup like you? I've seen you naked; I know it isn't because you have a massive schlong..."

"He uses it well," Jessie interrupted with a wink, causing Chivo to chuckle.

The rifle fire increased in tempo and ferocity.

"OK, kids, so we have a group of unknowns going full rock and roll up there. My guess is that Aymond and his Recon boys came down to help."

"So what do we do?"

"If we assume that to be true, then we stay on this level, clear it, and start working our way back up. Eventually, we should meet in the middle or we can put down their reanimated corpses."

"Or they can put down ours."

Chivo looked at Jessie. "Confidence, miss. We knuckle-draggers never fail because we don't believe in it."

Elsewhere In the facility

"Fucking blow it!"

Gonzo didn't have to be told twice. A moment later, a hard thump was heard after calling out to his teammates and the grenade's fury could be felt through the walls and floors. The fire team of Marines reinterred the cafeteria. Pieces of some of the Zeds were scattered, black scorch marks on the floor and tables, a dark red and black spray painting the low ceiling. Teeth gnashed and snapped at their boots from heads that were still reanimated as they stepped inside, quick and accurate shots putting the dismembered bodies down for good. Grenades weren't all that effective against the reanimated dead, not like living personnel, but in this case, the small clearing gave the special operations Marines the small foothold they needed to begin clearing the large room.

The team split into two groups as they entered the room, every other man peeling off to the left or right. Running the walls is what they called the technique and it was being done in excruciating slow motion compared to how they would do it against armed insurgents. The war against the Zeds was one of slow-motion attrition.

Muffled "clear" calls were heard around the room, which was filled with the smoke of battle. Tables and chairs were tumbled and covered in gore. Destroyed Zeds and pieces of bodies littered the floor, a horribly gruesome site if this had occurred before the rise of the dead. Aymond waved a small circle above his head and his team converged on him. Unlike traditional forces, his men didn't stand in a circle facing him as he talked, years of training and experience had each of them facing different directions while Aymond spoke. It wasn't out of disrespect but so any enemy snipers couldn't tell who the senior ranking man was. No Zeds held hidden positions waiting for a clear shot, but deeply ingrained training is hard to escape.

"Ammo check."

Each of the men double-checked their magazines. They kept count in their head as they fought, but the secondary check confirmed what they did and did not have left. Loaded magazines were passed around to rearm team members who were running low.

"Chief, we're not equipped well enough to finish this. We need to resupply."

Aymond didn't respond to Happy but keyed his radio instead. "Jones, ask Lampton what she knows about this facility. Is there an armory on site?"

A few moments later, Jones replied, "That's affirmative, Level 5, and she has a dozen cases of 5.56 in her MRAP."

Aymond looked at each of his men as they held up a number with their fingers, adding up the number of empty magazines his team had and dividing that by the number of rounds in a case of ammo. He keyed the mic. "Jones, I need you to run two cases down the hole, Happy and Kirk will meet you."

Without any further instruction, Happy and Kirk peeled off and began heading toward the entrance through the path of death they had cleared to get ammo from Jones. The rest of the team took a circular defensive position and knelt to rest while keeping watch. Beyond the cafeteria walls, the moans of the dead could be heard above the thumps and thuds of the bodies against closed doors and walls.

The Radio Hut

Wet thumps of the dead rattled the door which also rattled their nerves. Bill and two airmen pushed a desk against the door, which was locked, but like a child using a blanket to be safe from monsters, the desk helped them feel calmer. The spark gap radio buzzed and popped with transmissions. It had been offline since the attack and the noise generated once Bill got it working again attracted the dead.

"Should we take it down again, Bill?"

Bill looked at the airmen, then the radio, then the door, which visibly shook with each hit from the other side. The transmission being picked up was slow, slow enough that he didn't have to write down each of the letters to understand what was being said. Glancing at the map on the wall and all the push pins, Bill closed his eyes. *Montana...the guy in the silo, Dorsey.*

The transmission was confusing, wanting to pass a message to the president, something about a colonel showing up.

"No, Jon, we leave it up. We have a job to do and we can't stop now. Try raising the SSC again on the terminal; I have a strange feeling about this."

The Stairwell

The rifle fire had gone silent and the three of them stood quietly in the relative safety of the closed-off stairwell.

"Do we check on whoever that was or do we clear what we have?"

Bexar looked at Chivo who, after contemplating the question for a moment, looked to Jessie. "What do you think, Mrs. Bexar?"

Jessie smiled slightly. She hadn't been called Mrs. Bexar, always Mrs. Reed, but she kind of liked how cutely Chivo said it. "Everything is fucked, and there's only three of us. I say we try finding who that is."

Chivo nodded. "I agree. This is a monumental task for only the three of us. The other option is to get topside and bug the fuck out, which is probably the smartest option."

Chivo glanced at Bexar who looked at his wife. Jessie shook her head. "No, we can't do that. I couldn't live with myself if we abandoned these people. They're survivors but some of them aren't tough; they're here because they're not tough and they only made it this long through sheer luck."

"Mrs. Bexar, we've all made it this far only through sheer luck..."

Bexar began to speak, but Chivo held up a hand to stop him. "But I understand. My entire adult life has been spent in far-off places under a dark cloak of secrecy helping people who can't help themselves. Now those people are my fellow citizens, my brother and sister countrymen, and if we can push more luck into their favor, then maybe I'll earn my spot at the table in Valhalla."

Bexar shrugged as a form of acceptance. Jessie absentmindedly rubbed her hand across her growing belly and wore the hard look of determination. Chivo led the slow walk up the stairs, carefully clearing each corner.

"Valhalla? So what did you and your vatos call the god of thunder back in Cali?" Bexar whispered.

"El Thoro," Chivo whispered back.

The Blast Door

Jones had a stack of a dozen green metal cans of XM193, ammo for the M4 rifles the team carried. This was more than they had left over from their meager supplies in the MATVs. "Hey, buddy. Holy shit, where did you get all of this? Santa come early this year?"

"The president gave it to me."

"Fuck, Jones, she have anything else in her Mary Poppins bag of war?"

"Some MREs, a ruined MRAP, more ammo, and a bad attitude."

"I'm starting to like this president, like a fucking warrior princess."

Lampton stood on the concrete apron in front of the demolished hangar speaking to an animated guy who had flown the yellow plane in. Her M4 hung on the sling across her chest carrier, her right hand gripping the rifle, her finger indexed; she looked more like an unconventional operator than the first female president.

"What's the deal with that guy?"

"He's been all over the country. I think she's trying to get him to fly her back to Texas."

"Fucking Air Force One got downsized."

"Budget cuts, man, unless you assholes can find some of the missing UFOs."

"Did she tell you that?"

"Shit, I wish!"

After a quick fist bump, Kirk and Happy each picked up two of the green metal ammo cans by the handle in each hand and started back down below. Jones watched and wished he was going with his brother Marine, but his job was to babysit President Lampton, although he wasn't sure who was babysitting who.

The Suburban

Hours had passed since they crept out of Groom Lake and they seemed to be sitting still in the vast desert. Progress felt slow, but that wasn't the first thing on their minds. At this moment, Erin and Jason lay on the roof of the Suburban, the muzzle of her big .50-caliber rifle extended past the end of the roof and past the rear bumper. She was motionless, peering through the large optic on the rifle. Breathing slowly, she whispered to Jason.

"How many do you count?"

"Just four."

In the distance, heat shimmered off the asphalt of an airfield. Parked in the middle of the field, between the runways and taxiways, sat alone four-wheeled armored transport. It was the same as what they saw during the battle for Groom Lake; it was the invading forces.

"Do we kill them or do we sneak off?"

Jason wasn't sure. He wanted nothing more than to sneak off and hide out with Erin for the rest of their lives, surrounded by a simple life of the post-death apocalypse. He wasn't sure that such a life existed, not with an invading army, a new world order of death brought forth by the hatred and strife of another people.

"If we kill them, then there are four less. If we sneak off, they wouldn't know, but what about 10 years from now?"

Before Erin could respond, a faint dot in the sky grew in size as it flew closer.

"Is that a plane." Jason moved the spotting scope slightly to see.

"Yeah, babe, it is. Fuck these people, fuck this world..."Erin's finger slid onto the trigger.

"Wait."

"Why?"

"The plane."

Erin understood and indexed her finger, adjusting slightly to bring the aircraft's approach into view of her rifle optic. The runway that the aircraft appeared to be flying toward seemed to be nearly in line with her rifle, and a faint smile crept upward on the corners of her mouth. Watching the simmering heat waves coming off the runway, Erin clicked in the adjustments for a slight crosswind into the optic and waited in annoyed anticipation. Her mother flashed in her mind and then her father. His voice was in the back of her mind, coaching her shot, just like the first time she shot her own deer. Erin slowed her breathing, working hard to control her emotional arousal, to keep her heartbeat steady as she readied the shot.

The landing gear lowered, large tires reaching to the tarmac like a child reaching their toes toward the ground from a high swing. The first shot rattled their teeth, the windows in the back of the Suburban exploding from the pressure wave. Erin didn't wait to see the shot hit before adjusting and firing again, then firing twice more.

"Hit...another hit."

Smoke streamed out of the rear of the two engines on the right-hand wing. Jason watched in the spotting scope. Erin had already adjusted aim to the four soldiers near their armored vehicle, watching their reaction, wanting to kill them but waiting.

"Holy shit!"

Erin didn't see what Jason was reacting to; she fired twice and watched two of the big heavy tires of the armored truck collapse. The four men didn't seem to notice; they were pointing and yelling. Looking up from the rifle, she was just in time to see the impossibly large cargo aircraft fell the last 10feet to the runway, shuddering as it tried to stop. It bounded off the end of the runway, the nose gear collapsing in the dirt as it slid to a stop. The soldiers turned to their APC and found the damaged tires. They climbed in anyways and began driving toward the aircraft, which was lowering the rear cargo ramp. Other men scurried out of the fuselage and began taking defensive positions around the aircraft, which sat with its nose in the dirt, the two ruined engines still smoking.

"What are they doing?"

"Looks like they're getting ready to offload, Erin."

"Fucking thing has run flats.... I hate these assholes."

Erin fired again. A breath later, one of the men who was standing and directing the others fell to the ground, lifeless, a pink mist hanging in the air where his head used to be. Others raised their rifles toward Erin and Jason, although Erin was fairly sure that they were out of range and wanted to kill a few more of them.

"They see us. We've got to haul ass!"

Erin ignored Jason and fired again, punching a hole in the side of the aircraft, more out of anger than knowing what was behind it.

Jason climbed off the roof of the Suburban; Erin fired again and joined him. The windows were shattered, the windshield ruined from the concussion of the heavy rifle. After Jason kicked out the windshield and side windows so he could see, Erin climbed into the passenger seat. He turned and drove south, accelerating quickly. Glancing at Erin, he saw a tear roll down her cheek. Jason held her hand, intertwining their fingers. Erin slid across the bench seat closer to him, curled her feet up on the bench, and laid her head on his shoulder, crying into his shirt as the wind and the dust swirled through the cabin. Not entirely sure how to get to where they were going, Jason knew that it would be better to get lost and have to figure it out later than waiting for the Chinese and North Korean forces they just harassed to come visit them.

Groom Lake

"Aymond."

Aymond heard the soft whisper but couldn't see where the voice was coming from.

"Goat?"

Chivo smirked, although no one could see him. "Yeah, Master-Guns, the goat. There are three of us and we're going to come around to join you."

His eyes squinted in annoyance, but there wasn't much he could do. "OK, come on then."

Chivo waved Jessie and Bexar up and the three of them joined the Marines as they sat in a defensive position. Two of the men knelt in the middle, loading magazines out of ammo cans.

"What's the matter, goat? Things get too difficult?"

The annoyance and sarcasm in Aymond's voice was thick. Chivo had dealt with this sort of situation before, although never in a secret underground base overrun by the dead.

"No, mano, we heard your rifle fire and thought it better to team up for safety. We wouldn't want any friendly fire casualties; there are too few friendlies left as it is."

Aymond didn't respond.

"Besides, Master-Guns, this here is Jessie and she knows the layout. She and the people here set the security plan for this sort of situation."

Aymond looked at her, then Bexar and back to Chivo. Nothing about this situation was what he wanted, but nothing about the new world they lived in was what he wanted either. *Adapt and overcome.*

"Fine, let's get you guys topside and we can continue clearing out all the Zeds."

Jessie glanced at Chivo then back at Aymond. "Zeds?"

"Zeds, the dead that won't die; Zulu, Z as in zombie," Gonzo said with a sigh.

Chivo smiled. "Zeds, I like that...I agree, let's get Bexar and his pregnant wife topside and safe then I'll help you guys finish this job."

"Who the fuck are you?"

"Master Sergeant Arturo Rodriguez, 1st SFOD Detachment Delta, formerly and more recently, I was with the agency. I'd slap a challenge coin down for you but I don't see where you could buy me some cocktillios."

Aymond looked incredulous. People make wild claims and for Chivo to say he was formerly with Delta Force and then a CIA paramilitary operator wouldn't be uncharacteristic of someone who was full of shit, but there wasn't any way he could prove the claim one way or another.

Snow slid over next to Aymond and Chivo. "I thought you looked familiar. You said your name was Smith."

"Have you ever met a spook named anything besides Smith? That was in the Herat Province, wasn't it?"

"Yeah, it was and I met a couple of Johnsons too."

"So has your mom."

Bexar wanted to laugh but didn't quite understand what was going on; a few of the Marines grinned silently at the joke.

Snow gave Chivo a fist bump. "Chief, I'll vouch for him."

Aymond shrugged. He had to trust his teammate, but adding more unknown people into the mix wasn't ever a great idea during an operation. "What about your friend and his pregnant wife?"

"He's good, ex-cop, but he actually knows stuff."

Aymond's face didn't change, just a general look of annoyance remained as everyone stood silently. A single shot broke the silence.

"We should get moving, Chief; the natives are getting sporty."

"Right, Kirk. Chivo, why don't you have your friends go topside and we'll wrap this up."

Chivo turned around to face Bexar. "Hey, mano, this isn't worth the argument. You and Jessie head up top, your fight down here is on hold anyways since we found Erin's mom already. Stick around up there though and we'll figure out the next step in a few."

Bexar opened his mouth to speak but before he could, Jessie squeezed his arm and spoke for them. "OK, Chivo, be safe. Come on, babe, I'll lead the way."

Jessie turned and began silently sliding down the hallway toward the stairwell, her rifle ready. Bexar glanced at Chivo with a slight grin and followed his wife. He hated being shrugged off by people, but he trusted Chivo and his judgment. Besides, he didn't want Jessie down here in this fight in the first place, so in a roundabout way, he got what he wanted in the end.

As Bexar and Jessie left, the Marines and Chivo had a quick pow-wow to get on the same page before returning to their task.

The Radio Hut

Bill took the keyer and tapped a fast-repeating break message; he needed the band open to himself. Eventually, the frequency fell silent, the other stations waiting for Bill's message.

Groom Lake under attack...overrun...need help...trapped...invasion force... send help send help send help.

After repeating the message, some of the other radio operators on the frequency began transmitting on top of each other asking questions. Across the country, some survivors lost hope; if the last known stronghold of America could be shut down, what hope would they have trying to scratch out a life in the mist of so much death and destruction? Anger burned bitterly in other survivors. Anger at the first attack that destroyed civilization, anger at the Chinese, the Koreans, the dead. Months of frustration, weeks of fear, days and days of dread trying to live long enough that they might outpace this horrible new life fell with a crash of a thousand glasses. For all the survivors who cowered in fear, two more stood with faces red, nostrils flared, longing for the chance to see their tormentors and kill them.

"Think that will work, Bill?"

Bill shrugged at the airman's question, the locked door rattling with the bangs of the dead. "God I hope so."

The spark gap radio buzzed and popped with multiple stations transmitting on top of each other, the smell of ionized air from the current filling the room. Bill ignored all the transmission fragments he could understand, most of them questions about his transmission. He looked defeated.

"Even if it doesn't work, we should keep working. What else can we do but sit and wait for death? If we're going to die, we might as well try to go down with pride in our last mission."

"I know you're right," another hard wet thump against the door rattled the wall, "but fuck this is scary."

On The Surface

Amanda began walking toward Bexar and Jessie who had just exited the facility into the ruined hangar. Dirt and sand covered the concrete floor and the sun was low in the western sky.

"What are we going to do tonight, sleep in the FJ?"

"I still have a tent and I put it up near here."

"Really? One of the wall tents? That's amazing."

Amanda reached them. "How is it down there, Bexar?"

"Uh, pretty fucked really."

Jessie was a little surprised at the candor with the president. Amanda wasn't fazed.

"Think there are any survivors?"

Jessie answered first. "Yes, ma'am, I do. I'm not sure how many survived but it's worth fighting for."

"What about you, Jessie? Are you going to make it?"

"I'm beginning to remember all the bad things about being pregnant, but I have no choice. We have no choice but to make it. The hard part is what to do after she's born."

Amanda's eyes lit up. "You know it's a girl? They have an ultrasound here?"

"Oh no, I don't know, just sort of feels like it might be a girl."

"I understand." Amanda gave Jessie a hug.

Bexar left them to chat and walked toward the radar truck. He saw it earlier but didn't really know what it did. One of the Marines was near it, crawling around one of the big armored trucks that his group had arrived in. His leg hurt. It had only been a couple of months since he was shot in Terlingua and although the wound had healed fairly well and somehow didn't get infected again, it still ached and hurt. The fresh scar looked terrible.

The Marine stopped working for a moment and watched Bexar walk toward him. "Hey, guy."

"Howdy there. What's wrong with your truck? The name is Bexar." Bexar held out his hand.

Jones shook his hand. "Bear? How did you get that nickname? Terrance Jones, everyone just calls me Jones."

"It's actually my real name; spelled with an 'X' like the county in Texas."

"Huh. Well, nothing is wrong yet, nothing major at least, but if I don't keep up with some TLC on the M-ATVs here, then we won't have much truck left for longer."

"What's that thing?" Bexar pointed at the radar truck.

"Chinese truck. We took it from the PLA in San Diego. Uses the radar dome like a weapon; it zaps the Zeds."

"Wow."

"Yeah, no shit. Sucks while driving though; the fucking Zeds fall under the wheels. Everything is labeled in fucking Chinese, sucks. At least it runs on diesel so we don't have to fuck around with the shitty gas."

Bexar nodded. Gasoline was something that worried him. All the gas remaining was already months old and only getting older. They wouldn't have too much longer before it would be too old to burn and would only screw up anything they tried to run on it. Especially with the ethanol in most gas. Guillermo had a large cache of treated fuel at their compound in St. George and that gas has the chance of lasting for close to another year, but not much else would. That's why he, Malachi, and Jack had opted to not store gas at the cache site; too much work for too little of a return. The plan was to live there for the long haul. *Fuck, I miss those guys.*

"Come over here, little grizzly, and you can see the Zed-killing Chinese truck, but don't walk in front of the dome; we're not really sure how it would affect someone who is still living and I'm not too excited to find out yet."

Dusk was upon them by the time that Jessie walked to where Bexar and Jones were. They had crawled around the radar truck and now Bexar was standing on a wheel, bent over the engine of one of the M-ATVs helping Jones. Andrew and Oreo were walking back toward the hangar after visiting the wrecked C-130 out on the lake bed.

"Bexar, honey, it's time to stop for the night."

It took his eyes a moment to adjust to the darkness from the hard LED light he was using under the hood. "Yeah, sorry."

Bexar climbed down. Jones bid a good night and got back to work as the couple walked away.

"What is Lampton going to do?"

"She's going to sleep in her shot-up truck tonight; it's just you and me."

Jessie gave Bexar a gentle kiss on the cheek and smiled as they climbed in the FJ and drove toward the tent hidden up the hill.

CHAPTER 4

April 9, Year 1
Groom Lake

The tent shook, dust and dirt filtering in from under the door flaps, the roof of the tent beginning to glow with the rising sun. The previous night, Jessie found all the ammo and cases of MREs that she had cached in the tent were missing, most likely taken by Erin and Jason. Jessie was upset for a moment before guilt filled her body with sadness. Jessie had lost her best friend but Erin had lost her mother in the attack and she couldn't blame Erin for grabbing supplies to make a break for it. Bexar wasn't upset, which was odd to Jessie; this was the sort of thing that would have driven him mad before society collapsed. The unjustness of theft and the righteous need to be the sheepdog was central to his being—it was part of what defined the man she fell in love with years before. The last few months had changed him. All of them had all changed. Wrapped in surplus wool green Army blankets, they laid still, watching the tent shake, not wanting to get up, and not wanting to let each other go. The time they were separated felt like years and not weeks, so they stayed in the makeshift bed, holding each other tightly, shivering against the cold morning wind. The afternoons were warm, but the nights and mornings were still cold and felt even colder from the wind whipping through the mountains and across the open dry lake bed.

Jessie nuzzled her face into her husband's chest while he slowly ran his fingers through her hair. A gentle kiss was followed by another, the gentle caressing snuggle quickly changing to excited petting. Jessie unbuttoned Bexar's pants and pulled them to his knees before quickly removing her pants to climb on top of her excited husband, pulling a blanket over them both.

A few minutes later, Jessie lay with her head on Bexar's chest, still trying to catch her breath. They had no idea what time it was and didn't care; it had been so long since they had been together, since they could love each other and feel comfort in their embrace, that neither wanted to move, to get up and end their moment. Eventually, a side-effect of her pregnancy won out and Jessie got up to find a place to pee outside the tent.

Bexar dressed and followed her outside. "Nauseous?"

Jessie nodded, rubbing a hand across her growing belly. "We should head down the hill and see how Chivo and the Marines are doing."

The Hangar

Bexar and Jessie drove up in time to see the small yellow aircraft lumber into the sky after a short takeoff roll. The pilot's dog sat by the Marines, some of whom were eating breakfast, others sleeping, and a couple of them standing security watch. Chivo was one of those who were asleep on the concrete floor, using an ammo can for a pillow. After pulling to a stop and climbing out of the FJ, one of the Marines standing guard walked up to them and introduced himself as Happy. The pilot's dog trotted over with his tail wagging as well.

Jessie wasted no time to get down to business. "How far have you cleared and how many survivors have you located?"

Happy glanced over his shoulder at Aymond, who was asleep, and back at Jessie. "We've found 42 survivors. They opted to stay sheltered in place with some talk of beginning cleanup. We've also cleared down to the fifth level; the warehouse is a fucking mess, full of Zeds. That's where we stopped for a chance to get topside to re-arm and rest."

Bexar looked concerned. "What about the undead that were left in the warehouse? Can they get back up to the survivors?"

Happy shook his head. "No, it would seem that the Zeds have problems climbing stairs. Besides, we secured the doors and access points we could find for anything coming up from below."

"Where is President Lampton?"

"She flew out with that other guy just now. They're going back to Texas to some other facility she called the SSC."

Bexar nodded. He knew the facility and still had a rough idea as to where it was located. "Outside of Ennis, near Dallas, it was a big atom-smasher project from the '90s that was actually a cover story to build an underground facility like this one."

Happy shrugged. "Seems like they had a few of them. Surely one of them has a UFO."

A rare smile crept onto Bexar's face. "Maybe. Sorry to disappoint you, but I didn't see any when I was there a while back. What about this place? It is Area 51 after all. Find any aliens yet?"

"Roger that. Nothing here either...yet. The president left a directive for you, ma'am."

Happy retrieved a folded piece of paper from a pocket and handed it to Jessie, who quickly read it. She turned to Bexar. "She made me the director of the Groom Lake facility by presidential order."

Bexar appeared concerned. "Are you sure you want that? Are you sure you want to stay? We can bugout..." he said, his thoughts drifting to Guillermo and his friends in Utah.

Jessie ignored her husband for a moment. "What about you guys? What are Lampton's orders for your group of Marines?"

"We're to secure this facility then go to the SSC. She spoke with Chief for a bit before leaving and there is more in the works, but we expect to move out this afternoon."

Jessie shook her head slowly, frowning, before turning to Bexar. "We have to stay, at least long enough to get the survivors safe and the facility secured again. We can—"

The muffled sound of rifle fire coming from the entrance interrupted Jessie, who turned to face the ruined blast door. The Marines who had been sleeping were now standing and adjusting their gear. Chivo was awake and standing near the opening, the rest of the Marines gathering to form up and re-enter the facility.Aymond glanced at his team and Chivo looked back toward Jessie and Bexar with a shrug before joining his team at the entrance. A moment later they were gone, disappearing into the depths of the underground facility, leaving

Jessie and Bexar standing in the hangar with the pilot's dog and Jones, who waved them over to the radar truck.

"Good morning, you two." Jones handed them each an MRE from the stash that Lampton had left in the ruined MRAP. Bexar eagerly cut his open, ripping into the entire pouch before a puzzled look crept across his face. He glanced at the pouch and read that the offensive smelling meal was lemon pepper tuna and began eating without using the chemical heater. The color in Jessie's face drained. She dropped the MRE and stepped around the side of the truck, vomiting what little was in her stomach. Jones looked at Bexar who shrugged and ate quickly. Besides the hunger, he wanted to finish the meal before Jessie came back. Jessie returned and Jones handed her a canteen of water with a smile. Bexar handed her the pack of crackers from his MRE, although wisely not the thick cheese spread.

Feeling marginally better after some water and the crackers, Jessie sat on the truck's bumper while Jones told the story about how he and Simmons survived the initial outbreak while at Twenty-Nine Palms, the journey to San Diego, and the battle against the Chinese and Korean forces. Movement coming from the facility entrance interrupted their conversation; survivors from the overrun facility were coming topside. Jessie walked toward the first of the group of people who stood blinking at the bright morning sunlight. The woman was someone she knew as Mary but Jessie didn't know much else about her.

"Mary, are you OK? Is the rest of your town OK?"

Mary shook her head, her face dirty, dried blood stains on her clothes. "I didn't get bit if that's what you mean, but dammit," Jessie gave her a hug, and Mary choked back a sob, her voice cracking, "that place is a god-damned tomb. Not like before, much worse."

"I know. We were down there yesterday." Jessie could see the image of Sarah, the dead and reanimated Sarah in her mind. "I thought everyone was sheltering in place."

"We were. Some guys in camo told us to get up here, that it was clear behind them so we did. There are bodies everywhere, all our friends, all we worked for the past couple of months, all of it destroyed."

Jessie glanced at Bexar and tried to cover her fear and sadness at it all with a face of determination. "Nothing is destroyed. As long as we have a single survivor, we will make it work; we won't be beaten down."

"What about Jake? Where is he?"

Jessie slowly shook her head; Mary held her hand over her mouth in shock.

More survivors came out of the entrance, huddled in small groups. Jessie looked at them; all of them looked rough, bloodied, tired, faces with the look of defeat.

"Mary, would you mind asking everyone to gather up with us over here?"

Mary nodded and walked away slowly.

"What's going on?" Bexar asked his wife.

Jessie stood silently focused in thought for a moment before answering. "We did this before, only it wasn't this bad. We will need to organize work crews to drag the bodies topside, others to dig a mass grave, but before we can do any of those things, we have to see to all of these people's needs. They need a safe place to be sheltered, a meal, and fresh clothing. Meals and clothing are easy, sort of easy—a large storeroom is on the fifth level, MREs, clothing, blankets, ammo, all that we would need is there. We just need to be able to get to it."

"OK, let's say that Chivo and Aymond clear the floors all the way to where all of that is stored. What about the shelter?"

"Southwest of here, a couple of blocks are a couple dozen dorms. If we clear one, that's a start. That would be a place to give these guys shelter. Maybe we'll be lucky and they are powered by the same systems that power this facility or something like that."

Before Bexar could ask any more questions, the survivors that had come topside began forming around them, waiting silently. More survivors trickled out of the entrance and made their way toward the small crowd. Jessie didn't wait for the new arrivals to start describing her plan.

"I'm glad all of you are OK. What we know so far is that our facility was attacked by Chinese and Korean forces. The Marines that are clearing each of the levels of reanimates happened to arrive just in time to prevent a much worse outcome."

Some of the people grumbled amongst themselves. Some began asking questions of Jessie, who held up her hands and continued, "President Lampton was here, but left this morning to go back to the Texas facility. She left me in charge for now and we have a lot of work to do. We owe it to our lost friends to not give up; we can't give up. While the Marines are doing their job underground, we are going to begin clearing one of the dormitories near here."

Many of the people looked confused or puzzled.

"I know, I'm sorry. There are above-ground dorms that Jake and I had discussed clearing out to expand our quarters for some of the survivors after the last outbreak, the idea being that all of our eggs wouldn't be in one basket. Anyways, I'm sure that all of you followed the group bite inspection protocols, but I'm going to ask that we all check again. As you can see, the partitions along with most of this hangar were destroyed in the attack and I'm sorry, but if we're going to get everyone into new accommodations before sunset, we can't waste time. I'll be the first to be checked and then I'll need four volunteers to help Bexar and I begin clearing the first dorm."

Most of the survivors were exhausted and after the ordeal, the violence and fear of a massive outbreak contained in their underground bunker, the sight of Jessie stripping her clothes off gave rise to no reactions.

"What are you doing?"

Jessie gave Bexar a half-smile. "Bite check. One of the protocols we put in place after the last outbreak. We had a Typhoid Mary spark that one off and so we decided this would be a good attempt to keep that from happening again."

Fully nude, Jessie's pregnant belly was even more obvious even though she was only about twelve weeks along in the pregnancy. Jessie held her arms out and turned slowly; Bexar ignored the others, smiled at his beautiful wife, and remembered their morning together.

Deemed bite free, Jessie dressed and slung her rifle. "Who are my volunteers? Let's get you checked next so we can get started."

Four people stepped forward, one woman and three men. Each of them removed their clothing and were visually inspected. Once again dressed, Jessie began walking them toward the FJ. With six of them, it would be a tight fit, but they would make it work.

"What about that guy?"

Jessie didn't know who in the small crowd asked the question, but she knew they were talking about Bexar and she also knew they were right to ask. She turned to her four volunteers. "Get with Jones over there. He can get you something to eat and show you where to top off your ammo. Bexar, come back over here with me; you need to be bite checked as well."

Annoyed, Bexar did as his wife directed and set his rifle on the ground before shrugging out of his clothing. Jessie looked at his nude form; it had been weeks since she had really seen him naked. She hadn't spent much time looking over his body during their romp in the tent that morning. A bright, fresh scar filled a dent in his leg where he had been grazed by a round in Terlingua. Other scars, cuts, and bruises were present where they hadn't been before the attack and the start of this whole mess. The faded tattoos on his chest and back spoke to happier times, memories, and their family. Bite check completed and once again dressed, Bexar and Jessie walked to the waiting group by the FJ as the other survivors continued with the bite checks. Jessie climbed behind the wheel and started the engine. The sound of a commotion and yelling drew her attention back to the group. A half-nude woman ran from the group and toward the dry lakebed, an arm across her bare breasts, the other holding her bicep. Jessie realized it was Mary. A volley of rifle fire followed her before she tumbled to the ground, where she laid facedown and motionless. Another woman walked out of the group and toward where Mary's body lay. She drew a pistol and fired a single shot into the back of Mary's head. After holstering her pistol, the woman fell to her knees, her head in her hands, and sobbed. Some others helped the woman who put down Mary up and dusted her off, embracing her as she sobbed.

Jessie looked back at the group of survivors. The bite checks continued as she drove away toward the dorms. Bexar was surprised at the brutality of the scene but also impressed at how tough these survivors were. It takes a strong person to kill an infected friend for the good of the majority. He didn't expect people living in virtually a post-apocalypse five-star resort to be this hard; maybe there was hope for these people yet.

Ulm, Montana

"I don't see how the fuck you expect to accomplish that. Respectfully, sir."

Dorsey saw Col. Smith's plan for what it is, removing all the checks in place to prevent an unauthorized launch of the flight of ICBMs that the facility controlled. The obvious and most well-known safety feature is the launch keys, both of which have to be turned nearly in sync, and the control consoles were spaced far enough apart that no one person could accomplish the task. It takes two people, always has taken two people, and shouldn't be changed to allow for a single person to start a nuclear holocaust. Regardless as to the moral implications, what Col. Smith had in mind would take serious time and would require rewiring some systems. It would also require control of a purpose-built laptop that Smith claimed to have in the MRAP above ground.

Clint's expression didn't change; this sort of espionage was exactly what he was trained for, and playing the role of Col. Smith, he really could use Dorsey's help to accomplish the system changes. The hardware hack alone would take Clint a week to accomplish by himself.

Clint reached into his flight suit and retrieved an envelope and handed it to Dorsey. Dorsey turned the envelope over in his hands; the heavy stock paper had a blue embossed seal of an eagle, the seal of The President of The United States. Ripping open the end a single folded piece of paper, once again on heavy paper stock and also embossed with the president's seal at the top center of the sheet of paper, the letter contained exactly two lines of text with a signature. Under the signature was printed the name Amanda Lampton, and the two lines of text was a presidential directive to complete the retrofit of the ICBM launch systems. In his years of service, Steve Dorsey had never seen anything like this. Even during times of armed conflict, nothing in any of the top-secret briefings for the missions he had flown had been like this. Steve glanced at the pistol in the shoulder holster that Smith wore, skeptical of the entire situation.

"OK, Colonel, so how do we start? This is a monumental undertaking."

The Suburban

Wind whipped through the interior of the old SUV. Jason drove, and Erin sat in the back cleaning the big Barrett 50-caliber rifle. Since the morning of the attack on Groom Lake, she had flat-out abused the rifle and she was concerned that it would fail her if she continued to thump on it. The Suburban bounced along the deserted highway at a steady 50 miles per hour. Jason glanced at the fuel gauge and hoped that it was accurate. Not wanting to chance it, they would need to scavenge for gas soon. If they could find some spare fuel cans to carry, he would feel better about their journey. According to the highway signs, they were approaching the town of Pahrump. He hadn't heard of the town before, but the signs they passed were for a business he had heard of before, The Chicken Ranch. He always thought that was in Las Vegas, but he wasn't sure. As he continued to drive, Jason wasn't sure why any of it mattered at this point.

The sparse desert with distant mountains wasn't like anything he was used to from his hometown of Cortez, Colorado, but after the fight with the cult and his wife being killed, he never wanted to return to Cortez. Not really paying attention to the road and letting the Suburban drift, the rumble strip brought Jason's attention back to driving just in time to swerve hard to miss a reanimate that stood motionless in the roadway. Jason slammed on the brakes as the big SUV slid off the pavement and into the hard sand.

"What the fuck?"

"Sorry," Jason said sheepishly.

Erin, apparently finished with her rifle, climbed back into the front and next to Jason on the bench seat. The corpse that Jason nearly struck shuffled toward them, following the skid marks left by sliding off the road.

"We need to find some fuel."

Erin looked over the steering wheel at the fuel gauge and nodded, then looked toward the western horizon. "We should find a place for the night as well. I don't think I could sleep in this thing; I would be up all night watching for dead hands clawing through the missing windows."

The shuffling corpse was nearly to the rear of the Suburban when Jason turned the wheel and drove back onto the pavement, sand spitting from the rear tires peppering the reanimated dead.

"This is going to take forever; we're not exactly making great time on our drive."

Erin agreed. "But that's the only way to do it. We don't have the luxury of being picked up by a big cargo plane and brought to our new place. Shit, it took Mom and me weeks just to get across a few states."

Jason hadn't experienced an overlanding trip in the new world ruled by the dead. Although an obvious jab, Erin was right. Cliff and his crew of survivors flew a big C-130 to Cortez to pluck them out of the battle with the cult.

"I saw a sign for The Chicken Ranch. We could crash there tonight," Jason said with a sly smile.

"What the fuck is that?"

Jason laughed as he explained. Erin replied with a middle finger.

Groom Lake Dormitories

The northern-most dorms, closest to the destroyed hangar and the under-ground facility's main entrance, were the obvious choice to start with. The squat single-story structures looked just as one would expect for a government building, including the same dirty tan color that most of the other buildings on the surface had. Jessie and her small crew had cleared only a small fraction of the numerous random buildings and hangars that were scattered across the secret base. She had no idea what they all held or if some of the buildings may even contain useful equipment or gear. Even though she was standing in the middle of the most widely known top-secret facility that the government had, she still couldn't make heads or tails of what all was done at Area 51.

In just over four hours, the first pair of dorms was cleared with little fanfare or hassle, but a worse task remained before they could start the short migra-tion from the underground facility. Working in pairs, each of the terminated Zeds were drug out of the hallways of the dorms and into the dry sunbaked desert air. Still the beginning of April, it was surprisingly hot. Jessie had grown accus-tomed to the controlled temperatures and conditioned air of the facility. The pregnancy didn't help; piece by piece, she was remembering all the nuances of her pregnancy with Keeley. Gone was normal sweating to be replaced by what she called "man-boob sweatstains" on her shirt and that was only the tip of that iceberg. No wonder nature had conditioned women to forget the bad memories of bearing children; Jessie was sure if it hadn't that no woman would ever have more than one child.

Another 90 minutes and a stack of just over a dozen Zeds lay on the tarmac near the newly cleared dorms. They would add the bodies from underground to the bodies from the dorms once the work parties got started, but until then, they would sit in the open air and rot. The putrid smell of decomposing flesh was the real scent of the apocalypse. Jessie gave Bexar a high five as they walked to the FJ. The playful banter between them was reminiscent of their life in Brazos County, Texas, before the attack—a happy young family trying to make their way just as thousands and millions of others had every single day.

Thousands of families...my God, how many families are left? Erin without a family, so many others ripped apart.

One tear rolled down Jessie's cheek and then another. Quick on the uptake, Bexar put his hand on her back and rubbed it gently. She turned toward him, nuzzling into his chest and crying on his shoulder. Bexar glanced up at the others who stood by the FJ waiting and a little surprised at the Groom Lake woman warrior's breakdown. Bexar waved them on and after taking the hint, the four climbed into the FJ to drive back to the hangar. Bexar and Jessie would walk the short distance back in a few moments. Now alone with his wife, Bexar held her tight and looked at the scene around him. Standing in the middle of the famed Area 51, a stack of dead zombies near them and the complete collapse of all they held dear hanging over them...this was a future he had never planned for even though they had believed they were planned for the worst. Not once in the late-night whiskey-fueled campfire chats had he, Malachi, and Jack ever come up with this doomsday scenario. Yet here he stood, the only two survivors of their friends, a broken family trying to restart with a soon-to-be-born baby.

"What should we name him?" Bexar asked, gently wiping the tears off of Jessie's face.

A weak smile tried to hide the pain. "Who says he won't be a she?"

"If it is a girl, I hope she has your beautiful eyes."

Jessie squeezed Bexar tightly and let go. "We can decide names later, but we have a job to do before then."

After she let go and spun in place checking her surroundings, Jessie switched magazines in her rifle for a fresh and full one, press checking the round in battery before slapping the bolt assist a couple of times for good measure. Bexar smiled with surprise. His wife was proficient before, but in the time they spent separated, she had obviously become much more acquainted with her rifle and the new world they lived in.

"Come on, get your ass moving! You let those little shits drive off with our ride, leaving this pregnant chick to walk all the way back!"

Bexar smirked and took a few quick steps to catch up with Jessie, taking her hand in his and walking back toward the hangar like high school sweethearts.

"Do you have any idea when the due date is?"

"Yes, don't you remember the last time we had sex in Big Bend?"

Bexar looked at her blankly, the universal face of husbands around the world when they can't recall something important to their wife.

"It was on top of a damn mountain. Seriously? Early October should be our go time, sometime around the 28th."

The Radio Hut

Rifle fire grew in volume, both in rate of fire and loudness before a sudden silence reverberated through the heavy door. Three hard thumps shook the door followed by a man's voice.

"Anyone still alive in there?"

Before they could answer, the doorknob rattled.

"Yes, God yes, we're alive!"

"Great, unlock the door."

Bill unlocked the door, the other airmen stood back, weapons ready. The door swung open to the scene of bright weapon lights shining through the doorway, the shadowed shapes of rifle muzzles punctuating the blinding light.

"Safe your weapons. U.S. Marines, we're here to help you."

The command and statement was both comforting and jarring. The airmen lowered their weapons, the lights and rifle muzzles in the doorway moved, and a handful of men entered the radio room. Bill waved, the spark gap radio buzzing and cracking in the background.

"Thank you for coming. How did you get here? Who sent you? Are there more? Is our military back in action? What about the rest of the facility? Where is Jake?"

Aymond stepped forward. "Easy now, guy. We're here on President Lampton's orders. I don't know who Jake is and we're clearing the rest of the facility... what the fuck is that thing?" he asked as he pointed toward the device buzzing and cracking with radio transmissions.

Bill's eyes lit up. "Oh, a radio. That's a spark gap, historic radio technology. The frequency control is rough, noisy, and we can only transmit or receive CW but we're running on the HF bands, so when the propagation is good, we're coast to coast. We would be global but only the people who built one following the instructions we transmitted on the shortwave are able to send any transmissions."

Aymond looked over his shoulder and jerked his head toward Bill; another Marine stepped into the room. "Gonzo, what the shit is this guy yammering about?"

"It's a radio, Chief, like a stone age caveman radio. Works better than the shit we've got right now."

Bill stepped forward and offered his hand; Gonzo shook it. The airmen introduced themselves and handshakes were had all around—the usual service infighting was gone in the post-apocalyptic world, at least for the moment. After a few minutes of conversation, Bill elected to stay put in the radio shack and Aymond instructed Gonzo to stay with him to learn about the operation. The rest of the Marines peeled out of the room. Bill locked the door behind them before showing the spark gap radio to Gonzo, along with the chart to decipher the transmissions into letters. Bill sat down at the radio and waited for a short break in the transmissions. From the snippets, he was able to understand without writing down the transmissions the frequency was buzzing with speculation about the demise of Groom Lake.

Bill tapped at the radio key. "BREAK BREAK BREAK...GROOM LAKE SECURE... MARINES HERE...MORE TO FOLLOW SOON." After repeating the message twice more, Bill pushed his chair back away from the desk and turned to Gonzo. "Please tell me that there is a battalion of you all up there."

"You don't need a battalion, you have a handful of Marines. Now, we need to get to work. Tell me why the fucking SATCOM isn't working."

The Suburban

"This place is a ghost town." Jason nearly had to yell over the wind noise and noise from the engine.

"The whole fucking country is a ghost town!"

Jason wasn't joking and neither was Erin, except that Jason hadn't seen the cities and towns of America ruled by the dead as she had. Erin was surprised at the lack of reanimated corpses. They had seen a few dozen but she would have expected more. A dark stoplight hovered over the intersection; two wrecked cars sat in the middle of the road, crashed into each other. On opposing corners were two gas stations and to their right was, inexplicably, a bright white building built to look like a small castle.

Jason slowed to a stop. "How about a castle for my lovely Erin tonight?"

A rare smile snuck across her lips. "First, we gas in case we have to bugout."

Jason nodded but wasn't really sure what her plan was. Back in Cortez, they used a hand-cranked fuel transfer pump from the rancher's co-op. They seemed to be far away from any agricultural center here in the desert outside of Las Vegas.

"Pull into that one." Erin pointed at the gas station across the intersection on their right, and Jason drove into the parking lot and paused. Erin climbed out of the Suburban and walked to the side of the convenience store. Next to the building was a patch of now dead grass, what Erin assumed to be the only grass lawn in a 50-mile radius. As she had hoped, a water hose hung from a rack on the side of the building. A few minutes later and after some quick cuts with her knife, a four-foot section of hose was in her hands and she was ready to get to work. She motioned Jason to bring the Suburban close to a Honda parked in front of the dark store. After thumping on the windows a couple of times to make sure nothing would pop up from the floorboards and surprise her, Erin broke a window and unlocked the back door. She pulled up the rear seat and threw it on the ground before knocking the fuel pump assembly loose from the gas tank under the rear seat. The hose was inserted into the open tank; she took a couple of deep breaths before sucking on the hose. Spitting gas out of her mouth, she shoved the other end of the hose into the fuel filler of the still-running Suburban and watched the Honda's fuel tank, moving that end of the hose around trying to get every last drop of gas she could.

Once that tank was sucked dry, she asked for an update from Jason who answered, "Just over half a tank now."

"Fuck," Erin muttered under her breath.

Looking around, her next fuel siphoning victim to be chosen was a beat-up old Pontiac. She broke into the car and with considerable effort pulled the rear seat up only to find sheet metal. Erin walked around the car and didn't see any flaps for the fuel filler. Quickly becoming pissed off, she stood looking at the car. Jason called out of his open window, "Look behind the license plate on the trunk."

Erin looked at him and walked to the back of the car. After pulling on the license plate, she flipped it down and discovered the fuel filler cap.

"What the fuck?" Erin again muttered as she shoved the hose down the filler and into the tube. Jason brought the Suburban around and after spitting out more fuel, Erin put the hose in the SUV and let the fuel transfer.

"Nearly full."

"Nearly is good enough! Fuck this! I'm going inside to find a drink."

Erin turned and yanked open the door to the dark convenience store. After waiting for a moment, she banged on the door frame to be welcomed with the sound of a corpse crashing through the darkness. She backed away from the door, holding it open with a foot, and waited for the undead threat to come to her. A few moments later, a half-nude corpse of a middle-aged woman with comically large fake breasts shuffled through the doorway. Erin took a side step and shoved the corpse away from her. Jason fired a single blast from his shotgun and the woman's face disintegrated into a black pus-filled mist as the body fell to the ground. After opening the door again, Erin banged on the door frame and waited. No more reanimates could be heard, so the two of them walked slowly into the dark store. The shelves were mostly bare, picked clean by the people who had come before them. Large blank spots in the cooler were where beer was once stored cold and ready to be consumed, according to the advertisement clings on the glass doors. The smell inside was a mix of spoiled milk and rotting flesh. After weeks and weeks of living this nightmare out in the wilds of the American countryside, Erin was acclimated to the putrid smell. Jason pulled his shirt over his nose and tried not to dry heave as they walked through the store looking for something to drink.

A few two liters of warm cola was all that remained and Erin didn't care; old room-temperature cola left a better taste than gasoline. Erin took them off the shelf and handed them to Jason, asking him to put them in the Suburban for her. He took the armful of plastic bottles and walked outside. Erin rounded the aisle in the store and found what she was looking for. She wasn't sure what kind they would need so she grabbed a variety pack of condoms from the shelf, ripped open the box, and stuffed the foil-wrapped packaging into her back pocket before stepping back into the desert sun and Jason who waited next to the still-running Suburban.

"Let's get across the street and turn that damn engine off before we attract every undead corpse in the area."

They climbed inside the SUV, drove across the street, parked, and broke into the fake castle. The interior was empty of any persons living or undead and much to Jason's chagrin, the castle apparently used to be a strip club. Two stages with floor-to-ceiling poles were the centerpiece, along with a bar with liquor still on the shelves and VIP booths lining a wall.

In came some of their gear, a couple of MREs, and Erin brought in her big rifle, but much was left hidden in the Suburban parked around the back of the building. They needed the ability to bugout quickly if need be, but didn't want to leave all their gear in the SUV in case something happened to it.

The small round tables had tea candles in the centerpieces, so by candle-light they each ate an MRE for dinner, their first dinner alone together. Their first night truly alone together. Erin pulled a bottle of tequila off the shelf behind the bar and took a big drink before gagging and coughing then offering the bottle to Jason, who also took a long pull from the bottle. Late into the night, the two sat up passing the bottle back and forth, holding hands and telling stories about themselves, what sort of future they could have together if they lived long enough to have one. Erin's original plan for the night didn't work out as she had hoped, but she fell asleep in the arms of the man she loved more than she had ever loved anyone knowing, hoping that she would have many more nights with him before either of them were killed.

The Husky

The Grand Canyon looked as epic as ever. It had been 20 years since Amanda had visited, taking her then young children to the South Rim. As much as she tried not to, her lost family would flash in her mind, not knowing if they had survived or if their bodies were cursed to roam the countryside trapped in a ghostly life after death. The drone of the engine and the cool air that coursed through the narrow cabin made it hard to do much more than stare out of the windows at the peaceful-looking ground beneath them. The aircraft's radio didn't work and the intercom didn't work either. The pilot headsets protected their hearing but offered none of the usual communications ability. Having to shout over the sound of the engine, the wind noise, and to be heard through the hearing protection grew tiresome, so most of the journey was spent in silence, Andrew and Amanda each lost to their own thoughts.

Amanda knew, more so than many others, how perilous being on the ground was. The overland journey she took from Arkansas to Texas and then from Texas to Groom Lake was arduous to say the least. The first trip took much longer than anticipated, but was also immediately after the attack. As the dust had settled post-apocalypse, the Zeds became more dangerous and slightly more manageable, partly due to gaining the experience and instinct to avoid and fight the dead, but also because the dead had settled in a strange migratory pattern. Individual Zeds gravitated toward each other, possibly attracted by the movement and sound, Amanda believed. They were like a nebula of death at the center of the group and as they trudged along, they seemed to have a gravitational pull. More and more dead would congregate and follow the mindless pack, drifting across the landscape. The path of least resistance seemed to be the path of choice, which meant the interstates were plagued by huge swarms of dead passing through, destroying all that stood in their way. A positive effect of such a deadly swarm was that the roadways once clogged with the abandoned non-working vehicles as they sat after the EMP were now often clear of vehicles, obstacles, and debris, pushed aside by the mass of so much death pushing against them.

If we ever get on our feet again, if we can beat back the invasion, we will eventually rid the earth of the reanimated dead. The cleanup will take generations, but at least the roads will be clear to travel.

Amanda realized that Andrew was speaking to her, the voice behind her barging into her inner monologue.

"I'm sorry, I was distracted. What were you saying, Andrew?" Amanda yelled over the noise of the aircraft.

"Um, President Lampton, we're nearly out of daylight and we need to fuel, but we are near an airstrip that I used recently. There are friendly survivors nearby too."

"Please call me Amanda, and that sounds great. I trust you to make those choices for us."

"Awesome."

Andrew smiled, rolling the trim wheel to ease the Husky into a gentle descent. They were keeping to around 5,000 feet above ground level as they flew over the rugged terrain, high enough to fly efficiently but low enough to keep warmer and still be able to make out the details of the earth below them. They had flown over the Hoover Dam a few hours earlier. Amanda was excited to see the security lights illuminated, and she told Andrew that the dead didn't matter, just the fact that the hydroelectric dam was still producing power mattered. They had no idea if any survivors were inside the dam and keeping it running or if the systems were running automatically. Amanda hoped that there were survivors, not just for the hope of people, her fellow citizens surviving, but that there may be people trained and experienced in keeping the dam running. One of the biggest voids to fill in the coming months and years was that of knowledge and skill. The equipment at the SSC, especially the portable power generating stations, would help bring communities back into the modern world, if they could repair other damaged systems. She would need electricians, plumbers, and handymen, but she also needed skilled machinists, welders, engineers, black-smiths...the list continued ad nauseam. The modern world was woven in the fabric of highly specialized and skilled jobs; the concept of a master generalist, a renaissance man, was one lost on what civilization had evolved to become. But those persons, the men and women who had the skills to fight and survive and the skills to rebuild the country, had to exist. If not, she would need people to help her create those individuals from the survivors she had.

What she needed was a library of instructional material and the people to use the vast knowledge sitting stationary in the library stacks to create motion, a momentum of learning, but that wasn't a problem she would need to surmount today or tomorrow or maybe even next year. After the attack on Groom Lake, she reordered the priorities. The first threat was the invading Chinese and Korean forces; the second threat was ridding the nation of the dead.

As they descended closer to the ground, more details became visible. The wide-open expanses of New Mexico gave way to individual stories of survival and loss played out in every burned-out home, every car and truck abandoned on the roadway. Andrew pointed toward the right at smoke drifting lazily from some of the chimneys of the homes near the airfield. Andrew flew over the town before banking back toward the runways. After an uneventful landing, he taxied to where the fuel tank sat, shut down the engine, and opened the clamshell door. Amanda climbed out, rifle in hand, and scanned the area. Andrew climbed out of the plane and made use of the aircraft tie-downs before walking toward the hangar he and Oreo had slept in before.

Groom Lake

Jessie and Bexar arrived at the remains of the hangar in time to see Chivo appear from the underground facility. He was filthy and sweaty but wore the same smile he always wore as he slowly turned his head back and forth, scanning his surroundings. After he noticed Bexar and Jessie, Chivo waved them over, pointing toward the hulk of the shot-up MRAP.

By the time they joined Chivo, he was already tossing green metal cases of ammo out of the interior of Amanda's destroyed truck. "Hey, mano, lend a hand.

Start taking those to the Marines at the entrance. Mrs. Bexar, you want something to eat? I've got nothing but the finest MREs waiting for you."

"Thanks, Chivo, be back in a bit." Jessie grabbed the handles of two ammo cans and began walking with them, following Bexar toward the emerging Marines. After they dropped the ammo and the following return trips, the MRAP was now empty of any extra ammo. If they needed anymore, they would need to get it from one of the two supply rooms in the facility, the main warehouse on the fifth level, or the secret storage in the secondary facility.

Survivors trickled out of the entrance and gathered around Jessie; the other residents who helped clear the dorms stood to the side. Their faces showed exhaustion but resilience. They were tired but they weren't going to be beaten. They all looked to Jessie for direction. None of them had been necessarily informed of President Lampton's directive, but over the previous weeks, they had all grown to see Jessie as one of the leaders.

"I know that all of you followed the bite protocols while below ground, but we are going to have another round of bite inspections before moving to our temporary above-ground housing."

"Why does it have to be temporary?"

"Good question. I don't know that it does, we're just too early in the recovery from the attack and outbreak to know exactly what our future holds here in Groom Lake. Also, as you can see, our partitions have been destroyed. I'm sorry for the lack of modesty but we're going to have to take care of business out in the open. The sooner we get that done, the sooner everyone can pass out MREs and get in the dorms."

The original work party took charge of the bite inspections, the other survivors queuing up for their turn to strip and show a bite-free body. Unlike a few hours before, there were no mercy killings for someone who had been bit; all of the survivors were bite free. As the first group finished, they were handed one MRE each from the few cases that Amanda had left in the MRAP and were led across the tarmac on foot toward the dorms. More survivors made their way out of the underground facility while the sun drooped low on the western sky. By nightfall, the Marines, Chivo, and a handful of the survivors who volunteered to help along the way had resurfaced, confident that the facility was now devoid of living Zeds. A final sweep of the facility would be completed in the morning, but for now, the exhausted warriors were standing down for the night.

Some of the survivors wanted to stay below ground, but Jessie wanted everyone out. That would prevent a Zed that had been missed in the sweep to start up another outbreak. The only persons allowed to stay below ground were Bill and his handful of radio operators. Bill looked like hell, ragged and worn, but he was optimistic.

"The radio chatter is incredible. Numerous survivors asking if we needed more help, offering to make the journey across the country to assist. This facility is a beacon of hope to many." Bill sat on the dusty concrete floor, noisily eating an MRE. "And the president wants us to shut it down?"

"That's not the feeling I got. I think it's more of a 'we should consolidate facilities because this one has been compromised.'"

"Compromised? Hell, the Texas facility hasn't even been tested yet. We're survivors here, like a god-dammed Fort Apache, and we won't be beat."

Milan, NM

Amanda relaxed on the worn couch in the hangar before jumping to her feet at the sound of knocking at the side door. Andrew stood aside the door as a voice called out, "Andrew?"

Andrew smiled and answered. It was Jay whom he had met before. Once the door was opened, introductions were made and Jay was excited to meet the president. "We moved the radio into the FBO; did you get to Groom Lake? Did you know they were attacked?"

Amanda answered slightly, "He did, we both did, and were there for the attack."

"Amazing. Then you know they're safe now. People from all around the country were saddling up to be the cavalry, to go help. We spent most of today getting an old school bus running and were going to head out tomorrow but Bill gave the all clear."

Amanda was shocked, surprised, and excited. "What people? Where are they and how many are there?"

Jay motioned outside. "Come to the FBO. We have a map up that we've been using to keep track of things. People have taken to giving themselves call signs; we've made a list of them to go with the map too."

Amanda stepped outside. The sky glowed dark red with the setting sun, the mountains looked beautiful, and she hadn't been this excited about their chances of actually surviving as a country since she had been sworn in as president. After the short walk, they stepped into the FBO, the main office of the small airstrip. The candle-lit interior buzzed and crackled with the radio. She could smell the ionization of the air from the electrical sparking of the radio's reception. Occasionally, someone transmitted a message quickly, a person who had obviously been an amateur radio operator or an old military man with experience in Morse code. The rest of the time the transmissions were painfully slow with a lot of shorthand being used to shorten the length and complexity of the messages.

Jay pointed out the map and Amanda was amazed to see all the push pins that spanned the country; there were even some pins in Canada and Mexico.

"Have you heard from anyone outside of North America?"

"Not yet, but if they don't have a radio like this, I'm not sure how they would know to talk to us."

"There are even some regional communities setup that have some trade days and mutual assistance programs worked out."

This was all more than Amanda could have imagined. Clint had kept her in the dark for so long that she had no idea that so many people were doing more than just barely surviving.

"What are the details being talked about the attack on Groom Lake?"

"Not much except that Chinese forces had attacked, there was an outbreak, and now some Marines had taken back the facility. Like I said, some folks were discussing getting to Groom Lake to help, others were questioning the reasoning behind being locked into an underground building with no escape. The rest are trying to organize some sort of resistance for the invading Chinese forces."

"Really? Any other military units besides the Marines at Groom Lake so far? What are they saying that they are doing to prepare?"

"A bunch of vets have put out a call-to-arms, some are trying to rally people in their region to band together as a single community, a couple of guys who I guess are Vietnam Vets started naming their compounds Fire Bases."

"That's absolutely incredible; would you be able to transmit an official message for me?"

Jay glanced at Andrew and back at Amanda with a smile. "I would be honored."

CHAPTER 5

Jason blinked, blurry-eyed. He peered into the darkness and tried to remember where he was. Erin lay on the floor with him, curled up against him with her head on his arm, still asleep. His head hurt and it took a moment to remember the previous night. The two of them sat up sharing a mixture of a bottle of tequila and each other's deepest secrets, fears, and thoughts. The emotional intimacy was wonderful, the growing hangover not so much. Jason gently slid his arm free and stood slowly. The room felt uneasy but he was able to steady himself against a table. The abandoned strip club was dark and Jason had no idea what time of day it was, if the sun was up, or if it was even morning yet. That's the thing with strip clubs: very few seemed to have any windows. After stumbling to the restroom, Jason turned away in disgust, not sure why he had tried to go to the actual non-working restroom in the first place. This was their first night away from Groom Lake in a long time; he had become used to life's simple pleasures like running water and working toilets.

Peeing in a trashcan behind the bar seemed like the reasonable solution, not wanting to try opening the door to the outside for fear of sparking off a situation with the undead. He and Erin would need to do that together, ready to run for it, fight or hide as the situation may dictate.

Erin stirred in the shadows and whispered, "Jason?"

"Over here."

"Shit, I drank too much last night." Erin stood uneasily, wiping her hands on her pants. Trying to recall memories lost to a night in the bottle, Erin stuck her hand in her back pocket and found the condoms she took from the gas station. Slowly, her mind began piecing together the previous night.

"Did I say too much last night?"

Jason shook his head, which made his headache worse. "No, it was a special night together. We...I love you."

Crockett, Texas

Ken put the pencil down and read the transcribed radio message again. Candle-light flickered shadows into the darkness of the room, his shelter more like an overgrown shed than a house. Long before the tiny house movement gripped aimless hipsters, Ken and his friends called such homes what they were to them: hunting cabins. Against the far wall were bunk beds but he was the only one of his group that had arrived at the lodge near Crockett, Texas.

Four weeks after everything went to hell, he arrived in camp and was surprised to find it empty. The following weeks were spent in anticipation of his lifelong friends and hunting buddies arrival, but they never came. He no longer held out any hope for their safe arrival, assuming that they had succumbed to the dead like much of the country had.

This winter was a tough one, unsure if the weather was due to El Nino or La Nina and he frankly didn't care; what he knew was that it was cold, damn cold, and now that spring in central Texas had arrived, it was now soaking wet and getting hot. Central Texas had four seasons, like much of the world, except that the seasons consisted of winter, wet summer, drought, wet summer, and then back to winter again. There seemed to be two or three days a year of great weather. Today hadn't been one of them.

Most days were spent laboring to make or fix what he needed, hunting or trying to preserve the game he caught or killed, but Ken often ran out of daylight. Luckily, the days were getting longer. He still had time to have completely reread the heavily worn copy of Lonesome Dove that lived in the cabin and another thick book on the Lewis and Clark expedition. Lonesome Dove was a longtime favorite of his, although it had been a few years since he had read it last. The book on Lewis and Clark was one he hadn't read before and he hadn't realized how important the Native Americans had been to not just the success of the expedition but to keeping the explorers and their crew alive over the winter.

The only natives that Ken had found so far in Central Texas were reanimated dead. The Zeds weren't exactly like the helpful tribes that Merriweather Lewis had encountered in Northwest.

Alone, his friends' prepper caches had remained untouched, surviving out of what he had stored in their hunting camp and what he trapped, caught, or killed. A conscientious hunter, Ken wasn't one to waste much of the game he took, but the past few months he had conserved like never before. Antlers were kept not as trophies but for their usefulness as material for buttons, knife handles, and many other things, including trading if he ever had the chance and if there were any persons left alive to trade with.

The hand-cranked shortwave radio was a boon to his optimism, a voice; a real human voice appeared weeks ago, claiming to be in Area 51. He didn't really believe the transmission at first, but the following instructions on constructing a primitive radio gave Ken a new outlook for the world and his country. Slowly at first, people began transmitting messages back and forth, as the days wore on more and more people clogged the airwaves. It seemed that people were passing the instructions along to others who hadn't placed a survival radio in an ammo can for protection. Now Ken wished he could go back in time and put all sorts of electronics in metal protective containers and bury them. The camp generator didn't work and his attempts to repair it had failed—the walkie-talkies didn't work; nothing electronic worked except for the survival radio. At least he had that.

One of the camp's ATVs was sacrificed to construct the primitive radio he now stared at after reading the decoded message, again. Ken's mind spun with the possibilities. He wasn't sure what the outcome would be but he knew that the beat-up old diesel hunting camp truck that his buddy had purchased at a military surplus auction would be his exit. First, though, he had to dig up the other cached supplies and make a plan and he wouldn't do that until daylight. The dead seemed to be migrating and too many had spilled off the highway and too near the camp for Ken to feel confident moving during the dead of night.

CHAPTER 6

Heavy diesel trucks rumbled by outside, the low faint noise permeating the cinderblock walls as they passed. Erin and Jason were awake, hungover, but wide awake with rifles in hand. Erin slowly pushed the metal front door open just far enough for a faint sliver of the morning sunlight to pierce the darkness inside. Keeping her face back from the narrow opening and trying to stay in the shadow of the interior, she watched a narrow field of view of the intersection outside. The low rumbling of the trucks could be heard and it sounded like they were moving, but she couldn't see what or who was responsible for it all.

Suddenly, an armored truck rolled past noisily, the big tires kicking more dust into the already dirt-filled air.

"The fucking Chinese," Erin whispered over her shoulder to Jason, who stood at the ready. "What about our truck? Should we do something?"

"What can we do? It is hidden around back and looks like utter hell. Maybe they won't notice or if they do, they'll think it is long abandoned like every damn other thing in this world."

Erin knew Jason had a point. Even if they went out the back door and drove off, they would be up against APCs in their beat-up old Suburban. They wouldn't stand a chance. No, their best bet was to hide and hope their ride, as well as the meager supplies they had left in it, were still there once the enemy forces had passed by.

Transfixed, they watched and waited. Just in the time that they were watching, four APCs rolled by, commanders sitting high in an open hatch on the roof of each. It all looked like archival war film footage, quite surreal to them both. Besides the attack on Groom Lake that killed her mother and then the angst-riddled lashing out at the cargo aircraft unloading the same kind of APCs, neither Erin nor Jason had any experience fighting a *real* battle. Jason had fought the cult, but as heavily armed and motivated as those crazy people were, they weren't trained war-fighters like they assumed the PLA to be. It felt like hours and hours but in reality, it was probably closer to about 15 minutes for the convoy to roll by. After the sound of the last truck rumbled in the distance, Erin let the door shut and put a broomstick through the door handles if for no other reason than to feel slightly safer.

"Should we go or wait?"

Jason frowned in the darkness. "We should wait. We know they didn't stop here, there wasn't anything that caught their attention, but if we go, then we might run into them."

"What if it is the same group from yesterday? What if they come back through and recognize the Suburban? They'll level this fucking building with us in it, I think we should—"

Erin was cut off by the heavy sound of the walls being hit. The dead's haunting moans resonated in the walls. The sound of the dead hitting the wall sounded like thick bugs hitting a windshield, except that the frequency grew until the din of following dead was a constant roar. The heavy cinderblock walls shook with the onslaught. The bottles behind the bar shook, bar glasses rattled, it sounded like the whole damn place was going to fall in. It felt like an earthquake.

Jason and Erin would have had to yell at each other to be heard over the noise, but they were too scared to do more than sit holding each other in the middle of the main room, away from the walls, away from the metal doors of the front entrance, hiding and hoping that the Zeds would pass them by. The PLA force induced fear just from what they experienced during the attack on Groom Lake, but the fear of the dead came from deep in their bones. After months of dodging the dead, months of losing friends and loved ones, being surrounded by a massive swarm of Zeds was worst sort of nightmare fuel. Tears streaked down Erin's cheeks in the darkness. She knew her mother would never be doomed to be a mindless drone following a swarm. Erin had made sure of that herself.

Jason and Erin held each other in silence, waiting and hoping the Zeds would pass quickly.

New Ulm, Montana

"We need to go topside and do a fence check," Dorsey called over his shoulder, looking at the calendar hanging on the wall. Steve had made many pencil notations at intervals for each of the tasks that he had determined to be important. The CCTV security system allowed anyone below ground to see the barbed wire-topped fence surrounding the missile launch facility, but after he had to repair a fence that was rattled loose by a passing band of the dead, Steven made it a point to conduct weekly fence walks to physically inspect his first line of defense.

Clint looked up from the binder holding the launch system modification plans. "Mr. Dorsey, isn't that something you can complete on your own?"

"Colonel Smith, I could, but it would be safer to do with the both of us and we would complete the task in half the time...then we could get back to work down here. It would speed up your mission objectives for the day."

Dorsey watched Colonel Smith. He didn't need help checking the fences, but the task needed to be done and he did not trust Smith alone below ground; he could be locked out for good. Besides not trusting the colonel on a personal level, he didn't trust that the stated mission was real. Dorsey had one way to try to verify that the colonel was working under presidential order, but he didn't know how he would get a chance to use the radio or even if the guys in Groom Lake could get a response back to him in time to matter. The longer Smith was with him, the more he regretted letting the colonel into the facility, but now he was either stuck with him or would have to get him out somehow.

Slowly, a plan for each began to form, but Steve wasn't exactly sure which one would have to happen. He had to get a message out, but first they needed to check the perimeter fence.

Groom Lake, NV

Bexar stood just outside the tent, the air swirling with dirt, but he was on the downwind side of the tent trying to take a leak. The morning was crisp, not too cold, with the sun climbing out from behind the mountains. He knew the day would quickly warm up. They were quickly hurtling toward summer and its oppressive heat, but only if they could live that long.

He heard the rustling of the tent flap and Jessie appeared beside him. Bexar smiled at the growing baby bump, which had progressed past a bump. If it wasn't for the rifle and spare magazines, he could almost imagine they were camping in the high desert for a fun weekend. A fun weekend this life was not, and Bexar wasn't sure if he would get to experience a fun or even a lazy weekend ever again. As much as he hated yard work, he had a longing to work in his yard back in Texas, drink a beer, and spend a weekend chipping away at his honey-do list. Bexar shook his head; his honey-do list was simplified: keep Jessie and their unborn child safe. Yes, simple in list, but exceptionally difficult in execution.

"What are you scowling about, baby?"

Bexar realized he had been staring at Jessie. "Oh nothing, sorry. I'm trying to come up with a plan for us, for our baby."

"A plan like what?"

"I don't know, I'm not sure, I'm just, well, I don't know if this is the right place for us to stay."

"What would be better?"

"I'm thinking we should go to Utah and back to where I was. Guillermo's group. This is the second time you've had to unfuck this place and who do we have left here?"

Jessie thought about Sarah, but she always thought about Sarah. In their short time together, Jessie had felt closer to Sarah than she had ever felt with another woman. Sarah had felt like a sister, even closer than a real sister, and her death left a hole in Jessie's heart that wouldn't soon heal. The thought of Erin out on her own, without her mother even if she was with Jason, they were so young and the world was such a ruined place. Tears streamed down Jessie's face.

Bexar held his wife close. "I'm sorry. We've lost so much, so many people, I can't lose you again."

"I can't lose you again either. Whatever we choose, whatever we have to do, we have a little bit of time before we have to make a decision. If we leave—before we leave—I can't walk away from these people to let them dangle in the wind.

We have to at least get everyone safe and the facility secure before we make any decisions. I...we can't leave these folks to figure this out on their own."

"OK, baby, then that's what we'll do." Bexar wiped the tears from his wife's cheeks.

Crockett, Texas

Ken pulled the curtain back and peered out the dirty window. The trees moved from the wind, a hog was rutting around an old feeder, but there was no sign of the dead. With a sigh of relief, Ken slowly opened the door to the pre-dawn morning, scanned the area for any threat of the dead, and walked outside to relieve himself. The morning's task was a hard one, one of the admission that his friends were most likely dead, but it would be foolhardy to leave unknown supplies buried in their cache sites and set off on such a daunting task as traveling all the way to Nevada. Technology was a grand thing; a quick voice command to his phone and he would have turn by turn directions, GPS updates, overhead satellite photos of the area...everything he would ever need to travel the relatively short distance to Nevada, but that was before the end. Before the end of society, before the end of the living being the alpha-hunters on the planet. No, the earth was ruled by the dead and technology had failed. He was in a quasi-stone age, like some sort of bad made-for-TV movie. The only things missing were the outlandish costumes with football pads, leather, and spikes.

From the front door of the deer lease cabin, Ken counted off the paces. The whole group had been careful to conceal their individual caches, but each of them knew where the other buried caches were just for such an occasion.

Forty-one, forty-two...here.

The dirt looked slightly disturbed, like a place where vehicles turned around, but nothing like a secret location with important supplies. Ken looked around again, his rifle slung over his back, shovel in his hands, and he began digging. After some time, with sweat falling from Ken's brow, the shovel made the distinct sound of hitting wood, and Ken dug out around his hole. A half-sheet of inch-thick plywood protected the sealed aluminum cases. Once the protective cover was dug out and lifted free from the hole, Ken was able to drag the heavy cases topside and open them. The rubber weather seal had held well and the three Zarges aluminum storage cases had survived quite well. Resisting the urge to dig through each of the cases out in the open, Ken dragged them back into the hunting cabin before restarting the pace, counting to the next cache site and next group of heavy-duty aluminum cases.

The sun was nearing sunset by the time all the cases were dug up and in the cabin. Eight fingers from the horizon, Ken knew there were only about two hours of light left. The days were growing longer but they were still too short for all he had to get done before beginning his journey. Nine sealed Zarges cases now sat in the cabin. Ken left the holes exposed, the need for secrecy long expired. Now was the time for efficiency and expediency. One by one, the cases were opened, emptied, and organized by type of gear and use. Some of the gear was of no use to Ken, clothing that was too small for example. Some was cut into rags, the rest left in a heap in the corner. As strong as the urge was to leave nothing that could be of some use, Ken had to fit a lot of gear to travel a lot of miles and things like clothing cut into rags simply wouldn't be that beneficial. Other clothing like the 100 percent cotton underwear were cut up and set aside to turn into char cloth. One simply couldn't have enough char cloth to start fires with; he would set a fire before he went to bed to begin the process of making char.

Other things were incredibly useful, like the freeze-dried backpacking food. He could cold soak the food for the day to create a meal or warm water and prepare a meal in under an hour; regardless, the food was calorie dense and actually tasted pretty good, never mind that it was relatively lightweight, portable, and had a shelf life measured in epochs.

There were really no surprises except for a GPS unit that may or may not work. He would have to attempt to charge it with the truck on the drive. The rest of the caches comprised mostly of first-aid supplies, food, and ammo. Lots of ammo. After the end of the world and for the time being, he felt like a rich man due to how much ammo he had available. More than enough ammo to feed his group-standard 45-ACP pistol and his M1. At least when it came to protection and hunting, he was well set to make his cross-country journey.

Still, Ken felt uneasy, muttering to himself as he organized the gear he wanted to take back into the strong aluminum boxes. He wondered how badly he would be overloading the old deer lease truck and decided it didn't matter. Once he made it to Groom Lake, he should be set and the truck could rust into dust in the desert for all he cared. The problem was that the truck would have to make the journey or he would be in a bad spot.

Approaching Ennis, Texas

Amanda watched long shadows play across the landscape from a few thousand feet above the ground. After meeting Jay and becoming entranced with all the message traffic between different survivors and groups, she asked Andrew to stay an extra day so she could take it all in. Her official message took a little time to transmit, but once it had, the airwaves were a mess with different stations trying to transmit on top of each other. It was a radio pile-up of epic proportions and they could do nothing but wait. Long into the night, they all sat by the radio, answering questions and giving advice. Survivors, her fellow citizens, were ready to fight the living invaders just as they had been fighting the dead ones. Eventually, she excused herself to sleep on the sofa in the FBO, exhausted from her travels, the battle, the flying, and the enormous weight of the task ahead of her. Amanda just wasn't able to stay awake any longer.

That morning she felt hungover, even though she hadn't had a drink in some time. After reaching the smoother cool air of Andrew's chosen cruising altitude, she first tried to sleep, but the tight tandem seating and dual controls made that a challenge. Amanda gave up and took to writing down some notes and using the time to attempt figuring out what the next step would be.

The answer would be simple if she had some sort of military branch still functioning in some manner—to her untrained mind, even a single naval destroyer would be a game changer—but she also had no idea what capabilities that the mixed Chinese and Korean forces had. Checking off the things she knew to be true from the report that Aymond's men had given her, she knew that the PLA still had aircraft—at least cargo aircraft—personnel and ships—at least commercial ships—at their disposal. Strangely, they didn't appear to have any appreciable military strike aircraft or naval vessels. It would make no sense to leave cargo ships anchored waiting to off-load at a port without a significant naval presence to protect them.

They must not have them. Or those forces are engaged somewhere else... with reports being transmitted from the far-flung reaches of the United States, no one has reported anything of the sort. So the Chinese Navy was either disabled, trying to stay hidden for some unknown reason, or engaged in other conflicts elsewhere.

Amanda sat up straight at the thought and tapped on Andrew's shoulder before yelling over the engine noise. "Have you heard of anyone making contact with people in other countries or places like Europe?"

Andrew shook his head. "No, and I don't think Jay and them had either otherwise they would have pinned that on their map."

"Thanks." Amanda sat back against her seat and stared out the window as the airplane banked lazily. It took her a moment to realize that Andrew was circling overhead the above-ground park where her base was located, the HESCO containers and fortifications plainly visible, as Clint had said they would be. The sound of the motor changed, Andrew began his descent into the park, and Amanda thought he would land on the road between the farmer's fields leading up to the main entrance. She could do nothing but sit and hope that her pilot knew what he was doing.

The big tires bumped on the grassy surface before the engine spun up loudly and the Husky leapt back into the sky. Andrew yelled over the noise, "Sorry, we were out of position. I'm going to have another go at it."

The plane banked around the park before Andrew tried landing again, this time rolling to a short stop before cutting the motor off and opening the clamshell door. Andrew climbed out first, pistol in hand, before helping Amanda climb out. They scanned the area, but nothing moved. The wind seemed to have paused at the disruption, the world holding its breath for a moment. A single corpse broke through the tree line to the west, only a few dozen yards away. Amanda turned raised her rifle and fired a single shot, the corpse's head snapping back before it crumpled to the ground.

"Come on, let's get underground. We have to be ready to kill the closest thing I've ever met to an honest-to-god ninja when we get down there."

"First, we need to secure my plane. If we hope to use it again later, hold guard and I'll take care of it."

Amanda agreed and took a few steps out from under the shadow of the wing. Andrew dug around in the small luggage compartment before pulling a small canvas bag out, which had three corkscrew-looking metal stakes and three pieces of rope. After screwing each into the dirt, Andrew tied the aircraft down and put chocks under the main tires. He pulled the key from the dash. "Not having the key won't slow someone down much, but it makes me feel better."

Amanda's plan for Clint was to walk into the facility like nothing had happened, as if she hadn't left unannounced and disappeared a week prior. The first chance she had, Amanda knew she had to shoot first, fast and true, and kill him. If she didn't, there was no doubt that Clint would kill both she and Andrew without blinking. She knew that her plan was complete bullshit, but she really hoped it would work. It was all she had at the moment, so it had to work.

Pahrump, NV

Jason slowly pushed the door open, a growing sliver of light piercing the darkness sharply, painful to view. Slowly, his eyes adjusted and he could see past the blinding daylight. The awning over the gas pumps across the street was knocked over. Numerous bodies appeared to be trapped under it, and some were still moving. Even though their bodies were crushed, their skulls were intact and they were trapped under the awning. The enormous hoard had knocked it over like a toy. The convenience store appeared to be mostly intact and besides the reanimated dead under the awning, Jason could only find a half dozen or so moving in the street. It appeared the hoard had thankfully moved on. The direction the debris was pushed would mean that the hoard was following the PLA and that he and Erin could run into the back of them if they followed their previous path.

Before they could go anywhere, he had to check on their old Suburban parked around the back of their castle-shaped strip club. The sun was getting near the western horizon and Jason knew that any further travel or adventure would have to wait until morning. This night they would abstain from alcohol. He still felt lousy, but even sober it was impossible to tell time in the blacked-out, windowless building. Jason slowly closed the door, securing it shut for the night.

"What did you see?" Erin had been in the shadows with her M4 at the ready, but not able to see much of the outside.

"Well, the horde is gone, but they knocked over the gas pump cover. There are some trapped and moving. There are a few more in the streets but nothing like before."

"Then let's get moving."

"The sun is going down; there's only about an hour of daylight left. I think we should wait until the morning. Besides, I couldn't see the Suburban, we still have to check on that."

"Fine, I'll go out the back and check on our ride, but we leave at first light."

"How do we even know when first light is? There are no windows, no clocks that still work. I tried calling the front desk for a wakeup call but no one answered."

Erin flipped Jason off. "Drink two big cups of water before you go to bed. When you get up to piss, it'll be just before sunrise. That's how Native Americans did it to wake up before a battle."

Jason pointed his hands in the darkness. "What water? All of those bottles are alcohol; my stomach turned just thinking of the word."

"Go get some out of the truck."

"No, I don't want to waste that water on an alarm clock. We need to save that."

"Then go to the fucking store!"

"Fine, I'll go to the fucking store!"

"No, I didn't mean that, don't go."

Jason stood at the door he had just secured. A few moments later, he opened the door and stepped out into the sunlight. Squinting, he scanned for any immediate threats, turned right, and began walking toward the convenience store with the collapsed awning. Giving the wriggling mass of still moving undead trying to free themselves from under the awning, Jason made his way to what was the glass front of the store. In the shadows of the interior, he could see some movement and that some of the shelves were still standing. Shelves being upright were a good sign; that meant that the horde hadn't destroyed the entire store as they passed. The movement was obviously bad, as the only things still moving in this town besides he and Erin were already dead.

After banging the stock of his shotgun loudly against the ruin door framed, the movement in the shadows shifted. Jason could see the dead coming out toward him. Jason waved his armed and began walking quickly toward the near corner of the building. After waiting to make sure that the dead followed his direction, Jason turned the corner and headed toward the open field behind the store. The path ahead was clear, although there were a few new straggling dead joining the reined in shoppers. Jason turned and walked behind the store, certain that he was being followed. After a few quick steps, Jason trotted around the side of the building and toward the front from the other side.

Jason jogged around the corner and he bumped into the back of a walking corpse. Surprised and off balance, Jason fell backward as the undead turned trying to grasp him. The disfigured skull exploded in a dark gooey mist. Jason looked toward the castle to see Erin standing in the back by the Suburban, her rifle up and aimed at him. He smiled, got on his feet, and slid into the darkened store interior.

Quickly, Jason swept the front of the store for any lingering dead. Happy to find no threats, Jason grabbed a couple of plastic shopping bags from behind the counter and gathered up a few bottles of water. He also found some cans of Vienna sausages and a jar of ranch chip dip. The bags of chips looked worse for the wear and he didn't want to spend too much time digging around for better choices. The sound of Erin's M4 firing snapped his attention toward the outside. His previous group of trailing zombies had made the lap, and the parking lot was getting dangerously crowded. Erin was thinning the herd, but he needed to move quickly. Jason didn't want to catch a round meant for a corpse, so he eased out of the safety of the shadows. He could see Erin standing and firing her M4. Jason waved; Erin gave a thumbs up. He took a few big steps out of the store before turning and jogging back toward Erin. He made a rounded course to give Erin a better angle of fire for anything that followed, but her rifle stayed silent.

Jason jogged past Erin, opened the door, and waited for her to join him. Once the door was shut and secured, he took a deep breath.

"I'm sorry, Erin. That was stupid of me because of a stupid fight over nothing."

Erin gave him a kiss on the cheek. "Just don't do that again. I don't want to lose you."

"Did you check our ride while you were out there?"

"Yeah, it's beat to hell."

"It was beat to hell before, so what?"

"So I think it's fine. It hadn't moved so I don't think the dead or the PLA gave it much attention."

Jason smiled. "Would you like some Vienna sausages and chip dip for dinner?"

"Sounds awesome."

They sat quietly in the darkness and ate their dinner, Jason waiting to drink the water until right before he lay down for the night. The stillness was interrupted only by the occasional muffled bump of one of the meandering Zeds hitting the side of the building.

Groom Lake, NV

Jessie stood near the tent. Small fires below cast orange light across the open expanse of the runways, people's long shadows dancing across the ground. Most of the work for the day had been completed, so only the security watches would stay up for the night. The top-side dorms were now clear of the dead; all the survivors that had been found so far were staying top-side. They seemed surprisingly happy about being exposed on the surface, even though they didn't have a choice. No one was allowed to stay underground until all the levels had been fully swept and cleared of the dead, except for Bill and one other radioman demanding to be locked in the radio hut and left. Jessie let them; she believed that keeping in touch with outside survivors was paramount.

Against what she thought to be safe, the other survivors wanted to have a party of a campout. So like a driftwood beach fire, what little could be found and would burn had been rounded up for sunset. It was good that there wasn't any alcohol or an evening like this could go wrong for everyone, but she trusted that the "liberty rules" as one man had called them, would be heeded. For her piece of mind and much to Bexar's relief, they were in the canvas wall tent on the top of the hill by the tanks. It was unlikely that a Zed would come over the top of the mountain behind them, not that they had recorded many sightings as of late anyways. Before the attack, things had become mostly quiet and routine, insulated from the hard reality of being out in the wilds.

"Come on, babe, let's lay down. We have another long day ahead of us. Trust that the security patrols will do their job. Besides, Chivo is down there somewhere."

Jessie nodded, walking back to the tent, frowning.

"We can't stay."

"Well, we can't leave tonight, but we can go at first light."

"No, not tonight, Bexar. We should get these people through this, but we should leave after that. This is dangerous."

"So is being on our own. Where do we go?"

"I don't know, I'm just sure that staying here is a bad idea. We need to get somewhere safe, somewhere that isn't on the fucking Chinese hit list, and somewhere we can have this baby."

"Then we go to Utah."

"OK."

After taking care of the necessaries before bed, they closed the tent flap behind them to sparse accommodations. They didn't have their nice cots or much of their original gear—most of that had been lost or destroyed by the time they left Big Bend—but they still had one of the canvas wall tents and that was a good start. With a little work, they could live in the tent just about anywhere in the U.S. for months or even years. As close as Guillermo and Angel's compound in Utah was, Bexar was confident that they wouldn't need the tent for long. He just needed to help speed along the recovery process for the Groom Lake survivors so they could leave soon.

New Ulm, Montana

Dorsey walked along the tall chain-link fence, barbed wire strands running the length of the fence along the top. He wasn't too concerned with the barbed wire—the reanimated dead didn't try to climb fences—but they could push against one with enough force to cause it to collapse. Worse still would be any holes or failures in the fence line. He glanced up at the wire draped over the communications tower; it appeared to be unchanged since the last topside inspection. The day he climbed the tower to place the new loop antenna seemed like a lifetime ago even though it was quite recent.

There isn't a way to send a coded message. I can't sit and wait for a reply or even wait to hope that Groom Lake could get a message to President Lampton.... I have to trust the others to relay any messages so I can use the radio in secret.

Dorsey stepped back into the topside building, stamping the cold and snow from his feet as he walked through the entryway. He glanced at the entry to the bunker below. It appeared secure, but the problem could be the cameras; he could be observed from the colonel's position below ground. With a slight smirk, he remembered an old TV show where they used Polaroid photos on a bracket in front of a camera to fool anyone watching. It might work, but even if he wanted to try, he didn't have a camera or film. No, this was going to be difficult, but he had to figure out how to make it happen. Until a plan was formed, all he could do was stall Smith's efforts. Hindsight being what it is, Dorsey wished that he hadn't let Smith into the facility, but wishing for the past didn't make the future.

CHAPTER 7

The two convenience stores across the intersection from the gentleman's club castle were their first stops. This time, instead of Jason going alone and in anger, Erin held his hand as they crossed the deserted roadway, her short M4 rifle hung across her chest on the sling, and her left hand held the foregrip. Erin might be in love and her morning may have started happily with her head on Jason's chest as they woke up, but her eyes scanned the dark interior of the store ahead of them with laser focus. Some reanimated dead continued to writhe under the collapsed awning, but just as the day before, neither of them cared. Dead or alive, trapped is trapped and trapped isn't a threat. Their scavenging goals for the morning were dead simple: water, fuel, and food.

Now in the parking lot and alongside the exterior of the convenience store, Jason picked up a rock and threw through the shattered glass front with a loud crash into the shelves behind the counter. Jason stood with his shotgun ready, watching the dark shadows move inside the store, Erin standing about an arm's length away facing the opposite direction, her rifle ready for any threats from the outside.

"Looks like the first contestant is arriving," Jason said, smirking. The hard thump of his short-barrel 12-gauge tore open the still morning followed by the rhythmic crack-crack of the pump-action being worked, another round jacked into the breach. What was left of the reanimated dead's diseased body fell to the sidewalk with a wet thump. Jason took a loose shell out of his pocket and held it in his left hand with the pump of the shotgun, his eyes scanning for any more dead to come out of the store. Erin fired a half dozen rounds in a rapid but metered pace. Her breathing never increased, her face remained passive, the only part of her moving with any speed was her eyes, scanning for more threats as she smoothly drove the M4's barrel from corpse to corpse, center punching each forehead she found in the upright position.

After a moment of waiting, their ears ringing slightly, Jason turned his head toward Erin. "I think we're clear to go in." The loose shell in his hand was pushed into the magazine tube under the breech, topping off the shotgun with a full complement of 00-buckshot before he slowly stepped into the darkened interior.

Glass crunching beneath their feet, Erin stopped at the edge of the entrance, using the ICE freezer by the door as a reference and a place for cover. Her job was to protect Jason while he gathered everything on their shopping list. If he called for help, she would go inside, but her place wasn't that of the doting girlfriend: Erin's place was that of an alpha-warrior, a position she wasn't completely comfortable in yet.

Jason focused on his task. A hand truck was found in the storeroom, but the pneumatic tires were flat. Frowning at the flat tires, Jason stepped back into the front of the store and returned a moment later with a can of Fix-A-Flat from the store shelves. After making a huge mess, the small tires were pressurized and Jason began stacking some cases of Gatorade and water on the hand truck. He assumed those few cases were left in place because they were in the back and not on the shelves out front. Regardless, Jason didn't care and was happy to have them. The meager findings of canned food, soup, and beef jerky joined the stack on the hand truck, as did the remaining two cans of Fix-A-Flat, two jugs of antifreeze, and four quarts of oil. A five-gallon gas can was also found and added to the stack.

The rifle fire outside the store increased in tempo. "You doing OK out there, baby?"

After a few more rounds were fired, he heard Erin call back that she was fine. She didn't tell him to hurry up, although it was implied. Broken glass crunched beneath the tires of the loaded hand truck as Jason wheeled it to the parking lot.

"Holy shit, Erin!"

Whatever Zeds that had remained after the Chinese rolled through town had decided to all come welcome their newest members to be converted. The problem was that neither Erin nor Jason was ready to join their ranks. Erin calmly took shot after shot, missing very few of their intended targets, but calm wasn't something Jason could be when confronted with what appeared to be a few hundred approaching dead.

"Yeah, honey, we should probably skip the other store and haul ass."

Jason didn't even reply, already pushing his scavenging haul toward the Suburban as quickly as he could without upsetting the load. The beat-up Suburban started with a cloud of dark smoke that didn't bode well for the mechanical condition of the old SUV, but that was the only wheels that Erin and Jason had for the moment so it would have to do. Erin stood by the open driver's door while Jason threw everything they had and the newly acquired hand truck into the back, piled on the ammo cases and MREs. The empty gas container would need to be filled later.

"Erin, I'm loaded, it's time to haul ass!"

"As you wish."

The truck bounced out of the parking lot, over the curb and sidewalk, and onto the roadway before Jason could get his door all the way closed. Erin drove south, not because she wanted to go that direction, but that was the direction away from the approaching Zeds.

"Did you get a roadmap?"

Jason shook his head. "No, I forgot."

"Well, shit...that's OK. We'll stop at another gas station later. As long as we have each other, we can figure out the rest."

Erin and Jason held hands as they bounced down the road at a steady 45 miles per hour. They didn't know the name of the road, just that at some point they would need to take a left and head east to get back on the right track.

SSC

Eerie silence felt louder than possible. Amanda's own heartbeat and breathing felt so loud as to be heard by someone on the surface of the lake above them. She and Andrew quickly cleared the underground facility the previous evening after landing, but Amanda wasn't convinced that Clint was gone. She felt like there must be a trap, that he was lurking somewhere nearby and waiting to pounce on her for leaving. She was mostly sure that Clint wouldn't have tried to follow her to Groom Lake and Amanda was also mostly sure that once she turned up missing that Clint would have known she left for Groom Lake.

The room felt cold as the blood drained from Amanda's face. "Oh my God."

"What?"

Andrew wore new clothes and had enjoyed a ridiculously long shower the previous night and that morning after waking up. For some reason lost on Amanda, he didn't seem concerned about Clint in the least. His feelings were that the guy had left for destinations unknown after Amanda had left.

"The PLA, the Chinese, and Koreans. Aymond said that the PLA forces were in San Diego and that they had their hands full trying to simply get a foothold in the contiguous United States. Why would they divert men and equipment for a sabotage attack on a random facility in the middle of nowhere unless they knew. You know, unless they knew that a mass of survivors were there...unless they knew that I was going to be there."

"So they had listened to the radio transmissions offering sanctuary and you just happened to arrive as they attacked? So what? Sounds like bad luck to me."

"No, what if I was supposed to be there? What if I took too long to arrive? What if Clint told them I would be there?"

"I don't see how..."

"No, listen," Amanda interrupted Andrew. "This man, Clint, if that's even his real name, he's a manipulator. He has no emotion except the role he's playing and zero remorse. The asshole is a psychopath...he thought I would be killed and that's why we haven't found any traps yet. And we won't find any traps here. Clint didn't expect me to survive and I'm one of the few people left alive that knows exactly where this facility is, much less how to get in. That is except Bexar and Chivo. No one else left alive has been here."

"If that is true," Andrew looked like a parent explaining the Easter Bunny to a child, "then why were they killed or attacked?"

"They were attacked; I think they were supposed to be dead."

Andrew still looked incredulous.

"Look, Andrew, you don't have to believe me, but I'm telling you the truth. I think that whoever Clint really was before, he is now a clear and present danger to the United States and he must be stopped...no, he has to die. We will never be safe as long as he is alive. Damnit. I...we, have a lot of work to do, but the very first thing we must do is build a radio and make contact with Groom Lake, then we begin prepping for receiving survivors."

Groom Lake

The dust was bad and it was only just past breakfast. Wind whipped across the dry lakebed, sandblasting everything and everyone in its path. Near the runways, a work party continued to burn the bodies of their fellow residents turned Zed from the PLA attack. The gruesome task was nearly at a close. Chivo walked from the burn pile back toward the large hangars in which the survivor vehicles were stored. A small windbreak had been fashioned to protect the ruined blast door and entrance underground from the onslaught of the dust storm, but with the rest of that hangar destroyed, Chivo had made the next hangar over the top side command post. A familiar old FJ was parked near the hangar door and inside Chivo found Bexar and Jessie sipping coffee with a few of the newly designated top-side-staff.

Chivo gave Jessie a hug asked with a smile. "Are you supposed to be drinking coffee Momma Bexar?"

Jessie flipped him off and took another sip. "If you're going to be a dick, you could at least give me a status update on our progress."

"Yes, ma'am. Aymond and some of his guys have just finished the final sweep of everything below ground that we know of. The other Raiders have been rotating in and out of guard duty. All the Zeds have been neutralized and all the bodies have been brought topside, along with anything destroyed in the process. He even recruited a few civilians to police up all the spent brass and others to set the furniture back the way it should be. We should be able to begin repopulating the facility this afternoon. What do you say about having a welcome home dinner for everyone tonight? It might be just the thing to get morale and mood back on the right track."

"That's a wonderful idea. Do you know who to task with that?"

Chivo picked up a yellow pad of paper and flipped through a few pages of neatly written and organized notes. "Danny Cepeda is the highest ranking designated cook that survived."

Bexar interrupted. "Raiders?"

Jessie interrupted. "Cooks have ranks?"

"Marine Raiders...don't you know anything about history? And Jessie, how else would I describe our surviving cook?"

"I know plenty, but where is that from?"

Jessie held up her hands. "Awesome, well tell Danny he's promoted from the French fry fryer to head cook or director of food services or whatever you think we should title him and get him on board. Where is he now?"

"Dorm 7, room 213 is his current berth; he's probably there as I doubt there is going to be much exploring going on outside today."

Curiosity had taken hold with some of the survivors over the last bit, some of them using their downtime to walk around the once-secret facilities on the surface. Chivo secretly hoped that one of them would find a UFO.

"Speaking of exploring, Jessie and I are going to drive around the western side of the mountains and see what the deal is with that plane crash."

"In this weather, mano?"

It was Jessie's turn to interrupt. "Yeah, we know, but we're hoping that the mountains block some of this damn windblown dirt. Besides, we're itching to stretch our legs a little."

"Why don't I join you? I can have Aymond—"

"No, that's OK, buddy; take care of running the tribe. We'll be back before sunset."

"Alright, if you're sure, mano. Be safe out there...at least you two can't get pregnant again," Chivo said with a smirk.

Chivo turned to one of the other survivors who was working as a bit of a gofer for the facility reclamation process and asked him to find Danny Cepeda. As the gofer left, Aymond and few of his men walked into the hangar and toward Chivo.

If Aymond liked or disliked Chivo, he didn't let it show, but they all followed President Lampton's orders. The presidential directive prior to her departure was that Jessie was director of the facility and Jessie had placed Chivo in charge of operations, so minus using a flow chart, Chivo was the man in charge.

"Chief, I've been tasked with an operation and I need to borrow a man."

Aymond grunted.

"I also need to borrow one of your trucks."

"What sort of operation?"

Chivo filled in the group with the plan and mission objectives. Aymond's facial expression didn't change but he looked at Gonzo who nodded in response, understanding that he was to accompany Chivo on his little operation.

"Thanks, Chief, you have the conn until we return. Also, Jessie left with Bexar on their own operation, and they'll be back before sunset."

"Roger that." Aymond thought the whole situation was strange, but no stranger than standing in a hangar at Area 51 after being attacked by PLA forces and being swarmed by Zeds.

Chivo shrugged into his newly acquired tactical gear from the below-ground stores and walked outside with Gonzo for what was planned to be a quiet day of reconnaissance. Aymond watched them leave and turned to Happy. "Rally the guys, but leave one on fire watch; we need to come up with a plan to fortify our happy little firebase."

Happy acknowledged the order and left to get the rest of the MSOT together. Aymond stood quietly for a few moments looking around the hangar. They hadn't found any HESCO or even any sandbags, but there were a lot of things around the facility they could improvise with if they put their minds to it. Aymond smiled. All he needed now was a cigar and a van with a red stripe for his plan to come together.

Crockett, Texas

A handwritten note sat on the table explaining his plan, just in case one of his hunting buddies miraculously arrived; however, Ken really believed that they were either dead and deeply hoped that they were just sheltering in place in their homes. It was nearly four months since the world went to hell and it was now time to venture back out into it. The old truck coughed to life, dirty aluminum Kanz cases in the bed protecting all of the gear and supplies that he was bringing along. Assuming that he would never return, Ken took one last long look at the hunting cabin before shifting into gear and driving along the worn dirt driveway. Amazingly, the GPS still worked. After nearly 10 minutes of going through different options, Ken finally settled on pointing toward Roswell, New Mexico. After turning off the options for highways and tollways, Ken hoped the GPS would be helpful, but he didn't trust the directions, never had. Ken told himself that it would be helpful to keep him from getting completely lost, but to trust his gut instead of blindly following the device.

A small farm-to-market road would get him to the loop, which would connect with Texas 7 and take him to Centerville. From there, the plan was to follow Texas 7 to Gatesville and continue on the small highways to Nevada. The interstate was a mess when he first made his way to the hunting-cabin-turned-prepper bugout location and from all he had learned from the radio transmissions, he had no reason to believe it was better. There were, though, reports of massive hordes of reanimated dead following the interstates, pushing all that stood in their way clear. Reports all around the country said the same thing: "When the horde comes through, you better hope you're in a strong concrete-reinforced building or you're doomed."

It all seemed a little farfetched to Ken but to be frank, just six months ago the thought of the complete collapse of civilization was expected; it was the dead refusing to stay dead that was the problem. He was confident that if it hadn't been for the dead, this problem of an EMP attack wouldn't have been that big of a deal.

Mostly out of habit, Ken climbed out of the truck and closed the gate he had just opened and driven the truck through.FM 2065 appeared mostly clear. It was just far enough away from the big roads that only a handful of dead seemed to venture down this far. April in central Texas wasn't usually a cold affair and the morning sun was already baking the interior of the old truck. Ken cranked the windows down and tried to enjoy the warm spring morning. In a few short weeks, the daily temperatures would be in the 90s and the humidity would be nearly unbearable. Air-conditioning made this part of Texas bearable in the summer, and without it, if people weren't already dead, Ken believed the heat would kill some people, especially the elderly or the infirm. That was all part of his group's prepping discussion, but now Ken was fleeing his beloved country of Texas to drive to Nevada just in time for the summer. According to the radio traffic, the survivors were living in luxury underground, with running hot and cold water, hot meals, and climate control, so it was worth the try. Besides, as much fun as living in solitude sounds when you don't, some friends or even just other living people being near would be a huge improvement. Since the dawn of man, civilizations grew of the need for companionship.

SSC

Andrew followed Amanda as they continued to search the impressively large facility. Amanda's old bunk remained untouched; there was no sign that another person had lived below ground with her for all that time. Clint's presence was now less than a ghost. The control room was empty, although the computers were still on, the screens burst to life, and they showed a log-on screen when Andrew moved a mouse.

"Do you have a login?"

"I do, but I'm not sure what good it would do us. Before I left, all the communication with the outside had been lost. We didn't have access to any satellite imagery, no GPS data, and no communications at all. At one time, we had terminal access and could message back and forth with Bill in Groom Lake, but that quit working too."

"Do you know why?"

"Clint said the Chinese had hacked it or were jamming the signal, but he also said he was trying to protect me by keeping us hidden."

"And you believe him?"

"I did. But, if it wasn't true, why can't anyone else use the SATCOM radio?"

"What if Clint switched it off?"

Amanda shook her head, anger burning in her chest. Andrew hit a nerve and it wasn't his fault; it was her fault for trusting Clint in the first place. She could still be in Little Rock with her dogs. Even as the thought flashed through her mind, she knew it was wrong. She was a completely different person when she answered the knock at her door the day after Christmas. Now she was tough. She was a warrior and could take care of herself in the apocalyptic wasteland that her country had quickly become. No, if she had stayed in Little Rock, she would be dead.

"You're right, Andrew, he could have, but I don't know how to turn it all back on, so for now, we focus on what we can do instead of what we can't. Follow me, I have an idea, but first we need to check the tunnels."

Groom Lake

The FJ rattled and rocked in the wind like a sailboat as they followed the narrow ribbon of asphalt around the mountains. What began as driving through a flowing blanket of dirt and sand was beginning to get better. The wind still howled, but luckily the dirt and dust in the air was thinning. Still, visibility was limited as Jessie drove at what felt to be a walking pace.

"Have you been over here before?"

Jessie shook her head, her eyes still scanning what she could see of the roadway ahead of them. "No, not this far."

"Any idea what's over here?"

"I don't even know what all is over where we were. Sarah, Erin, Jason, and I spent some time clearing buildings over in the main area by the dorms and hangars, but even then we had a hard time figuring out what secret things went on in those buildings."

They drove slowly not because they were required to, but only because they didn't want to accidentally run over something that would disable their ride. The smattering of vehicles parked in the hangar that other survivors had brought was still there, but many of them were pretty rough. Vehicles that were old enough to not be affected by the EMP attack, tough enough to still be running and driven through the hellish landscape of the new modern America ruled by the dead, sat waiting for the next adventure, but the FJ was the best built of the bunch. Their friends were killed in Big Bend, but their purpose-built prepper bugout vehicle lived on.

Jessie stopped a few hundred yards shy of some buildings that appeared to flank an access gate, the buildings probably guard shacks of some sort. Silently, Jessie leaned over and kissed Bexar before pulling her goggles down over her eyes and her shemagh up over her face. Bexar did the same before they climbed out of the relative comfort of the FJ and into the wind. Luckily, the wind was at their backs, the peppering sting of the blowing sand slightly more bearable with it blowing against their backs instead of their faces. Bexar glanced at Jessie and smiled, not that she could see his face. They walked slowly on opposite sides of the blacktop, their rifles tucked neatly into the SUL position.

No cover was afforded them on the approach; all Bexar and Jessie could do was to have their rifles ready while being ready to immediately hit the dirt if ambushed. As they approached, a lone Zed shambled out from behind the larger metal building on their right. The reanimated corpse rocked unsteadily against a strong gust of wind, indifferent to the sand blasting what remained of its face. Jessie took aim and before the trigger could be pressed all the way to the rear, the Zed stumbled from the wind and fell backward as if it was some clumsy cartoon character. It slowly rolled over and with its butt in the air began to stand up like a disorientated toddler. Just as it began to stand all the way up, another gust of wind ripped through the air and knocked the Zed to the ground where it lay motionless for a moment as if it felt defeated. Bexar began laughing too hard to properly aim. Jessie glanced at Bexar, took a breath, and waited a moment for the corpse's head to get clear for a shot.

With a single shot muffled by the wind, blackened brain matter and bone spray across the pavement as the Zed fell to the ground for the last time. Jessie looked at Bexar who was still laughing and flipped him off. The tension gone with the threat, they walked the short distance to the buildings. Bexar tried a door of the building on his side of the road and found it unlocked. He looked at Jessie and pointed at his door; she gave him a thumbs up and waited. Bexar threw open the door and banged against the metal exterior of the building. Nothing appeared out of the darkness, and neither of them could see any movement in the shadows either.

Bexar switched on his rifle light and quickly entered the dark building more smoothly and more confidently than Jessie remembered seeing from Bexar during their rifle training days back in their past lives. Less than a minute later, Bexar reemerged and gave a thumbs up. Jessie tried the door to the building on her side, repeating the process Bexar had just completed. Less than five minutes later, they both sat in the FJ wiping dirt and sand off their faces.

"I didn't see any signs that they had been in there."

Jessie nodded. This whole expedition was a long shot, but she felt awful and had to try. Coming up empty with their first stop, they drove on as the road turned south. Slowly creeping behind the mountains, the wind seemed to be slightly better; at least the FJ didn't rock as badly even if it wasn't. She pulled to a stop at a split in the road. Unlike the driveways that split off the main road before, this junction looked significant. The paved road curved toward the right, an unpaved road continued straight.

"What do you think, Jessie?"

Slowly, Jessie moved her head left to right, scanning the desert features and the roadway. "From what I gathered from that pilot guy, the plane crash is probably down this dirt road."

"And?"

"And nothing. I have no idea. But my gut feeling is that we should try the dirt road first."

Bexar shrugged with a half-smile; it didn't matter to him. It was nice exploring and being away from the Groom Lake facility for a while. He couldn't figure out why but the place gave him the creeps. They could go down this dirt road today and tomorrow they could try the paved road. He didn't think that they would find what Jessie was looking for, but he didn't care.

Jessie drove forward off of the pavement and onto the dirt road. Even if the wind wasn't that much better, the visibility was significantly better now they were on the backside of the mountains. Bexar slid over and put his arm around his bride before gently rubbing her growing baby bump with a smile.

CHAPTER 8

April 11, Year 1
Nevada

"What the actual fuck is that?"

Jason pointed to a churning turmoil of darkness in the sky that billowed like smoke.

"I don't know, baby. I don't think it is a fire, it doesn't look like smoke, and it sure as shit doesn't look like a dust storm."

Erin press checked her M4. She knew there was a round in the chamber, there was always a round in the chamber, but the churning cloud on the horizon gave her pause and she wasn't sure why.

"Whatever it is, Erin, it can't be good. Think we should turn around?"

"No, we have Zeds to the back of us."

"Well, we can't really turn away. Um, well, we could stop and wait to see."

"I want to get closer. If we can't figure it out by the time we're within about a half-mile, then we stop, get to the high ground, and scope it out."

Jason nodded. It wasn't a great plan, but it was the only plan they had. Plan B didn't exist yet. He patted Erin's thigh which earned him a soft smile from the woman he loved.

"No matter what may come, we'll win or lose together."

"Forever?"

Erin kissed Jason on the cheek as an answer.

They rode in silence for the next 30 minutes, only the droning sound of the Suburban's old V8 rattling down the desert highway. Of the handful of vehicles they saw during the drive, they were all severely damaged, pushed off the roadway, and crumpled like tin cans. Jason took a deep breath to calm his nerves every time they passed another demolished car or truck. Even the lone semi-truck they saw was crumpled and tossed into the desert like a child's toy. Wind whistled through the broken windows of their SUV as they drove steadily at around 45 mph.

The churning dark mass seemed to grow in size as they neared. Jason stopped in the middle of the road and pointed at the mountains toward the north.

"I think we're close enough. Want to go up there and take a look?"

Erin nodded. "We need to find a place to hide our wheels."

"Yeah, looks like a bad neighborhood. I would hate for someone to steal our sweet whip."

Jason delivered the joke in perfect deadpan, which got the deserved chuckle. He drove off the roadway and up a worn dirt road that wound its way into the desert and the mountains.

Slowly, the heavy old Suburban jostled and bounced up the rugged dirt path; to say it was still a road would be a stretch. Eventually, they got to a point where they were confident that the old SUV wouldn't be seen from the road below. Jason turned the beast around and pointed back the way they had come in case they needed a quick getaway and they climbed out. The fact that the dirt path was now too narrow and rough to drive through was added motivation to get out on foot.

Erin slung her short M4 and grabbed her big .50-caliber rifle that was nearly as tall as she was. The heavy rifle went over her shoulders as she started up the path. Jason held his shotgun and followed, scanning their surroundings for any threats, living or dead, that may appear from around the sparse rugged moon-scape, a worn pack slung over his shoulders.

Sweating in the cool afternoon mountain air, they reached a point where a large rock provided a good surface to lay and observe the mysteries ahead. Erin snapped the bipod legs of her rifle open, pulled the covers from the large scope, and took a position lying on the rock, her rifle ready, her experienced eye scanning the area through the rifle's optic. Jason set the pack on the ground along with his shotgun and retrieved the spotting scope out of the pack. Sitting up, he scanned the area with the spotting scope.

"Holy shit, Erin. Those are flies, millions of flies!"

"Yeah, I noticed. Look under the flies then scan toward the right."

"Zeds."

Jason scanned right as instructed. "I've never seen so many dead upright and moving in one place, what the hell...oh."

The armored convoy was parked in a large circle like covered wagons, the vehicles touching nose to tail, four large square radar antennas erected pointing opposite each other like a compass rose. Arcing away from each of the radar trucks were piles of Zeds crumpled on the ground motionless. All the dead reanimates formed a crude wall surrounding their temporary fort.

"Damn, they have a Zed moat protecting their castle. Who could have come up with such a thing?"

"It isn't perfect; some of them are getting through to the trucks."

"Yeah, but then they fall like bugs on a bug zapper."

"That's exactly what it's like, Jason, what a good fucking idea. With enough of those radar trucks and some time, it would be possible to clear the entire country...or at least clear out areas for cities to take hold again."

"OK, so are we going to do that?"

"No, Jessie and her merry band of fuckwits can do that; we're going to ruin these asshole's day."

Jason looked at Jessie, who seemed to melt into her big rifle. Her breathing slowed and became rhythmic, purposeful.

After putting his eye back on the spotting scope and focusing in on the Chinese encampment, he asked, "Which one?"

"South is first, it's the closest. I'm not sure if I can hit it from here."

Jason shifted the spotting scope slightly to focus on the southernmost radar truck. The sudden hard thump of the rifle being fired bounced dirt in the air; the .50-caliber rifle was something you felt more than you heard. A breath later, he saw the plum of the big round slamming into the bottom right corner of the square antenna.

"Up and left, you hit the bottom right—"

Before he could say "corner," the rifle barked fire once again. Startled, Jason was able to regain his composure just in time to see the following round slam into the middle of the square dish.

"East" was all Erin said next, moving the rifle a hair and firing. Jason followed to the radar truck with the spotting scope just in time to see the round impact.

"Good hit."

"West."

"Fuck, Erin, they're—" Jason was interrupted by the rifle being fired again. "Erin, they're pointing at us!"

"Shit."

Erin stood quickly, pulling her rifle up with her. "Come on, we need to get the fuck out of here."

Jason tried to juggle the shotgun, his pack, and the spotting scope as he jogged down the trail following Erin, but he had to stop for a moment to get put together without dropping any of his gear. By the time he reached the Suburban, Erin was sitting in the driver's seat with the motor running.

Jason climbed in beside her and barely got his door shut by the time they were moving.

"Baby, they still have to claw their way through that huge herd of Zeds to get to us."

Erin nodded and slowed down a bit. It wasn't worth breaking their only vehicle for rushing when they didn't have to. By the time they reached the paved road again, the swarm of flies appeared to be getting larger.

"Is that getting bigger?"

"No, Jason, it's fucking getting closer!"

Erin turned right, back the way they had come, and accelerated sharply, as sharply as the old Chevy could.

"Are you going back to the strip club?"

"No, too obvious. If they come back through that town, they'll see the Zeds we killed and know someone was there. We'll find something else, we have to, or we'll keep driving back to Groom Lake, let those Marines handle it."

"OK, great, but we won't be doing much of either unless we find some fuel!"

SSC

Amanda walked slowly through the tunnel, the cool damp air hanging like a heavy curtain, muffling the soft sound of her footsteps. The M4 rifle tucked against her body in the SUL position, her hands relaxed but ready to move quickly. She reached the spot where the MRAPs were stored along with other vehicles and trailers. The spot where her now-destroyed armored truck had once sat remained empty, but the spot next to it was empty as well.

Relieved and annoyed, she now knew the next step of the story, but that answer only raised more questions.

OK, asshole, if you left, where did you go and are you going to come back?

There was no way to know for sure. She knew that Clint could evaporate into thin air if he wanted to, his training was too good, his experience too broad for someone like her to breach, but she had a feeling that he would reappear in her life sooner than later and it would be a problem.

A huge fucking problem.

Amanda walked the length of the tunnel to the ramp and door that she had driven through to leave. It was closed and appeared secure; she looked but couldn't find where she could bar the hatch any further than with the electronic control already in use. She bent her knees and stretched, peering back through the dim passageway. Her mind churned with the possibilities and what the next step would be.

First, radio contact, then Andrew can head back and ferry someone to run one of the MRAPs back to Groom Lake...or maybe Aymond could dispatch a couple of his men and one of their trucks to begin the arduous process of transferring survivors to Texas.

She shook her head. Her plan seemed so clear before, but now it didn't seem to make sense. If the survivors in Nevada were thriving and the PLA left them alone, what sense would it make to uproot their lives to drag them across the wilds of untamed country ruled by the dead? If the PLA came back, they were sitting ducks, but so was the SSC. No castle is perfect, no fort secure against a dedicated attack.

"Shit."

Amanda frowned at her runaway thoughts, a little bemused, wondering if past presidents had these sorts of dilemmas.

They didn't have the dead; no one has ever had the god-dammed dead.

With a shake of her head, Amanda took off in a light jog back toward the beginning of the tunnel. The light jog quickened in pace as she neared the halfway point and continued to get faster until she was in a dead sprint at the end. Slowing, she walked a few paces to her well-worn pull-up bar, the discolored athletic tape still wrapped around the grips. With her rifle and ammo carrier still being worn, Amanda hopped up to the bar and began ripping her body to the bar in perfect form. Six pull-ups later, she dropped to her feet, staring at the door that led back into the facility, sweat rolling down her face as she stood with her hands overhead trying to catch her breath.

Thirty minutes later, Amanda stepped through a billowing cloud of steam that followed her in wisps as she stepped out of the shower and into the barracks where her bunk and footlocker remained.

"Amanda, I think...oh shit, I'm sorry!"

Andrew spun in place to look away, not realizing when he came in looking for Amanda that he would find her nude. Amanda looked up and saw him facing away from her, the back of his ears were flushed red in embarrassment.

"That's OK, Andrew, what's up?"

"Uh, Amanda, well, I think we're ready to run the antenna up on the surface so we can test the radio."

"Outstanding. Give me five minutes and I'll meet you in the command center."

With a "yes, ma'am," Andrew walked out of the large room, shutting the door behind him. Amanda had to laugh; her modesty had fallen away shortly after Clint and Johnson had whisked her away back in December. She looked down at her body as she stepped into her panties. A lot had changed since that day, most of it for the worse, but she was in the best shape of her life and possibly the fittest president ever in office.

Amanda laughed; she was definitely the fittest woman president the United States had ever seen.

I hope there will be more women to hold this title in the future.... I hope that this title even exists in the future.

Groom Lake "SITREP."

The Marines stood in a loose circle, each of them looking in seemingly random directions and not at Aymond. It looked like disrespect, but in reality, it was their training and experience. Aymond wasn't in the middle; he wasn't distinguished in any way. If everyone was looking at him, then an observer could surmise that he was the leader. If he stood in the middle, the same, and it increased the possibility of Aymond being targeted. Not only those reasons, but it gave the men the chance to monitor the areas around them while they spoke and briefed on what they had found.

"Chief, there is a concrete production facility toward the south. I think they may have used it in the construction of the base."

"And?"

"And we'll have to figure out how to run it, but first, we'll have to figure out how to fix the machinery; we couldn't get anything to turn on or start."

"OK, consider that a long-term project, but we have certain urgency with what we have before us. Anything else?"

"Yeah, Chief," Happy chimed in. "To the west is a storage lot with some heavy machinery, backhoes, and the like."

"Do those work?"

"I couldn't get them started, and I don't know if it is because they are old or because of the EMP."

"Are they fucked up or just old?"

"No, they appear well-maintained; they just look like they were produced in the fucking Truman era."

Aymond nodded. "Well, maybe they did run and maybe they will run if they're old enough to have been built without electronics. Jones, go with Happy and scope it out."

"Aye, Chief," Jones replied. Jones and Happy walked toward the hangar to retrieve some tools and one of the vehicles to carry out the order.

"What else?"

Snow spoke next. "We don't have any HESCO in storage that we can find, but the storeroom has fourteen pallets of sandbags we can fill and place."

"Fan-fucking-tastic. See about organizing some civilians to make that happen. First priority is the blast door. If we have anything left over, put some emplacements in there and there." Aymond pointed. "While Jones is fucking with the heavy equipment, start with some fighting holes; get some other civilians to help. Get bags on them and make 'em right. We're stuck with this shithole for now; we have to make it work."

Groom Lake

Chivo rode up front, but for all the dirt and dust still in the wind, he might as well have been sitting in the back staring at the floor. Gonzo drove, which suited Chivo just fine, giving him time to think through the details of the different plans; he was war-gaming through the various scenarios he could think of. The problem with detailed plans is that they tended to fall apart just as the first round gets fired, but having plans made for more nimble responses since, usually, the harder parts and details have been accounted for. This afternoon for Chivo, that meant he had an armored truck that was fast and nimble off the paved road as well as his big sniper rifle.

Gonzo was a professional, not much chit chat and more importantly none of the questions that someone out of the SPECWAR community would be tempted to ask. Warriors in the Special Warfare community didn't ask each other personal questions, what their hometowns were, or anything else that held any substance to the person behind the tactical gear. The closest those questions came to being asked involved what the person's favorite beer was or if they chewed Skoal or Copenhagen. Those were the important questions; the rest was just business. Being that they were now months out since the last commercial beer was produced or the last can of dip was sold at a gas station, even those questions went unasked and unanswered. All that was left was business.

The nagging feeling that had bothered Chivo since sprinting into El Paso with a hoard chasing him from Mexico was finally answered. It wasn't enough that he survived the tour of duty—the tour would never end because it was simply life now. It wasn't enough that his friends survived—they had to thrive. Some sort of stability to life had to happen and that would only happen if the

Chinese and Koreans were stopped. In four months, they had mostly figured out how to scratch out survival amongst the Zeds. They were a constant and felt like a background nuisance more than anything. No, the problem of the new world were the Chinese and Koreans. If they could be stopped, then they could clear out patches of safe zones free of Zeds. Knock down the bad hombres that tend to appear in the voids of society and let the good folks live and survive. After losing his team and Lindsey to the dead along the way, his friends were Bexar and Jessie. They deserved a safe place to raise their child. Chivo thought of Erin and hoped she and Jason survived long enough to return to one of the safe communities that he now felt obligated...*destined* to create.

The dust storm was beginning to clear. After making the drive to the backside of the mountains, the wind had finally relented, visibility increasing with each minute. A few moments later, Gonzo kept driving off the paved road and onto the dirt road that the Marines said they had driven on to get to Groom Lake from the south. This was all new territory for Chivo. One would think that as a former Special Forces soldier who then worked for the CIA that he would know all the secret places in the United States, but he had never been to Area 51 and knew scantly more than what was in the public consciousness before the attacks.

Chivo and Gonzo continued to ride in silence through the desert. Large bomb craters were scattered in the distance, giving an appearance like what the moon looked like. The crumpled hull of the PLA cargo aircraft that had augured in on takeoff sat in the desert like an ancient ruin, which it would become one until the aluminum had all corroded away. Neither of them mentioned the wreck as they continued their journey in silence.

Groom Lake

This wasn't the worst dirt road that Bexar had driven down before, but it wasn't the best either. If his old Wagoneer hadn't met a violent end in Terlingua, he could have aired down the tires and aired them back up again once they drove back onto pavement. As it were, the FJ felt soft as they drove, so the tires were probably low on it as well. Not really sure what he could do to easily inflate the tires even if he did check them, Bexar decided to worry about it later. For now, the dust storm seemed to have cleared slightly, affording more visibility, not that there was much actually to see. The barren ground was pock-marked with enough craters that it looked like a bad moon landing movie set.

"It looks like they used this area for weapons testing or maybe to fake the Apollo moon landings."

Jessie gave him a playful angry look. "Really?"

"Oh yeah, everyone on the internet knows the moon landings were faked to cover up the presence of ancient alien ruins that the *real* moon missions found."

"Wrap your tin foil tight, lover boy."

"What's more likely, moon aliens or zombies? I'm going to say moon aliens because come on, dead walking?"

Bexar looked at Jessie and laughed, who rolled her eyes at him.

Out of reflex, Bexar cursed as he looked forward in time to see a face slap into the windshield, shattering it. Bexar slammed on the brakes, the FJ sliding to a stop on the dirt track. Jessie's door was already open by the time they came to a stop, stepping out she fired a single round into the skull of the Zed folded across their hood. She took a few steps, grabbed the Zed's jacket, and pulled the body to the ground. Inside, Bexar's feet were up on the dash as he kicked out the ruined windshield.

Jessie turned around and faced the direction they were heading. "What the hell is that?"

Bexar stepped out of the FJ and pulled the windshield off the hood, glass fragments falling in a crumpled mess on the desert floor. He looked at Jessie and followed her extended finger to what she was looking at.

"Oh fuck. That's bad. Get in! We've got to get!"

Jessie climbed in just as Bexar spun the tires in reverse to turn around. Sliding to a stop while shifting, the FJ lurched as the tires tried to find traction. Once moving, Bexar kept the needle at nearly 40 mph, which felt much faster as they bounced and shuttered across the uneven dirt road.

Wind whipping through the interior, Bexar shouted over the noise, "Those were flies, the cloud, but it isn't a cloud, its flies, millions and millions of god-dammed flies. That happens over the bad swarms or herds or whatever the fuck you want to call more Zeds than you've ever seen."

"Shit."

"Shit is right, babe. Me and Chivo 'bout fucking died in Utah due to a swarm of Zeds that had a cloud like that."

"What are we going to do? Go up to the tent, go underground, just go away?"

Bexar shook his head. He wasn't sure of anything except that it was stupid for the two of them to go fucking sight-seeing. Just because it was the holy grail of conspiracies doesn't mean that the world they now lived in was any different than the one that had killed their friends, their daughter. They didn't have enough gear, they didn't have enough water, enough food, and enough ammo...they had been stupid to be anything but 100 percent ready to bugout immediately if they had to. Bexar would change that, but first, they had to get safe.

Ulm, Montana

For all the high technology that the United States Air Force had, it would have been understandable to have expected a control center that could have been at home as a set piece on a science fiction TV show, but the reality was that most of the technology appeared to have been developed 50 years in the past instead of the future only because it really had been. The control room below ground for a Minuteman III installation had two comfortable chairs that were much like what was used in aircraft. Those were on tracks and could move across a workspace that had two large LCD monitors, but with inputs that consisted of not a keyboard and mouse, but rows of switches and a number pad. Racks of computer equipment and decidedly old-school electronics filled the room, minus the portion above the desk where the dual-locked safe resided and was flanked by numerous large binders that contained all the technical data that the attending Air Force officers would need to start World War III.

Dorsey sat in one of the chairs next to Col. Smith, who had a laptop sitting on the tabletop that pulled out of the desk between the two LCD monitors. Trying to listen, Dorsey's mind danced around the room, examining the space, which was mostly foreign to him. His eyes were still focused on Smith, a practiced trait of a career officer, but for all the experience Dorsey had, none of it was in missile command. Even still, something just wasn't right with Smith, not that a single problem could be listed; it was more of a gut feeling that Dorsey had.

I need to get a message out...more importantly, I'll need the reply and a plan of action.

The briefing that Smith was reading off of appeared to be an official one, at least the PowerPoint presentation was in the correct format; font and size to appear to have come from a high-level staff officer whose entire job was seemingly to be worrying about trivial details as those. The difference today was that instead of sitting in a meeting room or a flight briefing room, they sat below ground. Dorsey was sure that both of them were imposters appearing to be what they really weren't. The problem was that Dorsey knew what his motive was, but he didn't know what Smith's motive was, besides what appeared to be a plan to bypass the systems that prevented unauthorized missile launches. The briefing was complex, enough so that regardless of what plans Smith may have, he wasn't sure they could even accomplish the changes. The computer systems may be old, but they were tough and they were purposely made to be nearly impossible to bypass.

"Excuse me, Colonel Smith, how many other missile flights are being modified in this manner?"

Clint's expression still bore the mostly blank face of minor annoyance for the interruption, not the rapid "if, then" plotting of various plans that flipped through his mind in rapid succession trying to play out if he actually needed Dorsey or if he could simply kill him without jeopardizing the success of the mission.

"All of the flights that remain operational and manned."

"How many is that, sir?"

"One. Now, we must continue. There are a lot more slides to cover before we can get into the technical details."

These aren't the technical details? Jesus. Well, at least that means I have a little bit of time before the colonel could have his finger on the big red button.

Centerville, Texas

The outskirts of town appeared mostly normal. March in this part of Texas meant that the grass was turning green, even though the weather probably had one last good cold snap left in it before the temperatures began climbing steeply into summer. The old truck rattled with wind noise as Ken drove. Highway 7 was mostly smooth and the shoulders weren't bad for when he had to drive around a wreck or some abandoned vehicles. So far, the few Zeds that he had seen were off the road and there weren't that many.

On the bench seat next to him was his M1 Garand with wooden stock and iron sights. Ken had other rifles, but the M1 was his favorite rifle of them all. Ken's time in the jungles of Southeast Asia meant he lugged around an M14 for his first tour and an M16A1 for his second, but the Garand was the rifle he wished he could have taken to war, just like his dad and uncle had while island-hopping their way toward Japan in WWII. It was a battle rifle as God himself intended; sturdy, reliable, and with a round heavy enough to put a man down for good. Not one for much creative thought when it came to weapons meant for fighting, a well-worn 1911 was in a leather holster on his right hip. If it was good enough to carry in every modern conflict that Americans had fought in since WWI, then for Ken it was good enough to carry after the world ended.

Centerville wasn't a large and busy town before the virus hit, but now it was beginning to look worse for the wear. At the intersection of Highway 7 and Highway 75, the sign for the Leon County Expo Center still stood, but some of the old buildings on the square had burned. Since the attack was the day after Christmas, there weren't many cars in the parking spots along the street, but in the middle of the intersection stood alone black and white highway patrol car. The trooper was gone, the car was abandoned, but Ken just had to stop to check.

With the clutch pedal in, Ken jiggled the shifter to make sure he was in neutral before setting the parking brake and getting out while the truck idled. The rifle stayed in the truck, but the metal frame of the 1911 felt cool to the touch in his hands. Holding the pistol low, Ken made his way around the hood and found the driver's door of the patrol car closed but unlocked. The windows were tinted and hard to see in, but he didn't have to see much to see what happened. The interior of the car was destroyed—torn, bloodied, covered in pus, and stained. A body of a man lay across the center console and the front seats, his hands handcuffed behind his back with a large hole in the back of his skull. Someone had shot this prisoner. Behind the front seats was a rifle and shotgun rack, which was empty.

Ken assumed that the prisoner was killed after he had died and turned, which would explain the headshot and the condition of the car. Whoever did it took the trooper's rifle and shotgun or whatever else there was of value or use. The keys hung in the ignition switch on the steering column and that seemed peculiar. Ken slowly spun in place, his piercing eyes scanned the area, looking at every shadow before feeling confident he was alone for the moment. He held his breath, opened the driver's door, grabbed the keys, and quietly closed the door before letting his breath out. Even with the delay, the air that had escaped from the car was retched, the hard bite of rotten flesh that had been kept in a container too long. Ken flipped through the keys before unlocking the trunk. The trunk was more organized than Ken would have thought. Wires and electronic boxes were mounted around the interior wall of the trunk. Two big green ammo cans sat in the bottom. After checking, each contained a large number of loose 5.56 rounds. Although Ken didn't have a rifle that fired the round, he knew someone would and that ammo would be good bartering materials. A heavy black vest was picked up next. It had patches front and back that identified the wearer as a police officer. There were six large magazines for an AR-style weapon on the front of the vest, armor plates front and rear along with flex cuffs, a trauma medical kit, and an unopened can of Copenhagen in a pocket. Under the vest in the trunk was a thick black helmet meant to stop bullets. It was heavy, but it was still nicer than the steel pot that he took to Vietnam. Ken tried on the vest and the helmet, and after some minor adjusting, they fit. The AR magazines went in the truck with the ammo cans. The helmet sat on the bench seat next to the rifles, but the vest stayed on for now. The more Ken thought about it, the more Ken worried that he might encounter some shitheads or some end of the world religious whack jobs; either way, they might shoot at him. With the truck in gear, Ken turned the wheel and pointed north on Highway 75. His right hand shook with his finger thumping on the lid of the can of tobacco. He had quit dipping for his wife years ago, he even resisted starting again after she passed away, but Ken figured a dip would help him stay alert on the drive and who was left to care anyways.

Pahrump, Nevada

The dusty small town hadn't changed in the few hours since they left. The problem was that nothing had changed; if it was only the dead following, then all they had to do was get safe and let the raging storm of Zeds pass by. If the Koreans or the Chinese were following, they might recognize their vehicle— although probably not—but they would recognize Zeds killed by headshots. Their fake castle from before was an obviously bad choice for that reason, but as they drove through town, nothing from the highway looked like it would be a safe bet either. Low buildings, small casinos, and RV parks made for poor choices in a zombie apocalypse and they knew it.

Arguing over the wind noise that whipped through the holes in which they once had windows was tiresome and they settled on simply finding some more fuel for the Suburban and driving on until they found something better. They tried to find a good spot to scavenge for fuel away from the highway far enough to hide, but still be close enough to run if need be was tough. They passed the fake castle and the gas station with the collapsed awning. It seemed that fewer of the Zeds trapped under the awning were moving than had been this morning, but Jason really wasn't sure.

Nothing they saw suited their needs until they saw the big orange sign of a home improvement store that was set back off the highway. There weren't many vehicles in the parking lot, but there were some and a few of those were big pickup trucks, which meant it was easier to get to the fuel tank to siphon gas.

The sliding glass doors at the front of the building were shattered, the interior of the store darker than one would expect, but through the shadows, Erin could see movement. The idea to first think that the movement could have been caused by survivors had long been extinguished for Erin, her first and correct assumption that the shadows were caused by Zeds. As useful as the tool and raw materials could be to another survivor, they weren't useful enough to Erin to justify the risk. All they needed was gas for their ride; they weren't out to build a tiny home for the apocalypse.

Jason turned and drove along the far perimeter of the parking lot before stopping in the middle of a parking aisle with a lifted Jeep Wrangler on one side and a big gas-powered pickup on the other. The Jeep looked like it was strictly a mall crawler, as odd as that would be when the area was surrounded by off-road trails seemingly built for Jeeps to drive on, but there were two bright red jerry cans on the swing arm of the back bumper. Jason left the Suburban running while he went to check on the jerry cans. Erin went straight to the truck to cut the rubber hose off the filler neck to the gas tank and slid the end of a garden hose brought along for such a purpose into the tank. Jason broke the cheap brackets that locked the cans into their carriers by twisting them off with the Suburban's tire iron. Both of the cans were full of gas and one by one, each was fitted with the filler nozzle then tipped into the tank of the Suburban. While dumping the second can's gas into the Suburban's tank, Erin filled the empty with gas from the truck. Roughly 10 gallons of gas brought the fuel gauge needed back near the big F and they now had a spare 10 gallons of gas between the two cans. They were set for the rest of the day of driving, wherever that might take them, but for now, they had to get out of the parking lot.

While Erin had been filling the second jerry can, Zeds began coming out of the store and into the bright sunlight. Seemingly dazzled by the light for a bit, each of them zeroed in on their running shitbox of an SUV and began shambling their way toward the noisy intruders.

As for now, the numbers were few and they were staggered enough that Jason calmly dispatched each one by one with his pump shotgun, but the view coming from the store was bleak. The straggling dead were quickly becoming a churning riot of Zeds determined to destroy him and Erin. However, Erin finished filling the second can and the two of them were inside the Suburban and trying to drive away. Hundreds of Zeds poured out of the store and onto the parking lot with no end to their numbers in site. They threaded through some gaps in the groups of the Zeds before Jason was able to slam the accelerator to the floor to gain some distance and safety.

Jason drove over the curb toward the west and onto the empty section of desert between the store and the main highway. Dirt rooster-tailed into the air as he accelerated hard to gain some distance between their vehicle and the dead pursuers. Erin bounced out of her seat and hit her head on the interior ceiling as Jason launched through the roadside ditch, over the sidewalk, and slid to a stop on the paved highway.

After a quick glance to make sure his love wasn't hurt, he pointed the nose of the SUV north and back the way they had come from Groom Lake. When they got to the highway intersection from before, he would turn right and head east, away from Groom Lake. He wasn't sure how they would get around Las Vegas to get to Erin's chosen destination, but they'd figure it out when they got there. Erin slid across the seat and against Jason, taking his hand in hers. Jason looked at her. *She may be the toughest woman I've ever met, and I'm lucky that she has chosen me.*

Jason smiled as he drove. Looking at the sun in the western sky, he figured they would have to find shelter for the night in the next hour, but until then, it was just a pleasant road trip through the desert with the woman he loved.

Groom Lake

Dirt slid, small rocks rolling past the tires as the FJ ground to a stop. Bexar and Jessie were out and working fast to break camp. Faint gunfire could barely be heard echoing over the mountain's edge and over the rattling low hum of the Toyota's still-running engine.

"Hear that?"

Jessie nodded. "I can't tell where it was coming from, but it didn't sound close."

"No, it didn't, but it was also a full-auto burst."

"That's not good. Think that's still heading our way?"

"Reminds me of Maypearl," Bexar said while lashing the EMT poles of the wall tent together with bungee cords. The pole bundles went on the roof rack to be tied down when they were finished. The tent was stuffed in the back of the SUV, along with the cases of ammo, MREs, and other gear they had squirreled away in their tent away from the others. Another full-auto burst could barely be heard in the distance, almost like trees rustling in the breeze. Both of them picked up the pace and moved more quickly now.

Bexar climbed on the roof rack and Jessie tossed him a ratchet strap. "So what's the plan? Stay or go? If we stay, do we go below ground? If we go, then where do we go? St. George?"

"We need to go, but do we have enough gear to keep going if we have to?"

"Uh," Bexar stood on the roof rack and looked around, mentally checking through everything he saw go in and on the FJ, "no, we really don't. If we get cut-off, or something happens, we don't have enough to make our way anywhere else real. We need more water, like 10 more gallons to be safe, another couple cases of MREs would be smart too—"

"OK," Jessie interrupted, "we go down the hill, we park the FJ in the hangar so it's protected, maybe we can have it poised for escape if we need to, then we go below ground and start really prepping."

Bexar climbed off the roof rack while Jessie gave their site another quick walkthrough to make sure they weren't leaving anything important. They drove down the hill and north through facility, past the dormitory buildings and out onto the ramp, while making their way to the former flight line and the entrance underground.

Near The M-ATV

"You know some of these are craters from nuclear detonations."

Gonzo ignored Chivo as they walked.

"No, seriously, some of the most powerful explosions known to man were blown the fuck up out here, mano."

Chivo shook his head. Marines never seemed to have a sense of humor, and his friendly trip companion Marine Raider that just stopped in the middle of the road to stare at him seemed to fit the mold.

"Look, mano, we'll come back for your truck tomorrow, but for now, we have to outpace that cloud growing in the background back there." Chivo jerked his thumb over his shoulder.

"I get that, *mano*, but I don't get you. What the fuck are you for trying to play your stupid fucking spy games on the guy you're buddied up with. Trying to catch a glimpse of them fucking so you can beat off to it later, you sick fuck?"

Chivo shook his head. He understood why Gonzo was upset, but it wouldn't do either of them any good if he couldn't broker some sort of peace. Besides, Chivo suspected that if Gonzo was too annoyed that he might catch a round in the skull and have a harrowing tale of being overrun by Zeds told upon Gonzo's return to the facility.

"No, it was about security, making sure they stayed out of trouble."

"Why would they need your help if they obviously don't want it?"

"They don't know they need it. Look, mano, once I've got them set up in a good place and that baby is born safely, I'll feel better. Until then, I'm the guardian fucking angel they don't know they have."

"Well, a good fucking job you're doing of it. They've burned off and we're humping it like assholes."

The M-ATV sat at the bottom of a bomb crater. Chivo didn't think it was one of the nuclear detonations, but he didn't know for sure. Either way, the crater appeared to be much shallower and much less steep than it really was. They were caught off guard when the FJ stopped and reversed course without much warning and they needed somewhere to hide the big four-wheel-drive armored truck out in the desert flats. Chivo pointed and told Gonzo to go. They did, even with the Marine's objections, and now the truck was stuck for all eternity, or until they could bring the other M-ATV around and pull this one out. Before that could happen, they needed to walk back to the facility and where Aymond was, and before that, Chivo and Gonzo had to either outpace the looming cloud of flies or find a place to hole up. In hindsight, it wasn't Chivo's best decision, but they had some of the gear they brought, including the big .50-caliber rifle strapped to Chivo's pack.

The gate and the buildings were a bit odd. They were already on what used to be heavily patrolled and secured government property, but if someone had snuck onto the grounds they would have had to drive countless miles across a serious amount of open desert to reach another gate, with what were probably heavily armed guards. Chivo suspected this was the route that commercial truck traffic took to bring supplies and whatever else was needed onto the facility. The thought of being a truck driver making deliveries to Area51 was almost humorous in its absurdity. As it were, the squat cinderblock-made government buildings would be their best bet until the impending swarm had passed.

Chivo went to the largest of the three buildings and looked at the lone dark window on the side of the building along the road. It appeared to be made of thick glass, probably bullet resistant. The sharp rapping of his knuckles on the glass returned muffled thumps. Chivo smiled slightly; it was bullet resistant. So hopefully it would be Zed resistant as well.

With a few quick hand signals, Chivo made his intent known, and Gonzo nodded in response before sliding silently from across the road to form up with Chivo. The metal door was unlocked and Chivo pushed it open, slapping loudly against the door frame. If there were any Zeds in there, they would be coming to say hi soon. Silently, Chivo counted to 10 before stepping into the dark building, the light on his rifle snapping on, sweeping through the shadows with trained efficiency. The lone Zed trapped inside was destroyed and dragged outside the door.

A few moments later, the door was locked. If they had a drawbridge, they would have raised it, but for now, the deadbolt would have to do. The building was, in fact, a glorified guard shack. There was a front office with two metal desks, the window looking like a bank teller's window from the inside. Besides the restroom, there was a break room and two more offices. All in all, it was pretty sparse, but the big office water jug had water in it, cold water, because after flipping some fuses at the panel, the electricity came on. After some discussion about if it was the same electrical system as the underground base, to which neither of them had any real answers, Gonzo decided he didn't care. He did care about the coffee pot in the break room, which soon filled the building with the smell of a freshly brewed pot.

CHAPTER 9

"I'll check first."

Jessie held her rifle tightly tucked against her body as she eased around the corner to enter the hallway. She commanded herself to breathe after realizing she was holding her breath. After a painfully long silence, Jessie waved Bexar to follow as they walked into the hallway and up the stairs. After coming back below ground the previous evening, Bexar and Jessie found most of the survivors in the cafeteria holding a bit of a town hall-style meeting and there were serious problems.

Their first clue was that some of the survivors in the cafeteria were shouting at each other, but watching from just outside one of the doorways, Jessie and Bexar's curiosity turned to horror as time continued. Standing on a table at the front of the room was a man that Jessie had only spoken with once or twice: Trent. Jessie couldn't remember anything about where Trent was from or what he did before the Zeds, but standing on a table in the cafeteria, it was obvious the man knew how to handle a rifle. Athletic, late-30s with gray patches in his beard, he had the eyes of a man who was conditioned to violence and unaffected by empathy. Trent was a man who simply got what he wanted. Flanked on either side of him were about a dozen other men. They all had military bearing and the whole situation made Bexar feel unsettled.

"Who are they to rule us like a queen and her court?" one man yelled.

"They have risked their own lives to help save ours," a woman across the room yelled back.

Trent held up his arms, silencing the bitter back and forth. "Friends, we are safe here, but for how long? We have supplies, but for how long? We have survived, but for how much longer? It is time to retake control of our own destinies. We are not cattle to be herded to and fro. We are not beasts of burden to unwillingly take part in our owner's chores. No, we are a free people. We are still citizens of the United States, the *real* United States! Not one led by a self-appointed hack of a president! This will not continue, this will not stand." Trent paused for a moment, lowering his voice. "We will have our freedom, we will take back our rights, we will survive, and we will do it on our own terms!"

The room erupted in cheering and clapping and with that scene, any thoughts of staying were washed away from Bexar and Jessie's minds.

Safe and hidden, Bexar and Jessie later discussed how an uprising, a mutiny like this, could have happened under their noses and the answer was simple. Wright and the original crew of survivors had held this facility together. With their deaths and Jessie's attempt to recover the facility while making it safer for the future, she had been away from people for too long. All the work with the top-side dorms, the jaunt into the desert with Bexar, sleeping in their tent while trying to pretend that everything was fine, and all of it took Jessie away for too long and their group was too fragile to survive.

So now, early the next morning, the two and a half members of the Reed family snuck out of the secret facility that was built into the already-secret underground facility and toward the surface. Large, old-style ALICE packs bulged with the weight of the supplies they were taking from the secondary facility's own storeroom. Partially due to trying to be silent and use good tactics, but also due to their loaded packs, they climbed the stairs slowly, pausing on the false landings between floors to catch their breath and listen for anyone.

A facility clock on the wall of the secret internal bunker said it was 0300, not that they could have been able to tell being so far below ground. Regardless, the facility night crew should be on duty, if Trent hadn't ended the watch cycle. Jessie wrote the watch cycle list as well as the on-duty rounds and checks; she just hoped that they still used it.

Slowly and quietly, they crept higher and higher, closer to the exit with each step. Sweat dripped off the tip of Jessie's nose as they finally stepped into the cold dark morning air of topside. The moon shone brightly, casting long gray moonlight shadows. Moving with purpose, Bexar and Jessie moved into the shadows of the other hangars, edging their way to the door and to where they had left the FJ. There wasn't any sign of the Zeds that had been swarming on the other side of the mountains.

The FJ sat as they left it only a few hours before. Jessie dropped her ruck on the ground by the rear bumper and made her way to the large hangar door to open it. Bexar dropped his ruck and tossed it into the back of the SUV before picking up Jessie's ruck and doing the same. He shut the rear door and walked around the front toward the hood. They had left the plug going from the coil to the distributor disconnected before leaving the FJ unattended. Now that they were sure to leave, Bexar wanted to make sure that the FJ would be there upon their return so they could.

Bexar heard the slow rattle of the hangar door opening as he reconnected the plug and shut the hood. He turned to climb into the driver's seat when he was stopped in his tracks.

"Easy there, guy. You don't want to do this," Bexar said softly. Only about 18 inches away from his face was the dark muzzle of an M4. One of Trent's men stood on the other side of the rifle, night vision goggles flipped down in front of his face.

"Sure I do, but not as badly as I want to kill your bitch..."

That was the last word Bexar heard as the world went black around him.

New Ulm, Montana

Quietly, Steve Dorsey made his way topside to the Launch Control Support Building. He shouldn't be able to re-enter the launch control center below ground by himself, but in the weeks prior, he had made modifications to make sure he wouldn't be locked out of his new home.

Checking the interior of the building, which looked a bit like a large ranch-style home, Dorsey was confident that he was alone and the building was free of Zeds. He hadn't called them Zeds until everyone on the radio began referring to the dead as such. Moving quickly, Dorsey powered his home-built spark gap radio, which cracked and hummed to life. While listening to the sparse transmissions between two people he didn't know, Dorsey wrote out the short message and pulled his hand-written Morse code chart out of the pile of yellow paper pads stacked on the table.

After waiting for a short break in the radio traffic, Dorsey held the key down, blasting the radio spectrum with a continuous buzzing tone before keying "BK BK BK" to signal others to break the line for his transmission, followed by his chosen radio name and the call sign for the station at Groom Lake. After repeating the call sign, a return transmission of "GA" was transmitted from the Groom Lake station, signaling Dorsey that he was clear to transmit.

"URGENT COL SMITH ICBM REWIRE 4 ROGUE LAUNCH MM 3 SAYS PREZ AUTH ULM FLT 1 M 1"

Steve heard the elevator from the access shaft at the other end of the building and pulled the power lead to the radio, stood, and walked out of the room as calmly as he could. Walking back toward the access shaft, he was met by the colonel about halfway there.

"You're up and about early this morning, Steve."

"Yes, sir. Woke up and...had, was concerned that I hadn't checked that the doors were all properly latched and decided to check on it."

If Clint suspected that he was lying, Steve couldn't tell; the man's face showed no emotion, no reaction either way, like looking at a wax figure.

"Good idea. If you're done, we should get back down below. Since you're up, let's get some coffee on and we'll get to work. We have a lot to do."

"Yes, sir." Steve stepped into the elevator and pressed the appropriate button.

Groom Lake

Bill blinked hard. One of his radiomen stood in the open door to the office he converted into his own personal room, which was more like a tiny dorm room than an efficiency apartment. Light backlit the man, but Bill knew his voice. It was one of the civilians who had taken up some slack by working in the radio hut.

"I think this is urgent and we can't figure out some of what it says."

Sitting up on his green government cot, the dark figure stepped into the room and flipped the light switch before presenting the hand-written piece of paper to Bill. After reading the note once, Bill read it again and once more before bolting to his feet and walking toward the door. "I need to get a second opinion on this, uh, has Dallas checked on the net yet?"

"No, but we haven't reached your '*be concerned*' date, so we aren't too worried about Amanda yet."

"OK, fine, but if this means what I think it means, we need to make contact with her immediately."

Groom Lake

Walls shook from the onslaught, but the cinderblock and concrete-constructed hut of an office took the abuse, for now. The sound of the passing mass of the dead was terrible, a cross between a guttural inhuman noise and human moans. It stirred a primal fear in both Gonzo and Chivo, one so deep and ancient as to be nearly overwhelming. Both of them were seasoned special operators and war-fighters, pipe hitters of the highest order, so although fear raged below their skin, their faces never showed it. From the fear, a rage burned against the situation. For men of action, waiting was hard to do.

Neither slept. Instead, they slumped into the alert while resting false nap that combat veterans perfected. The noise of bodies slapping against the exterior walls had slowed in tempo, the passing moans of the swarming Zeds growing fainter until only few could be heard. Chivo's best estimation was that they had been sheltering from the dead for over 12 hours. Gonzo had tried his mobile radio with no success. There would be no rescue, no Quick Reaction Force to come to their aid; they simply had to wait and hope the Zed swarm would continue north.

The limited view out of the small bullet-resistant windows showed them both exactly what they expected. Stragglers remained, but compared to before, it was like finally being alone.

"Looks like it's nearly time to pop smoke, dude."

Chivo nodded. "Good. We have a long walk ahead of us, mano. If we want a chance to make it before nightfall, we're going to have to get moving."

The previous night had been spent in near silence. Gonzo watched Chivo field strip each of his weapons one by one to clean and inspect. Once Chivo had reassembled his pistol, the last firearm of the three to be cleaned, Gonzo began on his own M4 and pistol. Although the time was spent in silence, Gonzo spent the time trying to figure out who Chivo was simply by inferring what he could by the skills he possessed, trying to match up what he saw with what Chivo claimed to be. It was obvious to Gonzo that his new shipmate was well practiced with the weapons beyond just being a dedicated civilian shooter, down to the way he moved when clearing this building, but the most telling aspect was Chivo's eyes. His eyes burned with an intensity that would be lost on most, but Gonzo understood.

With purpose, they formed up, unsecured the outside door, and stepped into the blowing dust and bright sunlight. A few yards away was the first Zed, which was treated to a knee kicked through and broken by Chivo who was careful to keep free of the clawing grasp of the dead fingers as it fell. They had agreed to withhold from firing any of their weapons unless absolutely necessary for concern of attracting even more of the dead.

Spacing out on the roadway as they would on patrol in hostile territory, they set off at a comfortable but quick pace. Chivo took the lead, sweeping his eyes and head back and forth as he scanned the area for any threats.

What I wouldn't give for a sharp hatchet or a good tomahawk right now, something with an easy swing. Chivo made a mental note on that thought; he was going to dig through the storeroom on Level 5 for a hatchet, or maybe an entrenching tool. He could sharpen an edge of the folding shovel entrenching tool like the Soviets used to do. Whatever the solution, Chivo needed a quiet hand tool that he could swing for a Zed kill.

Groom Lake

It took most of the morning to figure out where the message was referring to, but the tiny town of Ulm, Montana, was found on a road atlas that someone had found, which made a lot of sense now that Bill could see it. Ulm was outside of Great Falls, which was home to Malmstrom Air Force Base, which was home to a bunch of flights of Minutemen III ICBMs spread across the area. The real problem now was figuring out what "FLT 1 M 1" meant in terms of specific location. It was suggested that the message stood for "Flight 1 of Missile 1," but even if it did, no one knew where that was. One survivor had been to the Minutemen III National Historic Site once and described what it would look like above ground, but without overhead photography, satellite imagery, or anything else to help, they had no idea where to look.

Earlier that morning, Bill made the decision that they would not transmit in the blind trying to reach President Lampton. He worried that those transmissions could strike panic in anyone else listening if there was no response from Dallas. Instead, they would wait for her or Andrew to contact them, assuming they would. In the meantime, they would try to figure out more of the details.

Hours before, Bill sent someone to wakeup Jessie, but so far no one could locate her. Her Toyota FJ was verified to be in the hangar above ground, so she had to be in the facility, but she was nowhere to be found. Two of the radiomen were still searching for Jessie so Bill walked into the cafeteria hoping to grab a light lunch before returning to his mission at hand and was surprised by the large crowd.

The tables were pushed aside, leaving an open area at the front near the serving lines. Rows of chairs filled most of the open area and it seemed that a majority of the survivors were sitting in attendance. At the front was Trent, making an impassioned speech while pointing at Bexar and Jessie. Bill looked at Jessie first and gasped. Her eyes were swollen, puffy, and bruised, blood crusted on her mouth and face, and her nose appeared to be broken. Her shoulders sagged and it took a moment for Bill to realize that her hands were handcuffed or tied behind her back. The hair on the left side of Bexar's head was matted and thick with crusted and seeping blood. Bexar's nose was broken as well. He stood with his hands handcuffed behind his back as well. It looked like someone had beat both of them with a pole and the other men who stood at the front with Trent appeared to be the ones who had given out the beatings.

Trent asked the gathered crowd for a verbal vote. Once completed, he turned to Bexar. "Well, there you go, sport. The majority has spoken."

Bexar spit blood and mucus in Trent's face. One of Trent's men hit Bexar in the head with a heavy leather sap, which sent Bexar crashing to the floor.

"Pick that trash up and bring them both topside; it's time to carry out the will of the people!"

The crowd parted to let Trent and his men through as they dragged Bexar and Jessie with them. Trent paused for a moment as he passed Bill and gave him a wink with a smile that seemed to suck all the warmth out of the room. After waiting for the following crowd of fellow survivors, Bill fell in behind them and followed everyone above ground. He wasn't sure what was going to happen, but Bill had a really good guess.

SSC

"OK, Amanda, I think it'll work this time. Flip it," Andrew yelled from down the hall.

Amanda Lampton flipped the toggle switch. Sizzling and humming, the radio came to life, followed immediately by a small electric spark that snapped across the leads. The air in the room began to smell from the ionization of the radio.

"Great job, Andrew," Amanda called over her shoulder.

Andrew smiled as he came into the room. After sitting next to President Lampton at the conference table with the newly completed spark gap radio, Andrew held a pen over a yellow pad of paper while glancing at a cheat sheet of Morse code. The transmission was slow enough that Andrew was able to transpose the sparking dits and dahs, the dots and dashes into letters and words, while waiting for the next letter to be sent. It felt like listening to a story being told by a three year old—confusing, out of context, and being told exceptionally slow—but eventually, they began to understand what the words were saying, even if they didn't understand the message.

"These guys have their own shortcut codes. I don't understand what 'MM3' is supposed to mean and why this guy is so concerned."

Amanda responded saying she didn't know either. The next transmission was garbled, multiple stations trying to transmit at once, their radio signals causing a flurry of noise.

Three hours passed before they were able to figure out that some of the transmissions were talking about a missile.

Groom Lake

Gonzo had point as they rounded the last mountain. Chivo wiped sweat from his face and checked behind them for any straggling Zeds. They hadn't seen one in an hour, which suited Chivo just fine, since he had been worried that the swarm had gone east instead of continuing north. A swarm of Zeds that large tearing through the hangars and old buildings of Area 51 could have wrecked it, although the underground facility shouldn't have been affected. Chivo estimated they were about a half a click from the destroyed hangar and the door back underground.

As tempting as it was to walk straight to the hangar and their home base, Chivo noted that Gonzo was leading them on a longer route around the edge, giving them a better chance to check for an ambush. Not that Chivo expected one, but better men than he had died for not following good tactics.

The old U-2 hangars were their last large piece of cover and concealment as they rounded the corner to have the ramp in view. Gonzo held up his hand to signal stop before giving the signal for enemy.

No shit, puentas set an ambush, Chivo thought to himself as he scanned his area of responsibility, which was the opposite direction of where Gonzo had been looking when he stopped. Chivo glanced over his shoulder at Gonzo and saw the signal for him to come forward. A moment later, Chivo nodded in response and retrieved the .50-caliber that was still lashed to the side of his ruck. Lying on his rifle, his heavy pack off his shoulders and by his side, Chivo surveyed the scene through the powerful optic mounted on the rifle. Gonzo quietly made a series of radio calls. Aymond, Kirk, Davis, and Jones were about one and half-clicks south trying to get a bulldozer running again. They were responding with the remaining M-ATV, but Hammer was up in the control tower. He hadn't seen the crowd of survivors pour out of the underground access but he turned and scanned the scene with the powerful binoculars they had found in the tower.

"There are two people in the middle of the crowd that appear to be prisoners...it almost looks like a fucking lynch mob, mano. Chivo continued to watch. The mass of people and his low position meant he couldn't see much detail in the crowd; there were too many people and too much movement. The doors to the hangar where the vehicles were parked were pushed open and two ropes were thrown over the extended door frame on the side of the hangar. A moment later, the ropes went taut as two writhing bodies were slowly pulled into the air as they kicked. Both people had black trash bags over their heads, their hands handcuffed behind their backs and their feet bound.

"It is a lynch mob, two victims; I can't tell who the people are...shit!"

Chivo didn't finish his sentence. The hard blast from the big rifle's muzzle brake and the concussive recoil caused sand and dust to bounce off the ground into the air. Gonzo could barely hear the radio, but thought Hammer said "pregnant" before another round was fired by Chivo. Hammer's big sniper rifle barked, the sound echoing off the buildings and mountains. Chivo watched as Jessie's rope slid off the ruined metal door track, the metal support ripped apart by two successive .50-caliber rifle rounds. Her body jerked and shook against her restraints. Chivo's aim shifted so he could see Bexar and was pleased to see Bexar's rope following Jessie's as they fell the couple of feet to the hard pavement. The rifle kept moving as Chivo scanned for hostiles. He saw a man pointing and yelling just before his head vaporized into a red mist, the rolling rifle report of another pipe hitter taking up slack.

Chivo could wait no longer and had barely leapt to his feet when he had started running toward the crowd and to where Bexar and Jessie had disappeared as they fell. The other M-ATV flew past, bounding across the ramp and sliding to a stop on the edge of the crowd. Four Marines burst out of the armored truck and took position, pushing the crowd back with their presence while Aymond gave loud stern commands. Chivo kept running until he reached where Bexar and Jessie were being sat up and tended to by Bill.

Bill pulled the trash bags off their heads and Chivo saw they both looked rough. Someone had done a number on them both. After retrieving the handcuff key from under his belt, as he had in New Mexico, both Bexar and Jessie's hands were freed before Chivo cut off the zip ties binding their feet.

"What the fuck, mano?"

Bill shook his head. Jessie spit blood out of her mouth and spoke first. "Like a fucking military coup, some asshole I don't really know named Trent somehow has everyone thinking we're dictators or despots or something. Had a kangaroo court and sentenced us to death."

"And they tried to overthrow you," Chivo finished.

Aymond walked up. "Chivo, SITREP."

"Chief, Situation Report is that they had a coup led by a man named Trent, decided to kill Jessie and Bexar."

Aymond's facial expression didn't change. "According to some of the others, Trent is down hard. Hammer center-punched his face."

"Good," Bexar replied.

There was still shouting in the crowd a few dozen yards away. Aymond helped Jessie to her feet while Chivo helped Bexar. Both were unsteady as they stood, red marks across their necks from the ropes. "Bill! Bill! We made contact! Bill!"

Bill turned and saw one of his radiomen, Brian, waving his arms frantically, the Marines not letting him out of the crowd or past them. Aymond looked at Bill and issued a quick command via radio and Brian was let past.

"Bill, we made contact, she made contact, the President." Brian held out a piece of paper, which Bill took and read quickly before handing it to Jessie.

"I don't get it, who is Clint?"

Chivo took the paper from Jessie and read the single line quickly.

Andrew coming 4 Chivo, kill Clint, stop launch.

Chivo looked up. "What launch, Bill?"

"Early this morning, we received a message from Montana that a Colonel Smith was sent on presidential orders to rewire a Minutemen III ICBM to be launched. I don't know who Clint is unless President Lampton knows him."

"Yeah, she knows him, I know him, and he isn't a colonel. He's a fucking secret squirrel like Cliff, same organization supposedly, but something is wrong with them. Cliff tried to kill us in Colorado then saved Bexar and I in Utah. Clint had been with the president at the SSC...rewire an ICBM, that sounds crazy. I didn't think you could do that."

Aymond shook his head. "It sounds like the plot of some damn bad late-night TV movie."

"It does, but the original message was very short. I think the guy meant that the launch controls were being rewired, not the missile."

"That still doesn't make any sense, Bill; those systems are really complex and robust."

"I assume they are, I have no idea, but if this Clint is some sort of secret agent, maybe he knows something we don't know, but what we're not asking is what the missile would then be aimed at."

Bexar's eyebrows arched. "How long will it take Andrew to get here from Dallas?"

Chivo answered first. "He could get here as early as tonight after dark, but I'm going to bet that it'll be tomorrow. So that means we have this afternoon to figure out what to do with this goat fuck before I go TDY so Bexar and Jessie are safe."

"Don't bother, we're bugging out. Fucking Trent and his cronies caught us as we were sneaking out with packs full of supplies. And once we get those supplies, Bexar and I are leaving." Jessie's face was dirty, dried blood and dirt crusted on the corners of her mouth and under her nose. Her cold gaze cut through whoever she looked at.

"You were just going to pop smoke like that, mano?"

"I didn't want to, but I didn't know where you were or when you would be back." Bexar pulled a folded and now blood-stained piece of paper out of his pocket. "I was going to leave you this note."

"Where are you headed?"

"Guillermo and Angel's compound, until at least after the baby is born."

Chivo smiled at Jessie. "Well, Mrs. Bexar, with the recent developments, I think that's a good idea. Where did they take the packs from you?"

Jessie described the location, the packs, and the rest of their missing gear. Brian went in search for the missing packs and weapons; Kirk followed along at Aymond's request to assist and give protection if needed. Chivo took a green notepad of waterproof paper out of his pocket, wrote a short note, and handed it to Bexar.

"Put that in your pocket. If you end up back in Texas, you might need it—plan B."

Bexar looked at the paper and saw a short series of directions and instructions with a long code. He folded it and put it in his pocket.

"Hey, mano, leave word if you move. I'll be there to visit your new baby in a few months if I don't see you sooner, but I need to get below ground and put together what I'm going to need to go after Clint."

Chivo hugged Bexar and then kissed Jessie on the cheek before jogging off back toward where he left his ruck and .50-caliber rifle.

Aymond turned. "We'll keep you secure until you leave, but what about this mess?"

Jessie shook her head. "You have the fucking conch, Piggy," and raised a middle finger toward the survivors who had been part of the lynch mob and were now milling about on the surface.

Twenty minutes later, Brian and Kirk reappeared with two bulky packs, Bexar and Jessie's rifles, pistols, and the rest of their gear. The couple re-armed, the gear stowed in the FJ that still sat in the hangar, and they drove off across the ramp and away from the dwindling crowd.

Aymond turned and looked at the survivors who were still milling around on the concrete ramp. "Well shit."

After a moment, he keyed his radio. "Hammer, good shooting; Jones and Davis, take the truck and get the bulldozer running. Kirk and I are going to go below decks and try to sort this shit out."

Aymond turned to Bill. "Get a message to the president. Inform her that we've stopped an uprising. I'm in charge and Chivo is ready."

Nevada

"Desert, town, or mountains?"

"Either town or mountains, baby, but not desert." Erin didn't have to yell at Jason over the wind noise because they were stopped at a stop sign intersection for two small highways. Surprisingly, the highway junction sign was still standing. The normal route to Las Vegas was out; the PLA soldiers and huge mass of Zeds took care of that.

Erin looked over her shoulder to see if they still had chasing Zeds. There were a few, but she couldn't see if the swarm was following or if the PLA was following. Jason turned right and accelerated. If he had turned left, they would have continued back the way they had come and back to the turnoff for Groom Lake. They needed to get east and they needed to get south so to get to Erin's chosen destination, so a right turn east it was.

They drove in silence for the next 20 minutes, holding each other's hand, Erin slid over to sit next to Jason. They passed a couple of abandoned buildings on the highway. One had a sign proclaiming "Cactus Springs Saloon," but with the sun still off the horizon and a known good location for shelter in reach, Jason decided to keep driving for a while longer to see if they found anything better. Something with supplies to raid would be ideal.

A serious fence appeared along the road to the north, with runways and a copse of government buildings. There were more fences within the fence line, tanks, and a control tower. Inside one of the inside fenced areas were a line of trucks that looked like the one that President Lampton had driven up in: big, armored, and painted in desert colors. Jason squinted against the wind of their destroyed beater of a Suburban and decided that was where he and Erin would spend the night and one of those trucks would be their new ride.

Jason turned and drove across the median of Highway 95 and up the drive to what appeared to be the main gate for the government airbase. The sign declared it to be the Creech Air Force Base and that they were in Indian Springs, Nevada. Really, Jason didn't care, but it's nearly impossible to see a sign and actually *not* read it.

The steel bar gates were shut. Jason stopped the Suburban in front of the entry gate and climbed out, Erin joining him. On top of the gates, on top of the brick walls next to the gates and along the entire perimeter fence, were three strands of barbered wire wrapped by concertina razor wire.

"Shit." Jason shook his head.

"No, it's fine, babe. Pull the Suburban between the gates across from the guard shack."

Erin pointed and watched as Jason turned and moved the big SUV broadside to the section of steel bar fence between the gates. The guard shack sat behind the fence, behind the barbed wire and beyond the razor wire. After handing her M4 to Jason, Erin climbed onto the hood and stepped onto the roof of the Suburban; Erin took a couple quick steps and jumped as hard as she could.

Her feet cleared the razor wire and she landed hard on the toccata tile roof of the small guard shack, slid off the side, and fell to the ground. Jason began to get out, following her over the fence, when Erin pulled herself to her feet and held up a hand. She limped to the control box behind the fence and rattled the padlock on the black box. "I need your shotgun."

Jason unslung his short 12 gauge and passed it between the steel bars of the gate to Erin. Erin flipped the safety and fired once at nearly point-blank range. The padlock fell, destroyed by the 00-buckshot barrage. She flipped open the box and released the clutch brake for the gate. The gate now slid open with ease. Once Jason drove the Suburban past the gate, Erin pushed it closed, secured the clutch brake, and shut the box. Just because they got in didn't mean that they should leave the gate open for everybody.

Ulm, Montana

A thick 3-ring binder sat open on the slide-out desk of the launch control cockpit. Steve wasn't sure if the seat for one of the officers in charge of launching a nuclear war was called a cockpit, but to his fighter-joke mind, it would only be so. To his left was a wall of electronic equipment mounted in an enclosed rack, handles sticking out on each of the boxy modules. Currently, the electronic module on the top row far left position was out. This was their first "hard wire" adjustment. To say it was "hard wire" would be wrong; the modules were mostly printed circuit boards with microprocessors and transistors. The piece looked nearly modern, but not quite current technology, like the motherboard from the old 386 computer Steve had purchased new in college.

However it appeared, the colonel had a small stack of 8" floppy disks, seriously old-school storage media that predated the 5 ½" and 3.5" floppies. Steve had only seen them in photographs. The 3-ring binder had exceptionally simple-to-follow instructions, but the wording was a little off, like the text had been machine-translated from a foreign language instead of originally being written in English.

In all the years that Steve Dorsey had been a professional military officer in the United States Air Force, he had never learned the technical details of how the Minutemen missile system really worked. He had no reason to and even if had wanted to, there was no way that Dorsey would have been given access to the documentation to learn even the basics. Yet here he was with Colonel Smith, whom Steve did not trust, and the monumental task of rewiring and then reprogramming a system designed specifically to prevent such a thing from occurring.

Dorsey flipped to the next page in the 3-ring binder, read the page, and returned to the first step. Screwdriver in hand, he stood next to the bank of equipment and began unscrewing the faceplate to the module that he located in the second position from the left on the third row from the top. The inside of the module was covered in thick dust bunnies that were held in place by the tangled web of cables and wiring over the circuit board. Steve shook his head and tried not to smile. *Damnit, this is going to be a pain in the ass, but a pain in the ass that will take a large amount of time. The more time I can waste, the more likely that I'll get a message back.*

The FJ

The cloud of dust trailing the FJ from the dirt road was like a giant red arrow in the sky pointed down at their vehicle, but so far the Zeds didn't appear to notice such things. Bexar hadn't seen any show any signs of intelligence like that. Not that it mattered now; they were back on the paved road, the same small highway that Bexar and Jessie had used to get to Groom Lake, although that had been two separate times and trips. The route that Bexar decided to follow was the same route that he and Chivo had taken to get to Groom Lake if only because he was familiar with it and he knew how to get to Guillermo's place via this route. A few minutes after riding on the smoother paved highway, Jessie was asleep. The adrenaline of their morning had long faded and the exhaustion of the ordeal took hold. A road sign indicated they were nearing Crystal Springs.

Bexar's eyes snapped open as he took a sharp breath, his heart racing upon the realization that he had been asleep at the wheel. As quickly startled as Bexar had been, the exhaustion began to lie heavily on his shoulders. This was not going to be the quick few hours long day trip that he had planned. If they were going to make it, Bexar would have to find a place to stop for a rest. If they had already driven through Crystal Springs, he didn't know, but at the T-intersection where the FJ idled, a sign across the highway advertised Alien Fresh Jerky. A large mural was on display behind it, along with a portable building that may not have looked much better before the end of the world.

After gently shaking Jessie awake, the FJ idled in the gravel parking lot while they cleared the building.

"This place is weird."

"Think about it. These guys are awesome. Where else are you going to find your alien souvenirs for visiting the famously secret Area 51?" Bexar held up a bumper sticker that had "I BELIEVE" printed on it next to a cartoon of a flying saucer. "I'm going to put this on the FJ."

Bexar turned and walked out. Jessie shook her head and began filling a shopping bag with what was left of the beef jerky selection when the sound of a single gunshot thumped through the thin walls.

"Shit." Jessie dropped the bag and ran outside.

The store was really just a manufactured building set in place on blocks off the desert floor, so the front door was a few feet off the ground with a handful of steps off the front landing. Jessie stepped into thin air where the ground would have been if she hadn't been at the top of the stairs. Bexar lay on his back near the FJ, one Zed already put down, dark pus-filled blood and brain matter soaking into the dusty lot. Another Zed had Bexar pinned to the ground while its rotted face and head stretched against Bexar's outstretched arms, blackened teeth gnashing and snapping while its hands clawed at Bexar's shirt and body. Bexar's pistol lay a few feet away in the sand near the other Zed.

Jessie took those details in as she fell down the stairs, hitting the ground hard. Her foot rolled to the inside with a hard pop and before she had even stopped falling, Jessie knew she had really hurt herself as pain shot through her leg and took her breath away. Unable to breathe, unable to yelp or cry, Jessie saw stars when she ended up on her back, motionless. She wasn't motionless for long. Rolling on her stomach, Jessie lay a little crooked from the growing baby bump. Jessie fired two rounds from her rifle, the first hit the Zed in the shoulder, the second catching the back of its skull. Its head erupted in a surreal fountain of dark brain matter, which showered Bexar with bits of skull and pus.

Bexar pushed the body off of him and lay on the ground gasping, trying to catch his breath. Jessie rolled onto her side and clutched her left foot and ankle. She yelped in pain with each ragged breath while poking her ankle, which was already swelling rapidly.

"All of this because of your stupid fucking bumper sticker! I hate this place, I hate this world, I hate everything that has happened!"

After retrieving his pistol, Bexar checked himself for bites. He couldn't find any, but he was slick with sweat and dark, ugly smelling blood. He helped Jessie up and mostly carried her back into the small shop.

"Do you think you broke it?"

Jessie shook her head no.

"Good, well at least we've got that. I'll get the med kit. I don't know if Jack kept any instant ice packs, but we'll figure something out and get your ankle wrapped. Bexar helped Jessie stand on her right leg while he pushed all the stuff off the top of a folding table to give Jessie room to lie down. A handful of T-shirts were used for a pillow and to elevate her left foot.

"I'll be right back."

Bexar walked outside and scanned the area more carefully this time before ripping off his own shirt and throwing it on the ground. It was covered in dirt, pus, blood, and sweat; if he needed another shirt, he would have a touristy souvenir. A few moments later, Bexar had Jack's medical bag and was back inside the store with Jessie. There was a single instant ice pack in the kit, which he handed Jessie while getting the ACE bandages out of their packaging. Jessie followed the instructions and broke the inside container, mixing the chemicals that created rapidly forming "ice." After prepping the bandages, Bexar unlaced Jessie's boot and pulled it off as gently as he could, with only one gasping yelp from his wife. He enjoyed making her scream, but not like this.

Her ankle was bad, already turning colors and already really swollen. Bexar wrapped the ankle as best he could before applying the ice pack and wrapping that in place with more bandages. After kissing his wife on the forehead, Bexar pulled Jessie's pistol out of her holster and placed it in her hands.

"I need your help to check for bites. I don't know if that last one got me or not. Make it quick if you have to...I love you."

After stripping nude, Bexar stood a few feet away from Jessie as he looked carefully at each arm and hand, and what he could see of his shoulders, chest, and stomach. Slowly, he turned in place, raising his arms away from his side; Jessie's hands shook while she held her pistol and watched, inspecting her husband's battered and bruised body.

"I don't know if I can do it if you're bit, baby," Jessie said.

The last few months have been incredibly hard, harder than anyone could have imagined, and their bodies were proof of that. Tears streamed down Jessie's cheeks. *Except that it is going to get much harder. How am I going to raise this child? What will I tell her?*

Buffalo, Texas

Usually, the drive from Centerville to Buffalo was a trivial matter, and the reality of Ken's situation was that the drive turned out to be no big deal. Upon arriving in Buffalo, Ken realized that the big deal was being in a town so close to the interstate. Sure, he was on Highway 75, but I-45 followed set off a few miles to the west and that had been a problem last night. It was still a problem this morning too. With all the Zed activity the previous afternoon, sleeping in his truck seemed like a safe bet, especially with how he had his truck parked. The previous afternoon, Ken had backed the truck into an open storage unit at one of those tiny mini-storage places. After checking that he could operate the latch from the inside, Ken had turned off his truck and lowered the roll-up door. This morning, he woke up to the sound of dead hands and bodies slapping against the metal door. The Zeds shook it so hard it nearly seemed like the door would cave in, but now he was safe in his truck, in a metal building with the only exit blocked. Dejected, Ken sat in the driver's seat trying to decide if he could roll up the door and get into the truck fast enough that he wouldn't be trapped or bitten. He knew that it would be impossible. With a heavy sigh, Ken opened his door and squeezed out to look and think.

Something bumped his elbow as he slid along the corrugated metal wall. Ken looked at the offending small lump and saw the head of a sheet metal screw. Looking up and down the wall, he saw the seam between two corrugated sheets and the smalls screws that held them in place against a metal stud. Smiling, Ken opened a box in the bed of the truck and retrieved a small socket and ratchet set. After a couple of tries, the correctly sized socket was found and the sheet metal screws were being extracted one at a time. Ken was careful not to drop the screws, since he would end up driving over them and ruining a tire. About 10 minutes later, Ken had the wall peeled back and was making his way into the neighboring unit, which was full of old furniture and black trash bags of clothing. He rattled the latch; it was locked from the outside.

After a few moments trying to come up with a plan, Ken made his way to the next wall by clearing away some furniture and he began removing the screws holding that wall together. Two more walls and nearly 30 minutes later, Ken stood in an empty unit that had an unlocked roll-up door. Satisfied, Ken made his way back to *his* unit, retrieved his M1 rifle, and started the truck. Unconcerned about the exhaust building up in that unit, Ken made his way through the peeled back sheet metal walls to his exit. After listening for a few seconds at the door, Ken slid the latch open and lifted hard on the door. It rattled open with a loud bang, just as Ken stepped into the sunlight. A few seconds later, the M1 was empty with a distinctive ping sound of the empty ammo clip being ejected and four Zeds lay ruined on the ground in front of the metal door with his idling truck behind it.

Ken retrieved the spent ammo clip and put it in his pocket. Before he could leave, Ken dragged the bodies away from the front of his truck. He didn't want to drive over one and accidentally damage a tire from one of the bones. Pointing north on Highway 75, Ken took the left turn on 164.He would have to cross under I-45, but once clear, he would be between I-35 and I-45 and still be able to drive to Waxahachie.

Worst case, Ken thought, *I have to backtrack and take a different route. As long as I'm safe and smart about it all, I'll get there.*

Groom Lake

This was the second meeting of survivors in the cafeteria in as many days. The first spurred the second, except that this time a real warrior stood at the front of the crowd instead of a person who Aymond considered to have been a coward.

"Until President Lampton orders otherwise, this facility is under my command. If you are unwilling to accept that fact, then the stairs to leave is that way. I will not tolerate another coup attempt. I will not tolerate any action that places the lives of your fellow survivors at risk. Some of my men are still up top creating a network of fighting positions and earthen walls. Knowing what we know now about the PLA and Korean forces, they should have been built a long time ago, but they weren't so we're building them now. At first light tomorrow, we begin training to fight and defend our position from another attack. We fought them in San Diego, we fought them in Yuma, and we've fought them here. We have to assume that they will be back and with greater numbers."

"Why don't we just shut the front door and keep it locked?" someone from the crowd yelled to the front.

Aymond took a deep breath before answering. "What front door? The blast door was badly damaged in the last attack. If we're going to keep the below ground secure, then we must keep the above ground secure too. I need a representative from each of the 'towns' of survivors to come to the front. They will bring the rest of the information and details back to your berths."

The assembled crowd grumbled as people stood and began filtering out of the room. Aymond didn't try to listen to the conversations; he gave some instructions to Kirk as he left the room. He needed to check the storage deck and see what sort of real supplies he had at his disposal.

CHAPTER 10

April 13, Year 1
Groom Lake

"Roger."

Chivo didn't have a radio, so he didn't know what Aymond just replied to, but he guessed it was time to get topside; his taxi was arriving. Aymond confirmed Andrew had just touched down and was taxiing toward the destroyed hangar and what remained of the facility entrance.

Once topside, Chivo found company waiting for Andrew to pull to a stop. Someone in the facility had been tasked with providing fuel for Andrew, so two dirty red fuel cans sat at the edge of the hangar's slab. Next to the fuel cans, Oreo sat patiently with his tail wagging until Andrew cut the motor and the prop lurched to a stop, then Oreo ran to Andrew.

Chivo had very little gear compared to what he could have taken after raiding the facility storage, with Aymond's blessing. Going to an underground ICBM launch control facility to kill a real-life secret agent wasn't the sort of mission profile that necessitated a comically large rifle that was over four feet long. It was the sort of mission profile that necessitated cunning and a close-quarters war-fighting kit. The kit was mostly worn on the carrier he wore, but the rest was in the small ruck that Chivo just tossed in the space behind his seat.

"Chico, do you mind? I need to go below to top off my water bottles, use the boy's room, and grab a snack before we go."

"No, mano, go ahead. I'll just wait up here."

Andrew smiled wearily and walked toward the entrance. Chivo smiled back seeing Oreo plod happily along next to his friend.

"Chico...huh." Chivo turned and walked around the yellow aircraft. It was dirty and looked worn, lovingly worn and maintained, but used.

I'm not sure how long into society's new future things like these will be able to survive and function.

A significant portion of Chivo's military and paramilitary career could be described as "hurry up and wait." The world had ended and yet here he was in full kit for a mission and waiting.

"No hay bronca," Chivo said as he sat down on the tarmac under the shade of the wing.

About an hour later, Andrew and Oreo reappeared and walked toward the plane. After a hug goodbye, Oreo sat away from the plane while Andrew walked around it, climbed in, started the engine, and began taxiing toward the dry lakebed. A few moments later, they were airborne and flying north. Chivo guessed that the flight might take two days, but flying a few thousand feet off the ground at what felt like a walking speed, Chivo decided to update his guess to three or four days of flying.

"Captain, how long will it take us?"

Andrew smirked at being called captain. "Well, I'm not really sure. I didn't have a chance to plot out a flight plan. I'm guessing three days, maybe two if we get good winds. Also," Andrew yelled over the wind and engine noise, "just so you understand, I don't know where this secret missile place is."

"Not at all?"

"No, I mean, I know it's in Montana and south of Great Falls, but we're going to have to find it once we get there."

Chivo quietly changed his guess from four to five.

Outside Buffalo, Texas

The topography sucked. He was downhill from the overpass, the sight distance was short, and if the Zeds had any sort of military bearing, then they would have easily spotted him and his truck. Ken shifted into reverse and gently guided the green truck backward. There was a church a few hundred yards behind him and the parking lot could give him a chance to figure out his next move. Ken wasn't sure what that would be. He might have to simply be patient and wait, but he wasn't sure if he would have to wait an hour or a month.

Some of the other survivors on the radio net had talked about massive herds of Zeds roaming from place to place, and he had seen some smaller groups in the initial weeks after the attack, but this was like nothing he had ever thought possible. The highway crossed under I-45 and that made things worse, at least it appeared worse to Ken. Besides the Zeds that trickled past on the access road, dozens and dozens of bodies fell over the side of the bridges as the writhing mass of corpses walked past above. The whole sight sent chills down Ken's back. It was possibly the scariest thing he had ever seen.

After backing into the driveway for the Baptist church, Ken realized he was much too close to the interstate to be safe. Ken shifted and drove pulled out of the driveway to go back toward Buffalo because at the very least there was a more manageable number of dead back the way he had come a few minutes before.

Once Ken reached Highway 75, he saw that the Zeds from the morning had mostly shambled off after whatever it was that caught their attention. He ran the stop sign that strangely survived thus far and still stood at the intersection and turned north. After a couple of minutes of driving, Ken slammed on the brakes. Through the trees, he could see a row of semi-truck trailers. The wheels were gone and the large box trailers sat on the ground forming a makeshift perimeter wall around what appeared to be the high school. Ken's mind filled in "makeshift" as he tried to accurately describe it to himself, but that didn't seem right. Improvised may be a better word because it appeared to have worked well. Dried blood and gore caked on the sides of the trailer-wall from what must have been a large group of Zeds gave testament to the wall's functionality.

Maybe there are other people still alive in there!

Ken began rolling forward when his windshield shattered. The crack of a rifle followed quickly. Ken slammed his foot down, pinning the gas pedal to the floor. The truck roared in protest and lurched forward as another round impacted the b-pillar near his head.

Shit! What the actual fuck?

The back glass of the truck cab shattered with the impact of another round. Ken ducked below the view of the dash. Although the thin sheet metal offered no protection from rifle rounds, it somehow felt better than being visible. Ken didn't hear any more rounds impact the truck and had miraculously kept the truck mostly on the road while fleeing. As quickly as everything had become exceptionally dangerous, Ken was clear of the attacker and alone in the countryside on an empty two-lane Texas highway. What few cars there had been were pushed into the fence lines and trees along the side of the road; they were badly damaged. After letting the truck settle into a safer speed, Ken decided that he would keep on until reaching Dew then see if I-45 was clear enough to cross, or maybe he could find one of the crossing roadways that goes over the interstate, but he couldn't remember which roads crossed over or under the interstate.

Crystal Springs, Nevada

Jessie woke with a start. Her ankle throbbed painfully; the Advil found behind the counter did little to ease the pain of her badly swollen ankle. Dried tears left crust on the edges of her eyes, and the previous night had been horrible. She couldn't believe how badly everything had gone in such a short time. Jessie no longer felt safe at Groom Lake—obviously after the uprising had tried to kill her and Bexar—where they were was unsustainable in the middle of the Nevada desert. The only extra supplies they had found was some of the different homemade jerky that the store sold.

Bexar was already awake, sitting up against the wall near the front door. He wore a silly souvenir T-shirt with a cartoon alien head on the front of it. Jessie had cried the entire time she checked him for bite marks. She was sure that after having her Bexar back, after losing her daughter, after losing Malachi, Jack, and Sarah, that she would then be left alone with a husband killed by the damn Zeds that she would have to shoot to save him from a death wandering the wasted world in which the now lived.

"Good morning, beautiful," Bexar smiled at his wife.

"Hey, sexy."

Bexar was filthy; dirt mixed with the dark, foul blood of the undead was still streaked across his face and arms. Jessie didn't care. She wasn't sure the last time that she had felt this in love.

"Baby, I need to pee."

Bexar smiled as he got up to help his wife. Jessie couldn't put any weight on her severely sprained ankle, and being a little off balance from the pregnancy didn't help. Gingerly, Bexar helped his wife up and outside. The landing by the door was made of wood, like a backyard deck, and it had arm rails on each side before the steps and the turnoff for the wheelchair ramp. That would have to do for a woman who now was unable to support her weight and squat to relieve herself. After sliding her pants down, Bexar picked up Jessie and helped her to the top of the rail, her bare ass hanging off the side.

"You better not let a Zed bite me in the ass."

Jessie steadied herself by holding onto Bexar and began laughing at the absurdity of their situation. If just six months ago someone would have described this scene to them, it would have sounded like a badly written novel; now they were living in one.

A handful of Zeds shambled in their direction from the highway, but it wasn't worth Bexar firing on them. Over a hundred yards away, they weren't an immediate threat yet and the rifle fire would attract even more. Bexar was amazed; the Zeds had a super-human ability to hone in on gunfire like no other. They may not get to the shooter very quickly, with their broken gait, but they would eventually get there. Then when more gathered together, even more arrived, like one of them sent the others a message about a happening party.

"That's it," Bexar said after helping Jessie off the rail and with her pants, pulling them up instead of down for once.

"What?"

"Aymond had that Zed bug zapper truck. If we had a few of those trucks and then were able to have a loud continuous sound, like an air raid siren to attract the dead, we could kill off huge numbers of the without having to fire a single shot."

"Great, but how do we get more than one of those trucks?"

"I assume we could from the Koreans or the Chinese or whoever these fucks are."

"Sure, you could walk up to the next group we find and just ask, 'uh, excuse me, I know you attacked us and invaded our country and shit, but could we have some of your Zed-Zapper trucks?' Yeah, I'm convinced that they would go for it."

"You know you can be a real bitch sometimes."

"And you still love me in spite of it."

"Maybe I love you because of it?"

Jessie had her arm around Bexar's shoulder so he could help carry her back inside as she hopped along with her one good leg. He smiled when she kissed him on his dirty cheek.

"Well, I'm sure that Aymond and President Amanda can figure that out. For now, we need to either get on the road to St. George or we need to prep to stay here longer."

"I'm not sure I could handle riding in the FJ very far. But more importantly, I know that I couldn't fight for shit like this."

Bexar helped Jessie lay down on the floor and slid an empty box under her swollen ankle to keep it elevated.

"OK, I'm going to hide the FJ and drag the Zeds we killed out of view. I'll probably have to drop the other Zeds out on the road before they start giving us problems over here. I'll be back in a bit."

Bexar knelt and kissed Jessie on the forehead before walking out the door.

The Zeds were shambling closer, following the last movement they had seen disappear into the lone building in the area. Now only about 25 yards from the building, Bexar still didn't want to use his rifle if at all possible. He took out his heavy custom CM Forge blade and walked toward the closest Zed. The knife had survived through a number of situations in which Bexar should have been killed and he was thankful to still have it. As heavy as it was to carry, its functionality in the post-apocalyptic world had been proven time and time again. It was worth the weight.

Getting closer, Bexar picked up his pace from a walk to a trot, closing the distance to the first Zed. Bexar kicked hard like he was kicking open the door to a crack house and plunged his knife into the bridge of the nose of the Zed he had knocked to the ground. Rocking the knife, he pulled it free, leaving a gaping, ragged hole where the heavy blade had ruined the undead's face and skull. Bexar stood and rotated, plunging the knife into the temple of the next Zed, this one falling with his knife planted firmly in the skull, ripping the butt of the knife out of his grip. Bexar turned, drawing his pistol, and shot the next Zed in the face, which was a few yards away. The back of its skull exploded outward as it crumpled to the dusty parking lot. The next Zed's jaw was missing, torn from its face sometime before. Unable to bite, Bexar still didn't trust that it couldn't hurt him and that Zed was shot in the skull.

Before holstering, Bexar tucked his pistol into the SUL position and turned in place, scanning the area for any more threats. Satisfied he was alone for the moment, Bexar retrieved his knife, wiped the putrid-smelling, pus-filled blood off the blade on what remained of the Zed's jeans before holstering the knife. With a heavy sigh, Bexar grabbed the arms of one of the Zeds and dragged it toward the large sign on the property. The sign was like a homemade billboard that he had seen in old movies. It wasn't elevated, but was more like a wooden wall erected in the middle of the parking lot and then painted for advertising. It would be a convenient place to hide bodies.

Thirty minutes passed as Bexar dragged bodies behind the sign and then drove the FJ around the back of the store to hide it. The tire marks in the dusty parking lot were still obvious, as were the drag marks and dark stains from the Zeds. Bexar wasn't sure what he could do about the dark fluid stains from the Zeds, but he did walk along the drag marks and the tire marks, kicking dirt and trying to obscure the marks.

They had water in the FJ, they had ammo and some MREs, and in the store they had some jerky made from a surprising mix of various animals. They also had time, with a few months to go before Jessie's due date. He and Jessie would be fine for a while hiding out where they were and time is what they needed for Jessie to begin to heal up. They didn't have any way to X-ray or image her ankle, so hopefully it wasn't broken. If it wasn't broken, it might be a few weeks before she was able to move and put weight on it if it was a really bad sprain. What they needed was Guillermo's expertise and the help of the rest of the awesome survivors at the compound.

We should leave in a few days no matter how Jessie feels. We need to get to Utah and accept their help.

Bexar knocked gently and announced himself before entering. He would hate to startle Jessie and get shot for it.

Indian Springs, Nevada

"That is the question, really."

Erin shrugged. "I think after what we saw before we should ditch that hunk of shit and get one of those armored trucks. Besides, who the shit knows if our beat-to-fuck Suburban will make it much longer."

"OK, but what do you know about driving one of those things? Even if we found one that started and has fuel?"

"A truck is a truck, how hard can it be?"

Jason smirked. "Tell you what, honey, we can go test drive one, but no promises."

Erin flipped him off and gave him a quick kiss before opening the door and stepping out into the hard light of the morning sun in the desert. Jason took the rear position with his shotgun; Erin took point with her short-barreled M4. The previous afternoon when they broke into the abandoned air base they only saw a handful of Zeds shambling between the buildings, but they had to assume that there were more. Even though what they saw of the facility's fence line appeared intact, they hadn't taken the time and they wouldn't take the time to check it. It wasn't worth the effort for an overnight.

Slowly, the pair made their way through the maze of buildings toward the fenced lot where they had seen trucks like the one President Lampton had driven to Groom Lake in. Neither could remember what the trucks were called, nor did they care.

What would have been a few minutes-walk took half an hour due to the stop and start movements, trying their best to avoid being noticed by the handful of Zeds out for their morning stumble. It went without saying that they would use their firearms as a last resort; the sound would be a huge beacon for all the Zeds in ear-shot. At the gate, they found it locked with a heavy-duty padlock. The lot was fenced and had barbed wire on top of the chain-link fence.

"If we're on a secure air base, why the fuck do they have a lock and barbed fucking wire?" Erin was agitated at the redundancy.

Jason shrugged. "Probably for the same reasons why there were locks on the doors underground at Groom Lake. I mean, how much more secret and secure do you get than that?"

"Fuck this. Blow the lock with your boom stick, babe."

Jason winked at Erin and placed the 12-gauge shotgun's muzzle next to the padlock. The shotgun blast echoed between the buildings and the ruined lock fell to the pavement. They quickly pushed the gate open and closed it behind them.

"How long do you think, Erin?"

Erin scanned the area, taking note of the movement in the shadows and between the buildings. "Uh, call it five minutes, maybe a little less?"

"Well, start kicking tires. I hope you know how to hotwire one of these things."

The first truck sat on two flat tires, but the other four had better-looking tires, and at least they appeared to be fully inflated. Erin opened the driver's door to the second MRAP and climbed in.

"There's no key, babe, just a switch to turn it on. Start it and shit."

Jason gave a thumbs up from the passenger's seat. Erin tried starting the truck and all they heard was the click of the starter.

"Shit, next in line," Erin said as she climbed down from the driver's seat. After climbing into the third truck, they were happy to find that the diesel engine coughed to life with a cloud of black smoke. Jason leaned over and scanned the gauges.

"Hey, check this out, there's an air system and it's leveling out the air pressure in the tires."

"That's cool as shit," Erin said with a rare smile.

The fuel gauge showed that they had about three-quarters of a tank. Neither knew how far that would get them, but before they could siphon any fuel, they needed the hose from the Suburban.

"Drive to the Suburban, transfer our gear, siphon fuel, and haul ass?"

"That sounds perfect, Erin. I'm going to dig around in the back and see what we've got on board," Jason said as he climbed over the center console and climbed up into the armored turret on the roof. Although Jason had high hopes, he wasn't surprised to find that the heavy gun that would have been mounted in the turret position wasn't there. After securing the hatch behind him, Jason dug around the Spartan interior of the rear. There was nothing in the truck.

"I guess they keep ammo and the guns and stuff separate from the trucks," Jason yelled up from the back.

"That's odd. Why do you think they do that?"

"Probably because we're in Nevada and not fucking Iraq or some shit."

The big armored truck rolled forward and stopped abruptly. "Sorry, it's going to take a little time to get used to this thing—get the gate, would you?"

Jason climbed back to the front and then out the passenger's door. Four Zeds bounced against the fence next to the gate. Jason pushed and slid the gate open quickly, which rattled loudly. Running away from the approaching Zeds, Jason climbed back into the cab of the MRAP, which felt deceptively safe. Even the doors were heavy with armor plating; they shut with a hard thunk almost like a door of a gun safe.

Erin drove the truck forward, the big diesel motor rattled and the turbo whined. For the first time since they left Groom Lake, they felt like there was no chance they could lose. A few moments later, they were outside of the still-running truck, tossing their gear from the beat-to-hell Suburban into the MRAP. Their task complete, they climbed back into the armored truck and sat for a moment.

"Should we get on the road or do some scavenging while we're here?"

Jason furrowed his brow as he thought for a moment. "We could spend months checking the different buildings and stuff. I say we go back to the other trucks, siphon enough fuel to top off our new truck, and then haul ass."

Erin nodded and put the truck into gear. A few minutes later, Jason spit diesel fuel out of his mouth after sucking on the end of the cut-up garden hose, starting the fuel transfer from the MRAP with flat tires to their truck. Once again, he had closed the gate behind them after driving into the small fenced lot and once again, Zeds bounced against the fence trying to get to him and the truck. Repeating the same process as before, they drove toward the front gate. Ten minutes later, they were on the road, bouncing down the highway toward their chosen destination to spend their lives together.

Jason held Erin's hand and smiled, yet his heart still ached for his wife. The scene of her death played in his dreams every single night; there seemed to be no relief. The sight of her body on the floor of the C-130, the blood, and then her reanimated corpse sitting up to attack the living, it was just too much. For all the death, all the destruction, the complete upheaval of reality, losing his wife, his best friend, and his soulmate was the worst of it all. With Erin, it felt different.

Jason knew he loved her, his heart leapt with happiness with each electric shock of her touch on his skin, but still he felt guilty, like he was somehow cheating on his true love. Jason turned his face away from Erin as a tear streamed down his face. No amount of heartache, no amount of longing, nothing he could do would bring his bride back to him; only the veil of death separated them now, but he knew it wasn't time to join her in whatever afterlife there actually was. No, Jason felt that as sad as he was, he was right where he was supposed to be. There was some destiny that he was to fulfill. He couldn't say that thought out loud for how silly and childish it sounded, but in his heart and in his mind, he knew it to be true. There was a reason he was still alive, there was a reason why he and Erin had fallen in love, and there was a reason they were doing what they were doing. Only time would reveal what his final destiny would be.

SSC

It didn't take long for Amanda to get back into her old routine, minus sleeping with who she thought was her trusted friend, not just her lover. Bruised and battered, her head was still a little tender from where she had been knocked out by Chivo before, but the knot had gone down. The steam filled the large locker room shower. A pair of scissors sat on the counter; her hair was really short once again. Somewhere in the facility had to be a pair of electric clippers, but she hadn't found them yet. Once she did, the plan was to shave her head. She didn't have the time or patience to keep up with long hair and being the President of the United States, or what was left of it, Amanda figured that any biting comments comparing her to GI Jane or calling her a dyke or whatever else the old world would have done would not happen. Even if it did, she didn't care.

Amanda's skin glowed pink from the hot water. Her workouts had quickly picked up where she had left off. She started every morning with runs in the tunnel along with pull-ups, pushups, and hanging leg raises. Today, she had used two ammo cans full of .50-caliber ammunition like kettle bells for her squats and presses. The workouts gave her mind time to work through the problems she faced. The steaming hot shower afterward was where her mind solved the problems and by the time she was dressed for the day, Amanda had a clear plan in her mind.

The uniform of the day was a pair of ACU pants, T-shirt, boots, belt, and pistol. Amanda carried her chest carrier loaded with full magazines for her M4 and pistol. She carried her M4 as she went about her day, but she only put the sling over her head if something set off the hairs on the back of her neck or if she went topside. She was confident that the underground facility was clear of Zeds, and she was mostly sure that there weren't any booby traps. She was alone, but there was a nagging thought that Clint may have left the facility intact and without any traps for arriving enemy forces. That meant she had to be ready. She had to keep the access points secure and she wanted to complete the topside improvements she had begun. HESCO barriers were in abundance and she had a front-end loader; that was going to be her afternoon task. Amanda figured that Clint had somehow kept his handlers informed of the status of the SSC, so outward appearances be damned. If the PLA was going to try to take out the facility, she was going to make it as difficult as possible.

However, that was this afternoon; the morning's task involved the computer systems. She had a basic working knowledge as to how to operate the facility, but she needed to have a better understanding of what she had available and how to use it. Maybe if God smiled upon her, Amanda might be able to figure out the issue with the communications between the SSC and Groom Lake, but that would be a huge stroke of luck. Her background and education wasn't computer security or digital communication. Luckily, the task of logging onto the system took no great feat of hacker skill. Clint had given her an ID card on a computer that was setup in a small office seemingly for only that task. Amanda took the plastic card out of a holder she wore on a lanyard around her neck. Her photo was on the card, along with the presidential seal and "POTUS" in bold letters under her name; the gold color chip on the end of the card was the important part. Amanda slid the card into a slot on the workstation and was greeted by a login screen. After entering her username and password, which Clint had setup for her as well, the system welcomed her and took her to the desktop screen.

The computer ran what appeared to be a normal version of Microsoft Windows. Amanda was sure, or hoped at least, that the operating system was beefed up for national security use and was more stable; a blue screen of death could be more than a little annoying during a battle. Amanda took the mouse and clicked through the system, taking notes on what each of the programs seemed to be. Like the movies, there were large monitors on the wall, a dozen of them, and she could display different information in different configurations on the screens. Sitting at what she assumed was the commander's desk at the back of the room, playing with the room displays was neat, but not what Amanda was really looking for.

The communications terminal was something she was familiar with, but it wouldn't connect with Groom Lake. In fact, it appeared to not be transmitting or working at all. Amanda knew that the satellite imagery had been working, new images being downloaded and seen well after she and Clint had arrived in Waxahachie, but the program Clint had used for that now displayed unintelligible error messages when trying to use it. Two more hours of frustration passed before Amanda decided her morning task was hopeless. She left for a quick lunch and to fill the Camelbak she was going to wear with her normal tactical kit. Amanda had an afternoon of hard work on a dusty piece of heavy equipment.

Groom Lake

Amazingly, the old Caterpillar front-end loader ran, not well, but his men had got it running with a little help from one of the survivors. Jones said that it was old enough that there wasn't an engine control module—a computer—that made it run. Aymond hadn't realized that even construction equipment could be taken out by an EMP.

After quelling the uprising, the other survivors had mostly settled down. There was grumbling and about a dozen had left, but things felt more settled than before. Aymond offered and allowed what Gonzo called party favors for those who wanted to leave. They received a case of ammo if their weapons were chambered in 5.56, which they all were for those who left, and a case of MREs. The reality of the situation was that Aymond didn't have to do anything of the sort, but he felt that the gesture would go a long way to help calm everyone down. This wasn't a military installation; well, it was, except that it was now a civilian community trying to survive the apocalypse. This took a different approach than what he typically had done in his long career in the Marine Corps. This was a job typically suited for what everyone called the Green Berets: organizing leadership and people in a population to help American interests.

The first task was the destroyed blast door. That gaping scar of battle allowed unrestricted access to the facility below and that was a serious problem. The immediate second task was to build a perimeter wall to what Aymond considered to be a firebase. Firebase on the surface, surreal government facility below ground...it was just the way things were in the new world.

However, Jerry Aymond knew that another attack may not be far behind the one they were able to stop before. They needed actual fighting positions, they needed the ability to secure the facility, and they needed it now.

HESCO is what he wanted. As much of an annoyance as it was in Afghanistan, it served an important purpose. They found some while in Yuma, but so far, his men had been unsuccessful at finding any here, at least so far. His men were in a tough rotation, pulling security, organizing the civilians, and overseeing the new construction project, and added to the mix were two two-man teams currently going building to building in search of anything useful. The upside is that they had dozens of pallets with ready-to-fill sandbags; the downside is that filling them took a lot of work. Work that a rotation of civilian *volunteers* was helping with.

Bill told Aymond that Jessie had a team that had been doing just that, except that he didn't really know what all had been cleared and he had no idea what were in those buildings. A man named Wright had been running the facility. Jessie and her crew took leadership roles and they did a reasonable job, but now it was time for a professional war-fighter to set things on the right track.

"Gonzo for Chief, over."

Gonzo and Happy had been checking some of the buildings, and Kirk and Davis were working on the others. Aymond wasn't 100 percent sure where each of the teams were at the moment, but he knew they were working their way outward from the main hangars using a series of concentric circles.

Aymond keyed his radio. "Go."

"Chief, you need to come check this out."

Aymond replied and confirmed the search grid location Gonzo relayed to him after checking the hand-drawn map he pulled out of his utility pocket and began walking their direction.

Ulm, Montana

So far, the work was tedious; hours were spent with each step. So far, they had worked through only the first few pages of the manual that the colonel had and that suited Dorsey just fine. At first, his thoughts centered around internal anger for letting Smith into the launch control facility, but late last night, Dorsey had a bit of an epiphany and that anger turned to satisfaction.

I gave him access to a Minuteman III launch facility, but with me being here, I have the ability to sabotage the operation. If Smith had gone to one of the other numerous facilities, then he might have had full reign.

As discrete as he could be, Dorsey pulled a ribbon cable off the electronic board, pushed the tip of a safety pin into the connector, and pushed the connector loose. He had no idea what this component did, or what effect that a couple of missing pinouts would do to the system, but Dorsey figured that if he continued to do little things like this that it might cause the system to fail. Failure wasn't just an option; failure was the only way to succeed.

SSC

Dust blew away in a thick cloud behind the armored front-end loader like smoke. Amanda was sure that it could be seen for miles, but her other option would be to wait until dark to complete the work. As confident as she was in her skills, awareness, and weapons handling, Amanda wasn't stupid. Trying to do much of anything at night with Zeds around was just stupid, although they were easy to kill with the heavy equipment. Amanda backed the front-end loader away from the now full HESCO container and turned to see a lone Zed appear from somewhere to investigate. She swung the bucket to knock it off its feet, backed up a little further, then lowered the bucket onto the dead thing that was once a man. His body squished under the enormous pressure like a roach.

In simpler times, such a maneuver would have landed Amanda in prison, never mind the personal repercussions of destroying a person in such a manner, but these weren't simpler times and that Zed was no longer a person. It was a diseased body set forth to destroy her. This wasn't personal, it wasn't even just business, it was the new reality; it was war, and the winners or losers wouldn't be defined by conquest. They would be defined by living or a fate worse than death.

Amanda paused and took a long drink from her Camelbak. The air conditioning in the cab worked fairly well, but this was still hot and dusty work in an armored cocoon that amplified all the sun's heat. She felt like an ant under a magnifying glass. She could try to prop open the door, but then what would the point be of being in an armored vehicle. She was by herself, she was trying to save what was left of the country, and the last thing she needed was to be killed for her own laziness.

Bouncing back into the dirt field across from the entrance, Amanda had the idea that since she had the time and the machinery, the HESCO barriers alone may not be enough. She stopped and let the heavy diesel engine idle while studying the terrain.

Behind us is the lake, which serves as a bit of a barrier, but not enough. I need to put HESCO along the shoreline and wall off the main area. If I leave the secret escape hatches unprotected, then they might not know about them and they could be used to our advantage, or to flee if need be. But Clint probably told them about the hatches; they probably know all the secrets of this facility. The damn Koreans and Chinese probably know more about it than I do. Fuck. So walls within walls, surrounded by what? Dig out tank traps like on the old war movies?

Amanda sat quietly and closed her eyes. She was in too far over her head, and she had no idea how to build a fortified position. She was never in the military; she hadn't even paid too close of attention to most of the old war movies her ex-husband used to watch.

A hard crack on the outside of the cab brought her attention back to focus instantly.

"Shit."

Another hard crack against the cab. This time, she saw the impact of the round on the armored glass windshield, Amanda raised the bucket to block the cab while scanning the area from where the shot would have come. After another round struck the bucket, Amanda drove and turned the loader to go through the zig-zag of HESCO containers into the front gate of the park and toward the main lift and entrance. Her first thought was to leave the loader topside, but she didn't want whoever was shooting at her to damage or destroy the loader. No, she needed to distract and outflank the attacker. Amanda realized she was assuming that there was only one person out there, which could be an assumption that was dead wrong. She needed to get safe and then figure out what the hell was going on.

Dew, Texas

Some days, 10 miles might as well mean trying to drive an old truck all the way to the moon and back, but the afternoon found Ken's luck had turned for the better, even if he had spent hours making sure he wasn't being followed. Although truth be told, his morning hadn't been all too bad. It had been a long time, decades really, since Ken had been shot at, but the old familiar feeling of elation, the rush of escaping death, was familiar and intoxicating.

The shiny new convenience store across the street had burned to the ground. Ken wasn't sure how or why, but there were at least a dozen charred bodies scattered in the parking lot and in the road. The only way he figured that the bodies could be arranged like they were that they were reanimated dead that caught fire. The old abandoned gas station across the street still stood as well as it had before everything happened, which suited Ken just fine. The truck was fairly hidden behind the overgrowth trying to reclaim the structure as a part of nature and the awning over the pumps gave him an elevated position to recon I-45. He wasn't sure if the huge mass of Zeds had passed through completely; there were some stragglers shuffling along the access road in the same direction, but those would be easy to evade. The bridge over the interstate appeared to still be standing, which was good, but he wasn't going to chance a crossing if the stampeding herd of Zeds was going past. The others on the spark gap radio had told of bridges collapsing and buildings being demolished by Zeds when in high numbers. It all seemed as if they were like fishing stories and the size of the fish that was caught and released, but seeing what he saw on I-45 this morning made him a believer.

Ken slid to the edge of the awning and climbed down the aluminum ladder. He found the ladder leaned against the house next door. No one was home and now Ken owned a ladder, which he hadn't thought to have prepped at the deer lease. He could have climbed up his truck and probably reached up onto the awning, but getting down would be difficult. Even something as simple as an ankle sprain could result in his death. With no medical care and no help, he was on his own.

The ladder went in the bed of the truck; quick work with some 550 cord and it was lashed down well enough to stay put. Ken started the truck and drove toward I-45 and the overpass on Texas 179. The interstate wasn't clear—there was still a seemingly endless number of Zeds shambling past—but there weren't as many as he saw a few hours earlier and the bridge was still intact. Swerving left and right, Ken dodged the Zeds on the roadway and drove across the bridge. The truck stop was still standing, but the windows were all broken out and one of the awnings over the fuel pumps was pushed over. A handful of big rigs sat in the parking lot, but there wasn't much movement from the building or from the semi-trucks. What may have still remained in the truck stop didn't interest Ken; it felt risky to attempt any scavenging so close to the interstate when he didn't need any supplies just yet. No, Ken scanned the road ahead for any movement or signs of trouble and drove on.

Groom Lake

Bill lay on the cot in the radio hut, his intent to nap a few hours, but he was too stressed and worried to do more than close his eyes and hope for his mind to slow down. They now had two spark gap radios popping and buzzing in the room, which smelled like ionized air. The door was open and an office fan blew fresh air into the room, but the room still stunk. Two airmen, or now former airmen with beards and not in uniform, manned the radios; a civilian volunteer manned the shortwave broadcast loops. The transmission of information had been disrupted with the attack and then completely stopped with the coup attempt, but now they were back in business under Aymond's orders.

With his eyes closed, Bill listened to the crackling pop of the radios, transposing the Morse code in his head as he heard the received transmissions. Never in his life had Bill been this proficient at Morse, but he never had to be. This was the current normal, and the current normal reminded him a lot of an ARRL Field Day, except that Field Day was in June and was a fun event where ham radio operators all met up to run exercises, hold contests, conduct testing for new licenses or operators upgrading their current license. Those weekends usually found him resting on a cot in some community center room with the sound of radios in the background. Not much had changed, except that now all the emergency drills were real and nothing anyone had planned would still work. The transmissions he could hear were between two other survivors; one was in Northern California and another was in Ohio. The pinboard map of survivors on the wall was full of pins; there were so many survivors that they nearly couldn't keep up. The radios had pileups often, people transmitting on top of others, sometimes unknowingly, perhaps sometimes on purpose. Some of that could be attributed to the propagation of the signal, where a transmitting station didn't know another station was transmitting because the radio signals were skipping over them off the ionosphere, but Bill thought that most of it was simply due to the number of people who have built radios. This was a good thing, but also a bad thing.

The good was that there were many more survivors than first thought and they were coordinating each other for assistance. Some simple trade routes had been established, as well as some safe zones. At least that is what they were calling the areas in which survivors had set hard perimeter walls and cleared out the Zeds. After the outbreaks in the facility and the PLA attack, Bill wasn't sure that there was such thing as a safe zone.

The bad was that Bill was waiting for priority transmissions from Dorsey in Montana, President Lampton in Texas, and Chivo or Andrew on the status of their mission. Before the collapse of society, no ham radio operator had priority over transmissions or frequency use, unless during a declared emergency. They most definitely had a declared emergency, but he couldn't claim the airwaves for himself, nor could anyone enforce it. He created this monster and now like Dr. Frankenstein, he no longer had any real control over it. Bill sighed. He would let it go, and he had to let it go for the good of the other survivors. He needed a better way for the president to communicate.

His thoughts returned to the idea that even back in the 1960s Strategic Air Command had overcome these same hurdles, except that had a lot of assets in place. There was a command and control aircraft aloft 24 hours a day, every single day of the year, that could transmit launch commands and other important information to the ICBM facilities across the country. Each of the ICMB control centers had High-Frequency radios, antennas, hardened antennas, including an Ultra-High radio antenna that looked like a little concrete and metal cone on the surface that could survive a very close nuclear detonation. Bill's eyes snapped open and he sat up with a start.

Hardened HF antennas.

Years ago, he had toured the Atlas II museum outside of Tucson Arizona and was intrigued by the radio antenna redundancy. The facility had antennas for High-Frequency radios that were mounted on masts located underground. The masts would rise through a hatch at the flip of a switch. If Groom Lake had a hardened and protected HF antenna mast, then so should SSC, and Dorsey most definitely had one at a Minuteman III ICBM control center. The spark gap radios would be wrecking the HF radio spectrum, but perhaps he could find some frequency ranges that weren't being overrun with the broad transmissions from the crude radios and that would still have good propagation. Bill put on his glasses and began his search.

On The Surface

"What is your plan to move them?"

Gonzo expected Aymond would ask that question first and was ready. "Simple. We drag them with the Cat," he said, referencing the old Caterpillar that Jones had working. The heavy diesel motor could be heard in the near distance as earth-work walls and fighting positions were being made.

"Make it happen, and gentlemen." Aymond paused as he turned to walk back to the main hangar. "Figure out how to stack them."

Happy and Gonzo watched Aymond walk off. "How are we going to do that without a crane?"

"We'll figure something out, but first we have to figure out how many CONEX containers they had exactly, and what is in them, if anything. Then we have to get them empty and get them moved while figuring out how large of a wall we can make."

"Roger that."

They went to work, using a shotgun to breach the heavy locks and opening each large metal shipping container one by one. The corrugated metal shipping containers were quite familiar to the Marines. They have been used by the U.S. military since the Korean War and they have had temporary shelters and walls made of them before, but they weren't the ones who usually put them together, arriving in theater or to training with all of them already in place. As an engineering challenge, it wasn't insurmountable, but before the attack in December, they would have had specialized equipment or even rotor wing support to lift and move the containers while out in the wilds.

These containers were going to be the inner ring around the entrance to the underground facility, basically replacing the hangar that has been significantly damaged. If they could fill them with dirt and build up the backside with a dirt berm, then they would have good fighting positions if the outer earthen walls were overrun.

The first CONEX they opened was empty; the second was full of weapons crates. Gonzo and Happy pulled one of the crates out, both smiling and hoping that the contents matched the markings on the crate. Happy opened the crate and were greeted by the site of a familiar weapon system.

"ADMS variant. You know what that means."

"Fucking PLA radar trucks are toast. Shit, I wish we had these back in Cali."

The Stinger missile system was well known to many, but the Air Defense Missile Suppression wasn't. It could home in on the radar transmissions that air defense missile installations used. It could hard-kill a radar.

"Think it would work. We don't know what frequencies the fucking Koreans and Chinese use and I'm not too excited to test it on our only radar truck."

"Who cares. We keep these, train up some folks on them, and when the time comes, give it a spin. If it works, great, if it doesn't, then they'll still blow some shit up. Besides, we could put down any of their strategic lift aircraft. We haven't seen any fighters or close air support aircraft, only the heavy lift shit."

"I say we close up this container, mark it, and drag it full to the hangar. Easier than humping each one of these fuckers one by one."

Gonzo gave Happy a fist bump and continued to the next container.

South of Twin Falls, Idaho

Andrew setup for a left-hand pattern, turned for the downwind, and overflew the center of the airport. He would not have done that before the attack, and the thought of an actual pattern made him smirk. There was no other traffic that he could see. Flying a pattern for landing gave him a chance to scope out the airport and what was or wasn't moving. They had enough AvGas to fly a few more hundred miles, nearly all the way to Great Falls, as long as nothing happened and the winds were favorable, but Andrew hadn't survived this long flying all around the country by cutting things close, and it would be dark soon.

Two Cessna Caravans sat on the ramp at tie downs; those were good bush planes and could land many of the same places he could land his Husky, as long as there was enough room. He could carry a lot more gear and people, but they had Pratt and Whitney turboprop engines. On the upside, the PT6 series of engines were some of the most proven and reliable turboprop fan turners ever made; on the downside, he would have to find Jet-A or the military equivalent for fuel. No longer would he be able to top off with a few gallons of unleaded gasoline if there wasn't any aviation fuel available. The other is the fuel burn. The Husky practically sipped fuel and flew like a camel compared to a Caravan. Andrew made a note on his aeronautical chart in pencil. Before he and Chivo flew out in the morning, he wanted to see if one of them would start.

Andrew turned base and absent-mindedly scanned the runways, the taxiways, and between the hangars. There were some Zeds turning to shuffle along following his flight path, but they were mostly between the hangars and not an immediate threat for landing.

Around southern Great Falls, I could land on a road with a Caravan. Nearly empty, I bet the landing could be done in less than 1,000 feet. I bet I could take off in about the same.

Andrew really didn't know. He rode in a Caravan years before with a pilot friend in Montana at the Lost Prairie skydiving boogie, but that plane had been loaded with sweaty skydivers doing their own brand of crazy. The rollout was surprisingly long as they bumped along at the high field altitude and where they were flying to would have a high field elevation.

But I could have Oreo with me even when playing tactical taxi driver.

Flaps down, Andrew gently pulled power as he slipped against a quartering headwind before setting down with a slight bounce. He opened the window as they taxied toward the fuel pumps, remembering that it was still April and now he was back in the part of the country that had cool temperatures and winter that seemed to last from August to June.

"Looks like we have some company coming up, Chivo."

"Yeah, mano. Once you shut down, I'll get out and take care of our friendly welcoming committee. Where are we?"

"Outside of Twin Falls, Idaho."

The flight had been mostly quiet. Shouting over the engine and wind noise was annoying and Chivo, being the experienced war-fighter he was, slept for long stretches of the flight.

"I thought we would cover more ground than that. We could have driven this far in a day."

"Headwinds and mountains. Things go slower for us with those two obstacles to overcome; you're not in a Herc or flying commercial."

Chivo flashed a smile at Andrew; there was a fine line between helping motivate someone and simply bitching. All bitching ever did was kill motivation and he couldn't do that. Chivo needed to get north, kill Clint, and figure out what the hell was going on, then haul ass to Utah to catch up with Bexar and Jessie. He worried about them, even though he knew they were tough and capable. Tough and capable, but Chivo had saved Bexar's life more than once in the past few months. Another smile crept across his face. *Bexar is a shit magnet. He means well and is talented and trained, but pandemonium and havoc follow his wake.*

Zeds were beginning to approach. Chivo walked toward the first of them, raised his rifle, and fired once. Chivo was moving before the first Zed's body had fallen to the tarmac, walking at a brisk pace. He was leading the dead away from Andrew and the aircraft while killing each of the Zeds one headshot at a time. Contrary to what the action movies from the '80s would lead someone to believe, headshots are difficult, even more so when everything is moving, but even Chivo had to smile at what he saw unfold in front of his eyes like a movie. He was the star of the show and the camera followed his movements, but each step, the step after that, and the step after that had already played out on the screen in Chivo's mind with a wake of destroyed Zeds following. The process of putting down small numbers of the dead had become so commonplace that Chivo was having difficulty focusing on the task; instead, he watched the movie like a disinterested teenager, but still amazed at how the constant target practice had improved his shooting skills.

That was it, target practice. This feels like on the range...maybe it is because no one is shooting back or maybe I'm just an asshole.

With an annoyed grunt, Chivo focused on his task and began actively scanning the full 360 around him while making a fast magazine change on his rifle. The above-ground fuel tanks were located on the northern end of the ramp and about 50 meters off the end of a long hangar. Chivo had walked around the southern end of the hangar, across the back, and back in view of Andrew during his dream-like shooting gallery jaunt. Chivo stopped and raised his rifle. The pilot's head and shoulder fit square in the optic on the M4, the reticle resting on the bridge of Andrew's nose from Chivo's view. Chivo's shoulders shifted slightly and he squeezed the trigger.

Andrew spun and fell to the pavement under the wing of his aircraft; Chivo sprinted across the tarmac to where Andrew lay. "What the actual fuck is wrong with you," Andrew yelled, his ears ringing.

Chivo pointed behind him. Andrew sat up and turned his head, seeing the rotten corpse of what appeared to have been a teenage girl lay in a crumpled heap on the tarmac, her head ruined.

"Holy shit, Chivo, the fucking crack of the bullet passing was LOUD. I can't hear shit out of my left ear."

"You're welcome, mano; now quit being a little punta and get up. I'm going to get a couple of rooms at the inn. You finish fueling, and I'll come get you in a few minutes."

All Andrew could hear in his left ear was a loud ringing; the crack of the bullet was so close that he first thought he had been shot himself. Chivo trotted off toward the northeast and the first row of hangars beyond the fuel tanks. A few minutes later, Andrew had finished fueling the Husky and Chivo came back. A few more minutes were all that was required to push the plane along the ramp and to the hangar that Chivo had secured. The resident Cessna 182 was pushed out of the hangar and up the apron to be replaced by the yellow Husky. Chivo slid the hangar doors closed, dropping the door pins in place to keep them from being opened again from the outside. The only light left filtered in from the open side door, which Andrew closed behind them after they both left to explore the airport and look for anything that might be useful.

Las Vegas, Nevada

"I don't know, babe, seems it is more risky than is prudent." Erin looked toward the west and the setting sun that appeared hazy through the bullet-resistant side window of the big MRAP. She held up her hand; the sun was four fingers off the horizon. "We only have about an hour of daylight left. Let's find a spot for the night."

Their MRAP sat in the middle of the roadway. They hadn't traveled very far on Highway 95 after spending a good deal of the day getting the new truck all put together. They were on the northwestern edge of Las Vegas where there were obvious signs of Zeds—a large number of Zeds—having come through the area, and Jason had to concede that Erin was right. It would be stupid to attempt to get past Las Vegas with only an hour of daylight left. Not only due to the likely chance of the city being completely overrun by Zeds, but that neither of them had ever been to Las Vegas, much less knew their way around the city.

"Do you want me to drive us closer and try to find us some shelter?"

"Nope, I want to find us a spot outside the city where we can keep the truck hidden. We can sleep in the back or even on the roof if it is too hot tonight."

Jason turned left and drove across the median of the highway, across the other lane, and down the hard-packed desert shoulder where it appears many people had done the same thing before. The vehicle path off the highway went around the end of a fence and then along a seemingly endless line of high-tension power lines. They could see some dark clouds rising over the mountains in the distance. The desert floor laid out between them and the mountains were as flat as a table, but he could see the towering mounds of dirt and rock just a bit further. They found that the mounds of dirt and rock were for some construction that had been going on before the end, but it didn't matter; the mounds gave a place for Jason to hide the armored truck from view until morning.

CHAPTER 11

"Fucking shit!"

Bexar burst back inside of the store, rifle raised and ready after the sound of his wife angrily cursing and the sound of stuff crashing to the floor. Jessie lay on the floor and she did not look happy. A low product display behind her had been knocked to the floor, which mostly explained the cursing, the anger, and the sound of a crash.

"What happened?" Bexar asked as he helped his wife off the floor. Her ankle looked like hell, swollen and badly bruised. Flecks of vomit were still on her shirt and Bexar could now see a small puddle of vomit on the floor next to the product display knocked askew. Jessie shook her head at his question as he helped her across the room to sit in a chair they had brought from the single office in a room behind the counter.

"I'm tired of this shit. Get us to your friends. I'll heal up after we're safe there."

"Are you sure we should travel?"

"No, but I'm done. I'm nauseous from this baby, I'm in a lot of pain, and all I want to do is sit in your old recliner at home and feel sorry for myself."

Bexar gently stroked the side of Jessie's face. "I don't know if we'll ever get to go back to our old home. I'm not sure I want to." His mind flashed to Keeley's room at their home in central Texas. Even if the home was still standing, he couldn't bring himself to set foot in her room ever again.

"We should be able to make it to Utah today. We'll want to leave soon to give us a buffer though." Bexar wanted to get there. He knew that even if Guillermo couldn't do anything for Jessie's ankle, they could get her in a bed, get her foot elevated, and he would have more hands on deck to help his wife. Jessie was pale and Bexar hoped that was mostly due to nausea from the pregnancy; at least her head didn't feel feverish.

"Give me a few minutes to prep for our departure then I'll help you get to the FJ."

Jessie gave a shallow nod and leaned forward in her chair. Her head in her hands, she took quick shallow breaths. Bexar was sure she was going to throw up again. "Can I help?"

His response was a flip of her hand shooing him away, so he walked outside to pull the FJ around to the front of the building. As Bexar walked down the stairs and scanned the area for more Zeds, he could hear Jessie throwing up. Bexar shook his head. He wished there was more he could do, he wished there was anything he could do, but there really wasn't except to get her to the compound in St. George.

Ten minutes later, Jessie sat in the passenger seat, still looking green in the face. Bexar took a right turn out of the parking lot onto Highway 93 and onward to a hopefully uneventful drive. Jessie rolled down her window and let the wind blow in her face, which seemed to help a little, except that pain shot up her leg from her ankle with every little bump in the road, which there seemed to be a lot of.

"According to the atlas, if we can keep the pace to about 50 mph, it might only take us about three hours. We'll have to refuel en route, though."

Jessie didn't reply with more than just a sideways glance, which Bexar correctly took as his clue to keep his mouth shut. The countryside was beautiful; they really were in a nice part of the country, although Bexar suspected that it was quite warm in July and August, seeing how warm the daytime temperatures already felt in mid-April.

A bit over an hour later, they drove past the small green sign next to the highway announcing that they were now in Caliente, Nevada. The speed limit sign still stood as well, which meant that one of the big herds of Zeds hadn't come through the town, at least on this road.

"Keep an eye out for a fuel source we can scavenge." Jessie nodded for a reply. They rounded a turn in the highway and saw a Family Dollar store on the highway across from the railroad tracks. The railroad could be an interesting thought. In Bexar's mind, it would be easier to get trains running again in some fashion more so than automobiles or semi-trucks. Then it would be easier to move a lot of gear or people without all the problems with driving on the highways. Even still, Bexar's mind wandered and began flipping through a list of problems they would have to overcome to do much of anything besides simply survive in small groups. He wasn't sure that the United States or any country of what was now the old world would rise from the ashes of the death and destruction the Koreans and Chinese rained upon the western world.

After passing the Dollar Store, they saw a volunteer fire department, a small hotel, and a gas station that appeared to have had served as the town's central social hub, restaurant, and daily shopping spot. Bexar stopped the FJ in the middle of the road across from the gas station. It appeared to be a disaster; the awning over the fuel pumps had collapsed, apparently from a truck crashing into the awning support and pumps. The building and store were partially burned and there was movement in what was left of the dark interior. Continuing, they slowly drove through more of the small town, passing more small restaurants and homes. Overall, the town wasn't in bad shape. Perhaps it was far enough off of the interstates and other major highways to be spared from the worst of dead's curse, but they didn't see any movement as they drove through the town except for a handful of Zeds.

"What if there are survivors in towns like these, but they keep hidden when a vehicle or people come through? Think about it. We've had absolute shit luck with some other survivors—I imagine others have as well—so when we drive through, if there is anyone alive, they watch us to make sure we don't stop and that we're not a threat. They're not going to show themselves though."

"That makes sense. It just seems like we should be finding more survivors out here in wilds."

There was no way that the question could be answered at the moment and Bexar slowly accelerated the FJ back to a better cruising speed of about 50 mph as they exited the town.

"Those poor cows." Jessie pointed out the window to a fenced pasture where dozens of heads of cattle lay rotted in the grass. Buzzards and the rest of the ecosystem had made good work of nature's reclamation of the dead cows, but sunbaked bone and hide lumps were still easily identified as they passed. Bexar didn't answer Jessie, too lost in the thought of how insurmountable survival seemed. Even if they made it and their baby lived to adulthood, what world awaited her? A desolate wasteland? The shadowed ruins of a once-great society that destroyed itself? Or would people be able to start up farming operations again?

"People will figure it out. For thousands of generations, our species has adapted and survived," Jessie said as if reading his mind. Bexar nodded and kept driving. She was still obviously in a lot of pain, but that didn't keep Jessie from holding Bexar's hand as they drove.

Outside of Las Vegas, NV

The morning began as normally as it could in the world they now lived in: just a young couple madly in love, standing armed, watching over each other as they took turns taking care of their morning business. Erin and Jason chatted, the difference being not just the lack of a bathroom door, but the lack of a bathroom. Sort of like the van life movement, they traveled the countryside, except that they were in a heavily armored truck instead of a beat-up old VW.

"The roadmap shows a loop, but you know it's still going to suck."

Erin agreed. Jason was on the roof of the MRAP standing watch for her turn to squat against one of the big off-road tires on their rig.

"You know, we could follow the dirt access road for the powerlines here. It heads east and we might get lucky."

"Well, you're not going to get lucky; I just started my period."

Jason was silent for a moment and smiled. "Do we need to run to the store?"

"Yes."

"Well, that settles our debate; we hit the edge of the city and find some supplies."

"Of all the prepper shit that we packed, I don't know why I left off any products to help with my period. This is so fucking annoying."

Erin's mind flashed to Jessie and her pregnancy. As annoying as dealing with her monthly cycle was, at least she wasn't bringing a baby into the world. Neither bothered to dig holes or cover their waste after using the outdoor facilities; they didn't care and they felt it wasn't worth the effort unless the plan was to stay in one place more than a night. With all the dead and rotting corpses, leave no trace seemed silly at this point.

"At least we have fucking toilet paper!"

"How does toilet paper fuck exactly?"

Erin chuckled at Jason's reply and climbed into the truck. Jason climbed down through the turret, and a moment later, the diesel rattled to life. They drove out from behind the rock piles and took a left onto Highway 95 with Jason behind the wheel.

"Too bad we can't get married since we're in Vegas."

Jason smiled in response. "Who is to say we aren't married if we say we are?"

"Really?"

Jason nodded.

"Forever?"

"Forever," Jason replied, smiling.

Erin squealed and climbed over the center console to kiss her husband.

"When we stop for my tampons, maybe we can find some rings to give each other."

The desert highway had suddenly given way to suburban sprawl, nearly without warning, causing Erin and Jason to fall silent. From the roadway, they could see hundreds if not thousands of homes built closely together. The highway was getting more crowded with semi-trucks and cars abandoned where they failed after the EMP, but so far, the number of Zeds on the roadway were sparse. As suddenly as the city began, they both quietly suspected that they would also run into a large number of Zeds.

"Maybe if we find a place to shop early we can turn back around and try the desert route?"

Erin's happy attitude had changed. She was back in her seat and she was checking the magazines to her rifle. Jason was amazed at the transformation. His new wife was a badass, and his warrior princess had flipped a switch and was now prepared for battle. If it wasn't so amazing, the transformation would have been scary.

Teague, Texas

The previous afternoon was spent passing pump jacks driving to the outskirts of Teague, Texas. Surprisingly, some of the jacks were still pumping, which was odd in that the nearly four months that had passed since the attacks, one would have assumed that they would have failed even if they had survived the EMP. It didn't matter, though. Ken knew that without people and processes in place to refine what was pumped out of the Texas dirt, the oil would be about useless to the machinery of the once-modern world. The metal shop that he and his truck spent the night in worked well enough. The oilfield trucking yard must have been idle the morning of the attack, or whoever was on duty had locked the place up before leaving, because the tall overhead doors were shut, no trucks were in the shop, and all the doors had been locked. The building was still dirty, the special kind of dirty that only oilfield workers can create. Dirt and grime didn't bother Ken too much; in his mind, it was a fair trade for the secure night's sleep he had. The truck was parked inside, all the doors secured, and Ken was hidden from anyone who might notice a living person. Yesterday was a big eye-opener for Ken, as getting shot at by a fellow survivor wasn't what he had hoped for. So hidden and secure became the touchstone of excellence for his nightly accommodations.

He was now on his third day of a journey that would have only taken a few hours of driving before. Ken felt lucky to at least have a working vehicle; it would have been a much longer journey to just get this far otherwise. After a snack of a breakfast, Ken started the truck and let the engine warm for a few moments while in the large metal shop. This gave him time to roll up the big overhead door and be ready to hop in and drive if something happened.

A few minutes later, Ken took a left turn out of the caliche drive onto FM 553. He cringed and sped up, passing the high school and athletic fields, but the shots never came. Another left and Ken was headed in the right direction while bypassing most of the small town. Teague didn't appear to have been too damaged during the past four months, but there were Zeds visible shambling near the highway, perhaps attracted to the sound of Ken's passing truck. Highway 84 would take him to Mexia and onward to Hillsboro, which might be a problem because he would have to cross I-35 somewhere near there. The mass of Zeds that Ken saw yesterday still gave him a chill when thinking about them. This journey was almost more frightening than the trip to the deer lease before. If anything the trip was worst due to knowing he was completely on his own unless he could get to Nevada.

Ken had the realization that his apprehension about trying to cross interstates might be sort of like what the early explorers felt about trying to cross some rivers. Safety was not guaranteed. Not one to borrow trouble, Ken focused on the present and played mind games to keep alert while he drove. The GPS lady was losing her mind, so Ken turned the volume off, but after a few minutes of listening to the wind rattle through the truck's cab, Ken turned the volume of the GPS back up so there was at least another voice to listen to while he drove, even if she was condescending and judgmental.

Like being married, Ken thought with a chuckle.

Twin Falls, Idaho

"How much room do you need?" Chivo yelled over the gunfire.

"Not far." Andrew glanced at the windsock between shots. The wind was in his favor for once, the ragged windsock popping in the wind and blowing straight up the tarmac between the hangars. "We can take off right here if we can get clear!"

"Light the fire, pendejo!"

Chivo and Andrew's morning was not going as planned.

Andrew turned to run and bumped into another Zed. Stumbling backward, he stitched rounds up the dead man's torso before finally landing a round to the head. Getting up, Andrew ran to his plane and pushed hard on the hangar door that was still blocking one of his wings. A few moments later, skipping any pre-flight checklist ever created for the Husky, the engine roared to life, the propeller's sound muffling the hard crack of Chivo's rifle fire. Dirt and trash in the hangar whipped through the air from the prop blast as Andrew taxied out and swung the tail wheel around. Feet planted firmly on the brakes, Andrew ran the engine to full power and hoped to God that nothing failed, or this would be a spectacularly short flight. The edge of another hangar was directly in their path about 1,500 feet in front of them.

"Get the fuck in, you crazy asshole!"

Chivo flashed a thumbs up, walking backward slowly, changing magazines in his M4 and continuing the Zed slaughter. The problem was that even if Chivo didn't miss a single shot, they didn't have enough ammo to put all the Zeds down and there were thousands coming. At least that was how many they could see coming through the airport fence to the north. Chivo spun in place, took a few steps toward the wingtip to clear the prop, and shot rapidly, killing the dozen Zeds that stood in their path.

Barely in the fuselage, Andrew released the brakes and surged forward, Chivo clambering get in his seat correctly without knocking any of the dual controls. The tail wheel picked up, Andrew held the yoke forward, keeping the main gear on the ground as they continued to pick up speed. More Zeds came around the edge of their hangar. Andrew deftly popped the yoke rearward, the Husky leapt off the tarmac, but continued in a straight line only a few feet off the ground, picking up more speed. Chivo finally righted, sat upright in his seat, and was now able to see out the windscreen.

"Shit," was all Chivo muttered as he saw the Zeds and the hangar followed by the fuel tanks in their path as they rocketed across the tarmac just feet off the ground.

Andrew quickly and smoothly pulled the yoke back hard, the view out the windscreen turning blue, only sky being visible. Chivo felt a thud and looked out the open window on his right. He saw a Zed tumbling across the tarmac as it quickly grew smaller, the aircraft quickly gaining altitude. The few gauges that were operational and still in the dash appeared normal to Chivo's experienced, but non-pilot eyes.

"What the fuck, mano?" Chivo yelled over the sound of the propeller and wind noise.

"We needed the airspeed. Sorry, that was so close."

"Close, what about that fucking Zed?"

"Hit the right side main gear, sorry. I thought we were going to miss. He must have raised his arms or some shit. It's cool though. Everything worked out."

Chivo smiled. Andrew may not have been a military pilot, but he would have fit right in with the men of the 160th or the old fucks from Air America, and that was just the sort of man Chivo needed to succeed when going against Clint.

Out of danger, Andrew trimmed the aircraft for cruising and backed the engine off a bit for what Chivo hoped to be a leisurely fight. With nothing else to do, Chivo unloaded his rifle, broke the upper off the lower, and pulled a bore snake, some CLP, and a small brush from his pocket. It wouldn't be a great cleaning, but a well-lubed and clean rifle was a happy rifle, and his life depended on keeping his rifle happy.

Groom Lake

Sporadic gunfire echoed across the dry lake. One of the civilian patrol teams encountered a group of Zeds coming around the mountains from the northwest, the same way the PLA had come, the same way Chivo and Gonzo had come. Aymond wished they had a way to block that pass between the mountains, but the Corps of Engineers he was not, and nor did he have the resources, the manpower, or the time. So for now, security teams would handle the problem with one thing they had a lot of: ammo. The primary storeroom was exceptionally well stocked, but they had found the secondary facility that also had well-stocked stores and that was just the small arms ammunition. The CONEX of Stinger missiles was a handy find as well. It wouldn't take long to train the civilians in how to use them.

Although the topside construction project had slowed overnight due to darkness, they hadn't stopped. Now that it was again daylight, the pace was back to where it should be, yet the process was still painfully slow. So far, the first earthen berm was nearly complete with fighting positions being put in place. The second berm was on hold while the first group CONEX containers were being dragged in position. The urgency hit the flashpoint just after dawn when a thick white contrail was seen crossing west to east to their north. There was no way to know what kind of aircraft was leaving the trailing water vapor behind, but everyone knew for damn sure where it had come from. Another attack on Groom Lake wasn't so much of a question if, but a question of when, and whatever progress they could make between now and then would be all they were able to make. Once the attack came, they would either succeed or would die, for the Marines all knew that the next attack would be made with much greater numbers and armament than before.

Outside Las Vegas, Nevada

Jason took the exit from Highway 95 onto the beltway and drove into a bad traffic jam. Cars and trucks were all stationary like the parkway had meant to be a driveway. Being in the desert was the only good thing about the situation, giving them ample room on the sides of the road to drive through the hard-packed dirt and sand. If they were just about anywhere else, trees and water-logged ditches might have been the end of them. Erin had experienced this before during her trek across the country with her mom, but Jason had only been in Cortez then flew to Groom Lake in the C-130 since the attack; this was a new experience for her husband.

"Smooth and steady, babe. The worst thing we could do is wreck. As long as we can keep, moving, we'll be OK."

Even as she told Jason that, she only half believed it. It didn't seem possible to ever be OK. What annoyed Erin the most of this situation is that it would be ludicrous to get down on the surface streets to look for a gas station or a drug store to pick up a supply of tampons. By the time they got through this, she would be a mess, which was exactly what annoyed her. Jason was doing a good job of swinging the big armored truck left and right, dodging cars and Zeds, mostly driving in the dirt on the side of the road at the blistering pace of about 20 mph.

"How are the Koreans and Chinese going to handle all of this? All of the Zeds? All of the abandoned vehicles clogging the roads?"

Erin shrugged. "Maybe they're in no hurry. Maybe they have huge versions of that radar truck the Marines stole...or maybe the Zeds will eventually die off on their own?"

"Shit, we could be so lucky. I doubt it though. If they were going to die off, why would they have already invaded? Seems like they would have sat back and waited."

"Maybe this is worse than they meant it to be. What if things hadn't gone as planned for them?"

Jason didn't respond immediately. He hadn't thought about the possibility that the PLA had made a mistake that things in the U.S were much worse than the planners had expected and now the invaders were simply trying to hold on just like the rest of the survivors.

"If that's the case, then maybe there's a chance for us, or maybe everyone is doomed and the human race is going through its own extinction event?"

"No, Jason, I won't believe it...we need to change our plan."

"How's that?"

"Instead of going to Big Bend right off, we should go to where Amanda is. Once everything is settled, we can go to our new home."

Jason nodded. "If that is what you think we should do, then we'll do it." It wasn't that he was a pushover, a leaf on the wind of Erin's whims, but he knew she was right and he hadn't felt right about running away. Although the thought of being able to roll into a beautiful national park with cabins, fresh water, solar panels, and game to hunt really was appealing. They would get there, they would have their utopia to live out the rest of their lives together, but first they had to do the right thing by their friends.

The MRAP nosed into a thick group of Zeds, swarming like clumsy ants that could kill you with a single bite. Slowly, Jason nosed the front of the truck through the crowd. Some of the Zeds fell under the truck, but most of them were pushed to the sides as the MRAP parted the sea of death at a slow walking pace.

"We would already have been killed if we were still in that old Suburban."

Erin agreed.

SSC

The armored front-end loader was secure, she was secure, and now Amanda sipped coffee while flipping through the different security cameras that were still functional. Surprisingly, some of the cameras above ground appeared to be working. Whether designed to withstand an EMP or luck, she had a view to the outside world. Clint hadn't shown her these systems, so finding the security system was fortuitous. It also made sense as to why he knew what she was doing and where she was, which really felt creepy now. Amanda felt even more betrayed and like she had been a foolish schoolgirl, taken by a cunning older boy, used and thrown away when he graduated.

At least the guy in Montana, Dorsey, had seen through Clint's bullshit early on. Hopefully, it was early enough for Chivo to take Clint out. Amanda didn't know what sorts of safety systems were in place for launching an ICBM. Years before, she had read "Command and Control" and knew that launch security was tight, but she was the first sitting president in the nuclear age without the nuclear football by her side. The policies of the United States since the USSR detonated their first nuclear weapon was that any weapon of mass destruction attack would be returned in kind; if she had the nuclear football, the launch codes, and that entire command structure was still in place, then Amanda would have launched a counter-attack against Korea and China, but she didn't have that capability. Unless what Dorsey sent in his last message was true, then Clint has a way to bypass the safety systems. That was a serious proposition, that it might be possible to launch a nuclear strike. With as much damage, as many deaths that have occurred, would a nuclear strike be worth the added destruction? Did Amanda even have any idea of what she would strike? Not without some more intelligence gathering, which she couldn't do at all.

Maybe Bill could figure out these systems? Maybe he could get the satellite imagery back online? Probably not. Major Wright would have been better experienced to do such things, but wanting for nothing since he was dead.

Movement on the computer monitor caught Amanda's attention. The screen was split into a dozen different camera views. With a click, the camera's view expanded and filled the screen. There was the movement; it was a person, a man. Even in the daylight, he was hard to see, the man sticking to the shadows. He wore camouflage of some sort, had a pack, and a rifle that looked like an oversized M-16. It was quite possible that this was the person who had shot at her yesterday. Anger flared and Amanda felt her cheeks flush. She stood and shrugged on her body armor and carrier, then slung her rifle. She was going to find out.

The man stopped, his head scanned the area, then he motioned off frame. A child came into view. The child had a smaller long gun; what it was Amanda didn't know, but it did look like the child was quite comfortable carrying it and his small pack. There was no way that the kid was more than 10 years old. Anger receded, replaced by concern. Except for some older teenagers, Amanda hadn't seen any living children since the attack, and the rotted faces of the dead children that reanimated that she had shot flipped through her mind like a rolodex of horrible death masks.

Amanda sighed and started toward the hatch nearest their position. The man and child, maybe his son, were near the houses on the south end of the lake, near where Clint had magically appeared that one afternoon and put down all the Zeds after she had snuck out. Amanda jogged through the facility to the tall ladder that took her topside. Once she reached the top, Amanda took a moment to catch her breath before slowly releasing the locks and cracking open the hatch.

Sunlight burst into her shadows through the small sliver of an opening. After a brief moment, Amanda's eyes adjusted and she could see the man and son. Their backs were to her. Cramped for space, Amanda drew her pistol and let the hatch snap open on the spring-loaded hinges, which clunked loudly. The man and boy spun toward the sound, to see Amanda a third of the way out of the hatch, her pistol pointing at them.

"Do not move. I don't want to hurt you."

The man motioned for the boy to lower his rifle, letting his own rifle hang on its sling. "We don't want you to hurt us either."

"Why did you shoot at me yesterday?"

"We didn't. We just made our way over here this morning. We ran into a scouting element of Asian soldiers. I think they might have been Koreans, but they had Chinese and Korean markings on their APC and uniforms."

Amanda was surprised, although she tried really hard not to show it. "They were probably mixed forces. The Koreans attacked us with the help of the Chinese; that's how this all started. Where are they? You and the kid need to get down here before they see you."

The man smiled. "They won't see us, and they didn't last night when I attacked their camp."

"What?"

"They were about two clicks that way." He pointed toward the southeast. "Unfortunately, their APC was disabled during the attack, and otherwise, we would be long gone."

Amanda lowered her pistol. It seemed like the man was telling the truth, and Amanda wanted it to be true.

"Where are you headed?"

"Area 51, if you can believe it. There's supposed to be a safe place there, a big underground bunker."

Amanda smiled and decided to follow her instincts. "Well then, guy, you're in luck. My name is Amanda Lampton and you've found the other underground bunker. Come below and let's get you two something to eat, hot showers, and some clean clothes."

The boy looked at the man who nodded.

Amanda holstered her pistol and descended the stairs. "Dog the hatch on your way down."

The man and the boy followed into the dark hole, closing and dogging the hatch behind them.

In The FJ

Not much had changed in the short time since Bexar had come through the area with Chivo. The highways showed damage from Zed herds, which was nice in that the vehicles that had been abandoned on the road were now off the road. Only the occasional Zed was swerved around.

The drive would have probably taken all of three hours before the attack, but with the slower driving speed, the need to stop and siphon gas out of abandoned vehicles, and Jessie's nausea, badly twisted ankle, and a growing baby pressing on her bladder, it was hard to keep the doors closed and the hammer down. It really didn't matter, though. After about five hours, the FJ drove up the hill toward Guillermo and Angel's compound. Bexar had spent the drive telling Jessie all that each of the wonderful people had done to help him and Chivo—the opposition, the battle and ambush, and the victory.

Cresting the hill and turning up the driveway, Bexar stopped at the gate. The big forklift was visible on the back of the property, but that was the biggest thing left standing. The home was a burned-out ruin, the shop further destroyed than it had been in the assault on the compound. Bexar turned off the engine and climbed out. Jessie opened her door and stayed seated, unable to really stand on her own yet. She headed her rifle and scanned the area for any threats. Jessie saw what was left of some gallows, a buzzard sitting on the last one, a body twisting slowly in the wind. Jessie watched Bexar walk toward a dark pile in the middle of the driveway in front of what was the house.

Bexar turned and scanned for threats in a full circle before focusing his attention on the bodies at his feet. Each of the bodies had their hands bound with flex cuffs, and each of them had single shots fired into the back of their skulls. Bexar rolled one of the bodies over, the pungent stench of rotting flesh filled the air.

Guillermo.

Most of his sweet little friend's face had been destroyed by the exit wound, but it was obvious who it was. Bexar counted the bodies and checked off the list of people who had been living at the compound when he and Chivo had left.

All of them. All of their bodies left out to rot, left out for someone to find... those motherfuckers.

Bexar stood and scanned the surroundings again before walking to the body hanging from a noose. The body was one he didn't recognize; it could have been another attacking group or a single interloper who tried to attack or steal from the group. Behind what was left of the house were a handful of graves. They hadn't been there when he left, clearly new. Each of the graves had an SKS rifle planted in the dirt muzzle down with a helmet for each. The helmets were on the ground, but Bexar assumed they had been left on the butt of each rifle. The helmets were the same that the Chinese and Korean forces wore.

Bexar kicked one of the helmets off the cliff's edge and walked back to Jessie and the FJ. Jessie was in the driver's seat, the FJ turned around pointing back the way they came, and the motor was running.

"Watching you, I knew that we would be bugging out and it might be in a hurry. I'd rather you drive. It hurt like a motherfucker trying to drive with this damn ankle."

Bexar helped Jessie to the passenger's seat, climbed in, and drove off in silence.

After reaching the access road for the interstate, Bexar turned left and drove the wrong way, not that it really mattered.

"It was the PLA. There were some soldier graves with helmets. They executed them, cuffed them all, and shot them in the back of the skull at close range."

Jessie held Bexar's hand, which was all she could do to help at the moment. "What should we do now?"

Bexar reached into his pocket and pulled out the piece of paper that Chivo had given him with an impossibly long access code. "We're going back to Texas."

The Skies over Montana

Before they left, Bill gave Chivo a single sheet of paper with all they knew about Dorsey and where he might be. In the hours after escaping the goat fuck that their stop in Idaho had turned out to be, Chivo had a chance to read the document, read it again, and commit it to memory. Some of the information was what Dorsey had transmitted via the spark gap radio, and some of the information is what Bill and the few remaining airmen knew about ICBMs, the Minutemen III launch facilities, and the area around Air Force Base in Great Falls. Still, the mission brief, which is how Chivo thought about the document, was really light on information.

It reminded him a bit like the early days in Afghanistan, bringing community leaders into the fold as fragile allies to get information. Actionable intelligence is what they called it; information that could lead to the capture or death of America's enemies. Now at about 5,000 feet above the ground, Andrew and Chivo had no tribal leaders to help, no allies except each other, to hunt down one of the craftiest traitors that history will record, if any history will exist in the future.

On the back of the single sheet mission brief, Chivo drew a map. It wasn't the best, and the cold air breezing through the cockpit didn't help. The aircraft's simple heater was on, an air exchanger that used the heat of the exhaust to warm air entering the cabin, but mostly it was cold. The plan for now involved an aerial survey, unless they saw a missile control center that was quite obviously the one. The problem was that although they were easy to stop, it would be hard to determine which one might house Dorsey. The facilities were remote, with a large ranch-style home looking structure, but they also had antennas, a tower, a helicopter landing pad, and a serious fence. The launch control facilities were separated from the actual missile silos, but if they found the heavy concrete pads of the underground silos, they would be close.

Chivo had one such facility marked on his hand-drawn map. He didn't think it was the right one; the fence was down, the above-ground structures were partially burned, and there weren't any signs of living persons. The site was near the interstate and for that proximity to the snow-covered ribbon of asphalt, Zeds moved through the snow inside what was the fence line of the facility. Next to the mark on the map, Chivo wrote the number three. He was grading the sites found as one, two, or three: one meaning that it was likely to be occupied, three being the opposite.

"Are you OK landing in the snow?" Chivo yelled over the engine noise. His breath hung as an icy cloud in the air.

"Kind of. Depends on how soft the snow is and more importantly it depends on what is under it. If we hit something, we'd be royally fucked. Hey, do those Zeds look like they're moving slowly, like slower than usual? Want to check it out?"

Andrew banked the aircraft left and pointed to the interstate. A small herd of Zeds, maybe a thousand strong, trudged through the snow, or what was left of it on the roadway. It appeared that Zed movements had plowed the road, or something akin to it.

"You're the captain of this spaceship; I'm just the door gunner. So if you think we should check it out, then go."

The aircraft's nose pitched down slightly as Andrew slowed the motor and began descending while banking to turn for a closer flyby of the Zeds. After a few moments, Andrew flew by the group fairly low, only about 100 feet off the deck, banking the Husky so they could see out the window.

"Good eye, Andrew, they are moving slow." Chivo flipped his map over to the mission brief and circled where it was said that Dorsey had relayed that extreme cold slowed the zeds, sometimes stopping them altogether.

Chivo decided that it didn't matter if living in the high altitudes of the Rockies meant a higher safety from Zeds. For him, it wasn't worth being this cold. He hated the cold. Chivo took a deep breath and focused his thoughts; he had a mission to accomplish. Besides, he had been on missions much colder and more remote than this. Andrew turned back toward their original path and slowly climbed toward 5,000 feet AGL.

There are a number of different ways and patterns to conduct a search. While en route to Great Falls, Chivo had asked Andrew to conduct a grid-pattern search and described how to accomplish the search.

Dorsey had transmitted that he was south of Great Falls in an early message, and Chivo was happy that Bill's crew kept good notes, because that shortened their search box by quite a bit. Although none of them knew if there were even any launch facilities north of Great Falls in the first place. Reaching the northern limit of their search box, Andrew turned east and flew approximately the distance to the next search grid. The grids were spaced out further than Chivo would have liked, but he felt like it would be OK. Chivo scanned the snowy scene out the windows, seeing patches of earth and grass sticking out of the snow like a leopard's spots. Once they found the right location or a handful of locations, they could either land nearby or land somewhere safer and try to find a vehicle that still ran. Humping it through the snow on foot was not Chivo's idea of a grand adventure.

Las Vegas, Nevada

Erin fumed in her seat, already not in the best of moods due to feeling like crap. The cramping really hurt this month and Erin dreamed of being able to soak in a hot bath to ease the pain.

"Every fucking month my uterus punishes me for not getting pregnant. It sucks, and I don't like it."

"I'm sorry, baby, but I do like you. Do you want to find a safe place to hole up for a couple of days?"

"I don't know, maybe. I mean, I'm not fucking sick, it's just being a woman sucks."

Jason took her hand. "Yeah, sure, it sucks right now, but if I've learned anything from my past life is that in another week, you'll have swung the other way and will feel great."

"That's the problem. In another week, my uterus will want to make a baby and will drive my hormones to make me make that happen, but after another cycle of not getting pregnant, I'll be back in the same place, with a body that hates me."

"In that case, maybe we should wait and find a safe place to hole up next week. That sounds like the right time to me," Jason said with a sly grin.

Erin slapped his shoulder hard enough it stung. "Let's do both. Find me a place to wallow in my misery now, and I'll find a place for you once I'm past this."

The thought brought a wide grin to Jason's face. He loved his wife and he practically exploded with happiness knowing how much she loved him too.

"OK, step one: we get off this god-damned highway and away from all of these Zeds. Once we're in place, then I'll go scavenge for some feminine products and Tylenol for you. Any requests?"

"Some chocolate if there is any, and if you're running to the store, maybe you should pick up some condoms so we're ready for stage two of our cunning plan." Erin reached across the wide center console and kissed Jason on the cheek.

Slowly, the MRAP continued to nudge through the enormous crowd of Zeds on the highway. They were past the first big group of housing developments on the north side of Las Vegas and were still making progress headed eastbound. The road signs were missing, knocked down by the shambling herds of Zeds, so neither of them were very sure what highway they had just run into, but they did guess that they should turn left and head northeast instead of turning right and pointing back toward the center of Las Vegas. Crossing the bridge to take a left on the feeder road, the new highway appeared mostly clear in the direction they wanted to travel; from what they could see on their right, it was most certainly not clear. A lone road sign stood on the edge of the right of way on the feeder road that informed them the highway was actually I-15. Erin sighed and shook her head.

"What? Are you OK?"

"Yes, it's just that fucking I-15...we spent a long time going the long way around to here. We could have gone out of the east gate of Groom Lake and ended up on I-15 in less than a day."

"It's OK, baby. We didn't realize we were going to end up here. Our plan was a much different route."

Erin shook her head, angry at their folly, and slightly annoyed that Jason wasn't annoyed. Now free of the thickest of the Zed formations, Jason sped up to a more respectable 45 mph, rocking the big truck around Zeds as they found them. They drove in silence. Jason was mature enough to know to be quiet and let Erin work through what was upsetting her without his futile attempt at helping.

Only the sound of the big diesel motor rattling the MRAP down the roadway filled the cabin. After a few minutes, Erin reached over and took Jason's hand, tracing the lines in his palm with her fingers.

Jason slowed and took the exit ramp. The sign for a Love's truck stop still stood triumphantly in the air in defiance to the collapse of the world around it. If the building still stood, if it wasn't burned or completely looted, it would be a good place to go shopping. After crossing the overpass, Jason was relieved to see that the Love's was still in good shape. There were a number of semi-trucks parked at the stop, which meant they could siphon diesel fuel from the truck's saddle tanks too.

Hillsboro, Texas

Sweat dripped off his face and fell onto the stock of his M1. Ken knew he was in trouble and he wasn't exactly sure what he could do about it.

Front sight, breathe, shoot and move. Front sight, breathe, shoot, move. Front sight, breathe, shoot move.

The deep and powerful voice of his drill instructor from decades before resounded in Ken's head. The tactics were simple and they were repeated so many times in training then reinforced in the jungles of Vietnam that Ken was nearly on autopilot while the rest of his mind spun at 10,000 RPM trying to come up with a plan to break contact and escape. Zeds weren't people any longer, though, and that meant they didn't react like people would. The reverberating ping of the M1's metal clip being expended and ejected enacted another automatic response: left hand to the bandolier belt for another loaded clip, insert into the rifle, and rip the charging handle to the rear. Ken couldn't stand to lose any more of the ammo clips for his rifle. As semi-expendable as they were before the attack, they were more precious than a magazine for an AR in that it might be hard to find replacements.

Ken spun in place and butt-stroked a Zed that had snuck up behind him, which knocked the dead body reaching for him off balance and to the ground, but it immediately began getting up. One fast shot and the heavy rifle round destroyed its skull.

"Fuck." Ken spun in place. The first time he looked up from behind the rifle sights in a few moments, which was a deadly mistake. He had to cross I-35 and trying to go through Hillsboro to do it was a bigger mistake than he had realized. His truck was stashed to the east about half a mile, so his quick escape wasn't so quick now that he saw the mass of Zeds coming from that direction. To the west wasn't going to work due to another passing herd of Zeds like he had seen on I-45. This herd was headed northbound, so Ken was trying to push south, which was proving difficult. Ken figured all he had to do was survive long enough for the herd to get past and then get far enough south to flank the Zeds keeping him from the truck. Evade, escape, and fight again tomorrow.

The problem was Ken was having a lot of problems trying to evade long enough to escape. "Fuck!"

Another metallic ping and another ammo clip was left in the dirt. Ken's bandolier was running seriously low and he couldn't restock until he got to the truck. He didn't think he would make it to the truck without more ammo. "Fuck!"

Zeds to the left of me, more fucking Zeds to the right, and I'm stuck in the middle with you.

In the midst of Ken's fight for his life, he couldn't help but snicker at the humor and inserted another clip into the rifle. The snicker turned to giggling which turned to loud almost manic laughter. Another metallic ping and another reload, except that this time Ken's left hand came up empty. Glancing down, Ken grabbed each empty pouch in disbelief. Ken looked up just in time to see a woman's rotting teeth snap at his arm. Ken spun and drove the hard butt-stock to her skull which impacted with a loud bone-breaking crack. The Zed stumbled but didn't die.

Fucking zombie shows are bullshit.

Ken drew his bayonet from his belt and drove it into the woman's skull. She crumpled to the ground, taking the knife stuck in her skull with her. Another Zed's fingers grasped Ken's shirt, but he spun and butt-stroked this one with the same results as before, this time drawing his pistol and firing a round at point-blank range. Then again with another, followed by another. The Zeds were closing in, some coming off the interstate drawn by the rapid gunfire, others coming from all directions. The barrel of his rifle smoked from the rapid-fire abuse, hot against Ken's skin through his clothes. Spinning again to the next threat, Ken pressed the magazine release and inserted his last pistol mag, thumbed the slide release, and put another Zed to the dirt. Then another round, followed by another, and another until the pistol slide locked back on an empty chamber. Ken stuffed the empty pistol into his waistband, unslung his rifle, and held it like a baseball bat, the barrel and forestock singeing the palms of his hands. Ken swung as hard as he could at the closest Zed, which fell to the ground and immediately began getting back up. Ken swung at the next one and then the next. His breath ragged and rasping, sweat poured off his face in defiance to his inevitable death.

Yelling loudly, Ken was swinging for the fences, anger rising and burning deep from within. Ken swung again and missed, spinning off balance, his rifle falling out of his hands. Ken looked up, hatred burned in his eyes, hatred at his arrogance that he could cross the country alone, hatred at the Koreans, hatred for the Chinese and their fucking attack. Another woman reached, teeth gnashing, jaw snapping in anticipation of a fresh bite. The side of her head exploded, showering putrid, dark, pus-filled brain matter and skull fragments down onto Ken. The sound of the rifle shot rumbled past as another head exploded, followed by another.

A car horn? What the actual fuck is going on?

Withering rifle fire rained across the landscape, echoing off the buildings nearby. Once again, the voice of Ken's old drill sergeant resonated in his mind. "Get your ass to the ground, Hull. Fucking Charlie is going to shoot it the fuck off you, fucking dickhead! Now move! Crawl, Hull! The VC aren't going to finger fuck you, they're just going to fuck you raw and then go after your slut sister."

Ken's rifle sling was in his right hand, dragging the rifle as he crawled faster than he had since his last combat experience. Whoever was directing fire was creating an escape route. Ken didn't have to wait for an invitation to go, crawling across the ground over destroyed Zeds, the blood, pus, and spent shells. The unknown gunmen kept up volley after volley, two car horns now blaring a constant note toward the north. They sounded close, but not too very close. After only100 feet of crawling like a new recruit, a woman on a John Deere Gator slid to a stop. "Let's go, old man, get your ass up. We'll come back for your truck later!"

He didn't have to be told twice. Ken jumped to his feet and sprinted the two dozen yards to his rescuer, unconcerned that they might not be a safe choice. They were a safer choice than sticking around with the Zeds.

The Gator was surprisingly fast. "I'm Allison, but everyone calls me Allie. Grab a fresh mag from the bed." Allie glanced at his rifle. "Or not. What the fuck rifle is that? Anyways, take this." Allie handed him a loaded pistol. "It's not a shotgun, but you're riding it so don't fuck up."

Ken took the pistol, press checked the slide to verify a round was chambered, and held it ready. The car horns continued to blow, but the sound was fading as they rapidly drove the opposite way.

St. George

Back in the FJ, Bexar drove toward I-15 and turned north.

"That's where we crashed the truck."

"Where?"

"We drove off the damn bridge. I thought we had royally fucked up—and we had. I don't remember anything after that, but according to Guillermo, Angel found us on the interstate near their compound. Chivo was dragging me behind him and fighting his way to safety. The fucking goat, I swear to God I've never met anyone like him. I'm not entirely sure he can be killed. Anyways, apparently, Clint drove up on us. I'm not sure if he was following us or what the deal was since he tried to kill us in Cortez, but he got into the fight and we would have still been fucked if Angel hadn't come down the hill on his horse like the fucking cavalry."

"Wow."

"Yeah, sorry, I guess I didn't really tell that story to the fullest before. Things got pretty sideways, but we made it. You and I will make it; we have to for our baby. Besides, love conquers all."

Jessie held Bexar's hand as he drove the FJ around small clusters of Zeds in the roadway. Since the last big herd had come through, the number of Zeds weren't manageable, but there was still the unknown of where the PLA that had attacked and killed his friends were. They couldn't fret about it; they would either bump into them or they wouldn't, and there wasn't anything they could do about it. First, though, they had to drive through Hurricane and Bexar's last trip through the town went quite badly, driving into a massive herd of Zeds coming out of the desert. It was the beginning of the sequence that resulted in him and Chivo crashing the truck.

Bexar was sad about the loss of his friends. He wasn't sure if his ability to have compassion or even if his capacity for real sadness was broken, but he wasn't as affected as he thought he would be (or maybe should be). Like old grizzled cops who had worked in the business too long, it was just another day and it sucked for others, but he and Jessie were fine. It was a tough attitude to have, but it was the only one he had at the moment. Perhaps in the future, after the PLA was run out, after the Zeds were conquered, he might once again find the ability to care about others, but at the moment, it wasn't going to fucking happen.

Hurricane thankfully turned out to be a huge letdown for as anxious as Bexar had been. The town was deserted; only a handful of straggler Zeds meandered through the streets of the deserted and destroyed town.

"Thank God. When we came through this town before, it was completely overrun and we were fleeing for our lives. It was bad."

Jessie didn't say anything; she continued to hold Bexar's hand, wincing in pain with some of the larger bumps in the road. Her ankle was a sickly green and purple color, still quite swollen and excruciatingly painful, but Jessie was tough and not complaining, even though Bexar was sure that he would have been if he was that hurt.

There wasn't much daylight left. It was already mid-afternoon, so there wasn't any way they were going to make their destination in Texas before nightfall, or maybe even the next day. They would need a safe place to setup for the night. Out in the middle of nothing Utah, they were surrounded by incredible landscapes and many national parks, but Bexar wanted a solid structure, something they could survive a siege of the dead in if they had to. Camping in Zion might be nice because there wouldn't be any crowds for once, but even if Jessie's ankle wasn't badly sprained, relaxing backpacking trips were not on their agenda for survival. The thought of low-stress, happy backpacking, easy meals, and Nalgene bottles of water in their packs sounded wonderful, but Bexar knew that world that life for them would never exist again in anything but a memory.

Outside of Las Vegas, NV

"Do you think that the Zeds are attracted to the smell of blood?"

"You know what? Why don't you go fuck yourself, dick!"

Jason smirked at his wife—*Wife? Was Erin really his wife?* He was confused but Jason felt deeply in love. Smiling, he slid past Erin toward the broken glass doors at the front of the Love's travel center, slapping her ass as he went by. Erin flipped him off with a grin. She picked up an unopened bottle of beer from the parking lot and threw it into the darkened store with a loud shattering crash. As expected, dark guttural moans erupted in response as the Zeds inside shambled into shelves and trash trying to get to the disturbance for the hope of a fresh meal.

Jason propped open one of the doors with a brick on the sidewalk that appears to have lived in that spot since before the rise of the Zeds, probably for the very reason of holding open the door. They took a few steps back, giving room for any new friends to stumble out of the store's interior, Jason standing nearly back to back with Erin. She watched the door, he watching behind them for any threats that might shamble up, living or dead. They weren't disappointed; a few breaths later, the first Zed fell through the door of the gas station and fell to the pavement with a hard crack of a melon falling to the floor as its head bounced off the pavement. Erin fired a single shot before it could get up, painting the concrete with the blackened pus-filled rot from its now ruined skull. It felt like an hour, but the reality was that only a few minutes had passed, and Erin had dispatched four Zeds that had come out to greet them. She threw a rock inside the store and waited; this time, there were no moans, no great crashes.

"Ok, lover-boy, in we go. Think the trucker's showers still work? I could use one."

"Heh...no, but maybe we'll find a bucket of water or something for you to use."

"Bitch bath, like some homeless hooker."

"To be a hooker, you'd have to have sex with people."

Erin smiled slyly. "Yeah, people who pay...maybe you should pay up."

"I was hoping to be put on an installment plan, like rent to own."

Erin smiled and slid inside the dark interior, broken glass crunching under her feet. The counter where the cashiers stood was a complete disaster. All the cigarettes seemed to have been taken, candy bars and bags of chips were strewn about the floor, and the store stunk, smelling of a mix of abandoned building, rotting flesh, and old poop. It was the perfume of the apocalypse, common enough that neither of them really noticed anymore. Twenty minutes later, they were done clearing the building. Not only did the showers not work, which was far from surprising, but in typical truck stop fashion, someone had shit all over the floor in the restrooms. It didn't matter, though, as they could sleep in their truck if they needed, but what did matter was that as ransacked as the store was, the limited selection of feminine products were still there. Without any embarrassment, they were far too close for that anymore, Erin pulled down her pants, cleaned herself up with a T-shirt from the store, threw that on the ground, and inserted a tampon.

"Now if we could find that mystical bucket of water to wash my panties and pants, I would really appreciate it."

Jason kissed Erin. "I'm on it."

They knew they were out of luck inside the Love's, as they had searched it for Zeds, but had also kept a lookout for things like a bucket of water. There were a few unopened bottles of water that were found, but those were too valuable as drinking water to be used for cleaning. A few minutes later, Jason returned. "It isn't the best, but I think I've got a solution for you. Follow me."

Walking out to the fuel pumps, Jason held out his hand. "Give them to me." Erin laughed and took her pants and panties off, handing the soiled pair to Jason. Jason pulled a squeegee out of the bin and plunged the clothes into the water used for washing windshields. Amazingly, it hadn't completely evaporated or been drunk by wildlife, which probably meant it wasn't just water.

Erin stood there, looking mean with her bemused look and rifle, half-naked in the parking lot. Clothed or not, Jason wouldn't want to get on her bad side. "Think we should let them soak for a bit? Maybe get them in the morning?"

"Uh, maybe? I usually just threw them into the washing machine. I don't know."

"OK, well I do have experience in such things. We should let them soak for a while. Why don't we figure out dinner, take a break, and then we can return to scrub on them?"

"So what should I do, just have my bare ass flying in the wind?"

Jason smiled. "I'm very OK with that."

They both went back into the Love's and scavenged for something to eat besides the MREs in their truck. As the sunset, they retrieved Erin's clothes from the stale water, scrubbed them with a stiff brush they found on the ground nearby, and rinsed them in another windshield washing water bucket. The pants and panties went on the roof of the MRAP to dry and the two climbed into their armored truck to sleep. They left the roof hatch open for fresh air and fell asleep in each other's arms, the cool breeze keeping the interior comfortable.

Hillsboro, Texas

The compound was impressive. It appeared to have been a large trucking yard or something like that before the rise of the Zeds, but since then, this group had used semi-trailers and shipping containers to build a heavy-duty wall. Guards manned observation towers, ready to kill as it appeared. A heavy gate slid open from the inside as they approached, and the UTV that Ken was riding in barreled into the courtyard without even slowing down. Once stopped inside, the heavy gate slid closed with a hard thunk behind them. A woman walked toward them. She was armed, but her rifle hung on a sling across her chest, a camou-flaged armor carrier with many rifle magazines in pouches covering her chest and midsection. She appeared to be middle-aged and had the look of someone who was once much heavier, but lost a significant amount of weight in a short time. Ken noticed her eyes in the light of the setting sun; they were hard and cold, and the blue-grey color of steel. Immediately, Ken knew that she was not someone to fuck with. On the perimeter wall, he noticed that two of the guards were staring at him instead of outside the wall, their rifles ready in their hands.

Ken didn't know if he was a prisoner or if these people were friendly, but it didn't much matter at this point because without them he would have died. Whatever came next, he would adapt and overcome as needed.

"You got yourself into a bit of trouble out there, guy."

Ken nodded, still unsure of the what was going to happen in this new and dynamic situation. The heavy gate slid open noisily and Ken turned to look. He saw his truck drive through and stop behind the UTV where he sat.

"Mister, we have a few rules here, one of which is that you're required to be armed and ready for a fight at all times. Do you have more ammo for your weapons in the truck?"

"Yes, ma'am."

A faint smile could be seen before she responded; not with her lips, but with her eyes, her face as unmoving as granite. "Good, go top off, then we'll chat."

Ken's face, however, was not the hardened face of a combat leader; his expression gave away his surprise, although the woman said nothing. First, Ken inserted a full ammo clip into his M1 and charged the weapon, then he topped off his empty pouches with fresh ones before reloading the few clips he was able to pick up and keep, replacing them in the ammo can with the others. He completed his task quickly, efficiently, and in silence. The leader watching from her spot in the courtyard, the woman who had driven the UTV, watched, as well as the two guards on the wall. Others filtered by, appearing to be completing chores, while a few others stood watch on the wall, facing outward.

"This reminds me of the firebase on Hill 354 back in 'Nam, except that we didn't have any women there. From the look of how things are going on here, we could have really used some women fighting alongside us back then."

The leader's face didn't change, but the woman who drove the UTV smiled at him the same way a girl smiles at her grandpa after he said something stupid.

Ken frowned and continued to load his pistol magazines, wondering what would come next, except that he didn't really think that he would be kept a prisoner since they were making him top off his weapons. He was worried that they would take his truck and supplies, though. If that happened, then he would be in trouble and getting to Groom Lake would be tough.

"What are you going to do with me?"

Finally, the leader's face changed, a thin smile appearing on her lips. "We're going to do nothing. If you would be kind enough to donate some gear or help out around the compound for a bit as repayment for saving your ass, that would be great, but if you want to leave now, you can. However, we won't save you again, and we're going to blindfold you to drop you and your truck off away from us. We don't need you coming back in an attempt to take what we have. My name is Samantha, but most call me Sam."

"Welcome to meet you, Sam. I'm Kenneth, but most call me Ken," Ken began, looking around again. "I don't think I could take what you have if I wanted too; y'all are setup quite well."

"We are, but we don't need any extra drama than we already have with the dead."

Ken nodded. "The Zeds have really fucked everything up, but not as bad as the fucking Chinese and Koreans that invaded."

The woman's smile vanished. "What?"

"The PLA, the invasion."

"What are you talking about? We know that we were attacked, we had the warnings right before everything went dark, and we saw the aircraft spraying the virus or whatever it was, but we haven't heard about an invasion."

"Do you not have a radio?"

The woman shook her head.

"OK, I could use some help setting mine up, and ma'am, we have a lot to talk about."

Great Falls, Montana

Chivo press-checked his rifle and looked out the windows, scanning for threats. He had to assume that something would go wrong and they would be on foot from this point on. Chivo obviously hoped that wouldn't happen. The aircraft descended closer to the snow-splotched landscape, which was the problem. Andrew was landing them for the night on a road that passed in front of a ranch. There wasn't much for them, except maybe shelter in the house or what looked like a utility shed or barn, but it was what they had for the night. The yellow Husky flared for landing, bouncing on the large tundra tires, snow blowing into the air and past the cabin from the propeller. Andrew stopped the engine and flipped open the clamshell door, climbing out with wheel chocks for the main gear. Chivo unfolded himself from the aircraft; as small of a person as he was, it was still cramped. Once out, he continued to scan the area, rifle in hand, but no threats appeared. There weren't any tracks in the snow and no signs of any movement, living or dead.

"I'm going to check the house. Don't chock the tires yet. Let me make sure we won't need a quick escape first."

Andrew flashed a thumbs up as Chivo turned and walked toward the house a few hundred yards away. There wasn't much for Andrew to do in the meantime, so he checked the leading edge of his wings for any icing and checked for any ice or snow building up in the petcock tubes. He didn't want them to end up like Buddy Holly. Chivo returned a few minutes later.

"House is clear. The owner is still there, killed himself on the back porch, and left some canned goods that look tasty, so score one for the good guys."

Chivo grabbed his gear out of the aircraft and started back toward the house. Andrew put the chocks in place and followed along shortly. The setting sun cast long shadows across the landscape, red and purple colors lighting up the bottom of the few clouds in the sky. Andrew smiled at the beauty. It was important to him to keep sight on the simple things now that the simple things were pretty much all he really had left. Their day was over and hopefully the next day would see them completing their mission. Andrew was ready to get back to Groom Lake and to Oreo. This was the longest he had been without his best friend since before the end of the world four months ago.

SSC

Amanda waited sort of impatiently for the man and his son to come back to the dining facility; they had enjoyed a light snack before heading off to shower and changed. He had said it had been many weeks since they had been clean. Their clothes were a filthy mess and if the powerful washing machines in the facility couldn't get the grime out, they would be thrown in the trash. Tired of waiting and figuring that the new guests could figure out how to eat the food, she left and went to the control room. Amanda toggled the view on the computer monitor between the different security cameras above ground, watching and looking for any sign of who the random attacker was who shot at her, but there wasn't any movement that she could see except for a handful of Zeds on the western side of the facility. They were shambling toward the main facility entrance, but posed no threat to them below. Even if a million Zeds stood on the ground above her, she would be fine.

Restless and giving up on the security cameras, Amanda flipped on the spark gap radio and waited as it came to life, popping and hissing as it did. On the table, she had a pad of paper and a pen along with a cheat sheet of Morse code letters and shorthand codes that people have been using. It appeared that people were excited, transmitting on top of each other; it was a pileup of popping buzzes. Amanda was able to catch snippets and slowly began to piece together what was being talked about. It was like being at a lively cocktail party in a foreign country, except that you couldn't see who was speaking or read their body language.

Amanda transcribed the transmissions and waited for her chance to get on the airwaves and set the record straight. It appeared that Bill, or someone from Groom Lake, was trying their best, but it was not going well for him. On the pad of paper, Amanda wrote out the message she wanted to send then drew the dashes and dots of how it would be transmitted above each letter. Once ready, and with some effort, she broke into the frequency and began transmitting.

BREAK BREAK BREAK
TRANSMISSION FROM POTUS
SSC - WAXAHACHIE TX SECURE AND READY FOR SURVIVORS
GROOM LAKE NV SECURE AND READY FOR SURVIVORS
PLA PLOT TO LAUNCH USA ICBM UNCOVERED AND STOPPED
PLA STILL A THREAT
REPORT ALL SEEN PLA TO GROOM LAKE
MILITARY RESPONSE PLANNING
NEED MORE VOLUNTEERS
NEED ALL CURRENT AND FORMER SERVICE MEMBERS HELP
WE WILL FIGHT
WE WILL WIN
GOD BLESS AMERICA
POTUS OUT

There was a pause at the end of her transmission then the radio practically exploded with all the received transmissions, all on top of the others. She could no longer decipher what was being transmitted so she stopped trying. The fight was that there was a rumor that the PLA had fled; there was also a rumor that their facilities had been overrun. Hopefully, this would help settle some of those fears, but Amanda wasn't sure. A Roosevelt fireside chat that was not and she felt slightly amiss for outright lying to the American public, but not much. She felt like they needed to be lied to, they needed hope and guidance, just as other wartime presidents had done.

Amanda looked up and saw Eric and his son Jacob standing in the room eating the dinner she left out for them with a puzzled look on their faces.

"It's a radio."

They both looked at her with blank expressions.

"There is another underground facility in Nevada. Actually, there were a lot more of them, and these are the only two left that are online and not overrun by the Zeds, but at the facility in Groom Lake, there's a radio guy who came up with this radio. We've transmitted plans and instructions via shortwave radio. Slowly, people began getting online and transmitting. It's amazing really; old technology working after everything else was wiped out from the EMPs."

"Is there anyone else here besides yourself?"

"Not for the moment. That's going to change soon."

"How is that? With your radio?"

"With that, but also with people in Groom Lake. There are enough survivors that they practically have too many. Besides, we're setup better here for future farming. Although the preserved food stores are extensive, they're not endless. We have to prepare for the next step of survival where we can no longer depend on what was made before the attacks."

"You don't look like a farmer."

"You're right, I don't, but I was the Secretary of Agriculture."

Eric gave Amanda a suspicious look.

"Well, none of that matters right now. I'm guessing the clothes fit, that your shower was nice, and the food was good enough?"

"Yes, ma'am, thank you, but now what?"

"You're welcome to stay, you're welcome to go. If you are willing to stay, there is work for us to do to get ready."

"Ready for more people?"

"No, ready for the attack." She held up her hand, stopping the question before it had come out of Eric's mouth. "The Koreans with the Chinese caused this mess. It was their attack, their EMPs in our atmosphere, and their development of the bacteria that caused the dead to reanimate that nearly wiped us off the map. That much you probably have figured out by now. The problem was that it didn't wipe us off the map. We think they expected less resistance, but they've invaded and are trying to take our country...what is left of it."

Eric stood quietly for a moment. "Well...even with all the destruction and death, the natural resources are astounding. It is still bat-shit crazy. Maybe they have a way to kill the dead for good?"

"They do. Some of our Marines captured a type of radar truck that basically zaps the Zeds and kills them for good."

"Huh." Eric gave his son a look. "Tell you what, we'll stay for a bit to see what we can do. Besides, it will be a nice break from trying to survive on the surface. What are you doing to prepare?"

"Did you see the earth-work topside?"

"Kind of."

"Groom Lake was attacked by a PLA team of what could best be described as some sort of special forces. We came out on top, but we wouldn't have without help and a bunch of luck. Part of the problem is that Groom Lake didn't have any above-ground defenses or fighting positions. It was a situation where they could lock down underground and hope to survive the siege or fight back. We all fought back with some losses, but we won. Not wanting to go through another siege scenario, since I'm 100 percent sure the PLA knows about this facility, I'm getting the above-ground portions ready to fight. At least I'm trying."

"I'm not a veteran, I was an engineer, but we'll help best we can."

Amanda smiled. "You know, there's a bunch of DVDs in the recreation room near the bunk rooms. Why don't we see if there's something your son would enjoy watching?"

CHAPTER 12

April 15, Year 1
Hillsboro, Texas

Ken woke up to the sound of car horns blaring in the distance. He didn't think that it was the same car horns from the previous night, from when the group had pulled his ass out of the swarming Zed death. *It could be someone else, or maybe they use the horns as distractions while they scavenge for supplies,* Ken thought, but he didn't know. What he did know was that his radio had been a huge hit and they had turned everything on just in time to catch the president's transmission. This group had no idea; they didn't know about the invasion and they didn't know about Groom Lake or President Lampton. Needless to say, Ken was kind of popular at the moment. Information in the post-dead world was a currency more valuable than gold.

April mornings were still cool outside in this part of Texas, but Ken knew that they wouldn't be cool and comfortable for long, so he should enjoy them while he could. He assumed that the underground facilities would have some sort of climate control so July and August wouldn't be too terrible.

Ken was already dressed—well, mostly dressed—his boots open and ready next to his cot. Shipping containers had been modified for use as the group's buildings. They would probably be quite hot inside of the containers, cooking in the heat come summer, but so far that morning, it wasn't too bad. After tying his bootlaces, Ken stood, stretched, slung his M1 Garand, and walked outside into the morning air. Toward the north side of the courtyard was a fire ring and a spit. A whole hog was dressed and spread over the smoldering coals, roasting slowly. They were going to eat well tonight! Feral hogs had been the bane of Texans for centuries, even though they were good eating, but now their abundance was a blessing. Between the hogs and deer, depending on what part of Texas someone was in, they had the ability to eat well if they could hunt. The problem would be food preservation, but there were enough people in this compound that eating most of a hog over the course of two days would probably be quite easy. *Either way,* Ken thought while gnawing on a hard MRE cracker, *a pig roast sounds delicious!*

The gate rattled open and one of the side-by-side utility vehicles rolled inside followed by billowing dust. One of the friendly faces from the previous evening saw Ken and waved him over to the UTV. They were smiling and pointed to the seemingly random pile of parts in the bed and Ken knew instantly what was going on and smiled too. They had a taste of the drug called information and they wanted more.

"Looks like you guys were busy after I went to bed," Ken said. He hadn't given them a parts list or any guidance last night. They must have examined his radio in detail to come up with what they needed.

"Yup, but with some changes. We charge car batteries using a system we put together with a homemade wind turbine, so we will be able to run a bank of batteries to keep the radio monitored at all times for now. Mostly, we use those batteries for our distraction noise makers for the dead now which we've used to save a number of lives, but a radio is worth the effort, too. There is too much we don't know and need to learn. We need to be ready for the PLZ, not just the dead."

"PLA. I think it stands for People's Liberation Army and we're not even sure it is really them, since the North Koreans are involved too. Anyways, yeah, what did you have in mind? Are you going to stay here or go to one of the facilities?"

"We had a council meeting last night and we want to stay here, but we want to make contact with President Lampton. I think we're close enough that we could be of assistance if needed. At the very least, we learned last night of so many other survivors all around the country; we want to be put on the map in case *we* need help."

Ken nodded and pointed toward the roasting hog. "Any chance I can stay and enjoy some of that when it is done?"

Samantha smiled. "We hoped you would. First, though, we would like it if you helped Brinson here build our own radio. He's our resident MacGyver and the one who built our battery-charging system."

Brinson and Ken introduced themselves and shook hands before agreeing to meet in the "shop" in 10 minutes. The shop was another shipping container, but with tools and workbenches. There weren't any power tools to speak of, minus some basic electronics gear like a multimeter that miraculously still functioned. Building the spark gap radio wasn't a hard task, and Ken was looking forward to the work nearly as much as getting the chance to actually chat and interact with another person for a while. *Everyone dreams of living alone in a cabin in the woods until it happens to them, then it is lonely as shit!* Ken smiled. He wasn't alone in his hunting cabin anymore and it felt great!

Outside of Great Falls Montana

Chivo stood back from the large window in the house, keeping his form in the shadows of the interior, but looked intently at the scene outside and frowned. They moved much slower than what he had seen in Texas and the southwest, but Zeds were still Zeds: they were still deadly and a serious problem. They were even more of a problem this morning, as they were against the plane.

Andrew was awake, shivering and slapping himself, trying to warm up. It was cold but Chivo didn't think that it was too terribly cold, not since his winter warfare training in Alaska and Greenland had he ever been that cold. Now, Montana in April felt sort of comfortable, but it was a fool who lost all respect for the cold or the heat because both will kill a man without any regard for who he is and what training he had done.

"What-t-t-t are w-w-we go-going t-t-to do?" Andrew's teeth chattered as he shivered.

"Distract them, kill them, and see what sort of damage they may have caused, if any. We repair your aircraft if we can. If not, then we move out with our alternate transportation."

"W-what alt-t-ternate?"

"Our feet, mano."

Andrew shook his head and stamped his feet like an angry three-year-old, except that he wasn't angry or throwing a temper tantrum, he was just cold. During the night, he began to start a fire in the fireplace—there was even wood on the back porch by the owner's body—but Chivo said no because the smoke would draw attention. To Andrew, there weren't any people to draw attention from, only Zeds, but a single glance from Chivo ended the conversation. For being surprisingly short, Andrew was a bit intimidated by the presence Chivo had. The guy really filled a room and there was no question that Chivo was not only the baddest dude there but also the guy in charge.

"When I go out there, give me a couple of minutes. I'm going to draw the Zeds away from your plane and dispatch them for good; you make your way down there and check for damage. Are you OK with that?"

Andrew nodded, still shivering and hoping that the movement and task would help him warm up. Chivo press-checked his rifle and walked out the front door. After walking a few dozen yards, he began yelling and waving his hands. A dozen pair of dead eyes turned and locked onto him as Chivo walked a line perpendicular to the Husky and the house, leading the Zeds away from both. The angle was still wrong, as he couldn't begin putting the Zeds down for fear of a round missing or over penetrating and striking the aircraft, so Chivo kept walking and occasionally yelling to keep the Zed's interested. Turning to head toward the road and the fence line, Chivo watched the Zeds and the aircraft, monitoring the angle and waiting for the time he could begin using his rifle to end this goofy dance of the dead.

They do move slower in the cold. I wonder if they're not as strong either... maybe, maybe not?

A hair-brained idea formed in Chivo's special-operations-soldier now turned mad-scientist mind. Now slightly more comfortable with the where he was with the Zeds in relation to the aircraft, Chivo stopped and shouldered his rifle, taking careful aim from a task well practiced. He smoothly pressed the trigger to the rear and watched as the second Zed in the group showered rotted brain matter and sickly black pus across the snow patch and fell in a crumpled heap. Chivo shot the third and the fourth, working his way back through the group of Zeds, the fire muffled by the snow still echoing across the landscape. A few moments later, all the Zeds were dead for good, except for the former leader, now alone. Chivo let his rifle hang on the slingers he drew his pistol and began walking toward the approaching Zed, closing the gap. He saw Andrew on the front porch, staring at them. Chivo flashed a thumbs up and kept walking toward the last Zed. As the gap continued to shrink between the two of them, the Zed's arms came up, reaching toward Chivo, its jaws snapping open and closed, teeth gnashing in excitement for a fresh bite, a fresh meal of living flesh.

Chivo stopped. The Zed was missing an arm and the remaining hand was frozen and black, some fingers missing, the others broken and bent at odd angles. Chivo shook his head, amazed at his own stupid luck. A single pistol shot put the mangled Zed down for good and now done Chivo set off the few hundred yards toward Andrew and the aircraft.

"How's the plane?"

"A couple of rips in the fabric, that's all. We can tape that up and we'll be OK until I can make more permanent repairs." Andrew reached into the small luggage compartment and retrieved a roll of black tape that looked slightly like duct tape, but stronger and made of cloth instead of plastic. A few minutes later, the two small tears were repaired, they were in the aircraft, and Andrew was trying to start the aircraft. The starter turned over slowly, too slowly for the engine to catch and start in this cold weather.

"See the pedals on the floor?"

"Yeah, mano, the rudder pedals?"

"Well, yes, push down on both on the bottom; that holds the brake. I've got to get out and hand prop my baby."

Andrew set the choke and throttle, set the master to on, turned on the magnetos, and climbed out, walking around the circumference of the prop.

"Turn off the master key for a second."

Chivo reached to the front and flipped the little metal key to off. Andrew slowly turned the prop over, the blades popping to a stop after each stroke of the engine. After a few revolutions, Andrew was satisfied. "Flip the key back on." Chivo did as he was told. Andrew took the highest blade of the prop, swung a leg up, and spun the prop hard with a full body swing. The prop spun over and the engine sputtered, but didn't start. Andrew tried again. Then he tried again. After two more tries, the engine coughed to life, the cold engine belching white exhaust for a few moments before the idle began to settle. Andrew walked around the spinning prop and climbed back into the cabin.

"Alright, well, we should be able to get the battery to charge while we fly today. We'll also get the fucking heat on. Let's get out of here and in the sky where it's safe," Andrew said, pointing to a new group of Zeds shambling down the road toward the loud aircraft engine. Before Chivo could answer, Andrew spun the aircraft around and into the slight breeze they had that morning before moving the throttle and running the engine up to take-off speed and releasing the engine choke. He switched between the two magnetos, testing each as he ran up the aircraft. Now at full power and holding, Andrew let the brakes go and they bounced down the country road, snow blowing up behind them like a smoke screen in the prop blast. After a few hundred feet, the yellow Husky lurched into the air and slowly climbed out, away from the Zeds and into the safety of the deep blue sky.

Pecos, Texas

Jessie's ankle looked worse and Bexar hoped that it was only the deep bruising from the injury coming up to the surface. She still couldn't put any weight on it and every bump, every jostle of the FJ, caused pain to throb through her entire body in waves from her ankle radiating up her leg. If Chivo's directions were correct, then they would have a reprieve soon. This part of Texas had always been sparse, populated mostly by oilfield workers and coyotes, but now in the early morning, with the horizon glowing bright yellow in the windshield, they found I-20 practically deserted. At some point, one of the massive herds of Zeds had come through, clearing the roadway of all the disabled vehicles. That made the drive nearly as quick as it would have been before the end of the world; the difference was still the need for top gas mileage, but if Bexar had wanted to, he could have driven 100 mph without worry of a trooper standing at his driver's window. Gas mileage or not, driving that fast would have been reckless, a quick way to take a Zed down with the grill of their vehicle. No matter what the movies had shown, hitting a person with a vehicle caused considerable damage, damage they couldn't afford to have. This FJ was the reason why they had a chance for their unborn baby and weren't stuck with the fanatical whims of others.

So far, the only group of survivors that Bexar would be OK with were killed, their bodies thankfully still in Utah and not reanimated. After Big Bend, after Groom Lake, after the disaster with Cliff and Clint, Bexar was through with others. He would have to convince Jessie, but it might work. He wanted to be close enough to evacuate to a fortified facility in case of a major attack, but far enough away to be left alone with his family. Family was all that mattered and Bexar intended to keep the remaining members alive as long as he could. Although with each passing day, Bexar seriously wondered if it was all just a losing battle.

Malachi was the lucky one. He didn't have to endure the crushing pain of loss, the fear, the fighting...no, he saw the end and was mercifully saved from the rest.

Bexar shook his head, trying to clear it. The images of Malachi's reanimated body, Keeley's little body, digging the graves flashed through his thoughts...but what chilled Bexar the most is that he had killed others, people who weren't Zeds, and he was OK with that. Their deaths didn't affect him at all. Those sorts of emotions were dead to him, but Keeley and Malachi kept appearing in his mind, like flashbulbs of views, gruesome and painful with each pop.

They rode in silence. Jessie grimaced with each bump on the road, but she still reached over and touched Bexar's arm. He wasn't talking, his dark thoughts contained to only himself, but Jessie knew when her husband, her lover, and best friend wasn't doing well. Bexar managed a weak smile for his wife. She caressed his arm and smiled back the best she could trying to soothe some of his stress and pain.

All the road signs were knocked down and gone, the mile markers as well. Bexar vaguely remembered there being an abandoned air base along the interstate, but he wasn't exactly sure where it was. The skeletal remains of a large aircraft hangar grew out of the distance toward the south and with that, Bexar was confident they had the right place. Bexar slowed and drove off the interstate through the desert median and to the frontage road...another driving stunt that a bored highway patrol would have loved to have seen. That life felt so long ago to Bexar that his career as a cop felt like a dream, something that wasn't even real. Bexar took a deep breath and tried to clear his mind to focus on his task of driving. Just because this leg of their trip had come and gone without any problems or damages didn't mean that it would stay that way. They could be driving into an ambush; there could be a pocket of Zeds waiting to tear the flesh from their bodies.

Bexar rolled the driver's window down, the cool morning air having a hint of the coming heat of the day on it. West Texas was not the place to be without air conditioning. It was amazing to Bexar that people have lived out in this part of Texas since before oil was discovered, since he couldn't imagine why anyone would want to live near Pecos on purpose.

He took another deep breath and stuck his head closer to the open window, hoping the rushing air would help wake him up enough to focus. Bexar turned onto the driveway and stopped. A gate blocked entry onto the abandoned air base, chains with locks wrapping through the pipe gate and post.

"I'll be right back," Bexar said over his shoulder as he climbed out of the FJ. Inspecting the gate, chain, and padlocks, Bexar tried to think through a solution. He didn't have a shotgun any longer, so the easy breach of the locks wasn't an option. The cattle gate was attached to the fence post via two hinges. It took a moment, but Bexar had an epiphany. Smiling slightly, Bexar lifted up on the gate next to the post and the gate slid off the hinges; either on purpose or by accident, the gate hadn't been installed correctly. Bexar pushed the gate to the side, still being held on by the chains and locks, drove the FJ through, climbed back out, and put the gate back on the hinges. They didn't need anyone else, dead or alive, meandering into the inside of the fence line if they could help it.

After a short drive along a dirt driveway, the tires of the FJ found the concrete of the expansive runways and taxiways. Bexar drove toward the remains of the large hangar. Chivo's directions were based on starting from that hangar to find the right place to enter. Traveling directly south from the hangar along what used to be the aircraft ramp, a non-descript concrete building stood. Following the instructions, Bexar found the access panel, entered the ridiculously long code, and waited. The entire building began to rise slowly with a deep hydraulic hiss. A lit entryway appeared with painted concrete floors and a ramp that would take them underground. Bexar tried to not act surprised, but Jessie knew he was. His eyebrows arched, Bexar looked like a bearded little boy on Christmas morning. A few moments later, they were driving down the ramp, pausing only to push the button that closed the entrance behind them before driving across the cavernous room, stopping next to the large blast door. Military vehicles sat in the shadows parked along the sides of the passageway. This was like a scene out of a bad sci-fi movie; Bexar was mostly sure that there was a guy with two talking robots making funny comments about them while watching on the movie screen.

Outside of Las Vegas

It was a zero day, like long distance hikers would do occasionally; this was going to be a zero-mile day. They were making terrible time to get to where they wanted to go, but the other days were out of their control; this one was their choice. Besides, the truck stop had things they needed and it was convenient to stay put while taking care of personal needs, fueling their big new MRAP, and taking some time to try to shed some of the stress they've been enduring. That was the problem with the end of the world that it seemed all the movies and books Jason had watched and read hadn't discussed: it was exhausting and the stress was incredible. There really wasn't any real downtime where someone could really let their guard down and just let the reality around them evaporate.

Erin made a sleeping area using some of the random stuff for sale in the truck stop: cheap Mexican-style blankets, that were made in China ironically, travel pillows, and other things; pretty much all the stuff that others hadn't looted already. However, up and awake, Jason went through the doors into the parking lot to observe what was around them and to take a leak. Toward the highway and coming from the direction of Las Vegas was an ominous low black cloud, churning and growing.

"Erin!" Jason yelled as he turned to go back into the Love's. "Errrriiin!"

Erin appeared in her panties and T-shirt. "Damn, Jason, what?"

Jason didn't say anything; he took Erin's hand, led her outside, and pointed toward the cloud.

"Fuuuuuck."

Erin stared at the cloud for a moment before turning to go back into the store. "Don't just stand there looking sexy. Get your ass in here and help me gather gear. We've got to get the fuck out of here."

Their zero day was no longer and they had some choices to decide on in the next few minutes.

"We're set back off the highway, so we might be OK."

Erin shook her head at Jason for that one. "No, we won't. If there are enough to have a cloud of flies, they will spread out and flatten this fucking place. No, we've got to bug out. The question is either the direction we were going or we take a perpendicular route away from this danger."

Jason rolled up their new blankets; cheap as they were, they were more blanket than they had, which was none. The pillows too. Erin took some plastic bags from behind the counter and began gathering all the things they should have gathered the previous night and put in their truck. She made a mental note about that. If they were going to live very long, they couldn't make stupid mistakes like that. She had become soft with the easy living at Groom Lake.

Twenty minutes later, they were in the MRAP, Erin now wearing pants, and they discussed their options while the truck warmed up a bit. The cloud was getting closer, and so were the Zeds.

They decided to push on ahead of the approaching herd, trusting that they would turn off the highway soon and get clear. They really didn't want to go well out of their way when there was always the chance to run into another herd of Zeds.

Driving toward the parking lot exit, Jason slammed on the brakes, the heavy truck rocking and the air brakes hissing in protest.

"What's up," Erin asked. Jason pointed toward the highway and left.

"Fucking Chinese."

Stopped on the highway was one of the four-wheeled APCs that they had seen being used previously. Jason slowly backed the MRAP away from the highway. There was a man sticking out of the top hatch of the APC, but he was looking the wrong way. After backing out of view, Erin crawled into the back of the MRAP and retrieved her big rifle.

"Come on, lover, we need to check this out."

SSC

Breakfast was a simple affair; it had to be because there didn't seem to be an easy way to make a hot breakfast for only three people. Three hundred? Yes, easy to do. Three? Not easy to do unless you want to waste a lot of food.

Industrial-grade commercial kitchens are purpose-built for the crowds, not family-sized meals.

"Next time I venture out, I need to try to find a camp stove, like a Coleman that burns gasoline as well as the special fuel, and maybe a couple of small pans. Then we can make a hot breakfast."

Jacob didn't notice; he was too busy eating his third helping of oatmeal and spacing out as only boys know how to do.

"Sure, but this is simply fantastic. For the first time in months, we are in a safe shelter that is well stocked and has modern amenities that actually still work. I'll give it five stars on Yelp," Eric laughed while saying.

Amanda smiled. Her life had been much too serious for far too long and it felt wonderful to have some humor and levity.

After another half hour of humorous banter, Jacob was finally full for the moment, so Eric and Amanda began the grand tour of the facility, as far as she understood it.

"You've already seen some of the highlights, such as the hot showers and you have new clothes from the storeroom, but through this door are the tunnels. This facility was originally a large public project to build the superconducting super collider, but in reality, the entire public project was a cover to build this facility. Anyways, the large tunnel still exists and it houses a bunch of equipment and vehicles."

Lights clicked on in sequence down the cavernous tunnel, flickering on one by one, slowly illuminating the dark void with hard shadows and flickering light like an old gymnasium. Eric let out a low whistle.

"Wow. Do these all work? You could go rescue people or bug out or build whatever you needed. I mean, I always suspected these sorts of places existed, but wow, unbelievable."

"This place is unbelievable. It was the best money could buy and now it is just about all that is left. There used to be a lot more facilities like this, this one and the one in Groom Lake—you know, Area 51—are the only two that are left. Others like the one in Denver were destroyed or overrun."

"If they're overrun, then it would be possible to go take them back."

"Um, yeah, I hadn't thought about it like that, but it could be. It would be dangerous."

"Sure, so is living, but...what did you call the biters?"

"Zeds."

"OK, but with the Zeds, everything is dangerous. At least clearing out another facility like this would open up an opportunity for hundreds of others to have a chance at surviving."

"We've offered for survivors to come find safety at Groom Lake, and the response has been good, but there are a lot of others who want to stay put and survive on their own."

"So what? They'll want to survive on their own until something bad happens. Once something bad happens, then they will want to have a safe place like this one to escape to."

"That's a good point."

"You said Groom Lake. Have you not offered...what are you calling this place?"

"The SSC."

"You've not offered the SSC to other survivors?"

"No, well no not until yesterday, and that's a long story involving what we thought was a government official turned double agent for the Koreans and Chinese was basically holding this facility hostage, keeping it a secret. He's being taken care of and is gone, so we can open things up. The problem is that I need help; I can't do it by myself. Also, there may be people who want to come from Groom Lake to here and need help getting here."

Eric took a long pause before answering.

"Those people aren't your immediate concern; they're safe or at least safer than a bunch of other people who are hacking it out of the wilds instead of sitting safely behind the walls at Fort Apache. Wait. That means that the enemy knows all the secrets about this place!"

"Yeah, I think so."

"Shit."

"Exactly. That's why I was building up the earth-works up top, to give us fighting positions. Groom Lake was attacked by some sort of Chinese and Korean special forces-type of team and it nearly was lost. There are a few Marines there and some really brave survivors who helped beat back the attack."

"We need people, as in hundreds of people, who can fight—people who know how to fight. We appear to have the equipment and arms, now it just takes bodies and trigger pullers."

Amanda's eyebrows arched. "What sort of background do you have?"

"Eclectic, but I deployed twice to Iraq and once to Afghanistan."

"That is simply marvelous. Thank you for your prior service, but your president needs you again."

Groom Lake

"Contact rear!"

Rifle fire erupted while the squad rapidly moved to counter the ambush. The heavy sound of the SAW gunner unleashing controlled bursts of withering automatic fire momentarily droned out the slower sound of the M4s being fired rapidly, but not on burst.

Happy slapped the man lying behind the SAW on the shoulder, the man immediately ceasing firing. Happy yelled over the continued rifle fire from the rest of the squad. "Gunner is hit! Break contact and recover the causality!"

Two of the others, a man and a woman, low-crawled to the gunner's position who lay slumped over his smoking automatic weapon. The man grabbed the causality and rolled him to his back while the other's rifle fire had increased in tempo and volume, some of the lead elements releasing semi-controlled burst shots.

"No pulse! He is dead!"

The man drew his right hand, placed the tip of his finger on the gunner's forehead, and mimed shooting him. The woman had already taken position behind the SAW and unleashed another controlled burst of heavy automatic fire, brass casings ejecting to the ground around them, hot to the touch. After "killing" the gunner and preventing him from becoming a Zed, the man yelled to break contact. The woman operating the SAW unleashed a heavy burst of fire, the can of linked ammunition running low. As the last lead element ran past, rifle fire erupted behind her, but offset. The woman leapt to her feet, the heavy M249

SAW in her hands, her M4 hanging by the sling across her chest. She heaved the weapon and sprinted toward the rear and away from the ambush. Heavy rifle fire covered her retreat as she ran, just like she had done for the others.

"CEASE FIRE, SAFE WEAPONS!" Happy yelled. The gunfire stopped. Even with the earplugs in, everyone's ears were ringing from the simulated firefight.

"Good job, but you guys were way too fucking slow getting that fucking SAW back into the fight. In a real firefight, you're going to need that weapon fucking up the enemy and stacking bodies to give you a chance to bug the fuck out. A long break in fire like that and the fucking PLA will destroy you and overrun your fucking position."

Happy smiled. The training was intense, more intense than most of these civilians had ever experienced, but they were getting better and the next time the PLA came knocking, they weren't going to like it. Happy was also a more intense person than most of the survivors had encountered in their previous lives. He looked up and longed for some air cover. If they could feed 9-lines to some fast movers, then the PLA wouldn't stand a chance, but for all the longing in the world, they would probably never have any sort of air support ever again. Even if they found pilots, even if they found aircraft, even if they found arms, there just isn't any way there were enough people left to maintain and fly complex war machines any longer. The crazy flying guy with the dog would get destroyed by enemy fire trying to do anything; it wasn't even worth asking. They were thrust back into the man-on-man fighting that killed so many in the First World War.

The squad of civilians looked exhausted, and with good reason. They had been training for most of the morning. "Get those fucking weapons clean, then you can get clean and grab some chow. Fucking tell D-Squad their ass is on deck for this afternoon."

Sure, they looked exhausted, but they also looked wired and happy, excited for successfully, if not sloppily, executing the training plan.

Outside of Las Vegas

Erin's breathing was slow, deliberate, and steady, her big rifle pulled into her shoulder, her body rigid, but relaxed lying behind the rifle's optic, her finger carefully indexed along the side of the weapon, safety on. Either through good luck or bad, the convoy had stopped on the highway only a couple hundred yards past their exit and past the truck stop.

Jason was near her, eyeing the scene through his spotting scope. Normally, they would be concerned with rear security, especially with random Zeds shambling up the highway, but they were on the roof of the truck stop, using the business facade as a sniper blind. The Zed stragglers had apparently followed the small convoy of four APCs. This group did not have a radar truck. Erin thought that they were a scouting element; so far, they had seen 23 soldiers, one of whom appeared to be a woman. She also appeared to be in charge.

"What do you want to do, babe?"

Jason took a moment to think before he responded. "We wait and watch. It wouldn't be smart to engage such a large number of them compared to us and the rifle fire would attract even more Zeds. So we wait. If they come up here, then we engage and run away; otherwise, we watch."

"I think they might be scouting routes for the larger force we saw a few days ago."

Jason nodded slightly, not that it was very noticeable; he was still peering through the spotting scope and Erin was still surveying the scene through the powerful optic on her rifle. They continued watching in silence. Jason was fascinated with the dynamics of the people below, trying to decipher what they were doing, what they were saying, even though if they could actually hear them neither he nor Erin would be able to understand what they were saying. This wasn't a bad action movie where the bad guys spoke English with an accent.

This felt more serious to Jason than dealing with the Zeds did. He wasn't sure if that was because he was used to the Zeds now or understood how to work around them unless they swarmed or if it really was more dangerous so it was more serious. It didn't matter. Jason shook his head to clear it. Dead was dead regardless of how someone got there. He had to focus and pay attention; the last thing they needed was to be surprised by the PLA.

"One of them is pointing toward us," Erin whispered.

Jason sat perfectly still, trying to will himself to melt into the roof of the truck stop. The man wasn't in view of his spotting scope, but Jason didn't dare move to adjust his view.

"He's looking at us through binoculars—fuck!"

Erin fired her rifle; Jason moved his scope in time to see the man crumpled to the ground, his head intact.

"You hit him center mass, not in the head."

"I meant to," Erin yelled as she shifted and fired again.

The scene below erupted into pandemonium. The other PLA apparently weren't completely sure where the sniper shot had come from, the sound of the rifle's report echoing across the desert. By the third shot, they knew and were trying to return fire. Erin fired rapidly, emptying the rifle's magazine quickly. Every single shot, every single man she killed was with a massive .50-caliber round to the chest instead of the head. Jason shimmed down the ladder at the back of the store—thankfully, the side opposite of the gun battle—and dropped onto the roof of the MRAP. After climbing through the gunner's hatch in the roof, Jason retrieved two loaded magazines for Erin's file and a pouch of loose ammo. Moments later, he was back on the roof and Erin had a fresh magazine in her big rifle. The gun battle had paused while the PLA tried to figure out if they had the right spot for the sniper or if they had killed him. Luckily for Erin, they hadn't hit her; unlucky for them, she was pissed and now once again had a loaded rifle. Silent with steady breathing, Erin made minor adjustments to her position and waited. A head popped out from behind one of the APCs, and it evaporated into a red mist moments later, eviscerated by the big round ripping through it. Blood sprayed in an arc out of the ruined neck of the nearly headless man as he fell to the highway.

"Holy shit, they're getting up!" Jason didn't realize that had been Erin's plan.

Erin only grunted, scanning and waiting for the next soldier to appear in her view. She watched as one of the reanimated soldiers dragged a living comrade out from behind an APC. It bit and ripped a large piece of flesh out of the man's neck and shoulder, thick red blood gushing and flowing, staining the pavement. The man appeared to be screaming, but Erin let him live, let him suffer through the brutal Zed attack, his fate now sealed for the arrogance of invading her country.

My country.

The words echoed and repeated in Erin's mind as she shifted and shot another soldier. The other handful of soldiers she had killed were up and shambling through the carnage, a battle erupting down below, a new battle. There were two remaining PLA soldiers, either Chinese or Korean, Erin didn't know or care, but they were no longer trying to hide and fight the unknown sniper: they were trying to kill their reanimated comrades before they were killed too. Erin made quick work of them as they came out of their places of cover. Both were killed with shots to the mid-section.

Erin got up, pulling her rifle up with her. "We need to get the fuck out of here, leave those fuckers for their friends to find."

"We could kill them and raid their vehicles for anything useful."

Erin paused. She hadn't thought of that, but Jason had better mind for such things.

Jason continued. "We only have a little bit of time before all that rifle fire brings all the Zeds to the yard for your milkshake anyways."

Erin looked at him. "Dude, what?"

Jason chuckled. "Never mind. Point being, we need to haul ass, but I think we should look inside those trucks first. Maybe we don't have to kill the new PLA Zeds; we can get them to move for a bit, use the MRAP as bate, honk the horn, that sort of thing."

Erin gave Jason a sly grin. "I like it. Let's go."

They climbed down the ladder. Erin passed the big Barrett rifle down to Jason after he was standing on the roof of the MRAP. He climbed into the gunner's hatch and set it inside, starting the truck's heavy diesel motor while Erin climbed inside and took her seat up front with him. A few moments later, they drove out of the parking lot and toward the highway. More Zeds were shambling toward them in the distance, so they didn't have much time.

Soon, they were on the highway and near the APCs. The new Zeds were already shambling toward the movement and sound of the approaching MRAP, but they really became interested after Jason honked the horn. Jason pulled alongside the first APC; he climbed onto the roof through the gunner's hatch and jumped across the short gap to the roof of the APC, only taking his sidearm for the excursion. Erin climbed into the driver's seat and drove forward and away from the APC at a walking pace. The trail of Zeds followed, unaware of Jason's movement.

Jason peered through the open roof hatch of the APC, using the light on his pistol to clear the interior; he didn't want to be surprised by anyone remaining. Satisfied he was alone, Jason climbed inside the dimly lit interior. The weapons and ammo weren't a lot of use to them, except that it would be smart to take some. There was one AK-47-looking rifle with a folding stock. Jason wasn't sure what model of rifle it really was and he didn't care. The boxes of ammunition were easy to identify, too. He opened the rear hatch, checked for any Zeds nearby, and placed the rifle and a few large boxes of ammo on the pavement. It wasn't easy to figure out what stuff was because Jason didn't know how to read whatever language was printed on everything. He assumed it was Korean but he didn't know.

After climbing out of the APC, Jason slung the new rifle and picked up the metal boxes of ammo, carrying the heavy load to a spot on the edge of the roadway away from the APCs. Jason, winded from the effort, quick-walked to the next APC, the rear hatch was already open, and he could see it was safe to enter. Inside, Jason found a handful of green canvas bags. He opened the first one, his heart quickened and he let out a low whistle when he realized what he held. The bag had four curved green devices, about 50 feet of coated wiring, and a device with a switch that had a safety. Jason had found the PLA version of a Claymore mine. Each of the five bags had the same kit. Excited and trying to imagine what he could do with them, Jason's thoughts were brought back to the present by the sound of rapid rifle fire. Two Zeds fell to the pavement just outside of the open APC rear hatch. He realized that fun time was over. Jason shouldered the satchels, drew his pistol, and came out of the vehicle. Erin was already loading the new rifle and ammo into their truck. Jason joined her, smiling, giddy like a kid on their birthday. The possibilities to use 20 anti-personnel mines, or whatever the PLA called them, seemed endless. As they drove away from the carnage they had caused, Jason told her what he had and a broad smile crept across her face.

"So do we start calling ourselves The Wolverines yet?" Jason asked with a smirk.

"What? No, fuck that movie! That was war porn that teenagers jerk off to. This is the real fucking deal. Besides, they all died; you and I are going to live forever."

Over Montana

Andrew banked, pointed out of the side window, and yelled over the engine and wind noise, "I'm going to put down there on the highway. We can check those cars for gas and check that tanker. Unleaded of any kind, unless we can find a sports car and get some high octane stuff, but I've got a limited amount octane booster too."

Chivo flashed a thumbs up and press-checked his rifle again. The act was nearly mindless a reflexive muscle memory action to get ready for insertion. That's what it felt like, every time they landed it was a potentially hot LZ; not a truly hot landing zone, but it could be. At least for the most part, they were only worried about the Zeds and not taking small arms fire, but if they had another group like the bikers in Texas, it could go sideways very quickly. With only the two of them, they would do better to avoid conflict that could be that intense, as they probably wouldn't fare well.

After a couple of deep breaths, Chivo focused on their task at hand. Andrew would handle the fueling, and he would provide security. It was a good arrangement that made perfect sense. Chivo scanned the landscape; it was stunningly beautiful, as Montana tended to be, and patches of snow still glistened in the sun, although it had begun to melt a little. Andrew banked and pulled power, the nose of the Husky pitching downward slightly, and Chivo felt the descent for landing in his seat more than anywhere. Another glance out the window toward the east and something caught his eye. They were still about 5,000 feet above the ground and descending, but Chivo saw what looked like an MRAP parked next to a ranch-style home. That was where they needed to go and it was only a few miles away. Chivo scanned the area again, memorizing details so he could find it easily after they took off again, and returned his focus to where they were going to land.

Andrew was going to land on the highway. A tanker truck was shining in the sunlight, a smattering of cars and pickup trucks near it. They had no idea what was actually in the tanker. It could have been fertilizer or it could be diesel and anything in between, but even if the tanker was a bust for a fuel stop, they should be able to scavenge gas from the other vehicles.

Snow flew into the air as they touched down, blown by the powerful propeller and kicked up by the tundra tires bouncing to terra firma, but soon, Andrew had spun the plane for a quick exit and turned the engine off. The area was quiet and still, nothing moved. Chivo pulled his shemagh over his face against the cold wind and climbed out of the cabin. He took a few quick steps away from the aircraft and took position behind a Subaru after glancing inside to check for Zeds or hostiles. After a few minutes, both he and Andrew were confident that they were alone for the moment and they got to work. Andrew retrieved a fuel can out of the plane and poured the contents into the wing tank. With a length of garden hose, Andrew went in search for more gas. The tanker had the wrong placards to be gasoline, and Andrew wasn't sure what the tanker held, but it didn't matter because it wasn't gas. Beginning with the car next to the tanker, Andrew unscrewed the gas cap and pushed the garden hose down the filler neck. Chivo walked over.

"Hang on; let me show you something Bexar showed me."

Chivo pulled on the back passenger's door handle and was surprised to find the car unlocked. A few seconds later, the bottom of the backseat was out of the car and thrown on the roof of the car. Shortly after that, the fuel pump was unscrewed, leaving easy access to the gas in the tank. There wasn't any dope in the fuel tank, which would have been funny, but there was about a half of a tank of gas. It took four vehicles to siphon gas from, but soon the Husky was full, Andrew's fuel can was full, and they were ready to fly off.

Before climbing into the aircraft, Chivo pointed the direction he had seen the MRAP. "I think that is the one. It appeared to be a launch facility and there was an MRAP parked out front. Even if it isn't the one we're looking for, someone is or was there and it's worth checking out."

Andrew agreed and a few moments later, they were airborne and climbing out toward their destination. They climbed to about 1,500 feet AGL and flew by the MRAP offset by about a mile so they could check it out and be out of range of small arms fire. Besides the MRAP, there was a big green heavy-duty truck-tractor that looked like something out of a Mad Max movie, but Chivo recognized it as a truck used in the recovery of armored trucks in theater. It was basically a semi-truck with armor and more axles, and it sat next to two large silver tanker trailers. Those were off to the side of the facility, but still inside the fence. The MRAP sat on the paved apron next to the above-ground, house-looking building.

The road that passed in front of the facility was small, but it appeared well built. Andrew banked and descended to land on the roadway after making a few orbits of the facility so Chivo could evaluate their target.

Once on the ground, Andrew turned the aircraft for a quick departure and put chocks on the tires. There wasn't anywhere to tie down, so they hoped that it wouldn't be too windy until they had a chance to better secure the aircraft later.

"What are we going to do? Go over the fence? Go through the fence? I have some small bolt cutters in the plane."

Chivo smiled and shook his head. "No, we have to assume that all the security systems are still functional. There's nothing that will hurt us above ground, but there are many alarms and sensors, so they would know we were there. I think we're better off knocking on the front door."

"What are we going to say? 'Hi, we're here to kill secret agent man and secure the nuclear weapons' or are you going to try to sell them a magazine subscription?"

With a smile, Chivo responded, "No, but you are."

Andrew looked surprised, but listened as Chivo laid out his plan. It was simple but might work.

⚬

Dorsey looked up at the monitor mounted on the wall near the desk. The desk was covered with one of the rack mount electronic components, which was in a state of disassembly. He was in the middle of the process of changing the system to allow a rogue launch. Not that it would; without fully understanding the process or the safeties against an unauthorized launch that were involved, the former fighter pilot had a vague idea as to what some of the systems did, but not all of them.

Clint walked near Steve Dorsey and stared at the man on the screen. The man was talking, but they couldn't hear anything inside yet. Steve pressed a button on the console and a speaker crackled to life.

"I'm hungry, lost, and need help. Any help you can give me, anything, and I'll be on my way. I'm trying to get to Wyoming."

The man had the look of someone who used to weigh more and had lost the weight quickly; his cheeks were gaunt and his eyes tired. The man kept pressing the call button and persistently asked for help.

Clint's expression didn't change, but he sighed when the man began shaking the gate and pleaded for help, nearly in tears. "Go topside, give him a case of MREs out of my MRAP, and make him leave. If he doesn't leave, kill him. If you can't kill him, I'll come kill him."

There was no emotion in Clint's voice, only minor annoyance, which gave Dorsey chills.

Steve nodded, slung his leather shoulder holster, and walked toward the staircase that led into the surface. He hadn't realized that Clint kept supplies in the MRAP; he hadn't had the opportunity to go in that truck and dig around. Inside the topside facility, Dorsey flipped through the different camera views. He hadn't dared while next to Clint just in case it was a responding force. It wouldn't have mattered, the only camera feed that still worked was the one by the gate, which was strange because the other cameras had been working just the previous afternoon.

After slinging his M4, which he kept topside, Dorsey cracked open the door and walked outside. The man by the gate waved with both arms over his head, excited to have someone to help when Dorsey heard a voice behind him. "OK, Colonel, do not turn around, do not move. I'm here on orders from President Lampton. What did Clint send you up here to do?"

"That's lieutenant colonel, and I'm supposed to give that man a case of MREs or kill him."

"I would suggest you give him the MREs then."

Dorsey didn't turn around; he stepped off the landing and walked toward the MRAP. It was full of cases of MREs, green ammo cans, a couple of wooden crates, and bottled water. Dorsey retrieved the MREs and walked toward the gate. Once at the gate and in view of the camera, the gate opened, activated by Clint on the inside.

"Here you go, buddy. This is all we have that we can give. I hope it helps you get to Wyoming."

Andrew smiled nervously at Dorsey. "Oh, it's more of a help than you can imagine!"

With the case of MREs in his arms, Andrew shook Dorsey's hand, turned, and walked toward his airplane. Dorsey smiled; the yellow Husky stood out of the beautiful landscape like a neon sign and was the most gorgeous thing Dorsey had seen since he landed his fighter back at base and nearly out of fuel late in the afternoon of December 26th. The gate closed behind him as Dorsey walked back toward the main building and the man standing in the shadows. While making the short walk back, Dorsey evaluated the man, whose name he didn't know yet. He was short and not overly muscular, but contrary to the movies, most of the Tier-1 operators he had ever met were under six foot and compact. They were guys who didn't know how to quit and what they might have lacked in size or strength they made up with effort and aptitude.

The man flashed a quick smile at Dorsey and shook his hand as he opened the door to the interior. Chivo held up a finger, gently took the door from Dorsey, and closed it softly.

"How many are there?" Chivo asked with a barely audible whisper.

"Just the guy called Clint and myself."

"Good, how is he armed?"

"Only a sidearm when I left."

"OK. This man is probably the most dangerous man you've ever met. Take me to where he is."

Chivo quickly outlined a plan that was so stupidly simple that Dorsey was sure it would fail.

Pecos, Texas

After the building lowered and the entrance had closed and they were fully enclosed underground, Bexar followed the directions and parked near the end of the rows of military vehicles. Some were quite impressive, armored and hulking in the shadows of the dimly lit parking area. At the end, Bexar found what was a cross between a golf cart and a John Deere Gator plugged into a charging station. It was similar to the motorized carts used inside the terminal of a large airport. He helped Jessie out of the FJ, her ankle still horribly swollen and throbbing in pain. After helping her to the seat on the motorized cart, Bexar laughed as he consulted a map of the cavernous facility, with a big red "YOU ARE HERE" dot, like they were at some large shopping mall.

"Where to first, babe?"

Bexar took one last glance at the map before driving into the dim rows full of boxes, crates, and gear. "Medical supplies first. We've got to get something done about your ankle before we do anything else."

The electric motor whined, the tires squeaking on the polished concrete floor. Dust covered a lot of the shelves and boxes, making it obvious that this was a seldom if ever used facility, or even visited often. He knew that Chivo and his crew used this facility to resupply on their way to Big Bend. Some of their trash and boxes were piled up near where the carts were stored and charged, but that might of been the very first time the facility had been used in that manner.

"This place is nuts. I wonder how many of these there are?"

"Malachi used to say these were all over the United States. He called them inland cache or supply or something like that. I never believed him, but it looks like he was right."

"I mean, this is in fucking nowhere West Texas. Seems odd."

"Well, it is away from the border, it is on a major interstate, and there is probably a rail line very near. If another country invaded from the south, this would be a great spot to support the front line."

"Maybe we should just live here?"

Bexar smiled. "That thought had crossed my mind, but for all the supplies, it would suck living here. We couldn't live completely underground forever. We would want to be on the surface often, and I never understood how early settlers decided that this part of Texas was where they would live. If it wasn't for oilfield work, I don't think anyone lives near Pecos on purpose."

"I bet some people did. Some probably love this area more than anywhere else."

Bexar smiled and held Jessie's hand. They had been driving for some time before they turned to travel down a long row of shelves. It was as if someone had taken two full-sized Costco stores, put them underground, and filled them with all the weapons and supplies of war.

"If you see an employee, could you flag them down and ask where the family-sized vat of dish soap is kept?"

Jessie stared at Bexar for a moment and began laughing; his comment was so unexpected it took a few moments for her brain to catch up.

"Screw dish soap. I think we should take this time to finish our baby registry; this seems like our kind of store."

Bexar laughed for a moment. "Maybe there are humanitarian supplies here. If there are, then maybe there are diapers and formula and such."

"There is the baby stuff in the FJ that I picked up before getting to Groom Lake."

"Yeah, that's a good start, but we're going to need..." Bexar was trying to figure out the number of diapers a month they would need. His mind spun with numbers and could only think of four diapers a day for three years, which didn't seem right, and it seemed low.

"So if this baby uses four diapers a day—"

Jessie cut him off. "Don't even start; the number is too overwhelming. We will probably need to do cloth diapers, but then we'll need to wash them. However, we will still want some disposable diapers too; I know we'll end up needing and using them. Formula is the big one. I'm planning on breastfeeding as much as I can, but I want to be ready in case we need to supplement, especially since we're not going to be able to pump and freeze the milk this time. Christ, this is why there used to be wet nurses."

They reached the shelf location the map indicated for medical supplies and found massive stacks of crates, boxes, and other bags and containers. Some of the boxes were labeled well, some not so much, only with numbers and letters instead of an actual name of some sort. After 10 minutes of searching, Bexar found readymade medical kits, what he would refer to as "bail-out kits" if he was in charge of marketing. Regardless as to what they were called, the large case held four duffels with various supplies for treating problems ranging from traumatic injury like gunshot wounds to sunburn and seemingly everything in between. The case had a manual with instructions, a guide of sorts showing what was in each bag and what you needed for most typical injuries and how to treat them. It seemed like the case was designed to be dropped or given to civilians or untrained persons and Bexar was impressed. Two of the cases came off the shelf and onto the back of the cart to take back to the FJ; a third case was opened on the floor and left there when they were done. Before they drove off in the cart, though, Bexar wrapped Jessie's ankle and activated an instant ice pack, which was wrapped onto her ankle as well. The rest of the instant ice packs in the open kit were taken out and placed on the cart along with an ankle splint, an ankle brace, more ACE bandage, and the entire bag of medications. That bag was in a duffle bag about the size of a loaf of bread and it contained a bit of everything including antibiotics and morphine. Luckily, it had Tylenol too, since that was all that Jessie should take being pregnant as far as they knew.

"How are you doing, baby? Do you want to ride in the cart while I go shopping to re-up our gear and ammo or do you want to take a break at the front?"

"I'd rather ride with you," Jessie said, smiling.

After dropping the medical gear by the FJ and checking the facility map again, they held hands as they drove through the seemingly endless rows of gear, stopping when they reached a row and shelf location. Jessie sat and watched, her sprained ankle resting on the dash, elevated slightly, while Bexar pulled crates and boxes, opening them and inspecting the contents. It seemed like a slow process, but neither of them knew for sure. There were no clocks that they could see; they had no watches and no other way to tell time. For all they knew, they could have been underground for an hour or a week; they had no idea. That thought gave Jessie an idea though.

"We should see if we can find a box with watches in it; the same for GPS devices, batteries, and all the other electronic gear we could want. All of this stuff should still work, shouldn't it?"

"Yeah, it should have been protected underground like this, but I would be surprised if it didn't though."

Nevada

It wasn't that it was a bad drive for the drive per se—this was turning into a bad drive due to everything else besides the Zeds. The interstate was basically clear, cars pushed to the side of the road, overturned by herds of Zeds; even the big semi-trucks were pushed to the side. That made the driving easier, having to dodge bodies and random debris, but that made life harder when it came to finding fuel to scavenge for the big, thirsty MRAP. So far, they had figured that they had about a 300-mile range, which Erin assumed was great for war, but sucked for cross-country interstate driving.

Mesquite, Nevada was a ghost town. It looked like it had been nearly one before the change, but neither of them had been there before, much less heard of the town before. If there were any survivors left in the town, they didn't see them or any sign of them. It appeared that most of the Zeds were gone too. It was eerie and unsettling when they stopped, like an old episode of the Twilight Zone. They were able to top off their fuel, though, so that made stopping worth the effort.

Soon they had entered the southern reaches of St. George, Utah. Bexar had told her and Jason about Guillermo and Angel; they sounded like good people, not that Erin cared about them as people. No, if Bexar thought they were good people, then they might give them a place to rest, fuel, and eat for a night on the way through. The afternoon was getting late and that was the best option they had, besides the typical random building they usually chose.

Part of the interstate was scorched; there had been a battle, a fire. A burned-out hull of an old pickup sat in the center median. Erin sat in the passenger seat, leaned up, and looked out of the thick windows trying to remember the details of where to find Guillermo's compound.

"Stop. We need to go up that hill." Erin pointed out the driver's side window. Jason nodded. The center barrier still partially stood and he wasn't willing to chance damaging the truck or getting the cabling wrapped up in the driveline to cross it. He drove northward until reaching an exit. Jason took the exit and drove under the bridge. There they found another smashed and burned pickup truck. Jason looked up at the bridge as he turned and it appeared the truck had driven off the edge. He shook his head, wondering if the person in the truck had survived or if they only lived long enough to become a Zed and shamble away.

Now southbound on the feeder road, they passed hundreds of homes. There was movement between the homes in the long shadows as they stretched across the landscape. Jason turned and drove up the narrow road toward the hilltop and took the last driveway on the right.

The scene that they found wasn't what they had hoped for. The buildings that had been there were burned, and what appeared to be recently dug graves stood in contrast to the destruction. A large forklift was overturned and appeared pock-marked from small arms fire. The fence that appeared to have stood around the property was also damaged and no longer useful.

"Fuck," Erin muttered as she climbed out of the MRAP.

Jason was silent, but agreed with his love's sentiment. He shut off the engine and climbed out as well. After a few moments of exploration and investigation, they had deduced that the PLA had attacked and killed everyone.

"Who do you think dug the graves? The Koreans?"

"I would be surprised if they had, Jason. That doesn't seem like them."

"What do you want to do?"

Erin looked at the horizon where the sun had just dropped below and the sky burned a dark red with the coming twilight. "We should stay here. It's too late for us to safely find and clear another place. We can sleep in the truck and figure things out in the morning."

Jason nodded. "I'm going to get the truck turned around in case we need to leave in a hurry, and then I'm going to set out our new defensive measures."

Erin smiled at Jason and walked off to explore the grounds a little more thoroughly. Jason turned the MRAP around and began setting out the claymores; the clackers would be run into the truck where they would sleep taking turns. If they were attacked during the night, the first response would be to detonate the claymores then to immediately drive through the carnage to escape. Jason wasn't sure if that was the right way to set a defensive position—in fact, he was quite sure it wasn't—but it was the best they could come up with. So far, they had survived through sheer will of luck, and they would continue to hope their luck held.

Once their camp for the night was set, they shared a quiet dinner comprised of MREs before Erin kissed Jason goodnight. He had the first watch and she needed to get some sleep before it was her turn.

"Baby, we should raid an outdoors store and pick up some hammocks to hang up back here. That would be much mo' better."

"Like a Bass Pro Shop or something?"

"Or an REI. I have no idea. It's just a thought."

"OK, sweetie, good night. I'll wake you up in four hours."

Jason climbed through the roof hatch to sit on the roof for a while, alternating between watching for any threats and star gazing. The night's cool air could be felt gently blowing into the truck from the open roof hatch. Jason's view of the driveway and the approach glowed in the moonlight, the stars overhead shining brightly.

When the light of these stars began their journey, the dead didn't stand up and walk...when the light of some of these stars began their journey, the human race hadn't evolved yet, much less fell to near extinction.

Jason's mind continued to wander as he laid back to have a better look at the night sky.

Groom Lake

Aymond surveyed the firebase, which is how he thought of the above-ground portion of the facility. The work that his men and the civilians had completed was nothing less than spectacular. Big metal CONEX boxes made two concentric rings, which were actually squares because the boxes were shaped like outsized Lego blocks. The security construction for the walls and fighting positions were nearly complete, not that they would ever be actually completed. There were always changes and improvements to be made, but they were quickly near being in a position of having good defenses for the next attack.

There was no question about it, everyone in Groom Lake knew they would be attacked again. They knew it would involve more troops and heavier firepower, they just didn't know when, so it was a race against the clock. Aymond continued to stroll around the outer perimeter. The Zed problem wasn't much of a problem here for the moment, but just like being in the Stan, he wore his kit and was fully armed just in case. Yelling coming from the other side of the metal wall snapped his attention back into focus.

"Chief! Bandits inbound!"

Aymond ran toward the entry, his eyes and head swiveling, looking for the approaching aircraft. The sky toward the east was growing dark, the sun hanging just over the edge of the mountains toward the west. Squinting, he could faintly see what one of the sentries had seen, two aircraft flying in formation descending with the sun at their backs.

"Get the fucking Stingers up! Everyone else, get below ground!" Aymond yelled as he cleared the entry. The entry was basically a tunnel made out of the containers, with another that slid into place to block entry after Aymond cleared it.

People were running toward the entrance, which was also capped with containers and heavily reinforced with what seemed to be hundreds of filled sandbags. His Marines stood ready, armed. Select civilians that they had trained stood ready with a half-dozen Stinger missiles, ready to engage. Oreo, Andrew's dog, ran up to Aymond and trod alongside, seemingly aware of the serious situation that was unfolding. Aymond scratched Oreo's ears quickly before returning his hand to his rifle.

"Chief, they look like fucking A-10s!" Happy stood behind cover, binoculars to his face.

"Roger! Everyone hold fire until we can confirm!"

The pair of aircraft seemed to hang in the air and didn't appear to be moving at all. Around him, Aymond could hear the electronic tone of a missile lock emitting from some of the Stingers that were aimed and ready to fire. The aircraft immediately broke formation left and right, wings banking over and diving for the safety of the mountains. Some of the tones were extinguished as the people aiming them tried to regain a lock.

As much as the aircraft seemed to hang motionless before, they seemed to be flying impossibly fast as they screamed by. Each taking a side of the firebase, they flew a simulated strafing run at incredible speed, diving even closer to the ground before banking and pulling out of the dive, splitting away from each other and away from the people. The aircraft were indeed A-10s and the markings were USAF.

"SAFE THE STINGERS!" Aymond yelled as the ear-splitting scream of the big twin turbines faded slightly.

Aymond climbed on top of the outer wall and waved both his arms over his head. One of the Thunderbolts orbited out of range while the other flew near once again, wagging its wings as confirmation of signal. The lead aircraft climbed and banked over sharply, ordnance clearly visible hanging under the wings. After banking out, the aircraft leveled, the landing gear lowered, and it landed on the ridiculously long runway. The second Thunderbolt in the flight followed and the pair taxied toward the firebase.

"Happy, Gonzo, you're with me. Someone get below and shake Jones out of his rack to come up here. Hammer and Kirk, you have overwatch. Fucking waste them and make sure they never fly again if things go tits up."

The heavy CONEX gate slid open just wide enough to let the trio out of the protection of the outer wall. The high loud whine of the big turbine engines stopped. The silence seemed louder than before with the absence of noise assaulting everyone's ears. The canopies opened and the built-in ladder extended from the fuselage of both aircraft. Two pilots in dirty flight suits climbed to the tarmac cautiously. Aymond gave them space, worried that crowding the pilots might cause undue anxiety.

Jones climbed out of the underground facility to face the waning daylight, excited and surprised at what he had been told. The Marine Corps didn't have A-10s, so he had never worked on one, but he would do what he could, if needed. After clearing the shipping container gate and stepping out onto the ramp, he saw them. Like angry wasps sitting on the tarmac, the aircrafts looked ready to kill at a moment's notice. Jones knew that if the massive GU-8 gun was out of ammo that there would be nothing he could do, especially in Groom Lake. For all the awesome things this facility had, A-10s was not one he had seen...although he did have a grand time crawling around the "red squadron" of foreign aircraft, especially the SU-27 that they found in the hangar behind theirs. Aymond stood on the tarmac with what appeared to be the pilots. Walking closer, Jones began to hear snippets of their conversation.

"Yes, sir, but everyone just calls me Chief, a nickname I was given when I was a young Marine and first attending jump school."

"Who is running this base? We expected to find someone at Tonopah, but didn't and so we decided to come here, hoping that there was some JP-8 on hand. We've found some survivors, but nothing really organized yet."

"I'm in command of this facility by order of the president."

The taller pilot laughed. "*The* president? Our understanding is that the president was killed in Denver. We saw the wreckage of Air Force One."

"You get around. I haven't been to Colorado since the attack. President Amanda Lampton, formerly the SecAg, is our new commander-in-chief."

Aymond continued the explanation and back story in the curt and quick explanation devoid of emotion that comes from experience in the profession of fighting for your country.

The major, a woman with the nametape of Pearce on her flight suit, spoke first. "We haven't seen any enemy activity yet, and do we have any intel on their strength or movements?"

"No, none. We have no assets in place except for a loose correlation of civilian survivors operating archaic radios made of used car parts. So far, they have reported some instances of what we believe to be reconnaissance elements, but no main forces except for what we fought in San Diego."

Major Pearce looked at Captain Hoose, her eyes burning with a hard intensity. "If we could get re-armed, we could knock the bastards down a few pegs. We've been hopping from airfield to airfield trying to find any."

Jones stood at ease just behind Aymond. The world may have ended but he wasn't going to break the military protocol that he had lived his life by. Aymond saw Jones approach and gave him a slight nod.

"Major, this is Jones, a mechanic we picked up at China Lake. I would like to offer his assistance to anything your aircraft needs. Jones, what are the chances we can re-arm their aircraft here?"

"Can't happen here, Chief. We haven't seen any ordnance we could hang off the wings, and we sure as shit don't have any rounds for that big Gatling on the nose."

Aymond nodded. "Major Pearce, where would we need to go to find what you need?"

CHAPTER13

Morning sun glowed yellow through the light fog and the trees. It was a beautiful Texas spring morning. Amanda wiped her palms on her pant legs. The AC was turned up in the cab of the heavy front-end loader, but that wouldn't help her keep cool right now; she was too nervous. Eric was in the tree line about a half mile up the way toward the highway, his son remaining down below watching a movie on DVD in the Rec Room. It was almost like nothing had happened. If they had been a family, they could be out mowing the lawn on a spring morning with their son watching TV in the living room, except that they weren't married, that wasn't Amanda's son, and she was working in her "yard" waiting for someone to shoot at her again. The last part was the clincher. The dusty impact marks on the up-armored heavy equipment, on the thick glass of the cab, were clearly visible, and the entire situation was more unnerving now than it was when she was originally being shot at.

Eric had found some handheld radios in the cavernous supply room. They still functioned and he knew how to work them. The thick handheld radio was propped up on the dash of the earth-mover for Amanda and she had instructions to maintain radio silence until, unless, she gets shot at. It was an attempt at an ambush and she was the rabbit to flush the dogs. Even if it was a tactical gamble on their part, Amanda was still using the opportunity to move dirt and continue to build up the above-ground defenses. So far, she had concentric dirt mounts, walls of a sort, with staggered breaks to allow vehicles to pass into the inner section built around the main gate and entrance. Now she was working on the section of fence line that was near the main entrance, the small building that rises to allow access to the entry ramp.

Amanda had calmed down some since she began working nearly two hours before, but every thump, every crack of a rock being tossed into the air by the tires made her flinch. She would rather face down 100 Zeds by herself than sit exposed in a metal and glass box. Amanda took another deep breath, wiped her sweaty palms on her pants again, and kept working. Groom Lake had informed her that they had taken big steps to increase the security against another attack, although they didn't really go into detail since everyone assumed at this point that the PLA were monitoring their communications. They had no proof, but according to Eric, COMSEC—communication security—was a big deal and they basically had none, which he explained after Amanda lost her cool trying to get a real status update and being given the runaround by the other radio operator.

She knew Groom Lake was in good hands. Although she hadn't had a chance to speak with Aymond for any real length of time, Amanda was confident he would do the right thing. Another point of stress was Andrew and Chivo. Chivo she knew would complete his mission even if he had to come back as a Zed and chew his way into the missile facility, but they hadn't made contact in a long time so she had no idea what was going on. Clint needed to die almost as much as they needed to stop a rogue nuclear launch. She had a plan, or, more accurately, the idea for a plan once they had made contact and eliminated the threat. She wondered if there would be a history of these events in the future and if there was what scholars would think of her actions during these events.

If there is a future history, if I do have a future legacy, then that means I was successful and so fuck what those people might have to say as long as we all survive to rebuild the nation.

Amanda took a deep breath. Lost in concentration, she had been holding her breath without realizing it. Smiling at herself, she wished there was a bottle of Merlot and a hot bath waiting for her when she was done, but there wasn't. There were no bathtubs in the facility that she had found and she had no bottles of wine, something, Amanda thought, she should remedy when they had a chance.

A hard thump against the windshield startled Amanda, the tell-tale sign of a round having impacted the bullet-resistant glass of the front of the cab right in her line of sight. Amanda stopped moving and raised the heavy steel implement, blocking her view but also blocking anymore rounds. Backing away from the threat, Amanda left the wide steel front loader, not sure what it was really called, up and blocking anymore rounds while she retreated. The plan was laughably simple. Eric was going to track and hunt the shooter, both of them having correctly assumed it would happen again, after using Amanda as bait to find where the shooter was.

She heard the distinct sound of rifle rounds striking the steel bucket, the right side mirror exploding in a shower of shattered glass and ruined metal. Using the remaining mirror, Amanda continued to back away, trying to get to the first set of dirt berms. The front right tire made sounds like someone was hitting a basketball with a bat, the hollow sounds changing when a round pierced the heavy rubber tread and the tire began losing air. More rounds impacted the tire and a few moments later, the tire was flat. Amanda tried to keep moving, dragging the ruined tire as the heavy hub turned and spun inside of the flat tire until she wasn't able to move any further.

More rounds impacted the earth-mover, the steel bucket, and the left side front tire.

"Eric, what the fuck? I can't move, over?"

"Be calm. Standby."

Amanda cursed loudly and waited. She could either wait and hope Eric was successful, or she could try to climb out and make a run for it, which would most likely result in her being shot or killed. She couldn't hear the rifle fire inside the cab, only the sounds of the rounds impacting hard on the armored equipment. Just as quickly as the assault began, it was over, only the sound of the heavy diesel motor rumbling behind the cab remaining. Amanda waited.

After what seemed like hours but was really only a couple of minutes, her handheld radio crackled to life. "Threat neutralized, two tangos killed, one captured, moving toward you now. How copy?"

Amanda keyed the radio with a sigh of relief. "Clear copy, two killed and one captured. The front-end loader is disabled in place, over."

"Roger."

Amanda decided to wait until she could see Eric and his prisoner before she climbed out of her safe-for-now armored steel and glass box. She didn't know if they had any tires or other parts to repair the damage done to this front-end loader. They did have another one, but it would be a waste to leave this one to rot out in the Texas weather.

"Coming into the open."

Amanda looked up and scanned the tree line and saw Eric appear out of the shadows with another man walking in front of him. The man had his hands on top of his head and Eric had his rifle ready to kill him if there were any attempts to escape or fight.

"Roger. I'm climbing out."

Amanda could see Eric nod. She shut off the engine and climbed down to survey the damage. She was two for two now, first being the destroyed and ruined MRAP that she left at Groom Lake and now the front-end loader. She couldn't keep this up or they would soon run out of things that had wheels and actually worked.

St. George

Erin woke with a start. Jason snored softly in the front of the MRAP. He was supposed to be sitting watch but had apparently fallen asleep. At first, Erin was annoyed that he had fallen asleep, but the reality of the situation was that it was exhausting trying to maintain a constant watch with only the two of them. She couldn't be mad at her love and best friend, instead trying to think of better solutions to their situation.

If we hide the truck from enemy forces, the Zeds can't hurt us. We're elevated and secure behind the armor, except for a massive herd of Zeds, and they would roll and push the truck out of their way.

Vague thoughts drifted in and out of Erin's mind as she shook the sleepiness and exhaustion from her head. They could discuss different plans and ideas after they had both woken up and got moving. St. George was of no use to them. The survivors they sought were presumably dead, along with the rest of the town. Erin sat up and made her way to the cab of the MRAP. She glanced out the windshield and froze. They were about to be swarmed by Zeds, a wall of death shambling up the driveway from the road. Terrible rotted faces, eyes missing in some, jaws snapping and gnashing in excitement. She couldn't smell them yet, but the swarm of flies above the approaching disgusting mass of bodies gave warning that they smelled horrible.

"Jason, wake up. We have a problem," Erin said in a quiet whisper. Her hand over his mouth, she shook him gently.

Jason's eyes blinked open. She could see his eyes slowly focus on her. Erin placed a finger to her lips to indicate to Jason to be quiet. He nodded and she removed her hand from his mouth.

Erin pointed out of the windshield. Jason sat up and looked, his eyes widening. They couldn't drive through that many Zeds, even in a big armored truck. Jason just smiled. He climbed behind the steering wheel and flipped on the master switches. Soon, the truck was ready to start. Jason pressed the button for the starter and the heavy diesel motor rattled to life with a loud roar. The Zeds became visibly excited; their jaws moved more quickly, arms were raised, fingers clutched at the air in front of them, trying to find purchase with their prey. Erin press-checked her M4 and sat up in the passenger's seat, ready to fight if they had to. Jason reached up to the dash and grasped a small box with a safe switch. He flipped the safety cover and then depressed the clacker. The clacker wires ran out of the truck through the roof hatch and into the gathering crowd of Zeds.

An intense explosion ripped through the massive herd of death. Bodies fell, some badly maimed, some killed by the steel ball bearings ripping through their skulls, launched by the Chinese-made Claymore mines. Jason had set out only two of them, unsure if they would be effective against the dead. Overall, they were effective in clearing a bit of a path, but many of the Zeds that had been knocked down were clambering back to their feet. Unlike the living, Zeds didn't really notice hundreds of ball bearings ripping through their flesh.

Jason took their closing opportunity and drove forward at a walking pace, trying desperately and failing to miss the Zeds with the tires. They both cringed with the feeling of bones crunching beneath the heavy-duty tires. Jason glanced back and forth from where he was driving to the gauges showing system air pressure and tire pressure. A flat tire would be a big deal at this moment in time. Jason wiped his sweaty palms on his pants, the intensity of his concentration and the nervous fear of the situation causing him to sweat.

What seemed like hours later, but was actually only a few minutes, the MRAP emerged from the main congregation of Zeds near the interstate. Jason turned and drove the wrong way on the access road. He drove around the wrecked and burned-out pickup truck, under the overpass, and drove up the on-ramp to the interstate. They were headed to Texas now. Their first stop was a bust and nearly a disaster, and they both hoped that their second destination was more successful.

Hillsboro, Texas

Ken stood near the group's main cooking fire, a large brick-lined structure, and the fire was stoked under the cooking surface like some sort of oven. He hadn't seen anything quite this involved before. Most of the outdoor oven or built-in grills he had seen in people's backyards were smaller and less elaborate. He was impressed, even more so at how well the brick oven seemed to function. Less fuel was needed to cook their food since the heat was captured and directed to the cooking surface instead of radiating in all directions like a campfire. It had only been a few days, but Ken was being accepted into the group of survivors. He was happy to help where he could; for not knowing him from Adam, the survivors had really taken care of him, besides saving his life.

After his morning walk around the camp to wake up, Ken walked toward his duty station for the next few hours in the radio shack. Others were monitoring the radio he helped build, but he took the main shifts because he was the most familiar with not only the radio, but the Morse code that was required to transmit and receive on it.

Ken walked into the metal shipping container that held the radio equipment. The other person, a teenager, stood and handed his notes over. The yellow pad of paper had a full page of tightly written notes for Ken. The notes were a synopsis of important conversations, information about other survivor groups, and other general information that their group wasn't aware of yet. It was basically a summary of all the radio traffic from the previous night.

After he read the notes, Ken sat at the radio and smiled, ripping off the top page of notes for a fresh sheet of paper. A few moments later, the teenager returned with a cup of coffee and sat down next to Ken, handing the steaming cup to him with a smile. Ken was amazed at how kind everyone seemed to be in the group, but there was an edge to the kindness, an edge that they wouldn't put up with any nonsense and they could easily and readily defend themselves.

The radio popped and crackled. Ken wasn't really sure what was being transmitted yet, and he wasn't ready to start transcribing messages, but quickly the pencil in his hand found the paper. The previous transmission paused for a moment and the rapid short broadcasted notice of an emergency transmission broke the silence. Ken sat up, his pencil ready. Brandon, the teenager next to him, hadn't heard the emergency notice broadcast before and his questions had to be hushed by Ken so he could keep up and transcribe the transmission.

F-O-R-THE-C-I-N-C-G-O-A-T-W-I-N-I-C-B-M-S-A-F-E

The transmission was a request to other stations to pass the message, which repeated two more times.

After the final transmission, the unknown station fell silent. Ken looked at the transcribed message, trying to make heads or tails of it.

For the commander-in-chief, goat win, ICBM safe.

"What does that even mean, Ken?" Brandon's face showed the confusion that Ken felt internally.

"Well, it appears to be a message for the president. ICBM is an intercontinental ballistic missile, you know, a nuclear missile. I don't know what "goat win" means, except that perhaps goat is a name for someone and that he or she won their objective, making the missile safe. Our task today is to now wait and repeat the message every hour or so, attempting to get it passed along to the president, if she doesn't respond."

"Isn't she close, like near Dallas? Why couldn't we just go deliver the message ourselves?"

"It's a damn hard life outside of these walls. My short journey nearly killed me more than a few times. I was shot at by unknown snipers, the Zeds nearly got me a couple of times, and frankly, I'm not too keen on leaving the walls of this compound until I rest up enough to be OK to make that journey. What used to be a couple hour's drive can easily be a multi-day journey now."

Brandon grunted. Ken could tell that he didn't think it would be that difficult, but that was the privilege of youth; a privilege lost with age and experience fraught with tough lessons.

Great Falls, Montana

"So I've been sabotaging the effort from the beginning."

Chivo nodded and smiled. "You did good, Steve. Clint and the others like him in the same program were good, damn good and well trained, so if you were sneaking failure points into the process unnoticed, you have scored a major triumph. He would have killed you once you weren't needed any longer, so besides averting a rogue ICBM launch, the added benefit is that you're still with us."

Steve Dorsey didn't react outwardly to the compliment. He was curious what else Chivo had in mind, because it was now obvious there was a plan he wasn't aware of. Andrew was still topside prepping his aircraft to fly back to Groom Lake. Clint's body lay outside the fence line of the launch facility, killed and verified to not return as a Zed.

"Steve, the president has another request for you."

Dorsey took a breath. The new pitch was to begin and he had to be emotionally ready for what he feared: that the president would want to launch a nuclear attack on the United States hoping to kill off Zeds. He wouldn't be able to comply with that order; he never would be able to help facilitate an attack like that on his own native soil.

"The president wants the ability to launch a counterattack against targets in North Korea and China. It won't do a damn thing about the destruction of our country, nor the massive amount of Zeds we have staring us down, but it might stop or slow the invasion forces and give us a chance to catch our breath...a chance to begin reclaiming our land for the living."

Dorsey sat still, trying to keep his face neutral. The president's plan was what he was secretly hoping for, but he hadn't expected it to be seriously considered and now that it was out in the open, Steve felt silly for not believing that a counterattack would be the plan.

Steve smiled. "I guess I have a lot of work to do."

Chivo nodded. "No, *we* have a lot of work to do."

The discussion broke into a detailed review of Clint's plans, Steve assuring Chivo that all the little mistakes he purposely made in the hacking process were remembered and correctable. Without the framework of Clint's double agent plans, they would not be successful. They would never be able to launch a nuclear counterattack. Chivo wasn't sure how long they had been chatting, but it felt to have been a significant amount of time when Andrew burst back into the room. They were in the kitchen of the above-ground structure of the launch facility, but hadn't heard Andrew come back inside.

"Chivo!" Andrew breathlessly entered and clutched a piece of paper in his hand. "A message from President Lampton. Wheels up in five minutes!"

Pecos, Texas

Laughable, Bexar and Jessie looked like a tactical store had thrown up on them. They found new clothes, including clothes for Jessie after the pregnancy. They packed the FJ with stripped-down MREs, ammo, spare magazines for their rifles, water, and water filters. Currently, Bexar sat at a folding table they had found with his AR-15 taken apart, going through it piece by piece. Beside him, new parts lay ready to be inserted if needed. This was in addition to the handful of "oops" kits of M4 parts that would interchange with his rifle that Bexar put together years ago. Jessie lay on a cot next to the table, her foot and swollen ankle elevated, a chemical ice pack wrapped around her ankle and held in place by vet tape.

Bexar held up a lower from a select-fire M4 and contemplated his decision. "I'm going to have to test fire this to make sure it all works and nothing breaks."

"OK, but I'm sure it's going to be fine. When you built your rifle the first time, it was with top-end parts."

"Top end-ish, really. No matter what I did with my AR though, I've never really messed with real M4s before and we can't have any issues. Our lives actually depend on it."

"And they didn't when you first built your rifle? You carried it on patrol."

"Well, yes, but that's different. I mean, yeah, my life depended on my rifle working if I had to actually use it and engage in a critical incident, but now it is every fucking day. I have no idea how many rounds I've fired since December, but I know it has been a lot, and every single one was because our lives were in immediate danger."

Jessie shook her head as Bexar continued to mumble to himself. It had been a long time since she heard him so stressed out and worked up. She wasn't sure that if they left this underground oasis in the Texas desert that they would survive, but she was sure that Bexar would consume himself if they stayed. Her Bexar would come apart for the lack of danger.

"We should leave tomorrow morning."

"We're not even sure what time it is, babe."

Jessie laughed gently, her ankle throbbing from the effort. "Then go topside and look. Get your new watch out, set it to the correct time, and come back down here to me. The next morning we have, we should leave."

Bexar finished assembling his AR and stomped off to test fire it. The rifle looked like a gun porn pinup rifle from a magazine—select fire, rail, optic, Magpul furniture, IR laser, weapon light, suppressor—it wasn't all new, but it was all clean and it looked sexy, if Bexar had even cared. His rifle wasn't a toy anymore and it hadn't been for some time; it was his daily tool of war against the dead and the dead's allies.

The large tire was new but with very large holes from what Bexar assumed to have been Chivo's .50-caliber rifle. After pacing off about 15 yards, Bexar shouldered his rifle and squinted through the optic, a glowing red triangle placed just right over his target. After a few dry runs, Bexar took a deep breath, exhaled, and fired a single round. The suppressor was quiet, but not movie quiet. It was practically nothing was like it had been in the movies, but even in the enclosed space, the noise wasn't overbearing. After firing a full magazine by ones and twos, getting a feel for the balance of the rifle and the stroke of the new trigger assembly, Bexar loaded a fresh 30-round mag, slapped the bolt release, and thumbed the selector switch all the way over. The action was smooth, the rifle easy to control, but 10 quick trigger pulls later, the bolt locked back on an empty magazine. Quickly, Bexar turned the rifle in front of his face. His eyes stared through the rifle at his target as the empty magazine fell away and a fresh one slammed into place in the magazine well. Bexar's thumb hit the bolt release and he quickly emptied a third magazine. This continued until the rifle was hot and smoking, a small pile of empty mags laying on the ground and spent brass rolling around the shiny concrete floor. With a faint smile, Bexar climbed back into the electric cart and drove back to where Jessie waited, still laying on the cot and reading the manual for one of the new "toys" they found.

Jessie smiled at her husband, who was noticeably more relaxed. He broke the rifle down on the table, set the magazines in a pile on the end, and began cleaning, inspecting each piece of his rifle for any damage or unusual wear, especially the new parts.

"Once I'm put back together, I'll go topside and use a GPS unit to update with the time from the satellites. With that, I'll set my watch and come back and we'll put a plan in place."

Jessie nodded.

"Also, I was thinking instead of Maypearl, we should find someplace closer to the SSC, maybe in Waxahachie or Ennis or Italy or something. I want to be far enough away to be hidden and not included in an attack, but close enough that we can get to a good facility when we have our baby or if anything happens."

"Mmm-hmmm." Jessie rolled from one side to the other, the pregnancy already far enough along to be uncomfortable lying on her back.

Bexar bent down and kissed her on the forehead before finishing with his rifle, loading the magazines, and heading out to get topside for a few minutes.

Groom Lake, NV

Aymond grunted. "That fucking place is dead and overrun. As I understand it, the remaining survivors were some PJs who came with a secret squirrel that reopened Area 51 here, but they were lost in enemy action in Colorado."

"So what you're saying, Chief, is that we can't do it?"

"Negative, Major, I'm saying it's going to be a full-on goat fuck, but we can do it. It'll be a damn sight better than trying to slug our way all the way to Tucson, that's for sure."

The nearest Air Force Base that had A-10s stationed there was Nellis outside of Las Vegas. It wasn't the good news that Aymond had wanted to hear when he inquired about rearming the deadly aircraft. Pearce and Hoose sat at the conference table, and after more discussion, a plan was beginning to come together. Hoose stood at the whiteboard and drew a rough sketch of the runways at Nellis as well as he could remember them. They were both stationed in Georgia, but had been to Nellis before. The mission planning would have gone much smoother with some overhead imagery or even a tourist map, but they had neither, so adapt and overcome they would. Two hours later, a primary, a backup, and a tertiary plan were agreed upon and they decided that they would leave at first light the next day. There was still much preparation before they could leave. It would be a full day of work, but with the threat of another possible attack by the PLA looming over their heads, they needed to act.

"Happy, would you take our guests to supply and get them kitted up for tomorrow? Test fire everything and get them safe. I'll get Jones to fuel and arm up the MRAPs for a road trip. We're also taking the radar truck."

Everyone rose and pilots Amanda Pearce and Henry Hoose followed Happy to get outfitted for a ground mission. Aymond walked out of the room to find Jones. They had a lot of work to do and a short time to do it. Oreo trotted out of the room following Aymond, his tail wagging.

Montana

"Unless otherwise directed Steve, the president needs this facility online and ready without delay."

"I'm on it, Chivo. The sooner you get your ground-pounding legs in that Husky, the sooner I can get back to work," Steve Dorsey replied with a smile.

Everyone shook hands, and Andrew and Chivo climbed into the yellow Husky aircraft. Dorsey heard Andrew call "clear" out of the window before engaging the starter. The motor whined and coughed to life, idling with the distinct rattle of an air-cooled motor. Dorsey turned and began walking up the drive toward the above-ground portion of the launch complex. He closed the gate behind him to the sound of Andrew running the engine up, going through his pre-flight checks while the engine warmed. When he heard the engine go to full power, Dorsey turned to watch the aircraft nimbly float off the ground after a very short rollout. He sighed; there was a lot of work to be done. At this point, Dorsey was sure that the only reason he had been kept alive was to be a helper due to the amount of work. The other concern is that he didn't know and Chivo didn't know if Clint had some sort of mission kill switch where his handlers would know if he disappeared or died. Like maybe he had to transmit a signal every few days to verify he was still alive and if he didn't, the PLA would send forces to investigate. After walking inside, Dorsey looked around and decided that he would need to be underground for his safety, for the safety of his mission, and only come topside for emergencies. The spark gap radio was too unwieldy to easily carry down below, so that would need to be left topside for the moment and that was pretty much the only thing of value that Dorsey needed remaining above ground. He opened the hatch and began the descent, hoping it wouldn't be his last time on the surface.

Hillsboro, Texas

Ken stepped out of the radio shack and blinked at the sunlight of the late afternoon. He hadn't realized how much time had passed since he got up that morning. He had forgotten to eat lunch, but the radio net was abuzz with reports of Chinese and Korean forces. The number of soldiers and vehicles reported were very low, like scouting elements reconnoitering the countryside before the full-scale attack. Some of the people reporting in didn't believe that a full-scale invasion was coming, that what they were seeing was all there was; others were fortifying their positions against a full-scale attack. President Lampton had been mostly quiet. All the official traffic seems to have been transmitted from Groom Lake, not that Ken had the equipment to really DX a signal and figure out where it was coming from. On the shortwave, Groom Lake was transmitting helpful guides on how to build up defenses and offer basic counterattack theories and practical suggestions. When Ken looked out over the CONEX-built camp of these survivors in his mind, he could see one of seemingly countless hilltop firebases in Vietnam; all they were missing were sandbags. Near the latrine were two 55-gallon drums ablaze with diesel fuel burning everyone's shit from the past few days. That was a smell he hadn't smelled in many decades and it really brought memories back.

The survivors had taken to calling their firebase Fort Apache, which was cute and he understood the reference, but he wondered if they would be better off relocating everyone to the SSC.

SSC

Amanda Lampton checked in on their prisoner. Fortuitous as it was, the designers had a small jail—a brig is what Eric had referred to it as—but it made things easier and safer to house their prisoner. *POW?* Amanda thought. She wasn't sure, and guessed that it would really depend on how the debrief with Chivo went. Amanda slid a tray of food through the slot in the door. The man didn't say anything, which was surprising to Amanda, but she assumed he would soon. After some deliberation, Amanda decided that if an international community existed at all, she'll figure out the definition of her prisoner with them long in the future. She couldn't worry about such trivial matters if she was going to get her country to survive, much less get on its feet again.

Her last task of the evening complete, Amanda went back to the control room where she found Eric and his son. Eric was hard at work over a yellow pad of paper, and Jacob was playing solitaire on one of the computers. Amanda smirked, glad that the government hadn't stooped so far as to take the most basic Windows game off the consoles.

"Amanda, I've cataloged the systems that I can find and know about in this place and although we're living OK with just the three of us—well, three plus one—we really need about 30 people to run the facility efficiently."

"What would that do about our food stores?"

"My best estimate is that with 30 people, we would have approximately two years' worth of food."

"What about with just the three of us?"

"About the same actually. Food is preserved in sealed stabilized containers, but they're very large. Once we open one, there is a limited amount of time we have to eat it before it begins to spoil and rot. There's no way even 10 of us could eat enough to keep on top of that."

"Wow, I hadn't thought of that."

"We can house a few hundred people and the food would probably stretch to a full year, but it's hard to say for sure."

Amanda nodded and thought quietly for a moment before responding. "So...what are you suggesting we do?"

"You wanted to bring in people from Groom Lake, which is fine, except that I think we should open the facility to survivors that are near us geographically. Eric and I bumped into dozens of other groups of survivors and some of them could really use our help. The problem is that none of them had a radio of any kind and have no idea about you or the SSC."

"What about bringing in a community killer like what had happened to Groom Lake where someone who was bit and infected and hid themselves, resulting in the facility nearly being overrun?"

"We take steps to prevent that. Full inspections of everyone who arrives, but then we would also have the manpower to build up the defenses like you want to do and begin agricultural operations in the surrounding fields. If we have two years of food, then we have two years of preparing, two years of working, and two years of action to put us in a safe place for survival once we reach the end of what we have readily available."

Amanda sat silently, suddenly aware that Jacob had stopped playing on the computer and was watching intently.

"OK," Amanda continued, "what do you suggest?"

Eric smiled. "First of all, there are numerous reports of PLA sightings, so I don't think we should broadcast it over the radio. Secondly, Jacob and I passed through a handful of survivor groups before we made it here. If you would let us take one of the trucks in the tunnel, we'll load up with supplies, gifts, aid, and set out to pass out invitations to the groups we found to be approachable."

"How many pounds of beads are you going to take with you, Merriweather Lewis?"

Eric laughed. "No—we don't have beads for the natives. Think more like Teddy Roosevelt with the Smithsonian. Are there gallons of whiskey available for our trip, Madam President?"

Pecos, Texas

Bexar returned to find Jessie lying on her cot snuggled in a green wool blanket, her rifle pointed toward him before he announced himself. She smiled and lowered the rifle.

"I heard someone coming, but couldn't see if it was you or not."

Bexar smiled. "No, that's good, honey. I want you to be safe. I should have announced myself better, but I didn't want to wake you. The sun is setting, nearly seven in the evening. I set an alarm on my watch for five in the morning to give us the most time. Until then, I'm going to finish loading the FJ and get you ready to travel."

Jessie smiled and pulled her blanket off, revealing her smooth skin, the baby bump much more than just a bump. Jessie radiated beauty. "I need you to do something else first." Jessie smiled lovingly at her lover, her husband, and her best friend.

"That's what got you in that condition in the first place."

"I know and I'm starting to feel better about it all. I think we're going to be OK. I think baby Scout is going to be OK too."

"You mean baby Bexar Junior? Can we call him Cub?"

Jessie rolled her eyes. "If you think so, lover."

A few minutes later, Jessie and Bexar laid on the cot together, holding each other and feeling each other's skin, both content and in love. Bexar ran his fingers through Jessie's hair. That it was dirty and greasy didn't matter—neither of them had a shower since leaving Groom Lake—but he didn't care, neither of them really cared; they were in love. Just neither of them knew that when they pledged their love together on their wedding day that their relationship would be required to survive the end of the world, the rise of the dead, and the death of so many friends and their daughter. Jessie sighed.

"I found a map—well, maps really—but we have complete Texas maps now. TOPO maps, too!"

Jessie raised her head off of Bexar's arm. "You found topographical maps of Texas? Holy crap, that's amazing."

Bexar smiled. "It is and we should really nail down our destination."

"That's probably a good idea." Jessie had been worried sick about details like birth. Even though the human race had been giving birth for thousands upon thousands of years, the mortality rate with childbirth was still surprising, even with modern medicine. Now, giving birth with even less support than tribes of humans had in the Stone Age, they didn't even have any tribal help, and the chances of this birth ending in death for the baby or Jessie or both were very real and very scary.

"The SSC is under Lake Bardwell." Bexar reached under the cot and pulled out a handful of large plasticized sheets of paper, the maps, flipped to the correct page, and pointed to a lake on the map. The contour lines on the map weren't very close together and there wasn't a bunch of elevation changes in this part of Texas.

"So I was thinking over here, on this hill. Then we're secluded, we have space, especially if they get attacked, but we are close enough to get there fairly quickly if we needed to."

"Baby, if that's what you think, then we should do it."

"Really? After everything that has gone wrong?"

"Yeah. I mean, how much of all of this is actually your fault? None. The fact that we're both alive is amazing and a testament to you."

"No, it's a testament to us both, together—love conquers all."

SSC

Amanda sat at the console, the radio humming in between messages, buzzing and crackling from the electrical spark. On a yellow pad of paper on the table, she had a message written out and a letter key below each word to show the transmission sequence so she would make fewer mistakes with the Morse code. After she took a deep breath, Amanda took the next break in traffic and transmitted the priority message identifier. Then after a moment, she transmitted the identifier again. After waiting to verify a clear channel, Amanda began the transmission with the number identifier to state that the traffic was from the president and for the people at Groom Lake. It all sounded complicated, but the reality was that the number identifiers greatly simplified how everyone acted on the radio. Bill had come up with it, but he said it was a variation of the codes that Western Union telegraph operators used to use.

A few moments later, Amanda was done and someone at Groom Lake, presumably, responded with the correct identifying code to indicate that they received the transmission and would reply with an answer quickly. The radio quietly hummed, absent of the sizzling and popping sparks as other stations waited for the priority traffic to release the channel.

Groom Lake

After a hard knock and before a reply, the door opened abruptly, and Bill stepped into the conference room.

"Sorry to bother you, Chief. Priority traffic from the president."

Aymond nodded and took the sheet of paper from Bill, read it twice, and handed it back. "Tell her we will leave at first light."

Bill turned and left to transmit the reply. Aymond leaned back in his chair, closed his eyes, and thought through the problem. They needed Jones for the new A-10 opportunity, but he also needed his men, and there simply weren't enough of them. They had a raid to Nellis in planning, hence this meeting with the pilots and with some of his men.

Aymond sat up and opened his eyes. "Gonzo, put together a squad with mostly civilians who are willing and ready to travel to the SSC. The president needs help prepping that facility to receive survivors."

"Roger that. How many Marines can I take?"

"Two, including yourself."

"Vehicles?"

"One M-ATV and scare up a couple of the civilian's vehicles. For the rest, you're in charge of planning and execution. Wheels up at first light."

"Aye, Chief," Gonzo said before turning and walking out of the door.

After the door closed, Aymond continued. "Major Pearce, your radios work between the aircraft?"

"That is correct."

"Jones, get with Bill and setup a test with our truck and some handhelds from supply."

Aymond made more notes and for all the details they needed to run down before they could leave for Nellis. Experience had taught him that all the planning in the world won't mean much once they had first contact. Regardless of those issues, they had a logistical nightmare, even with leaving their Warthogs secured in a hangar here at Groom Lake. They needed to move munitions and the specialized equipment used to load the ordnance on and in the aircraft. Luckily, some of the equipment that they needed to bring back could be towed on its own, although it would have been best to flatbed it. If they could get their hands on a Dragon and trailer, then they could make the process much easier. The semi-trucks that his men had found near buildings to the south wouldn't turn on or start. Jones said that the engines were all electronically controlled and not hardened against an EMP. So they needed military hardware that still worked or old trucks that would work regardless.

Aymond was a meat-eater. These sorts of logistical supply runs weren't his specialty, but this had to happen and it had to be successful with no losses. He couldn't afford to lose any more men, especially since the president needed them to fight the Koreans, the Chinese, and the dead.

CHAPTER 14

April 16, Year 1
Hillsboro, Texas

Ken was animated, excited, and was feeling out how the others felt. So far, most of them were unimpressed; they wanted to stay at their compound and understandably so. The group had worked hard and fought hard to build what they have, to establish their new way of life, and it was comfortable...as comfortable as it could be considering the state of the world at the moment.

"So what's this I hear about you trying to siphon our survivors off and spirit them away to another camp?"

Sam walked up to the central fire where Ken was standing, the president's message written on a piece of paper in his hand. The smile faded slowly from Ken's face when he saw her expression; she was serious.

"No, well, I'm sorry. I didn't realize that would be a problem. The President of the United States has control of a facility near Waxahachie and is opening it up for other survivors."

"Isn't that nice of her. Where was she three months ago? How about December 27th when she could have saved thousands of others?"

The sentiment took Ken back a little; he hadn't thought of the world in that fashion in some time. "I think she was the Secretary of Agriculture. A lot of people have to die before she would get a turn in the big chair. If all those other people were dead and they had hundreds or thousands of people working specifically to keep them alive, I think that things may have been more FUBAR than anyone had expected. She may not have even been named and sworn in as the president for weeks or months after the attack."

"But you don't know for sure."

"No, I don't, but I'm willing to give her a chance."

"Well, I'm not. If you want to leave, you are welcome to. If you want to stay, you are welcome to. But I will not tolerate sedition in my camp, so check your fucking attitude there, guy."

Ken was further taken aback. If Sam considered something as simple as a discussion treasonous, he knew that he was no longer safe.

"Thank you. You saved my life and I'm eternally grateful. If I did decide to leave, would I be allowed to take my truck and my gear?"

"Yes, of course. We're not monsters."

Ken smiled. "No, you're not, and you're kind people who are trying their best to survive." *Just like everyone else* was the rest of the sentence that went unspoken. Ken had serious concerns for his safety; something was wrong and he needed to leave immediately. He walked from the fire quietly back to his bunk. The stuff around his bunk was sparse, and most of his belongings remained in his truck, the few things he had left. Once packed, the ALICE pack of his clothes and basics went in the cab of the truck. Five minutes later, Ken was in the truck and driving out of the gate into the wilds.

Ken turned north and pointed toward Waxahachie. The president's message didn't give a good hard location for the facility, so he would get close and get safe then setup his own radio. He shook his head, mad at himself. He let his guard down with people he didn't know and it nearly got him into a bind. Luckily, he was able to leave and leave with all of his gear, and his spark gap radio setup sat in a case in the bed of the truck with some of the other supplies. So once he's close and safe, assuming he didn't stumble into a secret government base in the middle of Texas by accident, he would setup camp, setup his radio, and wait for information while staying shy of other survivors. Ken had been lucky that Sam and her compound of survivors were gracious and kind, but he couldn't afford to gamble with his safety like that again.

Cuba, New Mexico

The old roadside hotel on Highway 550 appeared to be well past its prime long before any attack, EMP, or the dead began hunting the living. It was, however, some of the more luxurious accommodations that Erin and Jason had the pleasure of sleeping in as of late. Amazingly, perhaps because it was a crappy hotel in a small town, they found a room that hadn't been ransacked or otherwise molested. Even the bed was still made, albeit a bit dusty. If the shower had worked, or better yet if the toilet still worked, then they wouldn't have known what to do with themselves.

It might almost be worth going to the SSC just for the chance to take a good shower, Erin thought while she sat in the bathroom trying to clean herself up and switch out her tampon. The fact that the toilet wouldn't flush when she was done didn't matter; they were leaving in a few moments. Jason had already used the toilet in an adjoining room. Having a place to sit in relative peace, even if it was dark in the room, instead of trying to squat in a parking lot or wherever they may be, was the true luxury of life.

They took a dozen rolls of toilet paper from the hotel since they would need it regardless of where they were. Soon after, they were in the big armored truck as it idled and warmed up as they ate their shared MRE breakfast. They used the chemical heater to warm some water for their instant coffee; quality coffee it was not, but it was still better than nothing.

Jason smiled at Erin. "We have it pretty good, baby."

Erin laughed. "What?"

"No, seriously, look at what we have compared to so many others. Not only do we have a vehicle that works, weapons, and food, we have each other forever."

Erin smiled warmly and took Jason's hand in her own, intertwining their fingers. She didn't have the heart to say the obvious that together forever might not last another minute, another hour, or another day, much less for the rest of a natural life.

It doesn't matter, Erin thought as she smiled at her love. *We have each other right now, which is more than we could ask for.*

Erin extricated her hand and unfolded their map. "We're going to skirt Albuquerque today, so we have to be careful. I don't want to be stuck dodging crazies again."

Jason knew the story, or he thought he knew the story, but the story didn't matter; what mattered is that when the last time she left Albuquerque, she had her mother and she had Jessie with her. As much as Erin appeared to be a rock-hard badass, Erin was really a kind and caring person. She wouldn't admit it out loud, but as much as she missed her mother, she missed Jessie nearly as much. Erin feared that something was going to happen to Jessie that she could prevent if they were together and worse, something might happen to her baby. Erin pulled her legs under her as she sat, folded the map to a more manageable size, and smiled at Jason. A tear snuck down her cheek, which she quickly wiped away before Jason could notice. They drove through the rest of Cuba and toward Texas. If they were lucky, they might make it today, but it would mean driving practically non-stop until dark. There were many difficulties to overcome when trying to drive cross-country—a trip that Erin had been on since just after the attack—but it was practically her way of life now. Erin felt perpetually trapped in a repeating loop of the most fucked-up version of the Oregon Trail anyone had ever envisioned. Hopefully, they wouldn't have to caulk their wagon.

Pecos, Texas

The inland supply cache had some unleaded fuel stored. It was nothing like the diesel fuel stores they found, but that made some sense owing to the fact that all the military vehicles they had seen ran on diesel and not gas. The stench of raw fuel was almost overwhelming. Bexar found a number of fuel cans mounted in racks on a lot of the vehicles. The fuel cans were empty, which was surprising except that it made sense for storage. Fuel goes bad fairly quickly, but stores better in larger containers if it was treated. They hadn't had much issue with bad fuel yet, but they both knew that it was only a matter of time and that time was quickly approaching. They were nearly four months from the EMP...four months since the fuel in all the vehicles and storage tanks available to them had been produced. They had maybe another two months of semi-reliable fuel available; after that, they had the advantage of driving a vehicle with a robust fuel and ignition system. A modern vehicle with precise injectors is usually more sensitive to fuel quality than some older and less fuel precise carbureted engine, just as the old FJ was.

All told, they had six fuel cans secured to the roof rack and a full tank of gas as the morning sunlight cut across the pavement while the ramp opened.

Squinting at the light, they drove up the ramp and toward their destination, or what they thought would be their destination. They wouldn't know for sure until they arrived. They might find what they thought was a good spot from their research with the maps was actually a bad spot. Without Google Earth, it was hard to guess, but they would adapt and overcome as needed, just like they always do.

Besides the fuel, the FJ was loaded out with more gear and supplies than they had since they first bugged out. Besides ammo, MREs, and clothing, they had new tactical gear, night optics, and a couple of new-to-them weapon systems that Bexar just couldn't say no to bring. The vehicle felt heavy to drive, but luckily they wouldn't be trying to keep up with highway speeds or get stuck in stop and go traffic. Jessie's ankle seemed to be improving. Their medical kit was now worthy of being a go bag in the back of an ambulance, including an incredible array of medications, the overwhelming majority of which they were sure that Jessie couldn't take due to being pregnant. They still had Tylenol for her pain, which she had begun referring to as candy for all the help they seemed to give her with the pain. Regardless, they remembered from their first pregnancy that Tylenol was safe to take, so that's what she took.

Their route should take them eight or nine hours, but it was hard to tell. They were avoiding the interstates as much as possible, planning on taking meandering highways to get to their spot sort of near Ennis, Texas, but that meant they were traveling through a bunch of small Texas towns and their experience taught them that those towns can be hit or miss. They had driven through many with no problems, and some they had serious problems with Zeds, but they had seen and avoided being ambushed by survivors too, which is what their discussion on the drive revolved around.

"But that was months ago. We can't assume that anyone like that has actually survived."

"Baby," Bexar began, "if anything, it might be worse. We're heavily loaded with supplies, and we're in a vehicle that runs, so we will attract a lot of attention if anyone sees us."

Jessie's hurt ankle was propped up on the dash, her AR across her lap, ready to be deployed in an instant. The weather was perfect for a road trip. They were well armed, well supplied, and might even have enough gas to get to their destination. They felt like if they were truly lucky, they might even get to their new homestead by sundown, but Bexar wasn't going to hold his breath.

Groom Lake

Three vehicles with an M-ATV in the lead represented the ragtag expedition force on the highway toward Las Vegas and Nellis Air Force Base. It wasn't ideal, but for what resources Aymond had at his disposal, it was the best they had and it would have to work. If it didn't work, then the A-10s secured in a hangar back in Area 51 would be about as worthwhile in battle as a paper airplane. The possibility to rain down fire upon their enemies, living or dead, was an opportunity too good to pass up.

The two civilian vehicles, not really technicals since they weren't upfitted with weapons like what they had fought in Afghanistan, had a handheld VHF radio in each. The M-ATV had the mounted radios still installed and once again working correctly. They were lucky to have found the handheld radios and other miscellaneous parts for their radios in the storage room underground in the facility. Even with the radios turned on, digital encryption between the radios enabled, they maintained radio silence. It wasn't for fear that a survivor might hear the radio transmissions—that possibility was remote and really didn't matter for their safety; Aymond was concerned that the Korean and Chinese forces might intercept their transmissions and be able to triangulate their position. None of the invasion force had been seen since the attack on Groom Lake, but that didn't mean they were gone. After Aymond's experience in California and in Arizona, he knew better, never mind his previous years of experience war-fighting.

Jerry Aymond hadn't visited Nellis in many years, not since a joint training exercise with some of the Pararescue Jumpers. Even then, his understanding of the layout of the base and how to get around was limited to the NCO club and the PJ's facilities on the northern end of the runways, so their plan was to establish themselves in the PJ's facility if they could then run operations down the flight line to gather the needed equipment and munitions. The hand-drawn map and the list of needed items with descriptions were folded and in his left breast pocket. The easiest course of action would have been to bring one of the pilots with them, but that wasn't the smart choice. Aymond had the last known A-10 pilots in the world sitting safely below ground. They were the only two officers that Aymond had seen in a very long time, so by tradition and training, Major Pearce was now the Officer in Charge, the OIC. Aymond should have stayed at the facility to run it "with direction" from the officers, but he decided it was more important for him to be on the supply run, which is why Happy stayed by her side as an "advisor."

So far, the ride was quiet and slow, the convoy averaging about 45 mph, but it was a safe speed to travel, especially if something unexpected happened. He hoped nothing unexpected happened, but the hope was weak, tempered by experience. Aymond expected this little expedition to have one hell of a time successfully completing the mission and returning to Groom Lake safely.

He heard and felt the turret above and behind him turn and stop before the intercom squawked. "Chief! We've got a problem!"

Jerry looked up and through the heavy windshield to see what appeared to be a dark churning cloud over the horizon, just barely visible in the distance.

West Texas

Bexar was sure it would be hard to tell the difference between BFE west Texas before the EMP and zombies and after if someone had before and after photos. The desert and nothingness seemed to stretch forever to the horizon, a never-ending sea of pumper jacks and mesquite bushes. Mostly Bexar and Jessie rode in silence. The new plan was to stop at practically every dollar store and pharmacy they came across to scavenge for baby supplies, but so far, they hadn't seen anything at all, much less a store with diapers and baby formula.

"Who the fuck would live out here on purpose?"

Jessie shook her head at Bexar. That sentiment was spoken a few times over the years and mostly in places like the west Texas desert. That Bexar enjoyed the Big Bend region so much was amazing for how much he did not like the area they were in at the moment. It didn't matter since it wasn't like they were house shopping there; as long as they were able to keep moving, they wouldn't be stuck here. Bexar pretty much assumed that the original settlers to regions he didn't like were there because their wagon had broken and there wasn't any wood to make repair parts from, so they built mud houses and hoped for the best, although Bexar did realize that the idea wasn't generally true.

Near Albuquerque, NM

The MRAP sat idling in the middle of the highway, indifferent to the handful of Zeds approaching from the dark businesses and strip centers from the suburban sprawl. Erin's facial features tightened, complete with pursed lips and frown. Albuquerque was the first step toward her mother being killed. If she hadn't saved Jessie when she was surrounded and about to be overrun by Zeds, they wouldn't have gone to Groom Lake and her mother would be next to her instead of Jason. Erin stole a glance at Jason, who had a concerned expression on his face as he scanned the area around the truck and the approaching Zeds. She felt conflicted. Her heart fluttered every time she looked at her love, but her heart ached for her mother.

Jason took Erin's hand gently into his own and said softly, "You're strong, you're awesome, and we can do this together and be OK."

Erin gave Jason a weak smile. They were only a few years apart in age, yet their lives had been so very different before they met. Now, she couldn't imagine her life without Jason in it. Erin remembered that for them to have met it took Zeds and Groom Lake; there was quite literally no way they would have met otherwise.

And even if we had, Jason was married to his high school sweetheart.

Erin was glad that the cult in Colorado had shot and killed his wife, but in a flash, before even finishing the thought, she felt guilty for even thinking such a thing. Sadness waved through her body at the thought of Jason's profound sadness and grief that he still felt, the guilt he felt for falling in love again and so quickly.

Angry at herself for being selfish about her emotions, Erin released the brake and began driving again. There were only about 90 minutes of sunlight left and they needed every second to find and secure a place for the night. They were still north of the city proper, but they were close enough that they might as well be in the city.

"I love you."

Jason turned his head and smiled. "I love you too."

They drove and looked for a good place for the night, discussing their options, before settling on a pharmacy on a corner of a large intersection. The glass doors and glass entryway were shattered, but the roll-down security gate inside each door appeared to be intact. If that was true, then they would have a fully stocked store to raid for supplies. That chance alone was worth checking it out. Erin drove around to the back of the business where deliveries were made. The strong metal door was locked, but Jason was able to breach the door with his shotgun after a few attempts. After Jason threw a couple of empty beer bottles into the dark interior, they waited. The only sound they heard was the sound of shattering glass from the bottles. Nothing else stirred, nothing moaned, and nothing lurched out of the darkness toward them.

"That's a good sign," Erin unnecessarily said. In her mind, a switch was flipped. No longer introspective, Erin was ready to fight and was focused completely on her task.

Twenty minutes later, they were confident that the large pharmacy was empty and their suspicions were mostly correct. The store had been looted, slightly—probably by an employee due to the lack of obvious entry by anyone else—but most of the store remained intact. It was exciting, like winning the post-apocalyptic lottery. The smell of rotted food wasn't too terrible, either due to the food decomposing far enough that it didn't smell too badly any longer or perhaps due to becoming acclimated to the smell of rot and death. Erin backed the MRAP up against the back door, effectively sealing themselves inside from the dangers outside.

"Shop first, sleep second."

Jason's smile was barely visible in the darkness pierced by their flashlights. "No, baby, shop first, eat second, sleep third."

The pharmacy area inside the main structure was further secured with a roll-down metal curtain and some locked heavy metal doors. Once again, Jason was able to breach the door with his shotgun, giving them access to medications that they might need for themselves or for trade. Painkillers, antibiotics, just about anything they recognized as a useful drug went into their basket and set by the back door for loading into the truck in the morning. Almost two hours later, after they both worked hard to load their newly scavenged goods into their truck, Erin and Jason enjoyed a meal of canned ravioli and Gatorade with some Oreos for dessert. For a brief moment, their life felt nearly normal.

CHAPTER 15

The convoy was officially detoured and stopped for the moment, the vehicles parked in a low spot below the crest of the hill the group was on. The civilians and some of the Marines were holding perimeter security while Aymond and Gonzo lay motionless further up the hill a few hundred yards away. Gonzo had his big rifle and optic, and Aymond had a spotting scope and a notepad.

The scene in front of them was bad, but it could have been worse; they might have run into a company-sized PLA element. After getting off the highway and setting their observation post on the hilltop a mile away from the paved road, Aymond had some tough choices to make. Aymond continued to jot important notes about the number and type of enemy troops, their vehicles, and movements. So far, through the night and into the early dawn, the company had stopped for the night, the personnel sleeping in shifts, as would be expected. There were four radar trucks visible, and the company had larger APCs than the four-wheeled variety they had seen so far.

"Do we have to assume that their ability to off-load container or cargo ships has been restored since they have larger equipment now?"

"Or they have their standard military transports working. My theory is that they used cargo ships at the start to put what they needed in place before the attack. A large overt military movement would have been too obvious and disrupted the surprise attack," Aymond whispered.

They both figured the leading edge of the company's position was approximately a half-mile away, about 900 yards. Swarming around the encampment were Zeds, thousands of them churning and moving, clawing at their prey only to die by the invisible fence that the radar trucks created. By the movements of the personnel, it appeared that they were ramping up to get the company moving again soon. The APCs were idling and warming. Some troops were still eating breakfast, some held security, but it didn't appear that any of them were still sleeping.

"Chief, what if we took out the radar trucks again? Think it would work?"

Aymond turned his head and looked at the sun; it was still low on the horizon and at their backs, which was fortuitous.

"I think we should. Give us a few moments to get the group ready to haul ass if we need to. Best case, the PLA are overrun; worst case, they are now down their protection and have to expend ordnance and time protecting themselves."

Without waiting for an answer, Jerry Aymond slid away from their position, staying low before getting to a point where he could move freely, the hill crest blocking any possible view of his silhouette against the sunrise.

"Look alive, folks. Get the engines warming and be ready to roll. We're going to engage the enemy troops and take out their radar trucks. If it works, we won't have to haul ass. if it doesn't, be ready to bug out."

Aymond made his way back to Gonzo's position, crawling on his belly the last bit and back to his spotting scope. "SITREP."

"As normal as any of this is, Chief, but their movement increased. They're probably going to be wheels up in 30."

"Then we better get started." Aymond glanced at his notes and the sketch of the PLA position with vehicle locations and ranges. "Target, radar truck one, 820 meters..." Aymond continued with the rest of the information that Gonzo needed to take the long shot and then the follow-up shot. The wind was calm, the temperatures moderate and comfortable. All in all, this would be an easy shot on the range, but this was not the range and they had to hit on the first shot or things could go poorly.

"Send it."

The rifle roared and a breath later, Aymond saw the round impact nearly center of the big square transmitter erected on the radar truck.

"Hit."

Gonzo shifted slightly as Aymond read off the information for the follow-up shot on the next truck. The second shot hit high right on the transmitter, but it appeared to be a good hit. The Zeds were already spilling through the large hole in the PLA's invisible fence. The soldiers on the ground scrambling to get into their APCs, while others were trying to engage the Zeds with small arms fire. Their training or discipline wasn't very good because the troops appeared to be panicking, letting loose with full auto bursts from their rifles. It all appeared undisciplined.

The third shot found the third radar truck. As planned, they left the fourth truck intact, hoping that they might be able to recover it at some point, but also hoping that it wouldn't be enough to keep the PLA alive. They would hard kill that truck if they had to though. The scene before them was exactly what they had hoped for. The sound of panicked uncontrolled rifle fire filtered up from the scene below. Men were running around, and APCs were trying to drive and get clear without any real direction or coordination. It was pandemonium and it was a lovely sight to behold for a professional war-fighter. A faint smile spread across Jerry's face; his day had just improved.

After the airport raid in San Diego and now the scene in front of him, Aymond really began to think of the Zeds as not necessarily an ally, but not an enemy to be feared any longer. He could control them, use them as tools to defeat the real enemy, just as long as he respected them and what they could do if fully trusted.

"Gonzo, disable some of those APCs. Box them in. We'll worry about any squirters after giving the Zeds a chance to catch them."

Gonzo smiled—well, as much a smile as the man ever had. He understood what Aymond was doing, and his first shot was already on deck before anything was said. The first shot boomed down range, and then another before Gonzo inserted a fresh magazine with the comically large rifle rounds.

Aymond watched one of the disabled APCs smolder and smoke before flames began licking through the commander's hatch. Another APC ran into it, becoming disabled from the wreck. Men poured out of the back hatch and into the waiting arms of the dead. If the A-10s were armed and airborne, a couple of strafing runs with the enormous rotating gun of death the plane was built around would have ended the PLA's slim chance of surviving the sniper attack.

Dark flies churned above the scene, obscuring the carnage. The mass of flies was so thick, but after about 10 minutes, the sporadic rifle fire had died down. The remaining radar truck appeared to still be functional; a swath of Zeds lay motionless on the ground arcing out from the erect transmitter. They would attempt to retrieve it, but first, they had to wait for their Zed-led war assistants to finish with their task of decimating the invaders and begin to filter off. With the excited frenzy of gnashing rotted teeth below them, Aymond knew it might be a while, maybe even be a day or two. There was no other option; they would have to wait.

Middle of Nowhere West Texas

Neither Jessie nor Bexar knew what the name of the last town was they drove through. It was small, and as one would expect, it was also destroyed. The fact that it was destroyed was odd since it was on a small Texas highway and not near the interstate. So far, most of the towns they had gone through that weren't on or near the interstate appeared to be mostly intact, vacant, some damage, but not devastated like this one. Entire buildings had collapsed, cars wrecked and moved; really, it appeared like a group of survivors had tried to make a last stand in their town and failed spectacularly. Picked-through corpses of various states of decomposition littered the streets, but all of them stayed on the ground, either never reanimated or after being killed for a second time. The carnage convinced them both, quite easily, to keep on driving and hope for shelter somewhere else for the night. They settled on an equipment shed set off from the road on some unknown ranch. It was cold, but they were prepared for the weather with their new gear and the shed was better than nothing.

Jessie was finally able to put a little weight on her foot again, but not much. She couldn't really walk at all, but she could now be helped to the spot and position and be left to use the impromptu restroom without Bexar needing to help and hold her. Bexar had a small book that came out of one of the larger crates in the back of the old FJ. If Jack and Sandra hadn't bought and built up one of the larger old FJ transports, there was no way they could have hauled all of this gear. At this point, Jessie sort of wished the vehicle was smaller, as it felt like they had too much stuff. Bexar read quietly as they both enjoyed the cold sunrise with mugs of hot instant coffee in their hands. This was more like a gypsy caravan than another bug-out maneuver.

"Good book, baby?"

Bexar looked up. "God bless the U.S. Government for writing comprehensive operating instructions for the common man."

"What?"

"It's the manual for a weapons system. Neat stuff."

Jessie was vaguely interested, but figured that Bexar could fill in the details later or she could read the manual. Either way, Jessie wasn't interested in Bexar's excited little kid-like rambling about his new war toy. She went back to scanning the area for any threats while finishing her coffee. They would get on the road in another half hour or so, and even though it was late in the morning, the sun was well overhead and they had hundreds of miles yet to travel. They both didn't want to leave their quiet morning for the dangers of the road.

SSC

Andrew banked the yellow Husky over the lake, which, if he had floats, would have been perfect to set down on, as the water was surprisingly smooth. They would have to settle for the roads near the lake. Above ground was a person, a man, who waved at the plane.

"Expecting some company," Andrew yelled over his shoulder to Chivo.

"No, but I'm not surprised either."

A few minutes later, the plane was on the ground between two plots of farm-land on a small country road. It was straight and a nearly perfect runway for the small bush plane. Chivo was surprised; quite a bit of work had been done above ground since the last time he was here. The man waved from the front gate, but stayed in position and close to cover, his rifle at the ready.

Moments later, the aircraft was secure and they were at the front gate.

"You must be Chivo and Andrew. Welcome back and good job. Is Clint dead?"

"Yes, and you are?"

"Eric. I arrived here recently. Amanda and I caught a sniper and we need your help debriefing him."

Chivo's facial expression didn't change. He liked that Eric was blunt and to the point with his SITREP, but that didn't mean that Chivo trusted him—especially alone with *his* president.

"Dad, Amanda says to bring them below so she can bring them up to speed."

The boy was peeking over the top of one of the berms near the main entrance toward the north. The head disappeared below the berm as the boy ran off.

"I like the improvements. Your idea and work?"

"No, sir, it was all Amanda's idea and work. I've mostly been trying to learn how to run the facility and explore all the nooks and crannies. There are layers of access, like secrets in secrets."

"Like an onion," Andrew piped up.

"Exactly. Also, Amanda said that once you're rested, fed, and fueled that you're free to head out. She said that your dog is still in Nevada?"

"Oreo, and yes. I need to get some food and fuel first, but I don't want to stay too long."

"We can whip you up something hot to eat; I imagine you've been eating like shit while away. Come on below, gentlemen. We need to discuss our other guest."

The trio walked through the park's main gate, which they had to zig-zag between dirt berms to reach. Chivo was happy to see it because it would help slow any attackers. Once inside the perimeter, they walked toward the below-ground entry. Chivo had a feeling he was going to be very busy for the next few days.

Area 51

Happy pointed toward the east. "Put in another tank trap there and there. Build the berms up with what is dug out."

"What about the runway and taxiway?"

With a shrug, Happy answered, "Lots of air traffic nowadays? Well, we still have all the other runways available and the entire lake bed; I'm not too fucking worried about it."

John, one of the survivors, worked construction in what felt like a past life. Even though he was more used to operating smaller equipment, the big Cat front-end loader wasn't too big of a leap to operate. So far, he had been instrumental in helping finish the CONEX wall around the main hangar and back-filling the metal boxes with dirt to keep them in place. Happy surveyed the scene and smiled...as much as a professional war-fighter would smile when his plans for fighting positions were coming to fruition.

The comically large front-end loader lumbered off, trailing black smoke from the exhaust. John reached the position, pushed the leading edge of the loader into the desert floor, and began the construction of another tank trap. It wasn't that the PLA had been seen operating tanks—they hadn't yet—but the traps should slow the APCs, as well as any personnel trying to get over the wall. If Happy's plans worked out the right way and the enemy cooperated, the remaining Marines and civilians would have fortified fighting positions and the PLA would have a hell of a time with their next attack. It wasn't that anyone was sure another attack was coming, it just seemed unlikely until after the invaders were defeated that Groom Lake would be safe from any more attacks. It would be suicidal in a military tactics sense to leave a frontier fort with resistance fighters after conquering a nation, and the modern history of the U.S. Military taught Happy this lesson time and time again.

A team of civilians worked in shifts to fill sandbags, hundreds and hundreds of sandbags, that were used to reinforce the CONEX boxes around the entry below ground. Jones found a maintenance shop that had some stick welders that still functioned, as well as a crate of welding rods. One of the civilians who had some welding experience, although she was not a professional welder, was cut loose welding the CONEX boxes together the best they could. She worked tirelessly and was a very quick study. Even if the PLA never came back, Happy was confident that the Zeds would never stand a chance against them. The radar truck remained inside the perimeter, standing by to protect the below-ground entrance in case of a swarm and a wall breach. The radar truck was far too valuable to let loose outside of "the wire." Wire was one thing Happy wished they had. Big spools of razor wire would have made the firebase, which is how he also thought about the above-ground reinforcements: nearly perfect, but compared to how they were operating in San Diego and in Yuma, this was a paradise of unlimited bounty.

Dust swirled in the air and felt like a sandblaster with each gust of wind. Groom Lake was a shithole in the middle of nowhere, but it was their shithole and they would fight to keep it. Oreo nudged Happy's leg, who absentmindedly scratched behind the dog's ears while surveying the above-ground improvements.

SSC

Chivo briefed President Lampton on Steve Dorsey's situation and how Clint had been killed. She approved and appreciated the dangerous work that Chivo accomplished. Andrew had already eaten and taken off pointed west. He missed Oreo dearly and couldn't wait to be reunited with his best friend.

"Madam President, I should warn you that you probably don't want to be involved with the interrogation. How far it goes, how intense things get, depend solely on this guy's responses and willingness to answer questions. Since you've already tried and he won't chat, I'm starting with some tactics to startle him into the reality of his situation."

"I appreciate that, Chivo. I'll take your word and advice on the matter under advisement. Is there anything I could do to help your process?"

"Yes, ma'am. I need to setup some things in the tunnel. I'm going to need help controlling the lighting while I get him to the tunnel for our sessions, and I need to hit the supply room for a handful of things that will be useful."

"Anything else?"

"I'll need a chair, some buckets, and a water hose."

Amanda looked at Chivo with a raised eyebrow, but his facial expression hadn't changed. He was well-trained and well-experienced in advanced interrogation techniques, and when he and his team had fought their way back to the border and into El Paso, Chivo would have never guessed he would be using that training and experience so often in such a dead world.

People are people regardless of the collapse of society and the dawn of the apocalypse.

The thought repeated in his mind, becoming truer with each playing.

Pecos, Texas

The big MRAP rumbled across the broken and failing concrete of the large ramp. Only the remnants of a large hangar remained from what was once a large Army airbase. Erin had the strange feeling of being somewhere so desolate that she was sure that someone was watching them. Jason drove toward the small concrete structure that was described in the notes Chivo had given them and found the access keypad. After the access code was entered, the whole building rose from the ground, revealing a lit concrete ramp that was surprisingly large, even large enough to fit their big armored truck in. The drive underground was reminiscent of something from the twilight zone. Neither Jason nor Erin had ever suspected such a place existed, but neither of them believed anything about Area 51 before going there either.

The entry to the ramp closed behind them, slowly lowering, the bright sunlight edging away to the shadows as it did. Lights overhead gave a warm glow much like a gymnasium, but it didn't chase away all the shadows around the surprising number of military vehicles and equipment already visible in the entryway.

"I can't even be surprised anymore. Seriously, what else is out there or underground or whatever the fuck. How many more are there of these sorts of things?"

Erin shrugged, wary that they might find something unexpected. Jason drove to the end of the parking area and parked next to an electric cart that reminded Erin of what they used at football games to cart off injured players.

"Think it still works?" Jason asked as he peered into the dark storeroom ahead that seemed to go on with no end. Jason turned their big truck around to be ready for a hasty exit if need be and pushed the button to shut off the ignition. Once the MRAPs diesel motor shut off, the silence of the underground supply cache seemed to echo with the ghost of noise. It was eerie. They climbed down from the cab and slowly inspected the space around them, weapons in hand, ready to fight, but no fight came. Next to the nearest electric cart were debris and some trash that was left behind by whoever had come before them.

"Who do you think has been here?"

Erin shrugged again. "I think Chivo had, but I don't know beyond that. Surely he's not the only person who knows about this place."

"He might be the only person still alive that knows."

Erin nodded and sat down in the passenger's seat of the cart; he had a good point. "Well, handsome, take your lady on a tour of her temporary new home."

CHAPTER 16

"Keep overwatch. I'll take a fire team down the hill to investigate and look for any intel. If we're clear, then we can make a path for our progress and move on."

"Rah, Chief," was Gonzo's not-quite-sarcastic reply. Aymond let it go, since it was only Gonzo being a smart ass and being a sometimes smart ass was basically a fundamental right for an NCO.

Gonzo shook it out and drank some water while snacking on his MRE crackers. Luck had smiled on the Aymond's favorite smartass and Gonzo had a huge blob of jalapeño cheese spread on his cracker. They were nearly inedible without it. It was an odd breakfast in normal society, but normal society didn't exist any longer, and Gonzo was in full-on, deployed-to-a-war zone mode, which is basically what they were. There would be no replacements, no help, and no rotation home next year. No, they either won or they died, and death, no longer being the escape from life, the end, held no appeal or promise of peace.

Twilight broke, the eastern horizon just beginning to glow a little brighter than the deeply dark night sky. These were the stars of their warrior ancestors, long forgotten by modern man, blotted out of the sky by the irritating glow of electric light's progress, but that was gone, a thing of the past and the night sky reigned supreme once again. It was a sky that Aymond associated with a war-zone deployment in a country very far away from North America.

Aymond, Happy, and Jones set off down the hill, taking a route that flanked the decimated PLA force and vehicles. The radar truck appeared to still be functioning, even after sitting idle all night long. The occasional Zed that approached fell silently to the ground as it shambled in front of the transmitter. It was a beautiful sight.

Thirty minutes later, Gonzo heard his earpiece for his radio squawk from Aymond depressing the push to talk button.

Click.

Nothing was said, just the squawking hiss of an empty transmission. Gonzo gave the scene one more really good scan for threats through his rifle's powerful optic and replied by pressing his radio push to talk button twice.

Click. Click.

There was no response from Aymond, but a few moments later, Gonzo could see Aymond appear from a shadow as if he formed from the melted dark form. Even if Gonzo was next to his friend and leader, he was confident that he wouldn't have heard a single sound coming from Aymond's footsteps or movement. The man was a complete professional and very good at his job.

Quickly, smooth and silent, Aymond and his fire team cleared the area of any threats. They found none and gave another click on the radio to signal the all clear. Gonzo gave two clicks in acknowledgment and gathered the rest of their band of merry miscreants to join the search down on the highway. A few minutes later, the M-ATV and the two civilian vehicles sat idling on the highway. The civilians dragged bodies from the roadway, clearing a narrow path of travel. The Marines pulled documents and wallets out of the pockets of all the uniformed soldiers. The interior of the APCs gave more intel to be sifted through. It would take some time to go through it all and decide what was valid, what was worthwhile, and what was nothing. Part of the difficulty is that none of them could read Mandarin. There wasn't anyone at Groom Lake that could, but that didn't mean that they wouldn't meet a new survivor who could. It was worth it, to Aymond at least, to keep all that appeared to be worth their effort just in case they did meet someone who could translate for them.

Really, Aymond was hoping for maps, and they found a few, but until they had a chance to look at them, he really had no idea what they were a map to. Only one of the APCs started and ran, which at least gave them the chance to use it to push the disabled APCs out of the way for their own vehicles. The remaining undamaged radar truck was low on diesel, which was no big deal after one of the civilians produced a section of garden hose he used to siphon fuel from one of the Chinese APCs. They took the opportunity to top off the M-ATV and the civilian vehicles as well. The other had a gasoline motor, so they would need to scavenge on the highway for that. That vehicle wasn't running too well, seeming to misfire and run rough. Jones said that unleaded gasoline was getting to the age now that it would begin to break down and go bad, especially if it had ethanol in it, which Aymond assumed most every vehicle did. Aymond made a mental note to stick to diesel vehicles from this point forward. If the gasser failed on this trip, they could come back for the remaining APC and bring that back to Groom Lake with them.

After a little trial and error, the transmitter for the radar truck was turned off and lowered. It took a position in their convoy behind the M-ATV so it might be protected in case of attack. Aymond wasn't as worried about deploying it while they drove as much as protecting it so they would have it to use later at Nellis. He assumed that the Zeds might be less than inviting just outside of Las Vegas; the swarms were bad when they came through the area on the way to Groom Lake and Aymond had to assume that they could be even worse now. So the addition of a new radar truck that they will be able to bring back to Groom Lake was incredible. Even more so because now they would be able to set a permuted and safe zone around the hangars and equipment stores while they gathered all they needed to re-arm the Warthogs.

Nothing they did seemed to be a trivial undertaking, everything seeming to be a monumental task, but with everything Aymond knew, he would have to put his head down and work their plan. If that plan failed, then they would move on to the next plan. There was no quitting; there was no possibility of failure.

Soon, the convoy plus the addition of the new-to-them radar truck was on the road and pointed toward Las Vegas. They didn't have any communication with Groom Lake because they were too far away and there were mountains in the way of the normal VHF/UHF radios, the SATCOMs were still assumed to be non-functional, and no one believed that there was any reason that the PLA would have stopped jamming the transmissions. Even Lincoln had the telegraph. Operating completely disconnected from all other forces was different than the typical mission radio silence that they used while deployed. No, this was more ominous, but thankfully their comm gear still worked between them and the team could split apart and stay in contact.

SSC

Muffled screams echoed down the tunnel into the darkness. Overhead, a single light was illuminated, flickering against the cold, empty tunnel walls. The vehicles parked in this section of tunnel had been moved further down toward the exit, near Amanda's pull-up bar and re-entry into the main facility, but the prisoner wouldn't know that. To him, they might as well be thousands of miles away, tens of hundreds of feet underground or on the space station. The man's entire world and future depended on his responsiveness and answers. Amanda's orders were simple. War-time powers gave her a large brush to paint policy with, a complete lack of oversight; no congress, no courts, gave her unlimited ability to do what she thought was best. Chivo thought she was being too soft still, but it was probably best that the sitting president who had practically unlimited power would have so much compassion, compassion even for someone who had tried to kill her.

"Tell me your name."

Chivo's voice was even, no emotion bleeding through the words, standing in contrast to the man's choked yelling. The metal chair from the mess hall was tilted back and braced against a large spare tire for one the MRAPs. The man was tied and duct taped to the chair. He writhed against the bindings and couldn't get free, couldn't breathe. Chivo pulled his head back with a pillowcase cut open. A garden hose ran to a spigot on the wall, two buckets of water sitting on the floor near them. Chivo counted silently to himself as he held the pillowcase tight, water from the hose pouring over the man's face.

This session could go on for a while, and if the man didn't answer the simple question of what his name was soon, then Chivo would turn out the light, take off the blindfold, and leave the man to shiver, dripping wet in the frigid subterranean tunnel for five minutes. Five minutes of uncontrollable shivering in complete darkness, bound to a chair, before they would start again. Chivo knew a few things to be true at this point. One, this man had some training; so far, he had resisted enhanced interrogation techniques that broke down men twice as strong as him. Two, there was no way the man found Amanda and tried to kill her by accident. And three, Chivo would kill him soon no matter what the man told him.

North of Hillsboro, Texas

"Fuck," Ken whispered to himself, his breath hanging in the air, steam rising off his bare head in the cool April morning. Things had not gone to plan, nothing at all had gone to plan. All of his hunting buddies group's prepping, all of their confidence in their survival, and here he was, stranded on the roof of a single-wide manufactured home that appeared to look better than it should due to the ruin around it.

Zeds swarmed around him and he lay still on his back, staring up at the crisp cold blue sky. His truck was a few hundred yards away still on the road. Ken had sprinted to safety for his life after he hit one of the damned things trying to swerve around other shambling dead bodies. Ken was confident he was fucked, he just wasn't sure how fucked or if he would be able to get off the trailer house before he died from exposure.

Ken's mentally reviewed his current inventory. *One pistol, one spare mag, one canteen of water, a rifle, and a bandolier with loaded spare clips for the M1. Food I can do without for a while...*

His thoughts drifted when he thought about the water. With the cooler temperatures, he expected at the hottest part of the day he would be better than if it was August, but water was a problem. Ken slowly rolled to his stomach, slowly and quietly lifting his head to peek over the edge of the flat roof. *Fuck.*

The swarm had mostly lost interested in the mobile home and where he was, but there were still hundreds or thousands of Zeds on the road, churning and writhing like maggots on rotted meat. It smelled about the same too. Ken knew that his truck was finished and that he either had to find a new ride or he would be on the shoe-powered express. He rolled back over and gazed at the clear sun-filled sky and sighed. All he could do is wait and hope he had a chance to walk out of the situation. Ken knew his odds were slim, razor-thin slim, but he also knew he wouldn't quit.

Fucking Charlie couldn't kill me, and the fucking Zeds don't stand a chance. I will not quit; I will win.

Comanche, Texas

That day felt like a lifetime ago. So much had happened since he flanked the ambush in Comanche while trying to get the four of them to Big Bend. Bexar never thought he would be back. Jessie and the FJ were hidden, along with her bad attitude. Bexar's wife was not happy that he left her to recon the town before they tried to drive through, but even though her ankle was getting better with each day, Jessie still couldn't really walk on it well and she sure as hell couldn't run. So her task for the day was to guard their ride and supplies. Unlike last time, they had radios. The radios were much more involved than Bexar knew what to do with, but the manuals with the radios helped him at least get them to talk to each other. All the other features were completely lost on them, but he didn't care.

If Bexar got into trouble, Jessie was going to swoop in and save him if she could drive there. If things went really badly, Bexar hoped that Jessie would continue on and go straight to the SSC. Amanda would help her; it was the best chance she had to have a baby. Bexar couldn't imagine Jessie trying to have their baby by herself in some abandoned home or in a tent or anywhere really. The possibility of her and the baby both being killed in childbirth was very real.

Click.

Bexar sighed. Jessie was worried.

Click. Click.

So far, there was no movement in the town at all that he could see. Slowly, using yards, buildings, and houses, Bexar made his way far enough into town to see the original roadblock and ambush point via his binoculars.

Nothing...it all sits as I remember it.

Bexar was on a roof, lying motionless, quietly peering through the binoculars and looking for any signs of danger, living or dead. There was nothing. Eerily still, not even the wind seemed to be blowing. After what seemed like the whole day, what was really an hour by his new watch, Bexar clicked the push to talk on his radio.

"All clear. Come forward." Bexar gave a brief description of the building he was on. A few minutes later, the FJ slowly drove into view, the sound of the running motor seeming horrendously loud in the stillness. Bexar climbed down and fell the last few feet to the ground onto the balls of his feet and climbed into the passenger seat of the FJ.

"Want to drive straight through?"

Bexar nodded in response, his eyes scanning the road ahead and around them for any new threats, his rifle ready.

"Where are the Zeds?"

"No fucking clue, babe. This place is a ghost town, literally. It's really spooking me out." Soon, they drove around the old roadblock and continued on the highway toward their destination and hopefully their last move for a while.

Pecos, Texas

A pile of trash and boxes made it obvious that someone had been here, perhaps someone besides Chivo and his crew. Erin had no way to tell; it wasn't like a secret underground inland supply cache for resupply in troops during an invasion and war in North America had a registrar's book.

That's too bad. I would totally sign it. I might not even use a made-up name...no, I would definitely use a made-up name.

"Mind if we drive around and explore before we try to do anything real or try to resupply?"

"Sounds great, baby." Erin held Jason's hand as the electric cart whirred down the deceptively long and not-very-well-lit canyons of shelves full of crates and boxes. Some of the crates and cases were obvious, like the seemingly thousands of cans of ammo. They would be able to leave with as much ammo as they wanted and could load into the MRAP, which almost made Erin smile...almost.

Aisle C2 had a black and orange stripe painted in the middle of the row that appeared to run the length of the dark shelving units. Jason turned the wheel and followed the line to the right.

"God, we should leave breadcrumbs or something. This place is massive."

"Maybe, but isn't that how the witch tracks you down to eat you?"

"No, that road is yellow and bricked," Erin said with a straight face. Her humor was dry, dry enough that Jason had to remind himself that she was often making a joke and not being weird, except that he liked her weirdness. Jason pinched her thigh, and Erin squealed and slapped his arm, her eyes smiling at him. Jason loved Erin. After he watched his wife die then reanimate, he really didn't think he would love like this again. He glanced toward the dark concrete ceiling, took a breath, and whispered quietly in his thoughts.

Is this OK, my love? I miss you dearly. Is it too soon to love again?

Jason felt like he knew the answer and that his wife wanted him to love again and love soon. Life was already too precious, too fleeting before people stopped staying dead, and now life was much too fragile to do anything but love.

Erin squeezed his hand, sensing Jason's internal conflict. Jason squeezed back and brought her hand to his face with a soft kiss. The cart stopped. They were at the end of the aisle and were looking at a cold concrete wall, but the dark grey wall wasn't smooth; a large, heavy-looking metal door that appeared reinforced stood starkly against the smooth concrete surface.

"What do you think is in there?"

"I don't know, Jason, but I do know there is only one way to find out."

The door didn't have a door handle like a house, but a handle to pull on and a metal latch that reminded Erin of doors on a ship. The latch flipped over with a hard tug, but it took both of them to pull the door open. The hinges glided effortlessly, but the door was so heavy it took a lot of force to get it moving. Thankfully, the door had thick hydraulic struts that slowed the door as it stopped and clicked all the way open. A narrow corridor stood before them, lights flickering to life one by one, fighting back the darkness.

"Wow. Erin, this looks like that secret area—"

Erin cut him off. "Yeah, it does, so be careful. We don't know if there are any others back there or anywhere in here, really."

"It really looked like the other vehicles in the garage area hadn't moved in a while."

"So fucking what, Jason? Survivors can't be trusted; no one can be trusted but you and I, only each other. There could be people who walked here or their vehicle failed out on the highway. There are so many ways we could be walking into a trap. We play this straight until we know for sure we are alone."

There was no use in arguing with her, so Jason retrieved his shotgun from the cart, Erin already holding her M4. They stepped through the blast-proof doorway and into the corridor. They left the door open behind them without really having a good reason why besides it felt wrong to close it. Slowly, they made their way along the corridor, expanded steel mats comprising the floor, piping and conduits visible below the metal floor. Massive springs were mounted along the walls every few feet.

"They're serious. These springs are like what they have the internal structures mounted with at Cheyenne Mountain. That's badass. I've only seen these on TV. I mean, I'm sure it was like this at Groom Lake, but I never saw it."

Erin grunted. She didn't really care and was more worried about what they would find through the smaller, yet still heavy metal hatch before them. Erin glanced over her shoulder at the door they had first come through then to Jason before unlatching the door and opening it. The room on the other side was dimly lit by red emergency lighting. As the door opened, lights began flickering to life, bathing the dark interior in humming electrical light. Nothing moved and the air inside was slightly stale. A heavy hum could be felt starting more than it could be heard, followed by a whoosh of air as the HVAC system apparently clicked on for the first time in a long while.

"That's a good sign, Erin."

She nodded and her shoulders relaxed slightly, a small amount of dust swirling in the room around them. The room before them was simply large even though the ceiling was low. Wide open with painted lines on the floor, it appeared to be setup to process hundreds of people. Chairs and tables were stacked against the far wall. A set of metal double doors stood on the opposite wall. Across much of the wall space were large patriotic murals and photographs of majestic patriotic places, like Mount Rushmore and the Washington Monument. Erin and Jason walked across the room and cautiously tried the set of doors on the opposite wall. The doors were not locked. The doors clicked into the open position and lights began turning on chasing away the darkness, revealing a long hallway with doors and openings along both sides.

"Further down the rabbit hole, my love?"

Erin gave Jason a sideways glance. He knew she was in the mode, but he couldn't resist the joke.

Las Vegas, Nevada

"We only have about an hour of daylight left, Chief."

Aymond nodded slowly, searching the scene ahead of them with binoculars. "There's a fence break about a half klick ahead. Take us up there to check it out." Aymond keyed the radio. "Stay put; we're going to check our entry spot." The M-ATV began forward with a lurch as they drove toward the damaged fence. After a few moments, Aymond keyed the radio again. "OK, all vehicles follow us through the hole in the fence."

They were near the runways after emerging onto the air base. The PJ's facilities were to their right and down a ways, but what they wanted were in hangars across the runways and near the flight line. With the feeling of being totally exposed, the convoy traveled quickly across the tarmac, across the runways, and to the flight line. A few dozen Zeds milled around near the hangars, but surprisingly, the undead population was light where they were. All of them knew that there had to be thousands and thousands of Zeds on base, many of them trapped inside by the perimeter fence and security measures. It only took a few minutes to break into the correct hangar. With only a short time to work, it was nearly dark by the time the group was able to push out the two aircraft that were partially disassembled for maintenance or repairs to make room for the convoy's vehicles. That was as much as they would get accomplished for the day. For an unknown and uncontrolled facility, Aymond wasn't willing to risk dealing with Zeds at night to locate the munitions storage and begin organizing for the return trip. For his team's safety, that work would have to begin at first light.

CHAPTER 17

Low clouds blotted out the stars, the moon, and any hint of impending twilight for the approaching day. The air was still, not even a breath of a breeze coming from the desert down to the lookout position on the heavy metal container-made-wall. Below ground, the last two days have been filled with drills, fire drills with all hands on deck to fight a fire and rescue trapped persons; it reminded Hammer of being aboard ship. Depending on the skipper, the ship may not be even out into blue water before drills commenced. Besides fire drills were other drills that would be expected, like battle stations and attack and others that were new, like containing an outbreak.

A distance sound grew in volume and intensity from a faint whistle to a full scream of protest.

"Fuck!"

Hammer keyed the radio. "MORTARS!"

He had just barely finished the radio transmission with the far corner of the CONEX wall exploded in hard thump, punctuated by the sound of twisting, ripping metal. Hammer knew the sound much too well. More mortars fell, the air ripped asunder by the blast of a klaxon horn emanating from the facility below ground and more falling rounds. The front gate and wall still stood, but the high-explosive rounds walked across the wall, tearing huge gaps in their protection from assault. More rounds fell, this time inside the courtyard as people ran to take fighting positions for the impending assault. These rounds appeared to be white phosphorus, bodies of men and women not blown off their feet erupting in flames as they staggered and fell.

Hammer scanned the edge of the mountains near where the first PLA observation post was found before and then the edge of the lakebed for where the mortar crews might be. The landscape glowed green in his NODS. Rounds continued to fall in the courtyard. Hammer lay prone at his still intact fighting position and picked up a FLIR scope. After flipping the NODS on his helmet up, Hammer powered the scope and scanned the same areas. This time in the darkness, the heat of mortar tubes glowed, blooming brightly with each launch, the bodies of the crews glowing early in the cool spring air. Hammer radioed the attacker's positions, which was relayed below ground by the repeater erected by Bill with the rest of the VHF communication gear below ground still wired to antennas above. The next round fell true, ripping Hammer's fighting position to pieces, along with his body, thankfully leaving a corpse that wasn't able to reanimate.

As suddenly as the onslaught had begun, the air fell silent. Bodies on fire popped and burned where the WP rounds had fallen in the courtyard. Kirk made it topside, scanned the scene, and sprinted toward the front gate and wall.

"We need men and women topside to repair and fight. We may not have much time. Guys, check in."

"Davis."

"Snow."

"Chuck."

Silence.

Kirk went toward where Hammer's position was and found the mangled remains of his body mixed with the twisted metal of the destroyed CONEX he had been on.

"Hammer is KIA. Snow, lead the repair party; Snow and Chuck, secure the perimeter."

Three "rogers" were the replies followed by Major Pearce. "Kirk, we are going to fly out to Nellis to protect the Hogs, and we don't have a hardened bunker."

"Whatever, Major," Kirk replied, annoyed. Those planes were worthless to him without any armament.

And so are the pilots, Kirk thought. He had more important tasks at hand.

"Incoming," an unknown voice yelled from across the courtyard. The first bone-jarring crunch of an exploding round mixed with the yelling. Kirk sprinted and slid to a stop hard against the metal wall, finding what little cover he had. Shrapnel hit the metal container just above his head with hard pings.

Kirk keyed the radio. "TURTLE, TURTLE!"

A moment later, a different horn sounded, the get-below-ground and get-secure horn. They were going to lock down the facility and try to get teams up through some of the more remote escape hatches. Small arms fire erupted around him, and Kirk realized that much of the wall he was hiding behind no longer existed. After a quick glance, Kirk rose off the ground, took aim, and began engaging the approaching PLA forces. After killing three combatants, a heavy machine gun answered his effort, ripping through the metal of the CONEX and through Kirk's body armor.

The loud whining scream of jet turbines in the distance filled the small pockets of silence punctuated by gunfire and explosions.

"No roll out, just fucking punch it and go, Hoose."

Major Pearce looked at her gauges as she ran up the engines, trying to get them to operating temperature quickly, taxiing through the shadows out of the hangar next to the battle. Her lights were off and she hoped no one noticed them, but she knew better. She heard rounds impacting her aircraft. Pearce glanced at the gauges. "Fuck it." She pushed the engines to full throttle. Still under temp, this wasn't good for the engines or generating power, but it was all she had.

Barely off the ground she retracted the landing gear and stayed low as she flew south, trying to give the enemy forces less time to shoot at her as she passed. If she had just a handful of JDAMs or even just a full drum of ammo for her big Gatling gun, then she could make a difference, but she didn't. All she could do is turn and run and it burned painfully in the pit of her stomach for doing so.

A couple of warning lights glowed in the dark cockpit, but Pearce knew her plane well and was confident she could make it to Nellis. She glanced over her shoulder and saw the dark shadow of Hoose followed by a glowing streak racing toward them.

"Fuck!"

Major Pearce keyed the radio. "SAM!"

Pearce slammed the control to the right while releasing flares and chafe, turning sharply. From the cockpit, it looked like she might drag a wingtip on the desert floor and there were mountains racing up toward her, but Pearce was calm, her eyes scanning her path as she banked hard the other direction. She glanced over her shoulder at where Hoose's aircraft should be in time to see the SAM explode, taking most of his starboard wing with it. Hoose's A-10 seemed to hang impossibly suspended in time and space before it tumbled and cart-wheeled in a fireball across the desert floor and into a building.

Anger burned hot in the pit of her stomach. Even after flying and fighting in Iraq and Afghanistan, she hadn't been this upset. A single sob escaped her outwardly cool demeanor before Pearce took a deep breath and focused on flying to Nellis so she could arm up and fly back to Groom Lake.

I'm going to kill each and every one of those motherfuckers.

North of Hillsboro, TX

A small diesel engine had a distinct sound, especially one that wasn't exactly new with all the emissions control. Ken blinked. He was tired, he was dehydrated, he was cold, and he was now really confused. Trapped on the roof of a manufactured home, Ken wasn't exactly having a good journey to find the facility where the president now resided. No, the trip from Crockett had been a complete disaster, *if not for being rescued.*

The rattling noise of an engine grew closer. Ken took a peek over the edge of the roof at his truck still in the middle of the highway. The two dozen Zeds that still congregated around the manufactured home, pawing at the walls, all turned and began shuffling toward the approaching vehicle. Ken tried to swallow but had difficulty. During the previous night, he had come to terms with dying on top of the manufactured home. He worried about his corpse reanimating after he died, but Ken couldn't bring himself to completely give up and eat a bullet.

Blurry-eyed, Ken saw an old beat-up Mercedes diesel sedan roll to a stop. It looked like a movie villain's car from a 1980s action movie, complete with the deeply tinted windows. The car stopped, and two men climbed out. Both wore tie-dye shirts, had long hair and beards. One man began pulling stuff out of his pocket while the other yelled, waved his hands, and began walking up the highway. Zeds in view all turned their heads toward the new people. If they hadn't already, the rest began to follow the man yelling and waving his hands like some sort of perverse pied piper.

The other man who had been digging items out of his pockets moved and Ken could see a slingshot in his hand. The man lit a firecracker and launched it with the slingshot. The pop sounded louder than Ken thought it should, thinking it sounded more like a rifle shot than a firecracker. A dozen yards away, the man who had been yelling and waving his arms stood as still as a statue while the Zeds turned toward the exploding firecracker. A few minutes later, the Zeds were herded away from the Mercedes, away from Ken's truck, and away from the manufactured home. Ken mustered his strength, emboldened by the strangers about to loot his truck. He slid off the far side of the roof to the ground with a muffled grunt. Ken snuck around the side of the home and watched the men walk up to his truck. He waited; Ken wanted to believe that they were concerned that someone might be in the cab and trapped. To his surprise, the men checked the cab first. He could tell they were talking, but they were apparently whispering so he couldn't hear what was being said. After checking the cab, the men looked around for where the owner might be. It occurred to Ken that they might know the area really well and they might know that his truck is a new addition.

Unable to find the driver, the men began looking in the bed of the truck. They were just beginning to open the aluminum cases when Ken stepped onto the road near the men's Mercedes.

"You two, stop there!"

Ken stood with his rifle ready, but with the muzzle held low. The men spun around, shocked and surprised to find a stranger standing by their car with a rifle.

"Hey, man, be easy, man. We can split it with you since we got the zombies to stagger off for a bit."

Ken looked around and saw that the Zeds were not staying away; all within sight had zeroed back in on them and were converging.

"Guys, look, my truck is in a bad way. That gear is my gear and the longer we stay here, the more likely we all die from the Zeds. So I can kill you both and take your car or we can quickly load what we can into your car—do you have a secure place near here?"

"Yeah?"

The other man started giggling.

"What's his deal, guy?"

"He is Keith, I'm Carl, and he's laughing for how outrageous all of this is. Just a few months ago, things were more normal. It's like a bad fucking trip, man, except that we never get to come down off it, so why not laugh at the absurdity of what man has done to itself?"

Ken looked from the men to the closest Zeds, turned, and raised his rifle. A single shot echoed off their surroundings, the nearest Zed's skull ripping open as it collapsed to the ground.

"Shit, man, that was a person, man."

"OK, then you stay here and hug it out with all the other persons walking up to say hi; I'm getting the fuck out of here. Or are you guys going to help me get my stuff and we can all go together?"

"Come on, Keith, get the zombies off our ass and then give me a hand to get this stuff put in the trunk."

Keith still giggled a little, but he took out another firecracker with a long fuse from his pocket, along with his slingshot. The trick didn't work this time. Some of the Zeds followed the diversion, but most had their dead white eyes locked onto the three men.

"Shit." Ken shouldered his rifle and fired. It startled Keith and Carl, but the Zed about to grasp Keith's shirt fell to the ground, never to rise again.

"Get to work, hippie. I've got the fucking Zeds!"

Both Carl and Keith nodded as they began moving stuff from the bed of the truck to the trunk of the car. Not everything fit so he took ammo and left food, as Carl said they had food to share. In a short amount of time, the three of them were in the Mercedes and driving off the highway into the countryside on a farm-to-market road. Ken kept catching a whiff of a smell that was like day-old french fries in the car.

Near Ennis, Texas

Sunlight broke over the horizon, which glowed red with thick clouds toward the northeast. Bexar walked the area, his AR-15 slung across his chest with his ammo carrier and pistol—his full tactical loadout. It didn't even seem odd anymore, much like remembering to put your cellphone and wallet in your pocket back before the world changed. The combat load, ammo, and weapons were his everyday carry and attire.

Red sky at night, sailor's delight, red sky in morn...

Bexar shook his head. The old limerick was often true and that meant they needed shelter sooner than later. They had parked for the night and slept in the FJ near the top of a hill in some pasture land. The fence appeared to be standing when they arrived last night and shut the gate behind them, which afforded them some limited protection from single Zeds. If a herd or swarm of Zeds hit the fence, it would crumble as if it was made of paper from the mass of bodies, but they did what they could with what they had. However, now they needed more. They needed a farmhouse near a lake or large pond that was set back from any major roadways. This was the area that he and Jessie had chosen while scouring maps in Pecos and so far, it looked promising. They should only be a few miles away from the SSC so they could flee there if they had to or for when the baby came. They weren't super sure on the due date, but Jessie thought the baby should be due in September or early October. They only had a few more months to prepare and if this baby was like Keeley had been, then time would zoom by in a blink and they would be holding a newborn with a slightly stunned expression on their faces.

There were a farmhouse and an outbuilding about a half mile to their south. It appeared to have a stock pond near the house and was worth checking out. Bexar thought about going back to get Jessie, who was resting in the FJ, or was supposed to be, but decided to clear the house and barn on his own. Her ankle was improving, but still very much injured and painful.

Dozens of long-dead cattle lay half-decomposed in the pasture between Bexar and the house. To Bexar, it seemed that thousands of years had passed since cows had been self-sufficient wild animals and they simply weren't able to survive as they were. Predators, diseases, and things Bexar was sure he didn't know about had killed off most of the cattle they had seen. Some even had bite marks from Zeds. Bexar laughed at the visual of a dead body trying to eat their steak very rare.

That must have really confused the cow.

Bexar chuckled then felt bad for laughing about something that was really inappropriate to laugh about. That was the nature of the world now, eat or be eaten as it were.

The house appeared to have been abandoned, but Bexar approached on a corner where there were the fewest windows just to be sure. Nearing the home, he scanned the windows for signs of activity. There was no movement; he didn't even see any flies inside the windows. Bexar's mind flashed to the church of bodies in Cortez and shuddered slightly. That was quite possibly the worst thing he had ever seen or experienced. A feeling of satisfaction waved over him at the thought of having extracted justice against the cult who had killed and tortured all those people.

After making a lap around the house and the barn with no sign of movement, Bexar checked the front door, which he found unlocked.

After a deep breath, Bexar pushed the front door open and backed away from the dark opening, using the door frame and wall as cover. He waited, staring into the darkened interior. No uniquely bad smells reached him outside, although the home smelled stale, which was actually a good sign. Maybe the people fled or maybe they weren't home when the attack had come.

Bexar yelled into the doorway and slapped his hand against the door frame a few times then waited, ready, rifle in his hands. He had to remind himself to breathe as he counted silently. Once he reached 60, Bexar slapped the door and yelled into the home again, waiting for any Zeds to shamble toward the disturbance. Checking his six, Bexar saw a single Zed stumble out of the barn and toward the house. The Zed appeared to have been an older man in coveralls, which seemed both cliché and appropriate for the homestead. Bexar let his rifle hang on the sling and he drew his heavy knife. After closing the distance, Bexar plunged the thick blade into the old man's skull before his hands could grasp the new prey. Bexar extracted the knife from the now truly dead man's skull, and wiped the pungent rotted gore from the blade on the man's coveralls and slid the knife back into the Kydex sheath on his belt before returning his attention to the open front door of the house.

Still no movement.

He walked back to the dark doorway, flipped on the bright light mounted on his AR, and began slowly clearing the house. A few minutes later, Bexar was done with the house and cleared the barn, which, after having killed the old man's reanimated body, was empty.

Bexar stepped back outside and looked up toward where the FJ was parked. He couldn't see it due to a rise in the landscape, but it should be down the hill from the house and on the other side of the next low hill. This house and barn were perfect for he and Jessie to bring a new baby into this fucked-up world in.

As he walked back toward the FJ, Bexar scanned the area and thought about ways to improve their security. If he could find a bunch of metal shipping containers, he could make a walled compound, but even if he found them, there was no way he could move them or put them in place. There was an ancient-looking tractor with a bunch of implements in the barn, including a front-end loader, so if he could get that working, Bexar knew he could make earthen walls or berms at least. Regardless, he had a case of empty sandbags to fill but he would need many more.

Nellis Air Force Base, Las Vegas, Nevada

Daylight didn't wait for the lazy, so just before sunrise, as the horizon glowed with twilight and the approaching sun, Aymond and his crew were awake and working. The new radar truck was up and functioning well. It kept the two dozen Zeds that meandered up during the night out of their hangar and let them keep from firing their rifles, of which the report of rifle fire echoing across the runway would almost certainly bring more Zeds. Quiet and calm, they worked quickly to prepare the convoy to return to Groom Lake. All they needed was munitions and some specialized loading equipment. Aymond didn't smile, his passive face as close to a smile as he would get while working a mission. He expected something unexpected to put a speed bump in their lane, but Aymond had no idea what it could be yet, just that it usually was that way.

The sound of big jet turbine engines and an aircraft flying at a high speed ripped over the roof of the hangar to a chorus of fucks being uttered from the surprise. The aircraft was low enough that some of the men ducked. Aymond looked outside the hangar doors and saw an A-10 bank and climb as it raced across the flightline and runways.

"Chief, is that—?"

Happy was cut off by Aymond's raised hand. Aymond keyed his radio and spoke tersely, the reply terse and quick as well.

"That's the major. Make ready to get that Hog into this hangar; she's going to land close and taxi fast."

The hangar erupted in activity. The vehicles were moved out, the radar truck moved aside to give room for the aircraft to taxi into the shelter of the hangar. A few minutes later, Major Pearce shut down the engines of her A-10 and yelled out of the open cockpit to close the doors and get hidden. The Marines and civilians looked to Aymond who nodded.

"The trucks! Get the fucking trucks hidden too!"

Aymond waved approval to the men as they scrambled to make the unusual directions happen. "What's the deal, Major?"

"Ambush and attack. Groom Lake is under siege and it's bad, really bad. Mortar teams destroyed much of the built-up perimeter and if everyone is smart, they're locked down and safe below the surface. We barely got off the ground.... Hoose got it from a SAM."

Aymond nodded and listened attentively to the brief. He wished he could raise Groom Lake on the radio, but they were too far away and there were mountains in their line of sight, so their VHF comms wouldn't work. His best-laid plans were now completely wrecked and now they were trying to organize a quick reaction force (QRF). The problem is that a QRF usually had a lot more men and weapons than they had, but they had a Hog and that was an advantage, as long as they could keep it from being shot out of the sky and keep it loaded. Their convoy to Groom Lake would have to wait; they couldn't setup shop where they had planned. There were other airfields in the Tonopah range, but they didn't know their status, if the Chinese and Korean forces had taken them, or even if they had fuel that could be salvaged and used.

"Major, we're going to setup a re-arm shop here in this hangar for you and leave enough of my men to make it work. Gonzo, Happy, and I are going to get back to Groom Lake and recon the situation. We will be on the same freq, so check in as you get airborne and into radio range."

Before Pearce could reply, Aymond yelled across the hangar, "Jones, Happy, Gonzo!"

The three men trotted over to where Aymond and Major Pearce stood. "Jones, you're in charge of the operation to arm, fuel, and keep the major's Hog flying. Happy and Gonzo, you're with me to recon Groom Lake."

He continued, understanding the confused faces. "Groom Lake is under siege, an attack just before sunrise. We have mortar teams and some may be armed with shoulder-fired SAMs. We're going to haul ass, get hidden, and relay information to the major here to conduct runs on their forces. We will also try to make contact with the remaining forces secured below ground."

Discussion continued quickly, hashing out the plans in slightly greater detail, but Aymond left most of the plans for how things were going to unfold in this hangar to Jones. Aymond had his own problems and mission to plan while on the drive. They simply didn't have time to wait.

A few minutes later, the M-ATV drove off with Aymond, Gonzo, and Happy. Major Pearce turned and began prepping her aircraft to be re-armed, specifically showing Jones the process of how to load the iconic GAU-8 sticking out of the nose of the aircraft.

Pecos, Texas

The odd facility in the already odd top-secret underground inland cache facility reminded Erin of the odd top-secret smaller duplicate facility at Groom Lake where her mother was found reanimated. It was small, purpose-built, and a secret inside of a secret. There were bunks in what looked like a hospital wing, food service facilities, and the large entryway that looked a bit like a processing facility.

The two of them explored the facility in greater detail. Erin started a checklist of items, gear, and weapons they could use and that she wanted. Jason had begun a checklist of clothing, food, and medical items he thought they would need.

"It's like a field hospital with supplies. Like some sort of secret re-up room in a fucking video game."

"Erin, if you see a section of wall that looks different, then we should blow a hole in it and see if it unlocks another secret passage."

Erin slapped Jason on the shoulder, who laughed at her. "Sure, act like you don't want to go on some sort of epic side quest."

"Baby, this is an epic fucking side quest, the entire damn world."

Erin kissed Jason gently on the cheek, slapped his ass, and continued walking down the aisle. For being underground, the facility was cavernous, like an entire gigantic warehouse box store selling five-gallon jugs of mayonnaise to preppers who have a lot of imagination and little practical skills. They walked because they wanted a chance to stretch their legs, but they also felt like they missed too many details as they whirred by on an electric cart. They would absolutely use the cart to collect supplies, but sort of like going to the Swedish flat box furniture store, they wrote down the aisle and shelf number of the items they wanted and kept the list going so they could find their new gear and supplies with ease. Lastly, they both felt safe, truly safe, and it's the first time in a very long time either had felt that way.

If anyone else showed up, that would probably change. If anyone else knew about this place, that would most likely change because they both realized that the feeling of safety was only because they were secured underground with no other persons there that could fuck up their new post-modern dream house.

"How long do you think we should stay here?"

Erin squeezed his hand, their fingers intertwined as they walked. "Really, the question is how long could we stay here?"

"We should probably go topside every so often to get some sunlight for our health and so we don't get too mentally fucked up from the lack of it."

"Probably, but I think we can put that off for a few more days, maybe a couple of weeks? Oh, I want to setup a shelter here. I would rather not stay in the hospital wing; it's sort of creepy."

Jason nodded, paused for a moment, and wrote an item on his list and marked down the item's location: a case of Life Straw water filters that they would absolutely need as society continued to get further and further away from having readily available municipality treated water, however safe and clean and good that was before the attack.

"We should see if we can find another bathroom somewhere out here besides the big one in the indoc area."

"Is that what you think all of that is?"

"Yes, I think so; it would make sense. They built this facility to be behind the friendly's front lines, assuming an invasion from Mexico from whomever, probably the Soviets when this place was first built, but they needed a place for supplies, fuel, and weapons, and they needed a safe field hospital as well. What I'm surprised about is a lack of other major entrances. Seems like there should be another large entry, but maybe that wouldn't be smart?"

"Well, in my extensive experience with secret underground military complexes, I would say maybe," Erin said with a snicker. They really had no idea, but this was the third secret underground complex that they knew about, and the second one to stay in.

"Imagine how many of these there are spread across the U.S. You know there has to be more along each of the two borders and on each coast."

"I would suspect as much. I wonder if our entry code works for all of them?"

"It would make sense to have a universal code for troops on the run, but maybe not? I mean, how in the hell will we find them? There's no way if Chivo hadn't told us about this one."

Erin stopped walking. "I mean, if we can find out where the others are, then we might find one close to our destination, a place we can really settle down and start a new life in our new world. Just you and me."

Jason had stopped walking as well and stood next to Erin. "It seems like a waste, though, that so many people could benefit from these supplies."

"It would be a waste to announce this is here and have it stripped and pillaged by assholes. No, we keep this close to the chest and it can serve us for the rest of our lives, which I think is more important than fuck sticks who lucked through survival due to the goodwill of others."

Jason gave Erin a hug. He suspected that her attitude had changed to one of an angry cynic after Sarah was killed and she still blamed Jessie, but Jason didn't blame Jessie at all. Just like he didn't blame the cult for killing his wife; he blamed the Koreans and the Chinese for ruining everything.

"Well, baby, for now, keep an eye out for a bathroom and we'll put up one of the tents near there with some coats, the whole works."

Erin laughed, which startled Jason. "It's like that home-buying TV show. 'She's a ruthless Zed killer, he's an adorable sexy prepper-supplies-logistics specialist. Together, they're searching for the perfect post-apocalyptic bungalow and their budget is 3.2 million.'"

Jason laughed, bending over with his hands on his knees. "Seriously, how did any of those people afford any of those homes? There is no way."

They needed that laugh, badly. With a faint hint of a smile, Erin took Jason's hand as they continued their leisurely shopping stroll.

SSC

Chivo walked into the command center and found Amanda sitting back with her feet on a desk leafing through a printout. Eric stood near her at another desk, operating a computer-projected display on one of the giant monitors on the wall. It looked like a set piece out of the movie War Games.

Amanda looked up. "Well?"

"We're finished."

"And?"

Chivo wore a clean uniform, with no insignia visible. "He gave us some good intel, and he won't be a problem any longer."

Amanda nodded, ignoring the obvious question. "And what is that good intel?"

"I would like to sit down at a computer and write a report so I can better organize the details and we can analyze it all, but the short version is that he was a North Korean agent who entered the U.S. via a false South Korean visa almost 36months ago. His job was to scout secret facilities in Texas for the coming attack and invasion. He hadn't known the date of the attack or even that there was one coming at all really—just a standard deep-cover recon mission—but he was notified via shortwave broadcast of the impending attack less than 24 hours before it happened."

"Wait, how was he notified via shortwave radio and we didn't know about it?"

"Encrypted transmissions. The radio stations play a continuous loop of voices reading numbers or letter or saying random words. All of those transmissions are for deep-cover operatives around the world and represent a number of different countries; we've used it too."

"Oh. OK, and what else?"

"Madam President, I'll have a full report coming to you by this afternoon, but we should prepare for a full-on battle here and more at Groom Lake. The PLA also know about the other facilities in Texas."

"Wait, back up for a moment. First, what battle? More attacks?"

"Yes, the PLA should be getting men and material on shore soon for the full invasion; that much we know from Aymond's crew of Marine Raiders. But the PLA are specifically targeting these facilities to convert to their use. I got the impression that they intend to take the facilities by force or destroy them so they can't be used by any survivors or government factions."

"Huh. Include recommendations with your written report, please. Now what other facilities?"

"Some of these I'm aware of, some I had heard rumors about, and a couple of them I had no idea they existed at all, but they make sense."

"And?" Amanda was getting slightly impatient.

Chivo walked to a dry-erase board and drew a bad outline of Texas with a dot near Dallas. "This is us" and he pointed to the dot. Chivo drew another dot, this one in West Texas, near where Midland and Odessa would be. "This is an inland supply cache near Pecos."

"Wait, a what?"

Eric interrupted, with his hand raised slightly for his question.

"During the 70s and 80s when the Soviet threat was the greatest, large underground facilities were constructed to serve our front lines in case of an invasion. They contain weapons, munitions, other supplies, and food. Some even have hospital facilities, others have command resources, but they all serve as a stop gap for our military for an invasion, before traditional war-fighting supply chains can get fully established."

Chivo drew lines across the state. "This is I-20, this is I-10, this is I-35, and this is I-45." He then drew a star for DFW, for Houston, San Antonio, Austin, El Paso, and Beaumont, labeling each. "Facilities were constructed on the major interstates, which is also near rail facilities to help with building and supplying the supply caches, but also for moving gear out and people in as needed."

"El Paso doesn't need one. They have Fort Bliss and the surrounding complex. Basically, anywhere there was already a base or a post, there isn't a cache site there." Chivo drew an X over El Paso and San Antonio. "But there are sites near them. This one in Pecos is where my crew resupplied on our way to get Bexar in Big Bend. There is another one here." Chivo drew a circle on I-20 in East Texas.

"Is that all?"

"No, these three facilities on I-10 I hadn't heard about. They are, or were, I guess, early warning tripwire stations: powerful listening posts to monitor and intercept transmissions from an invading force."

"OK. To summarize, our friend who shot at me was an enemy spy, he was sent here to recon secret facilities in Texas as a prelude to war, and he was captured by two regular survivors? That doesn't make any sense."

"He made a stupid mistake by trying to kill you. He had been watching and monitoring activity topside for nearly a week and had rightly deduced that the facility was occupied but by a small force. He didn't know how small, though."

"Did he get that information back to his, um...?"

"Handlers? Yes."

"Fuck."

"Exactly."

"What now, Chivo?"

"We have a lot of work to do, but we need manpower, we need people. We need able-bodied survivors to help us buildup defenses and to formulate a battle plan. It isn't a question of if we will be attacked, it is a question as to if we have time to prepare!"

"We're working on that already."

Chivo nodded. "There's more."

Amanda stopped and listened. "I found his camp on the northern side of the lake in the woods. I brought his gear here. It's in conference room C2002, you need to see it."

"Oh? OK then, let's go see it."

Amanda walked out of the room, Chivo clambering to keep up with her fast, determined pace. Shortly, she opened the door to room C2002 and saw that the large twelve seat conference table had the chairs pushed away and the table was covered in equipment and gear.

"Was he carrying all of this?"

"Sort of. He had a motorcycle; it's in the tunnel with the rest of the trucks. The obvious stuff, his shelter, sleeping bag, and similar items of no investigative value are piled over there." Chivo pointed to a large mound of what appeared to be high-end backpacking gear. "None of it has any logos or manufacture information. It all also appears to be well-made copies of commercially available gear from manufacturers like North Face, Osprey, and such."

Amanda sifted through some of the layers of nylon, all of which were muted earth-tone colors.

"The Chinese have been copying western goods forever, so have North Korea, but who cares? What is interesting is the gear on the table."

"What is this?" Amanda pointed at a backpack-sized plastic case.

"That is a SATCOM—satellite communication. That's how he was maintaining contact with his handlers."

"So their SATCOM system works and ours doesn't?"

"No, at least I don't think that is the case. I need to get Bill here to help, or someone else who is a radio geek. It appears to use our—the United States' military, that is—frequencies with different encryption keys."

"So their system uses the same frequencies as ours. Why does that matter?"

"No, I think they are actually using our satellites, that they took them over somehow and denied us access."

Amanda appeared surprised. "So..."

"Exactly, ma'am. Our assets might still be in place and usable. If we can overcome their control, or if we can simply use their keys or radios or something,

I have a limited working man's knowledge of how this all works. We need a radio guy."

Amanda nodded. "Then add Bill to the message and order...what about this one? A spare radio?"

Amanda pointed at another plastic case, but this one had an odd-looking antenna and transmitter on a stand next to it.

"No, I think that is a man-portable radar truck, like the Zed zapper that Aymond acquired."

Amanda's eyebrows shot up in surprise.

North of Hillsboro, Texas

As the hippies drove, Ken sat in the back seat, his pistol out and in his hand. He didn't trust hippies on principle, but these guys seemed harmless. The minute they had driven away, Keith had lit a joint and they were passing it back and forth. Ken's initial reaction was one of anger and annoyance, but then he decided to try relaxing and letting it go. He knew that if his new acquaintances were stoned when they got to their camp, he could easily kill them and move on with his life. Besides, maybe things would go differently. For the first time in his life, Ken was OK with pot smoke wafting around him. He had punched a guy in his platoon in Vietnam out cold for smoking a joint while on patrol, but this was a different place and a very different time.

Off of I-35 and down a couple of farm-to-market roads about 10 minutes later, the car pulled to a stop in front of a cattle gate. The fencing was very taut and well-maintained. Ken noticed that someone had recently made repairs to the barbed wire strands, and it looked like a couple of posts were replaced near the gate, too.

Keith must have noticed Ken looking at the fence. "Yeah, man, the fucking dead, man. They ganged up and pushed against our fence. I had to spend an entire fucking day fixing that mess. Very uncool, man."

Carl laughed. "That's their problem, the dead, they're just...very un-dude. They do not abide, although I'm pretty sure they were mostly lawyers."

Both Keith and Carl laughed heartily.

Ken was puzzled. "How did you know they were lawyers?"

Carl was giggling while trying to explain. "It's hard to tell the difference. The zombies have a better personality and are less selfish than any attorney I know!"

Keith climbed out of the car, opened the gate, and remained until Carl had brought the Mercedes through before closing the gate behind them before lighting another joint after climbing back into the passenger seat.

Even Ken laughed along with their stories and jokes; Keith and Carl's happy and relaxed attitude was contagious. They drove up the long dirt driveway, and Ken realized he was happier and more relaxed than he had been since the attack...and he was hungry. Ken didn't notice that the windows of the car were rolled up and that the interior was thick with pot smoke.

At the end of the driveway was a small ranch home with some old oak trees swaying gently in the wind in the yard. There was a metal outbuilding, which was expected, but there were also two large greenhouses, each with its own well-built and maintained fence around them. In fact, each of the buildings and the home was individually fenced.

"What's with all the fences?"

Keith answered, "Backups, man. If a zombie gets into place past the first fence, then we have more fences to slow them down while we pick them off one by one."

Ken was a little surprised at the planning and strangely he was really craving some fast food. He then realized for the second time that the car smelled like french fries and asked why.

"It's the grease fuel, man. This is an eco-friendly car. Instead of dinosaur bones, we're burning old fryer grease."

"Carl, how do you get fryer grease?"

"There are simply millions of gallons waiting for us in all the restaurants of the old world. Fast food joints are the best for it. They're setup with tanks and outside access for trucks to come remove the cooking oil and such, so we pull up and get our grease from there. We have a truck in the barn we use for that, big tank you know, man."

"Just like that? Put the oil in and drive?"

"No, man, we've got to refine it a little. Keith has us all setup in the barn; he's the mad scientist."

Ken looked at Keith, whose long hair and unkempt beard didn't look very scientific in his mind.

"Not a mad scientist, a mad engineer. Aerospace engineer by training and trade."

"No shit." Ken was surprised and he didn't do a very good job of hiding it.

Keith laughed loudly. "Yeah, well it doesn't matter now, but all of that schooling, training, and experience is sort of handy to have. We've been able to get things really setup around here with what we can find."

"What about you, Carl? Are you going to tell me you're a heart surgeon or something?"

"Naw, man, I'm not anything but me."

"He's brilliant and an excellent farmer. He gets it—the earth and dirt and plants and nature. All of it just makes sense to him. He had a lot of different careers over his life, but has really found his purpose with the new world we live in."

"Yeah, man, like we're making bio-diesel, more than we could ever hope to use, and we have our grow operations."

"Like corn and tomatoes or what?"

"Yes, sort of. Well, come on, let me just show you."

They parked the car in the large metal outbuilding, which was more of an industrial building than a barn or equipment shed. The floor was concrete and the interior was kept clean and clutter free. Once again, Ken was quite surprised. Large tanks dominated the back wall, each of which had piping coming out and go to other tanks and through other parts of what looked like a bit like a winery opened by a Bond villain, just minus the secret lair in a volcano.

"That's where we make the bio-diesel. These tanks over here we are small batching distilled spirits from grain. We cleaned out a farmers co-op recently and am currently making a corn whiskey."

They walked outside and to the first greenhouse. Large fans hung from the rafters inside, although they weren't spinning. Tubing hung from the ceiling and came down to where rows of green plants were in containers and on strange tables.

Carl began explaining, "Hydroponics, man. We keep the water circulating with nutrients and then keep the plants warm and sunned; they're happy for it."

One of the large fans kicked on with an electric whine. Ken looked up at stared at the fan for a moment. Keith answered his question before Ken could ask, "A combination of solar and wind power. We have a diesel generator we converted to run on bio-fuel, but we've only had to use it once so far."

"Wow."

Groom Lake, Nevada

Aymond peered through the binoculars, slowly and carefully scanning the scene from the mountain ridge west of Dreamland's main grouping of hangars and buildings. The dormitories were practically destroyed. *Luckily*, Aymond thought, *most of those survivors had been moved back below ground*. But there would still be casualties from their destruction, he was sure of it. The CONEX metal wall and fighting positions lay in smoldering ruins with large holes and numerous bodies in all directions. Some had reanimated and shambled through the fire, smoke, ash, and twisted metal; others lay blissfully dead. The Chinese and Korean forces held skirmish lines well over a kilometer away and there was a lot of movement in their ranks, but they were mostly holding their position and waiting, which couldn't be good.

An explosion erupted behind him and toward the north.

"Chief! Contact!"

The rest of the transmission was garbled, mixed with fast rapid fire. Happy tried to get the rest of the important information out, but fell silent. The explosion was the claymores they had set out along their perimeter for their observation post. This was not ideal, as the sun sat directly overhead. The safe blanket of darkness in the night would have been better, but it was far too late for wishful thinking now.

Aymond turned and, keeping on his belly, made his way toward the firefight, which was falling in intensity as quickly as it had started. It had been four hours since they left Nellis and it was as bad as Major Pearce had said, but now it was getting exponentially worse. Happy lay on the ground motionless, and Aymond saw Gonzo rip through an entire magazine and start on a second one before Aymond could get a target. They had the high ground and appeared to have stumbled into a security patrol, which would be the smart thing for the PLA to have done.

Rounds cracked as they tore through the air just inches overhead; other rounds impacted the dirt around Aymond, causing dirt to fly into the air like a geyser.

Fuck. Fuck all of this.

Aymond pulled a grenade from his carrier and yelled, "Gonzo! Cover fire! Grenade!"

Gonzo let loose with more multi-shot bursts, emptying one magazine and starting on yet another, which gave Aymond the chance to sit up slightly, pull the pin, and lob the grenade high over-head and down the mountain toward the enemy forces. After the explosion, they could hear pain-filled fearful screams mixed in with the hard clattering sound of their rifles firing on full auto.

The screaming subsided or was drowned out by a dramatic increase in the volume of rifle fire. Aymond heard Gonzo yell fuck as he pushed and began fighting Happy on the ground. Gonzo pushed and kicked Happy hard right in the face before moving his foot and firing a rifle burst into his friend's face.

Aymond didn't need an explanation; Happy had been killed and had reanimated.

Gonzo turned his attention back toward the firefight, emptying another magazine. Aymond was down to his last two loaded mags on his person. There were more in the truck, but that was a couple of hundred meters away, which might as well be in the next state for how likely it would be for him to make it that far without being killed. Between shots, Aymond glanced at Gonzo again, pulling magazines from Happy's gear; that did not bode well for their survival. Downrange, he could see that the PLA was advancing, a grenade exploding just a dozen meters from them, A small defilade protected Aymond from much of the blast and most of the shrapnel, but the situation was becoming dire. Aymond inserted his last rifle magazine and although he wasn't religious, he felt the need to say a little prayer over his last mag. "Please don't let me fuck this one up."

Carefully, Aymond lined up each shot, like a carnival game. Enemy forces seemed to appear magically before his front sight and every squeeze of the trigger made them disappear. Movement, people walking, Aymond could see their legs through his optic. Shifting up, he could see that they were Korean forces who had been killed and reanimated. The others turned and disengaged mostly from the fight with Aymond and Gonzo to protect themselves from their comrades turned Zeds. Before he could process that information, his earpiece squawked: it was Major Pearce and she was coming on station.

Aymond felt like yelling, but quickly and professionally contained himself. "Troops in contact, need immediate assist, danger of being overrun, low ammo, one KIA, how copy?"

A JTAC he was not. He couldn't give an accurate and fast 9-line, but he didn't care. "Pearce, popping blue smoke, tangos 50 meters northwest."

He couldn't see her, he couldn't hear her aircraft, but if Pearce said she was on station and was about to make a gun run on their position, he knew she meant it. From the south, Aymond saw a glint and looked: it was Pearce in her Hog flying low and fast across the desert floor to the west of the ridge where they were located. Aymond popped blue smoke.

Pearce climbed rapidly. Her gun with wings seemed to rip off the desert floor and into the clear blue sky, and the spec of her aircraft grew in size at a seemingly impossible rate before nosing over and diving toward his position with a lonesome scream from its two large engines. He could see the smoke from the huge canon of a gun before he heard the sound. A long *brrrrrrrrrrrrrrrrrrrt* sound filled the valley, the sound echoing across the mountains and from the sky, the sound that every modern ground troop longs for when everything had gone to shit. The hog pulled up through the smoke of the big machine cannon, dropping flares and chafe as it did. Pearce worried about shoulder-fired SAMs after seeing one kill her wingman and friend.

"Chief, I took a lot of small arms fire. Coming back around for another pass."

"Roger. Extracting toward the south to the truck during next run."

"Gonzo!" Aymond yelled across the battlefield, but Gonzo knew what was going on. He flashed a thumbs up and waited, coiled and ready. The A-10 banked back up and came screaming down on their position. Aymond leapt to his feet and sprinted toward Gonzo. They both grabbed Happy's armor carrier and pulled as a team, dragging his body with them back to the M-ATV. The sound of another gun run finished behind them and some sporadic small arms fire followed their exit. Once in the armored truck, Aymond pushed the button to start the engine and began driving down the mountain as quickly as he could. They would have to regroup and formulate a plan. What that could be, he had no idea yet, but he needed a little time to think it through.

"Chief, we have an unknown aircraft inbound, big one, four engine and its high, maybe angels-40."

Shit, Aymond thought. He was mostly confident that if this was a bombing run, it wouldn't be nuclear, since it would kill the PLA forces on the ground, but nothing good could come from this. This was also probably why the PLA forces had backed off so far.

"Pearce, do you have enough to make another run at the primary forces before bugging out?"

"Roger, Chief, can do."

Aymond drove as hard as he could and as quickly as he could. Gonzo began passing loaded magazines up from what they had brought in the truck, which Aymond took and began passing back empties from his dump pouch. Happy's body lay in the floor in the back. The floor was slick and the cabin was filled with the metallic smell of a large quantity of thick blood.

They couldn't hear the last run that Major Pearce took, but they saw her scream past overhead only a few dozen meters above them as she pointed back toward Nellis.

"OK, I'm winchester and headed back. See you all in a little bit."

Winchester; she was out of ammo that was fast. "Major, if you have the fuel, could you remain near for a bomb damage assessment?"

"Roger, only for ten minutes, then I'll be running on fumes when I land."

A few moments later, the shockwave, a single large shockwave, rocked the truck. They were on the backside of the mountains from Groom Lake and whatever the PLA had detonated had rippled through it all to them. A few minutes after that, he saw Pearce zoom past. "Total loss. I'll brief you when you get to the hangar," was all she said on the radio. Aymond replied affirmatively and drove in silence. Things were not going well.

Near Ennis, Texas

The home was clear, the barn was clear, and the FJ was parked by the front door. Jessie hobbled around their new home while Bexar unloaded the essentials and put them in the house. They weren't comfortable moving completely in yet. After their experiences, Jessie and Bexar both agreed that they should be ready to immediately bug out. Eventually, they would load out the FJ with bug-out gear and have their day-to-day stuff in the house, but it would take time to build confidence in their location and that they wouldn't be overrun by some crazy local religious cult—which seemed to be a strong possibility in their post-normal world.

Sweat dripped from Bexar's face as he bent over to get another shovel of dirt. With the rest of their needs currently handled, security improvements moved to the top of the list. Most of the windows were covered with sandbags with small gaps to fire a rifle through, but now Bexar was trying to bag the doors, which took more effort. All Bexar knew about how to build fighting positions with sandbags is what he had seen in documentaries about war, so Bexar wasn't even sure if he was doing anything right. It looked good, but he wouldn't know.

Maybe I can get word to Chivo and he can visit to help. At the very least, he'll probably want to visit after the baby is born.

For the first time in months, since they had been in Big Bend with Jack and Sandra, Bexar felt himself relax slightly. He couldn't relax completely because of how their stay in Big Bend had ended, but Bexar hadn't felt hopeful since the very beginning. Hope was a powerful state of being, but it was also fragile, cracking, and failing to despair with alarming quickness.

The sun was already nearing the western horizon; this would be the first night in their new home. When they had purchased their home in Brazos County, they went and sat in their new house the day they closed on it with no furniture. Jessie and Bexar had brought folding chairs, ordered a pizza, and watched a movie on a laptop to celebrate becoming *real* adults while enjoying the first dinner and a movie in their new home. Well, that, and they christened their new bedroom together. Bexar heard Jessie coming through the house. She stepped into the open doorway, using the door frame for support and keeping the weight off her ankle. It was still swollen and a sickly yellow bruised color, but it was getting significantly better.

Jessie was completely nude with a hungry "come hither" look on her face. "Are you almost done, lover? I could use some of your help inside."

Bexar laid his shovel on the ground and walked to his impatiently waiting wife. "I'm nasty, dirty, and sweaty, baby."

"I'm prepared for that, sexy husband. Come inside and let me help you get cleaned up." Jessie tugged on Bexar's T-shirt, which clung to his body. Bexar peeled his shirt off and draped it over a low sandbag wall.

Jessie tugged at his belt buckle. "Your pants are dirty too. You should lay them out to dry in the sun with your shirt."

Bexar grinned widely and did as he was told before following his pregnant and limping wife inside, helping her walk back to their bedroom. Jessie had worked really hard on cleaning up the house while he had been outside working. It wasn't that he expected his wife to take care of housework, quite the opposite, but Jessie wasn't able to fill sandbags and do the outside work with her ankle still injured. Soon, thoughts of sandbags and Zeds melted from their minds as they once again christened a new home together, restarting their family.

Groom Lake, Nevada

Dusk settled across the dry lakebed. Andrew flew over the mountain range and descended toward the lake bed and runways, excited and anxious to be reunited with Oreo. With his mission done, he was going to pick up his four-legged friend and haul ass back to the SSC in the morning. Andrew noticed a large group of vehicles and people moving on the surface near the hangars, except that the hangars were demolished, most of the buildings were in ruins, and smoke billowed into the sky.

"What the fuck happened?"

Where the four large hangars and the entrance below ground had been was only a significantly large crater. A flash and then a glowing orange ball raced toward Andrew from the ground. He stared at it for a split second.

"Fuck!" Andrew opened the Husky's throttle all the way open, retracted the flaps, and dove toward the ground. The orange ball screamed past at an incredible speed just past his port side wingtip. Andrew banked hard away from the missile and dove further toward the ground, nearly skimming his tires on the ground. Flying south, Andrew's mind raced.

Area 51 is a fucking crater; did something explode underground? Did the Koreans kill it, but how? Who cares how? They just did...like a bunker-buster bomb from the Gulf War.

Then the realization that Oreo was most likely dead and buried in the pile of rubble washed over him. Anger burned deep in the pit of Andrew's being. He was angry at Lampton, angry at Chivo, and most of all, angry at himself. Tears streamed down his face, mingling with his beard. Andrew pulled up gently on the controls and climbed out of the lakebed area to clear the mountains. He didn't see any more ground forces and he couldn't see any other aircraft. He leveled off and reduced power to save fuel. He wasn't sure where to go, he couldn't think clearly at all, so he let his mind go blank in grief while his hands and feet flew the aircraft to some other destination he wasn't sure of yet.

SCC

Amanda sat by the radio with her dinner. Chivo was still topside with Eric working on forming a battle plan for the attack they were now sure was coming and maybe coming soon. The radio was buzzing with talk about Groom Lake. The shortwave radio broadcasts were interrupted earlier that day and the last transmission from Bill was that they were under siege by Chinese and Korean forces, but now they had gone dark. Amanda hoped it was due to their ability to transmit being broken or blocked, but in the pit of her stomach, she had a feeling that they were all dead. She had no idea why, but dread waved over her. They had no way to verify anything quickly. Some chatter from other survivors in the general area—still a day's travel away from Groom Lake though—said that they were going to go check it out and help if needed, but so far no one had taken the literal first step out their door.

Worried and also considering the survivability of her own underground facility, Amanda waited for a break in the radio traffic and keyed the warning that a message from POTUS was about to transmit. After a few moments, the buzzing and crackling chatter was silent, her radio humming pleasantly.

Amanda began keying her message. "SAFE BASE IN TEXAS—OPEN FOR ALL—CLEAN SAFE UNDERGROUND STOCKED MEDICAL..."

She continued with her transmission and announcement that the SSC was open for business and welcoming all survivors, followed by directions from I-35 to the main gate. She was now making a considerable effort to get survivors to come to the facility. If the PLA had successfully destroyed Groom Lake, they would need all the help they could get to prevent a scenario where they would be under siege. Amanda had a realization: the reason why Clint wanted to keep the facility closed and secret wasn't for her safety, but so it could be taken over by the PLA with no fight. So they could have control of the facility. They could abandon and try to destroy the facility or they could try to recruit fellow citizen survivors to fight for the survival of what was left of their country. Her realization came too late, as the second option was what had just started, assuming people would want to come here. There were a thousand metaphors about trains, balls rolling, and all sorts of other colorful expressions that described her situation, but none of them fully described the weight of what had just happened that day.

Amanda signed off the radio, stood, and heard the radio erupt with transmissions walking all over each other. She felt nauseous. Amanda took a deep breath and looked around. *I pray that this won't be a modern Alamo. I don't know who would be left to fight a new battle of San Jacinto if we fail.*

Nellis Air Force Base, Las Vegas, Nevada

Andrew wasn't sure why he flew southwest and past the Tonopah range. His mind was in a fog and he hadn't realized where he was until he saw the sprawling desert city stretch out in front of his windscreen. This was not a city he would have enjoyed visiting before the attack and now he had even less of a desire to do so. However, he needed fuel and would need to put down somewhere, even to just fuel and lift off again. The afternoon had slipped away and there were only a couple of hours until sunset, so he didn't have much time to waste.

The small yellow plane banked over the expansive runways of the large air force base. He could practically land on the width of the main runway with room to spare, so Andrew took his time to attempt clearing his head enough to figure out where to put down to be near unleaded fuel or AvGas. AvGas wouldn't be found unless there was a general aviation side of the airbase, which Andrew didn't think there was. That feeling was reinforced with his flyover. Andrew didn't see any general aviation aircraft or tanks or an FBO that he could notice at least. A truck driving fast across the northern end of the runways caught Andrew's attention. It was a military truck and looked like the ones that he had seen at Groom Lake with Aymond's crew. He watched it stop at a large hangar. After a few moments, the hangar doors opened, the truck drove in, and the doors shut behind them. It was almost like watching the Batmobile driving into the Batcave and at this point, Andrew didn't really care if he found hostiles. He was angry, and he was sad; he felt the need to take ridiculous chances and feel the rush of life as it adventured by instead of the pain and darkness he felt closing around him.

Andrew pulled power and descended toward the hangar. There were a few Zeds shambling through the flight line, but they weren't grouped together and didn't seem to be aroused by anything or anyone. Andrew knew that was about to change with the noise from his engine and prop as he landed. He turned toward the north and came back around for a short approach to land on the flight line instead of the runways. After turning onto final for landing, Andrew lowered the flaps and killed the engine. The propeller turned a few last slow revolutions before engine compression kept it from spinning anymore. The only sound Andrew could hear now was the soft rush and swish of the aircraft gliding through the air. Compared to the engine and propeller noise, this was like hitting the mute button.

Andrew set down with a gentle thud and stayed off the brakes to coast to a stop near the hangar he saw the truck go into. As he climbed out of his plane, he heard a voice sternly whisper, "Do not move or I will kill you."

"Can I turn around?"

"Sure, bud, but slowly with your hands out and away from your body."

Andrew turned slowly while he held his hands out away from his side. He recognized the Marine as one of the ones from Groom Lake, but couldn't remember his name. The Marine spoke first, "Pilot guy...Andrew, right?"

The Marine lowered his rifle. His chest carrier was spattered with blood, and it did not appear to be his own. "Is Oreo with you?"

"No, he was at Groom Lake with the others; we were just there trying to figure out how to help because they're under siege by the PLA. We're re-arming and coming up with a plan to go back."

"There's no use. It's a huge fucking crater now and the PLA are still there. They shot a fucking missile at me."

"Crater, like craters along the ground? That's OK, there should be survivors safe underground."

"No, crater. Singular. It looked like the shit from the first Gulf War TV footage of bunker-buster bombs."

"Shit...get inside. Wait, we need to get your neon yellow 'come fuck with us' sign out of the open and hidden. Let me get the doors. Do you need help pushing it?"

"No, I can..."Andrew stopped speaking; his frazzled-looking Marine friend had walked off at a quick pace. After getting ready, Andrew waited for a few moments for the hangar doors to begin opening before he started pushing his plane inside. As Andrew's eyes adjusted to the darkness, he saw a hurried mess of activity around an A-10. The hangar door rattled closed behind him. A person, a woman in a dirty-green flight suit, hunched under a wing, pointing to each mounting location and explaining something to another. The Marine from outside stood next to Aymond. Aymond looked exhausted and a little angry; he looked up and glanced at Andrew before walking toward him.

"Gonzo says you flew over Groom Lake after we had left to re-arm and regroup and can give us a bomb damage assessment. Major Pearce warned us that a bombing run appeared to be en route as we bugged out, but we felt a single hard shockwave on the backside of the mountains from the base and we have no idea what happened yet. We're about an hour out from getting pointed back toward Groom Lake."

Andrew shook his head. "I only saw one crater. It stretched from past the far runways toward the east and nearly to the mountains to the west. The center appeared to be where the hangar with below-ground access was and the crater was really deep. No idea how deep, but I wouldn't want to try to climb down it!"

"What about enemy forces?"

"They were near the crater and very active. They fired a missile at me that I barely avoided."

Aymond stood silently for a moment. "It wouldn't have been nuclear if the PLA were at the crater's edge. At least I don't think even the Koreans are evil enough to radiate their own forces for no reason...fuck!"

Andrew stood quietly for a moment, and Aymond shook his hand. "Glad you made it. Now check in with Jones and get to work; we need to move quickly."

Aymond walked off and toward the pilot. Another man waved Andrew toward where he stood near the front of the aircraft. A large cart with odd-looking equipment was apparently rearming the machine canon, which was the only way Andrew could think to describe it now that he saw the scale and size of it in person.

"Hey, welcome back to our merry band of mismatched warriors."

Andrew nodded, numb by all the sudden changes, tragedy, and the loss of Oreo.

"Well, since you're a pilot, I think you would be best used to assist the major and what she needs to get back in the air to chew up some Korean and Chinese ass."

Jones pointed toward Major Pearce, who was now half hanging out of her cockpit. Andrew looked up. "Uh, Major?"

"Just a second."

A few moments later, Pearce lifted herself out of the cockpit and back onto the platform pushed next to it. "Jones, nothing appears to have penetrated fully into the cockpit, the armor held, so that's a plus."

"Major, this is Andrew the pilot."

"Oh, hi. What do you fly? Are you in the service?"

"Hi there, Miss, uh, Major. I have a Husky and no, I'm a civilian pilot."

"A Husky...bush plane? You have it with you, here?"

"Yeah, I had been flying around the country looking for survivors and places to lay low for a while with Oreo, but got sidetracked helping the president take a scary dude up to Montana and back."

"Oreo? Is he your dog?"

"Yup, good guy, but I don't think he made it. Groom Lake is a fucking hole in the ground now."

"You flew over?"

"Yes, right before coming here, apparently right after you guys left. They shot a missile at me, luckily missed, and here I am."

"Andrew, you and I have a lot to talk about." Pearce began climbing down the platform. "Mr. Jones, I'll be back in a few minutes. You're doing great."

"Yes, ma'am."

Aymond walked up to Major Pearce and Andrew as they walked toward Andrew's plane. "Major, we're just about ready to roll."

"OK, I'll be wheels up in three hours, as planned, but I have an idea for Mr. Andrew here, if he's willing to do it."

Pearce laid out her plan, which Aymond liked and Andrew reluctantly agreed after a few moments of consideration. Flying at night wasn't high on his enjoyable activity list any longer, not with so much unknown, no lights on towers, no lights on runways or roads, and Zeds filling every shadow.

CHAPTER 18

Andrew banked lazily in the dark sky. High clouds obscured the moonlight but didn't interfere with Andrew's ability to see. He trimmed the aircraft and softly held the coordinated turn with one hand and one foot, while the other hand held up binoculars. The night optic that Andrew gave him to use lay in the bag in the back seat. The PLA had floodlights setup shining inwards toward the crater and buildings, as well as outwards from their own encampment. Multiple radar trucks like what Aymond had sat in a ring holding perimeter against the Zeds and boy were there a lot of Zeds; Andrew was amazed at the swath of death that churned in the dry lake bed. In all of his travels, Andrew hadn't seen a swarm with so many reanimated bodies. It looked like there were hundreds and hundreds of thousands of Zeds. There were also a lot of Zeds on the highway where Aymond had driven his truck through a while earlier. It's strange: outside of the major cities, the number of Zeds seemed to have diminished. His best guess was that they grouped up in herds and shambled through the country-side via major roadways (where the terrain was easier and open), but this was bizarre. Pearce and Aymond said that the PLA had dropped a massive piece of ordnance, much like what Andrew suspected as a bunker-buster type bomb, so maybe the tremendous shockwave had attracted every Zed who felt or heard the explosion? If that was the case, then it would be possible to setup Zed traps with radar trucks and began culling the greater Zed population of North America, but that was something he could discuss in the future. Right now, he was concerned with Aymond.

He knew roughly where Aymond and Gonzo would be, on which ridge east of Groom Lake, but it was impossible to see them in the darkness and shadows, especially since this was what they were good at, and they were expert warriors, operators in every sense of the word. He couldn't even find their large truck even though there was no vegetation to speak of.

Careful not to fly near Aymond, Andrew stayed toward the southwestern edge of the complex and scanned the lit moonscape of death below him. Andrew had a radio that was usually carried on someone's back wedged into his aircraft, the handset dropped over the back of his seat so he could reach and use it.

Andrew clicked the mic once; two clicks was the reply. He had just informed Aymond he was on station and Aymond replied that he understood. Aymond would break radio silence with specific reports for gun and bomb runs once it was time, but for now, they needed to remain hidden.

More Zeds streamed into the lakebed as Andrew peeled off to take up his station further south at a higher altitude. He climbed to nearly 10,000 feet AGL and resumed his station, making lazy figure-8s in the dark sky.

Andrew's radio crackled to life. It was Major Pearce who had just taken off from Nellis and was en route to Groom Lake. After making contact, Andrew gave a situational report with general troop and material position and numbers. In her cockpit, illuminated by dim red light, Pearce made notes and formulated her own battle plan in case Aymond didn't give her what she needed to rain steel on the assholes that killed her wingman.

The overall plan was that Aymond and Gonzo would recon the area and give specific courses of fire to Pearce and that Andrew was going to act as a radio relay and initial recon for Pearce. It wasn't glamorous and fit the role that airborne communication and radar systems typically filled, but it was significantly important to coordinate everyone with continuous radio contact, unlike last time.

Back at Groom Lake, Jones had everyone ready to drive off if they needed to. They were also ready to drop the trailers loaded with munitions and parts for Pearce's aircraft to haul ass to Groom Lake as a ragtag QRF.

A few minutes later, movement caught Andrew's eye below him and he could see the shadow of Pearce's A-10 flying low and ridiculously fast. His radio crackled to life. "I'm on station."

Radio silence for Aymond was over and he gave a mission brief and his requested course of fire. Inside her red-tinted cockpit, a faint, cold smile crept across her face, her professionalism keeping her from having more of an outward reaction. Major Pearce flexed her fingers and made ready. Aymond scanned the southern ridgeline, watching for the most beautiful ugly aircraft he had ever seen, and he couldn't find it until a faint silhouette erupted from the ground shadows. The aircraft climbed hard and steep before winging over and pointing nose down. Fire belched from the plane's maw like a fiery tongue of death, screaming angry terror to the troops and equipment below.

Zeds swarmed thickly around the PLA lines, thick flies buzzing in a heavy cloud above the Zeds. The flies looked like static in the night optics that Aymond was wearing. The PLA had poor light discipline; they had large flood lights shining out and away from their encampment, showing all the zeds and any enemy forces that might try to approach. They obviously did not expect an air attack.

Pearce banked over and peeled off, diving for the lakebed. Chafe and flares dropped from the underside of the Hog while two missiles streaked toward her in a burst of trailing flame. Gonzo was waiting for that moment. His big .50-caliber rifle barked twice in relatively quick succession. Everyone who he saw with a SAM or who launched one was going to die.

Andrew called out movement and damage assessments from high above the lakebed, the need to relay radio transmissions being moot with Pearce on station and in radio range of Aymond. Major Pearce climbed and banked over for another run. Gonzo scanned the ground forces and fired three more times, after one of which a missile fired harmlessly skyward for a flash of time before detonating just a few yards off the ground, which appeared to kill many PLA near the blast. As the A-10 banked back over and began firing, two of the radar trucks exploded in a shower of fire. Instead of banking away, Pearce leveled her dive and released some of the gravity bombs she had under her wings.

More chafe, more flares, and another missile that streaked up, attempting to meet her. Aymond estimated troop strength at approximately 1,500 men and that the Zeds on the lakebed had to number at least 100 times that much. More zeds continued to stream through the mountains and desert to the dry lakebed. Gonzo switched magazines and killed the offender who had fired the latest missile. It was the scariest thing Aymond had ever seen. The sight of all of those Zeds chilled him deep within his bones.

"I have enough for one more, over," Pearce's voice crackled over the radio.

"Roger. Northeast quadrant and I think you'll have made their situation unrecoverable, over," Aymond replied.

After Pearce's positive reply, Aymond caught a glimpse of her aircraft across the mountains to the west as she setup for her last run before heading back to Nellis to re-arm and reassess their next move. The A-10 banked over and the main gun erupted, the sound echoing off the sky and ground around them. Pearce was angry. She wanted revenge more than anything else she had wanted before in her life. She pulled the nose up and began to release the last of her gravity bombs as three plums of fire streaked from the middle of the PLA forces. Flares and chafe fell from the aircraft as she banked it hard to the right and dove for the lakebed. Gonzo worked his rifle fast and hard to kill the men who launched at her. Aymond watched the dark silhouette of Pearce's aircraft through his night optics and squinted as he saw the bright plume of fire from the rocket motor come into frame. The explosion temporary blinded his night optic, but it recovered just in time for Aymond to see Pearce's aircraft tumble out of the sky; the entire starboard side wing appeared to have been destroyed. Major Pearce and her aircraft cart-wheeled across the dry lakebed in a ball of fire. The major was dead.

"Fuck." Aymond keyed the radio. "Andrew, Pearce is KIA, get to Nellis and organize the men to bug out; we no longer need any A-10 equipment. We will rendezvous near the halfway point and convoy to Texas. It's time for us to get to Firebase Bravo."

Andrew acknowledged the order and flew toward Nellis while Aymond and Gonzo watched the pandemonium below. Their plan had worked, the PLA lines had collapsed, Zeds flooded into their camp, and there was a complete loss of order. All but one of the radar trucks had survived to this point, but Gonzo was sure to put that one down for good, too.

"That sucks."

"Shit happens. OK, Gonzo, see if we can find any remaining leadership and put a stop to any attempt for PLA to reorganize."

Below them on the lakebed, it was complete chaos. Aymond was sure that eventually their ragtag tactic of taking out the PLA radar trucks with sniper fire and creating a confusing situation would stop working, but he was pleased that it still worked for them. He wasn't sure how he could help secure the SSC from an attack like the one at Groom Lake, except to hope that the lake above the core of the facility is enough to create problems for any munitions that the Koreans and Chinese could throw at it. He had no idea; Aymond's expertise was one of an alpha meat-eater, an apex predictor of evil men and not that of fortifying underground bunkers.

The eastern horizon glowed angrily in their night optics; it was time for Aymond and Gonzo to get out of dodge. Thirty minutes later, the pair had left the view of the dry lakebed and made it back to their M-ATV. The sound of sporadic gunfire grew slower and less frequent, which was music to Aymond's ears. That meant that there were few survivors and they were hopefully running low on ammo and very high on Zeds.

Near Hillsboro, Texas

Ken walked the property. Keith was up and tending to his grow house, and Carl was still sleeping in. The three of them stayed up too late the previous night drinking homemade wine while Ken's new friends smoked a copious amount of pot. He couldn't tell why, but Ken liked his new friends. The plan this afternoon was to return to his pickup and retrieve the rest of his gear and supplies. Carl talked about trying to get the truck back to their homestead so they could repair it for him. If they were nice enough to do that, then he might be on his way to the SSC sooner than he thought, except that he still didn't know exactly where it was. Neither Carl nor Keith knew either. They did think that they had what Ken needed to build them a radio, though. To top it off, the radio could run on the electricity they generated with renewable energy here on their homestead. They really had a veritable Garden of Eden in the middle of Texas; Sam Houston would have been proud. Maybe. Ken wasn't sure how the hero of Texas would react to marijuana, but it wasn't really popular back in 1836, so maybe it would have been OK.

Ken shook his head and kept on his rambling morning walk, while he tried to think through the things that mattered most to his survival. He hadn't left his hunting lease that long ago and he had already been shot at and been overrun by Zeds twice, which required someone to save him twice. *Perhaps*, Ken thought, *I shouldn't try to go to the SSC at all, but I could stay with Keith and Carl, maybe find a job I can do to help their trio-tribe of survivors.* Going outside the wire obviously was very dangerous to do alone.

The idea of staying with his new friends sounded better and better with every passing minute and by the time Ken had come back to the farmhouse, his mind was made up. He would ask to stay for a while, help around the farm, build them a radio, and possibly work on repairing his truck.

CHAPTER 19

Bexar stood on the roof of their house. He was sure that the sandbags were terrible for the shingles, but he didn't really care. Bexar was trying to improve the drainage of rainwater from the roof and direct more of that water to the water-collection barrels he had at every gutter downspout. A local co-op and some tractor supply stores gave him all the heavy-duty bags he needed to finish building up his bride's castle. The FJ barely ran; enough time had lapsed that all the gasoline had really begun to go bad. He was mostly sure that bad fuel had gunked up the carburetor. Since no one was making any more fuel or oil, much less drilling and pumping for oil, Bexar knew that their days of easy vehicle-based travel was behind them. During his scavenging excursions, he noticed a significant uptick in Zed activity in the last six weeks, but he didn't know why. It didn't really matter since they were far enough off the highways and off main roads that it seemed the roaming herds of Zeds didn't come close enough to be lured into their homestead.

The idea to find a diesel-powered vehicle had occurred to Bexar, in that diesel fuel should last longer than unleaded, especially unleaded with ethanol in it, but he decided it really didn't matter. They were still able to drive the FJ for a little longer, even if it ran like shit, then after that they would simply live on their homestead and make their lives matter for their soon-to-be-born child.

It was still hot outside; not the 100F weather they had during August, but the first real cold fronts of the year were still a couple of weeks away. They were ready for the cold. The sandbags added a lot of insulation and Bexar had gathered more than enough firewood for the entire winter's worth of heating and cooking. He had even found a wood-burning stove and installed it in the kitchen. The electric range sat out in the yard in the "could be useful parts" pile of almost-trash.

Jessie waved from by the barn. It was almost lunchtime and then Bexar would need to finish up his daily chores to get ready for nightfall. Poor Jessie looked miserable; she could give birth any day now, any minute really, and she looked beyond ready. He wished he could take photos of his wonderful bride. She might feel miserable and horribly pregnant, but Bexar had never seen a more beautiful woman. She glowed and radiated beauty. His beard was thick and longer than it had ever been. Jessie hadn't shaved her legs, or anything else for that matter, in months (she had surprised him for his birthday by shaving), and Bexar felt like this was what their lives should be. He was happier now than he could remember in his adult life.

The fall garden turned out to be more difficult than they had thought, but they had quite literally every seed of everything that Bexar could find at the garden supply in town on one of the weekly, sometimes twice weekly, scavenging excursions away from their ranch. It was a nice change of pace though. The summer was a hard transition, especially with no air conditioning or electric fans. This coupled with the Texas heat and a pregnant wife, Bexar was surprised that he lived through August. Tomorrow's plan was to assemble the new bicycles that he had out in the barn. Still in the boxes, Bexar had four bikes, two mountain-bike-type bicycles for him and Jessie, a utility trike with a cargo basket that could be really useful, and a child's bike. From their best guess for Jessie's due date and what the current date was, they would have their baby any day now. Jessie's projected due date was the 28th, but that was a guess. Also Keeley was born early, not that this baby was going to be the same as Keeley. Regardless, Bexar had a literal room full of diapers that he had spent most of the summer scavenging. All sizes ranging from newborn to pull-up-style training diapers. Wipes, clothes, all of it was stored and cached in large quantities; the only thing that they were really concerned about was baby formula. Most of the formula they had was in date, but they didn't have long and the formula would begin going out of date. Cow's milk or any fresh milk besides Jessie's breast milk was an impossible dream for them. To bridge the gap, Bexar had found and scavenged a serious quantity of powdered milk and condensed milk in cans. He worked quite hard this summer to prep for the fall and winter and the new baby. Bexar knew that once Jessie gave birth that he wouldn't be able to take long scavenging trips into the surrounding cities and that the fuel they had available would be going bad, which was why he had searched for and found the bicycles. Bexar cleaned out a bicycle shop, tires, helmets, inner tubes, chains, tools, a work stand...all of it was in the garage. He would make a work area to service their bicycles, but that was tomorrow and he needed to focus on today.

The breeze carried a faint sound that seemed familiar, but distant and incorrect. It took Bexar a moment to remember what it was.

"Jessie, get back in the barn! Aircraft coming!"

Jessie turned and ducked into the shadows of the barn. Bexar scrambled to get off the roof and under cover so he wouldn't be seen. It dawned on Bexar that the property would be really obvious when seen from the air. Anyone would be able to tell that someone was living there and making improvements. He really wasn't sure how to continue to make improvements and live without it looking like he was making improvements and that a family lived there. The engine noise grew louder. It didn't sound like a jet, but it didn't sound like a helicopter either. Now on the ground and hidden under the shadow of the front porch, Bexar waited anxiously. Soon, a small yellow aircraft flew over at a low altitude as it passed over the ranch, the wings seeming to save back and forth as if the pilot was saying "Hi."

As soon as it all had begun, it was over, and the plane was gone. Bexar came out of the shadows as Jessie came out of the barn.

"Who was that?"

"No idea. Maybe it was that guy that showed up to Groom Lake. Wasn't his plane yellow?"

"I mean, what are the chances of that, Bexar?"

"I don't know. Not a lot of aircraft out flying around nowadays and we are near the SSC, so maybe it isn't that odd of an idea."

Jessie winced and rubbed her pregnant belly.

"Feeling OK? You should go sit down."

"No, I'll be even more uncomfortable sitting down. I forgot how bad this last trimester sucked with Keeley."

"It'll be over soon."

"No, it'll all begin soon. We're about to get really busy, but at least neither of us will have to go back to work again and leave our baby in daycare."

With a sharp intake of breath, Jessie grabbed her belly and winced again. A moment later, the contraction passed, and it left Jessie panting.

"Jesus, that was a big one. I think we're going to have a baby very..."

Jessie didn't finish the sentence, another contraction waving over her body. Bexar grabbed his wife by the shoulders and helped steady her. Once the contraction was over, he began helping her inside the house.

"Oh God, my water broke." Bexar saw that Jessie's loose athletic pants were soaked and smiled before giving Jessie a gentle kiss on her forehead.

"I love you, baby. You can do this, we can do this; I'll be with you and we're about to meet our son."

"You mean our daughter."

Bexar kissed his wife again and helped her to the bed. They had a birthing plan, for all the good it would do them, but Bexar was committed to trying to stick close to that plan so Jessie wouldn't be stressed about it.

SSC

Andrew taxied to his spot and shut down the engine. After climbing out, one of the topside workers helped him push the yellow Husky back into the open-top hangar bay made out of walls of sandbags and cinderblocks. After thanking the man, Andrew walked to the entrance and began down the ladder to the underground facility. He had ended up here after flying around the country for a couple of months

The SSC was being run nothing like Groom Lake had been. Aymond implemented a command structure within the survivor groups that had taken residence at the facility. Instead of towns and mayors, civilians were organized into different-sized groups that eventually structured down to four-person "crews." It was a basic variation of a fire team and platoon structure from the Marine Corps, but so far, it had really worked. There were nearly200 people, civilians, military, and even some kids living and working at the facility now. Bill was dead, but another survivor who understood radios arrived a few weeks after Amanda had sent out her welcoming message, so he was placed in charge of all communications. It seemed like for most of their needs, a person with that skill set would arrive. It wasn't perfect, but it was so much better than they could have expected. Some of the survivors were from Texas, but some of them were from as far away as Maine and even Mexico.

After checking in with Bob, who was working door security that shift, Andrew walked into the main facility to make his way to Amanda's office. He reported directly to her. After knocking and waiting for a response, Andrew walked into her office and found Chivo already sitting on a stool in the corner. The Oval Office it was not, in fact, it was fairly small, besides having been constructed in a typical square shape.

"What do you have for us, Andrew?"

"Another survivor homestead that we should check out."

"OK, then why not give the information to the survivor contact team?" Chivo asked.

"Something is strange about this one. The entire home looked fortified, like covered completely in sandbags and built up with them too, like a fortress."

"Huh," Amanda began. "We've made contact with similar groups; what is so special about this one?"

Andrew took out his map and showed them roughly where the home was located in relation to where the SSC was. After some lively discussion, it was decided that Chivo would take whatever he felt was necessary and would check it out himself. There wasn't a lot of urgency, except that between Andrew's flying and the security patrols conducting recon in the surrounding area, they had noticed a serious uptick in Zed activity. It was like something was moving large numbers of Zeds in place in the region, which they assumed would be the PLA and that it wasn't just a coincidence. Figuring that some survivors might be caught unaware, they tried to make contact with groups to see if they could use any help, any food, any medical supplies, or weapons. Amanda knew that not everyone would want to be in a community bunker, but she was committed to helping every last one of her fellow citizens.

Near Hillsboro, Texas

Carl came into the barn. Ken was working on the filtering in the process to convert old nasty cooking oil into bio-diesel. "Hey, Ken, there was an airplane, man."

He nearly had to shout it, as the pumps made a lot of noise. Ken held up a finger to say "just a minute" and walked with Carl toward the door. Once outside and with his earplugs out, Carl repeated himself.

"Really? What kind of plane?"

"Small, man. Yellow."

"Like a private plane, not a military aircraft?"

"Yeah, Ken. How cool is it that someone is tooling around in an aircraft? Like Truman Sparks, man."

Carl was baked, but that was normal. Ken wasn't sure he had ever seen his friend not stoned. Ken realized that he didn't care; Carl was brilliant and a good friend. It was odd having personal epiphanies this late in life in a situation Ken could never have imagined.

"Ken, are you going to plot it and see if it is one of theirs?"

"Yeah, in a minute." Ken went inside and checked on the filtration process then decided to let the pumps run on a timer. They didn't leave the process unattended very often, but Ken figured he would only be gone a few minutes. A few moments later, Ken and Carl stood in the dining room inside the house, both standing in front of a large Texas map mounted on the wall. A red push pin was placed where the homestead was and another red push pin had been placed where the SCC was. On the table, the spark gap radio that Ken had built for them stood silent. He would check on the net tonight after his daily chores and dinner was done. Carl picked up a glass pipe sitting on the table, filled the small bowl with ground marijuana he kept in a pouch in his pocket, and began smoking.

"So, is it, man?"

Ken pulled a string from the red push pin at their location along the path that Carl said the plane had traveled; it led right to the SSC.

"It is." Ken picked up a notebook by the radio and jotted down some notes about the plane, location, and direction. Right now, they may not any use for the information, but it could be useful in the future. Regardless, Ken kept meticulous notes of sightings and meetings with other survivors. Survivor activity around the SSC had picked up considerably, which they knew from the radio traffic, but also from encountering refugees of the new world trying to make their way to the no-longer-secret underground facility.

Months ago, Ken decided that his test phase was over and that he was going to stay with Ken and Carl and not worry about trying to get to the SSC unless he needed to. These old hippies, surprisingly to Ken, seemed to be a much better fit for him and made him more comfortable than the group that had saved him further south. That feeling was reinforced over the past few months as the other survivor group had not survived a mutiny attempt. About half of the survivors in that group had died and the rest scattered to the wind. The secured facility with all the metal shipping containers was partially destroyed in their battle for leadership. Followed by Groom Lake being destroyed by some sort of Chinese and Korean bomb, the idea of hiding in a hole in the ground for the PLA to find and kill him or to be caught up in some survivor dick-waving contest did not appeal to Ken at all. He found a lot of peace and was quite content to live with his hippies on their compound and have a peaceful life.

The radio traffic sealed the deal for Ken. Survivors around the country, but mostly near the west coast, had begun radioing PLA sightings. Those had begun sporadically, but that all changed about six weeks ago. Those sightings grew into continual reconnaissance with some survivors trailing company-sized formations of Korean and Chinese forces as they worked their way across the countryside. Most of those trailing recon teams reported that any survivors that were encountered were killed. Also, the PLA's fighting style relied heavily upon the use of radar trucks, which anyone with a spark gap radio knew about in full detail now. Someone at the SSC had transmitted instructions on how to kill one of those radar trucks along with other instructions on how to operate one and what to do if you have the chance to steal one.

With the SSC's encouragement, a low-intensity conflict had begun with survivors banding together in loose mostly unorganized groups that led harass-ment raids on the invading forces. Trucks, vehicles, parts, food, weapons, and ammo were all stolen from supply convoys or recovered from killed forces. Ken knew how well-motivated people could be against an organized professional military force; he had experienced it all too well from the other side of the line.

Pecos, Texas

The date of Erin and Jason's invasion of the now foreign world above them had arrived. The calendar that hung on the wall had the days of the month crossed out with the corrected dates written in their place. There was nothing special about the date; it was just one they chose for being about the right time to head down to Big Bend for the weather. They were close, too, only a few hours to the north, at most a two-day drive from the park. The MRAP was fully fueled. They found that the facility had massive underground tanks of diesel fuel and jet fuel of some type. Neither of them knew much about it and didn't really care, except that the diesel was apparently treated because it still ran really well in their big armored truck.

Most of their day-to-day lives were spent below ground, but both of them made it a point to get topside for at least a few hours a week. They hadn't at first and the lack of sunlight and full-time living underground had really wrecked their emotional health. After some weeks of living in an emotional hell, Jason went topside to go scavenge for some liquor and maybe some drugs to help them cope and found that being in the sun had dramatically improved his mood. He recharged in the basking glow of sunlight, as it were, before returning below ground to retrieve Erin after he had found and raided a nearby trailer home for cheap booze. She was in a foul mood, but after a drink and a couple of hours of sunlight, Erin was feeling better. They sat on the roof of the MRAP at the end of the runway and watched the sunset before going back below ground that day. That was four weeks ago, the day that they decided to make a drastic change and leave for Big Bend. Erin had decided on the former National Park instead of heading back east to where she was from because of a few reasons. She knew how fucked everything out in Tennessee was and she knew what Jessie had told her about Big Bend and the area. If even half of the improvements that they had made while Jessie and Bexar had been in the park were still there, then Erin and Jason would be living on easy street. If those improvements were destroyed, they would still have a place to live with water and food to hunt or gather, far removed from population centers, far away from the interstates, and hopefully far away from the growing war.

The heavy truck shook slightly from the rumble of the big diesel motor, the exhaust echoing throughout the pristine concrete floor and ceiling. Slowly, the drive opened, rising out of the ground, sunlight crept into the darker space. A few moments later, they drove up the ramp, across the old airfield, and onto I-20 to head toward Highway 285 and south toward Ft. Stockton and onward to Big Bend.

"Stop!"

Jason slammed on the brakes and the MRAP shuddered to a stop. Jason scanned the area and his mirrors, looking for what Erin had seen to cause her to call a stop. Jason couldn't see anything.

"What is it, baby?"

"Jason, I don't...I mean.... Damnit, I'm worried about Jessie. She is due any day or had the baby or will soon. I need to know before we settle down for good."

"So we're going back to Groom Lake?"

Erin sat silently for a moment, the MRAP sitting stationary in the middle of the road on I-20 and a handful of Zeds beginning to take an interest in the rumbling, rattling intruder.

"No," Erin said quietly. "I fucking hate that place."

After another moment of silence, Erin continued. "Let's go to Dallas. We can ask them, they can ask Groom Lake, and then we can point to Big Bend. It'll probably only be an extra few days on the road."

"As you wish."

Jason turned the truck around and pointed eastbound. "You'll need to get the maps out and plot a route for us."

"I'm on it," Erin excitedly replied. She leaned over and gave him a kiss on the cheek. Jason was her favorite person in the world and she was thankful to have him by her side.

CHAPTER 20

"Madam President, we have received reports of PLA activity in our area."

One of the radiomen had come in from the radio shack to the control room, which is what everyone had taken to calling the main operations room that Amanda had been using since she first came to the SSC. In this case, the radioman was a radio woman named Sarah, a survivor from the Houston area that had somehow survived getting out of Houston, which from all accounts is a complete loss and overrun by the dead.

"What are the details, Sarah?"

"Ma'am, there appears to be a company-sized detachment heading north, roughly following I-35 from near the Austin area. Our contacts around Waco haven't seen or heard them yet."

"OK, let me know when the Waco tripwire triggers."

Sarah said she would and excused herself. Amanda picked up a handheld radio. "Chivo, over."

The radio crackled. "This is Chivo. Go ahead, Farmer, over."

"Check in with Control once you've finished topside, over."

"Roger, out."

Chivo was topside inspecting the current round of improvements. They had worked tirelessly to build concentric rings of security around the facility. It wouldn't hold an invading force forever, but it would slow them down enough to try to repel them. A few minutes later, Chivo walked into the control room wearing his full tactical loadout, armor, weapons, and magazines.

"Good morning, Madam President."

"Cut the shit, Goat."

Chivo cracked a rare smile. Amanda was the president, but she had also become his close friend.

"OK, Amanda, what's up?"

"PLA. Report just came in that they are headed this way following I-35 from around Austin, supposedly company strength of fighters."

"What about Waco?"

"Nothing yet. I want you to move up our timetable, get the completed security rings locked down, and get us ready."

"Roger that. We're nearly there already."

Amanda nodded. Chivo turned to exit and complete his task.

"Oh, Chivo?"

Chivo stopped and faced Amanda. "Yes?"

"Go make contact with those new survivors Andrew found. I think they're pretty close to being in the path."

"Can do. I think our security comes first, though."

"I agree, but don't task this one out. I want you to make contact.... I have an odd feeling about them and I don't know why."

Chivo flashed a thumbs up and replied in Spanish with a smile before leaving.

Amanda sat back and smiled at her computer screen. Chivo was an odd duck and she felt privileged that he considered her a friend. She felt like with Chivo as a friend, nothing bad could ever happen to her.

Outside of Waxahachie

The frantic, full-voiced cries that only a newborn can make filled the house. Jessie was exhausted. She had labored the entire night and just after sunrise, their daughter was born. They named her Scout Sandra Reed after one of their favorite books and one of their favorite people, who had died in Big Bend. After some difficulty latching, baby and Momma were learning each other and Scout's feedings improved.

They didn't have any of the big mesh panties and giant liners that the labor and delivery nurses at the hospital would use post birth for the mother, so Bexar had thick towels in place to attempt to contain the bleeding and discharge after giving birth. Jessie was sore, exhausted, and glowing with the glow that only a mother has immediately after giving birth.

Bexar had no camera, no way to take pictures, no way to share them, no way to make a baby book. No, all Bexar had was his ability to focus and hopefully remember these moments. He watched his daughter feed, and his wife smiled and talked softly to Scout while she caressed the tiny body. They didn't even know how much Scout weighed or how long she was. It didn't matter; Scout was beautiful. Bexar gently touched his newborn daughter and silently made a promise to her with the memory of digging Keeley's grave repeating again and again in his mind. Bexar promised would make sure she lived and had the chance to grow up. No matter what, no matter the consequences, Scout would survive.

North of Hillsboro, Texas

A high-pitched whistle caught Ken's attention. He stood outside the barn, waiting to go back inside to continue his chores. Looking around, he took his hearing protection off and heard the faint whistle grow quickly into a loud, piercing scream.

"Oh.... OH! FUCKING INCOMING!"

Ken ran toward the barn and slammed his body against the building, curled into a ball, and covered his head. Flashes in his mind, he felt like he was back on a hilltop in Vietnam.

"Fuck, fuck, fuck..."

Ken opened his mouth and waited from the crunch. He felt it more than he heard it. Disorientated, he looked up and saw part of the house was collapsed and smoking, quickly catching fire.

Another whistle and another, mortar rounds were falling and he wasn't able to get away from it. Keith and Carl never made any trenches or fighting positions and now Ken felt like a fool for not making them.

Carl lay in the open near the house, face down and not moving. Blood began to darken the dirt around him. Another round fell on the house and then the third. The house was in complete ruins. Keith had been inside and Carl was now very obviously dead to never rise again. Ken grabbed his rifle and looked at the old Mercedes before jumping to his feet and sprinting toward it. As he climbed into the car and the diesel engine rattled to life, the barn was struck by a round, which must have been an HE round because the entire thing exploded in a ball of fire. All of the bio-diesel in process and in storage added to the explosion. All the windows in the car shattered. Ken didn't slow down, he had to escape; it was his only chance at life. He took the butt of his rifle and knocked out the windshield so he could see and kept driving.

All he could do now was flee toward the SSC and hope he made it. In the car, he had his rifle, his pistol, and one bandolier of ammo and nothing. Ken felt royally fucked, fleeing for his life!

Near Italy, Texas

Jason stood on the roof of the MRAP and scanned their path. Their simple plan was once again ruined by the world they live in. The previous evening, they had stumbled across a small PLA force and they began loosely tailing them. This was trouble of the nth degree and as much as Erin and Jason wanted to point toward Big Bend and never look back, they both knew that they couldn't. Besides, their desire was to drive to the SSC to find out about Jessie and her baby. Even then it was most likely a losing proposition to try to fight such a well-organized invading force, following a smaller contingency of soldiers seemed less risky somehow. Really, they would love to flee and hide, but they could barely keep themselves from the cold, dead grasp of dead hands. If the PLA won, then there would eventually be nowhere safe to hide and it would be too late to fight. They didn't really have much of a plan except that they wanted to see where the PLA was headed and what they were doing. Erin and Jason thought that they could take that information to the SSC and it could be helpful.

They took shifts during the night to pull security and to watch the PLA forces. Even with three of those radar trucks creating a safe zone, the 25 soldiers Jason counted didn't seem to be active at night and only seemed to move during the day. Jason took that as the PLA being just as scared of the Zeds as they were, even though they had made them and created this whole shitstorm. It all seemed fairly crazy to Jason, and he hoped that it at least made sense to someone; otherwise, what was the point?

The eastern horizon glowed; sunrise would be in about 20 minutes. It was time to get Erin up and be ready to roll. It took two hours past sunrise for the soldiers to finally finish whatever it was they were doing and get moving. Erin and Jason were quite far away and couldn't see much detail, just some movement and the shape of their vehicles. The MRAP was parked behind a building and by sitting on the roof, Jason was able to use binoculars and observe more detail. They hadn't noticed them, so Jason figured his amateur tactics were working. He had never served in the military, but he had fought a deranged cult in Colorado. Strangely, the PLA didn't scare him as badly as the cult had.

The PLA convoy comprised nine vehicles, the three radar trucks and six APCs that had mounted weapons. To Jason, it reminded him of what he saw on the TV in places like Eastern Europe during conflicts; it was very surreal. They also drove surprisingly slow. The convoy was led by one of the radar trucks, with another in the middle and the other on the end. As they approached groups of Zeds, the undead would fall to the ground motionless and without a sound. That worked great except that they would swerve back and forth to go around all the bodies. If the lead truck had something like a plow blade on the front of it, then Jason thought the trucks could drive straight through. The visual gave Erin and Jason a long laugh.

Eventually, the convoy stopped outside of Waxahachie. The SSC was further north, and they waited. This was earlier in the day that they had stopped than the day before. It was only noon and there were hours left in the day. About a half hour later, another similarly sized convoy of PLA soldiers and vehicles arrived from the south. Now 50 strong, the convoy formed up with all six of the radar trucks and headed north toward the SSC. Trailing behind the second group were what appeared to be hundreds of Zeds, if not thousands. A dark black cloud of flies writhed and churned in the air above them, obscuring their view.

"Do you think that more will join up if they're going to attack the SSC?" Erin asked.

"I would think so, but maybe they're not going after the SSC. Maybe they're an advance force to prepare for that battle? I mean, they could zap all those Zeds following them and it's like they're leading them somewhere on purpose." Jason shrugged with his statement. He didn't know, but neither did Erin. They didn't really cover battle tactics in John Wayne's war movies, which were some of Jason's favorites.

SSC

"Alright, mano, just an easy meet and greet, but we have to be cool. Andrew said the homestead has been fortified with sandbags and maybe more."

Gonzo nodded; this wasn't their first rodeo or even their dozenth. They had become the community outreach coordinators of sorts, which was right in line with what Chivo had done most of his special forces career. Gonzo had similar experiences and training, even though his typical mission profile as a MARSOC Marine was a little different; he knew how to handle himself quite well. Regardless, this was an odd mix of feeling like traveling through war-torn Afghanistan while making peace with local leaders to build alliances and what a police officer would call a "knock and talk" with a suspicious home.

They climbed into the M-RAP and drove up the ramp on the northern end of the lake. These routes were well known to both of them, as was the surrounding countryside. Soon, they were rumbling down the road toward their day's mission. The topside improvements were coming along very nicely with security in place behind well-built fighting positions. The war was coming to them; it was only a matter of time.

The procedure that Gonzo and Chivo had established was a simple one: they would park a safe distance away and hump it to a good observation area so they could remain unnoticed. If after being watched and observed Chivo felt like they could make contact, they would walk from their observation post to the homestead and attempt contact. If they both felt it was unsafe to do so, they would wait and make contact in a neutral location outside of the homestead. Assuming the people left their compound, which they all almost always do.

The homestead in question was only a few miles away from the SSC and Chivo was surprised that they hadn't seen it yet, but there were still pockets of survivors that hide well. Overall, the response has been positive, the majority of survivors opting to come join their community of survivors underground. The process has been a huge boon for President Lampton's plan. All sorts of people with all different backgrounds had joined their community, including a couple of farmers who happily took over the farming operations topside. They were hoping to have their first good winter crop in a couple of months. It was all very exciting and gave everyone a lot of hope. Things were going much smoother under Aymond's steady leadership than it had at Groom Lake with a hodgepodge of people trying to do their best, which wasn't good enough. Chivo had real hope for the survival of everyone there, assuming that the PLA couldn't drop ordnance that would penetrate the lake and continue more than 50ft below that through layers of what he thought would be reinforced concrete.

An hour later, Gonzo pulled to a stop below the ridgeline of a hilltop in the middle of a pasture. An old oak tree stood defiant to the changes that had occurred around it during the past 75 years. The tree also broke up the silhouette of the armored truck, which was more than they would have anywhere else in farm country. After a harrowing experience a few months prior, the two of them were much more cautious when trying to make first contact with survivors.

They were approximately three miles from the homestead and according to their topographical maps, they would only have to cross one creek before reaching the hill that they would use as their observation post. The sun hadn't reached directly overhead yet and they still had half the day's sunlight left to get their mission completed. The sky was clear and the temperature outside felt to be in the low 80s, perfect weather to be topside and working.

I-35, North of Hillsboro

Ken pulled behind a ravaged truck stop, sat quietly for a moment, attempted slow his breathing, and attempted to control his runaway thoughts. Back in the 1970s, they didn't call it PTSD, but that is what he had battled his entire life. Mostly, he did OK, especially the last 20 years, but since the fall of society and the rise of the dead, the PTSD was particularly bad, bad enough that he was experiencing flashbacks. Smells were the worse. The smell of burning flesh and HE mortar rounds spun his mind back to a dozen different hilltops he fought for, was hurt for, and lost friends for in Southeast Asia. After a few more deep breaths, Ken pulled the Mercedes forward, out from between two abandoned semi-trailers and back toward I-35 before slamming on the brakes and waiting.

On the interstate, he saw a dozen APCs and some odd trucks that had large radar panels on them. What was odd was that the radar panels were up and appeared to be in operation while the trucks were driving. Ken estimated the convoy to be traveling about 35 mph northbound and wondered if it was the same element that had attacked his home and killed Keith and Carl. Trailing the convoy was a massive herd of Zeds, a staggeringly large cauldron of death moving and flowing while following, like some perverse mice of death following a magical flute.

Ken dug around in the car and found a handful of hand-rolled joints in the glove box, took one out, and lit it. He took a deep pull while watching the PLA continue past before he broke into a coughing fit. Ken had never tried marijuana until recently with Carl and it was the first time in his life since returning from Vietnam that the pain and images slowed down and relaxed their grip on his psyche. Now he understood why so many people swore by pot for their mental health.

He continued to sit there, after finishing the joint, for about 10 minutes after the PLA convoy had passed and the following Zeds began to taper off before he had a noble thought.

If that convoy is going to the SSC, then they should be ready for the attack, but if that was the same group that attacked his homestead unprovoked, then others are in serious danger.

Anger swelled up from the pit of his stomach and Ken knew what had to happen. He closed his eyes and said a prayer before accelerating out of the parking lot and toward I-35. He wouldn't let another survivor die without retaliation.

Accelerating sharply, Ken pushed the old deep-fryer-grease-smelling diesel wagon to 50 mph, which was much faster than he would have normally of traveled, but the PLA left a swath of dead Zeds in their wake. The radar trucks appeared to kill off all the Zeds within range, so Ken decided he could take the chance. He would follow the convoy and engage in harassing attacks until he could get the intel to the SSC and President Lampton. Ken had never felt so focused and sure of what he had to do in his life as he did at this moment.

This, Ken thought, *was what I was meant to do. I was meant to save his fellow citizens from the same fate as my friends.*

Near Waxahachie, Texas

Jason parked the big MRAP under a lean-to that housed two ancient-looking tractors. Erin was already wearing her normal tactical loadout, vest carrier, pistol, magazines, drop pouch, and other things in addition to her M4 rifle. Jason had his normal loadout with his shotgun, but he also carried an extra 100rounds of ammunition for the big .50-caliber rifle that Erin had thrown over her shoulder. That was a huge number of rounds and they were heavy, but they decided that when the convoy stopped, they would do their best to destroy the vehicles and kill anyone who appeared to be a leader before killing every last one of the invading assholes they could.

The PLA had stopped a short distance away from a farm that had a house and a barn along with a couple of lean-to-type structures. The PLA formed a protective circle with their vehicles in an inner circle and the radar trucks placed on points outside of that. Two rings of protection from the Zeds they brought to the party and any attacks. Erin shifted focus and peered through the binoculars at the teams setting up mortar tubes. She then shifted focus and tried to take in what was happening at the farm. The house appeared to be covered in multiple layers of sandbags; the same with the barn. Whoever had setup that home had really taken their security serious, very serious.

A distant "fwomp" sound came from the PLA and even though Erin had never heard the sound in person before, she knew instantly that was from a mortar being fired out of its tube. She watched as the first round landed near the barn and exploded in a fireball. Some of the sandbags were ripped apart, a lot of the surrounding ground was on fire, but the barn still stood. The sound of a series of mortar rounds being fired reached their ears. Erin had given up on her binoculars and was already lying on her big .50-caliber rifle and peering through its powerful optic.

More mortars were launched, this time targeting the house. The house did not fare as well as the barn. Four separate rounds screamed out of the sky and leveled the farmhouse. The sandbags appeared to work some, but even with the reinforcements, the house never had a chance. Erin hoped the people were alive still, but it didn't matter; she was going to kill every last soldier she saw. Zeds churned around the PLA position, but were kept at bay by the wagon circle of radar trucks. Erin watched a PLA soldier stand on the roof of one of the APCs with an odd-looking bazooka. It was large and gangly, not something that she had seen, even compared to those Stinger missiles they found in Pecos. She took aim at the man and waited, trying to figure out what the weapon was. Erin waited too long and he fired the rocket. A moment later, the round landed near the rubble of the destroyed farmhouse and began to emit a loud klaxon horn sound that hurt their ears even though they were so far away.

"Holy shit! Watch the house. I'm going to ruin these asshole's day."

Jason grunted his acknowledgment just as the first round from Erin's big rifle ripped across the pasture from their hilltop position and toward the mortar teams that were set out away from the circled vehicles on an adjacent hilltop. Dirt bounced into the air around them from the concussive blast. Erin shifted slightly and fired again, then again. A massive explosion waved over them. The blast made their ears pop even though they were close to 1,000 yards away.

"Got some of their explosives to set off, fuckers."

The PLA reorganized quickly. Some of the PLA survivors that had been assembled back in the circle of their vehicles took firing positions and killed off their compatriots that had begun to reanimate before they mounted their vehicles and began driving from their position toward the farmhouse. The rest were on foot, with the armored vehicles flanking them for protection as they walked, a radar truck at the front and rear of the advancing element to protect their own troops. Erin turned her rifle toward the house and saw movement through her optic. A man climbed out of the rubble and desperately began digging. Shortly after, he pulled a woman from the rubble who clutched a baby to her bare chest.

Erin gasped. "FUCK!"

Ken

Ken cursed the car his luck and the Germans; the old Mercedes wagon decided that it was done with this world. Smoke poured out from under the hood, thick black smoke that continued to grow in intensity. He abandoned the car and began walking as an explosion rumbled from a short distance away. He cursed under his breath and began walking faster. Twenty years ago, he would have jogged or run, but he was too beat up and felt too old to run like that.

Chivo and Gonzo

"What the actual fuck was that?"

Gonzo didn't know the answer to Chivo's question, but it sure sounded like mortar fire and the following explosion wasn't a good sign for their original mission.

Chivo began running toward the sound. They were about 500yards from their observation post. Gonzo followed. Eschewing safe tactics, he ran nearly to the hilltop and took out his binoculars and was still for a quick moment.

"Fuck. Goddamn it all.... FUCK! GONZO, GET THE FUCKING TRUCK!"

Chivo dropped the binoculars to the ground and began sprinting down the hill as fast as he could with his combat loadout. Gonzo hadn't asked any questions; he trusted his friend's judgment and had begun sprinting back toward the MRAP.

Ken

Ken wheezed, trying to breathe as he stopped; he saw a mounted and dismounted patrol approaching a destroyed farmhouse. It was partially on fire, and a barn near it was starting to burn as well. The smell of the battle, fire, and diesel fuel began to reach his nostrils and Ken began running toward the fight.

Anger burned white hot in his chest. He wasn't going to let it happen again, he wouldn't let it happen ever again. Ken stopped and raised his M-1, shouldered the rifle, and took aim at the trailing radar truck. Disregarding his limited ammo supply, Ken fired until the metallic ping of the ammo clip being ejected could be heard. Smoke had begun coming out of the large flat radar transmitter and Zeds began filtering past it into where the dismounted patrol was. Ken began running down the hill toward the farmstead; he needed to get closer if he was going to have a chance to hit man-sized targets.

Erin and Jason

Erin continued to fire, first destroying the lead radar truck and then taking aim on the front APC, not being able to get a clear shot at any of the soldiers between the armored carriers. One of the large mounted weapons on the lead APC fired. Erin shifted her hips and turning the rifle toward the house. She saw Bexar pulling Jessie and their baby out of the rubble. He was hurt, she didn't look great, and blood trickled out of her ears and mouth. Through the powerful scope, Erin could see the baby screaming. Erin had no way of warning her friends about the incoming round. A tear squeezed out from behind the scope and streaked down Erin's cheek.

Bexar stood and appeared to be screaming while rapidly firing his rifle at their attackers. He switched magazines and fired as fast as he could, moving from target to target. Advancing PLA and advancing Zeds were hit by his rifle fire. The PLA fell, but the Zeds kept marching toward the house, toward Bexar, Jessie, and their newborn.

The incoming round hit near the house and knocked debris into the air, knocking Bexar and Jessie off their feet. They didn't get back up.

CHAPTER 21

October 2, Year 1
The Farm House

Bexar.

Jessie fell back to consciousness like waking up to a terrible nightmare. Pain radiated through her body.

Jessie turned her head, smeared in dirt and blood. Bexar lay motionless on the ground, blood trickling out of his ears and nose, rifle clutched against his chest, dim, lifeless eyes staring back at her. Jessie moved to touch him and couldn't. She yelled as loudly as she could and no sound came out of her mouth. Silence engulfed her all but the ringing in her ears. Disoriented, she blinked hard, dirt seeming to hang weightlessly in the space around her. Time grinded ahead slowly as she lay on the ground.

Distantly, an infant screamed, the only sound she could now hear. The baby's cries penetrated her chest, and Jessie's heart burned in grief and anger. Anger at the world, anger at the invasion, the battle, and angry that for all they had overcome. For all that they were, it wasn't enough for the new reality. It wouldn't be enough for her Scout, her baby.

Louder, the infant cried. Tears streamed across Jessie's cheeks. A piece of metal lodged in the side of her rifle; it would never work again. She reached for Bexar and peeled his stiffening dead hands off his rifle, smoke wafting from the end of the barrel. Jessie ripped a fresh magazine from his chest carrier and loaded rifle. She pulled up to her knees. On the ground was an infant, her infant, covered in dust and dirt.

Her baby girl screamed in terror and pain.

Jessie glanced over the rubble and sandbags to see dozens of PLA soldiers advancing. Zeds rattled and pushed around the APCs as they approached. The sound of the rumbling diesel motors of the approaching soldiers felt distance even though they were only a few dozen yards away now. Jessie glanced back over her shoulder and saw Zeds tripping and falling through the debris of their ruined home. More came from each side.

She was trapped.

They were trapped.

"Oh God—forgive me, Scout, my child. I love you."

Blood obscured the red triangle in the optic; Bexar's blood. Jessie stood and fired as quickly as she could pull the trigger. Zeds, Chinese, and Koreans, the battle closed in around her until the lonesome howl of incoming ordnance grew louder with each millisecond that clawed past. She dropped the rifle, fell to the ground, cradled her baby girl tightly in a ball, and waited for the end.

Dirt, clumps of soil, rocks, and what was sure to be some Zed body parts fell from the sky above, the mortar overshooting her position and exploding behind her. The house was destroyed, the barn was on fire, and there was nowhere to run, nowhere to hide, and no way out.

Jessie stood, shouldering the rifle, and fired rapidly until the bolt locked back on an empty chamber. Bexar's empty rifle fell from her hands to the ground as she scooped her baby girl in her arms, clutched her tight, and began to run.

Jessie screamed in rage.

It was the guttural savage war cry of an ancient warrior princess as she sprinted toward the approaching PLA. She had a chance running forward. Behind her was certain death as the decrepit blackened teeth of the dead tore the flesh from her bones, from her daughter's bones.

She looked up, trying to pick the best route through the enemy soldiers ahead. The men were startled by the unexpected, but they were beginning to react, rifles shifting their aim.

Please no, I have to make it. She needs me...I can't lose another of my babies!

Her voice echoed through her mind. Jessie's feet felt like they were tied to the ground, and the harder she ran, the slower it seemed to be. Slowly, the invader's muzzles tracked her movement. She didn't know she was still screaming at the top of her lungs. Another glance up at the soldier ahead on her right saw his head vaporize in a pink mist. The next man was knocked off his feet, blood arcing through the air from the fist-sized hole in his chest as he fell.

I'm going to make it! Oh my God, I'm almost there.

"GO!"

Jason sprinted down the hill. His wife only said "go" and so he did. He could feel the pressure wave of the large-caliber rifle rounds passing his overhead as Erin tried worked to save Jessie, or just save the baby. They didn't have long. His shotgun sat next to Erin. He didn't have to shoot; Erin would protect him. Jason knew that he would be fine and they would win because his love would make sure they would.

Erin shifted aim quickly. One by one, she killed the enemy. They were confused as Jessie ran through the middle of the ranks, between the APCs and out the back of the patrol. The soldiers weren't firing their rifles for fear of shooting a comrade in the crossfire. In Jessie's path were some Zeds of the talented few who were trying to get a hand on her and drag her to the ground. One by one, each of them fell. The deep crack of the .50-caliber rifle punctuated each new death as it snapped across the field in rapid fire.

Closer and closer Jason came to Jessie. She had seen him; he saw the recognition of hope glint across her eyes, her desperation. Her baby cried and screamed, frightened at it all.

A heavy invisible fist reached out and struck Jessie.

She stumbled but managed to keep on her feet. Then another and another still. Through the rifle's optic, Erin saw dark stains appearing through the dirty tank top Jessie was wearing. She saw that an officer stood with a pistol drawn and was shooting Jessie in the back as she ran.

Erin pulled the trigger and exploded.

The rifle failed. Erin screamed in frustration and anger as she stood to run. Pain flashed and seared through her face and body. She felt blood running down her face and she couldn't see very well, but Erin saw well enough to see her ruined rifle on the ground.

The rifle magazine was blown out of the receiver; the bolt was peeled back like a cartoon banana. Erin realized she was lucky to be conscious after a catastrophic failure like that. Rage burned deep in her chest. Jessie, Jason, the baby she didn't even know yet...it wasn't fair. None of it was fair and she hated it all and she hated the PLA with every fiber of her being. She had never felt anger and hatred this deep and primal before.

Chivo ran like an Olympian, his head up, chest up, feet and arms pumping. He was indifferent to the full tactical kit weighing his body down, indifferent to his M4, which bounced and jostled against the tight sling. He couldn't breathe, his rapid pulse pounding in his ears. Breathing didn't matter to Chivo. Living didn't matter to him. Chivo wouldn't quit, he couldn't quit.

Chivo would never quit for his friends.

Jason caught Jessie as she fell. Blood traced out of the corner of her mouth. Panting, she couldn't breathe, couldn't talk. She didn't need to.Jason and Jessie locked eyes.

Jason knew what needed to be said just by the look in her eyes. He took the screaming infant from her arms, turned, and ran back the way he had come.

He didn't look up, didn't have to; he knew Erin was going to keep him safe. Jason glanced down at the baby. He didn't know if it was a boy or a girl, he didn't know the baby's name, and he never would. One look into its bright blue eyes and Jason knew that he would love this child for all time as if it was his own and would never let himself fail her.

The sharp crack of rifle fire snapping past him was the first time Jason realized that the PLA were shooting at him. He looked up and a few hundred yards away was Erin running toward him. Jason didn't know why she was running and wasn't using the sniper rifle. Pain like he had never felt before cut and burned in his back as Jason tumbled to the ground with his arms wrapped tightly around Jessie's baby. He didn't catch his fall.

It took less than a second for Jason to realize that he couldn't move his legs after he fell. No matter how hard he concentrated and how angry he was, he could not make his legs move.

"I'm sorry little one," Jason whispered to the baby as he tucked it tightly against his chest, hoping to protect its tiny body from the bullet impacts he continued to feel. "I'm sorry, Erin. I love you."

The next round hit Jason in the back of the skull.

Erin saw Jason fall, but was still too far away to see what happened. All she knew was that he hadn't got back up yet. Someone else was running toward Jason and she was startled to recognize who it was.

Chivo didn't break stride. He hit the PLA soldier closest to Jason as hard as he could, a brutal hit that led with the butt of his rifle. Chivo rolled and slid up to his feet with his rifle ready to battle. Rapidly he fired, shifting fire back and forth, killing the approaching men as quickly as he could aim. The first round hit Chivo in the thigh. He knew the feeling and knew that the wound wasn't immediately important, but Bexar's child was. He had to kill as many of these approaching assholes that he could and hope that Gonzo would get there in time.

Another round hit him in the ass. The PLA slowed their unorthodox advance at the sight of the crazed man with a rifle who was rapidly and accurately killing their comrades. The Zeds behind the PLA didn't slow; they continued to advance, entering the PLA's ranks, the soldier's attention being kept to the front and the rambling battle. Chivo shifted fire as he rapidly switched an empty magazine for a fresh one. The PLA weren't firing at him anymore, and his targets were now the growing wall of dead flesh that pushed on no matter what they did. Heavy rifle rounds cracked past Chivo. He didn't know who was firing, but they were helping him so he didn't care.Chivo turned and pulled Jason's body off of the baby. Bexar's child appeared OK, or at least it was still moving and crying. Chivo saw Jessie's eyes looking back at him in the little round baby's face. He clutched the baby girl—he was sure it was a girl just by her beautiful bright eyes—in his arms and tried to run. Being shot twice stopped any attempt to run very fast or much at all. Chivo glanced up and saw an old man with a rifle firing rapidly at him—around him—and saw a woman sprinting past the man and toward him. A woman he recognized.

Erin saw the Zeds and watched Chivo pick up the baby. Tears streamed down her face as she still ran toward the baby and Chivo. She knew her husband was dead. She failed him.

Rifle rounds fired by the old man snapped past them both. PLA and Zeds fell around them.

Erin reached Chivo. He held out the baby and handed her to Erin. "Please."

"For Jessie," was Erin's response.

Erin turned and began running back up the hill, away from the approaching Zeds, hoping like hell that she would make it. Chivo spun in place, raised his rifle, and began firing rapidly. Quickly, he inserted another fresh magazine and another, before dropping the empty and smoking rifle while drawing his pistol quickly and smoothly pressing the pistol into service. After some rapid hits, the pistol slide locked back on an empty chamber. Chivo thumbed the release as he grasped the last magazine with his left hand, before he was bit hard on the left shoulder.

No angry curse was yelled. Chivo knew his fate was sealed, but he still had to make sure Bexar's baby made it out safe. He turned and punched the Zed in the head with his pistol. Still trying to insert the last magazine into his pistol, still trying to fight, still trying to protect Bexar's baby, Chivo was pulled off his feet by more Zeds, their teeth pulling and ripping chunks of clothing and flesh with each hard bite.Chivo fought hard, angry he couldn't finish his mission, angry that he failed Bexar and Jessie.

Gonzo sped down the hill in the M-ATV, the long suspension of the armored truck bouncing with the speed and terrain. He was headed toward a woman running at the front of an enormous horde of Zeds. The M-ATV slid to a stop in front of Erin. She was startled but immediately opened the door and climbed in, cradling the baby in her lap. The old man with the rifle climbed into the back seat and began throwing up from the exertion. Neither knew who he was, but he had obviously been on their side.

Silently, Gonzo drove as quickly as they could. There would be time to talk later, but first they had to beat the Zeds to the SSC if they were going to survive, a dark cloud of flies and death following in their wake.

EPILOGUE

She stood atop Emory Peak and looked at the gleaming bronze plaque and read the inscription again. "The beginning of the fight by the most unlikely of people."

She was one of the oldest of the next generation, the new generation of people born after the attack. She also didn't know her exact birthday, just the date of her rescue from the PLA and the Zeds. Erin, her adoptive mother, refused tell her the story of her parents until she had been a teenager, just telling her that she had been adopted and that she was much loved. Erin named her after her mother and Erin's mother, who she had found out, had been friends. Before Erin died, she had admitted that she didn't know what her parents had actually named her and she still hurt deeply for not saving them. From what Erin had said, her mother Jessie and her father Bexar had been good people who had to overcome exceptional times.

Her childhood home, the facility under Lake Bardwell, was now a museum and she hadn't visited in many years, not since President Lampton had passed away from natural causes 10 years ago. It did serve as the capital of the United States for a number of years before moving the capital above ground.

The war against the Chinese and Koreans didn't last much longer past the attack on her parent's house. The siege and battle for the SSC lasted for over a month before Steve Dorsey radioed in that the modifications were done and President Lampton gave the launch order. Not surprisingly, the re-fit of the ICBM launch controls had worked and if the Korean spy had been successful, she was quite sure that they would have lost the war, their country, and their lives.

After the nuclear strike, PLA forces had eventually surrendered. Prisoners of war with no home to return to were conscripted to rebuild what they had destroyed, most of them eventually becoming citizens and becoming part of the communities they rebuilt. A dozen container ships at a dozen different ports all along the western coast and the Gulf of Mexico had been sitting ready for the full invasion, but President Lampton ended it before it could fully start. That PLA equipment helped rebuild America. Dozens and dozens of radar trucks were used to establish small safe zones for survivors to gain a foothold. The surviving PLA soldiers didn't know the real or full reason for the attack, only the propaganda given to them before it all started. At the root of the motivation for the attack was the communist party leadership. They had come up with the plan to attack and invade to seize global control. They hadn't expected the Americans to survive more than four to six weeks before succumbing to the Zeds, so the invading forces would easily clear cities and the countryside with their radar trucks with minimal effort or fighting. Obviously, that hadn't worked. The party leadership failed to take into account the self-reliance of the American people.

Eventually, those small safe zones expanded and Zeds were neutralized across the country. Some pockets were still infected, quarantined, and off limits; mostly larger cities, such as Miami and St. Louis, but much of the country was free from wandering dead. Regardless, Jessie still always carried a pistol. She didn't trust that all of the Zeds had been truly found and neutralized. Most of the major cities still lay in ruins and would for generations to come, but places like New Austin had popped up in the expansive stretches of land throughout the country. They had a bright future.

She hiked down from the peak, along the Pinnacles trail and toward the cabins. The cabins that had been destroyed were rebuilt on her order. A beat-up old MRAP sat idling in the parking area for the cabins, two men armed with rifles waiting for her.

"Ready to head back, Madam President?"

She nodded and climbed inside.

She didn't know her parents, and she didn't personally experience the sacrifices that were made in those early days after the attack, but Jessie Sarah Reed was grateful for the sacrifices that were made so that humanity could survive.

So she could survive.

The End

ABOUT THE AUTHOR

My name is Dave Lund. I hail from Texas and am a former Texas "motor-cop." My family and photography round out my usual day-to-day passions, but post-apocalyptic zombie stories really fire me up. Before my previous stint as a motor-cop, I was a full-time skydiving instructor and competitor (in Canopy Piloting, aka swooping) with over 3,000 skydives. I am no longer an active skydiver so I can focus on my family, photography, and writing.

The characters in the Winchester series comprise some personality composites of people I have known or met in my life, but no character is based on a single real person or even two people combined. They are a complete work of fiction and do not represent any actual people, living or dead. Yes, that includes Bexar! Many of the themes, objects, weapons, tactics, and locations in the Winchester Undead series are pulled from my past and experiences, as many writers are apt to do, including my love of Big Bend National Park in Texas; although I have to admit there is no secret cache site in the small Texas town of Maypearl. At least none that I had any hand in creating. Although the secret base from the SSC is probably true ...

ACKNOWLEDGMENTS

Without the support and love of my wife Morgan and our family, this would not have been possible. Also without the support of all my friends, fans and readers the Winchester Undead series would not have been able to come to a conclusion.

Thank you.

-Dave

Website: **http://www.talesofadventures.net**
Facebook: **https://www.facebook.com/winchesterundead**
Twitter: **@WUzombies**
Instagram: **https://instagram.com/f8industries/**

The *Author Dave Lund Tales of Adventures, Winchester Undead Newsletter* is the place for unique content. To gain access to the custom-made full Winchester Undead plot location map, special contests and tales of adventures, you have to sign up here:

http://talesofadventures.net/newsletter/

OTHER WINLOCK BOOKS YOU'LL LOVE

Winlock Press has a stunning range of post-apocalyptic adventures.

Craig Martelle's *End Times Alaska: Endure*
first in the *End Times Alaska* series!

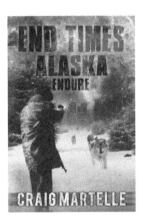

J. Rudolph's *The Reanimates: The Complex,*
first in *The Reanimates* series!

Available wherever books are sold.

PERMUTED
PRESS
needs **you** to help

SPREAD (THE)
INFECTION

FOLLOW US!

f | Facebook.com/PermutedPress
🐦 | Twitter.com/PermutedPress

REVIEW US!

Wherever you buy our book, they can be
reviewed! We want to know what you like!

GET INFECTED!

Sign up for our mailing list at
PermutedPress.com

PERMUTED
PRESS

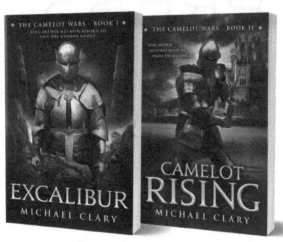

THE ULTIMATE PREPPER'S ADVENTURE.
THE JOURNEY BEGINS HERE!

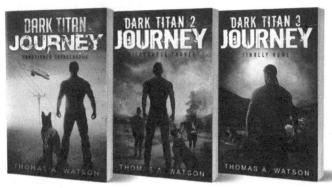

EAN 9781682611654 $9.99   **EAN** 9781618687371 $9.99   **EAN** 9781618687395 $9.99

The long-predicted Coronal Mass Ejection has finally hit the Earth, virtually destroying civilization. Nathan Owens has been prepping for a disaster like this for years, but now he's a thousand miles away from his family and his refuge. He'll have to employ all his hard-won survivalist skills to save his current community, before he begins his long journey through doomsday to get back home.

THE MORNINGSTAR STRAIN HAS BEEN LET LOOSE—IS THERE ANY WAY TO STOP IT?

EAN 9781618686497 $16.00

An industrial accident unleashes some of the Morningstar Strain. The doctor who discovered the strain and her assistant will have to fight their way through Sprinters and Shamblers to save themselves, the vaccine, and the base. Then they discover that it wasn't an accident at all—somebody inside the facility did it on purpose. The war with the RSA and the infected is far from over.

This is the fourth book in Z.A. Recht's The Morningstar Strain series, written by Brad Munson.

PERMUTED
PRESS

GATHERED TOGETHER AT LAST, THREE TALES OF FANTASY CENTERING AROUND THE MYSTERIOUS CITY OF SHADOWS...ALSO KNOWN AS CHICAGO.

EAN 9781682612286 $9.99   EAN 9781618684639 $5.99   EAN 9781618684899 $5.99

From *The New York Times* and *USA Today* bestselling author Richard A. Knaak comes three tales from Chicago, the City of Shadows. Enter the world of the Grey–the creatures that live at the edge of our imagination and seek to be real. Follow the quest of a wizard seeking escape from the centuries-long haunting of a gargoyle. Behold the coming of the end of the world as the Dutchman arrives.

Enter the City of Shadows.

PERMUTED
PRESS